DARK MATTER

Greg Iles is the author of thirteen international best-selling novels, including *Turning Angel*, *True Evil*, *Third Degree* and the *New York Times* No.1 bestseller *The Devil's Punchbowl*.

His novels have been made into films, translated into more than twenty languages, and published worldwide in more than thirty-five countries. He lives in Natchez, Mississippi.

www.GregIles.com

Books By Greg Iles

Praise for *Dark Matter*

"Alarming, believable, and utterly consuming . . . My favorite kind of novel—one that educates while it entertains. Ambitious in its scope and superbly satisfying in its execution, this story resonates long after the final page is turned"
Dan Brown

"Very impressive . . . this amazing and multi-layered story moves at quantum speed toward a breathtaking conclusion"
Nelson DeMille

"Impossible to put down . . . extremely compelling. This is Iles's best book yet"
Library Journal

"Keeps suspense and blood pressure high"   *Booklist*

"Greg Iles is a superb writer, and now he displays his genius and style in a stunning new direction . . . a powerful brew of science and suspense that will leave you dazzled!"
Linda Fairstein

"A riveting page-turner. Greg Iles brings imagination and vision to a novel as thought-provoking as it is thrilling"
Vince Flynn

GREG ILES

Dark Matter

US TITLE:
The Footprints of God

HARPER

Harper
An imprint of HarperCollins*Publishers*
77–85 Fulham Palace Road,
Hammersmith, London W6 8JB

www.harpercollins.co.uk

This paperback edition 2014
1

First published in Great Britain in 2003 by Hodder & Stoughton
A division of Hodder Headline

Copyright © Greg Iles 2003

Greg Iles asserts the moral right to
be identified as the author of this work

A catalogue record for this book is
available from the British Library

ISBN: 978 0 00 754657 2

Set in Sabon LT Std by Palimpsest Book Production Limited,
Falkirk, Stirlingshire

Printed and bound in Great Britain by
Clays Ltd, St Ives plc

MIX
Paper from
responsible sources

FSC **FSC™ C007454**
www.fsc.org

Acknowledgments

My deepest gratitude goes to Ray Kurzweil, a pioneering inventor whose insights into artificial intelligence did much to inspire this novel. I still remember the first time I played the grand piano sound on a Kurzweil synthesizer and realized what was possible in the field of electronic music. Kurzweil is a gifted futurist, and his book *The Age of Spiritual Machines,* should be read by all.

All my novels are enriched by the expertise and insight of many people. I owe them all an expression of thanks.

For his trip to Israel during difficult times: Keith Benoist.

For medical expertise: Salil Tiwari, M.D., Louis Jacobs, D.O., Michael Bourland, M.D., Jerry Iles, M.D., Edward Daly, M.D., Fred Emrick, M.D., Simmons Iles, R.N.

For military expertise: Major General Chuck Thomas, U.S. Army (retired). Chuck was of great help on very short notice, and he is not responsible for authorial invention as to military capabilities. Thanks also to Cole Cordray, and to S.B. for covert assistance.

For long nights discussing philosophy and religion: Robert Hensley, Michael Taylor, and Win Ward.

For contributions too numerous to name, the usual suspects: Geoff Iles, Michael Henry, Ed Stackler, Courtney Aldridge, Betty Iles, Carrie Iles, Madeline Iles, Mark Iles, Jane Hargrove.

For sticking with it anyway: Susan Moldow, Louise Burke, and Susanne Kirk.

Thanks also to the ladies at the Oak Ridge Chamber of Commerce.

As usual, all mistakes are mine.

Finally, to my readers. Writing about science and philosophy in a commercial novel is problematic. Write about them at their natural level and you leave the masses behind. Simplify too much, and you offend people conversant in those subjects. I trust you will enter this book as an exercise of the mind, and not judge too harshly either way. If we have learned anything in the past ten thousand years, it is that nothing is certain.

We should take care not to make the intellect our god.
—Albert Einstein

All things return to the One.
What does the One return to?
—Zen koan

ONE

"My name is David Tennant, M.D. I'm professor of ethics at the University of Virginia Medical School, and if you're watching this tape, I'm dead."

I took a breath and gathered myself. I didn't want to rant. I'd mounted my Sony camcorder on a tripod and rotated the LCD screen in order to see myself as I spoke. I'd lost weight over the past weeks. My eyes were red with fatigue, the orbits shiny and dark. I looked more like a hunted criminal than a grieving friend.

"I don't really know where to begin. I keep seeing Andrew lying on the floor. And I know they killed him. But . . . I'm getting ahead of myself. You need facts. I was born in 1961 in Los Alamos, New Mexico. My father was James Howard Tennant, the nuclear physicist. My mother was Ann Tennant, a pediatrician. I'm making this tape in a sober state of mind, and I'm going to deposit it with my attorney as soon as I finish, on the understanding that it should be opened if I die for any reason.

"Six hours ago, my colleague Dr. Andrew Fielding was found dead beside his desk, the victim of an apparent stroke. I can't prove it, but I know Fielding was murdered. For the

1

past two years, he and I have been part of a scientific team funded by the National Security Agency and DARPA—the government agency that created the Internet in the 1970s. Under the highest security classification, that team and its work are known as Project Trinity."

I glanced down at the short-barreled Smith & Wesson .38 in my lap. I'd made sure the pistol wasn't visible on camera, but it calmed me to have it within reach. Reassured, I again stared at the glowing red light.

"Two years ago, Peter Godin, founder of the Godin Supercomputing Corporation, had an epiphany much like that mythical moment when an apple dropped onto Isaac Newton's head. It happened in a dream. Seemingly from nowhere, a seventy-year-old man visualized the most revolutionary possibility in the history of science. When he woke up, Godin telephoned John Skow, a deputy director of the NSA, in Fort Meade, Maryland. By six A.M., the two men had drafted and delivered a letter to the president of the United States. That letter shook the White House to its foundations. I know this because the president was my brother's close friend in college. My brother died three years ago, but because of him, the president knew of my work, which is what put me in the middle of all that followed."

I rubbed the cool metal of the .38, wondering what to tell and what to leave out. *Leave out nothing,* said a voice in my head. My father's voice. Fifty years ago, he'd played his own part in America's secret history, and that burden had greatly shortened his days. My father died in 1988, a haunted man, certain that the Cold War he'd spent his youthful energy to perpetuate would end with the destruction of civilization, as it so easily could have. *Leave out nothing. . . .*

"The Godin Memo," I continued, "had the same effect as the letter Albert Einstein sent President Roosevelt at the beginning of World War Two, outlining the potential for an atomic bomb and the possibility that Nazi Germany might develop one. Einstein's letter spurred the Manhattan Project, the secret quest to ensure that America would be the first to possess nuclear weapons. Peter Godin's letter resulted in a project of similar scope but infinitely greater ambition. Project Trinity began behind the walls of an NSA front corporation in the Research Triangle Park of North Carolina. Only six people on the planet ever had full knowledge of Trinity. Now that Andrew Fielding is dead, only five remain. I'm one. The other four are Peter Godin, John Skow, Ravi Nara—"

I bolted to my feet with the .38 in my hand. Someone was rapping on my front door. Through thin curtains, I saw a Federal Express truck parked at the foot of my sidewalk. What I couldn't see was the space immediately in front of my door.

"Who is it?" I called.

"FedEx," barked a muffled male voice. "I need a signature."

I wasn't expecting a delivery. "Is it a letter or a package?"

"Letter."

"Who from?"

"Uhh . . . Lewis Carroll."

I shivered. A package from a dead man? Only one person would send me a package under the name of the author of *Alice in Wonderland*. Andrew Fielding. Had he sent me something the day before he died? Fielding had been obsessively searching the Trinity labs for weeks now, the computers as well as the physical space. Perhaps he'd found something. And perhaps whatever it was had got him killed. I'd sensed something strange about Fielding's behavior yesterday—not so easy with a man famed for his eccentricities—but by this morning he'd seemed to be his old self.

"Do you want this thing or not?" asked the deliveryman.

I cocked the pistol and edged over to the door. I'd fastened the chain latch when I'd got home. With my left hand, I unlocked the door and pulled it open to the length of the chain. Through the crack, I saw the face of a uniformed man in his twenties, his hair bound into a short ponytail.

"Pass your pad through with the package. I'll sign and give it back to you."

"It's a digital pad. I can't give you that."

"Keep your hand on it, then."

"Paranoid," he muttered, but he stuck a thick orange pad through the crack in the door.

I grabbed the stylus hanging from the string and scrawled my name on the touch-sensitive screen. "Okay."

The pad disappeared, and a FedEx envelope was thrust through. I took it and tossed it onto the sofa, then shut the door and waited until I heard the truck rumble away from the curb.

I picked up the envelope and glanced at the label. "Lewis Carroll" had been signed in Fielding's spidery hand. As I pulled the sheet of paper from the envelope, a greasy white granular substance spilled over my fingers. The instant my eyes registered the color, some part of my brain whispered *anthrax*. The odds of that were low, but my best friend had just died under suspicious circumstances. A certain amount of paranoia was justified.

I hurried to the kitchen and scrubbed my hands with dish soap and water. Then I pulled a black medical bag from my closet. Inside was the usual pharmacopoeia of the M.D.'s home: analgesics, antibiotics, emetics, steroid cream. I found what I wanted in a snap compartment: a blister pack of Cipro, a powerful broad-spectrum antibiotic. I swallowed one pill with water from the tap, then took a pair of surgical gloves from the bag. As a last precaution, I tied a dirty T-shirt from the hamper around my nose and mouth. Then I folded the FedEx envelope and letter into separate Ziploc bags, sealed them, and laid them on the counter.

4

As badly as I wanted to read the letter, part of me resisted. Fielding might have been murdered for what was written on that page. Even if that weren't the case, nothing good would come from my reading it.

I carefully vacuumed the white granules from the carpet in the front room, wondering if I could be wrong about Fielding's death being murder. He and I had worked ourselves into quite a state of suspicion over the past weeks, but then we had reason to. And the timing was too damn convenient. Instead of putting the vacuum cleaner back into the closet, I walked to the back door and tossed the machine far into the yard. I could always buy another one.

I was still eerily aware of the letter sitting on the kitchen counter. I felt like a soldier's wife refusing to open a telegram. But I already knew my friend was dead. So what did I fear?

The why, answered a voice in my head. Fielding talking. *You want to keep your head in the sand. It's the American national pastime. . . .*

More than a little irritated to find that the dead could be as bothersome as the living, I picked up the Ziploc containing the letter and carried it to the front room. The note was brief and handwritten.

David,

We must meet again. I finally confronted Godin with my suspicions. His reaction astounded me. I don't want to commit anything to paper, but I know I'm right. Lu Li and I are driving to the blue place on Saturday night. Please join us. It's close quarters, but discreet. It may be time for you to contact your late brother's friend again, though I wonder if even he can do anything at this point. Things like this have a momentum greater than individuals. Greater even than humanity, I fear. If anything should happen to me, don't forget that little gold item I asked you to hold for me one day. Desperate times, mate. I'll see you Saturday.

There was no signature, but below the note was a hand-drawn cartoon of a rabbit's head and the face of a clock. The White Rabbit, an affectionate nickname given Fielding by his Cambridge physics students. Fielding always carried a gold pocket watch, and that was the "little gold item" that he had asked me to hold for him one day.

We were passing each other in the hallway when he pressed the watch and chain into my hand. "Mind keeping that for an hour, old man?" he'd murmured. "Lovely." Then he was gone. An hour later he stopped by my office to pick it up, saying he hadn't wanted to take the watch into the MRI lab with him, where it could have been smashed against the MRI unit by the machine's enormous magnetic fields. But Fielding visited the MRI lab all the time, and he'd never given me his pocket watch before. And he never did again. It must have been in his pocket when he died. So what the hell was he up to that day?

I read the note again. *Lu Li and I are driving to the blue place on Saturday night.* Lu Li was Fielding's new Chinese wife. The "blue place" had to be code for a beach cabin at Nags Head, on North Carolina's Outer Banks. Three months ago, when Fielding asked for a recommendation for his honeymoon, I'd suggested the Nags Head cabin, which was only a few hours away. Fielding and his wife had loved the place, and the Englishman had apparently thought of it when he wanted a secure location to discuss his fears.

My hands were shaking. The man who had written this note was now as cold as the morgue table he was lying on, if indeed he was lying in a morgue. No one had been able— or willing—to tell me where my friend's body would be taken. And now the white powder. Would Fielding have put powder

6

in the envelope and neglected to mention it in his letter? If he didn't, who did? Who but the person who had murdered him?

I laid the letter on the sofa, stripped off the surgical gloves, and rewound the videotape to the point at which I'd walked out of the frame. I had decided to make this tape because I feared I might be killed before I could tell the president what I knew. Fielding's letter had changed nothing. Yet as I stared into the lens, my mind wandered. I was way ahead of Fielding on calling my "late brother's friend." The moment I'd seen Fielding's corpse on the floor of his office, I knew I had to call the president. But the president was in China. Still, as soon as I got clear of the Trinity lab, I'd called the White House from a pay phone in a Shoney's restaurant, a "safe" phone Fielding had told me about. It couldn't be seen by surveillance teams in cars, and the restaurant's interior geometry made it difficult for a parabolic microphone to eavesdrop from a distance.

When I said "Project Trinity," the White House operator put me through to a man who gruffly asked me to state my business. I asked to speak to Ewan McCaskell, the president's chief of staff, whom I'd met during my visit to the Oval Office. McCaskell was in China with the president. I asked that the president be informed that David Tennant needed to speak to him urgently about Project Trinity, and that no one else involved with Trinity should be informed. The man said my message would be passed on and hung up.

Thirteen hours separated North Carolina and Beijing. That made it tomorrow in China. Daylight. Yet four hours had passed since my call, and I'd heard nothing. Would my message be relayed to China, given the critical nature of the summit? There was no way to know. I did know that if someone at Trinity heard about my call first, I might wind up as dead as Fielding before I talked to the president.

I hit START on the remote control and spoke again to the camera.

"In the past six months I've gone from feeling like part of a noble scientific effort to questioning whether I'm even living in the United States. I've watched Nobel laureates give up all principle in a search for—"

I went still. Something had passed by one of my front windows. A face. Very close, peering inside. I'd seen it through the sheer curtains, but I was sure. A face, framed by shoulder-length hair. I had a sense of a woman's features, but . . .

I started to get up, then sat back down. My teeth were vibrating with an electric pain like aluminum foil crushed between dental fillings. My eyelids felt too heavy to hold open. *Not now,* I thought, shoving my hand into my pocket for my prescription bottle. *Jesus, not now.* For six months, every member of Trinity's inner circle had suffered frightening neurological symptoms. No one's symptoms were the same. My affliction was narcolepsy. Narcolepsy and dreams. At home, I usually gave in to the trancelike sleep. But when I needed to fight off a spell—at Trinity, or driving my car—only amphetamines could stop the overwhelming waves.

I pulled out my prescription bottle and shook it. *Empty.* I'd swallowed my last pill yesterday. I got my speed from Ravi Nara, Trinity's neurologist, but Nara and I were no longer speaking. I tried to rise, thinking I'd call a pharmacy and prescribe my own, but that was ridiculous. I couldn't even stand. A leaden heaviness had settled into my limbs. My face felt hot, and my eyelids began to fall.

The prowler was at the window again. In my mind, I raised my gun and aimed it, but then I saw the weapon lying in my lap. Not even survival instinct could clear the fog filling my brain. I looked back at the window. The face was gone. *A woman's face.* I was sure of it. Would they use a woman to kill me? Of course. They were pragmatists. They used what worked.

Something scratched at my doorknob. Through the thickening haze I fought to aim my gun at the door. Something slammed against the wood. I got my finger on the trigger, but as my swimming brain transmitted the instruction to depress it, sleep annihilated consciousness like fingers snuffing a candle flame.

Andrew Fielding sat alone at his desk, furiously smoking a cigarette. His hands were shaking from a confrontation with Godin. It had happened the previous day, but Fielding had the habit of replaying such scenes in his mind, agonizing over how ineffectually he had stated his case, murmuring retorts he should have made at the time but had not.

The argument had been the result of weeks of frustration. Fielding didn't like arguments, not ones outside the realm of physics, anyway. He'd put off the meeting until the last possible moment. He pottered around his office, pondering one of the central riddles of quantum physics: how two particles fired simultaneously from the same source could arrive at the same destination at the same instant, even though one had to travel ten times as far as the other. It was like two 747s flying from New York to Los Angeles—one flying direct and the other having to fly south to Miami before turning west to Los Angeles—yet both touching down at LAX at the same moment. The 747 on the direct route flew at the speed of light, yet the plane that had to detour over Miami still reached L.A. at the same instant. Which meant that the second plane had flown faster than the speed of light. Which meant that Einstein's general theory of relativity was flawed. Possibly. Fielding spent a great deal of time thinking about this problem.

He lit another cigarette and thought about the letter he'd

FedExed to David Tennant. It didn't say enough. Not nearly. But it would have to do until they met at Nags Head. Tennant would be working a few steps up the hall from him all afternoon, but he might as well be in Fiji. No square foot of the Trinity complex was free of surveillance and recording devices. Tennant would get the letter this afternoon, if no one intercepted it. To prevent this, Fielding had instructed his wife to drop it at a FedEx box inside the Durham post office, beyond the sight line of anyone following her from a distance. That was all the spouses usually got—random surveillance from cars—but you never knew.

Tennant was Fielding's only hope. Tennant knew the president. He'd had cocktails in the White House, anyway. Fielding had won the Nobel in 1998, but he'd never been invited to 10 Downing Street. Never would be, in all likelihood. He'd shaken hands with the PM at a reception once, but that wasn't the same thing. Not at all.

He took a drag on the cigarette and looked down at his desk. An equation lay there, a collapsing wave function, unsolvable using present-day mathematics. Not even the world's most powerful supercomputers could solve a collapsing wave function. There was one machine on the planet that might make headway with the problem—at least he believed there was—and if he was right, the term supercomputer might soon become as quaint and archaic as abacus. But the machine that could solve a collapsing wave function would be capable of a lot more than computing. It would be everything Peter Godin had promised the mandarins in Washington, and more. That "more" was what scared Fielding. Scared the bloody hell out of him. For no one could predict the unintended consequences of bringing such a thing into existence. "Trinity" indeed.

He was thinking of going home early when something flashed in his left eye. There was no pain. Then the visual

10

field in that eye swirled into a blur, and an explosion seemed to detonate in the left frontal lobe of his brain. A stroke, *he thought with clinical detachment.* I'm having a stroke. *Strangely calm, he reached for the telephone to call 911, then remembered that the world's preeminent neurologist was working in the office four doors down from his own.*

The telephone would be faster than walking. He reached for the receiver, but the event taking place within his cranium suddenly bloomed to its full destructive power. The clot lodged, or the blood vessel burst, and his left eye went black. Then a knifelike pain pierced the base of his brain, the center of life support functions. Falling toward the floor, Fielding thought again of that elusive particle that had traveled faster than the speed of light, that had proved Einstein wrong by traversing space as though it did not exist. He posed a thought experiment: If Andrew Fielding could move as fast as that particle, could he reach Ravi Nara in time to be saved?

Answer: No. Nothing could save him now.

His last coherent thought was a prayer, a silent hope that in the unmapped world of the quantum, consciousness existed beyond what humans called death. For Fielding, religion was an illusion, but at the dawn of the twenty-first century, Project Trinity had uncovered hope of a new immortality. And it wasn't the Rube Goldberg monstrosity they were pretending to build a hundred meters from his office door.

The impact of the floor was like water.

I jerked awake and grabbed my gun. Someone was banging the front door taut against the security chain. I tried to get to my feet, but the dream had disoriented me. Its lucidity far surpassed anything I'd experienced to date. I actually felt that I had died, that I *was* Andrew Fielding at the moment of his death—

"Dr. Tennant?" shouted a woman's voice. "David! Are you in there?"

My psychiatrist? I put my hand to my forehead and tried to fight my way back to reality. "Dr. Weiss? Rachel? Is that you?"

"Yes! Unlatch the chain!"

"I'm coming," I muttered. "Are you alone?"

"Yes! Open the door."

I stuffed my gun between the couch cushions and stumbled toward the door. As I reached for the chain latch, it struck me that I had never told my psychiatrist where I lived.

TWO

Rachel Weiss had jet-black hair, olive skin, and onyx eyes. Eleven weeks ago, when I'd arrived at her office for my first session, I'd thought of Rebecca from Sir Walter Scott's *Ivanhoe*. Only in the novel Rebecca had a wild, unrestrained sort of beauty. Rachel Weiss projected a focused severity that made her physical appearance and clothing irrelevant, as though she went out of her way to hide attributes that would cause people to see her as anything other than the remarkable clinician she was.

"What was that?" she asked, pointing to the sofa cushion where I'd stashed the gun. "Are you self-prescribing again?"

"No. How did you find my house?"

"I know a woman in Personnel at UVA. You missed two consecutive sessions, but at least you called ahead to cancel. Today you leave me sitting there and you don't even call? Considering your state of mind lately, what do you expect me to do?" Rachel's eyes went to the video camera. "Oh, David . . . you're not back to this again? I thought you stopped years ago."

"It's not what you think."

She didn't look convinced. Five years ago, a drunk driver

flipped my wife's car into a roadside pond. The water wasn't deep, but both Karen and my daughter Zooey drowned before help arrived. I was working at the hospital they were brought to after the accident. Watching the ER staff try in vain to resuscitate my four-year-old daughter shattered me. I spent hours at home in front of the television, endlessly replaying videotapes of Zooey learning to walk, laughing in Karen's arms, hugging me at her third birthday party. My medical practice withered, then died, and I sank into clinical depression. This was the only fact of my personal life I had discussed in detail with my psychiatrist, and this only because after three sessions she had told me that she'd lost her only child to leukemia the year before.

She confided this because she believed my disturbing dreams were caused by the tragic loss of my family, and she wanted me to know she had felt the same kind of pain. Rachel, too, had lost more than her child. Unable to handle the devastating effects of his son's illness, her lawyer husband had left her and returned to New York. Like me, Rachel had descended into a pit of depression from which she was lucky to emerge. Therapy and medication had been her salvation. But like my father, I've always been fiercely private, and I fought my way back to the land of the living alone. Not a day went by that I didn't miss my wife and daughter, but my days of weeping as I replayed old videotapes were over.

"This isn't about Karen and Zooey," I told Rachel. "Please close the door."

She remained in the open doorway, car keys in hand, clearly wanting to believe me but just as clearly skeptical. "What is it, then?"

"Work. *Please* close the door."

Rachel hesitated, then shut the door and stared into my eyes. "Maybe it's time you told me about your work."

This had long been a point of contention between us.

14

Rachel considered doctor/patient confidentiality as sacred as the confessional, and my lack of trust offended her. She believed my demands for secrecy and warnings of danger hinted at a delusional reality I had constructed to protect my psyche from scrutiny. I didn't blame her. At the request of the NSA, I'd made my first appointment with her under a false name. But ten seconds after we shook hands, she recognized my face from the jacket photo of my book. She assumed my ruse was the paranoia of a medical celebrity, and I did nothing to disabuse her of that notion. But after a few weeks, my refusal to divulge anything about my work—and my obsession with "protecting" her—had pushed her to suspect that I might be schizophrenic.

What Rachel didn't know was that I had only been allowed to see her after winning a brutal argument with John Skow, the director of Project Trinity. My narcolepsy had developed as a result of my work at Trinity, and I wanted professional help to try to understand the accompanying dreams.

First the NSA flew in a shrink from Fort Meade, a pharmacological psychiatrist whose main patient base was technicians trying to cope with chronic stress or depression. He wanted to fill me up with happy pills and find out how to become an internationally published physician like me. Next they brought in a woman, an expert in dealing with the neuroses that develop when people are forced to work for long periods in secrecy. Her knowledge of dream symbolism was limited to "a little historical reading" during her residency. Like her colleague, she wanted to start me on a regimen of antidepressants and antipsychotics. What I needed was a psychoanalyst experienced in dream analysis, and the NSA didn't have one.

I called some friends at the UVA Medical School and discovered that Rachel Weiss, the country's preeminent Jungian analyst, was based at the Duke University Medical

School, less than fifteen miles from the Trinity building. Skow tried to stop me from seeing her, but in the end I told him he'd have to arrest me to do it, and before he tried that, he'd better call the president, who had appointed me to the project.

"Something's happened," Rachel said. "What is it? Have the hallucinations changed again?"

Hallucinations, I thought bitterly. *Never dreams.*

"Have they intensified? Become more personal? Are you afraid?"

"Andrew Fielding is dead," I said in a flat voice.

Rachel blinked. "Who's Andrew Fielding?"

"He was a physicist."

Her eyes widened. "Andrew Fielding the *physicist* is dead?"

It was a measure of Fielding's reputation that a medical doctor who knew little about quantum physics would know his name. But it didn't surprise me. There were six-year-olds who'd heard of "the White Rabbit." The man who had largely unraveled the enigma of the dark matter in the universe stood second only to his friend Stephen Hawking in the astrophysical firmament.

"He died of a stroke," I said. "Or so they say."

"So who says?"

"People at work."

"You work with Andrew Fielding?"

"I did. For the past two years."

Rachel shook her head in amazement. "You don't think he died of a stroke?"

"No."

"Did you examine him?"

"A cursory exam. He collapsed in his office. Another doctor got to him before he died. That doctor said Fielding exhibited left-side paralysis and had a blown left pupil, but . . ."

"What?"

"I don't believe him. Fielding died too quickly for a stroke. Within four or five minutes."

Rachel pursed her lips. "That happens sometimes. Especially with a severe hemorrhage."

"Yes, but it's comparatively rare, and you don't usually see a blown pupil." That was true enough, but it wasn't what I was thinking. I was thinking that Rachel was a psychiatrist, and as good as she was, she hadn't spent sixteen years practicing internal medicine, as I had. You got a feeling about certain cases, certain people. A sixth sense. Fielding had not been my patient, but he'd told me a lot about his health in two years, and a massive hemorrhage didn't feel right to me. "Look, I don't know where his body is, and I don't think there's going to be an autopsy, so—"

"Why no autopsy?" Rachel broke in.

"Because I think he was murdered."

"I thought you said he died in his office."

"He did."

"You think he was murdered at work? Workplace violence?"

She still didn't get it. "I mean premeditated murder. Carefully thought out, expertly executed murder."

"But . . . why would someone murder Andrew Fielding? He was an old man, wasn't he?"

"He was sixty-three." Recalling Fielding's body on his office floor, mouth agape, sightless eyes staring at the ceiling, I felt a sudden compulsion to tell Rachel everything. But one glance at the window killed the urge. A parabolic microphone could be trained on the glass.

"I can't say anything beyond that. I'm sorry. You should go, Rachel."

She took two steps toward me, her face set with purpose. "I'm not going anywhere yet. Look, if *anyone* died while not under a doctor's supervision in this state, there has to be an autopsy. And especially in cases of possible foul play. It's required by law."

I laughed at her naiveté. "There won't be an autopsy. Not a public one, anyway."

"David—"

"I really can't say more. I shouldn't have said that much. I just wanted you to know . . . that it's real."

"Why can't you say more?" She held up a small, graceful hand. "No, let me answer that. Because to tell me more would put me in danger. Right?"

"Yes."

She rolled her eyes. "David, from the beginning you've made extraordinary demands about secrecy. And I've complied. I've told colleagues that the hours you spend in my office are research for your second book, rather than what they really are."

"And you know I appreciate that. But if I'm right about Fielding, *anything* I tell you now could put your life at risk. Can't you understand that?"

"No. I've never understood. What sort of work could possibly be so dangerous?"

I shook my head.

"This is like a bad joke." She laughed strangely. "'I could tell you, but then I'd have to kill you.' It's classic paranoid thinking."

"Do you really believe I'm making all this up?"

Rachel answered with caution. "I believe that *you* believe everything you've told me."

"So, I'm still delusional."

"You've got to admit, you've been having disturbing hallucinations for some time now. Some of the recent ones are classic religious delusions."

"But most not," I reminded her. "And I'm an atheist. Is *that* classic?"

18

"No, I concede that. But you've also refused to get a workup for your narcolepsy. Or epilepsy. Or even to get your blood sugar checked, for that matter."

I've been worked up by the foremost neurologist in the world. "That's being investigated at work."

"By Andrew Fielding? He wasn't an M.D., was he?"

I decided to go one step further. "I'm being treated by Ravi Nara."

Her mouth fell open. "Ravi *Nara?* As in the Nobel Prize for medicine?"

"That's him," I said with distaste.

"You work with Ravi Nara?"

"Yes. He's a prick. It was Nara who said Fielding died of a stroke."

Rachel appeared at a loss. "David, I just don't know what to say. Are you really working with these famous people?"

"Is that so hard to believe? I'm reasonably famous myself."

"Yes, but . . . not in the same way. What reason would those men have to work together? They're in totally different fields."

"Until two years ago they were."

"What does that mean?"

"Go back to your office, Rachel."

"I canceled my last patient so I could come here."

"Bill me for your lost time."

She reddened. "There's no need to insult me. Please tell me what's going on. I'm tired of hearing nothing but your hallucinations."

"Dreams."

"Whatever. They're not enough to work with."

"Not for *your* purpose. But you and I have different goals. We always have. You're trying to solve the riddle of David Tennant. I'm trying to solve the riddle of my dreams."

"But the answers are bound up in who you are! Dreams aren't independent of the rest of your brain! You—"

The ringing telephone cut her off. I got up and went into the kitchen to answer it, a strange thrumming in my chest. The caller could be the president of the United States.

"Dr. Tennant," I said from years of habit.

"*Dr. David?*" cried a hysterical female voice with an Asian accent. It was Lu Li, Fielding's Chinese wife. Or widow . . .

"This is David, Lu Li. I'm sorry I haven't called you." I searched for fitting words but found only a cliché. "I can't begin to express the pain I feel at Andrew's loss—"

A burst of Cantonese punctuated with some English flashed down the wire. I didn't have to understand it all to know I was hearing a distraught widow on the verge of collapse. God only knew what the Trinity security people had told Lu Li, or what she had made of it. She'd come to America only three months ago, her immigration fast-tracked by the State Department, which had received a none-too-subtle motivational call from the White House.

"I know this has been a terrible day," I said in a comforting voice. "But I need you to try to calm down."

Lu Li was panting.

"Breathe deeply," I said, trying to decide what approach to take. Safest to use the corporate cover the NSA had insisted on from the beginning. As far as the rest of the Research Triangle Park companies knew, the Argus Optical Corporation developed optical computer elements used in government defense projects. Lu Li might know no more that this.

"What have you been told by the company?" I asked cautiously.

"*Andy dead!*" Lu Li cried. "They say he die of brain bleeding, but I know nothing. I don't know what to do!"

I saw nothing to be gained by further agitating Fielding's widow with theories of murder. "Lu Li, Andrew was sixty-three years old, and not in the best of health. A stroke isn't an unlikely event in that situation."

"You no understand, Dr. David! Andy warn me about this."

My hand tightened on the phone. "What do you mean?"

Another burst of Cantonese came down the wire, but then Lu Li settled into halting English. "Andy tell me this could happen. He say, 'If something happen to me, call Dr. David. David know what to do.'"

A deep ache gripped my heart. That Fielding had put such faith in me . . . "What do you want me to do?"

"Come here. Please. Talk to me. Tell me why this happen to Andy."

I hesitated. The NSA was probably listening to this call. To go to Lu Li's house would only put her at greater risk, and myself, too. But what choice did I have? I couldn't fail my friend. "I'll be there in twenty minutes."

"Thank you, thank you, David! Please, thank you."

I hung up and turned to go back to the living room. Rachel was standing in the kitchen doorway.

"I have to leave," I told her. "I appreciate you coming to check on me. I know it was beyond the call of duty."

"I'm going with you. I heard some of that, and I'm going with you."

"Out of the question."

"Why?"

"You have no reason to come. You're not part of this."

She folded her arms across her chest. "For me it's simple, okay? If you're telling the truth, I'll find the distraught widow of Andrew Fielding at the end of a short drive. And she'll support what you've told me."

"Not necessarily. I don't know how much Fielding confided in her. And Lu Li hardly speaks English."

"Andrew Fielding didn't teach his own wife English?"

"He spoke fluent Cantonese. Plus about eight other languages. And she's only been here a few months."

Rachel straightened her skirt with the flats of her hands. "Your resistance tells me that you know my going will expose your story as a delusion."

Anger flashed through me. "I'm tempted to let you come, just for that. But you don't grasp the danger. You could *die*. Tonight."

"I don't think so."

I picked up the Ziploc bag containing the white powder and the FedEx envelope and held it out to her. "A few minutes ago I received a letter from Fielding. This powder was in the envelope."

She shrugged. "It looks like sand. What is it?"

"I have no idea. But I'm afraid it might be anthrax. Or whatever killed Fielding."

She took the package from me. I thought at first she was examining the powder, but she was reading the label on the FedEx envelope.

"This says the sender is Lewis Carroll."

"That's code. Fielding couldn't risk putting his name into the FedEx computer system. The NSA would pick that up immediately. He used 'Lewis Carroll' because his nickname was the White Rabbit. You've heard that, right?"

Rachel looked as if she were really thinking about it. "I can't say that I have. Where's this letter?"

I motioned toward the front room. "In a plastic bag on the couch. Don't open it."

She bent over the note and quickly read it. "It's not signed."

"Of course not. Fielding didn't know who might see it. That rabbit symbol is his signature."

She looked at me with disbelief. "Just take me along, David. If what I see supports what you've told me, I'll take all your warnings seriously from this point forward. No more doubts."

"That's like throwing you into the water to prove there are sharks in it. By the time you see them, it's too late."

"That's always how it is with these kinds of fantasies."

I went and got my keys off the kitchen counter. Rachel followed at my heels. "All right, you want to come? Follow me in your car."

She shook her head. "Not a chance. You'd lose me at the first red light."

"Your colleagues would tell you it's dangerous to accompany a patient while he chases a paranoid fantasy. Especially a narcoleptic patient."

"My colleagues don't know you. As for the narcolepsy, you haven't killed yourself yet."

I reached under the sofa cushion, brought out my pistol, and thrust it into my waistband. "You don't know me either."

She studied the butt of the gun, then looked into my eyes. "I think I do. And I want to help you."

If she were only my psychiatrist, I would have left her there. But during our long sessions, we had recognized something in each other, an unspoken feeling shared by two people who had experienced great loss. Even though she thought I might be ill now, she cared about me in a way no one else had for a long time. To take her with me would be selfish, but the simple truth was, I didn't want to go alone.

23

THREE

Geli Bauer sat within the dark bowels of the Trinity building, a basement complex lit only by the glow of computer monitors and surveillance screens. From here electronic filaments spread out to monitor the people and the physical plant of Project Trinity. But that was only the center of her domain. With the touch of a computer key, Geli could interface with the NSA supercomputers at Fort Meade and monitor conversations and events on the other side of the globe. Though she had wielded many kinds of power during her thirty-two years on earth, she had never before felt the rush of knowing that all the world bounded by electronics could be manipulated by the touch of her finger.

On paper, Geli worked for Godin Supercomputing, which was based in Mountain View, California. But it was her company's quasi-governmental relationship with the NSA that had lifted her into the stratosphere of power. If she deemed a situation an emergency, she could stop trains, close international airports, retask surveillance satellites, or lift armed helicopters into the skies over U.S. soil and order them to fire. No other modern woman had wielded such power—in some ways her authority rivaled that of her father—and Geli did not intend to give it up.

On the flat-panel monitor before her glowed a transcript of the conversation between David Tennant and an unknown White House functionary, recorded at a Shoney's restaurant that afternoon, but Geli was no longer looking at it. She was speaking on the headset phone to a member of her security team, the man who was watching Tennant's residence.

"I only heard conversation in the kitchen," she said. "That makes no sense. He and Dr. Weiss had to be talking elsewhere."

"Maybe they were getting it on."

"We'd have heard it. Weiss looks like a screamer to me. It's always the quiet ones."

"What do you want me to do?"

"Get in there and check the mikes."

Geli tapped a key on the pad before her, which connected her to a young ex-Delta operator named Thomas Corelli, who was covering Andrew Fielding's house.

"What are you hearing, Thomas?"

"Normal background noise. TV. Bumps and clatters."

"Did you hear Mrs. Fielding's end of the phone call?"

"Yeah, but it's hard to understand that Chinese accent."

"Are you out of sight?"

"I'm parked in the driveway of some out-of-town neighbors."

"Tennant will be at your location in five minutes. He has a woman with him. Dr. Rachel Weiss. Stay on this line."

Geli clicked off, then said clearly, *"JPEG. Weiss, Rachel."*

A digital photograph of Rachel Weiss appeared on her monitor. It was a head shot, a telephoto taken as the psychiatrist left the Duke University hospital. Rachel Weiss was three years older than Geli, but Geli recognized the type. She'd known girls like that at boarding school in Switzerland. Strivers.

Most of them Jews. She would have known Weiss was Jewish without hearing her name or seeing her file. Even with fashionably windblown hair, Rachel Weiss looked like she carried the weight of the world on her shoulders. She had the dark martyr's eyes, the premature lines around the mouth. She was one of the top Jungian analysts in the world, and you didn't reach that level without being obsessive about your work.

Geli had been against involving Weiss. It was Skow who had allowed it. Skow's theory was that if you held the leash too tight, you were asking for trouble. But it was Geli's head that would roll if there was a security breach. To prevent that eventuality, she received transcripts of Weiss's sessions with Tennant and recordings of every telephone call the psychiatrist made. Once a week, one of her operatives slipped into Weiss's office and photocopied Tennant's file, to be sure that nothing escaped Geli's scrutiny.

That was the kind of hassle that came from dealing with civilians. It had been the same at Los Alamos, with the Manhattan Project. In both cases the government had tried to control a group of gifted civilian scientists who through ignorance, obstinacy, or ideology posed the greatest threat to their own work. When you recruited the smartest people in the world, you got crackpots.

Tennant was a crackpot. Like Fielding. Like Ravi Nara, the project's Nobel Prize–winning neuroscientist. All six Trinity principals had signed the tightest possible security and nondisclosure agreements, but they still believed they could do anything they wanted. To them the world was Disneyland. And doctors were the worst. Even in the army, the rules had never quite seemed to apply to M.D.s. But tonight Tennant was going to step far enough over the line to get his head chopped off.

Her headset beeped. She opened the line to her man at Tennant's house. "What is it?"

"I'm inside. You're not going to believe this. Someone put painter's putty in the holes over the mikes."

Geli felt a strange numbness in her chest. "How could Tennant know where they were?"

"No way without a scanner."

"Magnifying glass?"

"If he knew to look for them. But that would take hours, and you'd never be sure you got them all."

A scanner. Where the hell would an internist get that? Then she knew. *Fielding.* "Tennant took that FedEx delivery. Do you see an envelope anywhere?"

"No."

"He must have taken it with him. What else do you see? Anything strange?"

"There's a video camera set up on a tripod."

Shit. "Tape in it?"

"Let me check. No tape."

"What else?"

"A vacuum cleaner in the backyard."

What the hell? "A vacuum cleaner? Take the bag out and bring it here. We'll chopper it to Fort Meade for analysis. What else?"

"Nothing."

"Take one last look, then get out."

Geli clicked off, then said, *"Skow—home."* The computer dialed the Raleigh residence of Project Trinity's administrative director.

"Geli?" Skow said. "What's going on?"

Bauer always thought *Kennedy* when she heard John Skow's voice. Skow was a Boston Brahmin with twice the usual brains of his breed. Instead of the customary liberal arts and law background of his class, Skow had advanced degrees in astronomy and mathematics and had served for eight years as deputy director of special projects for the NSA.

27

His primary area of responsibility was the agency's top secret Supercomputer Research Center. Skow was technically Geli's superior, but their relationship had always been uncomfortable. Short of taking a human life, Geli had independent responsibility for Project Trinity's security. She held this power because Peter Godin—citing security leaks at government labs—had demanded that he pick his own team to protect Trinity.

The old man had found her just as she was leaving the army. Geli believed heart and soul in the warrior culture, but she could no longer endure the bloated and hidebound bureaucracy of the army, or its abysmal quality standards for new recruits. When Godin appeared, he'd offered her a job she had wanted all her life but hadn't believed existed.

She would receive $700,000 a year to work as chief of security for special projects for Godin Supercomputing. The salary was immense, but Godin was a billionaire. He could afford it. Her conditions of employment were unique. She would follow any order he gave, without question and without regard for legality. She would not reveal any information about her employer, his company, or her employment. If she did, she would die. Geli could hire her own staff, but they would accept the same conditions and penalty, and she would enforce that penalty. She was amazed that a public figure like Godin would dare to set such terms. Then she learned that Godin had found her through her father. That explained a lot. Geli had hardly spoken to her father in years, but he was in a position to know a lot about her. And she could tell by the way Godin looked at her that he knew something about her as well. Probably the stories that had filtered out of Iraq after Desert Storm. Peter Godin wanted a security expert, but he also wanted a killer. Geli was both.

John Skow was not. Unlike Godin, who had fought as a marine in Korea as a young man, Skow was a theoretical warrior. The NSA man had never seen blood on his hands, and around Geli he sometimes acted like a man who'd been handed a leash with a pit bull on the end of it.

"Geli?" Skow said again. "Are you there?"

"Dr. Weiss went to Tennant's house," she said into her headset.

"Why?"

"I don't know. We got almost none of their conversation. They're on their way to the Fielding house now. Lu Li Fielding called him. Upset."

Skow was silent for a moment. "Going over to comfort the grieving widow?"

"I'm sure that will be their story." She wanted to gauge Skow's level of anxiety before giving him more details. "Do we let them go in?"

"Of course. You can hear everything they say, right?"

"Maybe not. There was a problem with the bugs at Tennant's house."

"What kind of problem?"

"Tennant put putty over the mikes. And there was a video camera set up on a tripod in there. No tape in it." She let that sink in. "Either he wanted to say something on tape that he didn't want us to hear, or he wanted to talk to Dr. Weiss without us hearing. Either way, it's bad."

She listened to Skow breathe for a while.

"It's all right," he said finally. "We're going to be okay on this."

"You must know something I don't, sir."

Skow chuckled at the contempt with which she said "sir." The NSA man was tough in his own way. He had the detached coldness of mathematical intelligence. "The perks of leadership, Geli. You did well this morning, by the way. I was amazed."

Geli flashed back to Fielding's corpse. The termination had

29

gone smoothly enough, but it was a stupid move. They should have taken out Tennant as well. She could easily have manipulated both men into the same vehicle, and after that . . . simple logistics. A car accident. And the project wouldn't be in the jeopardy it was in now. "Has Tennant actually talked to the president, sir?"

"I don't know. So keep your distance. Monitor the situation, but nothing more."

"He also took a delivery from FedEx. A letter. Whatever it was, he took it with him. We need to see that."

"If you can get a look at it without him knowing, fine. Otherwise, talk to FedEx and find out who sent it."

"We're doing that."

"Good. Just don't—"

Geli heard Skow's wife calling his name.

"Just keep me informed," he said, and rang off.

Geli closed her eyes and began to breathe deeply. She had made the case to Godin for taking out Tennant along with Fielding, but the old man had resisted. Yes, Godin conceded, Tennant had broken regulations and spent time with Fielding outside the facility. Yes, Tennant had supported Fielding's effort to suspend the project. And it was Tennant's tie to the president that had made that suspension a reality. But there was no proof that Tennant was part of the Englishman's campaign to sabotage the project, or that he was privy to any of the dangerous information Fielding possessed. Since Geli did not know what that information was, she could not judge the risk of letting Tennant live. She had reminded Godin of the maxim "Better safe than sorry," but Godin did not relent. He would though. Soon.

Geli said, "*JPEG, Fielding, Lu Li.*" An image of a dark-haired Asian woman appeared on her monitor. Born Lu Li Cheng, reared in Canton Province, Communist China. Forty years old. Advanced degrees in applied physics.

"Another mistake," Geli muttered. Lu Li Cheng had no business inside the borders of the United States, much less in the inner circle of the most sensitive scientific project in the country. Geli touched the key that connected her to Thomas Corelli in the surveillance car outside the Fielding house. "You see anything strange over there?"

"No."

"How easily could you search Tennant's car when he arrives?"

"Depends on where he parks."

"If you see a FedEx envelope in the car, break in, read it, then put it back. And I want video of their arrival."

"No problem. What are you looking for?"

"I'm not sure. Just get it."

Geli removed a pack of Gauloises from her desk, took out a cigarette, and broke off its filter. In the flare of the match she caught her reflection in her computer monitor. A veil of blonde hair, high cheekbones, steel-blue eyes, nasty burn scar. She considered the ugly ridged tissue on her left cheek as much a part of her face as her eyes or mouth. A plastic surgeon had once offered to remove the discolored mark at no cost, but she'd turned him down. Scars had a purpose: to remind their bearer of wounds. The wound that had caused that scar she would never let herself forget.

She punched a key and routed the signals from the microphones in the Fielding house to her headset. Then she drew deeply on her cigarette, settled back in her chair, and blew a stream of harsh smoke toward the ceiling. Geli Bauer hated many things, but most of all she hated waiting.

FOUR

We drove in silence, the Acura moving swiftly through the dusk. At this time of evening, it was a quick ride from my suburb to Andrew Fielding's house near the University of North Carolina at Chapel Hill. Rachel didn't understand my demand for silence, and I didn't expect her to. When I first became involved in Trinity, the xenophobic level of security had stunned me. The other scientists—Fielding included—had worked on defense-related projects before and accepted the intrusive security as a necessary inconvenience. But eventually, even the veterans complained that we were enduring something unprecedented. Surveillance was all-pervasive and reached far beyond the lab complex. Protests were met with a curt reminder that the scientists on the Manhattan Project had been forced to live behind barbed wire to ensure the security of "the device." The freedom we enjoyed came with a price—or so went the party line.

Fielding didn't buy it. "Random" polygraph tests occurred almost weekly, and surveillance extended even into our homes. Before I could begin my video today, I'd had to plug pinholes in my walls that concealed tiny microphones. Fielding discovered them with a special scanner he'd built at home and marked the bugs with tiny pins. He had made something of a hobby out of evading Trinity surveillance. He warned me that speaking confidentially in cars was impossible. Automobiles were simple to bug, and even clean vehicles could be covered from a distance, using special high-tech microphones. The Englishman's cat-and-mouse game with the NSA had amused me at times, but there was no doubt about who had got the last laugh.

I looked over at Rachel. It felt strange to be in a car with her. In the five years since my wife's death, I'd had relationships with two women, both before my assignment to Trinity. My time with Rachel wasn't a "relationship" in the romantic sense. Two hours per week for the past three months, I had sat in a room with her and discussed the most disturbing aspect of my life—my dreams. Through her questions and interpretations, she had probably revealed more about herself than she had learned about me, yet much remained hidden.

She'd come down from New York Presbyterian to accept the faculty position at Duke, where she taught a small cadre of psychiatry residents Jungian analysis, a dying art in the world of modern pharmacological psychiatry. She also saw private patients and carried out psychiatric research. After two years of virtual solitude working on Trinity, I would have found contact with any intelligent woman provocative. But Rachel had far more than intelligence to offer. Sitting in her leather chair, dressed impeccably, her dark hair pulled up in a French braid, she would watch me with unblinking concentration, as though peering into depths of my mind that even I had not plumbed. Sometimes her face—and particularly her eyes—became the whole room for me. They were the environment I occupied, the audience I confided in, the judgment I awaited. But those eyes were slow to judge, at least in the beginning. She would question me about certain images, then question the answers I gave. She sometimes offered interpretations of my dreams, but unlike the NSA psychiatrists I had seen, she never spoke with a tone of infallibility. She seemed to be searching for meaning along with me, prodding me to interpret the images myself.

"David, you don't have to drive around all night," she said. "I'm not going to hold this against you."

Right, I thought. *What's wrong with delusions of a secret government conspiracy?* "Be patient," I told her. "It's not much farther."

She looked at me in the semidark, her eyes skeptical. "What's the monetary award for a Nobel Prize?"

"About a million U.S. Fielding got a little less than Ravi Nara, because . . ." I trailed off, realizing that she was only probing again, trying to puncture my "delusion."

I focused on the road, knowing that in a few minutes she would have to admit that my paranoia was at least partially grounded in fact. What would she think then? Would she open her mind to my interpretation of my dreams, however irrational it might sound?

From our first session, Rachel had argued that she could not make valid interpretations of my "hallucinations" without knowing intimate details of my past and my work. But I couldn't tell much. Fielding had warned me that the NSA would consider anyone who knew anything about Trinity or its principals to be a potential threat. Beyond this concern, I felt that what I saw during my narcoleptic episodes had nothing to do with my past. The images seemed to be coming from *outside* my mind. Not in the sense of hearing alien voices, which was a marker for schizophrenia, but in the classical sense of visions. *Revealed* visions, like those described by prophets. For a man who had not believed in God since he was a boy, it was a singularly disturbing state of affairs.

My dreams had not begun with the first narcoleptic attacks. The first episodes were true blackouts. Holes in my life. Gaps

34

of time, lost forever. I would be working at my office computer, then suddenly become aware of a high-pitched vibration in my body. Generalized at first, it would quickly localize to my teeth. This was a classic onset symptom of narcolepsy. I'd begin to feel drowsy, then suddenly jerk awake in my chair and find that forty minutes had passed. It was like going under anesthesia. No memory at all.

The dreams began after a week of blackouts. The first one was always the same, a recurring nightmare that frightened me more than the blackouts had. I remember how intrigued Rachel was when I first recounted it, and how uncharacteristically sure she was that she understood the image. I sat in the deeply padded chair opposite her desk, closed my eyes, and described what I had seen so often.

I'm sitting in a dark room. There's no light at all. No sound. I can feel my eyes with my fingers, my ears, too, but I see and hear nothing. I remember nothing. I have no past. And because I see and hear nothing, I have no present. I simply am. That's my reality. I AM. I feel like a stroke victim imprisoned within a body and brain that no longer function. I can think, but not of any specific images. I feel more than I think. And what I feel is this: Who am I? Where did I come from? Why am I alone? Was I always here? Will I always be here? These thoughts don't merely fill my mind. They are my mind. There's no time as we know it, only the questions changing from one to another. Eventually, the questions resolve into a single mantra: Where did I come from? Where did I come from? I'm a brain-damaged man sitting in a room for eternity, asking one question of the darkness.

"Don't you see?" Rachel had said. "You haven't fully dealt with the deaths of your wife and daughter. Their loss cut you off from the world, and from yourself. You *are* damaged. You *are* wounded. The man walking around in the world of light is an act. The real David Tennant is sitting in that dark room, unable to think or feel. No one feels his grief or his pain."

"That's not it," I told her. "I did a psychiatry rotation, for God's sake. This isn't unresolved grief."

She sighed and shook her head. "Doctors always make the worst patients."

A week later, I told her the dream had changed.

"There's something in the room with me now."

"What is it?"

"I don't know. I can't see it."

"But you know it's there?"

"Yes."

"Is it a person?"

"No. It's very small. A sphere, floating in space. A black golf ball floating in the dark."

"How do you know it's there?"

"It's like a deeper darkness at the center of the dark. And it pulls at me."

"Pulls how?"

"I don't know. Like gravity. Emotional gravity. But I know this. It knows the answer to my questions. It knows who I am and why I'm stuck in that dark room."

And so it went, with slight variations, until the dream changed again. When it did, it changed profoundly. One night, while reading at home, I "went under" in the usual way. I found myself sitting in the familiar lightless room, asking my question of the black ball. Then, without warning, the ball exploded into retina-scorching light. After so much darkness, the striking of a match would have seemed an explosion, but this was no match. It blasted outward in all directions with the magnitude of a hydrogen bomb. Only this explosion did not suck back into itself and blossom into a mushroom cloud. It expanded with infinite power and speed, and I had the horrifying sense of being devoured by it, devoured but not destroyed. As the blinding light consumed the darkness, which was me, I somehow knew that this could go on for billions of years without destroying me altogether. Yet still I was afraid.

Rachel didn't know what to make of this dream. Over the next three weeks, she listened as I described the births of stars and galaxies, their lives and deaths: black holes, supernovas, flashes of nebulae like powdered diamonds flung into the blackness, planets born and dying. I seemed to see from one end of the universe to the other, all objects at once as they expanded into me at the speed of light.

"Have you seen images like these before?" she asked me. "In waking life?"

"How could I?"

"Have you seen photographs taken by the Hubble space telescope?"

"Of course."

"They're very much like what you're describing."

Frustration crept into my voice. "You don't understand. I'm not just seeing this. I'm *feeling* it. The way I might feel watching children, or combat, or lovers together. It's not merely a visual display."

"Go on."

That was what she always said. I closed my eyes and submerged myself in my most recent dream.

"I'm watching a planet. Hovering above it. There are clouds, but not as we know them. They're green like acid, and tortured by storms. I'm diving now, diving down through the clouds, like a satellite image zooming in to ground level. There's an ocean below, but it's not blue. It's red, and boiling. I plunge through its surface, deep into the red. I'm looking for something, but it's not there. This ocean is empty."

"A lot of things came to me when you described that," Rachel said. "The color imagery first. Red could be important.

37

The empty ocean is a symbol of barrenness, which expresses your aggrieved state." She hesitated. "What are you looking for in that ocean?"

"I don't know."

"I think you do."

"I'm not looking for Karen and Zooey."

"David." A hint of irritation in her voice. "If you don't think these images are symbolic, why are you here?"

I opened my eyes and looked at her perfectly composed face. A curtain of professionalism obscured her empathy, but I saw the truth. She was projecting her sense of loss about her own family onto me.

"I'm here because I can't find answers on my own," I said. "Because I've read a mountain of books, and they haven't helped."

She nodded gravely. "How do you remember the hallucinations in such detail? Do you write them down when you wake up?"

"No. They aren't like normal dreams, where the harder you try to remember, the less you can. These are indelible. Isn't that a feature of narcoleptic dreams?"

"Yes," she said softly. "All right. Karen and Zooey died in water. They both drowned. Karen probably bled a good bit from her hands, and where she hit her head on the steering wheel. That would give us red water." Rachel reclined her chair and looked at the ceiling tiles. "These hallucinations have no people in them, yet you experience strong emotional reactions. You mentioned combat. Have you ever been in combat?"

"No."

"But you know that Karen fought to save Zooey. She fought to stay alive. You told me that."

I shut my eyes. I didn't like to think about that part of it, but sometimes I couldn't banish the thoughts. When Karen's car flipped into the pond, it had landed on its roof and sunk into a foot of soft mud. The electric windows shorted out, and the doors were impossible to open. Broken bones in Karen's hands and feet testified to the fury with which she had fought to smash the windows. She was a small woman, not physically strong, but she had not given up. A paramedic from the accident scene told me that when the car was finally winched out of the muck and its doors opened, he found her in the backseat, one arm wrapped tightly around Zooey, the other arm floating free, that hand shattered and lacerated over the knuckles.

What had happened was clear. As water filled the car and Karen fought to break the windows, Zooey had panicked. Anyone would, and especially a child. At that point, some mothers would have kept fighting while their child screamed in terror. Others would have comforted their child and prayed for help to come. But Karen had pulled Zooey tight against her, promised her that everything was going to be all right, and then with her feet fought to her last breath to escape the waterbound coffin. For her to cling to Zooey while suffering the agony of anoxia testified to a love stronger than terror, and that knowledge had helped bring me some peace.

"Green clouds and a red ocean have nothing to do with a car accident five years ago," I said.

"No? Then I think you should tell me more about your childhood."

"It's not relevant."

"You can't know that," Rachel insisted.

"I do."

"Tell me about your work, then."

"I teach medical ethics."

"You took a leave of absence over a year ago."

I whipped my head toward her and opened my eyes. "How do you know that?"

39

"I heard it at the hospital."

"Who said it?"

"I don't remember. I overheard it. You're very well known in the medical community. Physicians at Duke refer to your book all the time. They did at New York Presbyterian, too. So, is it true? Did you take a leave of absence from the medical school?"

"Let's stick to the dreams, okay? It's safer for both of us."

"Safer how?"

I didn't answer.

By the next week's appointment, the dreams had changed again.

"I'm looking at the Earth. Suspended in space. It's the most beautiful thing I've ever seen. Blue and green with swirling white clouds. It's a living thing, a perfect closed system. I dive through the clouds, a hundred-mile swan dive into deep blue ocean. It's bursting with life. Giant molecules, multicelled creatures, jellyfish, squid, serpents, sharks. The land, too, is teeming. Covered with jungle. A symphony of green. On the shore, fish flop out of the waves and grow legs. Strange crabs scuttle onto the sand and change into other animals I've never seen. Time is running in fast-forward, like evolution run through a projector at a million times natural speed. Dinosaurs morph into birds, rodents into mammals. Primates lose their hair. Ice sheets flatten the jungles and then melt into savannah. Twenty thousand years pass in one breath—"

"Take it slow," Rachel advised. "You're getting agitated."

"How could I be seeing all that?"

"You know the answer. Your mind can create any conceivable image and make it real. That photograph of the earth from space is an icon of modern culture. It moves everyone who sees it, and you must have seen it fifty times since childhood."

40

"My mind can create animals I've never seen? Realistic-looking animals?"

"Of course. You've seen Hieronymus Bosch paintings. And I've seen the kind of time-lapse images you're describing on television. In the old days, *Life* magazine did things like that in print. 'The Ascent of Man,' like that. The question is, *why* are you seeing these things?"

"That's what I'm here to find out."

"Are you present in this surreal landscape?"

"No."

"What do you feel?"

"I'm still looking for something."

"What?"

"I don't know. I'm like a bird scanning the earth and sea for . . . something."

"Are you a bird in the dream?"

She sounded hopeful. Birds must mean something in the lexicon of dream interpretation. "No."

"What are you?"

"Nothing, really. A pair of eyes."

"An observer."

"Yes. A disembodied observer. T. J. Eckleburg."

"Who?"

"Nothing. Something from Scott Fitzgerald."

"Oh. I remember." She put the end of her pen in her mouth and bit it. An unusual gesture for her. "Do you have an opinion about why you're seeing all this?"

"Yes." I knew my next words would surprise her. "I believe someone is showing it to me."

Her eyes widened, practically histrionics from Rachel Weiss. "Really?"

"Yes."

"Who is showing this to you?"

"I have no idea. Why do *you* think I'm seeing it?"

She moved her head from side to side. I could almost see her neurons firing, processing my words through the filters that education and experience had embedded in her brain. "Evolution is change," she said. "You're seeing change sped up to unnatural velocity. Uncontrollable change. I sense this may have something to do with your work."

You could be right, I thought, but I didn't say that. I simply moved on. My silence was her only protection. In the end, it didn't matter, because the theme of evolution died, and what came to dominate my sleeping mind shook me to the core.

There were people in my new dreams. They couldn't see me, and I only saw flashes of them. It was as though I were watching damaged strips of film cobbled together out of order. A woman walking with a baby on her hip. A man drawing water from a well. A soldier in uniform, carrying a short sword, the *gladius* I had learned about in Mrs. Whaley's eighth-grade Latin class. A *Roman* soldier. That was my first real clue that this was no random series of images, but scenes from a particular era. I saw oxen pulling plows. A young woman selling herself on the street. Men exchanging money. Gold and copper coins with the imperious profile of an emperor upon them. And a name. *Tiberius.* The name triggered something in my mind, so I checked the Internet. The successor of Augustus, Tiberius was a former commander of legions who spent much of his reign leading military campaigns in Germania. One of the few important events of his rule—seen through the lens of hindsight—was the execution of a Jewish peasant said to have claimed to be king of the Jews.

"Was your father deeply religious?" Rachel asked, upon hearing about these new images.

"No. He was . . . he looked at the world in a more fundamental way."

42

"What do you mean by that?"

"It's not relevant."

An exasperated sigh. "Your mother, then?"

"She had faith in something greater than humanity, but she wasn't big on organized religion."

"You had no religious indoctrination as a child?"

"Sunday school for a couple of years. It didn't take."

"What denomination?"

"Methodist. It was the closest church to our house."

"Did they show films about Jesus's life?"

"It's possible. I don't remember."

"You grew up in Oak Ridge, Tennessee, right? It's more probable than not. And of course we've all seen the grand biblical epics from the fifties. *The Ten Commandments. Ben-Hur.* Those things."

"What are you saying?"

"Only that the accoutrements of these hallucinations have been sitting in your subconscious for years. They're in all of us. But your dreams seem to be moving toward something. And that something may be Jesus of Nazareth."

"Have you heard of dreams like this before?" I asked.

"Of course. Many people dream of Jesus. Of personal interactions with him, receiving messages from him. But your dream progression has a certain logic to it, and a naturalistic tone rather than the wildness of obsessive fantasy. Also, you claim to be an atheist. Or at least agnostic. I'm very interested to see where this goes."

I appreciated her interest, but I was tired of waiting for answers. "But what do you think it *means*?"

She pursed her lips, then shook her head. "I'm no longer convinced that this has to do with the loss of your wife and daughter. But the truth is, I simply don't know enough about your life to make an informed evaluation."

We were at a stalemate. I still didn't believe that my past

had anything to do with my dreams. Yet as the days passed, the scarred strips of film in my head began to clear, and certain dream characters to reappear. The faces I saw became familiar, like friends. Then more familiar than friends. A feeling was growing in me that I *remembered* these faces, and not merely from previous dreams. I described them for Rachel as accurately as I could.

I'm sitting in the midst of a circle, rapt bearded faces watching me. I know I'm speaking, because they're obviously listening to me, yet I can't hear my own words.

I see a woman's face, angelic yet common, and a pair of eyes I know like those of my mother. They don't belong to my mother, though, not the mother who raised me in Oak Ridge. Yet they watch me with pure love. A bearded man stands behind her, watching me with a father's pride. But my father was clean shaven all his life. . . .

I see donkeys . . . a date palm. Naked children. A brown river. I feel the cold, jarring shock of immersion, the beat of my feet on sand. I see a young girl, beautiful and dark-haired, leaning toward my face for a kiss, then blushing and running away. I'm walking among adults. Their faces say, This child is not like other children. A wild-eyed man stands waist deep in water, a line of men and women awaiting their turn to be submerged, while others come up from the water coughing and sputtering, their eyes wide.

Sometimes the dreams had no logic, but were only disjointed fragments. When logic finally returned, it frightened me.

I'm sitting beside the bed of a small boy. He can't move. His eyes are closed. He's been paralyzed for two days. His mother and aunt sit with me. They bring food, cool water, oil to anoint the boy. I speak softly in his ear. I tell the women to hold his hands. Then I lean down and speak his name. His eyes squeeze tight, expressing mucus. Then they open and light up with recognition of his mother. His mother

44

gasps, then screams that his hand moved. She lifts him up, and he hugs her. The women weep with happiness. . . .

I'm eating with a group of women. Olives and flat bread. Some women won't meet my eyes. After the meal, they take me into a bedroom, where a pregnant girl lies on the bed. They tell me the baby has been inside her too long. Labor will not begin. They fear the child is dead. I ask the women to leave. The young mother fears me. I calm her with soft words, then lift the blanket and lay my hands on her belly. It's distended, tight as a drum. I leave my hands there for a long time, gently urging, speaking softly to her. I can't understand what I'm saying. It's like a soft chant. After a time, her mouth opens. She's felt a kick. She cries out for the other women. "My baby is alive!" The women lay their hands on me, trying to touch me as if I possess some invisible power. "Surely he is the one," they say.

"These are stories from the Bible," Rachel said, "known by millions of schoolchildren. There's nothing unique about them."

"I've been reading the New Testament," I told her. "There's no record of Jesus healing a little boy of paralysis. No description of him eating a meal with only women, then inducing labor."

"But those are both *healing* images. "And you're a physician. Your subconscious seems to be casting Jesus in your image. Or vice versa. Perhaps the problem really is your work. Have you moved further away from pure medicine? I've known doctors who fell into depression after giving up hands-on patient care for pure research. Perhaps this is something like that?"

She'd guessed correctly about my moving away from patient care, but my lucid dreams weren't some strange expression of nostalgia for my days in the white coat.

"There's another possibility," she suggested. "One more in line with my original interpretation. These images of divine healing could be subconscious wishes that you could bring Karen and Zooey back. Think about it. What were two of Jesus' most notable miracles?"

I nodded reluctantly. "Raising Lazarus from the dead."

"Yes. And he also resurrected a little girl, if I'm not mistaken."

"Yes. But I don't think that's the significance of these dreams."

Rachel smiled with infinite patience. "Well, one thing is certain. Eventually, your subconscious will make its message clear."

That turned out to be our last session. Because that night, my dreams changed again, and I had no intention of telling Rachel how.

The new dream was clearer than any that had come before, and though I was speaking in a foreign language, I could understand my words. I was walking down a sandy road. I came to a well. The water was low in the well, and I had nothing to draw it with. After a time, a woman came with an urn on a rope. I asked if she would draw me some water. She appeared surprised that I would speak to her, and I sensed that we were of different tribes. I told her the water in the well would not cure her thirst. We talked for a time, and she began to look at me with appraising eyes.

"I can see you are a prophet," she said. "You see many things that are hidden."

"I'm no prophet," I told her.

She watched me in silence for a while. Then she said, "They speak of a Messiah who will come someday to tell us things. What do you think of that?"

I looked at the ground, but words of profound conviction

46

rose unbidden into my throat. I looked at the woman and said, "I that speak to you am he."

The woman did not laugh. She knelt and touched my knee, then walked away, looking back over her shoulder again and again.

When I snapped out of that dream, I was soaked in sweat. I didn't lift the phone and call Rachel for an emergency appointment. I saw no point. I no longer believed any dream interpretation could help me, because I was not dreaming. I was *remembering*.

"What are you thinking about?" Rachel asked from the passenger seat.

We were nearing the UNC campus. "How you got here."

She shifted in her seat and gave me a concerned look. "I'm here because you missed three sessions, and you wouldn't have done that unless things had taken a turn for the worse. I think your hallucinations have changed again, and they've scared the hell out of you."

I gripped the wheel tighter but didn't speak. Somewhere, the NSA was listening.

"Why don't you tell me?" she said. "What could be the harm?"

"This isn't the time. Or the place."

The UNC theater was up ahead on the left. To our right the Forest Amphitheater lay in the trees below the road. I made a hard right and coasted down a dark hill on a street that ran between two rows of stately homes, a single-entrance neighborhood that housed tenured professors and affluent young professionals. Fielding had lived in a small, two-story house set well back from the street. Perfect for him and the Chinese wife he hoped to bring to America.

"Where are we?" Rachel asked.

"Fielding's house is right up here."

I looked in the direction of the house but saw only darkness. I'd expected to find the place ablaze with light, as my own had been after I lost Karen and Zooey. I had a moment of panic, a premonition that I'd driven into one of those 1970s conspiracy films where you walk up to a familiar house and find it vacant. Or worse, with an entirely new family living there.

A porch light clicked on thirty yards from the street. Lu Li must have been watching from a darkened window. I turned my head and scanned the street for suspicious vehicles. I frequently spotted the NSA surveillance cars assigned to tail me. Either the security teams didn't care if we saw them or, more likely, they wanted us to know we were being watched. Tonight I saw nothing suspicious, but I did sense that something wasn't as it should be. Perhaps there were watchers who did not want to be seen. I turned into Fielding's driveway and pulled up to the closed garage door.

"A Nobel laureate lives here?" Rachel asked, gesturing at the modest house.

"Lived," I corrected. "Stay here. I'm going to the door alone."

"For God's sake," she snapped. "This is ridiculous. Just admit this is all a charade, and let's go get some coffee and talk about it."

I grabbed her arm and looked hard into her eyes. "*Listen* to me, damn it. It's probably okay, but this is the way we're going to do it. I'll whistle when it's all right for you to come up."

I walked up to the front door of my dead friend's house, my hands in plain sight, my mind on the .38 in my pocket.

FIVE

Geli Bauer listened intently as Corelli reported from the Fielding house.

"They're going inside now. Tennant went up first. The shrink is hanging back. Now she's going up. Wait . . . I think the doc is carrying."

"Which doc?"

"Oh. Tennant. He's got a gun in his pocket. Right front."

"You see the butt?"

"No, but it looks like a revolver."

What the hell does Tennant think he's up to? The cell connection crackled.

"What do you want me to do?" asked Corelli.

"Sit tight and make sure the mikes are working."

"The widow just answered the door. She's pulling them inside."

"Keep me posted."

Geli killed the connection to Corelli. If Tennant was carrying a gun, he was afraid for his life. He must believe Fielding had been murdered. But why? The drug that had killed Fielding caused a fatal bleed in the brain—a true stroke. Without an autopsy, murder couldn't be proved. And there would be no autopsy. Tennant must know more than Godin thought he did. If the FedEx letter he'd received had been sent by Fielding, it might have contained some sort of evidence.

She touched her headset mike and said, "*Skow. Home.*" Her computer dialed John Skow's house in Raleigh.

"What is it now?" Skow said after two rings.

"Tennant and Weiss hardly spoke on the way to Fielding's house."

"So?"

"It wasn't natural. They're avoiding conversation."

"Tennant knows he's under surveillance. You've always wanted them all to know that."

"Yes, but Tennant's never been evasive like this. He's up to something."

"He's a little freaked-out. It's natural."

"He's carrying a gun."

A pause. "Okay, he's a lot freaked-out. We knew he had one in his house."

"That's different than carrying the damn thing."

Skow chuckled. "That's the kind of reaction you inspire in people, Geli. Seriously, you need to calm down. Everything is context. We know Tennant was suspicious already. His best friend died today. He's naturally paranoid. What we don't want to do is make him *more* suspicious."

She wished she could talk to Godin. She'd tried his private cell number, but he hadn't answered or called back. It was the first time that had ever happened. "Look, I think—"

"I know what you think," Skow said. "Take no steps without my approval."

"Asshole," Geli said, but Skow was already off the line.

She pressed a button that connected her to NSA headquarters at Fort Meade. Her liaison there was a young man named Conklin.

50

"Hello, Ms. Bauer," he said. "You calling about the FedEx query again?"

"What do you think?"

"I've got what you want. The package was dropped into a collection box at a post office in Durham, North Carolina. The sender was listed as Lewis Carroll."

So, Fielding *had* sent something to Tennant. She knew he hadn't dropped it off himself, but his wife almost certainly had. Geli clicked off and leaned back in her chair, reassessing the situation.

Seven hours ago, she had killed a man on Godin's order, without knowing precisely why. She had no problem with that. Fielding posed a threat to the project, and under the conditions of her contract, that was enough. If she needed a moral justification, Project Trinity was critical to American national security. Executing Fielding was like killing a spy caught in the act of treason. Still, she was curious as to motive. Godin had told her that Fielding was sabotaging the project and stealing Trinity data. Geli wasn't sure. Rigorous precautions had been taken to prevent sabotage. No one could physically move data in or out of the building. And as for electronic theft, Skow's NSA techs made sure that not a single electron left the building without first being cleared by him.

So, why did Fielding have to die? Six weeks ago, he and Tennant had gotten the project suspended by raising medical and ethical concerns. If that were the motive, then why wait to kill Fielding? And why kill only him? Peter Godin had appeared almost desperate when he visited Geli last night. And she had never seen Godin desperate before. Was he that anxious to get the project back on-line? She knew little about the technical side of the Trinity research, but she did know that success was still quite a ways off. She could read that in the faces of the scientists and engineers who reported to work every day.

51

Project Trinity was building—or attempting to build—a supercomputer. Not a conventional supercomputer like a Cray or a Godin, but a computer dedicated to artificial intelligence—a true thinking machine. She didn't know what made this theoretical computer so difficult to build, but Godin had told her a little about the genesis of the project.

In 1994, a Bell Labs scientist had theorized that an almost infinitely powerful code-breaking computer might be built using the principles of quantum physics. Geli knew little about quantum physics, but she understood why a quantum computer would be revolutionary. Modern digital encryption—the code system used by banks, corporations, and national governments—was based on the factoring of large prime numbers. Conventional supercomputers like those used by the NSA cracked those codes by trying one key after another in sequence, like testing keys in a lock. Breaking a code this way could take hundreds of hours. But a quantum computer—in theory—could try all possible keys simultaneously. The wrong keys would cancel each other out, leaving only the proper one to break the code. And this process wouldn't take hours or even minutes. A quantum computer could break digital encryption codes *instantaneously*. Such a machine would render present-day encryption obsolete and give whatever country possessed it a staggering strategic advantage over every other nation in the world.

Given the potential value of such a machine, the NSA had launched a massive secret effort to design and build a quantum computer. Designated Project Spooky, after the description Albert Einstein had given to the action of certain quantum particles—"spooky action at a distance"—it was placed under the direction of John Skow, director of the NSA's Supercomputer Research Center. After spending seven years and $600 million of the NSA's black budget, Skow's team had not produced a prototype that could rival the performance of a Palm Pilot.

Skow was probably days from being terminated when he received a call from Peter Godin, who had been building conventional supercomputers for the NSA for years. Godin proposed a machine as revolutionary as a quantum computer, but with one attribute the government could not resist: it could be built using refinements of existing technology. Moreover, after a conversation with Andrew Fielding, the quantum physicist he'd already enlisted to work on his machine, Godin believed there was a strong chance that his computer would have quantum capabilities.

By dangling these plums before the president, Godin had been able to secure almost every concession he demanded. A dedicated facility to work on his new machine. Virtually unlimited government funds to pay for a crash effort modeled on the Manhattan Project. The right to hire and fire his own scientists. For government oversight he got John Skow, whom he had compromised years before by bribing Skow to choose Godin computers over Crays for the Supercomputer Research Center. The president's single demand had been on-site ethical oversight, which materialized in the form of David Tennant. And Tennant had seemed only a minor annoyance in the beginning. Everything had seemed perfect.

But now two years had passed. Nearly a billion dollars had been spent, and there was still no working Trinity prototype. In the secret corridors of the NSA's Crypto City, people were starting to draw parallels to the failed Project Spooky. The difference, of course, was Peter Godin. Even Godin's enemies conceded that he had never failed to deliver on a promise. But this time, they whispered, he might have taken on more than he could handle. Artificial intelligence might not be as theoretical as quantum computing, but more than a few companies had gone bankrupt by promising to deliver it.

Which was why Geli didn't understand the necessity of Fielding's death. Until last night, Godin had apparently viewed the brilliant Englishman as critical to Project Trinity's success. Then suddenly he was expendable. What had changed?

On impulse, she punched her keyboard and called up a list of Fielding's personal effects, which she had made after his death, at Godin's request. Fielding's office had been a jumble of oddities and memorabilia, more like a college professor's than that of a working physicist.

There were books, of course. A copy of the Upanishads in the original Sanskrit. A volume of poetry by W. B. Yeats. Three well-thumbed novels by Raymond Chandler. A copy of *Alice Through the Looking Glass*. Various scientific textbooks and treatises. The other objects were more incongruous. Four pairs of dice, one pair weighted. One cobra's fang. A mint copy of *Penthouse* magazine. A saxophone reed. A Tibetan prayer bowl. A wall calendar featuring the drawings of M. C. Escher. A tattered poster from the Club-à-Go-Go in Newcastle, England, where Jimi Hendrix had played in 1967, autographed by the guitarist. A framed letter from Stephen Hawking conceding a wager the two men had made about the nature of dark matter, whatever that was. There were store-bought compact discs by Van Morrison, John Coltrane, Miles Davis. The list of objects went on, but all seemed innocuous enough. Geli had flipped through the books herself, and a technician was listening to every track on the CDs, to make sure they weren't fakes being used to store stolen data. Aside from Fielding's office junk, there were his wallet, his clothes, and his jewelry. The jewelry was simple: one gold wedding ring, and one gold pocket watch on a chain, with a crystal fob on the end.

As she pondered the list, Geli suddenly wondered whether all this stuff was still in the storage room where she had locked it this afternoon. She wondered because John Skow had access to that room. What if Fielding had been killed for something in his possession? Maybe that was why they'd wanted him to die at work. To be sure they got whatever it was they wanted. If so, it would have to be something he carried on him. Otherwise they could simply have taken it from his office. Geli was about to go check the storage room when her headset beeped again.

"I think we've got a problem," Corelli said.

"What?"

"Just like Tennant's house. They're inside, but I'm not hearing any conversation. Just faint echoes, like spillover from mikes in a distant room."

"Shit." Geli routed the signal from the Fielding house microphones to her headset. She heard only silence. "Something's going down," she murmured. "What do you have with you?"

"I've got a parabolic, but it's no good through walls and next to useless with a window. I need the laser rig."

"That's here." She mentally cataloged her resources. "I'll have it to you in twelve minutes."

"They could be gone in twelve minutes."

"What about night vision?"

"I wasn't expecting anything tactical."

Goddamn it. "It's all on the way. Check Tennant's car for that FedEx envelope. And give me the address of the driveway where you're parked."

Geli wrote it down, then pressed a button that sounded a tone in a room at the back of the basement complex. There were beds there, for times when her teams needed to work around the clock. Thirty seconds later, a tall man with long blond hair shuffled sleepily into the control center.

"*Was ist* this?" he asked.

"We're going on alert," Geli said, pointing to a coffee machine against the wall. "Drink."

Ritter Bock was German, and the only member of her team handpicked by Peter Godin. A former GSG-9 commando, Ritter had worked for an elite private security service that provided bodyguards for Godin when he traveled in Europe and the Far East. Godin had hired Ritter permanently after the former commando averted a kidnapping attempt on the billionaire. Ruthless, nerveless, and skilled in areas beyond his counterterror specialty, the twenty-nine-year-old had turned out to be Geli's best operative. And since she had spent her early summers in Germany, there was no language problem.

Ritter sipped from a steaming mug and looked at Geli over its rim. He had the gray machine-gunner's eyes of the boys who had attracted her as a teenager, while her father was stationed in Germany.

"I need you to deliver the laser rig to Corelli," she said. "He's parked in a driveway near the UNC campus."

She tore off the top sheet of her notepad and laid it on the desktop beside her.

Ritter sniffed and nodded. He hated gofer jobs like this one, but he never complained. He did the scut work and waited patiently for the jobs he was born to do.

"Is the laser in the ordnance room?" he asked.

"Yes. Take four night-vision rigs with you."

He drained the steaming coffee, then picked up the address off the desk and left the room without a word. Geli liked that. Americans felt they had to fill every silence, as though silence were something to be feared. Ritter wasted no effort, either in conversation or in action. This made him valuable. Sometimes they worked together, other times she slept with him. It hadn't caused problems yet. She'd been that way in the army, too, taking her pleasure where she could find it. Just as she had at boarding school in Switzerland. There was always risk. You just had to be able to handle aggressive men—or women—and the fallout after you'd finished with them. She had always been up to both tasks.

"Corelli?" she said. "What are you hearing now?"

"Still nothing. Faint spillover. Unintelligible."

"I'm calling an alert. Ritter's on the way."

There was only static and silence. Geli smiled. Ritter made the others uncomfortable. "Did you hear me?"

"Affirmative. I'm at Tennant's car now."

"What do you see?"

"No FedEx envelope. He must have taken it inside with him."

"Okay."

"What do you want me to do?"

"Go back to your car and wait for Ritter."

"Right."

Geli clicked off and thought again about Fielding's personal effects in the storeroom. She had a feeling something was missing, and her instincts were usually dead-on. But she didn't want to leave the control center now. Once Ritter reached the scene, things could happen fast.

SIX

I pulled Rachel into the foyer of the Fielding house. The door closed quickly behind us, and we turned to face an Asian woman just under five feet tall. Lu Li Fielding had lived most of her forty years in Communist China. She understood English well enough, but she didn't speak it well at all.

"Who this woman?" she asked, pointing at Rachel. "You not married, are you, Dr. David?"

"This is Rachel Weiss. "She's a good friend of mine. She's a physician, too."

Suspicion filled Lu Li's eyes. "She work for the company?"

"You mean Argus Optical?"

"Tlinity," she said, substituting an *l* for the *r*.

"Absolutely not. She's a professor at the Duke University Medical School."

Lu Li studied Rachel for several moments. "You come in, too, then. Please. Hurry, please."

Lu Li bowed and led us into the den, which opened to the kitchen. I smiled sadly. When Fielding had occupied this house alone, it always looked as though a tornado had just blown through it. Books and papers strewn about, dozens of coffee cups, beer bottles, and overflowing ashtrays littering every flat surface. After Lu Li arrived, the house had become a Zen-like space of cleanliness and order. Tonight it smelled of wax and lemon instead of cigarettes and stale beer.

"Sit, please," Lu Li said.

Rachel and I sat beside each other on a pillowy sofa. Lu Li perched on the edge of an old club chair opposite us. She focused on Rachel, who was staring at a plaque hanging on the wall behind Lu Li's chair.

"Is that the Nobel Prize?" Rachel asked softly.

Lu Li nodded, not without pride. "Andy win the Nobel in 1998. I was in China then, but still we knew his work. All physicists amazed."

"You must be very proud of him." Rachel spoke with a calm that her wide eyes belied. "How did you two meet?"

As Lu Li responded in broken English, I marveled at the union of this woman and my dead friend. Fielding had met Lu Li while lecturing in Beijing as part of a Sino-British diplomatic initiative. She taught physics at Beijing University, and she'd sat in the first row during each of Fielding's nine lectures. Party bureaucrats held several receptions during the series, and Lu Li attended them all. She and Fielding had quickly become inseparable, and by the time the day arrived for him to leave China, they were deeply in love. Two and a half years of separation followed, with Fielding trying desperately to arrange an exit visa for her. Even with the supposed help of the NSA brass, he made no progress. Fielding eventually reached a point where he was considering paying illegal brokers to have Lu Li smuggled out of the country, but I convinced him this was too risky.

Everything changed when Fielding began delaying Project Trinity with his suspicions about the side effects we were all suffering. As if by magic, the red tape was cut, and Lu Li was on a plane bound for Washington. Fielding knew his fiancée had only been brought to America to distract him, but he didn't care. Nor did her arrival have its desired effect. The Englishman continued to painstakingly investigate every negative event at the Trinity lab, and the other scientists grew to hate him for it.

"Lu Li," I said during a pause, "first let me express my great sadness over Andrew's passing."

The physicist shook her head. "That not why I ask you here. I want to know about this morning. What *really* happen to my Andy?"

I hesitated to speak frankly in the house. Seeing my anxious expression, she went to the fireplace, knelt, and reached up into the flue. She brought out a sooty cardboard box, which she set on the coffee table. I'd seen the box before. It contained several pieces of homemade electronic equipment that reminded me of the Heathkit projects my father and I had worked on when I was a boy. Lu Li withdrew an object that looked like a metal wand.

"Andy sweep house this morning before work," she said. "Plugged all the mikes. Okay to talk now."

I glanced at Rachel. The subtext was clear. Lu Li knew the score on Trinity, or at least she knew about the NSA's security tactics. Geli Bauer would probably have this house torn apart as soon as Lu Li left for the cleaner's or the grocery store. I was surprised she had waited even this long.

"Have you left the house at all today?" I asked.

"No," Lu Li said. "They won't tell me what hospital they take Andy to."

I doubted Fielding had been taken to a hospital. He'd probably been flown to NSA headquarters at Fort Meade, Maryland, probably to some special medical unit for an autopsy, or worse. The British might complain later, but that would be the State Department's problem, not the NSA's. And the British—framers of the Official Secrets Act and the

"D" notice—had a way of falling into line with the United States where national security was concerned.

"I still think we should whisper," I said softly, pointing at the wand. "And I think I should take that box with me when I go. I'm afraid the N"— I stopped myself—"the company security people might search this house the first time you leave. You don't want anybody to find it."

Lu Li had been raised in a Communist country with ruthless security police. Her willingness to believe the worst was deeply ingrained. "Did they kill my Andy?" she whispered.

"I hope not. Given Andrew's health, age, and habits, a stroke was possible. But . . . I don't think it was a stroke. What makes you think he might have been murdered?"

Lu Li closed her eyes, squeezing tears out of them. "Andy knew something might happen to him. He tell me so."

"Did he say this once? Or often?"

"Last two weeks, many times."

I exhaled long and slowly. "Do you know why Andrew wanted to see me at Nags Head?"

"He want to talk to you. That all I know. Andy very scared about work. About Trinity. About . . ."

"What?"

"Godin."

Somehow I had known it would be Godin. John Skow was easy to hate—an arrogant technocrat with no moral center—but he did not generate much fear. Godin, on the other hand, was easy to like—a genius, a patriot in the best sense of the word, a man of conviction—yet after you worked with him awhile, you sensed a disturbing vibration radiating from him, a Faustian hunger to *know* that disdained all limits, disregarded all boundaries. One thing was plain: anyone or anything that stood between Godin and his goal would not remain there long.

Godin and Fielding had got along well in the beginning.

They were from roughly the same generation, and Godin possessed Robert Oppenheimer's gift for motivating talented scientists: a combination of flattery and provocative insight. But the honeymoon had not lasted. For Godin, Trinity was a mission, and he pursued it with missionary zeal. Fielding was different. The Englishman did not believe that just because something was possible, it should be done. Nor did he believe that even a noble end justified all means to attain it.

"Did Andy have papers to show me?" I asked hopefully.

"I don't think so. Every evening he make notes, but every night before bed"—she pointed to the fireplace—"he always burn them. Andy very secret. He always try to protect me. Always to protect me."

He did the same for me, I thought. Suddenly, I remembered the words in Fielding's letter. "Did Andrew take his pocket watch to work with him today?"

Lu Li didn't hesitate. "He take it every day. You no see it today?"

"No. But I'm sure it will be returned to you with his personal effects."

Her lower lip began to quiver, and I sensed another imminent wave of tears, but it didn't come. Watching Lu Li's stoicism, I felt a sharp pang of grief, familiar yet somehow new to me. I was no stranger to mourning, but what I felt now was different from what I'd felt after the loss of my wife and daughter. Andrew Fielding was one of the few men of his century who might have answered some of the fundamental questions of human existence. To know that such a mind had gone out of the world left me feeling hollow, as though my species were diminished in some profound and irrecoverable way.

"What will happen to me now?" Lu Li asked quietly. "They send me back to China?"

Not a chance, I thought. One reason Trinity was so secret

62

was the belief held in some quarters that other countries might be at work on a similar device. With its history of aggressive technology theft, Communist China ranked high on that list. The NSA would never let a Chinese-born physicist who had been this close to the project return to her native land. In fact, I worried about her survival. But I could do little to protect her until I talked to the president.

"They can't send you back," I assured her. "Don't worry about that."

"Andy say the government do anything it want."

I was about to answer when headlight beams shone through the foyer. A car was passing slowly by the house.

"That's not true," I said. "Lu Li, I don't like saying this, but the best thing you can do right now is to cooperate with the NSA. The less trouble they see you making, the less they'll perceive you as a threat. Do you understand?"

Her face tightened. "You say now I should let them kill my Andy and say nothing? *Do* nothing?"

"We don't know that Andy *was* killed. And there's very little you can personally do right now. I want you to leave everything to me. I've called the president, and I could hear back from him at any time. He's in China now, of all places. Beijing."

"I see on TV. Andy tell me you know this president."

"I've met him. He was a friend of my brother's, and he appointed me to my job. And I promise you that one way or another I'll find the truth about Andrew's death. I owe him that. And more."

Lu Li suddenly smiled through her anguish. "Andy was good man. Kind, funny man. And smart."

"Very smart," I agreed, though words like *smart* meant little when applied to men like Andrew Fielding. Fielding had been a member of one of the smallest fraternities on the planet, those who truly understood the mysteries of quantum physics, a field reserved—as Fielding's Cambridge students often joked—for those students who were "too smart to be doctors."

Rachel squeaked in surprise as a white ball of fur raced into the room and leapt into Lu Li's lap. The furball was a small dog, a bichon frise. Lu Li smiled and vigorously stroked the bichon's neck.

"Maya, Maya," she cooed, then murmured softly in sing-song Cantonese.

The bichon seemed anxious at the presence of strangers, but it did not bark. Its little brown eyes locked on me.

"You know Maya, Dr. David?"

"Yes. We've met."

"Andy buy her for me. Six weeks ago. Maya my baby. My baby until God blesses Andy and me with . . ."

As she lapsed into silence, I realized that my sixty-three-year-old friend had been trying to have a child with his forty-year-old wife.

"I'm sorry," I said uselessly. "I'm so sorry."

Rachel looked as though she wanted to speak, but there were times when even a gifted psychiatrist found herself at a loss for words. As Lu Li stared into space, my anxiety grew. If Fielding had suspected that he might be murdered, and he had voiced that fear to his wife, then the NSA might know he had done that. They almost certainly knew I was here now. If they were outside, they had probably photographed Rachel and would be trying to figure out what she was doing here.

"Maya looks like she could use a walk," I said brightly.

Lu Li started from her trance.

"I'll be glad to take her out for you," I added.

"No. Maya no need—"

I cut her off with an upraised hand. "I think the air would do us all good."

Lu Li stared at me for several moments. "Yes," she said finally. "Is good idea. Me inside all day."

Looking around for something to write with, I saw a message pad by the telephone. I went to it and wrote, *Do you have a portable tape recorder?* Then I pulled off that sheet and wrote my cell phone number on the next page.

When Lu Li read my question, she walked back to Fielding's study and returned with a Sony microcassette recorder, the type used for dictation. I put it in my pocket and led both women to the glass doors that opened onto the patio.

Maya followed us out but stuck close to Lu Li, who attached a leash to the dog's collar. About a hundred meters through the woods lay the University of North Carolina's outdoor amphitheater. On two previous occasions, Fielding had taken me there to talk.

"I know Andrew swept the house," I whispered to Lu Li, "but I still don't feel safe talking inside. I need to speak to Rachel alone for a few minutes. I want you to go back inside. Lock the doors, but leave Maya with us. We're going to walk through the woods to the amphitheater. We'll be back very soon. I have my cell phone, and I left the number on your message pad. If anything strange happens, call me immediately."

Confusion and worry wrinkled Lu Li's face. "You need Maya?"

"For cover. You understand? An excuse to walk out here."

She nodded slowly, then knelt, whispered something to the dog, and retreated into the house. I picked up the whimpering bichon and walked swiftly across the backyard to a narrow path that led through the woods. Rachel struggled to keep up as branches began to pull at our clothes.

"What are we doing?" she hissed.

"Keep quiet. I have to talk to you, and I don't think we have long."

I wasn't sure of the source of my fear, but I knew it ran deep. Without being aware of it, I had shifted the dog to my left hand and drawn my gun with my right.

SEVEN

"Ritter's here," said Corelli, his voice sounding tense in Geli's headset. "He's already got the laser trained on the front window."

"What's he hearing?"

"Definite sounds, but no conversation. Like one person moving around the house. They could be in one of the back rooms."

"Change position and put the laser on a back window. Hurry."

"Right."

Geli could hardly stay in her chair. Something was going down at the Fielding house, and she had only one way to know what it was. A minute passed, then Ritter's deeper voice said, *"Nichts."*

"You're not getting anything in back?" she asked.

"Nein."

"They know where the bugs are, and they've plugged them."

"Ahh," said Ritter. "How could they know that?"

"Fielding."

"That bastard," said Corelli. "He was always playing games with us."

Geli nodded. Around Trinity, Fielding had acted like an absent-minded professor, but he was the sharpest son of a bitch in the place.

"They've probably left the house," Geli said. "Fielding and Tennant did that twice before. Walking Fielding's dog. I'm going to put a team in the woods."

"*Nein*," said Ritter. "Tennant will hear them."

"You have a better idea?"

"I'll go alone."

"Okay, but I'm setting up a perimeter. Tennant could be trying to run."

"I don't think so. It's a stupid way to run. And Tennant's not stupid."

"Why stupid?"

"When you run, you don't take women with you. You move fast and light."

Geli smiled to herself. "Tennant's not like you, *Liebchen*."

Ritter laughed. "He's a man, isn't he?"

"He's American and he was raised in the South. I knew guys like him in the army. Born heroes. They have this romantic streak. It gets a lot of them killed."

"Like the English?" Ritter asked.

Geli thought of Andrew Fielding. "Sort of. Now get going. Tell Corelli to cover the front."

"*Ja.*"

Geli got out of her chair and began to pace the narrow alley between the racks of electronic gear. She thought of calling John Skow again, but Skow didn't want to be bothered. Fine. She'd call him when Tennant bolted, then see what the smug bastard had to say about not keeping the leash too tight.

EIGHT

I moved silently through the dark trees. Rachel sounded like a blind bear blundering along behind me. On a Manhattan street she probably maneuvered like a pro halfback, but the woods were alien to her. I slowed until she caught up, then told her to hold on to the back of my belt. She did.

When we were fifty yards away from the house, I said, "Do you believe me about Fielding now?"

"I believe you worked with him," Rachel said. "I'm not sure he was murdered. I don't think you are either."

I stepped over a fallen log, then helped her over. "I know he was murdered. Only two people at Project Trinity opposed what was being done there. Fielding was one, and now he's dead. I'm the other."

"Are you going to tell me about Trinity now?"

"If you're willing to listen. I think you understand now that it could be dangerous for you."

She sucked in her breath as briers raked her arm. "Go on."

"When you came to my house today, I was making a videotape to give to my lawyer. He was to open it if something happened to me. I never finished it. And the truth is, I'm worried about seeing tomorrow morning alive."

Rachel stopped in the overgrown track. "Why don't you just call the police? Lu Li clearly shares your suspicions, and I think there's enough circumstantial evidence to—"

"City police can't investigate the NSA. And that's who oversees Trinity."

"Call the FBI then."

"That's like calling the FBI to investigate the CIA. There's so much ill will between those agencies that it would take weeks to get anything done. If you really want to help, become my videotape. Listen to what I have to tell you, then go home and keep it to yourself."

"And if something happens to you?"

"Call CNN and *The New York Times* and tell them everything you know. The sooner you tell it, the safer you'll be."

"Why don't *you* do that? Tonight?"

"Because I can't be sure I'm right. Because the president could be trying to reach me as we speak. And because, as juvenile as it may sound, this is a national security matter."

Holding Lu Li's whimpering bichon in my left arm, I put my gun in my pocket and pulled Rachel forward. Forty yards on, I saw a deeper darkness ahead. The trees gave way like thinning ranks of soldiers, and then a man-made wall stopped me in my tracks. When my eyes adjusted, I saw the door I had known was there. I opened it with my free hand and led Rachel through. We emerged into a moonlit bowl, lined with cut stone.

"My God," she said.

The amphitheater looked as though it had magically been transported to the Carolina woods from Greece. To our right was the elevated stage, to our left a stone stairway leading up through the seats to the top row. Not far above that lay Country Club Road. The view down from the road was almost completely blocked by pines and hardwoods, but I could see the broken beams of headlights passing high above us.

I took Rachel's hand, stepped onto the stone floor, and led her to the edge of the stage. There I tied Maya's leash around a low light stanchion. While the dog sniffed an invisible scent trail, I set the tape recorder on the edge of the stage and depressed RECORD. "This is David Tennant, M.D.," I said. "I'm speaking to Dr. Rachel Weiss of the Duke University Medical School."

Playback gave me a staticky facsimile of my words. I looked at my watch. "We need to do this in less than ten minutes."

Rachel shrugged, her eyes full of curiosity.

"For the past two years, I've been working on a special project for the National Security Agency. It's known as Project Trinity, and it's based in a building in the Research Triangle Park, ten miles from here. Trinity is a massive government-funded effort to build a supercomputer capable of artificial intelligence. A computer that can think."

She looked unimpressed. "Don't we already have computers that can do that?"

This common misconception surprised me now, but when I went to work at Trinity, I hadn't known much better myself. For fifty years, science fiction writers and filmmakers had been creating portrayals of "giant electronic brains" taking over the world. HAL, the speaking computer of *2001: A Space Odyssey,* had entered pop consciousness in 1968 and remained firmly embedded there ever since. In the subsequent thirty-five years, we had witnessed such a revolution in digital computing that the average person believed that a "computer that can think" was just around the corner, if not already within our capabilities. But the reality was far different. I had no time to go into the complexities of neural networks or strong AI; Rachel needed a simple primer and the facts about Trinity.

"Have you heard of a man named Alan Turing?" I asked.

"He's one of the men who broke the Germans' Enigma code during World War Two."

"Turing?" Rachel looked preoccupied. "I think I've heard of something called the Turing Test."

"That's the classic test of artificial intelligence. Turing said machine intelligence would be achieved when a human being could sit on one side of a wall and type questions into a keyboard, then read the answers coming onto his screen from the other side and be certain that those answers were being typed by another human being. Turing predicted that would happen by the end of the twentieth century, but no computer has *ever* come close to passing that test. Using conventional technology, it's still probably fifty years off."

"Didn't that IBM computer finally beat Garry Kasparov at chess? I know I read that somewhere."

"Deep Blue?" I laughed, the sound strangely brittle in the amphitheater. "Yes. But it won by using what computer scientists call brute force. Its memory contains every known chess game ever played, and it processes millions of probabilities every time it makes a move. It plays very good chess, but it doesn't *understand* what it's doing. As a human being, Garry Kasparov never has to consider the billions of possibilities—many of them ridiculously simple—that the computer does. Kasparov's acquired knowledge allows him to make intuitive leaps, and to learn permanently every time he does. He plays by instinct. And no one really understands what that means."

Rachel sat on the edge of the stage. "So, what are you telling me?"

"That computers don't think like human beings. In fact, they don't think at all. They simply carry out instructions. All those TV commercials you hear about 'software that thinks'? They're bullshit. Serious AI researchers are afraid to even use the term *artificial intelligence* anymore."

"Okay. So what's Project Trinity?"

"The holy grail."

"What do you mean?"

"Everyone wants to build a computer that works like the human brain, but we don't understand how the brain works. Everyone concedes that. Well . . . two years ago, one man realized this didn't have to be the obstacle everyone thought it was. That we might be able to *copy* the brain without actually understanding what we were doing. Using existing technology."

"Who was this man?"

"Peter Godin. The billionaire."

"Godin Supercomputing?"

Now she'd surprised me. "That's right."

"They have a Godin Four supercomputer in a basement at TUNL, the Duke high-energy lab."

"Well, Godin is the man who conceived Project Trinity."

Rachel looked as though the accumulating details were starting to persuade her. "What kind of existing technology can copy the brain?"

"MRI."

"Magnetic resonance imaging?"

"Yes. You order MRI scans every week, right?"

"Of course."

"There's a lot of information on those scans, isn't there?"

"More than I can interpret sometimes."

"Rachel, I've seen MRI scans that contain a hundred thousand times the information of the ones you see every day. A hundred thousand times the resolution."

She blinked. "But how can that be? How much more can you see?"

"I've seen reactions between individual nerve synapses, frozen in time. I've seen the human brain working at the molecular level."

72

"Bullshit."

Any doctor would have said the same. "No. The machine exists. It's sitting in a room ten miles away from us right now. Only nobody knows it."

She was shaking her head. "That makes no sense. Why would a company keep something like that secret?"

"Because they're legally bound to by the government."

"But an MRI like that would make whoever developed it hundreds of millions of dollars. It could detect malignant cells long before they even become tumor masses."

"You're right. That's been my main problem with this project. It's unethical to keep that machine from cancer patients. But for now, just accept that there's an MRI machine that can produce three-D models of the brain, with resolution to the molecular level."

"Molecular snapshots of the brain."

"Basically, yes. Ravi Nara calls them neuromodels.'"

"Neuromodels. Okay."

"Rachel, do you realize what one of those neuromodels is?"

"I know that a single one of them would revolutionize neuroscience. But I get the feeling that's not what this is about."

"A neuromodel is the person it was taken from. Literally. His thoughts, memories, fears—everything."

"But . . . it's just a scan, right? A high-resolution map of the brain."

"No. It's a coded facsimile of every molecule in the brain, in perfect spatial and electrochemical relation. Which means that—"

"Hold on. Are you about to tell me they can load one of these neuromodels into a computer?"

"No. But that's what they've been working around the clock for two years to achieve. Godin predicted it would take fifteen to twenty years, but they got halfway there in *nineteen months.* I've never seen anything like it. The only historical precedent is the Manhattan Project during World War Two."

Rachel started to speak, but I held up my hand. High above us, a pair of headlights was cruising past at less than half the speed of the other cars. They slowed still more, then sped up and disappeared.

"We need to hurry."

"If Trinity is everything you say it is," she said, "then why in God's name would it be based in North Carolina?"

This I hadn't expected. "Aren't you the top Jungian analyst in the world?"

"Well . . . one of them."

"Why are *you* based in North Carolina?"

She frowned. "Because Duke University is here. That's different."

"Not so different. Peter Godin wanted Trinity based at his R and D lab in Mountain View, California. The NSA is footing the bill, and they wanted it based at Fort Meade, Maryland. Research Triangle Park was the ultimate compromise. High-tech, but out of the way."

"What's the end point, here? What does the NSA want to do with Trinity?"

"Our government sees most scientific revolutions in terms of weapons potential. If such a machine can be built, our government wants to be the first to do it."

"What kind of weapon can this computer be?"

"Think Desert Storm, Afghanistan, Iraq. Everything's computerized in modern war. Code-breaking, nuclear weapons testing, information warfare, battlefield systems. But a Trinity wouldn't be merely an advance. It would make today's supercomputers as obsolete as Model Ts. And if Fielding was right about it having quantum capabilities . . .

then present-day encryption is *gone*. That's why the NSA has spent close to a billion dollars on Trinity."

Rachel processed what I'd said. "But this isn't just a faster supercomputer. We're talking about a computer that thinks like a person."

I shook my head. "We can't build a computer that thinks *like* a person. We're talking about copying an individual human brain. Creating a digital entity that for all practical purposes *is* a person. With his or her cognitive functions, memories, hopes, dreams . . . everything except a body. Only it would run at the speed of a digital computer. One million times faster than biological circuitry."

She spoke almost to herself. "This is why Andrew Fielding and Ravi Nara would be working together."

"Exactly. Nobel laureates in quantum physics and neuroscience. Peter Godin brought them together." I checked to see that the spools on the recorder were still turning. "But I've only told you part of Trinity's potential. Once your neuromodel is loaded into the computer as Rachel Weiss, speed isn't the only advantage it will have over you—the original."

"What do you mean?"

"Say I decide to learn to play the piano. It takes me three years of intensive study. You're impressed by that. You want to learn to play the piano too. It's going to take you three years as well, give or take. That's the disadvantage of the human brain. Each one has approximately the same learning curve. But the computer model of your brain doesn't have that problem. The sum total of music theory can be digitized and downloaded into its memory—*your* memory—in about three seconds. There's no learning curve at all."

She shook her head. "You're saying you could download the sum of human knowledge into this computer—into me—all in a few hours?"

"In theory, yes."

"David, you're talking about something like . . . like a god, almost."

"Not almost. Because that computer model would not only be Rachel Weiss. It would be Rachel Weiss *forever*. It could be backed up and stored, or downloaded into another Trinity computer. It would never have to die."

She pursed her lips to speak, but no words emerged.

"Are you starting to believe me now?"

"What's *your* job at Trinity?"

"I was appointed by the president to evaluate any ethical dilemmas that might arise. During the Manhattan Project, some scientists turned against the atomic bomb for moral reasons, and they had no real voice. The president wanted to minimize the public controversy that was bound to come if Trinity became a reality. He knew my brother in college, and he'd read my book on medical ethics—or watched the *NOVA* series based on it, more likely. That's what made him pick me for the project. It's really that simple."

Rachel looked off into the dark trees. "This sounds anything but simple. In fact, it sounds crazy." She looked back at me, her eyes glinting. "You said Trinity got halfway to success in nineteen months. What's holding up the second half?"

"Building a computer powerful enough to hold a complete neuromodel in its circuitry. The human brain is fairly slow in terms of speed, but it's massively parallel. It contains over a hundred trillion possible connections, all capable of simultaneous calculation, and that's just for processing. It also holds the equivalent of twelve hundred terabytes of computer memory."

She shrugged. "That means nothing to me."

"Six million years of *The Wall Street Journal*."

Her mouth fell open.

"When Trinity began, no computer on the planet had that kind of capacity. The Internet as a whole does, but it's far too dispersed and unreliable to be controllable."

"And now?"

"IBM is building a computer called Blue Gene that will rival the processing power of the brain, but it'll still be unable to do things any five-year-old child can."

"And Trinity is different?"

"You could say that. Blue Gene will fill a fifty-by-fifty-foot room and need three hundred tons of air-conditioning just to function. Trinity will be about the size of a Volkswagen Beetle. And Godin thinks that's still too big. He's always saying that the human brain weighs three pounds and uses only ten watts of electricity. He believes the solutions to great problems must be beautiful. Elegant."

Rachel gazed up the incline of stone seats, trying to grasp a future that was crashing headlong into the present. "How close is Trinity to becoming a reality?"

I thought of the black mass of carbon and crystal growing almost like a life-form in the basement lab of the Trinity building. "There's a prototype sitting in our lab right now with one hundred and twenty trillion connections and practically unlimited memory."

"Does it *work*?"

"No."

"Why not?"

"Because even if you succeed in loading a neuromodel into the computer, how do you talk to it? The human brain interacts with the world through a biological body with five senses. Imagine your brain downloaded into a box. It's deaf, dumb, blind, and paralyzed. A quivering mass of fear. And thank God for it. Because once a machine like that *can* talk—and listen and act—there's no telling what it might do."

Rachel looked up at me with interest. "What could it do?"

"Do you remember HAL from *2001: A Space Odyssey*?"

"Sure. The most reliable computer ever made. Urbana, Illinois, right?"

I chuckled softly. "He was until he murdered the crew of his spaceship. Well, imagine what HAL could do if he were connected to the Internet."

"Tell me."

"One Trinity computer connected to a phone line could hold the industrialized world hostage. It could disrupt power grids, rail lines, air traffic control, missile systems, NORAD, Wall Street. It could demand whatever it wanted."

She shook her head in confusion. "But what would it *want*?"

"What does any intelligent entity want? Especially one that's essentially human?"

"Power?"

"Exactly." I jumped as my cell phone rang. The ID said "Andrew Fielding." I pressed SEND. "Lu Li? Has something happened?"

"Nothing happen," Lu Li replied in a shaky voice. "I worry about Maya. I think I hear noises outside. You bring her back, Dr. David."

The bichon stopped sniffing the ground, looked up at me, and cocked its head as though listening.

"We're coming. Right now."

"Is she all right?" Rachel asked as I ended the call.

"Yes. She wants us to come back, but we're going to wait a bit."

"Why?"

"Because the NSA heard that call. If they have people in the woods, they'll probably move now. And we'll hear them."

Rachel glanced anxiously at the wall that separated us

from the trees. "Do you really think there's someone out there?"

"That's not what scares you," I said. "What scares you is that now *you* think there might be."

She slid off the stage and looked at the door we'd passed through. It was easy to imagine someone waiting behind it.

"You said Fielding was murdered because you and he resisted the project. How exactly did you resist it?"

"We didn't just resist it. We stopped it cold. Suspended it, anyway. Fielding was the driving force, but it took me interceding with the president to accomplish it. It was like trying to stop the work on the atomic bomb during World War Two."

"Why did you want to stop it?"

"I'm not completely sure about Fielding's reasons. I think he kept a lot from me—to protect me, I mean. But my reasons were simple.

"Six months ago, we tested the Super-MRI machine. We used animals first, and there were no problems. The first humans to be scanned were the six of us in the inner circle. Within a week, we all developed strange neurological symptoms. Side effects from exposure to the machine. Fielding believed—"

"MRI doesn't cause side effects," Rachel broke in.

"Not the machines you use. But the magnetic fields generated by the Trinity MRI are exponentially more intense than those in present-day machines. They use superconducting materials that allow massive pulses—"

Maya was growling deep in her throat and looking up the slope of stone seats. I hadn't heard anything in the woods, but maybe the dog had. I put the tape recorder in my pocket, picked up Maya, then drew my gun and pulled Rachel through the stage door.

Darkness enveloped us.

"Stay right behind me," I said, ducking under a branch.

"Did you hear something?"

"No."

If I hadn't had Rachel with me, I would have used stealth to safely reach the house. But speed was the only option now. I plowed through the underbrush, warning Rachel whenever I hit branches likely to whip back into her face. She cried out twice and stumbled once, but she got back up and somehow managed to stay on my heels. As we neared the house, I saw the yellow square of Fielding's patio doors. Lu Li stood silhouetted inside them, a perfect target. The image made me shiver.

When she slid open the door, I pulled her deep into the room. Maya barked wildly until Lu Li bent and held out her arms. The dog leapt into them as Rachel closed the glass door.

"Call a taxi," I whispered over my shoulder.

Rachel went to the phone.

Lu Li's eyes were wet. I touched her elbow, and the dog snapped at me. "I wish I could stay the night with you," I said quietly, "but that would look more suspicious than my going home. I'm going to go to work tomorrow and try to get some answers, so I want everything to look as normal as possible. Do you understand?"

"Yes."

"I'll take Andrew's box of toys with me. I don't want anyone to find it here. Is that all right?"

Lu Li nodded, stroking the bichon as lovingly as she would a child.

"I'm going to pull into the garage when I leave, so no one sees me take the box. If anyone asks you what I was doing here, tell them it was a sympathy visit. If they somehow overheard some of our conversation, just act like what you are. A distraught widow."

"What means distraught?"

"Grief-stricken. Grieving."

She smiled bravely. "I no need to act this."

I laid my hands on her shoulders and squeezed, then spoke almost inaudibly. "In the FedEx letter Andy sent me, there was some white powder. Almost like sand. It's in those plastic bags on the couch. Do you know anything about that?"

Lu Li's gaze went to the couch, and her face wrinkled in confusion. "No. Nothing."

"Did you drop it off at the FedEx box?"

"Yes. How you know?"

"It doesn't matter." I knew Lu Li had dropped off the envelope because I had been inside Fielding's head during my last dream. I felt a sudden compulsion to get out of the house. "Rachel? The taxi?"

"Any minute," she said from behind me.

"I want you to go into the garage," I told Lu Li. "When you hear me tap the horn, open the door for me. After I pull in, close the door."

"Okay." She left the room without a word.

I picked up the Ziplocs, then led Rachel to the darkened living room, where wide windows looked onto the street. I dropped the Ziplocs on a chair, then sat on a sofa opposite the window to wait for the cab.

"Is the taxi for me?" she whispered, sitting beside me.

"Yes."

"But my car's parked at your house."

"You don't want to go back to my house. You can get it in the morning if you want to. I'd rather you take a taxi to work."

"Did I hear you tell Lu Li you're going back to work tomorrow?"

"If I don't hear from the president tonight, I am."

"*Why?* If they killed Fielding, why won't they kill you, too?"

Her question gave me a perverse satisfaction. "It sounds like you're buying into my delusion."

Her lips tightened, and I could see that she was genuinely afraid.

"Look, if they really wanted to kill me, I'd be dead already. And if they decide to kill me before tomorrow, nothing will stop them. But I think they're too worried about how the president would react to try that. If I'm alive tomorrow morning, it's all right for me to go in."

Rachel sighed and rubbed her temples with her fingers.

"I don't know what's going to happen," I whispered. "If anyone questions you, tell as much truth as you can. You came to my house because I missed three sessions. I got a call from the wife of a friend who died today. She has no family here, so you offered to help console her. We calmed her down and walked her dog. That's all you know."

She studied my face in the dim light. "This isn't what I expected."

"I know. You really thought I was crazy."

She bit her lip, the gesture almost girlish. "I suppose I did. Part of me hoped I was wrong. But now I'm frightened. I know about psychiatric problems. This is something else."

I pulled her close and spoke into her ear. "I want you to forget it all. Unless something happens to me. Then you remember. Remember and scream to high heaven." I pulled back and looked into her eyes. "I won't be coming back to your office."

She stared at me as though I'd said, "We're never going to see each other again," which deep down was what I felt.

"David—"

"Here's your taxi." I stood as headlights rolled to a stop in front of the house, looking close to make sure there was a taxi light on the roof.

She was shaking her head, almost helplessly.

"Don't worry," I said. "I'm going to be fine. You've helped a lot."

"I didn't do a damned thing for you."

I pulled her out of sight of the window, then took the recorder from my pocket, removed the tape, and put it in her hand. "If you want to help, here's your chance." I started to send her on, then hesitated. "There is one more thing you could do."

"Tell me."

I pointed to the Ziploc bags on the chair. "Is there someone at Duke who could safely test that powder for infectious agents and poisons?"

"Of course. There are guys over there who live for that kind of thing."

There was a slipcover on one of the sofa pillows. I took it off the pillow, then put the Ziplocs inside it and handed it to her. "Be very careful with those."

"You're preaching to the choir."

I squeezed her arm. "Thank you. Now, go."

She didn't go. She stood on tiptoe and kissed me gently on the lips. "Be careful. Please, please be careful."

As I stared, Rachel slid the slipcover under her blouse, then walked to the foyer. I heard the front door close softly. Through the front window I watched her get into the taxi. The cab pulled into Lu Li's driveway, then backed out and rolled up Gimghoul Street.

I went out to my car, pulled up to Fielding's garage door, and tapped my horn. Lu Li opened the door from inside, then closed it behind me.

She pulled open my passenger door and set her husband's cardboard box on the front seat. I reached across it and gripped her wrist, my eyes boring into hers.

"Tell me the truth, Lu Li. Do you know what they're trying to build at Trinity?"

83

After several seconds of eye contact, she nodded once.

"Don't ever tell anyone that," I warned. "*Never.*"

"Me Chinese, David. Know what can happen."

For an instant I flashed back to her standing silhouetted in the patio doors, a target awaiting an assassin.

"Come with me," I said suddenly. "Right now. Just get in with your dog and we'll go. I'll keep you safe."

A sad smile touched her lips. "You good man. Like Andrew. Don't worry. I already make my own arrangements."

Arrangements? I couldn't imagine what these might be. I didn't think she knew anyone in the States. "What are they?"

She shook her head. "Better you don't know. Yes? I be okay."

For some reason, I believed her. The revelation that Lu Li had not been rendered helpless by her grief made me ask one more question.

"In his letter, Andy told me that if anything happened to him, I should remember his pocket watch. What's so special about that watch?"

Lu Li studied my eyes for what seemed a long time. Then, in a nearly inaudible whisper, she said, "Not watch. Fob."

"Fob?"

"Watch fob."

I closed my eyes and pictured Fielding's watch. It was a scarred but precious heirloom, and at the end of its chain was a small, diamond-shaped crystal.

"The crystal?" I asked.

Lu Li smiled. "You smart man. You figure it out."

NINE

Geli Bauer was on her feet, pacing the control center and shouting into her headset at John Skow. She'd never lost her temper with him before, but without Godin backing her up, Skow was proving maddeningly obstinate.

"Haven't you heard a word I said? Can't you see what's happening?"

Skow answered in a condescending voice, "This is what you've told me. Dr. Tennant and Dr. Weiss visited the grieving widow and walked her dog. Dr. Weiss kissed Tennant, then she went home in a cab."

Geli closed her eyes and tried to suppress her anger. "Tennant pulled into the garage and closed the door before he left the Fielding house. He obviously took something that he didn't want us to see."

"That's possible," Skow said. "But as far as you can tell, he's headed home now. What's the problem?"

"We couldn't hear a damn thing! They plugged the bugs, same as they did at Tennant's house. And Weiss left her Saab at Tennant's house, instead of taking the cab there to pick it up. Why would she do that? Tennant might be planning to run or even to go public. Maybe both."

"I think you're projecting your own paranoia onto him."

"Ritter heard them talking about MRI side effects."

"That's small potatoes. You couldn't know that, of course. The Super-MRI unit is Tennant's pet ethical concern, and it's got nothing to do with the central issue."

"But they talked for ten minutes before that. And Ritter thinks he saw a tape recorder."

Skow sighed. "What would you have me do about that?"

"Take them out."

The NSA man caught his breath. "Did I hear you correctly?"

"You know you did. We have to assume Weiss knows the full details of Trinity and about Tennant's suspicions regarding Dr. Fielding's death."

"Dr. Weiss is a private citizen who's broken no law."

"If you won't take them out, then bring them in for interrogation with prejudice."

The resulting silence seemed interminable. Then Skow said, "Do you have someone following Dr. Weiss's cab?"

Ritter was covering Weiss. "My best man. He could easily stage an accident."

Skow's voice, when it came, was like shaved ice. "Listen to me, Geli. Your man will follow the cab to Dr. Weiss's residence, then break contact. He will not let her see him. He will not even breathe hard in her direction."

"*What?*"

"Call off your dog. And your team on Dr. Tennant will follow him to his residence and set up a static surveillance post as per normal procedure."

Geli could barely control her voice. "Project security has been breached. If we allow things to proceed, we'll lose control of the situation, if we haven't already."

"Ms. Bauer, tomorrow the president of the United States could ask to see David Tennant in the Oval Office. Do you understand that? They may *already have talked*. So you do whatever you have to do to calm down. Take a tranquilizer. Get laid. I detest crudeness, but that's the bottom line. Now . . . I'm with my family. Don't bother me unless Tennant tries to reach the president or he shoots somebody in a public place."

"I want to go on record as protesting this decision."

"Fine."

"I want to talk to Godin."

"Impossible. He can't be reached right now."

"Where is he?"

"In Mountain View, handling a crisis."

"He was still in town at lunchtime today."

"Peter didn't buy a G5 to leave it parked in the hangar."

Geli could hear Skow's teenage sons arguing in the background, and the mindless babble of a television. "I'm afraid I can't accept your assessment of the situation. I can't ignore my responsibilities because you haven't got the balls to do what's necessary to protect Trinity."

"Are you out of your mind? I've spoken to Peter twice this evening. I know what he wants done and not done. And if you take matters into your own hands . . . not even your father will be able to protect you."

Geli hadn't liked Skow before, but she hated him now.

She hung up and stared at her computer screen, which still displayed the list of Fielding's personal effects. Why the hell would somebody keep a cobra's fang? She wanted to go to the storage room and check the actual objects against the list, but she was too pissed off to deal with that.

She had always worked with incomplete information at Trinity. It hadn't bothered her much. The army was good training for that. You could guard a building for twenty-four hours without knowing whether it contained nuclear bombs or cases of underwear. But now there was too much she didn't know. The mystery at the heart of Trinity was taking control of everyone and everything around it. Yet there was nothing she could do. She had to talk to Godin, and he was incommunicado.

Faced with this impasse, she called Ritter Bock and told him to break contact with Weiss. The taciturn young German was needed back at the control center. Skow had ordered her to calm down, and Geli knew only one way to do that. She needed to take some orders rather than give them.

TEN

Dreamless sleep evaporated in a rush of pounding blood and the memory of Fielding lying dead in his office. Sunlight knifed through a crack in the curtains. I had survived the night, but still I reached beneath my pillow for my .38. Only then did I slap the top of my clock radio, killing the alarm.

My phone had not rung during the night, so the president hadn't tried to reach me. I checked my answering machine in case I had slept through a call, but there were no messages. Trying not to think about the implications of this, I dialed Lu Li Fielding's house. A machine answered. The taped message still had Andrew's voice on it, brimming with humor. Hoping Lu Li was a hundred miles from Chapel Hill by now, I hung up and carried my gun into the bathroom, then locked the door behind me.

I shaved quickly. A surveillance car had been parked nearby when I got home from Fielding's house last night. It pulled away as I approached. After removing the sensitive items from my trunk, I called Rachel at home to be sure she'd made it. Then I lay awake for two hours, listening for the sounds of a break-in and thinking of Fielding's pocket watch. It had a dull gold case, worn from rubbing, and a yellowed face with Roman numerals. *Not the watch,* Lu Li had said. *The fob.* I'd asked Fielding about the crystal on his watch chain once. He told me a Tibetan monk had given it to him near Lhasa, promising it would ensure an unfailing memory. Fielding belly-laughed when he told me that story, but I hadn't gotten the joke. Now I did.

One new computer technology perfected by the Trinity team was holographic memory storage. Rather than storing data in microchips, Trinity engineers stored it as holograms within the molecules of stable crystals. Using lasers to read and write data, they could store enormous amounts of information within the crystal's symmetrically arranged atoms. The crystals I had seen in the Trinity holography lab were the size of NFL footballs, but I saw no reason that a smaller one could not be used. Like the one on Fielding's watch chain.

Somehow, the Englishman had been downloading Trinity data into his crystal watch fob. And because no one outside Trinity's inner circle of scientists and engineers knew this was even possible, Fielding could walk it in and out of the building every day without anyone suspecting a thing.

But *why* would he steal information? To sell to the highest bidder? Fielding was old school. Even if he were desperate for money, he was the last person I would suspect of corporate espionage. Had he secretly embraced some ideology? Or abandoned one? Was he a politically naive scientist who believed all nations should share access to the latest technology? Possibly. But I didn't think he would want a rogue nation to possess something as powerful as a Trinity computer. To hear Fielding talk sometimes, you would think he didn't want *any* country to possess one.

Was that it? Had he been working to prevent Trinity from becoming a reality? That scenario seemed the most likely, but I didn't have enough information to make an accurate guess. And without the watch, I couldn't prove anything.

I showered in near-scalding water, then dressed in chinos and a sport jacket and walked quickly to my car, trying not to think too much about what I was doing. My primary goal in returning to Trinity was to find Fielding's pocket watch, but in truth I saw little choice. Staying home would only invite closer NSA scrutiny, and running—as I hoped Lu Li had done—would bring the full resources of the agency down upon me. But if I could preserve the illusion of normalcy a little longer—until the president got back to me—I might be able to avenge Fielding's death.

On a good traffic day, the Trinity complex was a twenty-minute drive from my house in suburban Chapel Hill. Research Triangle Park, the manicured haven of corporate research known locally as the RTP, lay between Raleigh and Durham and was named for the triangle formed by Duke University, UNC at Chapel Hill, and North Carolina State. Its quiet lanes led through expansive lawns that suggested an exclusive country club, but instead of golf links, the seven-thousand-acre RTP boasted labs owned by DuPont, 3M, Merck, Biogen, Lockheed, and dozens of other blue-chip names. Forty-five thousand people reported to work within its borders every day, but less than three hundred knew what lay behind the walls of the Trinity building. I drove slowly, hoping in some juvenile way that I would never arrive at my destination.

The Trinity lab stood two hundred yards back from an understated sign that read ARGUS OPTICAL. A forbidding five-story block of steel and black glass, it sat on sixty wooded acres with extensive subbasements and a heliport. The steel and glass was just a shell constructed for show. Behind it, high-tech copper cladding code-named Tempest encased the inner building, preventing electromagnetic radiation from passing in or out of Trinity. The same stuff protected the NSA operations buildings at Fort Meade.

Because the building had been sited in a sort of bowl, its first two floors lay out of sight. The main entrance was on the third floor. To reach it, staff had to cross a roofed catwalk forty yards long. Inside a fortified archway at the far end, they confronted a narrow passage guarded by a security officer and lined with sensitive metal detectors, electronic bomb-sniffers, and fluoroscope machines. Authorized entry required photo ID, a fingerprint scan, and a mandatory search of all bags.

A sentry buzzed open the archway door, and I walked up to the security desk, my face revealing none of the anxiety I felt.

"Morning, Doc," said a middle-aged guard named Henry.

I sometimes thought Henry had been hired through central casting. The other security personnel were all in their late twenties, lean young men and women with smooth faces, avian eyes, and zero body fat. Only Henry, the gate man, ever said a word of greeting.

"Good morning, Henry," I said.

"There's a meeting in the conference room at nine."

"Thanks."

"You got four minutes."

I looked at my watch and nodded.

"Still can't get over Professor Fielding," Henry said. "They say he was dead before the ambulance got here."

I took a careful breath. This exchange was being recorded by hidden cameras. "That's the way it goes sometimes with strokes."

"Not a bad way to go out. Quick, I mean."

I forced a smile, then laid the pad of my right forefinger on a small scanner. After the unit beeped for a match, I passed through the gauntlet of threat-detection equipment and took the stairs to the fifth floor, which housed the administrative offices and conference room.

Yellow police tape stretched across the closed door to Fielding's office. Who had put it there? Surely the NSA hadn't allowed local or state police to enter this facility. Glancing up and down the empty corridor, I quickly tried the knob. Locked. And not with some lightweight mechanism from a hardware store. If Fielding's pocket watch was inside his office, I couldn't get it.

I walked a few doors down to my own office, closed the door, and sat down at my primary computer. Part of a closed network that served only the Trinity scientists, it had no connection to the outside world. To access the Internet, I had to use a second computer that had no ports or drives through which files could be exported from the building.

My primary screen showed one interoffice e-mail: a reminder of the meeting scheduled to begin in the conference room in two minutes. With a macabre chill I realized that I'd half-expected a humorous e-mail from Fielding. He often sent me little jokes or ironic quotes from dead scientists or philosophers: *Scientists over 60 do more harm than good!*— *T. H. Huxley*—like that. But today there was no message. And there would never be another. I looked blankly around my office. Fielding was gone, and I was profoundly disoriented. Together, we had stopped Project Trinity for six tense weeks, angering our colleagues while we tried in vain to discover the cause of the MRI side effects experienced by the six Trinity principals. Today that issue remained unresolved.

I hadn't volunteered to be scanned by the Super-MRI unit out of stupidity. The theory was simple: since *Homo sapiens* had evolved in the earth's magnetic field, an MRI's magnetic energy did not pose a health risk. This had been proved countless times by conventional MRI machines, which generated fields thirty thousand times more powerful than that of the earth. But the Super-MRI developed at Trinity—using superconductivity and colossal magnets—generated fields up to eight hundred thousand times greater than that of the earth. Gross side effects such as tissue-heating had been solved in animal tests, but within days after undergoing our "superscans," all of us had begun experiencing disturbing neurological symptoms.

Jutta Klein, the designer of the Super-MRI, suffered short-term memory loss. Ravi Nara endured extreme sexual compulsions (he had several times been caught masturbating in his office and in the rest room). John Skow developed hand tremors, and Godin himself had suffered epileptic seizures. Fielding had developed, of all things, a form of Tourette's syndrome and frequently blurted out inappropriate words or phrases. And I had narcolepsy.

Ravi Nara, our Nobel-winning neurologist, could find no medical explanation for this sudden flurry of symptoms, so all Super-MRI scanning had temporarily been halted. Work on the Trinity computer continued, but with the Super-MRI removed from the chain, Godin's engineers had only the six original scans to work from, and no one knew whether those were of sufficient resolution to "make the leap" into the prototype computer. With Nara at a loss, Fielding began investigating the side effects in his spare time. Six weeks later, he suggested that they had been caused by a disruption of quantum processes in our brains—and backed up his theory with twenty pages of complex mathematics. Nara argued that nothing in the history of neuroscience suggested that the human brain carried out quantum processes. Only a few physicists subscribed to this "New Age" theory of consciousness—Roger Penrose among them—yet Fielding toiled on, trying to prove his theory.

Peter Godin initially supported Fielding, but before long he resumed MRI testing on primates. Chimps and orangutans suffered no ill effects. Fielding argued that primates weren't conscious in the human sense, and thus their brains had no quantum processes to be disrupted. Godin ignored him. I then reported Fielding's suspicions to the president, who officially suspended the project pending an exhaustive investigation of the side effects.

That was six weeks ago. Since then, Fielding and I had worked almost around the clock to prove his theory of quantum disturbance. I felt like an assistant to Albert Einstein, sharpening pencils and taking notes while the genius worked beside me. Yet despite Fielding's formidable intellect, he could not prove his theory. Too much remained unknown about the brain. Now he was dead, and without a demonstrable link between the MRI unit and our "side effects," I couldn't hope to hold back the collective tide of wills set on resuming the project. Without proof of foul play, Trinity would continue.

The battle would begin in minutes, after a few hollow words of regret over Fielding's "untimely passing." Perspiration filmed my face as I walked toward the conference room door.

The room was empty.

I had never arrived first at a meeting. The other principals were compulsively punctual. I poured coffee from the urn on the credenza, then sat at the far end of the table and tried to stay calm.

Where the hell was everybody? Watching me from the security room? Where would they hide the camera? Behind a picture? Hanging to my right was a rare black-and-white photograph of the core physicists of the Manhattan Project: Oppenheimer, Szilard, Fermi, Wigner, Edward Teller. They stood in a friendly knot before the Oscura mountains of New Mexico, giants of science, each destined for fame or infamy, depending on one's point of view. Some, like the hawkish Teller, had wound up wreathed in glory and the flag; others were not so fortunate. Oppy was stripped by lesser men of the security clearance he needed to work, and lived but a shadow of the life he might have had. But in 1944 they stood together, wearing dark European suits in the stark white sand of the desert. They gazed over the Trinity conference table like patron saints, their eyes communicating an inscrutable combination of humor, humility, and hard-won wisdom. The only Trinity scientist who displayed those qualities had died yesterday on his office floor.

Voices filtered from the hallway into the conference room. I straightened in my chair as my colleagues began to trickle in with an air of forced casualness. I had a feeling they had just adjourned a private meeting whose only order of business had been "handling" me.

First in line was Jutta Klein, the team's sole woman. Chief research scientist for the Siemens Corporation in Germany, the gray-haired Klein—also a Nobel laureate, in physics—had been loaned to Trinity for the duration of the project. With assistance from Fielding and a team of engineers from General Electric, she had designed and built the fourth-generation Super-MRI machine. Now she oversaw the smooth operation of the temperamental behemoth.

"*Guten Morgen,*" she said stiffly, and sat at my right, her matronly face impossible to read.

"*Morgen,*" I replied.

Ravi Nara followed Klein through the door. He sat three chairs away from me, emphasizing the distance that had recently marked our relationship. The young Indian neurologist held a chocolate doughnut in one brown hand, but his right protruded from a cast. I suppressed a smile. Four days ago, he had taken a coffee mug partly made of lead into the Super-MRI room and set it on a counter. When Klein activated the machine for a test on a chimpanzee, the mug had flown across the room and smashed Nara's arm against the machine's housing, shattering his ulna. Klein told him to consider himself lucky. On the day the Super-MRI went

96

operational, a technician on loan from Siemens had been killed by a metallic EKG cart that slammed her against the machine and crushed her skull.

"Good morning, David."

I looked up to see the trim, Brooks Brothers-clad figure of John Skow take the chair at the head of the table. A deputy director of the NSA, Skow was America's foremost authority on information warfare, and the titular director of Project Trinity. Yet it was Peter Godin who determined the direction and pace of Trinity research. The relationship between Skow and Godin mirrored that of General Leslie Groves and Robert Oppenheimer at Los Alamos. Groves had been a ruthless taskmaster, but without Oppenheimer's co-operation, he could never have delivered the atomic bomb. So, the ultimate power had lain with the civilian scientist, not the soldier.

"Skow," I said, not even attempting a smile.

"Yesterday was a terrible blow to all of us," he intoned in his aristocratic Boston accent, his thin lips barely moving. "But I know it's a particular loss for you, David."

I searched for genuine grief in his voice. The NSA man was a practiced bureaucrat, and his sincerity was hard to gauge.

"Peter will be here in a moment," he said. "I guess he'll be the tardy boy from now on."

I smiled inside. In the past, Fielding had always been last to arrive, when he bothered to show up at all. Some days he went AWOL, and I would be sent in search of him. I usually found him poring over equations in his office.

A faint curse drifted through the open door, announcing Peter Godin's approach. Trinity's lead scientist suffered from rheumatoid arthritis, and merely walking was a burden to him on some days. At seventy-one years old, Godin was by far the senior scientist on the project. Vacuum-tube computing machines had not even existed when he was born, yet for the past forty years, the "old man" of Trinity had pushed the envelope of digital computing further and faster than any CRT-dazed savant who ever skateboarded out of Silicon Valley.

Like Seymour Cray—the father of the supercomputer—Godin had been one of the original engineers at Control Data Systems in the early 1950s. In 1957, he left the company with Seymour to help found Cray Research. Godin had been part of the teams that built the famed 6600 and the Cray 1, but when Cray began to lose control of the bloated Cray 2 project, Godin decided the time had come to step out of his mentor's shadow. He quietly made the rounds of investment bankers, raised $6 million, and sixty days later opened the doors of Godin Supercomputing in Mountain View, California. While Seymour struggled to bring the revolutionary Cray 2 into being, Godin and a tiny team built an elegant and reliable four-processor machine that outperformed the Cray 1 by a speed factor of six. It wasn't a revolutionary advance, but it was one government weapons labs were willing to pay for. At $8 million per machine, Godin quickly paid off his debts and began designing his dream supercomputer.

Competing against national governments and Seymour Cray himself, Peter Godin had gained a foothold in the supercomputing market, and he never looked back. When the end of the Cold War virtually wiped out the supercomputing business, Godin switched to parallel-processing technology, and by the midnineties his computers had augmented or supplanted the Cray machines at NORAD, the NSA, the Pentagon, Los Alamos, Lawrence Livermore, and in missile silos across the country. In his day, Peter Godin had been both pioneer and follower, but he was first and foremost a survivor.

Everyone looked up as the old man entered the conference room, but I nearly got to my feet. When I joined the team two years ago, Godin had looked scarcely older than Andrew Fielding, who was sixty-one at the time. But two years leading the Trinity team had aged Godin at a shocking rate. His face sometimes had the swollen look of a cancer patient on steroids. At other times, it was thinned to skeletal hollowness, and his hair almost disappeared. Today he looked as though he might collapse before reaching the table. He'd told me that during times of creative stress, his body always underwent physical changes. Godin often worked without sleep for fifty or sixty consecutive hours, and though he knew this was taking years off his life, he felt that was a fair price to pay for what he had achieved during his years on earth.

His light blue eyes scanned the room, resting longer on me than on the others. Then he gave a general nod and settled into the empty chair beside Skow.

"Now that we're all here," Skow said with an air of ceremony, "I would be remiss if I didn't begin this meeting with a few words about the terrible loss that we—and this project—suffered yesterday. After a complete autopsy, the pathologist has confirmed that Dr. Fielding died of a massive cerebral hemorrhage. He—"

"Pathologist?" I cut in. "The state medical examiner?"

Skow gave me a look of forbearance. "David, you know we're not in a conventional security situation. We can't involve local authorities. Dr. Fielding's cause of death was certified by an NSA pathologist at Fort Meade."

"The NSA has a pathologist?" I understood why the agency might need psychiatrists. Code-breaking was a high-stress profession. But a pathologist?

"The agency has access to a full complement of medical specialists," Skow said in the voice of a government tour guide. "Some directly on the payroll, others fully vetted consultants." He glanced at Godin, whose eyes were closed. "Do you have some doubt about what killed Andrew, David?"

There it was. The gauntlet on the table.

"After all," Skow said in a condescending tone, "you *are* an experienced internist. Perhaps you saw something inconsistent with a stroke?"

I felt the tension in the air. Everyone was waiting for me to speak, especially Ravi Nara, who had diagnosed the stroke as Fielding died.

"No," I said at length. "Ravi said he observed paralysis, speech impairment, and a blown pupil just prior to death. That's consistent with stroke. It's just . . . it usually takes a while to die from a bleed. The suddenness took me by surprise."

It was as though the air had been let out of a balloon. Shoulders sagged with relief, buttocks shifted position, fingers began drumming on the table.

"Well, of course," Skow said generously. "It took us all by surprise. And Andrew was, quite simply, irreplaceable."

I wanted to strangle Skow. He had wanted to replace Fielding for the past six months, but there was no one remotely as qualified as the Englishman available for the job.

"And to show how serious I am about that," Skow said, "we will not try to replace him."

Only Jutta Klein looked as shocked as I. Fielding had known more about Project Trinity than anyone but Godin. He'd got us through a dozen major bottlenecks. Problems that had stumped software and materials engineers for weeks were but puzzles to the eccentric Englishman, something to be solved in a quarter of an hour. In this sense, Fielding truly was irreplaceable. But the quantum aspects of Project Trinity could not be ignored. Quantum physics was akin to alchemy in my mind—alchemy that worked—and to push ahead without someone qualified to handle problems like quantum entanglement and unwanted tunneling would be madness.

"But what do you plan to do about the MRI side effects

100

we've been studying?" I asked. "As you know, Fielding believed they were the result of quantum disturbances in the brain."

"*Ridiculous*," barked Nara. "There's no proof there are any quantum processes in the human brain. There never has been, and there never will be!"

"Dr. Nara," Skow said.

I gave the neurologist a look of disdain. "You didn't sound half so sure when you were in the room with Fielding."

Nara shot silent daggers at me.

Skow gave me his patient smile. "David, both Peter and I feel that you and Ravi are quite capable of continuing to explore the medical anomalies. Bringing in a new physicist at this time would be a needless security risk."

I wasn't going to argue this. I would save my efforts for the president. "Will Fielding's body and personal effects be turned over to his widow?"

Skow cleared his throat. "We can't seem to contact Mrs. Fielding. Therefore, Andrew's remains will be cremated as per his written wishes."

Along with any evidence of murder. I struggled to keep my face impassive. So Lu Li had made her escape. On the other hand . . . would they say anything different if they'd caught or killed her?

Godin touched Skow's wrist.

"Would you like to add something, Peter?" Skow asked.

Godin rubbed his nearly bald pate under the indirect lights. He sat with a Buddha-like centeredness, only the blue eyes in detectable motion. He spoke rarely, but when he did, the world listened.

"This is no time to talk about trivialities," he said. "We lost a giant yesterday. Andrew Fielding and I disagreed about a lot of things, but I respected him more than any man I've ever worked with."

101

I couldn't hide my surprise. Everyone at the table leaned forward, so as not to miss a word. The hypnotic blue eyes made a quick circuit of the room. Then Godin continued, his voice soft but still deep and powerful.

"From the dawn of history, the driving force of science has been war. If he were here today, Fielding would argue with me. He would say it is mankind's innate curiosity that has driven the upward surge of science. But that's wishful thinking. It is human conflict that has marked the great forward leaps in technology. A regrettable reality, but one that every rational person must recognize. We live in a world of fact, not philosophy. Philosophers question the reality of the universe, then look surprised when you hit them with a shoe and ask if they felt *that* reality."

Ravi Nara snickered, but Godin gave him a withering glare.

"Andy Fielding was not that sort." Godin nodded to the black-and-white photo on the wall. "Like Robert Oppenheimer, Andy was something of a mystic. But at his core, he was a gifted theoretician with a great practical bent."

Godin brushed a wisp of white hair off his ear and looked around the table. "The weaponization of science is the inevitable first step that brings countless peacetime gifts in its wake. Oppenheimer's superhuman efforts to give us the bomb ended the Second World War and gave the world safe nuclear energy. We here—we five who remain—face a task of no lesser importance. We're not trying, as Fielding sometimes suggested, to assume the mantle of God. God is merely a part of the human brain, an evolutionary coping mechanism that developed to make bearable our awareness of our own deaths. When we finally succeed in loading the first neuro-model into our prototype and communicating with it, we will have to deal with that part of the brain, just as with all the rest. For those who favor anthropomorphic expressions, we will have to deal with *Him*. But God, I predict, will prove no more troublesome than any other vestigial element of the brain. Because the completion of Trinity will render that particular coping mechanism unnecessary. Our work will end death's dominion over humanity. And surely there can be no more noble goal than that."

Godin laid his crooked hands on the table. "But today . . . today we mourn a man who had the courage of his convictions. While we, out of grim necessity, focused on the military and intelligence possibilities of an operational Trinity prototype, Fielding looked toward the day that he could sit down and ask the computer man's oldest questions: 'How did life begin? Why are we here? How will the universe end?' At sixty-three, Andy Fielding had the enthusiasm of a child, and he wasn't ashamed of it. Nor should he have been." Godin nodded soberly. "And I, for one, will miss him."

My face felt hot. I'd expected the crocodile tears of John Skow, then a rush back to full-scale research and development. But Peter Godin was classier than that. His words showed that he'd known his adversary well.

"After the cause of our neurological symptoms has been found," Godin concluded, "the project will resume. If we need another quantum physicist, we'll hire one. What we will *not* do is charge forward without knowing the dangers. Fielding taught me the importance of prudence."

Godin carefully massaged his right hand with the fingers of his left. "We've all sustained a severe shock. I want everyone to take three full days of rest, beginning at lunch today. We'll meet in this room on Tuesday morning. All the usual off-site security precautions will be observed during this period."

The resulting silence was total. The man who drove himself twice as hard as anyone else was suggesting time off? Such a "vacation" went so against Godin's nature that no one knew what to say.

103

Skow finally cleared his throat. "Well, I, for one, could use some time at home. My wife is about ready to divorce me over the hours I put in here."

Godin frowned and closed his eyes again.

"Meeting adjourned?" Skow said, glancing at Godin.

The old man got unsteadily to his feet and walked out without another word.

"Well, then," Skow said needlessly.

I stood and walked back to my office, my eyes on Peter Godin's retreating back. The meeting had gone nothing like I'd expected. Ahead of me, Godin started to turn the corner, but instead he stopped and turned to face me. I walked toward him.

"You and Fielding were very close," he said. "Weren't you?"

"I liked him. Admired him, too."

Godin nodded. "I read your book two nights ago. You're more of a realist than I would have guessed. Your opinions on abortion, fetal tissue research, cloning, the expenditures on last-year-of-life care, euthanasia. I agreed with all of it, right down the line."

I couldn't believe Peter Godin had worked with me for two years without reading the book that had brought me to Trinity. He looked over my shoulder for a moment, then back at my face.

"Something occurred to me during the meeting," he said. "You know the old hypothetical about history? If you could go back in time, and you had the opportunity to kill Hitler, would you do it?"

I smiled. "It's not a very realistic formulation."

"I'm not so sure. The Hitler question is easy, of course. But imagine it another way. If you could go back to 1948, and you knew that Nathuram Godse was going to assassinate Gandhi—would you kill him to prevent that assassination?"

I thought about it. "You're really asking how far down the chain of events I would go. Would you murder Hitler's mother?"

It was Godin's turn to smile. "You're right, of course. And my answer is yes."

"Actually, I think your question is more about causality. Would murdering Hitler's mother have prevented the Second World War? Or would some other nobody have risen from the discontented masses to tap German resentment over the Versailles Treaty?"

Godin considered this. "Quite possibly. All right, then. It's 1952, and you know that a clumsy lab technician is going to ruin the cell cultures of Jonas Salk. The cure for poliomyelitis will be greatly delayed, perhaps by years. Would you kill that innocent technician?"

A strange buzzing started in my head. I had a sense that Godin was toying with me, yet Peter Godin never wasted time with games.

"Thankfully, real life doesn't present us with those dilemmas," I said. "Only hindsight allows us to formulate them."

He smiled distantly. "I'm not so sure, Doctor. Hitler could have been stopped at Munich." Godin reached out and patted me on the arm. "Food for thought, anyway."

He turned and carefully negotiated his way around the corner.

I stood in the corridor, trying to read between the lines of what I'd heard. Godin never wasted words. He hadn't been idly reflecting on history or morality. He had been talking quite frankly about murder. Justifiable murder, in his mind. I shook my head in disbelief. Godin had been talking about Fielding.

Fielding's murder was necessary, he was saying. *Fielding was innocent, but he was interfering with a great good, and he had to be eliminated.*

As I walked back toward my office, I realized I was shivering. No one had asked about my call to Washington. No one had mentioned my visit to Fielding's house. Not one word about Rachel Weiss. And three days off would give me plenty of time to speak to the president. I might even be able to fly to Washington. What the hell was going on?

I froze in my office doorway. A tall, sinewy blonde woman with electric blue eyes and a stippled scar on her left cheek sat in my chair, gazing at my computer screen. Geli Bauer. If anyone in this building had murdered Andrew Fielding, it was she.

"Hello, Doctor," she said, a trace of a smile on her lips. "You look surprised. I thought you'd be expecting me."

ELEVEN

I stood speechless in my office doorway. Relief had turned to paralyzing anxiety in less than a second, and the fact that Geli Bauer was a woman did nothing to slow my racing pulse. Like her handpicked subordinates, she was lean and hard, with a predatory gleam in her eyes. She radiated the icy confidence of a world-class alpinist. I could imagine her hanging for hours from a precipice, her body supported only by her fingertips. Her intelligence was difficult to judge in an incubator filled with geniuses, but I knew from previous conversations that she was quick as mercury. She treated all but the top Trinity scientists like prisoners working under duress, and I attributed this to her being the daughter of a powerful army general. Ravi Nara had crudely called her "a terminator with tits," but I thought of her as a terminator with brains.

"What can I do for you?" I said finally.

"I need to ask you a couple of questions," she said. "Routine stuff."

Routine? Geli Bauer had visited my office a half dozen times in two years. I mostly saw her through a sheet of glass, observing the polygraph tests to which I was randomly subjected.

"Godin just gave us three days off," I told her. "Why don't we do this when I get back?"

"I'm afraid it can't wait." She had the stateless accent of elite overseas schools.

"You said it was routine."

A plastic smile. "Why don't you have a seat, Doctor?"

"You're in my chair."

Geli didn't get up. She thrived on conflict.

"You don't usually handle this kind of thing personally," I said. "To what do I owe the honor?"

"Dr. Fielding's death has created an unusual situation. We need to be sure we know as much as possible about the circumstances surrounding it."

"Dr. Fielding died of a stroke."

She studied me for a while without speaking. The scar on her left cheek reminded me of some I'd seen on some Vietnam vets during physicals. The vets described how shrapnel from a phosphorous grenade burned itself deep into the skin and then self-cauterized, only to reignite in the air and wound the operating surgeons when they attempted to remove the fragments. Soldiers lived in terror of them, and Geli Bauer looked as though she'd suffered intimate contact with one. I had been predisposed to like her because of that scar. A beautiful woman marked by such a thing might have earned some insight about life that few of her sisters possessed. But my interactions with Geli had convinced me that whatever hell she had survived, she'd learned only bitterness.

"I'm concerned about your relationship with Dr. Fielding," she said.

Always *I* with Geli, never the bureaucratic *we,* as though she felt personal responsibility for the security of the entire project.

"Really?" I said, as though shocked.

"How would you characterize your relationship?"

"He was my friend."

"You saw him and spoke to him outside this facility."

To concede this was to admit a violation of Trinity security regulations. But Geli probably had videotape. "Yes."

"That's a direct violation of security protocol."

I rolled my eyes. "Sue me."

"We could jail you."

Shit. "That'll really help keep this place secret."

She ran her long fingers through her blonde hair. I thought of a hawk preening itself. "You could lose your position here, Doctor."

"Now I get it. You're here to fire me."

Her smile slipped a notch. "There's no need for drama. I'm trying to learn what I can about Dr. Fielding's situation."

"His situation? He's dead. Deceased. No longer with us."

"What did the two of you discuss outside work hours?"

"Soccer."

"Soccer?"

"Fielding called it football. He was 'football mad,' in his words. He followed Arsenal, an English team. It bored the hell out of me, but I liked talking to the guy."

"You're being disingenuous, Doctor."

"Am I?"

"Both you and Dr. Fielding opposed further work on this project."

"No. I had ethical concerns about one aspect of it. Fielding had other concerns."

"He wanted the project stopped."

"Only until the cause of the neurological side effects we're all experiencing could be determined."

"Did he discuss those side effects with anyone not cleared for Trinity information?"

"I have no idea."

"His wife, for example?"

109

I strained to keep my face impassive. "I can't imagine that he would."

Geli raised one eyebrow. "You spent nearly an hour with her last night."

So they had been watching. Of course they had. They'd just killed Fielding, and they needed to see how his best friend would react. That meant they knew about Rachel.

"I made a condolence call."

"You discussed sensitive Trinity information with Lu Li Fielding. A Chinese physicist."

"I did nothing of the kind." I had thought Lu Li's marriage to Fielding made her a British citizen, but I didn't want to get into that discussion now.

"Mrs. Fielding has vanished. We need to talk to her."

"Sounds like a personal problem."

Geli ignored my sarcasm. "If you helped her flee, you could be charged with treason."

"Has Lu Li committed a crime?"

Geli's face gave away nothing. "That has yet to be determined. She may be an accessory to treason."

The crystal, I thought suddenly. *This has to be about Fielding's watch.* "So both Fieldings are missing now. That's embarrassing, isn't it?"

Geli didn't look embarrassed. She looked unflappable.

"Last night Lu Li told me she'd received no word about her husband's body," I said. "She was very upset."

"That's not my area of responsibility."

"What about Fielding's personal effects? Lu Li particularly mentioned a gold pocket watch. An heirloom."

Geli pursed her lips, then shook her head. "I don't recall a pocket watch. But as soon as Mrs. Fielding turns up, all this will be sorted out."

Geli was lying. She hadn't worked here for two years without seeing that watch a hundred times.

"We're going to need a polygraph this morning," she said.

Cold sweat broke out on my trunk. "Sorry. I won't be taking one."

Her eyes narrowed. This was the first time I'd ever refused such a request. "Why is that?"

"I just lost a good friend. I didn't sleep well. I feel terrible. My dog ate my homework."

"Dr. Tennant—"

"And I don't feel like submitting to your fascist bullshit today. Get it?"

She settled back in my chair and regarded me with increasing interest. "The employment agreement you signed permits polygraphs to be taken at any time. You've already agreed to submit."

The fear in my belly made me want to punch her in the face. I'd lived all my life with an extraordinary amount of freedom. As an internist, I'd owned and managed my own practice. As an author I'd been limited only by my subject. But in the oppressive atmosphere of Trinity, I'd developed a kind of spiritual claustrophobia. My father had experienced similar feelings when working on nuclear weapons at Los Alamos and Oak Ridge. And he'd submitted to his share of polygraph tests in his day. But times had changed since the Cold War. Today the NSA had lie detectors based on MRI technology, and unlike conventional polygraphs, they were accurate 100 percent of the time.

The principle was simple: it took more brain cells to lie than to tell the truth. Even a pathological liar first thought of the true answer when asked a question. Then he invented or recited his lie. That activity lit up the liar's brain like Christmas lights, and the MRI detector imaged and recorded the result for his interrogators. It was Fielding who'd stopped the MRI polygraph sessions, arguing that our strange

111

symptoms could be aggravated by further MRI exposure. It was a victory in Fielding's war against the invasion of our privacy, but conventional polygraph sessions were unnerving enough. Taking them on a surprise basis gave you the feeling you were living in an Orwellian dystopia, especially when you had something to hide.

"Are you going to sedate me?" I asked. "Tie me down?"

Geli looked as though she'd like to.

"No? Then forget it."

She raised a finger and idly touched her scar. "I don't understand why you're so combative, Doctor."

"Sure you do."

"You're hiding something."

"If I were, that would make two of us."

"You're trying to subvert this project."

"How could I do that? And why would I? The project's already been suspended."

Geli studied her fingernails, two of which were gnawed to nubs. Maybe she wasn't unflappable after all. "By going *public*," she said finally.

There it was. The deepest fear of the paranoid military mind. "I haven't done that."

"Are you considering it?"

"No."

"Have you spoken to the president?"

"In my life?"

Annoyance crept into her voice at last. "Since Dr. Fielding's death."

"No."

"You left a message at the White House yesterday."

I felt my face flush. "Yes."

"You used a pay phone."

"So?"

"Why?"

112

"The battery on my cell phone died." An easy lie, and impossible to check.

"Why not wait and call when you got home?"

"I was in the mood right then."

"In the mood to talk to the president of the United States?"

"That's right."

"About Dr. Fielding's death?"

"Among other things."

She seemed to weigh her next words carefully. "You told the White House you didn't want the other Trinity principals informed of your call."

My blood pressure dropped like a stone. *How did they know what I'd said during that pay phone conversation?* It had to be wiretapping surveillance, and not the local police or FBI variety. The NSA recorded millions of private telephone calls every day, the disk drives in the basements of Fort Meade triggered by key words like *plastique, Al Qaeda, strong encryption, RDX,* or even *Trinity.* I recalled that I'd said "Trinity" as soon as the White House operator answered, to make her switch me to the proper contact. The NSA probably had a recording of my conversation from that point forward.

I drew myself up and looked Geli hard in the eyes. "I was personally appointed to this project by the president. Not by the NSA or John Skow or even Peter Godin. I'm here to evaluate ethical problems. If I determine that a problem exists, I report directly to the president. No one here has any say in the matter."

The gloves were off. I had just drawn a line between myself and everyone else in the Trinity building.

Geli leaned forward, her blue eyes challenging me. "How many cell phones do you own, Dr. Tennant?"

"One."

"Do you have others in your possession?"

113

Clarity settled in my mind like a resolving chord. They knew I'd called the White House, but they *didn't* know whether or not the president had gotten back to me. They had my phones covered—the ones they knew about—but they were worried about channels of communication they didn't know about. If they were worried about that, they had no inside line to the president, and I still stood a chance of convincing him of my suspicions.

"Rachel Weiss owns a cell phone," Bauer said, her eyes alert for the slightest reaction on my part.

I took a slow breath and kept my voice even. "I don't know a doctor who doesn't."

"But you know Dr. Weiss rather better than you know almost anyone else."

"She's my psychiatrist, if that's what you mean."

"She's the only person other than Trinity personnel to whom you've spoken more than fifty words over the past two months."

I wondered if this was true.

"The same is true for Dr. Weiss," Geli said.

"What do you mean?"

"She sees no one. She lost her son to cancer last year. After the boy died, her husband left her and returned to New York. Six months ago, Dr. Weiss began accepting occasional dates with male colleagues. Dinner, a movie, like that. She never saw anyone more than twice. Two months ago, she stopped seeing men altogether."

This didn't surprise me. Rachel was an intense woman, and I couldn't imagine many men meeting her expectations.

"So?" I said.

"I think you're the reason for that, Doctor. I think Dr. Weiss is in love with you."

I laughed, really laughed, for the first time since I'd seen Fielding's body. "Dr. Weiss thinks I'm delusional, Ms. Bauer. Possibly schizophrenic."

This didn't faze Geli. "She kissed you last night. At the Fielding house."

"That was a sympathy kiss. I was upset about Fielding."

Geli ignored this. "What have you told Dr. Weiss about Project Trinity?"

"Nothing, as you well know. I'm sure you've found some way to record every one of my sessions."

She surprised me by conceding this with a slight nod. "But lovers are resourceful. You may have managed unauthorized contact. Like last night."

"Last night was the first time I ever saw Rachel Weiss outside her office." I folded my arms across my chest. "And I refuse to discuss her further. She has nothing to do with this project. You're invading the privacy of an American citizen who has signed no agreement waiving her rights."

This time when Geli smiled, a little flash of cruelty burned through. "Where Project Trinity is concerned, privacy means nothing. Under National Security Directive 173, we can detain Dr. Weiss for forty-eight hours without even a phone call."

My frustration boiled over. "Geli, do you know what Project Trinity *is*?"

My use of her first name wiped away her smile, and my question put her squarely on the defensive. It would kill her to admit that she didn't know the inmost secrets of Trinity, but to say otherwise might cost her her job. She glowered but said nothing.

I took a step toward her. "Well, I *do* know. And until you do—and you fully understand its implications—don't be so damn eager to follow orders like a good little German."

The insult struck home. Geli tensed in the chair as though about to spring at me. I took a step back, instantly regretting my words. There was nothing to be gained by earning the personal enmity of Geli Bauer. In fact, it was a singularly

115

bad idea. She had probably killed Fielding herself. *And that's why I'm baiting her,* I realized.

"We're done," I said, taking my car keys from my pocket. "I'll be back on Tuesday morning. Keep your human Dobermans away from me until then."

I turned my back on her.

"Dr. Tennant?"

I kept walking.

"Tennant!"

I pressed the elevator button. When the door opened, I got in, then stepped out again. Geli could probably turn the tiny cubicle into a cell with the push of a button. She could seal the entire building just as easily, but I took the stairs anyway.

As I hit the fourth-floor landing, an image of Fielding sitting in a cloud of smoke filled my mind. The Englishman smoked like a chimney, but smoking was forbidden everywhere in the Trinity complex, even for the top scientists. This wasn't due to federal regulations; Peter Godin couldn't stand a hint of smoke in the air. Ever resourceful, Fielding had found a place where he could indulge his habit. In the materials lab on the fourth floor was a large vacuum chamber that had been used during the project's early stages, for testing the properties of carbon nanotubes. There were smoke detectors in the lab, but none in the vacuum chamber. Fielding had managed to pile enough boxes around the chamber that most people had forgotten its existence. When I couldn't locate him anywhere else, I'd always known I could find him there.

If Fielding were in the Trinity building and afraid for his life, I reasoned, wouldn't he have tried to distance the crystal watch fob from himself? He wouldn't hide it in his office, which would certainly be searched. But the vacuum chamber was only one floor away, and he could be fairly sure that I would eventually search his informal sanctum sanctorum.

116

I exited the stairwell and made my way down the hall to the materials lab. Two engineers recruited from Sun Microsystems walked out of the lab and separated to pass me, heading toward the elevators. I forced a smile, then slowed my walk so that I would reach the materials lab after they rounded the corner behind me.

The lab was empty. I moved swiftly to the pile of boxes that obscured the steel vacuum chamber and began uncovering the door. The forbidding machine was like a large decompression chamber for scuba divers, with a porthole window and a large iron wheel set in its hatchlike door. I turned the wheel that unlocked the hatch. The lights came on automatically.

My heart thudded when I stepped inside. I remembered wide shelves cluttered with tools, clamps, and old scraps of carbon. There was nothing in the chamber now. Even the shelves were gone. The entire room looked as though it had been steam cleaned.

"Geli Bauer," I breathed.

If Fielding's pocket watch had been hidden here, Geli had it now. I hurried out of the chamber, half-expecting her to confront me in the lab. But the lab was still empty, as was the hall. Slipping back into the stairwell, I descended to the third floor and walked toward the security desk, where Henry awaited me.

Upon exiting Trinity, staff had to submit to a body search to prove they weren't trying to remove computer disks or papers from the building. How Fielding must have laughed inside every time Henry ignored his crystal watch fob. As I approached the desk, I realized that Henry was speaking into his collar radio.

"What's up, Henry?" I said, pausing to wait for his pat-down.

"Just a minute, Doc."

My heartbeat accelerated. I imagined Geli Bauer giving him orders: *Don't let Tennant out of the building . . .*

"I really need to get moving," I said. "I have an appointment."

Henry looked at me, then said into the mike, "He's right here."

Jesus. If Geli had to ask if I was at the door, that meant she wasn't watching me on camera from the security office. She was probably on her way here. My limbic brain was telling me to run like hell, but how far would I get? Harmless-looking Henry was armed with a 9mm Glock automatic. Still, it took a supreme act of will not to bolt for the door.

Henry listened to his ear-bud for a few seconds, looking confused. "Are you sure?" he asked. "All right."

He came around the desk, and I suddenly knew that if Henry reached for his gun, survival instinct would dictate the next few seconds. I tensed for action when his hands dropped, but then he squatted and began his normal pat-down, starting with my pant legs.

Geli had decided to let me go. Why? *Because she can't be sure whether I've talked to the president.*

"Good to go, Doc," Henry said, patting me on the shoulder. "For a second I thought she—I mean *they*—wanted me to hold you here."

As I looked into Henry's face, I saw something in his eyes that I didn't understand. Then I did. He didn't like Geli Bauer any more than I did. In fact, he was afraid of her.

The minute I cleared the armored-glass doors, my cell phone began ringing. I hit SEND and held the phone to my ear.

"Hello?"

"*David!* Where the hell have you been?"

"Don't say your name," I snapped, recognizing Rachel's voice.

"I've been trying to reach you for an hour!"

No cellular transmissions could pass through the copper cladding that encased the Trinity building. "Just tell me what's wrong."

"Did you come to my office this morning?"

"Your office? Of course not. Why?"

"Because someone practically tore it to pieces. Your file is missing, and everything's out of place."

I sucked in a lungful of air and forced myself to keep walking toward my car. "I haven't been near your office today. Why do you think I'd do something like that?"

"To bolster your delusions in my eyes! To make me think they're real!"

She sounded close to hysteria. Had she understood nothing last night? "We need to talk. But not like this. Are you at your office now?"

"No, I'm on Highway 15."

Rachel could take 15 all the way from the Duke Medical Center to Chapel Hill. "Are you in a cab?"

"No. I went and got my car this morning."

"Meet me where you saw me making the videotape."

"You mean—"

"You know where. I'm on my way. Hang up now."

She did.

It took all my self-control not to run the last few steps to my car.

TWELVE

Rachel's white Saab was parked in front of my house. Rachel herself was sitting on my front steps, her chin in her hands like a college girl waiting for a class to begin. Instead of her usual silk blouse and skirt, she wore blue jeans and a white cotton oxford shirt. I tapped my horn. She looked up, unsmiling. Waving once, I pulled into my garage and walked through the house to open the front door.

"Sorry you got here first," I said, glancing up the street for unfamiliar vehicles.

Her eyes were red from crying. She went into the living room but didn't sit. Instead, she paced around my sparse furniture, unable to remain still.

"Tell me what happened," I said.

She paused long enough to fix me with a glare, then continued pacing. "I was at the hospital, checking on a patient who attempted suicide two days ago."

"And?"

"I decided to run by my office and dictate some charts. When I got there, I realized someone else had been there. I mean, the office was locked, but I could tell, you know?"

"You said the place was torn to pieces."

She averted her eyes. "Not exactly. But lots of things were out of place. I know, because I like my things a certain way. Books arranged from small to large, papers stacked . . . never mind."

"You're obsessive-compulsive."

Her dark eyes flashed. "There are worse problems than having OCD."

"Agreed. You said my file was missing?"

"Yes."

"Any other patient records missing?"

"No."

"That's it, then. What I don't understand is why they would steal my file. Why not just photocopy it? I'm sure they've read it before. They probably read it every week."

Rachel stopped pacing and looked at me in disbelief. "How could they do that?"

"By sneaking someone into your office. Probably the nights of my appointment days."

"Why didn't I notice anything before?"

"Maybe this time they were in a hurry."

"Why?"

"They're frightened."

"Of what?"

"Me. Of what I've done. What I might do."

She sat on the edge of my sofa as though to collect herself. "I need to be clear on this, David. Just who is *they*? The NSA?"

"Yes and no. They're the security people for Project Trinity, which is funded by the NSA."

"And this is who you say murdered Andrew Fielding?"

"Yes."

She closed her eyes. "I had a friend at the medical center test that white powder you gave me. It's not contaminated with anthrax or any other known pathogen or poison." Her eyes opened and looked into mine. "It's sand, David. Gypsum. White sand. No threat to anybody."

My mind began spinning with the possible significance of that. Microchips were made of silicon, a kind of sand. Was gypsum the basis of some new semiconductor Godin had discovered? Maybe Fielding was trying to tell me something like that without being overt—

"Have you tried to reach the president again?" Rachel asked.

I opened my mouth in surprise.

"What?"

"I forgot to check my answering machine. Excuse me."

I went to the kitchen. The machine's LED showed one message waiting. When I hit the button, a New England accent crackled from the tiny speaker:

"Dr. Tennant? This is Ewan McCaskell, the president's chief of staff. I remember you from your visit a couple of years ago. I just received your message. I'm sure you understand that we're very busy over here. I can't involve the president until I know what this is about, but I do want to talk to you as soon as possible. Please remain at this number, and I'll call back as soon as time permits."

My relief was almost overwhelming. I put my hand on the counter to steady myself. The caller ID unit showed that McCaskell's call had come in twenty minutes ago.

"Who was that?" Rachel asked.

I replayed the message for her.

"I have to admit," she said, "that sounded like Ewan McCaskell."

"Like him? That *was* him. Didn't you understand anything you saw last night?"

She pulled a chair away from the kitchen table and sat in front of me. "Listen to me, David. Do you know why I'm here? Why I helped you last night?"

122

"Tell me."

"Your book."

"My book?"

"Yes. Every day in the hospital I see things they never told me about in medical school. Cases that fall into the cracks between reality and legality. Dilemmas the government hasn't got the guts to face. I do what I can about them . . . maybe I complain to another doctor, but that's it. You wrote it down for the world to read, without giving a damn what would happen to you. Abortion. Last-year-of-life care versus pre-natal care. Euthanasia. My God, you wrote about assisting your own brother to die."

I closed my eyes and saw an image of my older brother, unable to move anything but his eyelids due to the ravages of ALS, then unable to move even those. We'd made a pact. At that point I would help him end what remained of his life.

"I nearly left that out," I said.

She gripped my forearm. "But you didn't. You took the risk, and you helped countless people by leaving it in. People you'll never know. But they know you. I know you. And now *you're* ill. You've needed help for months, and conventional therapy wasn't working. I couldn't break through the walls you'd put up." Her hand tightened on my arm, and she smiled encouragingly. "I believe you're involved in some kind of special work, okay? But tell me this. If the Trinity computer is all you say it is, then why you? You know? You wrote a great book. The president knew your brother. But does that qualify you to make judgments about the kind of science you've told me about?"

She was right. There was more to it. I'd kept my past secret for so long that to speak of it now required a surprising act of will.

"My father was a nuclear physicist," I said softly. "He

123

worked at Los Alamos during the war. He was the youngest physicist to work on the Manhattan Project."

Her dark eyes flashed. "Go on."

"My undergraduate degree is in theoretical physics. MIT."

"My God. I really know nothing about you, do I?"

I touched her shoulder. "Sure you do. Look, my father was part of the group that began to protest using the bomb. Leo Szilard, Eugene Wigner, those guys. The Germans had surrendered, and the Japanese just didn't have the resources to build an atomic bomb. My father's group wanted our bomb demonstrated for the Japanese army, not used on civilians. Their dissent was ignored, and Hiroshima became history.

"But we live in a different world now. Once the president realized the implications of Trinity—we're talking about liberating human intelligence from the body, for God's sake—he knew he'd be vulnerable politically if the public learned he'd gone ahead without concern for ethics or morality. Look at the craziness that surrounds cloning and fetal tissue research. So he demanded ethical oversight. He knew my book, he knew the public trusts me to tell the truth, and he trusted me because he'd known my brother. Beyond that, my pedigree for conscientious objection went back to my father and the Manhattan Project. So, who better than I?"

Rachel was shaking her head. "Why did you become a doctor rather than a physicist?"

She couldn't stop being a shrink. Or maybe she was just being a woman. "After Hiroshima, my dad led a troubled life. Edward Teller was gearing up to build the hydrogen superbomb. Oppenheimer opposed it. So did my father. Dad requested a transfer. General Groves didn't want to release him from weapons work, but they agreed to give him a more technical job, one more removed from the actual warheads. They moved him to the national lab at Oak Ridge, Tennessee."

"Why didn't he just quit altogether?"

"Eventually he did. But this was the Cold War. There were different kinds of pressure then. Oppenheimer was persecuted for years for his opposition to the hydrogen bomb. Dad also met my mother at Oak Ridge. Things were better there. They had my brother. I was born much later. An accident, really." I smiled at the memory of my parents revealing this fact to me. "I grew up in Oak Ridge, but when I was a teenager, Dad quit nuclear physics and moved us to Huntsville, Alabama, so he could work on the space program."

"I still don't see the medical connection."

"My mother was a pediatrician in Oak Ridge. She did a lot of good. It didn't take a genius to see that she was a lot happier in her work than my dad had been. That's what influenced me."

I glanced down at the phone, willing it to ring again. "Last night, I only told you part of the truth. When the president offered me this position, it felt oddly like poetic justice. I was being given the opportunity my father never had at Los Alamos. The chance to exercise some control over a great undertaking that was likely to change the world forever. For good or evil. I sensed that on the day I visited the Oval Office, and that's what put me here."

Rachel took a deep breath and slowly blew out the air. "It's all real, isn't it? Trinity, I mean."

"Yes. And I'm damned glad McCaskell called me back. We need the president badly."

I stood up, half wanting to replay McCaskell's message, but a wave of fatigue rolled through me. I hoped it was just exhaustion, but then the familiar high-pitched humming began in my back teeth. Remembering I had no amphetamines left, I took a can of Mountain Dew out of the fridge, popped it open, and drank a long pull for the caffeine.

"David?" Rachel was watching me strangely. "Are you all right? You look shaky."

"I may go out," I said, taking another gulp of the soda.

"Go out?" Her eyes widened. "Narcolepsy?"

She'd never witnessed one of my episodes. As I nodded, a shadow seemed to pass over my eyes. It left me with a vague feeling of threat, as though someone were in the room with us, there but unseen. "I'm missing something," I thought aloud.

"What are you talking about?"

An image of Geli Bauer came into my mind. "We're in danger."

Rachel looked worried, more about me than any external threat. "What kind of danger?"

"There's something about the way all this is happening. Godin giving us time off . . . my chart being stolen from your office . . . McCaskell's call. I'm missing something, but I'm too tired to think of what."

"I thought McCaskell's call was good news."

"It is. It's just . . ." As drowsy as I was, I felt a desperate need to have my gun in my hand. "I want you to do me a favor. Wait here for two minutes."

"What?" Worry darkened her eyes. "Where are you going?"

"To my neighbor's house." I hurried to the back door.

"David! What if you pass out?"

"Don't answer the door!" I called. "But if the phone rings, answer it and say I'll be right back."

I ran outside and crashed through the thick hedge that bordered the backyards of the houses on my street. I sprinted the length of three backyards, then cut back through the hedge behind a neighbor's utility shed. I'd slipped out of my house last night about 2 A.M. and hidden Fielding's box beneath it. Inside the box were Fielding's electronic gadgets, my partially recorded videotape, Fielding's letter, and my pistol. I got on my knees and retrieved the box, then crawled back through the hedge and sprinted back to my own yard. By the time I reached it, I felt like a drunk running through an unfamiliar city.

Rachel was waiting just inside the back door. "That's the stuff from last night," she said. "Why do you need that?"

I tilted the box so she could see the gun.

She stepped back. "David, you're scaring me."

"You need to get out of here. You'll be fine for the time it takes me to tell my story to McCaskell." I set the box on the floor, put the gun in my waistband, then led her to the front of the house. "Spend the rest of the day somewhere public, like a mall. Don't go home until you hear from me."

She pivoted and stopped me from pushing her toward the door. Her assertiveness seemed to bring us eye to eye. "Stop this! You're so out of it right now you could shoot yourself by accident."

I started to reply, but my words went spinning off into the dark edges of my mind. I would be unconscious in less than a minute.

"I'm about to go under."

She grabbed my arm and dragged me into the hall, looking for a place to lay me down. I pointed to the door of my guest bedroom. Sensing that I was about to fall, she rushed me through the door and let me fall facedown across the mattress.

"Do you have any medication?"

"I ran out."

Her footsteps moved away. I heard cabinet doors banging, then Rachel's voice talking to herself. When the voice seemed closer, I managed to roll over. There was a dark silhouette in the doorway.

"Coffee's brewing," Rachel said. "You're still awake?"

"Sort of."

She watched me like someone observing an animal during an experiment. "There's no food in your kitchen. Nothing but rock-hard saltines. When was the last time you went to the market?"

I couldn't remember. The last few weeks had been an endless parade of hours working with Fielding on experiments I barely understood.

Rachel sat on the bed and put her fingers against my carotid artery. Her fingertips were cool.

"I was like that for a while," she said, looking at her watch. Her lips moved slightly as she counted pulse beats. "After I lost my son. Not going to the market, I mean. Not paying bills. Not bathing. I guess it takes a man longer to get back to those kinds of things. In the end, I used those small chores to enforce some order in my life. It kept me from going completely mad."

I felt my lips smile. I liked that she didn't let psychiatry get in the way of using words like *mad*. I also liked the way her fingers felt against my neck. I wanted to tell her something about her touch. It reminded me of someone, but I couldn't think who . . .

"When's your birthday?" she asked.

I couldn't remember.

"David?"

A black wave rolled over me, covering me in darkness.

I'm walking up a suburban sidewalk, studying the perfect houses in their perfect rows. It's Willow Street. I live on Willow—sleep on it, anyway—but it has little in common with the street I lived on as a boy. On Willow Street, I don't know my neighbors well, and some not at all. The NSA told me not to make friends, and that has turned out to be easy. On Willow Street, no one makes an effort. In Oak Ridge the houses were smaller, but I could name everyone who

128

lived in them. My little neighborhood was a world unto itself,
filled with faces I knew like those of my own family. On
Willow Street the children stay inside more than outside. The
fathers don't cut the lawns, hired men do. In Oak Ridge,
the fathers cared for their lawns like little fiefdoms, spent hours
discussing various mowers and fertilizers with each other.

I walk around a curve and see my own house. White with
green trim. From the outside it looks like a home, but it's
never felt like home to me. A black Labrador retriever lopes
across the street without its master, a rare sight here. A Lexus
rolls toward me, slowing as it passes. I wave at its driver, a
tall, imperious woman. She stares at me as if I'm a dangerous
interloper. I cross the street and walk up to my front door.

My hand goes into my pocket for my key, then to the
doorknob. I insert something into the lock, but . . . it's not
my key. It's thin and metallic, like a file. I jiggle it in the
lock. There's a moment of resistance, then the lock gives. I
open the door, slip inside, and quickly close it behind me.

My hand digs into my other pocket, brushing against some-
thing cold. My fingers close around wood, and my hand
emerges gripping the butt of a gun, an automatic. I don't
recognize the weapon. From my other pocket I withdraw a
perforated silencer and slowly screw it onto the gun barrel. It
seats itself with satisfying finality. From the hallway, I hear a
tinkle of glass. Someone's in the kitchen. I take one careful
step forward, testing the floorboards, then begin to walk—

I snapped awake in panic and jerked my pistol from my
waistband. A revolver, not an automatic. And no silencer. I
wanted to call out to Rachel, but I suppressed the urge. In
a single motion I rolled off the bed, landed on my feet, and
moved to the bedroom door.

At first I heard only a soft humming in a female register.
The tune sounded like "California" by Joni Mitchell.

The hardwood floor of the hallway creaked.

I drew a silent breath and held it.

The floor creaked again. Someone was passing my door from right to left. I closed my eyes and waited. Another creak. I counted slowly to ten. Then I reached down with my free hand and slowly turned the knob. When it had turned far enough, I yanked open the door, leapt into the hall, and aimed my .38 to the left.

A long-haired blond man stood six feet away, his arms extended through the kitchen door. I couldn't see his hands, but I knew they held a gun.

I pulled the trigger.

There was no boom or kick. I'd forgotten to cock the hammer, so the double-action trigger only went halfway back. As I jerked it home, the blond man whirled and a silenced automatic whipped into view, its bore black and bottomless. Then my trigger broke, and an orange flash illuminated the hallway. I blinked against it, and when I opened my eyes, the blond man was gone.

A woman was screaming an ice pick through my eardrums.

I looked down. The blond man lay on the floor, blood pouring from his skull. I moved forward and stepped on the wrist of the hand holding the gun. The screaming wouldn't stop. I glanced to my right. Rachel was standing with her back against the sink, her face deathly gray, her mouth open wide.

"Stop it!" I yelled. *"Stop!"*

Her mouth remained open, but the scream died.

I pulled the automatic from the blond man's hand, then checked his brachial pulse. Thready. The bullet had entered the skull just above the right ear. His gray eyes were glazed, both pupils fixed and dilated. Leaning down, I saw exposed brain matter. He wouldn't last five minutes.

I sensed more than saw Rachel moving. Looking up, I saw her holding the kitchen telephone, preparing to dial.

"Put that down."

"I'm calling for paramedics!"

"He doesn't have a chance."

"You don't know that!"

"Of course I do. Examine him, if you don't believe me." I straightened up. "Even if he did, we couldn't risk it."

"*What?* What do you mean?"

"Who do you think this is? Some street punk? A crackhead breaking into my house in broad daylight? Look at him."

Rachel glanced down for perhaps a second. "I don't know who he is. Do you know him?"

As I stared down at the ruined young face, I realized that I did. At least I'd seen him before. Not often, but I had passed him in the parking lot at Trinity, a tall, lanky blond with the look of someone you'd meet on a mountain trail in Europe. Like Geli Bauer, he had the physique of a climber, or an elite soldier.

"I do know him. He works for Geli Bauer."

Rachel squinted in confusion. "Who's that?"

"She's Trinity. She's Godin. She's the NSA." I laid both guns on the kitchen counter. "Someone ordered her to take me out too. You, too, apparently."

Something in me still resisted the idea that Peter Godin had ordered my death. Yet nothing at Trinity happened without his approval.

"We have to call the police," Rachel said. "We'll be all right. He was about to shoot me. This was self-defense, or justifiable homicide, whatever they call it."

"The police? You can't call local police to investigate the NSA. I told you that."

"Why not? He was going to kill me. That's a state crime."

I almost laughed. "The NSA is the largest and most secret

131

intelligence agency in the United States. *Everything they do* is classified. It would take a court order to get a cop past the front gate at Fort Meade."

"This isn't Fort Meade."

"To the NSA, it is. Look, until I talk to the president, we're on our own. Do you understand?"

She looked down at the growing pool of blood. "Maybe he *is* a street punk."

"Don't you get it? This is why they stole my file from your office!"

"What?"

"They already knew they were going to kill you."

She opened her mouth but said nothing.

"Otherwise they would have photocopied the file and left it in place. They wanted nothing left in your office for the Durham police to connect you to the project."

She was shaking her head, but my logic was difficult to refute. I stuck the automatic into my waistband and picked up my .38.

"We have to get out of here. Fast. There could be others close by."

Her eyes went wide. "*Others?*"

Suddenly I saw it all. "The NSA taps my phones. When they heard Ewan McCaskell leave his message, they knew I hadn't spoken to the president yet. That's all they were waiting for. I was too excited to see the implications."

I grasped her hand. It was cold and limp. "We have to run, Rachel. Right now. If we don't, we'll die here."

"Run where?"

"Anywhere. Nowhere. We have to disappear."

"No. We haven't done anything wrong."

"That doesn't matter." I pointed at the man on the floor and saw that he was no longer breathing. "Do you think that corpse is one of my hallucinations?"

132

"You killed him," she said in the voice of a child.

"And I'd do it again. He was about to fire a bullet into your head."

She wobbled on her feet. I steadied her, then led her to the guest bedroom where I'd lain unconscious only minutes ago.

"Stay here. I have to get something." I tried to put my .38 in her hand, but she recoiled. "Keep it," I insisted, closing her fingers around it. "If you leave this house alone, you'll be killed."

She stared hollow-eyed at me.

I took the silenced automatic from my waistband and checked to make sure the safety was off. "Promise me you won't leave."

"I won't leave," she said dully.

I left the guestroom and raced upstairs. My bedroom was on the left side of the landing. On the right was a bedroom I used for storage. I pulled an old chair into the closet of that room and stood on it. With my arms stretched high, I could just reach the plywood panel that gave access to the attic. I pushed out the wooden square, then lifted myself by main strength and wedged my body through the space.

Standing half-erect to avoid the roofing nails jutting down from above, I balanced on two rafters and looked around to get my bearings. Enough light was showing through the eaves and soffit vents to show my way. I crept twenty feet to my left and knelt. Lying on pink fiberglass insulation were a hammer and crowbar I'd left there four weeks ago, as though dropped carelessly. I picked them up and moved quickly to an area floored with quarter-inch plywood.

Jamming the crowbar into a seam between two pieces of wood, I hammered it deeper, then leaned heavily on the bar. The plywood splintered. I shoved the end of the bar through the resulting hole, then jerked upward, ripping open a two-foot section of wood. From the dark cavity below I removed a small nylon gym bag and unzipped it. The light filtering through the eaves illuminated the rectangular outlines of a passport and two thick bundles. The bundles were stacks of hundred-dollar bills. Twenty thousand dollars' worth.

Five weeks ago, when Fielding told me I needed to cache a bag like this, I'd laughed at him. But he had known this day would come. Zipping the bag shut, I crab-walked across the rafters to the access hole, then dropped the bag onto the closet floor. My arms quivered from strain as I lowered myself back down to the chair and pulled the plywood square back over the opening.

When my feet hit the floor, an image of Rachel running from the house in panic filled my mind. I grabbed the bag and ran downstairs.

She was still sitting on the bed, her eyes blank with shock.

"Time to go," I told her. "Are you ready?"

She blinked but said nothing.

I took her free hand and pulled her to her feet. "I need you to keep it together for five minutes. After that, you can collapse if you need to. Here we go."

I led her through the hall and kitchen to the laundry room, which opened into the garage. Leaving her there, I retrieved Fielding's box from the back door, then returned and took my .38 back from her.

"Hold this," I said, giving her the box. "Wait here till I call for you."

Without pausing long enough for fear to take hold, I threw open the door from the house to the garage and charged through with the automatic extended, traversing it right and left to cover all angles of fire.

The garage looked empty.

I made a quick circuit of my Acura, then dropped to my knees and looked beneath it. "Come on!" I shouted. "Hurry!"

Rachel's shoes hissed on the smooth cement. I opened the passenger door for her, then took Fielding's box and set it on the backseat. "If anything bad's going to happen, it's going to happen right now," I said, getting behind the wheel. "Get down in your seat."

She slid to the floor. The top of her head showed above the doorframe. I pushed it down, then started the engine and put the car in reverse.

"Stay down."

I touched the remote control clipped to my visor. The garage door motor groaned above us, and the wide white door began to rise. With the killer's gun clenched in my hand, I watched for the silhouette of legs in the growing rectangle of sunlight.

I saw nothing.

The instant the garage door cleared roof height, I gunned the engine. The Acura shot backward over the cement and into blinding sunlight. I hit the remote to lower the garage door, then spun the wheel left. I didn't touch the brake until the car was pointed up Willow Street.

"What's happening?" Rachel cried, alarmed by my sudden stop.

"Stay down!"

I'd planned to drive calmly if the street was clear, but as we stopped, I could almost feel an unseen marksman taking aim. I shifted into DRIVE, floored the accelerator, and fishtailed up Willow, leaving six feet of rubber on the pavement behind us.

THIRTEEN

In the Trinity building's control center, Geli Bauer stood absolutely still and spoke into her headset.

"We heard a shot. In Tennant's house."

"Isn't that what you expected?" Skow asked.

Idiot. "No. Ritter had a silenced weapon."

"And Tennant was carrying his gun last night."

"Right."

Skow processed this in silence. "That doesn't mean Ritter failed."

"No. In fact, I can't imagine a scenario like that."

"Good. What do you want to do?"

Geli had always pegged Skow as a theoretical warrior, and now that bullets were flying, he was looking to her for guidance. "I pulled my other assets back so nothing would look suspicious. But if I don't get confirmation of success within five minutes, I'm putting in a team to check things out."

"You have cover?"

"A carpet-service truck."

"Is there any chance the shot might have been reported to local police?"

"Some. If a patrol car shows up before we've cleared the scene—"

"Use your NSA credentials to quarantine the house," Skow finished, showing some balls at last. "Then contact me immediately."

"I will."

"I'm out."

"Wait."

"What is it?"

Geli was tired of being in the dark. "Tennant asked me about the pocket watch."

"What pocket watch?"

Her bullshit detector pegged the meter. "I checked the storage room this morning. Fielding's personal effects. Everything was there except his pocket watch."

Skow was silent for a time. Then he spoke almost to himself, "Fielding must have told him something about it."

"You want to tell *me* something about it?"

"That knowledge isn't necessary for you to do your job."

Anger flashed through her. "If it's on Tennant's mind, it may be important."

"It is important. Just not to you. Keep me posted on the situation at the house."

Skow hung up.

Geli sat in her chair. She hated the mushroom treatment, but that was the nature of intelligence work. *Keep them in the dark and feed them bullshit*. She understood the value of compartmentalizing knowledge. And for the past two years, she hadn't really needed to know what the scientists were working on. But things had changed. Since the project's suspension, Peter Godin had been spending a great deal of time away, supposedly visiting his corporate headquarters in California. Geli no longer believed that. Sometimes Godin took Ravi Nara with him, and that made no sense. Nara had nothing to do with Godin Supercomputing, and Godin didn't even like the neurologist.

Now Godin had dropped off the face of the earth. Had Fielding's pocket watch gone with him? How could the watch be so important? When Fielding first came to work at Trinity, an NSA engineer had disassembled the pocket watch to be sure it contained no data-recording device. He'd pronounced the watch clean. It was disassembled again this year, on a day chosen at random. The watch was clean again. So why had it been taken from the storeroom? Geli pictured the watch in her mind. A heavy gold case, scarred from use. There was a chain attached, and a crystal on the end of the chain. But the crystal was transparent. Nothing could be hidden inside that. At least nothing she knew about.

Her direct line to the NSA flashed red. She routed the call to her headset. "Bauer."

"Jim Conklin here." Conklin was her main contact in Crypto City at Fort Meade.

"What is it?"

"We're still running those intercepts on the pay phones around Andrew Fielding's house. All pay phones within three miles, twenty-four hours a day. You never rescinded the order."

"I never meant to."

"Well, with all the intercepts we're doing for the anti-terror effort, we're running a few days behind on screening for voiceprint matches."

Geli's heartbeat quickened. "You have something?"

"Andrew Fielding made a call four days ago from a service-station convenience store. I think you'll want to hear it."

"Can you send me the audio file?"

"Sure. I'll use Webworld." Webworld was the NSA's secure intranet, and Geli was one of the few outsiders linked to it. "You want the spectrograms of the matches?"

"No. I know Fielding's voice."

"Two minutes."

Geli clicked off, looked at her watch, then said, *"JPEG, Fielding, Andrew."* A photo of Fielding filled her computer screen. The white-haired Englishman had an angular, handsome face that bloomed red in the cheeks. Fielding had liked his gin. But it was his eyes that got you. Sparkling blue, they held a childish mischief that almost blinded you to the deep intelligence beneath it. As Geli looked into those eyes, she realized how formidable an adversary Fielding was. He might be dead, but he was still controlling events.

An audio file icon popped onto the corner of her screen. The NSA was nothing if not efficient. She was about to open it when her headset beeped an alert code from her team in the carpet-service van.

"What is it?"

"There's a police cruiser coming up the road. Somebody must have reported the shot."

Geli closed her eyes. She would have to invoke her federal authority and quarantine Tennant's house. The NSA's presence in Chapel Hill was about to become the knowledge of municipal police.

"I'm on my way."

"We're gone."

Geli hit an alarm button on her desk, alerting every member of her security teams, whether inside the building, on surveillance duty, or sleeping at home. In two minutes a net would close on David Tennant's house from every direction.

FOURTEEN

I was about to drive out of my subdivision when I realized I was making a mistake. The open highway looked like escape but wasn't. I knew Geli Bauer better than that. Yanking the wheel left, I did a 180 in the middle of Hickory Street, then turned onto Elm.

"Why are you turning around?" Rachel asked from the floor on the passenger side.

"Have you ever hunted rabbit?"

She blinked in confusion. "Rabbit? I'm from New York."

A woman on a mountain bike rode by us and waved, a toddler in a baby seat perched on the back fender. In our present circumstances, the image looked surreal.

"When a rabbit runs for its life, it takes a zigzag course at lightning speed. But it always circles back to where it started. It's a good escape strategy. Of course, rabbit hunters know that. That's why they use dogs. The dogs chase the rabbit while the hunter stands there waiting to shoot him when he comes back around."

Rachel's face showed disgust. "That's barbaric."

"It puts food on the table. The point is, the people hunting expect us to run like humans. But we're going to take a lesson from the rabbit."

"What do we gain by doing that?"

"A car, for one thing. We wouldn't get five miles in this one. Yours, either."

"Whose car can we get?"

"Just sit tight."

Elm Street circumnavigated my subdivision. When I came to the east entrance of Oak Street—which paralleled Willow—I turned left. As I drove, I watched between the houses to catch a glimpse of the roofs on my street. When I saw my own, I began scanning the lawns ahead. A hundred yards up Oak Street, I saw what I wanted. A blue-and-white FOR SALE sign. The house it advertised had a long, curving driveway with no cars parked in it. Turning into the drive, I pulled quickly off the cement and rolled behind a thick stand of boxwood shrubs.

"Follow me," I said, getting out.

Rachel climbed off the floor and opened her door. Her face was pale, her hands shivering. The shooting at my house had put her into shock. It had rattled me, too. I had killed before. I'd injected my own brother with narcotics and potassium, then watched the last spark of consciousness wink out of his eyes. But blowing a man's brains out was something else. And when Geli Bauer learned that I'd killed one of her people, she would move heaven and earth to take her revenge.

I walked over to Rachel and pulled her against me, hugging her as I once had my wife and daughter. "We're going to be all right," I said, not really believing it. Her hair smelled familiar. My wife had used the same shampoo. I put the memories out of my mind. "But we have to run. Do you understand?"

She nodded into my chest. I stroked her hair, still not quite believing what had happened myself. Thirty minutes ago, I'd believed the nightmare was over. Ewan McCaskell would call back, and the president would take control of Trinity. Now that hope was blown to hell.

"We're going to walk a little ways," I said, "and then we're going to borrow a car. Nobody will bother us. With me carrying Fielding's box, it'll look like we're selling something. Can you do it?"

She nodded.

I got Fielding's box from my car and started down Oak Street, Rachel beside me. "There's a hedge in these backyards that runs behind the lots on my street. You'll see it in a minute. We're going to cut through it to my street. I'll tell you when."

Using the sidewalk, we quickly covered the hundred yards back to where I'd seen my roof. I walked her past two more lawns, then said, "Right here. Cut between the houses."

A wooden privacy fence blocked the space between the two houses I'd chosen.

"If the gate's locked, we'll climb over," I said.

"What if someone's in the backyard?"

"I'll deal with it."

The gate opened easily. The backyard contained some plastic playground equipment and a parked lawn mower, but no people. With my hand in the small of Rachel's back, I guided her across the yard. There was no gate in the back fence, so I bent and interlocked my fingers, boosted her over, then slung myself up and dropped to the ground beside her.

The space between the fence and the hedge was only a couple of feet wide. I crawled through an opening at the bottom of the bushes, then got to my feet behind the utility shed where I'd hidden Fielding's box earlier. Rachel followed, grabbed my hand, and pulled herself up. I didn't know what the shed's owner did for a living, but I assumed he had some sort of sales job, because he was hardly ever home.

The interior was dim, and it stank of dead mice and motor oil. A row of tools hung from hooks on a pegboard. I was looking for a crowbar like the one in my attic, but I saw nothing like that. Kneeling, I scanned the area beneath the shelves. The owner stowed fishing gear there. Nothing heavy enough for my purpose.

"I feel sick," Rachel said.

"It's the smell. Go outside."

As she left, I saw a twelve-pound sledgehammer leaning in the corner. I picked it up and walked outside. Rachel was bent over with her hands on her knees.

"What's that for?" she asked.

"Stay close."

I trotted up to the back door of the house, drew back the sledge, and swung it in a roundhouse arc at the lock. The door caved in. Dropping the hammer, I ran into the dark house. Rachel followed. I didn't hear an alarm, but it could be silent. Wired straight to a security service.

"We want the kitchen," I told her.

"This way. I smell garlic and dish soap."

"Look for wall hooks. We need car keys."

"It would help if you turned on the lights."

I hit a wall switch and flooded the kitchen with light. It was a showplace, filled with professional Viking appliances in stainless steel. While Rachel searched the walls for hooks, I pulled open drawers. One held dishrags. Another practically spewed coupons, which seemed odd. Someone who could afford Viking appliances didn't need to cut out coupons.

"Key!" Rachel cried, grabbing something off the countertop.

I took the key and examined it. "That's for a riding lawn mower. Keep looking."

143

The next drawer contained jars of nails, screws, glue sticks, and paper clips. No keys.

"Why did you pick this house?" she asked.

"The guy's single and never home, but I know he has two cars."

"Got it!' She pulled a square black key from a hook under a cabinet. "It's for an Audi."

"That's it."

Just as in my house, you had to go through the laundry room to reach the garage. The same contractor had probably built both homes.

"How did you know the key was for an Audi?"

"My ex-husband drove one."

I opened the door to the garage and saw a silver A8 sitting there like an answered prayer. The guy's other car was a Honda Accord. He probably took the Accord to the airport to sit in the Park & Fly and saved the flagship Audi for his road trips.

"Anybody with an eighty-thousand-dollar car has a security system in his house," Rachel said over my shoulder.

"The cops are definitely on their way. Key?"

She slapped it into my palm like a nurse passing a scalpel to a surgeon, and twenty seconds later we were pulling onto Willow Street, the garage door sliding down behind us. I looked up and down Willow, being careful not to turn too far right when I looked toward my house. I didn't see anybody. Not even a yardman.

"What good is stealing this car if the police come check out that guy's alarm?" Rachel asked.

"The police won't know what was taken. They don't know this car was there. They'll have to track down the owner, and he's probably on a business trip to God knows where."

I made two quick turns and swung onto Kinsdale, headed east toward Interstate 40. Traffic was fairly heavy, and I was glad of it.

"Where are we going now?"

I reached into the backseat and grabbed Fielding's Ziploc-sealed letter from the box, then laid it on her lap. I pointed to the line, *Lu Li and I are driving to the blue place on Saturday night.*

"The blue place?"

Steering with my knee, I searched the Audi's console and found a ballpoint pen. Then I pulled the letter out of the Ziploc and wrote *Nags Head/The Outer Banks* beneath Fielding's cartoon White Rabbit.

"Why can't you tell me out loud?"

I scribbled, *They could be listening.*

She took the pen and wrote, HOW? WE JUST STOLE THIS CAR!

"Trust me," I whispered. "It's possible."

She shook her head, then wrote, *Is there something at Nags Head? Evidence?*

An image of Fielding's pocket watch came into my mind. I took the pen back and wrote, *I hope so.*

She wrote, *Cell phone in my pocket. Try to call President?*

I took the pen and wrote, *It's not that simple now.*

"Why not?"

There was no way to write all I needed to say. I pulled her close and whispered into her ear. "Once they heard Ewan McCaskell's message, they knew they could eliminate me and tell the president whatever they wanted to explain my death. Yours, too."

"What kind of lie would explain that?"

"An easy one. By now the president has been told that my hallucinations have progressed to psychosis. Ravi Nara will write a formal diagnosis. He'll say I've become danger-ously paranoid, that I believe Andrew Fielding was murdered when he clearly died of natural causes. Your own office records say I've been having hallucinations and may be schizophrenic. They'll be used to support Nara's position." I took my eyes off the road and looked at her. "Do you think that would be a hard sell?"

She turned away.

"Not a very optimistic picture is it?"

"No. But you have to put it out of your mind for a few minutes. You're all over the road. If you insist on driving, you need to calm down."

"That's not what's getting to me right now."

"Then what is?"

By answering this honestly, I would be asking for trouble, but I didn't want to keep it to myself any longer. "I saw it."

"Saw what?"

"The guy who was going to kill you."

"Of course you did. You had to see him to shoot him."

I swung onto the I-40 ramp and merged with the traffic headed toward the RTP and Raleigh. "That's not what I mean. I saw him walking up the street. Willow Street. Before he ever got to the house. He walked right up to the door."

"What do you mean?"

"I dreamed it, Rachel."

She stared at me. She had never been with me when I'd experienced one of my hallucinations. "*How* did you see him? Like your Jesus hallucinations? Like a movie? What?"

"I saw it the way you see what the criminal or the monster sees in B movies. I saw it through *his eyes*."

She sat back in her seat. "Tell me exactly what you saw."

"The houses on my street. My feet walking. A dog trotting by. I thought I was dreaming about myself. But when I got to my house and reached into my pocket for my key . . . I brought out a lockpick."

"Go on."

"I picked the lock and went inside. I heard you in the kitchen, and then I took out a gun."

146

Rachel stared through the windshield, but her mind was clearly elsewhere. "That doesn't mean anything," she said finally. "Dreams of someone invading the house or bedroom are almost universal in narcoleptic patients. Even if you weren't narcoleptic, that would be a typical dream, a distortion of reality caused by anxiety."

"No. The timing was too perfect. I saw a threat in my dream, and when I woke up, the threat was there in the real world. Just as I saw it."

She squeezed my shoulder. "Listen to me. You're accustomed to the sounds of your own house. You were already in an anxious state. You heard something unfamiliar, something that triggered your fear of a break-in. The front door opening. A window going up. A creaking board. In response to that stimulus, your mind generated a dream of a break-in. It frightened you enough to wake you. Your dream was a reaction to external stimuli, not the other way around."

I did remember a creaking board. But I was already awake when I'd heard that. "I saw his gun in the dream," I said doggedly. "An automatic. It had a silencer." I tapped the gun in my waistband. "Just like this one."

"Coincidence."

"I've never seen a gun with a silencer before."

"Of course you have. You've seen hundreds of them in films."

I thought about it. "You're right, but there's something else."

"What?"

"That's not the first dream I've had like that. Where I was someone else, someone from the present day. I had one the day Fielding died."

"Describe it for me."

A Durham police cruiser passed us in the westbound lanes. My heart clenched, but the cruiser didn't slow or blink its lights.

147

"Yesterday, when I was making my videotape—just before you came in—I dreamed I was Fielding just prior to and during his death. It was so real that I felt I'd *actually died*. I couldn't see . . . couldn't breathe. When I answered the door for you, I didn't know which way was up."

"But Fielding had already died that morning."

"So?"

She held up her hands as if to emphasize an obvious point. "Don't you see? Your Fielding dream didn't *predict* anything. It could easily have been a grief reaction. Have you had any more dreams like that?"

I looked back at the road. We had reached the Research Triangle Park. I-40 ran right through it. Less than a mile away, Geli Bauer was directing the hunt for me.

"David, have you had other dreams like that?"

"This isn't the time to discuss it."

"Will there be a better time? Why did you skip your last three appointments with me?"

I shook my head. "You already think I'm crazy."

"That's not a medical term."

"Descriptive, though."

She sighed and looked out the window at the perfect green turf on her side of the road.

"That's Trinity," I said. "Coming up over there."

The lab was set so far back from the road that little was visible.

"The sign says Argus Optical," she said.

"That's cover."

"Ah. Look . . . what's the point of keeping a hallucination from me? What part of yourself do you think you're protecting?"

"We'll talk about it later." I could see that she didn't intend to drop it. "I need drugs, Rachel. I can't afford to be passing out five times a day while we're on the run."

"What have you been taking? Modafinil?"

Modafinil was a standard narcolepsy treatment. "Sometimes. Usually I take methamphetamine."

"David! We talked about the side effects of amphetamines. They could be exaggerating your hallucinations."

"They're the only thing that can keep me awake. Ravi Nara used to get me Dexedrine."

She sighed. "I'll write you a prescription for some Adderall."

"A scrip isn't the problem. I could write that myself. The problem is that they know I need it. They'll be watching all the pharmacies."

"They can't possibly cover every pharmacy in the Triangle."

"They're the NSA, Rachel, and they know I need drugs. These are the people who recorded the cockpit chatter of the Russian pilots who shot down that Korean airliner over Sakhalin Island in 1983. That was twenty years ago, and it was a *random* incident. They are actively searching for us. You read *1984*?"

"Twenty years ago."

"When I say *NSA*, think Big Brother. The NSA is the closest thing we have to it in America."

"But you still need your drugs."

"You must know somebody."

"I could get it at the hospital pharmacy."

"They'll be watching for us there."

"Well, *shit*."

I'd almost never heard her use profanity. Maybe it came with the blue jeans. Maybe she shed her demure exterior with her silk skirts and blouses.

"I know a doc in North Durham who'll give us some samples," she said.

We'd already left Durham behind and were well on our way to Raleigh. My knowledge of Geli Bauer made me reluctant to linger in the area longer than necessary. Also, paradoxically enough, something in me did not want the dreams to stop. My last one had saved our lives, and though I'd never confess it to Rachel, I felt somehow that my dreams—however frightening they might be—were giving me information about our plight, information I could gain in no other way.

"We're not going back," I said.

"What if you pass out at the wheel?"

"You saw how it works at the house. It doesn't happen instantly."

"You weren't driving then."

"I usually have a couple of minutes' warning. I'll pull over the second I feel something wrong."

Rachel was clearly unhappy. As though to drain off some anger, she put one foot up on the dash, untied her shoe, then retied it. Then she did the same to the other. This compulsive ritual seemed to calm her.

I took the 440 loop around Raleigh, then merged onto U.S. 64, which would take us all the way to the Atlantic Ocean. The highway was generic Southern: two broad strips of cement running through pine and hardwood forest. It would be another two hours before the land started to drop toward the Outer Banks. Fielding would have been traveling this road today if he hadn't died, a road he had traveled before, to a destination my wife and I had visited twelve years earlier. Thoughts like that showed me the needless ambiguity of words like *space-time*. The average person heard a word like that and figured he'd never understand it. But it was so simple. Every place you ever saw was linked to a specific time. The Nags Head cabin Fielding and his wife had honeymooned in appeared to be the same one my wife and I had used—but in reality it was not. In the fabric of space-time, it was altogether different. The school you visited twenty years after you graduated, the football field you played on,

150

the track you ran—none of them was the same. If they were, you would collide with the generations that had run on them before and after you. The lover you kissed was not the same person he or she was sixty seconds before. In that minute, a million skin cells had died and been replaced by new ones. The smallest slices of space-time separated thought from action. Life from death.

"I don't want to make things worse," Rachel said, "but since you can't call the president anymore, what exactly can you do? Where can we go?"

"I'm hoping something at the cabin will give me a clue. Right now I'm just trying to keep us alive."

"Why don't we just go public? Drive to Atlanta and tell it all to CNN?"

"Because the NSA could just say I was lying. What can I really prove at this point?"

She folded her arms. "You tell me. Would a Nobel laureate like Ravi Nara perjure himself to cover all this up?"

"He wouldn't hesitate. National security is the ultimate rationalization for lying. And as for the Trinity building, it could be totally empty by now."

"Lu Li Fielding would support you."

"Lu Li has disappeared."

Rachel's face lost some color.

"Don't assume the worst yet. She had a plan to escape, but I have no idea whether she made it or not."

"David, you must know more than you're telling me."

"About Lu Li?"

"About Trinity!"

She was right. "Okay. A couple of weeks ago, Fielding decided that the suspension of the project was just a ruse to distract the two of us. He thought the real work on Trinity was continuing elsewhere, and maybe had been for a long time."

151

"Where else could they be working on it?"

"Fielding's bet was the R and D labs at Godin Supercomputing in California. Godin's been flying out there quite a bit on his private jet. Nara's gone with him several times."

"That doesn't prove anything. For all you know, they're playing golf at Pebble Beach."

"These guys don't play golf. They work. They'd sell their souls for what they want. When you think of Peter Godin, think *Faust*."

"What do they want?"

"Different things. John Skow was about to be canned by the NSA when Godin asked that he administer Project Trinity. That resurrected his career."

"Why would Peter Godin want a man like that?"

"I think Godin has something on Skow. He probably compromised him a long time ago and knows Skow will keep quiet about anything he's told to. Working at the NSA doesn't make you rich. But being the man who delivered a Trinity computer to the agency would put Skow in the director's chair. And after that, he'd be invaluable to private corporations. Skow will do anything necessary to make Trinity a reality."

"And Ravi Nara?"

"Nara demanded a million dollars a year to come on board. What the government wouldn't pay, Godin made up in cash. Beyond that, Nara's contribution to Trinity would give him a lock on another Nobel. Shared with Godin and Jutta Klein, of course. Fielding would deserve it the most, but the Nobel committee doesn't give posthumous awards. Tack on unlimited research funds for life, Nara's name in the history books . . ."

"And this Jutta Klein?"

"Klein is straight. She's an older German woman, and she

152

already shared a Nobel with two other Germans back in 1994. She's on loan to Trinity from Siemens. That's the way it's set up with several companies. Godin wanted the best people in the world, so he borrowed them from the R and D divisions of the best computer companies. Sun Micro. Silicon Graphics. In exchange, those companies will get to license certain parts of the Trinity technology once it's declassified. *If* it's declassified."

"If Jutta Klein is straight," Rachel said, "maybe she's the person who can help us."

"She couldn't if she wanted to. They'll have her sewed up tight."

Rachel gave a frustrated sigh. "And Godin? What does he want?"

"Godin wants to be God."

"What?"

I eased into the left lane to pass a motor home. "Godin doesn't care about Trinity making a profit. He's a billionaire. He's seventy-two years old, and he's been a star since he was forty. So forget being the father of artificial intelligence or anything like that. He wants to be the first—maybe the only—human being whose mind is ported into a Trinity computer."

Rachel pushed a dark strand of hair out of her eyes. "What's he like? An egomaniac?"

"He's not that simple. Godin is a brilliant man who believes he knows what's wrong with the world. He's like the people you knew in college who thought *Atlas Shrugged* was the answer to the world's problems, only he's a genius. And he's made major contributions to science. So far, America is truly a better place because Peter Godin lived here. His super-computers played a significant role in winning the Cold War."

"It sounds like you admire him."

"He's easy to admire. But he scares me, too. He's

153

practically killing himself to build the most powerful computer in the world, and he doesn't care that he won't understand how it works when it finally does. Godin's building Trinity to use it himself. And I don't know if there's anything more dangerous than a powerful man obsessed with remaking the world in his own image."

As I reached out to set the Audi's cruise control, my vision started to blur. A wave of fatigue washed through me, and Rachel's last words slipped out of my head. My eyesight cleared, but the familiar high-pitched humming had begun in my head. I braked and swerved onto the shoulder.

"What is it?" asked Rachel.

"You need to drive. I may go under."

She sat up. "Okay."

I got out and walked around to her side of the car. Rachel climbed over the console and slid behind the wheel. Before getting back in, I looked up and down the highway. Traffic was moderate but steady, and no drivers showed any interest in me.

She studied me closely. "Are you all right, David?"

"A little shaky."

She reached over and fastened my safety belt. "Is it an episode?"

The humming had descended to my back teeth. "Yes."

"Close your eyes. I've got the wheel."

"Just keep going east. Our destination is about"—I held up three fingers—"hours away." In the glove compartment was a map of the Carolinas. I located Highway 64 and pointed to Plymouth, near where the Roanoke River ran into Albemarle Sound. "If I don't wake up by the time we reach here, wake me up."

Rachel put the Audi in gear and began accelerating along the shoulder. When she reached fifty, she pulled onto the highway and goosed the pedal.

"Is it getting worse?" she asked.

In my mind I said, *I'm fine,* but some part of my brain realized that my lips had not moved. I was about to go under. My palms were tingling, and my face felt hot. Rachel laid a hand on my forehead.

"You're burning up. Does that always happen?"

I tried to answer, but I felt as I had as a boy in the Oak Ridge swimming pool, trying to talk to my friends underwater. We yelled as loud as we could, but we couldn't make our words understood. Rachel's hand seemed to be melting into my forehead. That pleased me somehow. I wanted to check the visor mirror and see if her hand really was melting, but I couldn't move. A woman was calling my name from far away. Before I could answer, the deep blue swell of a wave broke over me and I went under, rolling and tumbling into darkness.

I'm sitting outdoors in a circle of sleeping men, leaning against a wall. Banked embers glow at the center of the circle. The sky is on fire with stars. A robed man named Peter sits beside me. He seems upset.

"Why do you want to do this?" he whispered. "If you go, you'll suffer all manner of indignities. Even if the people listen, you'll be rejected by the priests and elders. And what of the Romans? I fear you will be killed."

Though he does not name the place, I know he's speaking of Jerusalem. "Go away," I tell him. "You value what the dog values. Your body, your next meal, your life."

He takes hold of my arm and shakes it. "You don't drive me off so easily! I've seen it in a dream. If you go, you will be executed."

"Whoever will save his life shall lose it," I reply.

Peter shakes his head, his eyes filled with confusion.

The scene changes suddenly. I'm on a high mountain, looking out over a plain. Three men sit with me.

"When you go into the towns," I ask, "who do you say that I am?"

"We say you are the anointed one."

I shake my head. "Do not say this of me. Speak from your hearts of what you have seen. No more."

"Yes, Master," answers a man named John, whose eyes are large and brown like a woman's. He looks at Peter, then speaks cautiously to me. "I'm told you mean to go to Jerusalem."

"Yes."

John shakes his head. "If you do this, the priests will not know what to do with you. They will fear you, and they'll condemn you to death."

"This cup has been passed to me. I must drink."

The men fall silent. As I contemplate the plain below, fear simmers in the pit of my belly. To know the gift of this life, this body, and then to give it up . . .

I snapped awake and grabbed the dashboard, my eyes on the rear of a tractor-trailer ahead. Rachel grabbed my knee.

"It's all right, David! I'm here."

My hands were shaking, the fear of the dream still palpable. "How long have we been on the road?"

"An hour and twenty minutes. We just passed Plymouth."

"I told you to wake me up!"

"You were sleeping so hard, I hated to do it."

"Have you seen anything suspicious?"

"We passed a state trooper a half hour ago, and a couple of Plymouth cops, but none of them looked twice at us. I think we're okay."

Rachel looked anything but okay. And once our immediate goal of escape was accomplished, her composure would crack. I was no different. My reaction to killing Geli Bauer's assassin had been blunted by a flood of neurochemicals evolved for

156

my survival. Images from my dream returned in flashes of color and light, but the fear was fading, and in its wake I felt a strange sort of relief. After months of vagueness and mystery, the dreams were finally localizing to a specific place. Jerusalem. Logically this made no sense. I had never been to Israel, and I knew little about it beyond the bloody conflict I'd seen for decades on the evening news. But where had logic led me so far?

"David?" Rachel said. "Maybe we can hole up for a while at the—"

I clapped my hand over her mouth. "Don't. I'm sorry, but I warned you already."

She nodded, and I took my hand away. "If the NSA is so all powerful," she whispered, "what were you doing making that videotape in your own living room? Wouldn't they hear that?"

I reached into the backseat, lifted Fielding's box of home-made electronic toys, and set it on my lap. From it I withdrew a metallic wand about ten inches long. "Fielding showed me where their bugs were. In tiny holes in the Sheetrock."

"What was he doing with equipment like that? Don't you think that's a little suspicious?"

"I can see how it would look that way. You had to know him."

Even as I said that, I wondered if I really had known the eccentric Englishman. I poked through his box, looking for signs of a secret agenda. Most of the home-built devices looked like the projects of a teenager who spent his weekends at RadioShack. One resembled the old View-Master toy of my youth, a plastic frame with tubular eyepieces and a switch on the right side. I held the makeshift goggles up to my face, aimed them at Rachel, and flipped the switch. An amber haze fell across my field of vision, but beyond that, nothing happened.

"What are those?" Rachel asked.

"I'm not sure." I turned the goggles toward the windshield and looked out over the road.

My heart turned to ice. A thin, green beam of coherent light—a laser—was hitting the Audi's front windshield at an angle almost perpendicular to the ground. I'd seen many such beams in physics labs at MIT. The only other places I had seen them was in films, on laser-gun sights. Someone was aiming a laser at us from the air! I wanted to scream a warning to Rachel, but my throat was glued shut. Shoving my foot across the floor, I hit the brake, throwing the Audi into a skid.

Rachel screamed and tried to control the spinning car. I turned the goggles and searched for the laser. It was about forty yards away, tracking back toward the car like the hand of God. The Audi shuddered to a stop on the grassy shoulder.

"Why the hell did you do that?" Rachel yelled.

Our nearest cover was a line of trees fifty yards from the shoulder. Someone with an automatic weapon could easily cut us down before we reached the tree line. I held the goggles up to Rachel's eyes.

"Someone's going to shoot at us! Get under the dash. As far as you can."

As she tried to fold herself under the steering column, I reacquired the laser beam. I expected it to move onto me, but instead it froze on the windshield glass. The beam didn't penetrate the glass; it terminated at the windshield's surface. By extending the beam in my mind, I realized it would not intersect with either me or Rachel, but the dashboard.

"If they wanted to shoot us," I thought aloud, "they could have done it before I ever turned on the goggles."

"What?"

"It's not a gun sight."

"What are you talking about?"

158

The laser could be a bomb designator, but not even panic would drive the NSA to drop a smart bomb on the shoulder of an American highway. They had too many other options. Suddenly I understood. The laser was a surveillance device. By bouncing the beam off the windshield and measuring the vibration of the glass, eavesdroppers in a plane or helicopter could hear every word we said inside.

"Get up! Get up and drive!"

Rachel struggled back into her seat, shifted the car into drive, and pulled onto the highway. The green beam stayed locked on our windshield like a satellite weapon aimed from space. Taking the map off the floor, I folded it down to a small rectangle and tapped a spot three times to indicate our location.

She nodded.

I then followed 64 eastward for a couple of miles, to a small rural road that broke to the left. There I wrote, *Take this turn.*

When Rachel nodded again, I leaned down to her ear and said, "Take the turn no matter what happens. Understand?"

"I will. Is whatever you saw still there?"

I checked through the goggles, then squeezed her shoulder. "It's there. Speed up."

She pressed the accelerator to the floor.

FIFTEEN

Geli Bauer stood alone in David Tennant's kitchen, alone with the corpse of her lover. The carpet-cleaning-service truck was still parked outside, its vacuum equipment running loudly. By any operational standard, she should have moved Ritter's corpse long ago. But she couldn't. She wanted to understand what had happened here. From the wound in Ritter's head and the way his body was lying, it seemed he had been shot from the front or slightly to the side. She couldn't imagine an untrained man winning a shootout with a former member of Germany's most elite counterterror unit. That left two options.

One: Tennant had somehow surprised Ritter and fired very accurately as Ritter whirled to shoot him.

Two: Tennant was not what he seemed.

He had been raised in the rural area around Oak Ridge, Tennessee, which might make him proficient with a hunting rifle, but not with a handgun. And where had he learned to sweep rooms for microphones? Had Fielding taught him that, or had he learned it elsewhere? His escape from the crime scene raised more questions. The team in the carpet van had arrived to find Rachel Weiss's Saab parked out front but

Tennant's garage empty. A second team had combed the neighborhood and discovered Tennant's Acura parked behind some hedges at a vacant house. It had taken a half hour of police liaison to learn that a silver Audi A8 had been stolen from the house down the street.

Without the voiceprint analysis that had turned up Fielding's covert call from a convenience store, Tennant and Weiss might have slipped through her net. But four days ago, Fielding had reserved a cabin at Nags Head on the Outer Banks in the name of Mr. Lewis Carroll. This, combined with Tennant's having received a FedEx letter from Fielding yesterday, had been enough for Geli to put air assets over Highway 64, the route to Nags Head. And that had put Tennant back into her hands.

As she looked down at Ritter's shattered skull and blood-matted hair, her cell phone rang. "Bauer," she said.

"This is Air-One. They know we're following them."

"How high are you flying?"

"Ten thousand feet. There's no way they could have made us from looking at the sky. They had to see the beam."

"That's impossible without special equipment."

"They must have some."

"What are they doing now?"

A crackle of static. "They ran off the road like they saw the beam and panicked. They ducked under the dash for a while, then got back on the highway. They're doing about ninety now, still headed east."

"What are they saying?"

"Nothing about a destination."

"Where are our ground units?" Geli asked.

"Closest is fifteen minutes away, give or take two."

"I'll call you back." She speed-dialed Skow's scrambled cell phone. He answered after eight rings.

"What is it, Geli?"

161

"Tennant detected our airborne surveillance. He's taking evasive action."

"You must be joking. Have your people lost him?"

"The plane has the Audi now, but they could lose it."

"I suppose you want to terminate them now?"

Geli sensed Skow's finger on the chicken switch. "That's my standing order from you."

"The situation has changed."

"The geography has changed. Not the situation."

"I don't like it. How will it play?"

The bureaucrat's mantra, Geli thought scornfully. "Tennant went psychotic. He killed his Trinity guard and kidnapped his psychiatrist. We're attempting a rescue."

There was a long silence. Then Skow said, "Peter was right to hire you. Good luck with that rescue."

"Fuck you very much," Geli muttered, and hung up. She opened her connection to the plane and her ground units.

"Air-One, do you still have the Audi in sight?"

"Affirmative. And they definitely know we're here. Tennant leaned out and looked up at us."

"Ground units, when you get there, wait for low traffic, then box in the car and take them."

"Take them out?" asked a voice with the eerie calm of a fighter pilot on a mission.

Geli looked down at Ritter's corpse, remembering last night. He was still alive inside her. "Tennant may have kidnapped his psychiatrist. We're not sure. We do know that he's highly unstable, armed, and he's already killed one of ours. Ritter Bock, which should tell you something. Nobody take any chances. Protect your own lives first."

There was a chorus of "Affirmative."

"Am I understood?"

The responding silence said more than the subsequent acknowledgments. This was why she hired former soldiers.

162

"Ah, that's a rog," said a cold male voice.

"Call it play by play for me, Air-One."

"Will do."

Geli smiled. Tennant and Weiss wouldn't live to see nightfall.

SIXTEEN

As the Audi roared eastward toward the turn, I scanned the highway behind us. The nearest vehicle was two hundred yards back. It looked like a pickup truck. I doubted it was NSA, but you never knew. With aerial surveillance, ground units wouldn't have to follow closely to stay up with us. They could even drive ahead of us. There was simply no way to know who or where our pursuers were. If we were lucky, whatever aircraft was up there had acquired us only minutes before I saw the laser.

Rachel reached out and pulled me close enough to whisper. "I think I see the turn. Is it Highway 45?"

I checked the map. "Yes, but it's no highway. Take it."

She slowed to fifty, then screeched left onto 45.

"Punch it," I said.

She hit the accelerator and shot down the two-lane blacktop at seventy miles per hour. I put the goggles up to my face and looked for the laser. It had lost us at the turn, but it quickly tracked back onto our rear windshield. I leaned over to Rachel's ear.

"We're going to cross a bridge over the Cashie River where it flows into Albemarle Sound. Take the next left after that."

"Just tell me when to turn."

The A8 devoured the road like a starving tiger, racing up and over the high bridge that arced across the Cashie. I leaned far enough out the window to look skyward. A small plane was flying over the road at about five thousand feet. A wave of relief went through me. My fear was a helicopter that could set down on the road and deploy a SWAT team armed with submachine guns. A fixed-wing aircraft could land on a highway, but not on the twisting road we would soon be driving.

Rachel pointed at an intersection ahead. I nodded. She slowed just enough to make the turn, then whipped onto a much smaller road that was heavily forested on both sides.

"Look at those trees," I said, bracing my hands on the dash.

A hundred yards ahead, towering oaks closed over the road, turning it into a shadowy tunnel. When we entered it, I rolled down my window and leaned out again. First I saw nothing but branches. Then I caught a silver gleam as the plane swooped over the road behind us at about two thousand feet.

"Go!" I yelled. "We're losing them!"

"If I go any faster, I'll lose control."

"You're doing fine."

Law enforcement used fixed-wing aircraft for surveillance because they could stay on station much longer than helicopters. Today they would pay a heavy price for that strategy. A plane couldn't crisscross the sky in tight enough patterns to maintain contact on a twisting road with heavy cover.

The Audi's big tires squealed as Rachel took another tight curve at seventy-plus. My right shoulder compressed against the door. Struggling to hold the map steady, I searched for an escape route. If we took the next tiny rural road to the left, we would quickly recross the Cashie River, but not by bridge. The Cashie looked scarcely wider than a creek at that point, and an italic legend said, *Ferry*. That could mean anything from a free-floating vessel to a cable barge.

I picked up the goggles and scanned the road ahead. The laser was dancing erratically about seventy yards in front of the car, breaking and re-forming as the operator in the plane tried to contend with the branches shielding us from above.

"There's a ferry up ahead," I said. "If we can get over to it, we may be able to cut off ground pursuit."

"All right."

"You've got a left turn any second."

"Okay."

"There!"

Rachel stepped on the brake. I thought we were going to spin out, but the all-wheel drive held the car to the pavement, and she just managed the turn. As the tunnel of oaks thickened, the one-lane road quickly petered out into gravel and mud, dropping at a shallow angle that told me we were nearing water.

"Careful," I said, dreading the scrape of gravel against the undercarriage.

With the car listing to starboard, we rounded the last curve and came to rest behind an ancient green Chevy Nova parked in the middle of the track. Beyond the car I saw a dark, slow-moving river about eighty yards across.

"I don't see a ferry," Rachel said.

A beat-up aluminum canoe was tied to the roof of the Nova, but I saw no people. I covered my gun with my shirttail, then got out and walked toward the river.

The sound of an acoustic guitar floated back to me, reminding me of *Deliverance*. When I rounded the Nova, I saw not two inbred hillbillies but a pair of college-age boys sitting on the ground. One was blond and wore a bandanna as a headband. The other was dark-haired and fingerpicking a beat-up dreadnought Martin guitar. I waved casually and walked past them to the river's edge.

A ferry built to hold three or four cars was making its way across the water from the opposite bank, a dark column of exhaust rising from its rumbling engine. A house trailer stood on the far bank. Beside it was a small ramp, and a road that disappeared into the woods.

"We already called the ferry," said one of the boys behind me.

I turned and smiled at them. The blond with the bandanna wore a UNC T-shirt and had quick green eyes The guitar player looked stoned and had a bad sunburn across his shoulders. I smelled the unmistakable odor of marijuana.

"You guys been running the rivers around here?"

The blond laughed. "We take it pretty slow. We floated the Chowan this morning. We're headed home now. Tarboro. We just wanted a look at the Cashie here."

I put my hand over my eyes and looked skyward. The surveillance plane droned out of a cumulus cloud and flew across the river.

"Sounds good," I said to the guitar player, who was still picking softly. Then I walked back to the Audi and got inside.

"The ferry's on the way."

"Is the plane still up there?" Rachel asked.

"Yes."

She looked as though she'd endured about all she could in one day. As I stared morosely at the Nova's rear end, an idea hit me.

"I'll be right back."

I got out and walked around the Nova, then squatted in front of the college boys. "I've got a proposition for you guys."

"What kind of proposition?" asked the blond.

"My wife's never done any canoeing. She saw your boat

167

and got a wild idea. She'd like to float down the river to the sound."

The guitar player stopped picking. "We're on our way home, man."

"I remember. Tarboro. But I was thinking . . . how much do you figure your canoe is worth? It looks like an old Grumman to me."

"That's right," said the blond. "Used to be my uncle's. I guess she's worth about four hundred bucks."

We all turned as the ferry's deck hit the ramp on our side of the river.

I reached up and twanged the inverted V of rope that bound the bow of the canoe to the car's front bumper. "Two hundred would be closer," I said with a laugh. "But I like to keep my wife happy. How about five?"

The blond swallowed hard. He was calculating how much weed he could buy with five hundred in cash.

"The thing is, I don't want to leave my car here. I'd like you to drive it up the road a ways."

"Where to?" asked the blond.

"How about Tarboro?"

He looked confused. "But how will you get there to pick up your car?"

"Get aboard!" shouted the ferryman, a white-haired beanpole in faded overalls.

I took out my wallet and counted out ten $100 bills. "For a thousand bucks, what do you care?"

"Shit," said the guitar player, getting to his feet. He looked over the Nova at the Audi. Rachel's face was a blur behind the sun's reflection. "Is that your car?"

"That's it."

"What's the deal, man?"

"The deal is a thousand bucks for the canoe and a quick drive. You up for it?"

Both boys looked at the Audi, then at each other. "Fifteen hundred," said the blond, turning to me. "For fifteen hundred I'll drive it to Tarboro. Call it hazard pay."

I smiled. "Fifteen hundred it is. But here's how we have to do it."

We loaded the cars on the ferry, and the old man guided the shuddering vessel back into the slow current. As agreed, the boys sat in their Nova during the crossing. Rachel and I stayed in the Audi. The NSA plane remained on station, flying a tight circle over the river. I could almost feel Geli Bauer's security teams converging on this little corner of North Carolina.

When the ferry reached the far bank, the Nova drove slowly off the deck and down the ramp onto the road. Rachel followed. Then suddenly she swerved around the Nova and raced into the woods like a woman pursued by demons. As soon as the oak branches closed over us, she braked and waited for the Nova to catch up. Twenty seconds later, the old Chevy rounded a curve and pulled up behind us.

"Move fast!" I yelled to the boys as they got out.

Their canoe sat on yellow foam squares that protected the car's roof from the metal gunwales. I started to untie the bow ropes, but the blond whipped a knife out of his pocket and cut the lines at both ends of the canoe. I took hold of the bow, the guitar player took the stern, and together we slid the boat off the roof, inverting it as we lowered it to the ground. At the last minute we lost hold and the canoe hit the gravel with a ringing *blang*.

The blond reached into the backseat, took out two long wooden paddles, and dropped them into the canoe. When he looked up, his eyes focused on something behind me, and he blushed. I turned and saw Rachel standing behind me in her jeans and white button-down.

169

"Hey," she said. "I appreciate this." Then she smiled in a way I'd never seen her smile before.

"Uh, no problem," said the blond.

The guitar player waved at Rachel but said nothing, and I saw that even at thirty-five, Rachel Weiss still impressed boys in their twenties.

"We've got to get going," I said. "So do you guys."

I handed the blond fifteen $100 bills.

"You're either paying me too much or not enough," he said. "But it's cool." He pointed into the trees. "If you carry the canoe through there, you should hit the river after fifty yards or so."

"Thanks."

He trotted back to the Audi and slid behind the wheel. As I got Fielding's box from the backseat, I touched the kid on the shoulder. "If anyone stops you in this car, tell them exactly what happened. The money, everything. You'll be fine."

He nodded. "No sweat."

The Audi roared to life and tore off down through the tunnel of oaks. The guitar player in the Nova laughed, shook his head, and slowly followed. I tossed Fielding's box into the canoe, wrapped the bow line around my right hand, and started dragging the boat toward the trees.

"Should I push?" asked Rachel.

"I've got it. You watch for snakes."

From that moment forward her eyes never left the ground.

The trees grew almost too close together to pull the canoe between them, and I was soon dripping sweat. But the blond kid was right. Before long, I smelled decaying plants, and then I sighted a yellow flash of sunlight on water. Fifty more feet and I was shoving the canoe between two cypress knees and into the river.

"Get in," I told Rachel. "All the way to the front."

She climbed into the stern and made her way carefully to the bow seat. I shoved the canoe into deeper water, then jumped into the stern as it arrowed away from the shore. Settling on the hard seat, I picked up a paddle and propelled the boat along the snaky-looking bank.

"I'm going to keep us under the trees," I said. "Watch for the plane."

Rachel looked up and squinted. I listened hard as I paddled, but I heard only the frothy whisper of wood cutting water.

"See anything?"

She shook her head.

I looked down the long, dark bend of river, bounded on both sides by thick stands of cypress and pine. At this moment, the vast resources of the NSA were focused on finding us. But here, those resources were largely useless. For the first time in many hours, I felt some peace.

"Any idea where we're going?" Rachel asked.

"No. But I'll know when we get there."

SEVENTEEN

Geli Bauer sat in her zero-gravity chair in the security basement of the Trinity building, her right hand squeezing a pair of weighted dice she'd taken from Fielding's personal effects in the storeroom. She'd taken them for luck, but so far they had brought her little.

On the bank of monitors to her right, dozens of NSA personnel with forklifts and dollies were moving sensitive equipment and files to trucks waiting at the back of the building. If Tennant went public, she wanted nothing left here for nosy congressmen to find.

"Tennant just pulled onto the shoulder and stopped," said a female voice in her headset. It belonged to an ex-navy warrant officer named Evans, who was in the first ground unit to sight the stolen Audi.

"Did he try to run at all?" Geli asked.

"Negative. When he realized we were pursuing, he just pulled over like it's a traffic stop."

Geli didn't like the sound of that. "Are they in plain sight?"

"Only the man."

"Do you have a megaphone?"

"We don't need it. He just got out of the car. He's holding his hands up."

"Dr. Tennant?"

"I don't think so." The line crackled. "This looks like a kid."

"A kid?"

"A hippie. College kid."

"You stopped the wrong car!"

"No, the plate's right. Wait . . . they must have pulled some kind of switch."

"Who?"

"There were two college kids in a green Chevy on the ferry. Tennant and Weiss must be in that car."

"Question the goddamn kid! Find out!"

"Hang on."

She glanced at her monitors. The NSA movers were rolling stacked computers onto the loading dock on the ground floor. Moving the equipment was a pain in the ass. If they had let her kill Tennant at the same time as Fielding, none of this would be happening.

"Evans here," said the voice on the headset. "They're on the river now."

"They're *what*?"

"The college kids had a canoe on their car. Unpainted aluminum. Tennant bought it off them."

Geli felt like she was about to stroke out. "Find the Chevy and nail it anyway! And impound the Audi."

"Will do."

"Air-One, do you read?"

"Affirmative."

"Start making low passes over the river. Start at the ferry and move toward Albemarle Sound. Even Tennant wouldn't try to get away by paddling upstream."

"We'll be back over the river in five minutes."

"Get ground units started down the river on both sides."

"There's only a road on one side. The north side."

"Jesus Christ."

"We'll cover the other side."

Geli killed the connection and said, "*Skow, home,*" into her headset. After one ring, Skow said, "Tell me you have them."

"They're gone."

"What does that mean?"

"Tennant pulled a switch on the ferry. He and Weiss are now in a canoe somewhere on the Cashie River."

"Damn it, Geli. How could you screw this up?"

Her cheeks burned. "Do you want to have a conversation about who fucked this up?"

"Don't be insubordinate."

"If Tennant slips through our fingers here, you can kiss control good-bye."

"That's not necessarily true. Give me a moment."

As Skow pondered the situation, Geli punched up a map of North Carolina on her screen. What would Tennant do after getting on the river? Where could he go? There were five miles of water between the ferry and the sound, and no road on the south bank from which to surveil the river. If Tennant knew that, he could beach the canoe anywhere.

"What do you want to do?" Skow asked.

"I want real-time satellite imagery of that river right now. Highest possible resolution. You authorize it, I'll give the NRO the coordinates."

"What else?"

"I need more manpower. I don't have near the tactical strength to carry out a wide-area search in wooded terrain."

"That's a problem. Until we go public with some form of this story, we're low on manpower."

"Then you'd better think about going public, and fast."

"Listen, Geli, if we lose him here, we still have a good shot. I'm going to be giving you some information that could put you one step ahead of Tennant."

Her internal radar went on alert. "What kind of information?"

"You'll see when you get it. It's from an unimpeachable source."

"There's no such thing. Is this an NSA source?"

"Yes."

"The agency hasn't given me anything reliable so far."

"That's about to change. I'm in a hurry. Have we covered everything?"

"No. Rules of engagement."

Skow took an audible breath. "I'm comfortable with your rescue scenario."

"I'll bet you are. I want a shoot-to-kill order."

Skow did not reply.

Geli felt her temper rising. "Look, we've waited—"

"Give me a moment to think."

"Why are you so damn wishy-washy about this?"

"Look . . . this is a hostage situation. You have the tactical experience. I have to leave the rules of engagement to your discretion."

Geli shook her head and muttered, "Be careful what you wish for, right?"

"The burden of command, Ms. Bauer."

"Command isn't a burden, Skow. It's nirvana. The burden is putting up with ass-covering bureaucrats second-guessing every move after the fact."

Skow chuckled softly. "You sound exactly like your father. I'll mention it to him."

This comment stopped Geli cold. "You do that," she said, covering.

After Skow hung up, she sat in silence, lightly touching the scar on her cheek. So Skow and her father had more than a passing acquaintance. She didn't like that idea. Not at all.

EIGHTEEN

I had been paddling steadily for an hour when I spotted the boat ramp. It lay at the foot of the high bridge over the Cashie River, the one we'd crossed on our way to the ferry. The river had widened since the ferry, and sooner or later it would open into the vast expanse of Albemarle Sound. In open water we would be easier to spot from the air. I'd seen no further sign of the surveillance plane, but that gave me limited comfort.

Drifting under the overhanging trees on the right bank, I thought about the ramp. There would be a parking lot there. Trucks and boat trailers. Probably fishermen returning from their day of sport.

Rachel turned on her seat and sat facing me, watching intently as I paddled. "You've done this before."

"What? Been on the run?"

"Paddled a canoe."

I nodded. "My brother and I camped a lot with my dad around Oak Ridge. Hunted and fished, too."

She looked into the trees on the bank. The sun hovered stubbornly behind us, but the shadows under the limbs were already deepening to blue-black.

"Are we safe now?"

"For a while. The people who are hunting us depend on technology. If we were out in the world, in a city or on a highway, we'd already have been caught. Here the playing field is more even."

She toyed with the blue-and-white nylon stern line. "Who is this Geli Bauer person you talked about?"

I was surprised she remembered the name, but I shouldn't have been. She'd never forgotten anything I told her. "She's a killer, and she's hunting us now."

"How do you know she's a killer?"

"She was in the army for a while. Geli's fluent in Arabic, so they dropped her into Iraq with some commandos before Desert Storm. To interrogate captured Republican Guard troops. She executed two Iraqi prisoners because they couldn't keep up with her unit behind the lines. Cut their throats. Even the Delta Force soldiers with her were shocked."

"I guess women have come further than feminists think."

"No. Female assassins are an ancient tradition. Geli gave Ravi Nara a lecture about it one day."

"She sounds like a sociopath." Rachel dropped the stern line and wearily rubbed her neck.

"She'd make an interesting case study for you."

"Do you think she killed Fielding?"

"Yes. She'd know all about drugs that could cause death by mimicking a stroke, and she has constant access to everything at Trinity. The food, the water, everything."

I paddled harder, and the bridge over the Cashie came steadily closer. Rachel looked over her shoulder at the massive structure. Cars drove onto it every few seconds. That bridge represented civilization. I stopped paddling to give my burning back muscles a break. The silence was almost total.

"Listen to the birds," she said.

I listened, but the sound my ears picked out of the silence

178

was not natural. A faint rumbling drone was floating down the river. It could have been a boat motor, but my gut told me it wasn't.

"What is it?" Rachel asked. "You look scared."

I scanned the right bank, looking for a place to beach the canoe. If a small plane flew right down the river, overhanging branches wouldn't give us any cover. The engine was growing louder. Even Rachel heard it now.

"That sounds close," she said.

Just ahead, a diseased tree had fallen into the river. It lay half in and half out of the water, its dead branches and leaves fanning out like ghostly wings. The space between the tree and the bank was the kind of spot where you could expect a water moccasin to drop into your boat if you were stupid enough to pull under it looking for fish. I guided the canoe straight into the narrow chute, feeling a little like Hawkeye in *The Last of the Mohicans*. I only hoped I had some of his luck.

Seconds after the bow plowed into the bank, the rumble of the approaching engine became a roar. I peered through the trees and saw exactly what I'd feared: a small plane flying twenty feet over the water, like a Vietnam pilot giving support fire to riverine troops.

"They can't see us, can they?" Rachel asked.

"Not without thermal-imaging equipment. But they may have that. Get down low in the boat."

She slid off her seat and lay flat in the bottom. I lay beside her. The plane's engine vibrated the aluminum skin of the canoe. We stayed in the bottom of the boat, waiting to see if it would circle back for another look. It didn't.

I climbed back onto my seat and stroked toward the bridge.

"I can't believe this is happening," Rachel said. "I can't believe a woman I've never met is trying to hunt me down and kill me. How could she do that?"

I thought back to my last meeting with Bauer. "She thinks we're too close. She thinks you're in love with me."

Rachel's cheeks colored in the fading sun. "Because of the kiss at Lu Li's?"

"Not just that. When Geli questioned me yesterday, she told me that you never see anyone."

"How would she know that?"

"She knows everybody you've dated and when you stopped seeing them. She knows who your third-grade teacher was and what your mother used to cook for you when you were sick."

"What did you tell her when she said I was in love with you?"

"That you think I'm schizophrenic."

Rachel smiled, her eyes full of sadness.

I panned my eyes across the broad expanse of river, searching for other water craft. I saw none, which didn't surprise me too much. Fishermen bought big outboard motors to take them to distant fishing spots as fast as possible. I dug in my paddle and pointed the canoe toward the boat ramp.

"We're stopping?" Rachel asked, looking at the gentle slope of the ramp.

"Yes. When we hit, stay in the boat. I won't be long."

"What are you going to do?"

"Take a look around."

I beached the canoe beside the ramp, then jumped into the shallow water and splashed onto shore. The oyster-shell parking lot stretched from the woods on my right to the huge concrete bridge pilings on my left. I saw no people, but a line of pickup trucks with boat trailers sat parked about forty yards from the ramp. I walked over to them and moved between two trucks.

Ducking low, I felt along the tops of the tires of both pickups, searching for stashed keys. I found none. Moving around the truck on my left, I checked its other two tires. Nothing. I had no luck with the next two trucks either. The next in line was a maroon Dodge Ram. There was no key sitting on its tires, so I changed tactics. Squatting between the rear of the truck and the empty boat trailer behind it, I reached under the bumper and slid my fingertips along the inside of its metallic lip. Something slid toward the fender with a scratching sound.

A magnetic key case.

I opened the small black box and found a key to the Dodge and one for the locking trailer hitch. Quickly disengaging the trailer from the truck, I got behind the wheel and started the engine.

Rachel ducked down in the canoe as I drove up, not realizing I was behind the wheel. I swung left so that my window came to face her.

"Bring Fielding's box!" I shouted. "Hurry!"

Cradling the cardboard box in her arms, Rachel climbed out of the canoe and splashed out of the river. I ran to the bank and grabbed a handful of mud from the shallows, which I spread across part of the truck's license plate. Then I washed my hand in the river, set Fielding's box on the backseat, and helped Rachel onto the bench seat beside me.

"Did you hot-wire this thing?" she asked.

"I wouldn't know how. Fishermen are honest people. They trust each other. I hate to take it, really."

"I'll say a prayer of penance. Let's go."

We left a white cloud of oyster-shell dust behind us as we raced out of the lot.

"Are we still going to Nags Head?" Rachel asked.

"No. They could be waiting for us there. Let me use your cell phone."

She pulled a silver Motorola from her pocket and gave it

to me. I dialed the White House number from memory; Fielding had told me long ago to memorize it.

"Who are you calling?" Rachel asked.

"The president, I hope."

"But you said—"

"I want to see what happens."

An operator answered on the second ring. I said, "Project Trinity." There was a silence, then a click, and the man I'd spoken to yesterday said, "State your business."

"This is David Tennant. I need to speak to the president."

"Hold, please."

A hissing silence followed, and I knew that every ticking second gave the NSA longer to track the location of Rachel's cell phone.

"Well?" she said.

"Count to forty. Out loud."

She had reached thirty-five when a voice with a New England accent said, "Dr. Tennant?"

"Yes."

"This is Ewan McCaskell. I'm talking to you from Air Force One."

My heart thudded. "Mr. McCaskell, I need to speak to the president."

"He's talking to the British prime minister now. He should be able to come to the phone in about five minutes."

I couldn't sit on an open cell phone for five minutes.

"Will you wait?" McCaskell asked. "The president knows there have been confusing events at Project Trinity. He wants very much to speak with you."

"I can't wait. I'll call the White House again in seven minutes."

"We'll have it routed to us."

I clicked END, my heart pounding.

Rachel touched my arm. "Good or bad?"

182

"I don't know. That was McCaskell. He said the president wants to talk to me. But they've obviously been talked to already. By John Skow, probably. They only know what Godin wants them to know."

"Are they back in the U.S.?"

"They're on Air Force One."

"On their way back from China?"

"No. That's a five-day trip, plus a one-day stopover in Japan. I checked yesterday. This summit is sort of a celebration of Nixon's visit in '72. A repeat performance, without the Cold War tension."

"What are you going to say when you call back?"

I shook my head. President Bill Matthews had been the senior Republican senator from Texas when he was swept into the White House on a tide of anti-Democrat frustration. No one had been more surprised than my brother, James, who had known Matthews since their days at Yale. Matthews was a charismatic figure, but not the sharpest arrow in the quiver, according to my brother. As a senator, he had relied heavily on his advisers, and that had not changed in the White House. Still, the general opinion was that he was doing a solid job on both the domestic and foreign fronts. I'd met Matthews once in the Oval Office, then again at a Georgetown reception, when I was filming the *NOVA* series based on my book. How did he remember me? As a levelheaded physician whose brother he had liked? Or as the delusional paranoid Skow had undoubtedly described?

I drove anxiously along Highway 64 until it was time to call back. This time, when I identified myself, the connection was almost immediate.

"Dr. Tennant?" said the president.

"This is David Tennant."

"This is Bill Matthews, David. I know it's been a while

183

since we last saw each other, but I want you to know you can tell me anything. Now, talk to me."

I took a deep breath and went straight to the point. "Sir, I know you've already heard some things about my supposed mental state. I want you to know that I'm as sane as the day we met in the Oval Office. So, please listen with an open mind. Andrew Fielding died in his office at Trinity yesterday. I believe he was murdered. Today there was an attempt on my life. A man came into my home with a gun, and I had to shoot him in self-defense. Project Trinity is completely out of control, and I think Peter Godin and John Skow are to blame."

There was a long silence.

"Mr. President?"

"I heard you, David. Look, the first thing we need to do is get you to a safe place."

"There is no safe place."

"Well, somewhere has to be safe, doesn't it?"

"Not when the NSA is trying to kill you."

"Don't worry about the NSA. I can arrange for the Secret Service to pick you up somewhere, and they can take you to a safe house while you wait for me to get back."

This sounded attractive, but I knew I couldn't risk such a rendezvous. Getting to it alive would be close to impossible. "I can't do that, sir."

"You don't trust the Secret Service?"

"It's not that. The point is that I don't know any Secret Service agents by sight."

"I see." Silence. "Well, couldn't we set up a code or a signal or something?"

"It wouldn't be secure from the NSA. Nothing like that will be safe."

"We could pick one right now."

"We have to assume the agency is listening to this call. They can pull it right out of the ether over China."

Mathews sighed. "All right, David. Tell me this. Do you trust Ewan McCaskell?"

I thought about that. There'd been no attempt on my life until McCaskell returned my call at my house, which had told the Trinity security people that I hadn't yet talked to the president. If McCaskell was tied to anyone at Trinity, he would have communicated this to them long before that phone call. "I trust him. But I'll have to see his face."

"Well . . . it looks like you're just going to have to lie low until we get back. McCaskell and the Secret Service will pick you up then. Can you get to Washington in four days?"

"I can. Mr. President, could I ask you one thing?"

"Of course."

"Do you believe anything I've said?"

Matthews replied in a less folksy voice. "David, I won't lie to you. John Skow says Dr. Fielding died of natural causes, and that you shot a Trinity security officer outside your house without provocation. He also says you've kidnapped your psychiatrist."

I blinked in disbelief. Skow had finally made a mistake.

"Hold on, sir." I handed the phone to Rachel. "Tell him who you are."

She hesitantly took the phone and held it to her ear. "This is Dr. Rachel Weiss. . . . Yes. . . . No, sir. I came with Dr. Tennant of my own free will. . . . That's right. Yes, people are trying to kill us. . . . Yes, sir. I will."

She handed me the cell phone.

"Mr. President?"

"I'm here, David. Look, I'm not sure what to think. But I know you come from good people, and I want to see you and hear you out."

The first tiny fillip of relief went through me. "Thank you, sir. All I ask is a fair hearing."

"You'll get that as soon as I get back. Keep your ass in the grass, Dave."

A bubble of laughter burst through the lump in my throat. That saying was right out of my older brother's mouth. "Thank you, Mr. President. I'll see you then."

I clicked *end*.

Rachel was watching me expectantly. "What do you think?"

"I think we're better off than we were five minutes ago. What did he ask you?"

"Whether I was under duress. He also told me to take care of you. My God . . . I can't believe this. What are we going to do for the next four days?"

I pressed down the accelerator and sped up to seventy. "We're going to Oak Ridge."

"Tennessee?"

"Yep. I know that place like nowhere in the world. Five miles outside of town, you're lost in the wilderness. No police. No TVs to broadcast photos of wanted fugitives and stolen trucks. Nothing."

"How far away is it?"

"Eight hours." I passed a slow-moving car and settled back into the right lane. "Settle in and get some sleep."

"I can't sleep in a car."

"This is a truck."

"Wiseass."

Escaping the plane and reaching the president had produced a sense of elation in both of us, but that feeling wouldn't last long. "I'm not kidding about the sleep. You're going to need every bit of energy you have in the morning."

"For what?"

"Mountains."

NINETEEN

Geli was running on adrenaline, her body charged by the chase. Between the hunt for Tennant and Weiss and the search for Lu Li Fielding, her resources were stretched to the limit. But when the lack of manpower vexed her, she thought back to the Iraqi desert, where her total force had numbered only eight Delta Force commandos.

Her latest headache was Jutta Klein, the German MRI expert. Klein had apparently taken advantage of her reduced surveillance and driven to Atlanta, where she'd boarded a Lufthansa flight for Germany. The German government had pledged to "assist in any way possible," but Geli knew they would welcome Klein and her newfound expertise with open arms.

Geli spun in her chair. Someone with the day's access code had buzzed through the door of the control center. John Skow stepped out of the shadows, clad in his unvarying Brooks Brothers suit, his eyes glinting with fear or excitement.

"What are you doing here?" she asked. "What's happened?"

Skow straddled a chair opposite Geli and folded his almost feminine hands on its back.

"Tennant just spoke to the president. Matthews was in

Air Force One, en route from Beijing to Shanghai. Our routine intercepts over China picked it up, and I just broke the executive comm codes."

Geli felt as though she'd opened the door of a hot oven. No wonder Skow hadn't wanted to talk on the air. "What did they say?"

"The president tried to arrange for the Secret Service to pick up Tennant somewhere, but Tennant wouldn't bite."

"Did Matthews buy our story? Or does he believe Tennant?"

Skow bit one side of his lower lip, like a man weighing odds. "I'd say he's leaning toward us. But he told Tennant he would get a fair hearing."

"And how will that happen?"

"Ewan McCaskell and the Secret Service will meet Tennant and pick him up when the president gets back. Tennant trusts McCaskell."

"When does the president get back?"

"Four days."

"Are we talking D.C.?"

"Yes."

"Perfect."

"Why?"

Geli had already foreseen that Tennant might run for Washington. "D.C. gives us a perfect cover story to take Tennant out. Starting now, we maximize our effort to discredit him, expanding on what we've already said. Tennant's side effects worsened to psychosis. He shot his security guard and kidnapped Dr. Weiss."

"And?"

"Now he's threatened the president's life."

Skow's eyes narrowed. "But he just talked to Matthews. And he didn't make any threats."

Geli rolled her eyes. "Tennant is saying whatever he has to

say to get access to the man he wants to kill. By painting him as a deranged assassin, we can use every metro cop in D.C. to hunt him down. And once you give him the Lee Harvey Oswald treatment, the Secret Service won't let him near the president."

"That's an elegant strategy. What do we use for evidence?"

"We have hundreds of hours of recordings from Tennant's house and phone. Is the Godin Four still running upstairs?"

"I didn't notice. Why?"

"With the right programs from the NSA—and our Godin Four—you could piece together a verbal threat against the president that no one could prove was fake."

Skow smiled with appreciation. "That's good, Geli. Very good."

"That's why I'm here. The question is, will Tennant go straight to D.C. or wait the four days?"

"My source says no," said Skow. "I've got a short list of places Tennant might run, and Washington is at the bottom."

Anger tightened Geli's jaw muscles. "Who is this source, damn it?"

"I can't give you that. I'm sorry."

"But he says Tennant will run somewhere besides D.C.?"

"Yes. Isn't it just common sense? Why should Tennant risk going straight to Washington when the meet is four days away?"

"Because he knows people there who have access to POTUS. The surgeon general. The director of the National Institutes of Health. The politicians from his home state. Senator Barrett Jackson heads the Select Committee on Intelligence, for God's sake. He can get access to the Oval Office with a phone call. And if Tennant convinces someone like Barrett Jackson that he's sane . . ."

"I see. All right. But we can't be sure *where* he'll run. And our assassin story will allow us to bring in other federal assets to cover the other locations."

"Good. You take care of the media. You also need to hit everyone Tennant knows inside the Beltway with a classified NSA security warning. Emphasize his mental instability. Can you do that gracefully?"

Skow's thin lips flattened into something like a smile. "That's why I'm here."

Geli nodded, feeling better than she had in hours. "You'd better get upstairs and make sure they keep the Godin Four fired up. Or get it moved back here quick."

Skow had never touched Geli before, but he reached out and laid his hand on her wrist. "You have four days to kill Tennant and Weiss. After that, the Secret Service will be running things, and they'll work very hard to trap Tennant rather than kill him."

"That's why you're going to make sure nothing he says will be believed."

Skow nodded. "Right."

"Don't worry," Geli assured him. "The president will never see Tennant again. In twenty-four hours he'll be as dead as his brother."

TWENTY

It was dark by the time we reached Raleigh. Highway 64 turned to I-40, and then we were rolling back through Research Triangle Park, moving west toward Tennessee.

"Look at that," Rachel said, watching the familiar lights drift by. "When it's dark like this, I can almost believe you could drop me off at my house in Durham, and I could go inside and make a cup of tea."

"You know better now."

She looked at me for a long time, then sighed in the dark.

"I'm sorry I got you into this," I said. "I haven't really apologized yet."

"I got myself into it."

"No. I did that when I chose you as my analyst."

The weariness in Rachel's face told me she was accustomed to dealing with other people's guilt. "Don't start trying to figure out the vagaries of fate. If a butterfly had flapped its wings in Malaysia before you called, you would have found someone else. That's the way life is."

I'd said that kind of thing to myself before, but in this case I didn't believe it. "No. I sought you out because you're the best at what you do. And Jungian analysts aren't like psychologists, one on every corner. I know it sounds juvenile, but I have this feeling I was meant to find you."

She looked at me with infinitely perceptive eyes, but beneath her perception I saw pain. Somehow, I had prodded a deep nerve. When she spoke, it was in a voice devoid of emotion.

"It's easy to tell ourselves that whatever happens to us was meant to be. It's comforting. It gives us a sense that there's some larger plan. I thought my husband and I were meant to be together. But we weren't. It was just a bad choice that I rationalized as fate. It's pathetic, really."

"Pathetic? That marriage gave you your son."

"Who died frightened and in pain at the age of five."

Her tone had a warning edge to it. I'd seen many children die during my years practicing medicine, and I knew how it could affect parents. They could be shattered beyond recovery. Even hospital staff weren't immune. The exoskeleton of professionalism melts easily in the presence of a suffering child. For me that suffering—the agony of innocents—was one of the primary obstacles to believing in God.

"You and your son gave each other five years of unconditional love. Would you rather he'd never lived, to spare you both the pain at the end?"

She fixed me with an indignant glare. "You'll say anything, won't you? You don't observe *any* boundaries."

"Not when I've earned the right to cross them." I was speaking of the loss of my own child, and she knew it.

She looked out the window again. "Let's not talk about this."

"We don't have to talk at all. But we need supplies. I'm going to stop at an all-night Wal-Mart in Winston-Salem or Asheville. That gives you a couple of hours to sleep."

"I am exhausted," she admitted.

"Come here."

192

"What?"

"Lean over here."

"On your shoulder?"

"No. Be brave. Curl up on the seat and lay your head on my lap."

She shook her head, but not in refusal. I kept my eyes on the road. After a few moments, she pulled off her shoes, then folded her legs on the seat and laid her head on my right thigh. I sensed that her eyes were open, but I didn't look down. I lowered my right hand and began to stroke her forehead, sliding my fingers back into her hair.

"This reminds me of when I was a little girl," she said.

"I'm not talking to you. Close your eyes."

After a while, she did.

We hit Asheville at 10:30 P.M. A brightly lit Wal-Mart store appeared like an oasis out of the dark, and I pulled off the interstate. Rachel's head was still in my lap, and my right leg was nearly numb. She didn't respond when I spoke. I was tempted to leave her in the truck while I went into the store, but I didn't want her to wake up alone in the parking lot. There was also a chance that the local police had received an APB on the fisherman's stolen pickup. To avoid being ambushed when we came out of the store, I awakened Rachel and posted her just inside the glass doors, where she could see anyone who took an undue interest in our maroon Ram.

I went straight to the sporting goods department and began piling items beside an unattended cash register. A two-man tent. Sleeping bags. Backpacks. A Coleman lantern, a stove ring, and fuel. From another aisle I selected two Silent Shadow camouflage jumpsuits, camo headgear, rubber camo boots, and insulated underwear. One aisle over again, I chose a compound bow, eight arrows, and a quiver. I topped off my pile with a compass, a pair of binoculars, a Gerber knife, water purification tablets, a Maglite, and two battery-powered walkie-talkies. Then I went in search of a salesperson to ring it all up.

The young Mexican woman I found was suspicious of my cash. While she checked each hundred-dollar bill for authenticity, I went to the toiletries section and got toothpaste, toothbrushes, and soap. The total purchase came to $1429.84. After paying, I pushed my cart to the front of the store and left it with Rachel, then took another to the grocery section and grabbed enough basics to keep us alive for a couple of weeks, plus some bottled water. As I went through the checkout aisle, I thought how amazing it was that I could pull off the highway late at night and in one stop outfit myself for long-term survival in the wilderness. My father wouldn't have believed it.

Rachel made an "okay" sign with her hand while I checked out, and I breathed a little easier. The rent-a-cop at the exit stopped me, but only to check my receipt against what was in my cart. Ten seconds later we were walking through the parking lot. I tossed everything behind the seat, then helped Rachel inside and started back toward I-40.

Just before we reached the interstate, I turned into the parking lot of a Best Western motel and parked between two trucks on the back side. One was a blue Dodge Ram with a horse trailer attached. Using a screwdriver from our glove box, I removed the Texas license plate from that Ram and exchanged it for the plate on our maroon one. Then I drove up the access ramp to I-40 and headed west toward the Tennessee line, which lay somewhere in the Appalachian Mountains before us.

Soon Rachel was snoring softly, her head on my lap again. I tuned the radio to a station playing David Gray and let my eyes blur until all they tracked were the edges of the road. We were driving into my past, into the forests of my youth, a world of strange contrasts and indelible memories. The Oak Ridge National Laboratory was one of the most high-tech installations in the country, yet it was nestled in thickly forested wilderness. There I had gone to school with the children of brilliant men and women from Chicago and New York, and the children of emaciated men and women who'd never left the county where they were born. Some of the scientists found the rural setting boring, if not downright disturbing, but for my family the wooded mountains surrounding Oak Ridge had been a paradise.

There were several isolated spots around Oak Ridge where we could hide, but one was perfect for us. Last year, I'd heard from a boyhood friend that because of budget constraints, the government was closing the Frozen Head State Park. My brother and I had camped there countless times, and by now the mountainous park would be deserted but for a few fanatical hikers who wouldn't bother anyone enjoying the same illicit recreation they sought.

We crossed the Tennessee line at the south end of the Pisgah National Forest. Then we broke out of the big trees, and by midnight we were passing through Knoxville. I continued west on 62 and in less than thirty minutes we were driving through Oak Ridge, America's "secret city" of the Second World War. Today it is known worldwide for its nuclear facilities, but during World War Two it hadn't even existed on maps. Between 1945 and 1975—the year I left it for Alabama—Oak Ridge had grown into something resembling a normal American town. But it never quite was. There was always a shared sense of mission in Oak Ridge, and the proof of the town's value was invisible but ever present. We who lived there knew that in the event of nuclear war, we would be vaporized in the first few minutes. Even in the dark I could see that the city had grown since I'd left it. There were more franchise restaurants on the strip, more chain stores, but the town's heart was still the laboratory and the old wartime uranium piles, which drew tourists curious to see the tools that had won the war against the Japanese.

Leaving Oak Ridge on Highway 62, ours was the only vehicle on the road. We skirted the base of Big Brushy Mountain, on the far side of which lay the state penitentiary. Three county lines intersected in this isolated area, a mist-shrouded world populated by the descendants of coal miners and moonshiners. They clung tenaciously to existence in the shadowy hollows and along the abandoned strip mines that still scarred these mountains.

I turned north on 116, a narrow road that wound past the hamlet of Petros and then the prison, a starkly depressing enclosure lit by a harsh mercury glow and surrounded by razor-wire fences. North of the prison, the road began to twist back upon itself like a wounded snake. I turned left on a track that had no map number, but which I remembered well. Before long, I would come to the gate of the abandoned state park, which would probably be barricaded now.

A half mile from the gate, I slowed and began looking for an opening in the trees. When I saw one, I braked and turned off the road, and in ten seconds we had vanished. I drove until the woods became too thick and the grade too steep to go farther. Then I parked and shut off the engine.

Rachel hadn't stirred. I reached back and pulled our sleeping bags from the gear behind the seat. As I unrolled them, she snapped awake and popped up out of my lap, staring wide-eyed in the dark.

"*What are you doing?*"

"Take it easy," I said. "You're fine. We're there."

"Where?" She tried to look out the window, but there was no light beneath the trees. We could have been in a cave.

"We're outside Oak Ridge, at a place called Frozen Head. It's an abandoned state park."

"Frozen Head?"

"You've been asleep for hours."

She shook her head. "I can't sleep in cars."

"Well, keep on not sleeping. I'll wake you just before dawn."

She blinked as though coming out of a trance. Then she put her hand to her mouth and grimaced. "Did you buy us toothbrushes?"

"Yes. You can do that in the morning."

"I need to pee."

"You've got the whole forest."

"Is it safe out there?"

I thought of telling her to watch for timber rattlers, but she probably wouldn't get out if I did. "This is the safest you've been in twenty-four hours."

She climbed out of the truck and moved out of the light but didn't close the door. This illuminated us like a lantern in the woods. She took a long time, and I started to feel anxious. Then raindrops began hitting the windshield, and I heard her squeal. She scrambled back into the truck with her jeans unbuttoned and yanked the door shut.

"It's pouring!" she cried, fastening her pants.

"Rain's good for us. It deadens sound when you walk in the woods."

She pulled a sleeping bag over her chest and shuddered. "I don't want to offend you, but this sucks. We couldn't stay in some cheap motel?"

"No one in the world knows where we are now. So no one can find out. That's the way we want it. Go to sleep."

She nodded and settled against her door.

I sat listening to the symphony of rain and the ticking engine, recalling predawn vigils with my father and brother, waiting for our chance at ducks or deer. I was exhausted, but I knew I'd wake before the sun. Some primitive part of my brain that lay dormant in cities awakened in the wilderness and whispered the forest rhythms to me with unfailing accuracy. That whisper told me when dawn was close, when rain was coming, when game was moving. I pulled my sleeping bag up to my chin.

"Good night," I said to Rachel.

Steady breathing was her only reply.

I woke as the first dim shade of blue showed through the trees. I blinked several times, then surveyed the scene without moving my head. Seeing nothing, I gently shook Rachel awake. Again she jerked erect, but not in quite the panic of last night.

"Time to go," I said.

"Okay," she mumbled, but she looked ready to go back to sleep.

I got out and relieved my bladder, then unloaded the gear from behind the seat. I put most of it into my own pack, giving Rachel only her sleeping bag, some canned food, and a couple of fuel bottles. When she got out, I handed her a Silent Shadow camouflage jumpsuit, heavy socks, and boots.

She made a wry face, but she took the clothes and went behind the truck. While she changed, I fixed the quiver and compound bow to my pack. Then I slipped into my jumpsuit and boots. As I shouldered my pack, the forest seemed to grow lighter all at once, and I knew the sun was topping Windrock Mountain to the east.

Rachel came around the truck looking like photos I'd seen of female Israeli soldiers. She shouldered her pack without much trouble, and she didn't complain about the weight.

"If your friends could see you now," I said, clipping a walkie-talkie to her belt.

"They'd be rolling on the ground laughing."

I stuffed our street clothes into her pack. "Watch the

ground. Step where I step, and watch for briers catching your clothes. If we get separated, use the walkie-talkie, but very quietly."

"Okay."

"Don't speak unless it's an emergency. If I hold up my hand, stop. Grab my belt if I go too fast. We're not in a hurry. You're going to see animals out here. Move calmly away from snakes, and ignore the rest."

She nodded. "Where exactly are we going?"

"There are caves on the mountain. Hikers know about some, but there's one that's almost unknown. My dad and I found it when I was a kid. That's the one we want."

She smiled. "I'm as ready as I'm going to get."

We followed the path left by the truck's tires until we reached the road, then piled some brush over the open place. I crossed the road and began looking for a spring-fed tributary of the New River, a small creek that cut its way down the mountain through a rocky defile about fifty feet deep. That defile would be our route up the mountain. The park service had blazed a trail that paralleled the creek, but I didn't want to risk running into any hikers. I also worried about locals growing marijuana in the closed park. During lean times, that temptation was great for the descendants of moonshiners, and they tended to frown upon trespassers. They booby-trapped their fields and shot before asking questions.

I soon found the creek, and by the time daylight illuminated the forest we were shin-deep in water, picking our way up the defile. Gnarled tree roots threaded through its walls like arthritic hands, and boulders big as cars lined the ravine. The creek was shallow and wide in some places but narrowed to gurgling channels in others. I saw deer tracks and scat, and once what looked like the track of a bear. That made me a little anxious about the cave. There was constant scuttling in the brush, rabbits and armadillos flushed from cover by our passing. Every few minutes I turned to check on Rachel, but she seemed to be holding up well. She slipped on wet rocks a few times, but moving uphill on slick stone was no task for beginners.

I was stepping over a waterlogged branch when I smelled smoke on the wind. I stopped in my tracks, hoping the smell was a hiker's campfire. It wasn't. It was good Virginia tobacco. I held up my hand, but there was no need. Rachel had halted the second she saw me stop.

Without moving my head, I scanned the rocks and trees ahead. Nothing moved but creek water and raindrops sliding off the leaves overhead. I raised my gaze and searched the low limbs of the forest canopy. A poacher in a deer stand was a possibility. But a real hunter would know that smoking a cigarette would kill his chances of bagging a deer, even out of season. I saw nothing in the trees.

Moving my head slightly, I searched the rim of the defile. First the right side, then the left. Nothing. I sniffed the air again. The odor was gone.

Rachel tugged at the back of my belt. "What's the matter?" she whispered.

I turned and saw fear in her face. *Be quiet,* I mouthed. *Stay still.*

She nodded.

Another wave of tobacco scent wafted past me, stronger than before. I turned very slowly and for some reason looked up. Forty yards away, a man dressed in black ballistic nylon leaned over the rim of the defile and flicked a cigarette butt down into the creek. My heart clenched, but I remained still. The butt tumbled in the air, a flash of white against green, then hit the water and floated toward us.

The man followed the butt with his eyes. I was certain we were about to be seen, but the man suddenly looked away and took something off his shoulder. A black assault rifle.

200

An M16. He leaned it against a tree, unzipped his fly, and began to urinate off the small cliff. He played like a little boy, aiming his stream for the creek but not quite reaching it. A boy would have been able to reach it. This was a man in his late thirties, and he was wearing body armor.

I prayed that Rachel wouldn't panic. She might not have seen the rifleman at first, but she couldn't miss the long golden arc glinting in the early light. The man stopped urinating with a few desultory flourishes, then shook himself, zipped up, and picked up the M16. As he shouldered the rifle, he looked down the creek, right at us.

I held my breath and waited for our eyes to lock.

The rifleman's gaze passed over us, then returned. He squinted, then looked farther down the creek again. It was the camouflage suits and headgear. He couldn't distinguish us from the background of creek and brush. As I watched, he moved his head to the right in a strange way, as though he had a nervous tic, but then I realized he was speaking into a collar microphone. I heard the faint metallic squawk of a reply but couldn't make out distinct words. Then the rifleman turned and walked back into the trees.

Numb with disbelief, I turned back to Rachel, who was staring at me in confusion.

"What's the matter?" she whispered.

"You didn't see that?"

"What?"

"The guy up there pissing off the cliff!"

Her eyes went wide.

"He had a rifle."

"I didn't see anything! I was watching you. I thought you'd seen a snake or something."

"We're going back to the truck. Now."

Her face had lost its color. "What about the cave?"

"It's blown. They're waiting for us up there."

"They can't be."

"They *are*. The guy was carrying an M16 and wearing body armor. Deer hunters around here look a little different."

"But we've come all this way."

Prickly heat covered my skin. "What do you care?"

"I don't. I mean—that cave just sounded safe."

"It's not."

A new awareness smoldered in the dark of my mind. *They knew we were coming.* Before my thoughts could go further, I found myself listening with absolute concentration. I wasn't sure what I'd heard, but it was something. A movement that didn't fit the usual sound track of the forest. I cursed silently. The rain that had dampened the sound of our steps was now giving cover to our enemies. Or were they only *my* enemies?

As understanding flashed into my mind, another faint squawk broke the silence, and I knew there was another rifleman within fifty feet of me. Stepping quietly behind Rachel, I clapped one hand over her mouth and whipped my other arm around her chest, pinning her against me with all my strength. She tried to scream, but no sound passed her lips.

I stood in the creek without moving, water pulling at my legs. Rachel struggled against me. The backpack made it hard to hold her. I was afraid she might bite my hand, but she didn't. That alone kept alive doubt that it was she who had told the NSA where to find us.

"I'm going to uncover your mouth," I whispered. "If you scream, I'll cut your throat."

TWENTY-ONE

When I let go of Rachel, she whirled in the creek, her face a mask of terror and fury. Then she saw the knife in my hand, the Gerber I'd bought at Wal-Mart.

"Walk," I told her. "Back down the creek. You know how to do it."

She stared at me a moment longer, then turned and started over the rocks. I sheathed my knife and unslung my bow. I would stand little chance against a man with an M16, but if I saw my opponent first, I might get off a quick shot.

"Stick close to the right wall."

She moved to the right, quickly picking her way from stone to stone. As I followed Rachel down the steep water-course, my mind filled with questions I should have asked her before but hadn't. That first day, when she'd awakened me from my dream about Fielding's death . . . how had she unlocked the door? I'd locked it after the FedEx man left, yet I'd awakened to find the door banging against the chain latch as Rachel yelled my name. And finding my house without me telling her my address? *I know someone in the UVA personnel office,* she'd said. The university would have been warned about giving out information on a Trinity principal. And the surveillance plane over the highway? How had they known which of the thousands of cars between Chapel Hill and Nags Head to train their laser on? One phone call from Rachel while I was unconscious could have given them the Audi, the Nags Head cabin, everything.

As for Oak Ridge, she could easily have called them from the Wal-Mart in Asheville, when I'd posted her by the door. She hadn't known about Frozen Head then, but she did have a cell phone. With a little nerve, she could have called the NSA when she got out of the truck last night to pee. On the other hand, I still remembered leaping into the hallway of my house and finding an assassin pointing a gun at Rachel's back.

She paused as she came to a deep channel in the creek. I moved close behind her in case she fell or tried to run. As we negotiated the channel, I thought back to how I'd chosen her. Skow had resisted my going to a non-NSA psychiatrist, but had he resisted vigorously enough? Friends at UVA had told me Rachel was the best Jungian analyst in the country. Had Geli Bauer been walking in my footsteps, talking to everyone I talked to? Had she briefed Rachel before my first appointment? How could Geli have compromised her? An appeal to patriotism? Blackmail? There was no way to know.

I reached out and grabbed Rachel's pack. The creek had leveled out. The road wasn't far away.

"We're close to the truck," I said softly. "Veer left here, and don't step on any branches."

She looked back at me, her eyes still furious. "You don't really think—"

I poked her in the back. "Walk."

She picked her path through the dripping trees with surprising agility. After about forty yards, I grabbed her pack again, then scanned the trees ahead.

"David, you don't think I betrayed you."

204

I nodded. "No other explanation."

"There *has* to be."

I peered between the wet trunks, searching for anything out of place. "They might have figured out Oak Ridge, but not Frozen Head. I could have picked a dozen other spots in the mountains around here."

She held up her hands helplessly. "I don't know what to tell you. I haven't spoken to anyone."

"How did you get into my house that day? The first day?"

"Your house? I picked the lock."

"Bullshit."

"You think so? My father was a locksmith in Brooklyn. I grew up around the trade."

Her explanation could be a facile lie, but it had the outrageous ring of truth. "What's a Chubb?" I asked off the top of my head.

"A high-quality, British-made lock. I also know what a spiral tooth extractor is. Do you?"

I had no idea. "Turn around and keep walking. The truck's a hundred yards ahead."

Rachel turned and walked quickly through the trees. With my bow unslung, I had to be more careful. The bowstring seemed to attract briers, and the broadhead I was holding along the shaft of the bow kept catching on branches and shaking water onto me.

Suddenly, I heard a *swish* like a big buck leaping through wet foliage. Then I saw a flash of black between two trees.

"Freeze!" barked a male voice.

Rachel stopped, her back just visible between two glistening trunks. Beyond her stood a man wearing black nylon and a bulletproof vest. He held an automatic pistol, and it was trained on Rachel's face.

"Where is he?" asked the gunman.

"Who?"

"You know. The doctor."

I nocked the arrow and slowly raised my bow.

"I don't know what you're talking about," Rachel said. "I'm out here shooting a wildlife spread on deer."

The lie sounded effortless. Was she signaling the gunman with her hand?

"Where's your camera?"

I pulled the bowstring to full draw against my right cheek and peered through the peep sight. Rachel's body partially blocked my shot, and I didn't want to shift my weight for fear of making noise.

"I lost it in the creek," she said. "Are you a game warden?"

"Red Six to Red Leader," the gunman said into his collar radio.

"I'll tell you!" cried Rachel.

I leaned to my right, straining for a shot.

The gunman looked up from his radio. "All right. Where is he?"

Some bulletproof vests will stop a bullet but not a knife point. A razor-sharp broadhead should pierce what a knife would, but if it didn't, Rachel's face—or mine—would disappear in a cloud of red mist. I aimed for the V of the gunman's throat, just above the top of his vest.

"What will you do if you find him?" Rachel asked.

"That's not your problem."

"*Red Six,*" crackled the radio receiver in the man's ear, loud enough for us to hear. "*This is Red Leader. Repeat your message.*"

As he reached up to key his radio, Rachel screamed my name, and I loosed the arrow.

Rachel's scream masked any sound of impact. For a moment I was afraid I'd hit her. She'd fallen to her knees, but the gunman was still standing and holding his pistol. Why hadn't he fired? Had my arrow passed him without a sound? My bowstring was silenced. I jerked another arrow from my quiver and tried to nock it with shaking fingers.

"Red Six, this is Red Leader. This better be good."

I expected a pistol shot, but instead I heard a heavy thud that I instantly recognized. When I looked up, the gunman was gone. I'd heard deer fall like that after a spine shot. First came the sing of the bowstring, then the knee-buckling impact and the cement-sack thud of a clean kill. The delay was what had thrown me. This man had hung in the air like a statue, unwilling to die.

"This is Red Leader, respond immediately."

Rachel's face was streaked with tears. As adrenaline poured into my system, I shoved her aside and looked down. The black-clad man lay flat on his back. The broadhead had pierced his throat and punched through his cervical spine. He couldn't have remained standing more than a second with that injury, which only proved how subjective time was in the heat of action.

"Get in the truck," I told Rachel.

"Where is it?"

"Thirty yards on. *Move!*"

She staggered over the fallen man and disappeared into the trees.

"Red Six, this is Red Leader, what the hell are you doing?"

I heard someone else talking through static. *". . . goddamn no-count radios. Go find the son of a bitch. Tell him we got coffee up here. That'll bring him."*

The dead man's eyes were open but already as cloudy as antique glass. I picked up his automatic and stuffed it into my jumpsuit pocket. Then I got to my knees and hefted his corpse over my shoulder. I had to grab a thick branch to pull myself to my feet, but I managed it, and then began trudging toward the truck. Anyone within a hundred meters would think Bigfoot was lumbering through the forest.

Rachel was waiting by the truck, her face almost blood-less. I staggered to the side of the pickup and dumped the corpse into its bed. When she pulled at my sleeve, I spun her against the truck and untied the sleeping bag from her pack. This I unzipped and threw over the dead body. To anchor the opened bag, I tossed both loaded backpacks on top of it.

"Get inside," I snapped.

She did.

I climbed into the truck bed to retrieve the ignition key from my backpack, then got behind the wheel and backed out of the trees. Twice I hit patches of mud I thought would bog us down, but by slowly rocking the truck, I managed to get clear of the woods. The SWAT team must have heard the truck's engine by now. I hit the accelerator and headed back toward the Brushy Mountain State Prison.

Only after I'd covered the first mile did I look at Rachel. She'd set her back against the door and was watching me as she would a violent patient.

"What's your story?" I asked. "How did they get to you?"

She said nothing.

When we reached 116, I didn't turn toward the penitentiary but toward Caryville, where the road intersected I-75.

"You think I've been telling them where we are?" Rachel asked.

I nodded.

"Why would I do that?"

"Only you know that."

"If I'd wanted them to find you, I could have betrayed you long before now."

It started to rain again, big fat drops that splatted like bugs on the windshield. I switched on the wipers and slowed down.

"Maybe they didn't want to capture me until you'd got

all the information you could out of me. Did you call them from Wal-Mart?"

She looked at me with scorn. "When that guy with the gun asked me where you were, I could have told him you were right behind me."

"You knew I had an arrow pointed at your back."

Frustration tightened her face. "*Think,* David. I could have hit you in the head with a rock just now. While you put that corpse in the truck."

"I'll think later. Right now I have to run."

We drove in silence for a while, heading toward the deep divide that marked the line between Morgan and Anderson Counties. A bridge appeared ahead. Despite the rain, there wasn't much water under it, but the gorge was deep, cut by years of water flowing from strip mines higher up. About a third of the way across, I pulled the truck close to the rail and stopped.

Taking the key out of the ignition, I got out and climbed into the bed of the truck. The sleeping bag covering the corpse was soggy with rain. I kicked it aside, wrestled the corpse onto my shoulder, then stood and heaved it over the bridge rail. It crashed through some branches and hit the rocks below. The sleeping bag was bloody, so I tossed it over as well. Then I got back into the cab and drove on, staying right at sixty on the twisting road.

"I didn't know you had that in you," Rachel said in a dead voice. "I can't believe you're the man who wrote so movingly about compassion and ethics."

"This is survival. Everybody has it in them. You included."

"No," she said quietly. "I won't kill."

"You would." I looked her full in the face. "You just haven't been put in the right situation yet."

"Think what you want. I know myself."

The road was gradually straightening. I accelerated to

seventy and shut Rachel out of my thoughts. I felt alone again, as alone as I had on the day Fielding died. I hadn't realized the degree to which Rachel had been a comfort. The hardest thing to accept about her betrayal was that it meant she had never seen me as anything more than a patient. A sick and deluded man.

A wave of heat rolled through me, leaving deep fatigue in its wake. I hoped it was a postadrenaline crash, but the ringing vibration in my teeth told me otherwise. I would soon be unconscious. And this time I couldn't trust Rachel to take care of me.

"What's the matter?" she asked, looking intently at me. "You're weaving over the center line."

"Nothing."

"Get over! You're in the wrong lane."

I jerked the wheel back to the right. Maybe the strain of dumping the corpse had made me especially vulnerable to an attack. There was nothing gradual about this one. I had to stop the truck.

"Pull over!" Rachel yelled.

Trying desperately to keep my eyes open, I swerved onto a small logging road and managed to cover about a hundred yards before I had to stop. I got the truck into PARK, then pulled the dead man's automatic from my jumpsuit and aimed it at Rachel.

"Get out."

"*What?*"

"Get out! And leave your cell phone in here. Do it!"

She looked out the window as though she were being asked to leap off a cliff. "You can't just put me out here!"

"I'll let you back in after I wake up. If you're still here."

"David! They'll find us. Let me drive!"

I jerked the gun at her. "Do what I said!"

She laid her cell phone on the seat, then climbed out of

the truck and closed the door. Her dark eyes watched me through the rain-spattered glass. As I leaned over and locked her door, the black wave rolled over me.

A city gate stood high before me, a plain arch in a wall of yellow stone. People lined the road, some waving palm fronds and cheering, others weeping. Men held a donkey for me, and I climbed upon its back. The symbolism was important. There was a prophecy to fulfill.

"This is the eastern gate, Master. Are you sure?"

"I am."

I passed through the gate on the donkey's back. I heard horns blowing. Roman soldiers watched me with wary eyes. Women ran into the street to touch my robe, my hair. The faces in the narrow street were hungry, not for food but for hope, for a reason to live.

The road vanished and became a columned temple. I sat on the steps and spoke quietly to a large group. They listened with curious, uncertain faces. The words they spoke were not the words in their minds. The words in their minds were all the same: Is he the one? Is it possible?

"You know how to interpret the appearance of earth and sky," I told them. "Why do you not know how to interpret the present time? I have cast fire upon the world, and I am guarding it until it blazes."

I watched the faces. Words meant different things to different people. Men seized upon what they wanted, discarded the rest. Someone asked from whence I came. Better to answer in riddles.

"Split a piece of wood and I am there. Lift up the stone, and you will find me."

I left the temple and walked the alleys of the city. I wanted privacy, but I was accosted from all sides. Priests came to me and questioned me. Blind men could see more.

"*By what authority do you say and do these things?*" they asked.

I smiled. "*John baptized the people. Did his authority come from heaven or from men?*"

The priests answered out of fear of the mob. "*Of this we are not certain.*"

"*Then I shall not tell you by whose authority I do these things.*"

I left them seething in the street, but it did no good. They came to me upon a hill and questioned me at length. My answers drove them mad.

"*Only a little while am I with you,*" *I said.* "*Then I go back from whence I came. Whither I go, you cannot come. You shall seek me and not find me. You are of this world. I am not.*"

They called me a liar.

"*Yet a little while the light is with you,*" *I said.* "*Walk while you have the light, lest darkness come upon you. He that follows me shall never walk in darkness.*"

Even as I watched them, I saw my doom in their eyes. Yet I could not turn from my path. In one priest's eyes I saw hatred, and also the death that he saw for me . . . a Roman punishment. But pain was not my greatest fear. A strong man could stand pain. What I could not endure was to be alone, alone again for all time—

Rachel was screaming. I blinked in confusion, and then the door at my left shoulder was yanked open. I tried to turn and see who was there, but sleep closed over me again like quicksand.

TWENTY-TWO

Geli Bauer rubbed her eyes with one hand and poured strong coffee into her mug with the other. She was waiting for John Skow's wife to bring him to the phone. She had slept three hours on the cot where she and Ritter had made love last night. She almost never dreamed these days, but an old recurring nightmare of pursuit by soldiers had returned. In the dream she always killed herself before they reached her. The terror before that act of release was nearly unbearable.

"Geli?" Skow said in her headset, his voice exhausted.

He had spent all night with the Godin Four supercomputer, piecing together a threat to the president from digital recordings of Tennant's voice. Geli had already awakened him once, to tell him she'd received a report of a man missing from one of their SWAT details. At that point there had been no proof that Tennant had been there, but now . . .

"The SWAT team at Frozen Head found their missing man," she said. "He'd been dumped into a creek bed from a highway bridge. He had an arrow in his throat."

"Did Tennant do it?"

"I think so. I've been reviewing his background. He did

a lot of hunting when he was a kid. Probably bow-hunted in the early season."

"Where the hell would he get a bow and arrows?"

"We're checking the security tapes of stores along the routes between the ferry and Oak Ridge. He was obviously planning to hole up for a while on that mountain. What I want to know is this. How did *you* know where he would be?"

"I told you, I can't give you that."

"Your secret source is Dr. Weiss, isn't it?"

"Geli—"

"Who else could it be? How else could you know about Frozen Head Park?"

"If it was Dr. Weiss, you'd know it already."

Geli knew better. "That's why you were so skittish about a shoot-to-kill order. You knew your informer might be killed. What I don't get is why you didn't tell me she was helping us. I could have protected her."

"You have a habit of asking questions above your pay grade."

"I don't have a fucking pay grade! I make ten times what you do."

"But you still take orders from me."

She wanted to reach through the phone and crush his windpipe, but self-discipline slowly reasserted itself. "When did you last talk to Godin?"

"It's been longer than I'd like," Skow admitted. The NSA man sounded nervous, and he wasn't trying to hide it.

"What are the extended trips Godin and Nara have been taking for the past few weeks? They fly west and disappear for three and four days at a time. Where are they going?"

"You must have dug deeper than that."

She would not be drawn in so easily. "Whoever's handling security on that end is very good."

A dry chuckle from Skow. "You have no idea."

"Why aren't you with them?"

No answer.

"How is all this related to Fielding's pocket watch?"

"I'm sorry, Geli."

Things she had noticed over the past few weeks began to push themselves to the forefront of her thoughts. "Zach Levin and his Interface Team were laid off five weeks ago. They seem to have dropped off the face of the earth. Why would a whole technical team be dropped?"

Skow didn't reply.

She searched for a question he could answer. "Does the person handling security wherever Godin is control your ultrasecret source?"

In the ensuing silence, she realized that Skow's reticence was not meant to offend her. He had the paralysis of a man trapped between duty and fear.

"Has this secret source told you where Tennant is going next?"

"You'll get another list of destinations soon. I'll get it to you as soon as I have it."

"You do that." She tried to push the mystery of Peter Godin's location from her mind. "How public is our deranged-assassin story now?"

"It's still inside the Beltway, but it'll spread fast. The D.C. police will get it this morning. I didn't want to go wide with it until I finished last night's project."

"I listened to the recording again a few minutes ago. It's rock solid."

"It better be. What are you going to do now?"

"Wait here for something. Anything. A whisper of where Tennant might be."

"And then?"

"I'm going to go there myself. I don't trust anyone else at this point."

"Go there how?"

"Godin's JetRanger is still on the helipad. You have any problem with me taking it?"

"No. I'll keep the pilot on standby for you." After a pause, Skow said, "Getting Tennant is personal for you, isn't it?"

Geli took a sip of hot coffee and held it in her mouth.

"I think you cared more for Ritter than anyone knew," Skow added.

She swallowed. "You're a shrink now?"

"Something just hit me. If you're so sure that Weiss is my secret source, Tennant may conclude the same thing. I mean, as you said . . . how else could that SWAT have been waiting at Frozen Head?"

"Go on."

"If Tennant decides Weiss is informing on him, he'll dump her. We should put out an APB on her and cover the phones and homes of everyone she's close to."

"I've already covered everybody she might call, but not for that reason. Tennant won't leave Dr. Weiss anywhere."

"Why not?"

"He's in love with her."

"He can't ignore logic that obvious."

Geli laughed softly. "Of course he can. People do it all the time."

216

TWENTY-THREE

I snapped awake with a rush of terror. Rachel was behind the wheel of the pickup truck, and we were moving. I lay crumpled on the floor on the passenger side. Pulling myself onto the seat, I saw that we were racing down a deserted rural highway. There was nothing behind us but empty road.

"How did you get in?" I asked. "Did I not lock the door?"

She didn't look at me. "You locked it. There was a piece of heavy wire in the truck bed. I made a hook and pulled the lock from inside the doorframe."

"Where are we?"

"Almost to Caryville. From the signs, it looks like I-75 runs through there."

I shook the remnants of the Jerusalem dream from my head. How long had I been unconscious? "Where's the SWAT team?"

"Looking for us, I'm sure."

I was certain that Rachel had betrayed our destination to the NSA. So why was she driving me down a deserted road? Maybe she was driving back *toward* Frozen Head.

"I know what you're thinking," she said. "But you're wrong. Someone else had to know about Frozen Head Park.

217

Maybe you told someone at Trinity about it. Ravi Nara? Before you started hating each other?"

"No. You're the only person alive who knew about that cave. At least about its connection to me."

I rolled down the window, leaned out, and scanned the sky. I saw nothing, at least in the space visible between the trees that lined the narrow blacktop. Was there any reason Geli Bauer's people wouldn't move in if they knew where I was? I couldn't think of one. Anything Geli wanted from me she would get quicker by torturing me than by following me.

"If you're not helping them, why are you still with me?"

Rachel looked at me then, her eyes filled with sadness. "I'm not even going to answer that."

I wanted to believe in her, but I'd be a fool to do so. "Look . . . if you didn't tell them about Frozen Head, they could not have been waiting there."

"You're missing something," she insisted. "You have to be."

"No. My father and brother are dead. The NSA would have to be able to read my mind to know—"

I froze with my mouth open. Revelation had stunned me like a blow to the head.

"David? What's the matter?"

"They've done it," I whispered. "Good God."

"Done what?"

"Trinity. They've got a prototype up and running."

"How do you know?"

I put a shaking hand to my forehead. Somewhere in America, the Super-MRI scan of my brain had been loaded into a Trinity computer. And that neuromodel now existed— at least to some degree—as David Tennant. I felt as if the people hunting me had discovered I had a twin brother, an evil twin who shared all my memories and would betray me on demand. The feeling of violation was absolute. My

218

mind was my most sacred refuge from the world. I felt raped in some incomprehensible way, robbed of my individuality.

Where else are they waiting for me? I wondered.

"David, don't shut me out," she pleaded. "Talk to me."

"They have my memories, Rachel. They have *me,* loaded into their computer. That's how they knew to be waiting at Frozen Head. They don't have to chase us anymore. They know what I'll do before I do it."

"That's impossible."

"No. That's exactly what they've been working toward for two years. I know these people. I know Peter Godin. And I know it's true."

She slowed the truck for a hairpin turn. "You're saying that Fielding was right? They've been working on the computer somewhere else all along?"

"Yes. While Fielding and I screwed around trying to figure out the MRI side effects, they were building the goddamn thing at some secret location." I slapped the dashboard. "*That's* why they laid off certain teams during the suspension."

"What are you talking about?"

"After we suspended the project, groups of engineers were told to take paid leave. Sometimes there were only skeleton crews in the building. The team most conspicuously absent was the Interface Team, led by a guy named Zach Levin."

"What's the Interface Team?"

"The team responsible for trying to communicate with the neuromodels once they're successfully loaded. Remember what I said at the amphitheater? If you download a human brain into a computer, what do you really have? A deaf, dumb, blind, and paralyzed human being, scared to death. Half the battle is giving that brain eyes, ears, and a voice. That's the job of the Interface Team. With the project suspended, it made sense for them to be laid off. But now I see. God, I wish Fielding were here."

Rachel glanced at me. "But if they were that close to success, why kill Fielding? If Godin actually made Trinity work, would anyone really care about medical side effects or anything else?"

"You've got a point. If they've really done it, Godin will be almost invulnerable. We don't have enough information. Maybe—" My hands went cold. "Oh, God."

"What is it?"

"I know why they killed Fielding."

"Why?"

"They could afford to."

"What do you mean?"

"Yesterday, John Skow announced that he wasn't going to replace Fielding. I thought he was crazy. But now I understand. If they have a prototype computer up and running, Fielding *isn't dead*."

Rachel turned to me in confusion. "What does that mean?"

"I mean they can load Fielding's neuromodel the same way they've loaded mine. They'll have Andrew Fielding's mind at their fingertips. He can solve their remaining problems for them!"

She drove for a few moments without speaking. "Okay. Let's just say this is possible for a minute. Why would Fielding help the people who murdered him?"

An eerie feeling of admiration came over me. Peter Godin was more ruthless than I ever imagined. "Fielding's neuromodel will help them because it won't know he's been murdered. It was made six months ago, when Fielding was scanned by the Super-MRI. It has no memories of anything that's happened since then. *That* Andrew Fielding doesn't even know he married Lu Li."

"David, this can't be happening."

"Sure it can. We just happen to be standing close to a revolutionary leap in science. Splitting the atom. Unraveling the human genome. Cloning a sheep."

"What you're talking about isn't like those things. Liberating consciousness from the human body?"

I thought about it. "You're right. This is bigger because it will give us the ability to make those kinds of advances at an exponential rate. Or not us, exactly. Whatever you call the new form of consciousness that Trinity will evolve into. And it will evolve *very* fast."

"You don't know for sure that they've done it."

"They're at least part of the way there. Maybe they just have a crude version up and running. Maybe they can access my memories—pull out images, for example—but not actually operate the model as a functioning mind. Human memory is Ravi Nara's specialty, and they made a lot of progress in that area early on. There's just no way to know."

Rachel touched my arm. "If you're right, what do they know about what we're doing now?"

"Nothing, I hope. They can't read my mind in any mystical way. They probably have my memories from childhood up to six months ago, when I was scanned by the Super-MRI. As for my thought processes, my judgment, my personality— that would take a fully functional computer. And if they have that . . ."

"What?"

"The president won't care what happened to a couple of doctors. The nation accepts more casualties to build a skyscraper or a bridge. You and I are a negligible price to pay for the strategic superiority Trinity will bring. If they've truly completed Trinity, we're dead."

She pointed through the windshield. "There's Caryville. And I-75. Are we going north or south?"

"Pull over."

She slowed gradually, then turned the wheel and stopped on the shoulder, just short of the northbound on-ramp.

"I'm trying to escape from myself," I thought aloud. "To do that, we have to make utterly random choices. But how random can my choices be? I suppose we could flip a coin every time we come to an intersection like this."

Rachel was shaking her head. "They don't have a scan of *my* brain. They can't predict anything I would do. I'll just make the choices from now on."

She saw doubt in my eyes. "You still don't trust me?"

"It's not that. But by now Geli Bauer knows everything there is to know about you. She knows things even you don't remember."

Rachel's lips compressed into a white line. "I hate her. I hate her, and I don't even know her."

"I know. But hate's not going to save us."

"Why can't we just disappear into nowhere? Pay cash at a no-name motel in a no-name town? Back this truck up to a fence and go to sleep for three days. America is a big place. Even for the NSA."

"You ever watch *America's Most Wanted*? They catch criminals every week who try what you just suggested. Television makes America a lot smaller than you think."

I leaned back in my seat and tried to let instinct take over. Cars and trucks passed in both directions, some slowly, others shaking the truck with the wind they threw off. As I sat there, the situation began to clarify itself.

In three days, we would get a chance to see the president. Our problem was staying alive long enough to talk to him. The odds of that were long and getting longer. Even if we did reach Matthews, I'd have to convince him that I was telling the truth and that everyone else involved in Project Trinity was lying. To do that, I needed hard evidence. And I had none. My other option—going public—would only

222

convince the president that I was the loose cannon everyone at Trinity claimed I was and alienate the one man who could save us. *Three days . . .*

"How long are we going to sit here?" Rachel asked.

"Give me a minute."

Hiding was not the answer. Running wasn't either. Not in any conventional way. We needed to take a step so radical that no entity in the world could predict it. But what?

As I stared through the windshield at the oncoming traffic, I realized I was sitting here with Rachel for one reason: my dreams. My dreams had brought us together. Without my dreams, we would both have been shot back at my house. Yet I was no closer to understanding them than I had been on the day I first walked into Rachel's office.

For months they had progressed, like a persistent message being sent from a distant radio source. In the beginning, the incomprehensible images had troubled and even frightened me. But over time—and especially during the past three weeks—a conviction had begun to crystallize within me that something important was being communicated to me. Of course, schizophrenics felt the same conviction. What separated me from them?

I closed my eyes and tried to blank my mind, but the opposite happened. I suddenly saw a walled city on a hill, its stones glowing yellow in the sun. There was a gate set in its face.

The eastern gate, whispered a voice in my head. *Jerusalem.*

Never had I experienced a vision while awake. I opened my eyes and saw Rachel staring at the dashboard. I closed my eyes again, but the city vanished like the afterimage of a flashbulb.

"David? What's wrong with your eyes?"

"Nothing."

I rubbed my temples and tried to open my mind to

whatever was coming. I'd felt drawn to specific places before. During my twenties, I'd traveled a lot, and while I was usually driven by student wanderlust, there were times when something deeper had pulled me off my planned track.

While visiting Oxford University, I'd awakened one morning with a feeling that I needed to get to Stonehenge— not just to see it, but to be in the presence of the sarsen stones. My companion assured me that there was no rush; the stones had been standing for five thousand years and would surely wait another few days. But still I rented a car and drove south until I reached Salisbury Plain. After darkness fell, I approached the ancient ring alone and did what tourists can do no longer: walked among the stones in the moonlight and lay upon the sacrificial altar. I was no New Age dilettante, but a medical student from the University of Virginia, looking toward a stable career. Yet this wasn't the only time such a thing had happened. I was drawn to Chichén Itzá the same way. And on a drive to the Grand Canyon, I changed course and camped at Chaco Canyon in New Mexico for a week instead. In Greece it was Delphi over Athens. In all these situations I had felt an external pull, as though something were calling me to a specific place.

What I felt now was different, an internal compulsion to travel to Jerusalem, whatever the consequences. That the city was sacred to three great religions was irrelevant. I had nothing in common with the faithful millions planning pilgrimages to the Holy Land. I sensed only that the city held answers for me, answers that could be found nowhere else.

"Where are we going?" Rachel asked irritably.

"Israel," I said.

"*What?*"

"Jerusalem."

"David—"

"It's because—"

"Don't tell me. Because of your hallucinations, right?"

"Yes."

She reached out and lifted my chin, then looked deeply into my eyes. "David, people are trying to kill us. The *government* is trying to kill us. You've been having hallucinations for reasons we don't understand, but which may have been caused by damage to your brain. And you want to use those hallucinations to guide you in trying to save our lives?"

"Whoever will save his life shall lose it."

"What?"

I turned up my palms. "I'm not saying this will save our lives. I'm saying that if I'm going to be hunted down and killed, I'd rather it happen while I'm trying to learn the meaning of something I believe *has* meaning."

"You truly believe your hallucinations have meaning?"

"Yes."

"Why?"

"I can't explain it logically. It's just something I know. Like a bird flying south."

She sighed like an exhausted mother talking to a child. "*Try*, okay? Try to explain."

I closed my eyes and searched for words to explain the inexplicable. "I feel as though I've been chosen."

"For what?"

"I'm not sure."

"Chosen by whom?"

"God."

"*God* God?"

"Yes."

She took a deep breath and folded her hands in her lap. She was clearly struggling to remain calm. "I think it's time you told me what these recent hallucinations have been about. Are you still dreaming that you're Jesus?"

"Yes."

"What's different about these visions as compared to the older ones? Why have you hidden them from me?"

We'd finally arrived at the line between sanity and the rubber room. I was glad we were in a truck on a highway and not in Rachel's office. There was no one she could call to have me committed. "Because I no longer believe they're hallucinations. Or dreams. I think they're memories."

She expelled air in a frustrated rush. "*Memories?* My God, David. What's happening in these dreams?"

"I'm reliving parts of Jesus' life. His travels to Jerusalem. His experiences there. I hear voices. My own . . . the disciples. Rachel, what I see in my head is more real than what I see around me. And events are moving rapidly. I'm approaching the crucifixion."

She was shaking her head in disbelief. "How could you have two-thousand-year-old memories that only entered your mind in the past six months?"

"I don't know."

"These dreams make you feel some urgency to get to Israel?"

I hadn't thought of my feeling as urgency before, but that was what it was. What I'd perceived as generalized anxiety was really a slowly developing compulsion to travel to the setting of my dreams.

"To the Holy Land," I said. "Yes."

"Are you afraid you'll die in real life if you don't get there before you dream of the crucifixion?"

"Maybe. Mainly I have a sense that if I don't get there soon, I'll lose the chance to understand what my dreams are trying to tell me."

Rachel stared at the oncoming traffic, her head rocking back and forth. Then she suddenly turned to me, her eyes bright and wide.

"Do you realize what day it is?"

"No."

"We're less than a week away from the Easter holiday."

I blinked. "So?"

"We're approaching the traditional dates of Jesus' death and resurrection. Not only in your dreams, but also in the real world."

"You're saying the two are connected?"

"Of course. Somehow, the approach of Easter is causing you to have these dreams, this anxiety. You're like the people who thought the world would end when the millennium turned. Don't you see? This is *all* part of a delusional system."

I shook my head and smiled. "You're wrong. But you're right about the dates. They could be important."

Rachel was watching me as she would someone who was playing an elaborate joke on her. "What about meeting the president?"

"We'll do it when we get back. What difference does a couple of days make? Especially if it keeps us alive?"

She closed her eyes and spoke softly. "Did you tell Andrew Fielding about your hallucinations?"

"Yes."

"What did he say?"

"He told me to pay attention to them. Fielding always said that in trying to build Trinity, we were walking in the footprints of God. He didn't know how right he was."

"Perfect. Two peas in a pod." Rachel put her hands on the wheel as though to pull onto the road, but she left the truck in park. "You really intend to follow these hallucinations to Israel?"

"Yes."

"And you admit they might be the result of brain damage?"

"Not brain damage, as you think of it." I thought of Fielding's excitement as he expounded his theory of consciousness. "Disturbances to the quantum processes in my brain."

Rachel was squeezing the steering wheel so hard that her knuckles were white. "You're like someone who dreamed he was once a pharaoh deciding to go to Egypt to find the meaning of his life!"

"I suppose I am. I know how crazy it sounds. The thing is, we don't have a better alternative. If it makes you feel better, we're going because we need to do something the Trinity computer can't possibly predict."

"It can't predict you'd go to Israel?"

"No. It was my Super-MRI scan that caused my dreams to start. My neuromodel has no memory of dreams that occurred after that. There's not even any mention of Jerusalem in your medical records, because I stopped going to you before the city took center stage in my dreams."

Rachel looked thoughtful. "Going to Israel isn't like going to Paris, you know. The country's in a permanent state of war. I've been there. They pay close attention to who goes in and out. El Al has four times the security of other airlines. And we're being hunted by the American government. As soon as we tried to book a ticket, they'd be waiting for us at the airport."

"You're right. We need fake passports."

She laughed bitterly. "You say that like 'We need to pick up some bread and milk on the way home.'"

"I have eighteen thousand dollars left. There has to be a way to get fake passports with that."

"Fake passports won't cut it in Israel. Those people deal with terrorists every day."

"Being jailed in Israel is better than being murdered here."

Rachel leaned back in her seat and sighed. "You've got a point."

"I'm going to New York. With eighteen grand, I can find a fake passport there. I know it."

"What about me?"

"You can go. You can not go. It's up to you."

She nodded as though she'd expected this. "I see. What will happen to me if I don't?"

I thought about Geli Bauer. "You want me to lie to you?"

Rachel put the truck in gear and pulled onto the northbound on-ramp, accelerating fast.

"New York?" I asked.

"No."

"Where, then?"

She looked at me, her face less guarded than I'd ever seen it. "Do you want me to come with you or not?"

I did. More than that, I felt she was *supposed* to go with me. "I want you with me, Rachel. For a lot of reasons."

She laughed dryly. "That's good, because you couldn't make it without me. Passing out by yourself in the street isn't very healthy. If I'd left you back there in the truck, you'd be dead now."

"I know that. Are you coming?"

She passed a tanker truck and eased back into the right lane. "If you want to go to Israel, we have to go to Washington, D.C., first."

I stiffened in my seat. All my doubts about her had returned in a nauseating rush. "Why Washington?"

"Because I know someone there who can help us."

"Who?"

I wanted to probe her eyes for deception, but she kept them on the road. "I treated a lot of women when I practiced in New York. Mostly women, actually."

"And?"

"Some of them had problems with their husbands."

"And?"

"Sometimes the courts gave husbands access to their children despite evidence of physical abuse. Some of the wives were so afraid of what might happen that they felt they had no alternative but to run."

I felt a tingle in my palms. "You're talking about custody situations. Kidnapping your own children."

She nodded. "It's not difficult to hide from the police if you're alone. But with children it's tough. You have to enroll them in school, get medical care, things like that." She glanced at me, her face taut. "These women have a network. Sort of an underground railroad. That takes resources."

"New identities," I said.

"Yes. For a child, the foundation of a new identity is a birth certificate. For an adult, a social security card and a passport. I don't know many details, but I know that the people who help these women are in Washington."

"These women buy fake passports in Washington, D.C.?"

Rachel shook her head. "They're not fake. They're real."

"*Real?* What do you mean?"

She cut her eyes at me, reluctant to give up what she knew. "There's a woman who works in one of the passport offices in D.C. She had a problem with her husband years ago. She's sympathetic to the cause. I don't know who she is, but I know someone I can call. A former patient."

"The cause," I said. "This is still going on?"

"Yes. I sent a woman from Chapel Hill to them. A doctor's wife."

"Wow."

"There's only one serious problem I can see," Rachel said.

"What's that?"

"You're a man. I don't know if they'll do anything to help you."

230

TWENTY-FOUR

When the security door buzzed open this time, Geli knew it was Skow. She also knew it was bad news, because she hadn't been off the phone with him long, and the NSA man had sounded too exhausted to get out of bed. She spun her chair and saw him striding toward her, for the first time wearing something besides his Brooks Brothers suit. Today it 'was khakis and an MIT sweatshirt. Skow's eyes had dark bags under them, but he still looked more like a university administrator than an expert on information warfare.

"You look like shit," Geli told him.

"I feel worse."

"You wouldn't be here if this was good news."

"You're right. Ravi Nara called me as soon as you and I hung up." Skow flopped into the chair behind her. "Give me one of your cigarettes."

"You don't smoke."

"Oh, Geli, the things you don't know about me."

She shook a Gauloise from her pack, lit it, and passed it to him.

Skow took a deep drag and exhaled without coughing. "These are nasty."

"Where did Nara call from?"

Skow shook his head. "Everything in time. I want you to listen to me now."

She crossed her legs and waited.

"You and I have always held back a lot from each other. But now is the time to come clean. Or as clean as we can."

"I'm listening."

"Godin has always compartmentalized everything at Trinity, so I don't know what you know. You know we're working on artificial intelligence, but do you know exactly how?"

"Tell me."

"We're using advanced MRI technology to make molecular scans of the brain, then trying to load those scans into a revolutionary type of supercomputer."

"Go on."

"Our goal is to create artificial intelligence not by reverse-engineering the brain, but by digitally *copying* it. The result, if it works, is not a computer that works like a human brain, but a computer that for all practical purposes *is* a specific person's brain. You understand?"

Geli had thought the MRI scans were being used to study the brain's architecture, not as the actual basis of a machine. "The principle sounds fairly straightforward."

Skow gave a hollow laugh. "In theory, it is. And it *will* be accomplished, sooner or later. But the difference between sooner and later is critically important to you and me."

"Why?"

"Because Peter Godin is dying."

Something fluttered in her chest at this confirmation of an unacknowledged suspicion. Images of Godin flashed behind her eyes: facial swelling, his drooping mouth, his clumsy gait.

"Dying how?"

"Peter has a brain tumor. Ravi Nara discovered it six months ago, when the original scans for the neuromodels

232

were made. That's why you haven't been able to contact Godin these past two days. When he's not working directly on Trinity, he's under treatment."

Geli shifted in her chair. "How close to death is he?"

"It's a matter of hours now. A day at most. The tumor was inoperable even at the early stage where Ravi found it. Peter thought if the government knew he had a terminal cancer, it wouldn't commit the resources necessary to make Trinity a reality. So he and Ravi made a deal. Ravi would keep the tumor secret and treat Peter with steroids to keep him functioning long enough to complete Trinity. I hate to think what Ravi asked for in return."

"Nara's a weasel."

"Agreed. The point is, there's been a hidden agenda at Trinity from the beginning. Peter Godin has been building Trinity to save his own life."

"What do you mean?"

"If the Trinity computer were to be completed before he died, Peter's neuromodel could be loaded into it. His body would die, but he would continue to exist in the computer as Peter Godin."

Geli blinked in disbelief. "There's no way in hell I believe that."

Skow laughed. "Not only is it possible, it's inevitable. It's just not going to happen this week."

"If that's true, then couldn't Godin's neuromodel or whatever be loaded into the computer after his death as well? Whenever Trinity is finished?"

"Of course. But in that scenario Peter would have to die without being certain it would happen. He'd have to die the way every other human being in history has. And he'd have to trust us to resurrect him in the machine."

"I see." She was trying to absorb the implications of Godin's imminent death. "So why exactly are you here?"

Skow took another drag on the Gauloise and fixed her with a no-bullshit stare. "I'm here to save your ass. Right along with mine."

"I wasn't aware it needed saving."

"It does. Because Project Trinity is about to fail."

Now she understood. The ship was sinking, and the rats were looking for lifeboats. "But you said success is inevitable."

"Eventually, yes. But Godin's going to die before he can get the computer operational, and there's no one left who can take it to the next level. Fielding's dead. Ravi's already contributed what he can. The remaining work is out of his league. And if we fail to deliver a working Trinity computer after spending almost a billion dollars—"

"A *billion?*"

Skow looked impatient. "Geli, the Trinity prototype is built largely of carbon nanotubes. That's not just cutting-edge technology. We've had to create a whole new science. The expense of the materials R and D alone is staggering. Same for the holographic memory research. We—"

"Okay, I get it." Her brain was working in survival mode. "You said that when Godin's not under treatment, he's working on Trinity. Where is he working? Mountain View?"

Skow shook his head. "There's another Trinity research facility. I won't tell you where that is until we come to some agreement. But it was set up two years ago, right after we learned that the president was going to insist on having Tennant here for ethical oversight. Godin knew the day might come when he needed to work on Trinity without Tennant or the government knowing what he was doing. So he made it happen."

Her perception of the situation changed with each sentence. "So where does Trinity stand right now? A total write-off?"

"No. At this moment, we're partly operational. It was

the Trinity prototype that predicted Tennant would run to Frozen Head. Tennant's neuromodel basically told us where he would be."

Geli could hardly believe this. "You saw this yourself?"

"No. But I've seen the prototype. And it's beyond imagination."

"That's where you got Frozen Head. Not from Dr. Weiss?"

"Right."

"My God. If it can do that, why do you consider it a failure?"

Skow held up a hand and tilted it back and forth. "*Part* of Trinity works. But it's only been working for twenty hours, and I can't even begin to explain the complexities of completing this machine. They're having success with the memory area, but the main processing areas are something else altogether."

"It was the crystal, wasn't it?" Geli thought aloud. "Fielding's crystal watch fob. That's what you needed to make it work."

"Yes. Fielding was sabotaging the project, but he was also keeping a record of everything he did. Even as he corrupted other people's code, he saved the original code to his crystal. Idealists make terrible saboteurs. Fielding was simply incapable of destroying real scientific progress. Anyway, once we had the crystal, we got back all the computer code Fielding had corrupted. But the real bonus was original work that Fielding had done himself. He couldn't resist trying to solve our remaining problems, even while he sabotaged our progress to date. Fielding's new work put Trinity within reach. Without that crystal, the prototype wouldn't be functioning at all."

"But if it's partly working now, why can't the government just use other scientists to take over and complete it?"

"They could, if they knew about it. But they don't.

Everything Godin has done since the project's suspension has been unauthorized and illegal."

"So move the prototype back to this building."

"Peter won't allow that. He wouldn't survive the move now."

"You said he'll be dead soon."

"Not soon enough." Skow's anxiety showed in his eyes. "If we had produced an operational Trinity computer, no one in the American or British governments would have worried about the cost of delivering it—financial or human. But in the wake of failure, hard questions will be asked."

"What are you saying?

"Failure requires a scapegoat."

"I've had nothing to do with building that computer."

"No, but Fielding's death might be blamed for its failure. And who killed Fielding?"

Now she saw where Skow was headed. "You're starting to piss me off."

The NSA man turned up his palms. "I'm only painting a possible scenario. You're an easy fit for the role. Known to be overzealous—"

"Do you want to leave this room alive?".

Skow smiled. "I'm only showing you your personal stake in this. Now, Tennant and Weiss are still running around loose. And Lu Li Fielding is still missing."

"Those are three problems I can solve."

"All evidence to the contrary."

She gave him a look that would shatter glass.

"Take it easy," Skow said. "I don't want Tennant dead now anyway. It's stupid to keep piling up bodies. It makes things exponentially harder on us."

She sensed that they had arrived at the point of this meeting. "Okay. If I'm not the scapegoat, who is?"

"Peter Godin."

"*What?*"

Skow blew a perfect blue smoke ring between them. "Think about it. After Peter dies, everything can be explained by a mere exaggeration of the truth. He's been dying of a brain tumor all along. None of us knew it. Peter was a great man, but the tumor affected his mind. He became obsessed with saving his own life. He saw the Trinity computer as the only possible means of doing that. When Fielding and Tennant suspended the project, Godin panicked and ordered their deaths."

Geli leaned back and let the plan sink in. The logic was perfect. It was the Big Lie, which turned everything black to white.

"If we go this way," Skow continued, "Tennant can't hurt us no matter what he says. This is a much more elegant solution than murder."

"There's one problem," Geli said. "If we leave Tennant alive, he'll tell the world that I was the one trying to kill him."

"Will he?" Skow smiled and shook his head. "Who went to Tennant's house to kill him? Whom did Tennant and Weiss see?"

"Ritter."

"Exactly. And Ritter Bock was an employee of Godin Supercomputing before you came on board. Correct?"

Skow seemed to have thought of everything. "Yes."

"Does anyone know you gave Ritter the order to kill Tennant?"

"I never gave such an order."

Skow grinned. "Of course you didn't. I couldn't imagine such a thing. Peter gave the order directly to Ritter, his own private Doberman. Dr. Tennant got lucky and killed Ritter in self-defense. You're as pure as the driven snow, Geli. All you've been doing is following Godin's orders."

"And you?"

"By the time I realized that Fielding didn't die of natural causes, Ritter was already dead and Tennant was on the run. I've been trying to get to the truth ever since."

Geli kept trying to punch a hole in the story. "And the reason we cremated Fielding's body so quickly?"

"Once we realized he'd been murdered, we suspected a highly infectious biological agent. Nara's advice was to burn the body and all blood samples immediately. That was the only way to maintain the safety of this building."

"Will Nara verify this story?"

"He'll do anything to save his reputation."

Geli got up and began to pace the control center. Skow turned his chair and followed her with his eyes.

"What if Godin succeeds?" she asked. "What if he delivers Trinity before he dies, and it's everything he promised?"

"Ravi says it won't happen. Peter's fading too fast."

The irony of the situation depressed her. "You know, I like Peter Godin. I respect him. You, on the other hand, I don't like at all. I didn't respect you either, until you came up with this. This could work."

"It's going to work. The only missing piece is you."

She saw no option but to cooperate. "Tell me where the other Trinity facility is, and you have a deal."

The confidence left Skow's face. "I'm not at liberty to do that."

"Why not?"

"You'll understand in a minute. I'm going to give you the name of the person who handles security at the other site. You can ask him your questions."

Geli stopped and stared at him. "What kind of game is this?"

"That's the way he told me to handle it, and he's not the kind of person I like to make an enemy of."

238

"Who the hell is he?"

Skow shook his head. "I'll give you his number."

"I'm not calling anybody until I know who I'm calling."

Skow drew on his cigarette, looking at her with something like pity. "General Horst Bauer."

Geli's face felt hot. Every bit of pride she'd felt at her Trinity job drained out of her in a sickening rush. "My father is in charge of the other Trinity site?"

"Yes."

"You son of a bitch. Why are he and I both involved in this?"

Despite obvious reluctance to speak, Skow seemed to sense that she wouldn't cooperate further until he had answered.

"It's simple," he said. "Every aspect of Trinity has been stage-managed by Godin from the beginning. Because of your father's military intelligence background, he always had influence on what types of computers the army used at certain facilities. The Pentagon, various bases, and now Fort Huachuca."

Fort Huachuca, Arizona, was the center of U.S. Military Intelligence, and her father was its commanding officer.

"General Bauer helped secure contracts for Godin Supercomputing from the army," Skow said. "His influence helped Peter beat out Cray, NEC, all the rest."

"You mean he took money."

"Wads of it. He's got a numbered Cayman account padded by Godin, same as me. The NSA doesn't pay near enough to finance my lifestyle."

"That hypocritical son of a bitch. I thought at least where his country was concerned, he'd—never mind. I should have known better."

"Your father didn't damage the country by pushing Godin supercomputers. They were as good as anything out there. The general just took a little bonus where he found it. That's the way business is done these days."

239

The scar on Geli's face seemed to pulse with fury. "The army is a service, not a business."

Skow chuckled. "I'd never have pegged you as a romantic."

"Fuck you."

"Anyway, when Peter decided he needed a secret research site, he called your father. Some money changed hands, and the general found us a nice secluded spot where no one would bother us."

"Why was I brought in?"

"Peter was looking for a certain kind of person for your job. Your father suggested you."

Geli began to pace again, blood pounding in her ears. "He knows about all this, doesn't he? Godin dying, the project going down the tubes?"

"Yes. And he's on board. He has a career to save, too."

"Well, fuck him. And fuck you."

"Call him, Geli."

"Is the secret Trinity site at Fort Huachuca?"

"No."

She didn't believe him. There were thousands of acres set aside for weapons testing at the remote Arizona base. On the other hand, her father was an expert at covering his ass. He'd have wanted some deniability if Trinity became a liability and so would have been unlikely to put it at his own base.

She slipped on her headset, hit a computer key, and said, "Major General Horst Bauer. Fort Huachuca, Arizona."

Skow breathed an audible sigh of relief.

The general's aide-de-camp answered the phone.

"General Bauer," Geli snapped.

"The general is unavailable. Who's calling, please?"

"Tell him his daughter is on the phone, Captain."

"Hold, please."

Skow was clearly enjoying this spectacle. She spun her

chair so that she wouldn't have to look at his aging Ivy League face.

As she waited, images of her father rose in her mind. Tall and imposing in the Germanic mold, Horst Bauer had been described by his enemies as a blond version of Burt Lancaster's General James Mattoon Scott from *Seven Days in May*. This was a fair comparison. Yet the stiff martinet seen by the public was not the man Geli knew. She saw the womanizer who had cheated ceaselessly on his wife and left several illegitimate children abroad. She saw the brute who, upon finding himself embarrassed by his daughter's "wildness," beat her remorselessly with whatever was close to hand. The irony of her life was that she had followed in the footsteps of the man she hated. The reason was simple. She'd hated her father for scarring her so deeply, but she'd despised her mother's passiveness even more.

"Well, Geli," said a deep voice that tensed every muscle in her body. "You must be in trouble. That's the only time I hear from you."

She wanted to slam down the phone, but she needed answers. "What do you know about a certain artificial intelligence project?"

"So much for pleasantries. That's a vague question you asked."

"You want specifics? I'm in charge of security for Project Trinity in North Carolina. I'm told there's a secret facility carrying out research for that project. What do you know about that?"

A moment of silence. "I might know something."

"And you never told me about this because . . . ?"

Dry laughter. "I wasn't aware we'd started a father-daughter rehabilitation program."

"You gave Godin my name for this job?"

"How else did you think he found you? But as for telling

241

you about my involvement, Godin wanted everything compartmentalized. You can't be angry about that. You haven't told me anything about your life since puberty. What I learned, I learned from gossip or doctors or the police."

Some battles never end, she thought. "There's no point in rehashing the past. I know what I needed to know."

"And you understand the situation? What has to be done?"

"I've been made aware."

"Skow has no balls, but he does have a talent for damage control."

"I'm going now," she said, yet she remained on the line.

"Go ahead," said the general. "I have a feeling I'll be seeing you soon."

She yanked off her headset and glared at Skow.

"Well?" said the NSA man. "Are we all on the same page?"

"Get out."

"You haven't answered my question."

"What choice do I have? But it sickens me that a man like Godin will be torn down so that scum like you and my father can skate. You're not fit to carry water for Peter Godin."

Skow colored at last. "You agree about Tennant and Weiss? We bring them in alive? Tell them it's all been a misunderstanding?"

"Godin's not dead yet."

"True."

"And we have no idea where they are. We can't communicate with them unless we go on TV and tell the whole world."

"Also true."

"I'm still not sure I want Tennant running around telling everyone what he thinks went on here. He knows some powerful people."

Skow nodded thoughtfully. "I tell you what. I'll leave

Tennant and Weiss to you. If they have to die, we'll make it play."

"You're damn right you'll leave them to me."

He got up and moved toward the door. "Any last questions?"

"Just one. Why was Fielding sabotaging the project?"

Skow smiled. "He didn't believe scientists should create things they don't understand."

"Then why did he sign on for the project?"

"I don't think he believed it would move nearly as fast as it did. He thought we'd have to earn the requisite knowledge about the brain before we could make Trinity work."

"And did you? Earn that knowledge?"

"Are you kidding? If Trinity does go a hundred percent operational, it will be completely beyond us."

TWENTY-FIVE

We chose a cheap motel in Arlington, across the Potomac from Washington, one where the desk clerk didn't raise an eyebrow if a guest preferred to pay in cash. One room, two double beds, a bathroom, a television, a phone. Rachel stripped off her camouflage jumpsuit the minute she got inside and went to the bathroom to shower. I found myself watching her until the bathroom door closed. Her informal attire of the previous day had been startling enough after weeks of seeing her dressed only in skirt suits. To see her walking unabashedly away from me in her underwear transformed my perception of her. Rachel's body was taut and well muscled in a way that only strenuous exercise could maintain. This didn't square with my impression of her as an academic physician, but maybe it fit with her obsessive-compulsive tendencies.

I retrieved our street clothes from the truck, then bought a *Washington Post* and two bottles of Dasani from machines in the parking lot and returned to the room. The crack beneath the bathroom door exhaled puffs of steam. I changed into my regular clothes, propped myself against the headboard, and switched on CNN. There was no mention of any federal fugitives, so I started scanning the stories in the *Post*.

We'd begun preparing for our trip to Israel during the eight-hour drive from Tennessee. The first step was to arrange for the illegal passports. We used a truck stop near Roanoke for Rachel's first phone call. A former patient of hers from New York gave her a contact number in Washington, D.C., and told her to wait an hour before calling it. During that hour, someone would vouch for Rachel to the person at that number.

She made her second call from Lexington, Virginia, where she received instructions to go to the Au Bon Pain café in Washington's Union Station at eleven tomorrow morning. She was also told to choose two full names and birth dates, and to obtain passport photos for the "friends" involved. She should deliver the photos along with cards bearing the names and physical descriptions of the "friends" to the person at the Au Bon Pain meeting. When Rachel asked how long it would take to obtain what she required, the source told her forty-eight hours was the usual delay.

Between Lexington and Interstate 66, we realized we had another problem. Credit cards. Buying air tickets to Israel for cash would raise concerns, as would the fact that we had no advance hotel reservations. Friends or relatives would have to make reservations for us in our new names, using legitimate credit cards. My parents were dead, and all my friends would be covered by the NSA. Rachel's parents, ex-husband, and friends would be covered as well. In the end, she chose to call a doctor to whom she'd almost become engaged when she was attending Columbia. He was Jewish, traveled often to Israel, and was utterly devoted to her. I thought a request to make flight and hotel reservations in names he didn't know might worry the man, but Rachel assured me that anything she asked would be done. She tried three times to phone him before we reached D.C., but had no luck. His answering service refused to give out his cell number, and Rachel couldn't leave a number for him to call back.

The bathroom door opened with a rush of steam, and Rachel emerged with one towel wrapped around her body, another around her head.

"There's still some hot water left. And one towel. You should try it. I feel human again."

"We need to try your doctor friend one more time. I brought in your clothes. They're pretty dirty."

She smiled wearily. "I'd give a thousand dollars for my flannel pajamas."

"We'll get some new clothes tomorrow. Or tonight, if you really want some. After we make that call."

Her shoulders sagged. "Can't we just sleep for a while?"

"We need that hotel reservation to date from as early as possible before our departure. Most reservations like that are made weeks in advance."

"You're telling me to get dressed?"

I nodded.

She sat on the edge of the bed and began drying her hair.

"I was thinking," I said. "If you don't have any problem with it, we should travel as husband and wife."

She turned and looked at me. "Do I look like I have a problem with it?"

"Good. We'll give your friend married names for the reservations. Should we use Jewish names?"

"No. You wouldn't fool an Israeli for five seconds. I'm a good Jewish girl who broke down and married a goy. I'll do all the talking."

She picked up her shirt off the bedspread and walked back into the bathroom. I heard the wet towel land on the shower rod; then she returned wearing only the shirt. Its tail hung

246

halfway down her thighs, but there was nothing beneath, and it left little to the imagination.

"I have to lie down," she said. "Wake me up when you're ready to go."

I looked at my watch. It was 5:45 P.M. Letting her fall asleep would be a mistake, but it was probably better to wait for dark. I didn't think I could get up yet either. I'd had no real sleep for two days, and I ached in muscles I hadn't used for years.

Rachel pulled back her bedcovers, climbed under them, and lay on her stomach, her face turned toward me. Her dark eyes were cloudy with fatigue, but there was a trace of a smile on her lips.

"I can hardly think," she said. "You?"

"I'm barely here."

"Do you know why I'm really here?"

"Because you're afraid of dying?"

"No. Because I'm more afraid of not living than I am of dying. Does that make sense?"

"Some."

She slid deeper under the covers. "You don't understand. My son is dead. My marriage is over. What do I have to lose?"

Rachel had always surprised me, but maybe this time she was delirious. "I'm sure your patients—"

"If I died tomorrow, my patients would get another shrink. I sit in that room for days on end, listening to people who are depressed, afraid, angry, paranoid. I listen to other people's lives and try to make sense of them. Then I go home and write about them for the journals."

She smiled strangely. "But today is different. Today a man I diagnosed as delusional has pulled me into his delusion. I'm Alice through the looking glass. People are trying to kill me, but I'm still alive. And now I'm going to fly to Israel *because* of a hallucination. Because a man I actually respect has suddenly decided he's Jesus."

"You need sleep."

She shook her head, her eyes never leaving my face. "Sleep won't change how I feel about this."

In that moment I wasn't sure what she was referring to. I slid down the headboard, rested my head on my elbow, and looked across the space between the beds. Her shoulders were dark against the white sheet, and her damp hair spilled across her eyes.

"What are you really talking about?" I asked.

Her eyes looked through mine the way they sometimes had in her office, as though all the walls I had put up since my family's death were nothing to her. Then, very deliberately, she smiled.

"I have no idea. Why don't you go take a shower?"

The look in her eyes spoke more directly than her mouth. I got up and went to the bathroom, stripping off my dirty clothes as I went. After two days of running for my life, the steaming water felt more nourishing than food. My hands and neck stung from brier scratches, but my muscles began to relax under the spray. As I washed my hair with shampoo from the tiny hotel bottle, I thought of Rachel's dark hair spread over the pillow, and I hurried to finish. She had to be as exhausted as I was, and sleep would be hard to fight. I toweled off in the bathroom, then tied the towel around my waist and walked out to the space between the beds.

Rachel still lay on her stomach, but now her eyes were closed, her breathing deep and regular. I looked down at her, wishing she had managed to stay awake, but I couldn't blame her. She had seen too much in the past two days, and run too far. I pulled off my towel, then sat on the edge of my bed and started drying my hair. After a few moments, I wanted only to fall back on the bed and sleep until I could sleep no more.

A dark, slender arm crossed the narrow space between the beds. Rachel's hand touched my knee, then opened and closed in the air, as if grasping for something. When I put my hand in hers, she pulled me over to her bed with surprising strength. I slid in beside her and looked down into her eyes, which were open wide, like dark pools.

"Did you think I was asleep?" she asked.

"You were."

"Am I dreaming, then?"

I smiled. "Hallucinating, maybe."

"Then I can do anything I want."

"That's true."

She raised her head and kissed me. Her lips were firm and filled with blood, and her mouth opened with a hunger that told me she had wanted this for a long time. I undid the buttons of her shirt and pulled her over onto me. She laughed as her damp hair fell across my face.

"Did you think about this during our sessions?" she asked.

"Never."

"Liar."

"Maybe once or twice."

She kissed me again, and the way she molded her body to mine told me there would be no fumbling of first-time lovers. Her touch was as knowing and confident as her eyes, and as she focused all her attention upon me, I remembered that there is nothing so thrilling as a woman of words when she decides that the time for words is past.

I jerked awake in a panic, certain that we had waited too late to make our call. The glow of the television illuminated the motel room. The bedside clock read 11:30 P.M. Rachel

249

lay on her back beside me, one arm thrown over her face, the other lying along my body.

She was a different woman to me now. After three months of professional distance, she had given herself to me without reservation. My memories of what we had done before giving in to sleep seemed more like hallucinations than any of the visions I'd had during my narcoleptic episodes. Yet they were real.

Rachel needed sleep, but I had to wake her. I sat up and drank a bottle of Dasani in one long series of swallows, then gently shook her upper arm. I was afraid she would awaken in a panic, as she had in the truck, but this time she stirred slowly, then reached out and squeezed my wrist.

"Hey," I said. "How do you feel?"

She opened her eyes but did not speak. Instead, she took a deep breath, then sat up and hugged me. I hugged her back, wishing that this had all happened long before, in some other place.

"We have to try to call your friend again," I said.

"Can't I just do it from here?"

"No. If you were that close to this guy in medical school, the NSA could know. And if they've tapped his line, they can trace our location in seconds. If we do reach your friend, we should stake out the phone booth we used and wait to see if anyone shows up. That will tell us if his line's safe or not."

"Okay." She leaned forward and kissed me lightly on the lips. "Let's get it over with."

Five miles west of the motel, I saw a pay phone outside a gas station on the Columbia Pike that looked private enough. I parked so that I could watch the road while Rachel made her call.

She went straight to the phone, carrying the phone card

we'd bought at a Quik Stop near the motel. After a few moments, she smiled, gave me a thumbs-up sign, and began talking. The conversation lasted a long time, but I thought it must be going well, because I saw her reading our fictional names off the motel stationery. *Mr. and Mrs. John David Stephens*. Rachel's "maiden name" was Horowitz, and her passport would list her as Hannah Horowitz Stephens. As she talked, I thought about how deeply this doctor must have loved her, that he would do this for her after fifteen years. She hung up and came back to the truck.

"Well?" I said.

She closed the door. "No problem. He'll make reservations for everything. The plane, the hotel, even a couple of sightseeing tours."

"Out of New York?" We couldn't risk staying in Washington an hour longer than necessary.

"JFK."

"Who is this guy?"

"Adam Stern. He's an OB in Manhattan. He has four kids now."

"He must have liked you a lot in the old days."

She gave me a sly smile. "They never get over me."

I drove a hundred meters up the road, parked, and left the engine running. I could still see the pay phone Rachel had used.

"Adam says this is the busiest week of the year for tourism in Israel," she said. "Easter in Jerusalem is like Mardi Gras in New Orleans."

"That may be good for us."

"If we can get a flight at all. He's going to try for something besides El Al, but there are no guarantees."

"Anything's good. They don't seem to be hunting us publicly yet."

We sat awhile in the drone of the idling engine, but no

one approached the pay phone. I slid my hand across the seat and closed it around hers.

"Are you okay?"

She nodded but didn't look at me. "It's been a long time since I felt good about doing what we did."

I squeezed her hand, and she turned to me. Her eyes were wet. I knew then how long she had lived without real intimacy. Probably about as long as I had.

"I'm glad you're here," I said. "And I'm glad you're coming with me to Israel. I couldn't do it without you."

She took back her hand and wiped her eyes.

I glanced at the phone. There was no one near it. "I think we're okay. You ready to get some real sleep?"

"I'm ready for a cheeseburger. *Then* sleep."

At nine-thirty the next morning, we were crossing Memorial Bridge, rolling toward the Lincoln Memorial. I'd last visited Washington to film part of the *NOVA* series based on my book. The contrast between that visit and today did not bear thinking about.

We found a Kinko's copy shop southeast of Capitol Hill and in twenty minutes had the passport photos we'd been instructed to drop off at the Au Bon Pain café in Union Station. As I drove toward the station, pedestrian traffic increased, and I began to get nervous. With Washington topping the list of terrorist targets, there were bound to be surveillance cameras near all important public buildings. They might not be visible, but they would be there. And the NSA had the computing power to do visual searches of those surveillance tapes. I kept well clear of the Mall and parked in a lot on the east side of Union Station.

As we walked toward the massive white granite building, we moved quickly toward the main entrance. Rachel kept abreast of me all the way, a Kinko's bag swinging from her right hand. She didn't know that I was carrying my revolver in the small of my back, beneath my shirt. If there were metal detectors at the station's entrance, I would have to return to the truck. Dozens of people were lined up at the entrance, but after watching the flow of visitors, I breathed a sigh of relief. They were moving too quickly to be passing through serious security.

Once through the doors, we joined the throngs moving through the renovated beaux arts rail station. We passed an elevated restaurant standing in the middle of the floor, then moved farther into the cavernous main hall. This led into a multilevel mall area where tour groups, travelers, and shoppers jostled each other on walkways and curving staircases, marveling at the statuary and pointing into store windows. I could tell by the rumbling under my shoes that trains were running nearby, yet my surroundings looked as pristine as a museum.

"There's the Au Bon Pain," Rachel said, pulling me to the left.

A huge B. Dalton bookstore anchored this end of the mall, and the Au Bon Pain café was on its right. People moved quickly in and out of the café, and I could see that our contact had chosen well.

Rachel walked through the wide entrance and joined a queue before some coffee urns on a marble table. I joined her, casually scanning the tables to our right. She'd been instructed to look for a woman carrying a copy of *The Second Sex* by Simone de Beauvoir. I figured I would be able to guess which woman would carry that book by appearance alone.

At a table near the back I saw a red-haired woman of fifty with no makeup and a hard line of a mouth. She kept her eyes on the table, as though afraid she might be accosted by a stranger. I was preparing to wager a hundred dollars that this was our contact when Rachel pulled at my arm and pointed at a fortyish African-American woman standing by the pastry racks and reading *The Second Sex*. Rachel left the queue and approached her.

"I haven't seen that book in years!" Rachel said. "Not since college. Is it still relevant today?"

The woman looked up and smiled, her eyes bright and welcoming. "It's a bit dated, but valuable from a historical perspective." She offered a brown hand bejeweled with rings. "I'm Mary Venable."

"Hannah Stephens," said Rachel. "Very nice to meet you."

I was amazed by how easily she slipped into her role. Maybe psychiatrists were natural liars. As I walked forward, I heard Mary Venable say softly, "It's an honor to meet you, Doctor. You've helped so many."

"Thank you," Rachel replied. Then, much louder, she said, "I never knew how Simone stood being Sartre's lover. The man looked like a *frog*. And that's no slur on the French. He truly did!"

Mary Venable laughed so naturally that I almost didn't see her take the Kinko's bag from Rachel's hand and drop it into a big woven African purse at her feet.

"If I finish this tonight," Venable said, "I'll lend it to you tomorrow. I'll be here about this time."

"I might see you then," Rachel said.

Mary Venable leaned in close and said, "Tell your man he needs to hide his piece a little better."

While Rachel stood puzzled, Mary Venable squeezed her hand with affection, then picked up the purse and walked away. As she passed me, she caught my eye for only a moment, but in that moment I read her message loud and clear: *You'd best take care of that woman, mister.*

I walked up to Rachel, who looked oddly at me. "Was she referring to something anatomical?"

"I'll tell you later." I took hold of Rachel's arm and led her out of the store.

"I didn't know there was a mall here," she said. "Can we get some clothes?"

"Not here. I don't really see the kind of place we need. We want one big department store that carries everything."

"Maybe on the upper level?"

"Not here," I insisted.

As I led her back toward the main entrance, a D.C. cop walked past us. My heart flew into my throat. I was sure he had started a double take just as we passed. I wanted to turn and check, but I didn't dare.

"What's the matter?" Rachel asked, sensing my tension.

"I think they're looking for us here."

"Of course they are."

"I mean *publicly*. I think that cop just recognized me."

She started to turn, but I shook my head hard enough to stop her.

"You mean it's not just the NSA anymore," she said.

"I'm afraid not. Stay beside me, and be ready to run."

We passed a tree growing from a huge planter in the middle of the floor. I pulled Rachel behind it and looked back from cover. The cop was walking in our footsteps and craning his neck, trying to see around the planter. He was also speaking into a collar radio.

"We're blown," I said. "Come on!"

TWENTY-SIX

I grabbed Rachel's hand and doubled my walking speed. Instead of making for the main entrance, I veered toward a staircase that swept up to the next level, using the crowd for concealment.

"Up?" Rachel asked, pointing at the stairs.

"No." My goal was the trains. I moved toward the ticketing area to our left, but a female voice over the PA stopped me.

"Attention, all travelers. Attention. All incoming and outgoing trains will be stopped immediately for maintenance reasons. Please remain on the platforms, and we will issue further bulletins as we have more information. Thank you for your patience."

Adrenaline flushed through my body. The announcer was repeating the message in Spanish.

"Back to the stairs," I said, reversing direction.

"Up or down?"

"Up!"

We took the steps two at a time. On the next floor, I leaned far enough over the rail to see the cop who had spotted us. He was still on the main floor, trying to decide which way we had gone. He looked up, shielding his eyes against the lights, then started toward the stairs.

"Why did they stop the trains?" Rachel asked.

"Us."

"They're shutting down all the trains in Union Station to find us?"

"*Attention, please,*" said the PA announcer. "*The police have asked that all shoppers and travelers move in a calm and methodical way to the exits. We apologize for this inconvenience. There is no danger of any kind to persons or property. You may pay for your purchases, but we ask that you move to the exits as soon as possible. Thank you.*"

I could see the effort it was taking for Rachel to stay calm.

"We're not going to get out, are we?" she asked.

I looked over the balcony rail again. The cop was trying to decide whether to come up or go down. "They must have triggered some sort of terrorist alert. That's the only way you could evacuate this place. There could be a hundred cops surrounding the building."

Rachel looked along the mezzanine. Clusters of people were hurrying toward us. We stepped away from the stairs and let them pass.

The cop below moved toward the ticketing area and spoke into his collar radio again.

"We've got two choices. One, we change our appearance and try to get out with the crowd."

"Change our appearance how?"

"Go into a store and put on all black clothes, maybe. Find some scissors and cut off your hair. Mousse mine up. Try to look ten years younger."

Rachel didn't look encouraged. "That'll get us nailed in the airport. We won't match our passport photos."

"You're right. Then we do the simple thing. Go into the

257

back of a store, find a couple of big cardboard boxes, and hide in them until all this dies down."

"Simple is good."

"But the police might bring dogs."

"God."

"Come on," I said, suddenly sure what to do.

I ran down the curved staircase, watching for police uniforms. I'd seen a marquee for a theater on our way in, and from the station's layout, I guessed it was on the lower level. The staircase terminated in a food court. People were rushing to finish their meals, anxiety on their faces. Through a jumble of orange and yellow chairs I saw a line of moviegoers filing out of the theater doors.

"Where are we going?" Rachel asked.

"The cinema."

"They're evacuating it."

As we moved toward the theater entrance, a section of wall opened about ten yards in front of us, and a frightened-looking young couple walked out, squinting their eyes. Before the tire door's spring could pull it closed, I darted forward and blocked it with my foot.

The houselights were on in the theater, but the seats were empty. Up the sloping floor to my left, a man in a sport jacket was ushering the last moviegoers up the center aisle toward the main exit. To my right, a ten-foot-tall Hugh Grant walked dejectedly along a London street, his hands in his pockets. Rachel leaned against my back.

"What's in there?"

I pulled the door open wide enough for us to slip through, then lifted the bottom of the heavy red curtain that ran along the wall and let it fall over us. We flattened ourselves against the wall and separated, so as to fit more naturally into the billow of the fabric. I could no longer see Rachel, but I realized with surprise that we were holding hands. The instinct

258

was as primitive as that of two Neanderthals comforting each other against a cave wall.

"Why here?" she asked. "Why not the back of a store?"

In my mind's eye, I saw police converging on our stolen truck.

"Dogs," Rachel whispered. "A minute ago, this room was full of sweating people. Different scents. Not like the stockroom of some store."

"Right." The soundtrack of the movie died with a groan. I expected to hear voices, but none came. Fifteen minutes passed. Twenty. Rachel clung to my sweating hand. As I wiped perspiration from my forehead, a male voice penetrated the curtain.

"I got the center aisle!"

Rachel's hand clenched mine.

Police radio chatter echoed through the theater.

"Okay," called a second man. "I'll shine my light under the seats."

The men didn't worry me much, but the rapid panting that followed nearly stopped my heart. I might soon have to choose between surrender and a shoot-out with city police.

"She's got something!" cried the first man. "Look, she's on a scent. Go, girl!"

I tried not to breathe.

"Shit, it's half a hot dog."

"Wait, she's onto something else."

The voices were closer. Rachel's hand was shaking. How would she react if I fired my gun? These weren't assassins sent by Geli Bauer. They were probably D.C. cops doing their duty.

"She's going in circles," said the second voice. "Too many scents. I'm smelling some BO myself. We're gonna have to come back later."

"Okay. They want her down by the tracks anyway."

The voices receded.

"What are we going to do?" Rachel whispered.

"Wait."

"How long?"

"They can't keep Union Station closed all day."

"You think the dog is coming back?"

"I don't know."

"I think I peed in my pants."

"Don't worry about it."

"Won't the dog smell it?"

She was right. "Just try to be quiet."

An hour and forty-five minutes later, a male voice came over the PA system. *"Dr. Tennant, this is Officer Wilton Howard of the Washington, D.C., police department. We want you to know that we know this is all a misunderstanding. We've been made aware that the shooting in North Carolina was self-defense, and we are prepared to offer you protective custody and unlimited communication with anyone you wish to speak to. Please step into plain sight with Dr. Weiss, put down any weapons, and turn yourself in to any officer. You will not be treated as a criminal."*

"What do you think?" Rachel asked.

"I hear Geli Bauer in that message."

"Maybe it's for real. I mean, all the cops in the building heard that, too."

"If they've been told I'm a terrorist or something like that, they think anything is justified to bring me out. Plus, they think I'm armed."

"Are you?"

I started to lie, but she needed to know the truth. "Yes."

"Oh, God."

The police message began again.

"David . . ."

I reached out and squeezed her hand. "Stay quiet."

Another hour passed, with more and varied messages

coming over the PA system. On instinct, I told Rachel to lie flat on the floor and remain against the wall. I did the same.

The dog didn't come back, but more cops did. It sounded as if they were walking every row of seats. Now and then I felt the heavy curtain sway as one of them checked it. As footsteps neared us, I pulled my gun out of my pants and prayed that Rachel could hold her nerve. Heavy steps approached me, and then the fabric lifted off my face.

A pair of black boots was inches from my eyes. I held my breath, unsure whether I'd been seen or not. The curtain danced along my right cheek. Then it dropped, and the boots walked away. The cop had only hit the wall a few times with his hand to check behind the curtain.

My heart felt as though it had turned to stone.

The boots approached again. The cop checked the curtain the way he had before, one row down. I tried to shut out the sound of his footsteps. After a seeming eternity, I realized he had passed us by. The search continued for another five minutes, then the radio chatter died. I thought Rachel must be close to cracking, but I didn't risk trying to speak to her. After twenty minutes with no further appeals over the PA system, I heard a mechanical hissing and clicking that I recognized as rewinding film.

"Is that the projector?" Rachel asked.

"Somebody's rewinding the film. They must be reopening the station. We should go."

"Maybe we should wait until tonight."

"No. There'll be guards posted at the exits tonight. Right now, we can count on a lot of confusion as they reopen the station. This is our best chance."

We got up and moved down the wall to the exit door. After listening and hearing nothing, I opened the door a crack. Two women walked past wearing street clothes. I thought they might be cops, but then the PA announced a rescheduled train. An empty terminal needed no such announcement. I pulled Rachel through the door.

The escalators and staircases were filling with people, and the clangs of kitchen equipment reverberated across the marble floor of the food court. We walked to the escalator and started up.

"When we hit the main floor, walk twenty yards behind me," I said. "If someone spots me, blend into the crowd and disappear."

The escalator terminated near the entrance of the B. Dalton store. I kissed Rachel on the cheek, then struck out across the floor, scanning the crowd for uniforms.

Angry travelers were pouring into the station like water through a dam. Most were heading for the trains. I couldn't have asked for better cover. I glanced back to make sure Rachel was following, then prepared to turn right, toward the main entrance. If the police were funneling people through a single checkpoint, I'd double back and search for an alternate escape route. If not, I'd gut it out and trust to the anonymity of the crowd to get us through.

I veered right and headed into the barrel-vaulted chamber that led to the main entrance. The river of humanity flowing against me was hard to navigate, but I was glad for every person there. By shutting the station for three hours, the police had created an almost impossible situation for themselves.

Between me and the entrance stood the circular restaurant I'd seen on the way in. Two stories high, the open-air café was like an island in the center of the floor. It had tables on its second level and a wrought-iron balcony that allowed its patrons to watch the pageant below. It also provided a bird's-eye view for anyone wanting to surveil the huge hall. I started around it on the left side, keeping my face downcast.

"Dr. Tennant!" shouted a female voice.

I glanced up.

Geli Bauer was staring down at me from the café's second level. Her scarred face and electric blue eyes were impossible to miss, and her presence here had the inevitability of fate. The three hours we'd hidden in the theater had given her time to fly here from North Carolina. The police had reopened the station, but Geli had waited in the hope of spotting us. As I whirled to see if Rachel saw the danger, I realized my mistake. Geli instantly spotted her and raised a walkie-talkie to her lips.

"Run!" I shouted to Rachel.

Geli dropped her radio, whipped up an automatic pistol, and aimed down at me.

A woman beside her screamed. As others joined the panic, Geli darted onto a staircase that curved down to the main floor. I slid my hand behind me, toward the gun at the small of my back.

"Don't!" Geli shouted, moving quickly down the stairs. *"I'm not going to fire! The order to kill you came from Godin! Godin's lost his mind!"*

She stopped three-quarters of the way down the steps, holding her pistol in a two-handed combat stance.

"If that's true, put down your gun!"

She didn't.

Why hasn't she shot me? I wondered. Then I knew. Rachel was far enough away that if Geli shot me out of hand, she might escape with the terrified mob.

"Drop your gun, Doctor!" Geli yelled, continuing down the stairs. "Drop it now and lie prone on the floor! I won't fire!"

She couldn't miss from where she was. I dropped my gun on the gleaming floor. Her eyes flashed with satisfaction.

The crowd reacted to this disturbance like an ant colony perceiving danger in its midst. Waves of panic radiated into preoccupied travelers farther from the center, creating a cyclone of people rushing for the exits. Police stationed there would have to battle their way here foot by foot.

"Get over here, Dr. Weiss!" Geli shouted.

"David?" Rachel called tentatively.

Geli's automatic had a silencer on its barrel. *"Run!"* I screamed. *"Get out of here!"*

Geli shifted her aim toward Rachel. I lunged up the steps. My hands closed around her wrists as the gun spit a round past me. The fury in her face told me she'd missed.

Geli drove a knee into my stomach, knocking the wind from my lungs. I wrenched at her bones like a man trying to break green sticks. She threw herself backward and spun, flipping me onto the steps with her sitting on top of me. I fought to keep her gun pointed away from me, but she had the leverage on her side. The silencer inched steadily toward my face. Geli's scar went white as the strain of combat filled her cheeks with blood.

"Let go of the gun!" screamed a female voice. *"Both of you! Let go and stand up!"*

Ten feet away, Rachel stood with both hands clenched around my revolver, her eyes wide with terror.

"Put down that weapon!" Geli yelled. "You're interfering with a federal officer in performance of her duty!"

"Shoot her!" I shouted, trying to rip the gun from Geli's grasp. "She killed Fielding! Shoot!"

Geli slammed the point of her elbow into my solar plexus, and the silencer jammed into my cheek. An explosion rang my eardrums like gongs, and something wet spattered my face. Geli's blazing eyes seemed to fill my vision, but then a river of blood flooded down her shirtfront.

I grabbed her gun and rolled her off me.

Rachel was still aiming the smoking revolver and shaking like an epileptic. The bullet had hit Geli in the neck, but she'd managed to stuff her fingers into the wound to stop the bleeding. Never had I seen such rage in human eyes. I grabbed Rachel's wrist and ran back toward the main hall.

As we rounded the corner, Geli's voice echoed though the hundred-foot-high chamber: *"You're dead, Tennant! You're fucking dead!"*

I sprinted toward the B. Dalton store at the end of the mall. Cases of books were bulky and heavy. That meant a loading dock.

Customers scrambled out of our way as I hustled Rachel into the stockroom of the bookstore. The tile floor was piled with boxes, and sure enough, there was a loading bay with a motorized door to handle deliveries. I hit a red button on the wall, and the door began to rise.

Sunlight flooded into the room. I lowered Rachel to the cement of the loading bay, then jumped off myself. A delivery truck was parked at the entrance to the bay, and two men stood talking beside its cab. As we ran up the incline, I saw a white Toyota Corolla parked by the truck. Its driver's door was open, but no one was inside.

I aimed my revolver at the two men, then jerked it toward the Toyota. "I need that car!"

The truck driver held up his hands, but the other man looked at the Toyota. "That's my car."

"Give me the keys!"

The man looked blank.

"Give him your damn keys!" said the truck driver.

"They're in it."

I pulled Rachel around to the passenger door and put her inside, then scrambled into the driver's seat and started the engine. The owner of the car yelled something, but his words were lost in the roar as I sped away. Forward momentum slammed my door, and it took all my self-control to slow down. I'd have to drive at normal speed to get us clear of the station, then ditch the car to get clear of the city.

"Oh, God," Rachel said, her face white.

Wailing sirens were converging on Union Station.

TWENTY-SEVEN

I stood behind Rachel at the food court at JFK airport in New York, watching her for signs of a breakdown. She was wearing a blue dress, part of a new wardrobe she'd bought in New Jersey, but the dress did nothing to mask her pale skin and hollow eyes. Shooting Geli Bauer had rattled her badly, and though news reports had revealed that the "federal officer" shot at Union Station had survived, Rachel had remained shaky throughout the drive to New York.

I would never have got her out of Washington without help. After ditching the Toyota five blocks from Union Station, I hailed a taxi and had it carry us back over the Potomac to Alexandria, Virginia, to an upscale shopping center. There I called the phone number that had led to the café rendezvous with Mary Venable. I told the woman who answered that Dr. Rachel Weiss was in mortal danger and desperately needed help. Forty-five minutes later, a woman in a blue Toyota Camry picked us up and took us back into Washington, to a private residence on the south side.

The house was a sanctuary run by the feminist group that provided new identities for battered women on the run with their children. We were installed in a bedroom at the back of the safe house, and after a brief wait, Mary Venable arrived. She questioned Rachel at length—she didn't seem to trust me—then made arrangements for a car we could use to drive to New York the following day. She told us to leave it in the long-term lot at JFK, where it would be picked up by one of their New York "sisters."

There was a television in the bedroom, and the Union Station shooting was all over the news. The temporary closing of the station seemed to have caused as much of an uproar as the gunfire. Early reports speculated that a bomb threat had forced evacuation of the station, but by the late-news broadcast, the story had changed. D.C. police sources had leaked that a potential presidential assassin had been tracked to the station. My name wasn't given, but the anchor said that the woman who had done the shooting in the station, formerly believed to be my captive, was now believed to be my accomplice.

We slept little, and by morning *The Washington Post* had my name and photograph. In the article, a Secret Service spokesman characterized me as an idealistic physician who had snapped after years of grief over the tragic loss of my family. Driven by paranoid delusions, I had threatened the president's life, and my appearance in Washington with a gun proved how dangerous I was. The identity of my female accomplice remained "unknown," but several witnesses had seen her fire the shot that downed the federal officer. What frightened me most was that the article's closing comment came from Ewan McCaskell, the president's chief of staff, who had been reached in China:

"Dr. Tennant actually met the president in the Oval Office on one occasion," McCaskell said. "The president admired his book on medical ethics. He regrets that this noted physician has apparently suffered some sort of psychotic break, and hopes Dr. Tennant can receive treatment before something tragic happens."

I worried that Mary Venable would see the story and turn me in, but an hour later she dropped off our new passports, two Virginia driver's licenses, and the keys to our "borrowed" car. She had seen the article, but her loyalty to Rachel was stronger than her belief in media stories. I lost no time in getting on I-95, headed for New York.

Having my name and face broadcast nationwide only strengthened my resolve to leave the country. The NSA believed I was planning to meet the president in Washington tomorrow, so leaving the country was the last thing they would expect me to do. Going through JFK airport would be risky, but if we made it, we would be far safer than in the United States.

Rachel hardly spoke during the first leg of the drive, and nothing I said seemed to register. By the time we reached New Jersey, she'd regained enough of herself to go into a mall with a list of clothing sizes and outfit us for our trip. Other than that, we stopped only for gasoline, and I never got out of the car. Just before we reached New York, Rachel telephoned Adam Stern and gave him a cover story I'd scripted to explain the doctor's third-party reservations for us.

With the Easter crowds, Stern had been forced to book us on a midnight El Al flight, which worried me quite a bit. I wore a Yankees cap into JFK, praying that my "six-foot white guy" looks were generic enough not to attract attention. Things went surprisingly well at the El Al ticket counter, but I did most of the talking. My worry was the informal security interview. According to Stern, at some point before you boarded an El Al plane, one or two plainclothes security officers would strike up a conversation with you, to get a feel for your intentions. There was no way we would get through that without Rachel handling some of the talking.

"The chicken with broccoli looks good," I said, pointing

through a glass screen in front of the Chinese food counter. "What do you think?"

"Fine," Rachel said in a dead voice.

I touched her shoulder. "Are you all right?"

She didn't answer.

I stepped in front of her and ordered two chicken and broccoli plates. As I paid, I heard a man's voice behind me.

"Hi, there. We were in line with you at the El Al counter. You going over for Western Holy Week?"

"Uh . . . no," Rachel replied.

I glanced back and saw two dark-skinned men of medium height standing behind us. They had quick eyes and easy smiles. They looked like brothers.

"Visiting family then?" said the second man, who wore a gold chain around his neck.

"No," Rachel said awkwardly. "It's a private matter. A health problem."

Concerned looks. "Oh. Sorry to pry."

They're looking for terrorists, I told myself. *Not presidential assassins.* I turned around and nodded to the two men.

The silence was uncomfortable, but suddenly Rachel straightened up and came to life. "I guess it's nothing to be embarrassed about," she said. "My OB-GYN is sending me over. I was just diagnosed with ovarian cancer. It's advanced, but he has a friend at the Hadassah Hospital in Jerusalem. There's a clinical trial for culturing your own T cells and reinjecting them to fight the tumors. My doctor's an old friend. He made all the arrangements for us, thank God. Planes, the hotel, all of it." She put her hand over her heart. "I'm sorry to run on. It's just the first ray of hope I've had, and it feels better to talk about it."

"Quite all right," said the man wearing the chain. "I'm sure you'll do very well. The doctors at Hadassah are the best in the world."

"The trial looks very promising," I chimed in, not wanting

269

to appear awkward. "The lead researcher did his training at Sloan-Kettering."

"You sound like a doctor yourself," said the shorter man, and I lost any remaining doubt that they were El Al security. Suddenly all I could think about was the $16,000 in cash in the money belts concealed beneath our clothes.

"Food, mister," snapped one of the Chinese clerks.

"Thank you," I said, glancing back at the plates. "Yes, I'm an internist."

"You know about arthritis?" asked the shorter man. "They tell me I got psoriatic arthritis. You know about that?"

Answer him? I wondered. *Act arrogant?* "Well, there are five types. Some are relatively mild, others crippling."

"What's the bad kind?"

"Arthritis mutilans."

The man grinned happily. "That's not me, thank God. I got something about phalanges."

"Distal interphalangeal predominant." I lifted his hands and looked at his fingernails, which showed marked pitting. "It could be a lot worse."

He pulled back his hand. "Good, good. Well, enjoy your food."

"Good luck at Hadassah," said the one wearing the chain. "You're going to the right place for a cure."

I put both plates on a tray and carried it to a vacant table. Rachel followed me, looking shell-shocked. I glanced back at the food counter and saw the two men walk away without ordering.

"You did great," I said softly. "Academy Award caliber."

"Survival," she said, taking her seat. "Everybody has it in them. You told me that in North Carolina, and I didn't believe you. Now I know better."

I picked up my fork. "There's no point feeling guilty about it."

270

"They'd already talked to Adam. That's the feeling I got."

"No doubt. He must have given them the same story. If we make it onto the plane without being arrested, I'm going to send that guy a case of champagne."

Rachel closed her eyes. "Are we going to make it?"

"Yes. Just keep it together for another half hour."

The 747 was crowded despite being a late flight, but we were insulated from our nearest neighbors by two empty seats and an aisle, and that gave us some privacy. I sat by the window with my Yankees cap on, taking care not to make eye contact with anyone as I retrieved two blankets and covered us both to the neck.

We sat at the gate for what seemed like two hours, but it was only forty minutes by my watch. While passengers around us talked excitedly about their upcoming visit to the Holy Land, Rachel and I pretended to sleep, holding hands under the blanket. At last the El Al jetliner taxied out onto the runway and lumbered into the night sky.

"Thank God," she whispered as the wheels lifted off the concrete.

We would have to clear security at Tel Aviv in eleven hours, but making it into the air was half the battle, and I tried to focus on that small victory. "Are you all right?"

She opened her eyes, which were separated from mine only by the bill of my Yankees cap. In them I saw emotions I could not read.

"I need to ask you some things, David." She sounded more like the psychiatrist I had known before we made love. "We're going to Jerusalem, and I need to get to the bottom of why. I'd like you to treat this as a session."

"No. If you ask me things, I can ask you things. And you have to answer honestly. That's where we are now."

She hesitated, then nodded. "Fair enough. You've told me

you're an atheist. You said your mother believed in something greater than humanity, but not in organized religion. What about your father? Was he a declared atheist?"

"No. He just didn't believe in the conventional concept of God. A God who focused all his attention on man. Dad was a physicist. They're a skeptical bunch, as a rule."

"Did he believe in a supreme being of any kind?"

My father wasn't the type to "get cosmic" very often, but on a few occasions—camping in the mountains under a star-filled sky—he had talked to my brother and me about what he'd really believed.

"Dad had a simple conception of the way things are. Simple but profound. He didn't see man as separate from the universe, but part of it. He always said, 'Man is the universe becoming conscious of itself.'"

"Have I heard that before?"

"Maybe. I've heard New Age gurus like Deepak Chopra say it. But my father was saying it twenty-five years ago."

"What do you think he meant?"

"Exactly what he said. He always reminded us that every atom in our bodies was once part of a distant star that had exploded. He talked about how evolution moves from simplicity toward complexity, and how human intelligence is the highest known expression of evolution. I remember him telling me that a frog's brain is much more complex than a star. He saw human consciousness as the first neuron of the universe coming to life and awareness. A spark in the darkness, waiting to spread to fire."

Rachel looked thoughtful. "That's a beautiful idea. Not exactly a religious view, but a hopeful one."

"Practical, too. If we're the universe becoming conscious of itself, we have a moral duty to survive. To preserve the gift of consciousness. And to do that, we have to live in peace. From that you can derive a workable set of laws, ethics, everything."

Rachel reflected on this. "Do you subscribe to his view of the universe?"

"I did until a couple of weeks ago. My latest visions don't exactly fit into it."

She laid her hand on my knee. "We don't know where they fit, all right? And I don't think your father's view precludes the existence of a creator. Do you still have anxiety that you'll die if you don't reach Jerusalem before you dream of the crucifixion?"

The immediate threat of capture by police had distracted me from this concern. "I still feel some urgency, but not like before. The fact that we're going there seems to have eased the pressure a bit."

"If you do dream of the crucifixion, you shouldn't worry about it. A dream never killed anybody."

I wasn't so sure. "Let's talk about you for a minute. You say you believe in God. What exactly do you believe?"

"I don't see how that relates to what we're doing."

"I think we're both on this plane for a reason. And I think what you believe matters."

A look of ineffable sadness entered her face. "I came to God very late. As a child I was never taken to synagogue or church."

"Why not?"

"My father turned his back on God when he was seven years old."

"Why so young?"

"He turned seven inside a concentration camp."

Something inside me went cold.

Her gaze became unfocused, as though she were looking years into the past. "My father saw his father murdered in front of him. It wasn't a normal event, even by camp standards. The Allies were approaching, and the SS guards were liquidating the prisoners. One guard invented a game with his small work detail. He killed one prisoner a day. He tried to get the starving prisoners to kill each other and offered them survival if they would. My grandfather refused, of course. He'd been a surgeon in Berlin. He'd met Freud, corresponded with Jung."

My mind spun as Rachel's career choice came into perspective.

"The guard beat my grandfather to death in front of his little boy—my father. My father decided then that a God who allowed what he'd seen deserved curses, not prayers."

I wanted to say something, but what words would mean anything?

"He was one of the lucky ones allowed to emigrate to America. He was taken in by distant relatives in Brooklyn." Rachel smiled sadly. "Uncle Milton was a locksmith. My father's refusal to worship angered him, but Milton knew the boy had been through a lot. When he came of age, my father changed his name to White, moved to Queens, and stopped seeing his family, though he did send them money. He married a gentile who cared nothing for religion, and they raised me in a secular house."

I listened in amazement. You saw a face on an American street, or in an office, and you had no idea that a tragic epic lay behind it.

"I always felt like an outsider because of that. All my friends went to church or synagogue. I got curious. When I was seventeen, I sought out my Uncle Milton. He told me everything. After that . . . I embraced my heritage."

Many small mysteries of Rachel's personality suddenly made sense. Her severe dress, her professional distance, her abhorrence of violence . . .

"The thing is," she went on, "I think I became Jewish more out of emotional and political identification than a desire to do God's will."

274

"There's nothing wrong with that."

"Of course there is. If you ask me what I really think about God, it has nothing to do with the Torah or the Talmud. It has to do with what I've seen in my own life."

"What do you really think?"

She folded her hands on her lap. "I believe that to create means to make something that didn't exist before. If God is perfect, then the only way he can truly create is to make something separate from himself. So by definition, his creation must be imperfect. You see? If it were perfect, it would *be* God."

"Yes."

"I believe that for human beings to be distinct from God, we must be able to make our own choices. Free will, right? And unless bad choices resulted in real pain, free will would have no meaning. That's why we have such evil in the world. I don't know what religion that adds up to, but whatever it is, that's what I believe."

"That's a good explanation for the world as we find it. But it doesn't address the central mystery. Why should God feel compelled to create anything at all?"

"I don't think we'll ever know that."

"We might. Our sun is going to burn for another five billion years or so. Even if the universe ends by collapsing inward on itself—the Big Crunch—the earliest that could happen is about twenty billion years from now. If we don't destroy ourselves, we'll have plenty of time to answer that question. Maybe all questions."

She smiled. "You and I will never know."

Looking into her dark eyes, I realized just how little I knew about her. "You're not nearly as conventional as you pretend to be. I wish you could have talked to Fielding."

"What did he believe about God?"

"Fielding had a big problem with evil. He was raised a

Christian, but he said that neither Judaism nor Christianity had ever faced evil head-on."

"What did he mean?"

"He'd recite three statements: 'God is all powerful. God is all good. Evil exists.' You can logically reconcile any two of those statements, but not all three."

Rachel nodded thoughtfully.

"Fielding thought the Eastern religions were the only truly monotheistic ones, because they admit that evil flows from God, rather than trying to blame a lesser figure like Satan."

"And you?" she asked. "Where do you think evil comes from?"

"The human heart."

"The heart pumps blood, David."

"You know what I mean. The psyche. The dark well where primitive instincts mix with human intelligence. When you look at the atrocities man is capable of, it's difficult to imagine a divine plan behind any of it. I mean, look what happened to your grandfather."

Rachel gripped my arm and looked at me with almost desperate urgency. "On the day my grandfather was murdered, there was a moment when he could have killed that guard. They were alone at a rock quarry, one guard and three prisoners. The Americans were only a day away. But he didn't do it."

"Why not?" I asked, stunned by her passion.

"I think he knew something that we've forgotten."

"What?"

"That if you take up the weapon of your enemy, you become like him. Jesus knew that. Gandhi, too."

"Even with your son standing there beside you? Needing your protection? You turn the other cheek and sacrifice yourself?"

"You don't commit murder," Rachel said firmly. "If my grandfather had killed that guard, he *and* my father might have been executed that night. We can't know the future. That's why what I did yesterday shook me so badly. I picked up your gun and shot a fellow human being. What did I really do when I did that?"

"You saved my life. Yours, too."

"For a while."

I squeezed her hand tight. "We're *alive,* Rachel. And I believe I have something very important to do before I die."

"I know you do."

A male flight attendant appeared in the aisle beside us. I didn't want to look up, so I motioned for Rachel to turn.

"Yes?" Rachel asked in a sleepy voice.

"Are you going to want dinner tonight?"

She looked back at me, and I nodded. "Yes," she said. "Thank you."

The flight attendant glanced at me, then walked away.

Rachel was holding her breath. "What do you think?"

"I don't know. It seemed odd, but maybe he was checking to see if we were going to sleep through dinner."

She shook her head. "I can't do this."

"Yes, you can. We're fine."

"What about the Tel Aviv airport?"

"We'll make it through."

"You don't know that."

I touched her cheek and spoke with conviction I had not known was in me. "I do know. There's something waiting for me in Jerusalem."

"What?"

"An answer."

TWENTY-EIGHT

WHITE SANDS, NEW MEXICO

Ravi Nara revved the throttle of his Honda ATV and drove toward what Godin's technical staff was deluded enough to call the hospital. The New Mexico air parched his throat, and the scorching sun left the neurologist so drained that he tried to stay indoors as much as possible. A white-coated technician crossed his path on foot and raised an arm in greeting. Ravi braked angrily and drove on.

It had taken all his nerve to telephone John Skow, even with the scrambled cell phone the NSA man had given him. But with Godin close to death, he'd had to take the risk. Skow had made it clear that if Godin died before Trinity became a reality, all their careers—and maybe their lives—could be destroyed. Zach Levin, Godin's chief engineer, had predicted that the Trinity prototype could go fully operational in seven to ten days. But that estimate assumed the continued participation of Godin himself. Ravi knew he'd be lucky to keep the old man alive for another twenty-four hours.

He doubted that any doctor had ever worked so hard to keep a patient alive. At thirty-six, Ravi Nara was already a revered scientist. In his native India he was treated as a hero, despite his having become an American citizen. But if Trinity failed under a cloud of scandal caused by the murder of a fellow Nobel laureate, nothing would save his reputation.

Again he wondered if someone had overheard his call to Skow. The security in North Carolina had been intrusive, but White Sands was a bloody military reservation. Still, no one had confronted him yet. Maybe the remoteness of the place made the security people less paranoid.

White Sands was bigger than Delaware and Rhode Island put together. The parcel fenced off for Trinity research was a mole on a white elephant, part of a larger tract administered by the U.S. Army Intelligence School at Fort Huachuca, Arizona. Before Ravi visited the base, Godin had described the living conditions there as "spartan." A transplanted New Yorker, Ravi had thought North Carolina was the middle of nowhere. White Sands was a hole in the world, a moonscape of white gypsum and rock with only rattlesnakes for company. He half-expected Indians to come riding over the dunes with John Ford cowboys in pursuit, but they never did.

The Trinity compound was laid out with geometric simplicity. There were four major buildings: the research lab, the hospital, Administration, and Containment. There were also barracks, a machine shop, a massive electrical power plant, and an airstrip that could take military jets. The buildings weren't really buildings, but converted aircraft hangars assembled by army engineers in five frantic weeks of construction. Only Containment was different. Containment housed the Trinity prototype.

Ravi could see the strange building to his right, standing alone at the center of the compound. Built like a World War Two pillbox, Containment had four-foot-thick concrete walls reinforced with tempered steel and shielded with lead. It was served by four giant electrical cables, two plumbing pipes, and a residential air-conditioning system. No telephone lines, coaxial cables, or cat-5 network cable ran to it. No antennae or satellite dishes sprouted from its roof, as they did from all the other buildings. Containment was like a structure built to hold Harry Houdini, if Houdini could have digitized himself and escaped through wires or beamed transmissions. If the Trinity prototype ever went fully operational, no one—not even Peter Godin—wanted it connected to the Internet.

Ravi had avoided the hospital today. Godin had been dying by inches for weeks, but two days ago he'd finally begun the slide toward eternity. Ravi was convinced that Fielding's death had done it, a ruthless necessity that hit the old man harder than he'd expected. Of course, Fielding's death had given them the crystal, so any doubts about the rightness of killing him were pointless.

Within hours after getting the crystal, they had made up all the ground lost to Fielding's sabotage, and after discovering the independent work Fielding had done, they'd found themselves within spitting distance of a working prototype. The euphoria of this success had been undercut by the problems with Tennant and his psychiatrist. Godin could ill afford the stress of dealing with that, yet in the final analysis, it was the cancer that was killing him, as it killed everyone who got his type of malignancy.

Ravi parked the ATV in front of the hospital hangar and walked inside. The hangar was divided into "rooms" by partitions. None had ceilings—not even the bathrooms—so foul smells drifted throughout the building with annoying regularity. Peter Godin was not bothered by this. He occupied an airtight chamber with positive pressure that no infectious agent could penetrate. Served by filtered air and water, the plastic cubicle known as the Bubble sat like an incubator at the center of the hangar floor.

To spare Ravi and the nurses from having to waste time with protective suits, a UV decontaminator had been installed near the Bubble's door. To sterilize himself, Ravi had only to scrub his hands, don a mask, then stand in the radiation long enough to rid his skin and clothing of dangerous organisms. The process only took two minutes, but lately it had begun to get on his nerves. Still, he couldn't blame Godin. Steroids and chemotherapy had beaten the old man's immune system into submission, and Godin wanted what every man had wanted since the beginning of time: to cheat death.

The humming UV unit finally went dark. Ravi stepped on a button that opened the Plexiglas hatch in the Bubble and stepped inside. Godin lay unconscious on a hospital bed, surrounded by monitors and resuscitation equipment. His body was pierced by a central IV line and coupled to the monitors by thin wires. His commanding head had scarcely more color than the white sheet it lay on.

Two nurses bookended the bed, watching for the slightest change in their patient's status. Ravi nodded to them, then lifted the chart from its slot at the end of the bed and gave it a token look. *Brainstem glioma, diffuse and inoperable.* He'd made the diagnosis six months ago, when he'd first seen the Super-MRI scan of Godin's brain. It was eerie to see a tumor growing inside one of the most gifted minds on earth. When Godin asked Ravi to keep his cancer secret, Ravi hadn't hesitated. Revealing Godin's condition might have ended his chance to take part in the greatest scientific effort in history. Of course, Ravi had exacted a price for his cooperation. It was only proper. Peter Godin was rich, Ravi Nara relatively poor. That imbalance had now been addressed, if only in a small way. Yet the fortune in cash and stock Ravi had received now seemed trivial in the face of what might happen.

"Ravi?" croaked the old man. "Is that you?"

Ravi looked up from the chart and saw the intense blue eyes fix upon him.

"Why am I so tired?" Godin asked.

"Your seizures, probably." Godin still suffered from epilepsy caused by his exposure to the Super-MRI.

Ravi walked around the bed and looked down into the slack face. Peter Godin had been one of the most vital men he'd ever known, yet cancer had laid Godin as low as it would any street beggar. Well . . . that wasn't quite true. No street beggar had Ravi Nara and almost limitless wealth keeping him alive. Even near death, with his hair and eyebrows gone, Godin retained the hawklike profile that had made the driven young computer designer so recognizable in the late 1950s, and for five decades afterward.

"Your tumor is very advanced, Peter. There's only so much I can do. It's a battle between keeping you conscious and keeping you free enough from pain to function."

"Damn the pain." Godin clenched one arthritic hand into a fist. "I can stand pain."

"That's not what you said last night. Last night you told me your face was on fire."

Godin shuddered. "I'm conscious now. Send Levin to me."

Zach Levin had led the R&D department at Godin Supercomputing in Mountain View until he was brought to North Carolina to run the Interface Team, the group responsible for communicating with the Trinity computer. Levin was a tall, cadaverous man of thirty-five, and prematurely gray. Like his master in his healthier days, Levin seemed to live without sleep.

"I'll send him in," Ravi said.

Godin held up one hand. "What have you heard about Tennant and Weiss?"

"There's been no sign of them since Union Station."

The old man closed his eyes and sighed with a rattle, a hint of what lay in the near future. "The woman shot Geli?"

"They say it was Dr. Weiss, yes."

When Godin frowned, a nest of lines formed in the lower half of his face. Though married to one woman for most of his life, Godin had no children, and he'd always displayed a paternal affection for Geli Bauer. The notion made Ravi's skin crawl; it was like having paternal affection for a cobra.

"How is Geli doing?" Godin asked.

"Remarkably well, I hear. They transferred her to Walter Reed. Her father arranged that."

A trace of a smile touched Godin's lips. "If she'd known that, she wouldn't have gone." The smile vanished. "What do you think Tennant was trying to accomplish in Washington? The president's still in China."

Ravi wished he knew. For most of the project, the internist had been his biggest headache. Hiding cancer from laymen was easy, but Tennant was always noticing Godin's fluctuating weight, his gait disturbances, and the body changes caused by steroids. The old man's rheumatoid arthritis explained some of that, but for the last six weeks Ravi had been forced to keep his patient practically isolated from Tennant.

"I have no idea, Peter. It worries me."

As a nurse gave Godin a sip of water, Ravi tried to gauge the time left to the tenacious old man. It wasn't easy. He hadn't worked directly with patients for years, and Godin was well past the mortality tables for his type of tumor. Predicting survival in these circumstances was the kind of augury at which doctors like Tennant excelled. Years of clinical experience gave them a sixth sense about life and death. But any Madras midwife might do as well.

A buzz and a purple flash made Ravi turn. Through the Bubble's transparent hatch he saw Zach Levin standing in the UV decontaminator.

Levin spent most of his time in the concrete womb of Containment, but he always seemed to sense when Godin had regained consciousness. Levin and his technicians were like a priesthood, tending their master as he died and his creation as it was born. *Priests of science,* Ravi thought. *What a contradiction in terms.* He waved to Levin and thought, *You get on my last bloody nerve—*

"There's Levin now," he said, and forced a smile.

"How long will I be conscious?" Godin asked.

"Until the pain gets unbearable."

"Send Levin in on your way out."

Ravi suppressed his anger. He'd been a wunderkind all his life, but for the past six months he'd felt more like a royal physician tending the bed of a king. The whims of a tyrant ruled his days. He stepped on the button that opened the hatch and walked out of the Bubble.

Zach Levin nodded from the decontaminator. Technically, Levin and his team were Ravi's subordinates. But the hardware and software of the Trinity computer were so complex that Ravi could not hope to lead Levin's people in any meaningful way, except where the brain itself was concerned. Even when they approached him with neurological questions, he felt more used than listened to. They swam like piranhas through his mind, devouring what they needed for their excursions into the labyrinthine neuromodels—

"How's he doing?" Levin asked loudly.

The UV decontaminator buzzed and shut down.

"He's awake," Ravi said. "Lucid."

"Good. I have some exciting news for him."

But not for me, Ravi thought bitterly. "Have you put any more questions to Tennant's model?"

Levin's seemed to consider his reply. "I dumped Dr. Tennant from the computer an hour ago."

"Who told you to do that?"

"Who do you think?"

Godin.

"At this point," said Levin, "bringing Trinity to full

284

operational status is more important than any damage Dr. Tennant could do the project."

Ravi felt the same way, but he didn't want the engineer to know that. "How does dumping Tennant's model help you to do that?"

"Peter thinks some of the problems we're now experiencing could have a quantum etiology. He thought perhaps Andrew Fielding might be able to help us."

"Fielding? You mean you've loaded Fielding's neuromodel into the prototype?"

"That's right."

"Do you really think his model can help you solve your remaining problems?"

"To tell you the truth, I don't see why his model should perform any differently than Dr. Tennant's. But it's interesting. Dr. Fielding is going through the same acclimatization problems Tennant experienced—terror, confusion, feedback loops from his biological survival circuits having incorrectly balanced relief outlets—but he seems to be adapting to them at a significantly faster rate."

Ravi shivered. Levin spoke as if Fielding were still alive. "What do you think that means?"

The engineer shrugged. "Maybe nothing. But Peter's intuition has been accurate too many times to ignore it. And it was the work stored in Dr. Fielding's crystal that brought us this far. If the processing areas of his model perform at a higher efficiency level than Dr. Tennant's . . . it could be a whole new ball game."

Ravi's heartbeat quickened. "What are the odds of that happening?"

Levin didn't answer.

Ravi felt like slapping the taller man's face, but the implications of what he'd learned drove such thoughts from his head. "Well, carry on."

Levin's arrogant smile told Ravi just how little weight his words carried now.

Ravi walked out of the hangar, climbed aboard his ATV, and gunned the engine. If what Levin said was true, then his phone call to Skow had been premature. Trinity might quickly become a reality despite Godin's death. And if that happened, it would change everything. Instead of looking for scapegoats, the president would be looking for chests to pin medals on. And if Ravi played his cards right, he could be first in line.

As he rode back toward his office, he glanced at the Containment building. Half-buried in sand, the concrete block exuded a sense of power he had felt nowhere else in the world. He'd experienced unease standing in nuclear power stations, but the danger in a nuclear reactor was quantifiable. Even the worst-case scenario was predictable, because nuclear fuel, however dangerous, obeyed natural laws.

Trinity would be different.

Fifty miles north of this facility, the first nuclear explosion on earth had turned the desert floor to glass. Robert Oppenheimer had stared awestruck into the eye of the resulting fireball, but his awe had been at himself as much as at the new machine he had built. But if the computer inside Containment reached its full potential—if every problem were solved and a neuromodel hit 90 percent efficiency—then Peter Godin's creation would dwarf Oppenheimer's deadly toy. For when men looked into the eye of Trinity, Trinity would *look back*. And it would know what it was looking at.

An inferior form of life.

TWENTY-NINE

I came awake in a sweat-drenched T-shirt with no idea where I was. A sticky film covered my face, and a dark-haired woman lay in bed beside me. I could tell it was a woman by the shape of her shoulder. Afternoon sunlight spilled through a curtain to my left, falling across two suitcases standing on the floor. Then I remembered . . . *Jerusalem*.

A dream had awakened me, and no normal dream. All I could see was the face of a man leaning close to kiss me. The image made me shudder, but I fought the urge to push it from my mind. *Soldiers,* I remembered. *Soldiers with swords.* I was standing in the dark, beneath a tree in a fragrant garden. Men slept around me on the ground. Their snores made me feel alone. Fear was working in me, a fear that death was approaching. I heard a commotion to my right, and then soldiers burst among the sleeping men, shouting and searching the trees. A robed man walked toward me from the shadows. With the paralysis of nightmares, I stood there as he kissed me on the cheek. His lips were waxy and cold. As he pulled back, the soldiers seized me . . .

Rachel shifted beneath the bedcovers. I looked at my watch. Three-thirty P.M., Israel time, seven hours ahead of New York.

I couldn't believe it. We'd slept almost eighteen hours. I picked up the phone beside the bed, called the lobby, and requested a car and an English-speaking driver for the afternoon. The price was 130 shekels per hour, whatever that was. Rachel stirred at the sound of my voice but did not awaken.

I should go alone, I thought, looking down at her. Then I saw an image of myself falling unconscious in the street, lost in a narcoleptic dream. I couldn't risk that. I went to the bathroom and got into the shower.

Israel was nothing like my dreams. From the moment we'd entered Ben Gurion airport in Tel Aviv, we were assaulted by modernity from every side. Radios, metal detectors, submachine guns, the odor of jet fuel. We rode from Tel Aviv to Jerusalem in a *sherut,* a hired minivan with six other people. I kept quiet most of the way, and Rachel occasionally squeezed my hand in reassurance. She could tell I was disoriented, that the scenery outside the van was not what I'd expected to find.

As we neared Jerusalem, though, I caught sight of the Old City on its hill, pristine in the dying sunlight, and my disappointment faded. Whatever I had come for, it awaited me behind those ancient walls.

It was nearly dark by the time we reached our hotel. We gave our passport numbers to the desk clerk and followed our bags up to the sixth floor. The room was clean but small. We'd planned to go out for food, but when we sat on the bed to catch our breath, jet lag and the exhaustion of the past two days caught up with us. Rachel had slept a little on the plane, but I had not. The warmth and silence of the hotel room were like a narcotic poured into my veins. I ate an orange Rachel had bought at Ben Gurion and fell into oblivion. Only the dream of the garden had brought me out of it.

I shut off the shower nozzle, toweled myself off, and

walked back into the room. Rachel had rolled onto her stomach. Her bare shoulders still showed above the covers. I went to the window and pulled back the curtain in the hope of seeing the Old City, but nondescript buildings blocked my view.

I walked to the bed and shook Rachel's arm. She didn't respond. I shook her again. She blinked several times, then stretched and got up on one elbow.

"Is that clock right?"

"Yes. We've got a car coming."

This did not seem to please her. "You still want to go today? It's late already."

"I had another dream."

"What about?"

"The Garden of Gethsemane."

She lay back on the bed and stared at the ceiling. "That's a lot further in the chronology than you were before, isn't it?"

"Yes. Gethsemane begins the countdown to the crucifixion. I have to get to the Old City. It can't wait until tomorrow."

She pulled the sheet around her, then stood and gazed into my eyes. "I think we should wait until tomorrow."

"Why?"

"We're safe in this room. It's a miracle that we even got here, and I think we need some time to recover from all we've been through."

"But my dream . . ."

She reached down and took my hand. "Nothing is going to happen to you, David. Not even if you dream of the crucifixion. You're here with me, and I know how to take care of you."

She dropped her other hand to mine, and the sheet fell around her feet. I tried not to drop my eyes, but she meant for me to see.

"Rachel, I have to go today."

"We can go. Just not yet." She laid her head against my chest and put her arms around me. "The world isn't going to end if we take a few minutes for ourselves."

She kissed my chest, then nuzzled my neck and pulled me against her waist. Her professional persona had been shed like a dead husk of skin. This new woman was a revelation to me, and I wanted her. I bent to her upturned face and kissed her. Her lips were warm and elastic, nothing like the waxy lips in my dream. A shudder passed through me at the memory.

She drew back and looked into my eyes. "What's the matter?"

"I'm okay." I leaned down to kiss her again.

She shook her head. "You're not. You're not going to be all right until we put this Jesus business to rest once and for all."

The phone rang, startling us both.

I picked it up. "Yes?"

"Your car is here, sir," said an accented voice.

"Thank you." I hung up.

Before I could explain, Rachel kissed my cheek, then turned and began to dress.

Our driver was a mustached old Palestinian named Ibrahim. His English-speaking qualification was marginal, but he understood that we wanted the Old City, and that was enough to get us to the Jaffa gate. As we approached the sun-bleached stone wall, I felt my first wave of déjà vu. Behind that wall, in that blood-drenched repository of history, lay a secret for me alone. For two thousand years it had waited, invisible to those who came with shovels, toothbrushes, files, and dental picks. What that secret was, I didn't know, but I would know it when I found it.

290

"Where do you want to start?" Rachel asked.

"Jesus' last day."

"Yes," said Ibrahim, looking back at me. "Mount of Olives, Garden of Gethsemane, place of the skull."

A motorcycle honked angrily and shot past us.

"Place of the skull?" I asked.

"In Hebrew, *Golgotha,* in Latin, *Calvary.* Where Jesus was crucified."

"That's what we want."

"Church of the Holy Sepulchre. Nine stations of the cross outside the church, last five stations inside. I take you there now."

"Why there?" Rachel asked me.

I felt a wave of heat pass through me, and for a moment I couldn't breathe. "I don't know."

"David? What's the matter?" She put a hand to my forehead. "You're burning up."

Thirty seconds ago I'd felt fine, but she was right. "Let's just hurry."

Ibrahim pulled into a parking place as a Citroën backed out. A huge tour bus blocked out the light behind us.

"Are we stopping outside the wall?" Rachel asked.

"Yes," Ibrahim replied. "Is customary to walk from here. See landmarks of the city."

"How far away is the church?"

"Holy Sepulchre? On day like today, half hour to Via Dolorosa, maybe little more."

Rachel looked doubtful. "Can you get us closer?"

"Is the mister sick?"

She hesitated. "Yes. He's come to Jerusalem in the hope that it will help."

"Ah. Many sick people go to Jesus' tomb and kiss the rock where he rose up from the death."

"Can you help us?"

"Of course. For a hundred shekels more I get you there very fast."

"Whatever it takes."

Ibrahim backed up, then honked his horn and stepped on the gas, earning curses from a shawled woman who had to dodge his front bumper to save her life. Another wave of heat rolled through me. I was afraid I might pass out.

"Is it narcolepsy?" Rachel asked.

"No. Different."

"We should go back to the hotel."

"No. The Via Dolorosa."

"Via Dolorosa," echoed Ibrahim. "Way of Sadness. Christians here call it the Way of Flowers. First station Jesus condemned to death, second station the cross was forced upon him, third station he stumbled for the first time, fourth station . . ."

Our guide's voice quickly became a drone I couldn't follow. Sweat poured from my skin, and I felt suddenly cold. As our car whipped through the narrow streets, I saw stone walls, bright shutters, market stalls spilling knick-knacks from their shelves, and tourists dressed in the apparel of a hundred nations. Ibrahim rolled down his window to curse someone, and the scent of jasmine filled the car. When it entered my nostrils, I felt a sudden euphoria, and then everything went white.

THIRTY

"David? Wake up. We're here."

Someone was shaking my shoulder. I blinked and sat up. Rachel was leaning in through the back door of the car.

"Where are we?"

"The Via Dolorosa. It's a surrealist painting in motion. Do you still want to see it?"

I pulled myself out of the car and stood gazing in awe at the throngs of tourists, four of whom carried large wooden crosses over their shoulder. Two of the would-be Jesuses wore white robes, the others street clothes. The crosses had wheels to ease the burden, which to me made the act of carrying them almost pointless.

"Do you recognize anything from your dreams?" Rachel asked.

"No. Let's go."

Ibrahim led us along a cobbled street, weaving through the tourists with practiced ease. I had expected to find reverence here, but the atmosphere was more like a circus. A babel of voices reverberated between the walls: German, French, English, Russian, Hebrew, Arabic, Japanese, and Italian, and those just the languages I recognized. A man with a crew cut and an Alabama accent preached fire and brimstone to a group of Japanese pilgrims. Ibrahim talked all the way, his spiel honed to an emotionless monotone over years of guiding.

"Wait," Rachel said, stopping him. She turned to me. "What do you want to see?"

"Where are we?"

Ibrahim smiled. "Sir, up there at the blue door is the Omaria School, site of the first station of the cross, where Jesus was condemned to death."

"Do you want to see that?" Rachel asked.

"No. What's the second station?"

Ibrahim pointed down the cobbled street to a half circle of bricks set in the street. "There is where Jesus began to carry the cross. Down the street is the Chapel of Flagellation, where the Roman soldiers whipped Jesus, set on him a crown of thorns, and said, 'Hail, King of the Jews!' Then Pilate led him to the crowd and cried, *'Ecce homo! Behold the man!'*"

Ibrahim delivered this information with the excitement of a man reading bingo numbers in a nursing home.

"Go on," I said. "To the church."

Our guide continued down the street. We passed a black door set in a white stone arch, and Ibrahim said something about Jesus falling for the first time. I stared at the door but felt nothing. Perhaps what I sought lay buried beneath this warren of streets and shops and awnings. Jerusalem was probably like Cairo, built upon its own bones, a place where any new construction unearthed lost chapters of history.

Ibrahim led us to another semicircle of bricks and started his spiel again. "This is the fifth station, where the Romans soldiers compelled Simon of Cyrene to help Jesus carry the cross."

Rachel glanced at me. "Keep moving."

A smiling boy wandered by selling thorn crowns. He took my stare as a sign of interest, but Ibrahim shooed him away.

As I watched the bundle of thorns bob down the street on the boy's arm, blackness filled my vision, and my knees went to water. Rachel slipped under my right arm, and together we stumbled after Ibrahim.

The next few stops were a blur, the Palestinian's words blending in a rush of strange images: *Here Veronica wiped Jesus' tormented face, at which his true likeness was miraculously imprinted on the veil . . . here Jesus fell the second time . . . here he said, "Daughters of Jerusalem, do not weep for me, but weep for yourselves and for your children" . . .*

We passed over a rooftop and through a dark chapel, and then I found myself in a crowded courtyard before a Romanesque church. Pilgrims, priests, and nuns moved under the watchful eyes of a dozen Israeli soldiers with submachine guns.

"This is Church of the Holy Sepulchre," Ibrahim said, waving his arm toward the building. "Built by Crusaders over fifty years between 1099 and 1149. Original basilica was built by Queen Helena, mother of Constantine, who came here in 325 and discovered pieces of the true cross in cave below the earth."

I looked with dismay at the line of tourists before the door.

"This not bad," Ibrahim said. "Tourism very bad for this time of year. The fighting scare everyone away, even in Western Holy Week. Good for you, bad for me. Do you feel all right, sir? I could get you some water while we wait."

"I'm fine."

"You can put more weight on me," Rachel said, repositioning herself under my arm.

I leaned a little harder on her. "Thanks."

She touched my cheek with the back of her hand. "I wish I could take your blood pressure."

"To the right of the entrance is tenth station," said Ibrahim. "There Jesus was stripped of his clothes. Last five stations of the cross are contained within the church itself."

295

"It's strange, isn't it?" Rachel said quietly. "Millions of people traveling to see an empty tomb?"

All I could manage was a nod.

"This is only empty tomb in any Christian church on earth," said Ibrahim. "The angel asked the Marys, 'Whom do you seek?' 'Jesus of Nazareth,' they said. 'He is not here,' said the angel. 'He is risen.'"

The courtyard suddenly faded before me, and my limbs grew less heavy. I seemed to float on Rachel's arm.

"David?" she asked. "Can you hear me?"

I blinked and found myself looking at a stone ceiling. "Are we inside the church?"

"You were *sleepwalking*," she whispered, her eyes filled with anxiety. "We have to get you back to the hotel."

"We're here now. We made it. I have to see it."

"See *what*?"

And then I knew. "The tomb."

She turned to Ibrahim. "Where is Jesus' tomb?"

"This way. All the sites close together in this church." He pointed at a reddish marble slab on the floor. Several men and women in street clothes knelt with their faces pressed to the stone. Above them, a woman poured something on the slab. A sickly sweet wave of perfume hit me.

"What's that?" I asked.

"The Stone of Unction," said Ibrahim, "where Jesus' body was anointed with oils and wrapped in a shroud after he was taken down from the cross."

I moved closer, but I felt nothing. "Is this the original stone?"

"No, sir. This stone dates from 1810 and replaces stone from twelfth century. Nothing certain is known beyond that time. This way, sir."

He led us to the left, into the rotunda of the church. Light cascaded down from a spectacular gold and white dome. Below the dome stood a large rectangular edifice of marble that seemed to have been boxed for shipping in great metal bands. It was topped by a cupola that looked like it belonged on the Kremlin.

"What's that?" I asked.

"This is the Holy Tomb, sir. Called the Edicule, or little house. Because Jesus was very important man, Byzantines and Crusaders spent a lot of money to make this tomb for him. It is fourteenth and final station of the cross. By the customs of Jews, always they buried the people outside the city. The present marble exterior is disintegrating and must be held together by iron bands. Come, sir? Get in the line? Madam?"

Ibrahim continued his unrelenting recitation, but I was too disoriented to process it. I'd expected the tomb of Jesus to be a cave of some kind, situated in an open place, not this mausoleum in a dungeon-like medieval church.

"The line's moving," Rachel said, helping me forward.

Soon we were standing before the door of the Edicule. Here Ibrahim spoke with the respect I had expected from the beginning.

"Inside the tomb we will see two rooms. Let us go in now."

In the first room I saw a podium with a glass case atop it. Inside the case lay a piece of stone.

"This we call the room of the angel," said Ibrahim. "Where the dead person wait until they prepare place to bury him. Here is kept a piece of the rolling stone where angels opened the tomb and Jesus raised up from the dead."

I noticed two holes in the wall to my right. Ibrahim said, "When the people have no fire for their Easter candles, the priest he stand here and give them from the Holy Fire, gives light from his big candle to theirs."

My attention had been drawn to a low door in the thick marble wall of the inner tomb. I stooped and moved through the door into a small inner chamber. A man and woman knelt in prayer before what appeared to be a marble altar slab. They had placed crucifixes on the stone, as though the objects would be blessed by contact. Above them hung ornate silver lamps on chains, and everywhere burning candles threw flickering light around the room. Vases of white roses scented the air, their odor cloying in the small space.

"David?" Rachel whispered. "Is this what you came to see?"

I leaned down and touched the marble stone before the praying couple. I didn't know what I'd expected, but something. I'd felt more at Stonehenge when I climbed over the barrier and touched the sarsen stones. "This isn't the place."

"What?"

"Nothing happened here."

The kneeling man and woman looked up at me, their eyes wide.

"Sir, you must not say this," Ibrahim said from behind me. "This is most holy place."

"This isn't the place," I repeated. I ducked down and hurried back onto the floor of the rotunda.

Rachel came after me. The people waiting in line stared at us, sensing trouble. I didn't care. A wild feeling of panic had gripped me. Soon it would be dark outside, and I had not found what I'd come for.

"Tell me what's happening," Rachel whispered.

"Nothing happened in there. That's not the place."

Someone in the line gasped.

"What place?" asked Rachel.

I turned to Ibrahim, who now had a walkie-talkie in his hand and seemed to be debating whether to call for help. "Is that the original stone in the tomb?"

"No, sir. Marble stone was put there to cover the actual stone where Jesus' body lay."

"You can't see the actual stone?"

Our guide's face brightened. "Yes, you can see this. Touch also. Follow me."

He led us to the rear of the Edicule. There stood another chapel, much less ostentatious and open to the rotunda. It was far more colorful than the marble tomb we'd left, with bright wall hangings, wrought iron, and a casually dressed young man with a five-o'clock shadow tending it.

"This is the holy tomb from the other side, sir," Ibrahim said in a whisper. "Part of the Coptic chapel. Coptics are Christians from Egypt. Very devout."

The queue here was much shorter. It disappeared into the shallow chapel and stopped where a small curtain shielded something.

"Sir, beyond that point lies exposed part of the actual stone where Jesus lay. Here the sick come to be cured, people to be blessed."

As I waited for the line to move, my skin began to itch as though from hives. At last my turn came. I went through the curtain, knelt, and laid my right palm on the bare stone.

"David?" Rachel whispered from behind me.

I shook my head. "Nothing." For the first time in six months, I began to truly doubt my sanity.

"I think we should go back to the hotel," Rachel said. "Ibrahim is close to calling for help."

I scrambled up and left the chapel, my mind racing. Ibrahim was staring at me as though I might start shouting blasphemy, which the old guide had probably seen in his day. The walkie-talkie was still in his hand.

"Nothing happened there either," I told him. "That's not the place."

"But, sir, this is the holy tomb."

"There's no doubt of that?"

"Well . . . some Protestant Christians believe the garden tomb outside the city is the site of Jesus' tomb. But no archaeologist believes this. You have seen the actual tomb, sir."

A tall, plain woman carrying a King James Bible stepped out of the line before the chapel and said in English, "Does it really matter where the tomb is, brother? 'He is not there. He is risen.'"

"Does it matter?" I asked her. "Of *course* it matters. What if you found the actual tomb with Jesus' bones still in it? It's the difference between a legitimate religion and mass hysteria."

The woman almost jumped backward.

Ibrahim looked stricken. "Sir! You must not say these things!"

"You're a Muslim, Ibrahim. You don't believe any of this."

"Please, sir—"

I walked away from the Edicule, not knowing where to turn or what to do.

Rachel appeared at my shoulder. "David, what is it you're looking for?"

"The place where Jesus was resurrected."

"But you don't believe in God. How can you find the place where Jesus was resurrected when you don't believe that he was?"

Ibrahim had caught up to us. "Sir? Some people believe Jesus rose from the death at another place. I will show you."

He led us across the rotunda to the door of a large church wholly contained within the bounds of the greater one.

"This is the Catholicon." He pointed toward a chandelier. "Below the cupola of this church is a marble basin called the Omphalos. The navel of the world. Some Greeks believe Jesus was resurrected here, and will return here to judge the world one day."

"Can we see it?"

"This church is usually closed, but I can take you to it."

He led us past a chain toward a stone chalice standing on

an inlaid floor. High above stood a dome with an ethereal image of Christ painted in pastel hues. I looked down at the stone hemisphere, essentially a large bowl. Then I leaned down and touched it. I felt no more than I would had I touched a birdbath in someone's backyard.

Rachel instantly read my reaction. "What are you hoping for? An electric shock? A voice from heaven?"

I turned to our guide, who was shaking his head. "What have I not seen, Ibrahim?"

"Many things. Most important is Golgotha. In Latin called Calvary. The place where Jesus was crucified."

"It's inside the church?"

"Of course, sir. Follow me."

He led us out of the Catholicon and over to a steep staircase. I counted eighteen steps as I plodded upward, my spirits sinking lower the higher I climbed.

The moment I reached the top of the stairs, I felt a quickening in my blood. The room was crowded, but to my left, above the heads of the people, I saw a life-size sculpture of Jesus hanging on a cross. He wore a silver cloth around his waist and a crown of silver on his head. It wasn't the sculpture that moved me, but something in the room itself. I felt as if I were standing close to a high-voltage cable, with static electricity raising every hair on my body.

"What?" Rachel asked. "What is it?"

"Something in me is vibrating."

"You've felt that before. That's a textbook precursor to a hypnagogic hallucination."

"No . . . this is different."

"Ibrahim?" said Rachel.

"Yes, madam?"

"We're going back to the car."

"Yes," he said with relief.

I stepped away from them. To my right, a mural showed

Jesus lying on the cross, which lay flat on the ground. Some people standing before the mural parted, revealing a cabinet with panels of hammered silver. As I walked toward the mural, pain radiated up my arm from my left hand. For a moment I thought I was having a heart attack. Then pain shot up my right arm as well. I clenched both hands into fists, but it did no good. I turned to Ibrahim.

"What is this place?"

"This is the eleventh station, sir. Where Jesus was nailed to the cross."

I moaned.

"We have to get him out of here," Rachel said. "Can you get help?"

"He is walking," Ibrahim said. "Let us go now."

"I don't think he'll go."

Some people in the room were staring at me as if I might be mad.

"I can get soldiers," Ibrahim said. "But I would rather not do this."

"No," Rachel said quickly. "I mean, yes. That's not necessary."

A group of pilgrims moved away from the sculpture of Jesus, revealing a fantastically ornate altar. I stepped forward, my eyes locked on a silver-clad Madonna standing below the cross. The altar before her seemed to be sitting on a large glass case, and under the glass I saw rough gray rock.

"What's that?"

"Golgotha," Ibrahim answered. "The place of the skull. That is the mountain itself, where the rock cracked when Jesus' blood fell down from the cross. Then came the earthquake."

Searing white light blotted out the scene before me. I saw the mountain as it had been before the church was here, a bare, rocky hill beside a mountain riddled with tombs. Three crosses stood on the hill, but no one hung from them. The sky darkened and went black, and I fell to my knees.

I found myself staring at a shining silver disk with a hole in it. The disk lay on the marble base of the altar, a foot off the floor. I put out my shaking right hand and laid my palm on the disk.

The pain in my hands instantly eased.

"This is the place," I said. "This is where Jesus left the earth."

"He is right," said Ibrahim. "That disk marks the spot where the cross stood in the ground. To the right and left are black disks where the thieves' crosses stood, one being good, another being bad. Afterward, Jesus was taken away to the tomb of Joseph of Aramathea and rose from the death three days later."

"No," I said.

Ibrahim blanched. "Sir, you cannot say such things here!"

"Whisper," Rachel pleaded.

"What's the hole in the disk for?" I asked, my hand caressing the cool silver.

"You may put fingers through and touch Golgotha. The rock of Calvary."

I closed my eyes and slipped two fingers through the hole. My fingertips scraped rough stone.

"Did you dream of this?" Rachel asked.

I couldn't speak. Something was flowing into me from the living rock. Rachel's voice receded and did not return. I felt as if my bones were singing, vibrating in sympathy with something in the earth. At first the feeling was something like joy, but as the intensity built, I began to shake, then to jerk spastically.

It's a seizure, said a familiar voice in my head. My medical voice. *A tonic-clonic seizure.* Through the fog of receding consciousness, I heard people yelling in several languages. Then I fell, and Rachel screamed.

The impact of the floor was like water.

THIRTY-ONE

WHITE SANDS

At 7:52 A.M. mountain standard time, Peter Godin went into code blue. Ravi Nara wasn't in the hospital hangar, but he was sleeping nearby, and he got to Godin's bedside in less than two minutes. He'd been expecting the old man to crash. Without a shunt to relieve the pressure in the fourth ventricle of the brain, hydrocephalus was inevitable. But when Ravi arrived in the Bubble, he found the old man suffering a garden-variety heart attack.

Godin's two nurses had already intubated and bagged him, and one was defibrillating his heart. Ravi read the EKG and confirmed their diagnosis: ventricular tachycardia. They were using the paddles because Godin had no pulse. It took two drug combinations and a 360-joule shock to bring the heart back to a sinus rhythm. Ravi drew blood to check for cardiac-specific enzymes that would tell him how much damage had been done to the heart muscle. Then, since Godin remained unconscious, Ravi sat down for a moment to decompress.

He hated clinical medicine. Something was always coming out of left field to surprise you. Godin had had a coronary bypass fifteen years ago, and a cardiac stent implanted in 1998.

304

The risk of an MI was constant, but under the strain of treating the brainstem glioma, Ravi had let the cardiac risk recede in his mind. The nurses had noticed his hesitancy during the code. Not exactly what they expected from a Nobel laureate in medicine. After years in research labs, he was out of practice. So what? A veterinarian could run the protocols of a code blue.

As a nurse started to attach the ventilator to Godin's breathing tube, the old man tried to speak, but his effort produced only squeaks.

Ravi leaned down to his ear. "Don't try to talk, Peter. You had a little arrhythmia, but you're stable now."

Godin held up his hand for something to write with. A nurse gave him a pen, then held a hard-backed pad up to his hand.

Godin scribbled: *DON'T LET ME DIE! WE'RE SO CLOSE!!!*

"You're not going to die," Ravi assured him, though he was far from sure himself. Hypoxia could easily trigger the fatal hydrocephalus he'd been expecting. He squeezed Godin's shoulder, then ordered the nurses to put him on the ventilator. It would make the old man furious, but he would endure it.

To avoid Godin's protests, Ravi left the Bubble. As he closed the hatch, he saw Zach Levin rush into the hangar.

"What is it?" Ravi asked. "What's happened?"

Levin had to catch his breath before he could speak. "Fielding's model is cracking the final algorithms! He's got the memory area linked to the processing areas, and he's creating all new interface circuitry. I've never seen anything like it."

"You mean Fielding's *model* is doing all that."

"Yes, yes. But I've got to tell you, even with the machine running at only fifty percent capacity, I can feel him in there. It's like talking to the man I worked with for the past two years. Like he's alive again."

"You're at fifty percent efficiency?"

Levin grinned. "And rising. I should have had more faith in Peter's instincts."

Ravi tried to conceal his shock. Ninety percent efficiency was the point at which Godin had predicted that a neuro-model would become fully conscious—a condition he had termed the *Trinity state*.

"You said 'talking,'" Ravi thought aloud. "Is the voice synthesizer working? Is Fielding talking to you?"

"He's trying. He can't really explain what he's doing, but the efficiency is creeping steadily upward. We've got a definite timeline now."

Despite the complexities of his personal situation, Ravi couldn't suppress his excitement. "How long?"

"Twelve to sixteen hours."

"To Trinity state?"

Levin nodded. "And I'd bet closer to twelve. We've got a pool going in Containment."

Ravi looked at his watch. "How certain are you?"

"As certain as anything gets in this business. I've got to tell Peter what's happening."

Ravi didn't want Godin hearing about this until he had talked to Skow. "You can't go in right now. He won't hear you. Peter coded twenty minutes ago."

Levin stiffened in alarm. "He's not dead!"

"No, but he's on the ventilator."

"Conscious?"

"Not enough to understand you. And he can't speak."

"But he has to know this! It will double his will to fight."

Ravi tried to look sympathetic. "He's never lacked that."

"No, but this will change everything."

"I'm sorry, Zach. I can't allow you to go in."

Levin looked down at Ravi with disdain. "You don't

306

make decisions like that. Limiting Peter's access to critical information?"

"I am his physician."

"So, do your fucking job. It doesn't take a doctor to see that the best thing anyone could do for Peter's health right now is to give him this information."

Levin turned away and stepped into the UV decontaminator. Ravi started to argue, but the engineer stamped on the start button, making conversation pointless.

If Levin insisted on entering the Bubble, Ravi couldn't stop him. Godin would probably ask for him soon anyway.

Ravi hurried to the exit. He needed to talk to Skow immediately. Because Zach Levin was right: with Trinity twelve to sixteen hours from becoming a reality, Godin would almost certainly live to see it. And that changed everything. Skow was preparing the president for Trinity's failure, setting up to blame Godin for everything, and using Ravi to help him do it. If Skow went too far—and Godin at the eleventh hour delivered the revolutionary computer he had promised—Ravi could find himself in a precarious position. Peter Godin would not take betrayal lightly. He would exact his own form of justice. An image of Geli Bauer came into Ravi's mind. He was damned glad she was lying in a hospital in Maryland.

JERUSALEM

Rachel braced herself against the side of the ambulance as it tore through all but impassable traffic. David lay unconscious on a gurney on the floor. The paramedic in the back spoke enough English to communicate with Rachel, but he could tell her little and do even less, given his patient's condition.

When David collapsed in the church, Rachel had known instantly that he was having a seizure. She'd knelt and cradled his head to keep him from banging it on the floor, but that was all she could do. Seizure victims swallowing their tongues was a myth, and you could lose fingers trying to prevent it. Ibrahim had used his walkie-talkie to call the ambulance, and Rachel got the feeling he'd done it before.

Israeli soldiers quickly cordoned off the chapel. By the time the ambulance arrived, David's seizure was over, but he had not awakened. The paramedics checked his blood sugar and found a normal glucose level. With coma, that was the limit of what they could do at the scene, so they fitted a collar on him, put him on a backboard, and had the soldiers carry him out to the ambulance in the courtyard.

As they careened though the streets, Rachel mentally raced through the possible causes of coma. Drugs were the most common cause after hypoglycemia, but David had no history of substance abuse. He hadn't hit the floor hard enough to cause head trauma, and forty-one was old even for late-onset epilepsy, though she'd suspected it ever since hearing about the hallucinations. *Ravi Nara ruled out epilepsy,* she recalled.

A stroke could cause seizure and coma, but only rarely. Poisoning? She thought of the white powder from Fielding's FedEx envelope. Had there been some toxic agent in the "sand" that the Duke scientists had failed to detect? West Nile encephalitis was a possibility. David could have been bitten by a mosquito in Tennessee and only now have developed brain swelling. He could also have picked up a meningitis bacterium in JFK airport. A brain tumor was possible, but Trinity's Super-MRI unit should have detected any masses.

Even as she made mental notes to relate all this to the emergency physician, Rachel cursed herself for not insisting that David submit to a full workup while under her care. Actually, she *had* insisted. He had refused.

The ambulance finally broke out of traffic and accelerated up a long green hill toward a building that looked like a

308

fortress. Its roof was studded with more satellite dishes and antennae than a television station.

"Is that the hospital?" Rachel asked.

The paramedic nodded. "Hadassah. The best."

They screeched to a stop in a concrete receiving area, and the paramedics rolled David into the emergency department. They didn't waste time with triage; they took him straight to a treatment room. Rachel had told them she was a physician, so they allowed her to follow them. She took a chair against the wall and stayed out of the way.

A nurse checked David's IV, then switched him from bottled oxygen to hospital oxygen. Another undressed him and attached leads from a heart monitor to his chest. Seeing David naked and helpless pierced Rachel in a place that her professional armor did not cover. She took his money belt and clothes and put them into a plastic bag.

A man in white came to the door and spoke Hebrew to the paramedics. He glanced at Rachel, then entered and in heavily accented English asked her to summarize what had happened at the church. She complied, then gave David's medical history as best she knew it.

He had been unconscious for thirty minutes. Most patients suffering a grand mal seizure would be coming out of it by now. The doctor ordered blood work; X rays of the chest and cervical spine; a CT scan to rule out stroke, tumors, or subarachnoid hemorrhage; and a spinal tap to rule out meningitis.

After a nurse drew the blood, an aide moved David to radiology for the CT scan, which took nearly an hour. When he returned to the treatment room, he was still unconscious. Next the ER doctor performed the spinal puncture. The escaping spinal fluid had normal pressure, and Rachel breathed much easier when she saw that the fluid was clear. Infection was highly unlikely.

The next step was a referral to neurology, and at that

point Rachel began to panic. A neurology referral meant admission to the hospital, which would bring questions about medical insurance and payment. There was $15,000 in the two money belts, but she didn't want to raise suspicions by showing that kind of cash. She nearly hugged the ER doctor when he informed her that there were no beds available in neurology. David would have to remain in the emergency department.

When an EEG tech wheeled in a portable machine to do an electroencephalogram of David's brain, Rachel saw instantly that he was sharp. He switched off most of the electrical equipment in the room before performing the test, which eliminated background interference and made for a much clearer tracing.

As the tracing emerged from the machine, the tech looked concerned, and Rachel soon saw why. David's brain showed only alpha wave activity, of uniform frequency and amplitude. The tech leaned forward and clapped his hands near David's right ear, but the alpha waves did not desynchronize. They didn't change at all.

Rachel's heart sank. David appeared to be in a state known as alpha coma. Few patients emerged alive from alpha coma.

"Are you a doctor?" the tech asked, noticing her expression.

"Yes."

His eyes softened. "I'm sorry."

As he reached to shut off the machine, Rachel saw a theta wave appear on the screen.

"Wait!" she cried, pointing.

"I see it."

The theta waves increased steadily in amplitude. Then some beta waves appeared.

"He's *dreaming*," Rachel said, hardly believing it. "Could he only be asleep?"

The tech pinched David's arm. There was no response. He leaned down to one ear and yelled, "Wake up!"

Nothing.

"He's not sleeping," the tech said thoughtfully. "But those thetas are definitely increasing in strength."

"What do you think is happening?"

"This guy's definitely in alpha coma. But his brain is doing something. What, I don't know." The tech walked to the door, then looked back at Rachel. "I'm going to leave the machine connected and get a neurologist down here. Okay?"

"Thank you."

She sat alone beside the bed, her hands shaking as she watched the screen. Until she'd seen that theta wave, she'd believed David was as good as dead. Now she had no idea what was happening. But *something* was going on in his head. Could he be hallucinating in coma as he had during his narcoleptic attacks? Maybe he wasn't really in coma at all. Sometimes a patient could appear to be comatose when he was actually having small seizures. Yet the EEG didn't show that. It showed an alpha coma state, interrupted by inexplicable theta and beta intrusions.

She didn't want to think about what David had been doing prior to his seizure, but she couldn't stop herself. In the medieval gloom of Holy Sepulchre, he had been searching for some remnant of Jesus' life on earth. Or of his death. He had scorned the traditional places venerated by pilgrims—the anointing stone, the tomb itself—but at the place marked as the spot where Jesus died on the cross, he had fallen to his knees and whispered, "*This is the place.*" Then the seizure had started.

The incident had actually begun before that. When David looked at the mural depicting Christ being nailed to the cross, he had clenched his fists as though his hands were in agony. What had been going on in his mind? Did he really believe that he was Jesus Christ? Believe it so completely that he felt

311

Jesus' wounds? She'd heard of cases of stigmata caused by the mind, but she had never really believed them. Was she witnessing something similar?

She grasped David's limp hand. Despite the EEG, she half-expected him to open his eyes. Yet they remained closed. She silently thanked God that the ER doctor had ordered a CT scan rather than an MRI. How could she have talked him out of what he would see as a harmless imaging test? How could she protect David from anything here? She didn't know what her enemy was. The only person she could think of who might have answers about this strange coma was Ravi Nara. But according to David, Nara was part of the group that wanted to kill them.

"Wake up, David," she said softly in his ear. "For God's sake, wake up."

THIRTY-TWO

WHITE SANDS

Ravi Nara parked his ATV outside the hospital hangar and walked to the door. In his pocket was a syringe of potassium chloride that would stop Godin's weakened heart as surely as a bullet.

He paused at the hangar door, unable to open it. It had taken hours to steel himself for this visit, and without Skow threatening him, he would not have made it this far. *They're watching this on monitors somewhere,* he said to himself. *Move.*

He entered the hangar, slipped on a fresh lab coat, then walked into the decontaminator and stepped on the floor switch. High-intensity UV light bombarded him from all sides. As he stood in the purple glow, he stared through the hatch in the Bubble. Godin's nurses sat like guard dogs on either side of the bed. *It's him or me,* he told himself. *Remember what Skow said. . . .*

The NSA man had not shouted with joy when he'd learned that the computer might reach Trinity state within twelve hours. He'd asked how long Godin was likely to live. When Ravi answered more than twelve hours, Skow told him that could not be allowed to happen.

"Why not?" Ravi had asked, afraid he already knew the answer.

"Because it's too late," Skow snapped. "The president called me from China, very upset about the Tennant situation. Very suspicious, too. I had to tell him something that made sense."

"Something besides the truth, you mean."

"Exactly. I told him that Peter has been ill all along, and that I was afraid he might be responsible for Fielding's death. I told him that Peter had disappeared, and that there might be a secret research facility somewhere. The FBI is tearing apart the Godin Supercomputing complex in Mountain View as we speak."

Ravi shut his eyes and prayed this was a nightmare. In the conference room in North Carolina, the decision to end Fielding's life had seemed almost an official government act. Trinity existed to strengthen America's strategic position in the world. Fielding had sabotaged its progress. But when you stripped away the window dressing, Fielding's "termination" had been plain old murder.

"Ravi?"

"I'm here." He knew what Skow was going to ask of him. And he dreaded it.

"You know what has to be done."

Ravi made one last stand. "You said that if we delivered Trinity, no one would care who had died to make it happen."

"That was before the mess with Tennant. We've had a shooting in Washington, for God's sake. I've painted Tennant as a dangerous psychotic, but that's all right. I have medical evidence to support that."

"Those are problems for *you,* not me."

Skow spoke calmly, but his words chilled Ravi's blood. "You're not the only person who knows you were part of Fielding's death. I have recordings of you. Very incriminating recordings. We're all in the same boat, Ravi. You, me, Geli, and General Bauer. If we all tell the same story, no one can touch us. But Peter has to die."

Ravi closed his eyes in anguish.

"Our lives are in your hands, Ravi. A few seconds of courage will wash you clean."

Clean? he thought. *I'll never be clean again.*

Was it morally wrong to kill Godin? The man was only hours from a natural death, and without Ravi he would have died days ago. Godin had ordered the murder of Andrew Fielding without any visible compunction. And beyond that, there was the almost fantastic reality that killing Godin's biological body would not really end his life. As long as his neuromodel existed, his mind and personality could be resurrected in the Trinity computer.

The problem was not one of morality, but of opportunity. When a man was as sick as Godin, there were a half dozen ways to push him over the edge. But Godin's nurses never left him alone. Ravi had tested them twice today; in both instances they had taken cell phones from their pockets and awakened sleeping relief nurses for assistance.

After considering several options, Ravi had prepared the syringe of potassium chloride. As a diversion, he would trigger an alarm on one of the monitors, then inject the potassium into Godin's IV line. A code blue would follow—one that Godin would never survive.

The UV lights of the decontaminator buzzed and went dark. Ravi saw the blur of nurse's whites through the Bubble's Plexiglas door.

Where the hell is Geli Bauer? he thought. *This job is tailor-made for her.*

Ravi opened the Bubble's hatch and stopped, his throat sealed shut. Standing beside one of Godin's nurses was Geli Bauer. She wore black from head to toe, and she looked

315

every bit as dangerous as she had when he had last seen her in North Carolina.

"Hello, Ravi," she said. "You look surprised to see me."

Ravi could not speak. Geli wore an armored vest over her black bodysuit, and a web belt laden with pistol, Taser, and knife.

Godin raised the upper half of his bed with a switch, his blue eyes locked on Ravi. Only then did Ravi realize that Godin had been taken off the ventilator.

"What do you have to say, Ravi?" the old man asked.

"I'm surprised to see Geli up and around," he stammered. "I'd heard it was a neck wound."

Geli smiled, then pulled down her black turtleneck, revealing a white pressure bandage. "Just another scar to add to my collection. I had a good surgical team."

Ravi's heart thumped against his sternum. What the hell was Geli doing in White Sands? And why was she guarding Godin? According to Skow, she'd accepted the necessity of Godin's death and was on board with Skow's plan.

The old man seemed amused by Ravi's discomfort. "Well, here I am, back from the dead," he rasped. "They tell me it was my heart this time."

"Ventricular tachycardia," Ravi confirmed.

"I hear it was my nurses who brought me back."

All Ravi could think about was the syringe in his pocket. He felt sure that Geli was going to walk over to him, pull out the syringe, and jam it into his jugular vein.

"They did everything perfectly," Ravi said.

Godin nodded. "Would you have done the same, Ravi? If you were alone with me?"

Ravi's stomach flipped over. "I don't understand, Peter. Of course I would have."

Godin ignored his answer. "As for Geli . . . I wanted her with me. I feel safer when she's around."

The piercing blue eyes fixed Ravi with a relentless stare. "What are you doing here, Dr. Nara?"

"I was hoping to take you off the ventilator. But I see your nurses have already done that."

Godin glanced at Geli. They seemed to be sharing a private joke.

Ravi searched for something to support his lie. "Levin told me the prototype could reach Trinity state soon. I knew you'd want to be as alert as possible when that happens."

"And all due to Andrew Fielding," Godin said. "The ironies are breathtaking."

Ravi glanced nervously at Geli. "It's a miracle, Peter. You're going to live to see your dream come true."

Godin's lids descended until his eyes were slits. "Really? Have you heard from Skow lately?"

Ravi's blood pressure plummeted. "I spoke to him earlier today. He's very excited. He's going to fly out soon."

Godin snorted. "He wants to be present at the creation?"

"I suppose so. I mean, naturally he does."

The ensuing silence became almost unbearable. Ravi couldn't bring himself to look into Geli's eyes. He was searching for an excuse to leave when Godin said, "How long do I have left? Worst case?"

Ravi was too frightened to speak anything but the truth. "You could code again in the next half hour. If you chew your food wrong, it could trigger fatal hydrocephalus."

Godin nodded soberly. "What's the longest I could live?"

"Maybe . . . twenty-four hours."

Ravi marshaled all his courage and stepped toward the bed. "I'd like to do a quick examination, if you don't mind."

Geli blocked his path. She did nothing overtly threatening, but her very posture seemed dangerous. Ravi could hardly believe he'd once spent hours fantasizing about having sex

317

with her. The idea that he could satisfy a woman of such strength and power seemed ludicrous.

"Search him," Godin said.

Ravi knew then that he was lost. He wanted to bolt, but he was like a man facing an attack dog. If he ran, Geli would pounce and rip his throat out.

She knelt before him and patted him down. She gave his groin a taunting scratch with her fingernail, but as her hand passed over his right thigh, her eyes lit up like a mischievous child's. Reaching into his pocket, she pulled out the loaded syringe, which she held up for Godin to see.

"What's in that?" Godin asked.

"Epinephrine," Ravi said. "In case of another code. I wanted to be ready."

Geli shook her head. "I just reviewed a surveillance tape of you in the dispensary earlier this afternoon. It shows you filling this syringe from a bottle marked KCl. Potassium chloride."

Ravi's hands began to shake.

Godin spoke in a neutral voice. "Dr. Thomas Case from Johns Hopkins is being flown here as we speak. You will brief him when he arrives. Dr. Case will perform any hands-on treatment that is required after that point."

Ravi's face felt numb.

Godin's eyes sought him out, refusing to let him hide. "You couldn't wait one day for the cancer to take me?"

What could he say? Would blaming Skow spare him anything?

"Don't answer," Godin said. "Despite past glory, you want more. You look at your achievements not with pride, but with fear that you might never repeat them. You're a pygmy in your soul, Ravi. Andrew Fielding was worth ten of you."

"And of you," Ravi said, surprising himself. "Is that why you killed him?"

The blue eyes closed, but Godin answered in a clear voice. "Fielding was a great physicist, but no man can hold back the future. He'll have another chance at life. He's partly alive in Containment now, and one day his model will reach Trinity state. On that day, he'll understand what I've done. Now . . . it's time for you to go."

Ravi had never seen Geli Bauer smile with more pleasure than she did now. Taller than he by three inches, she draped her arm around him like a lover. Then she looked down into his eyes with chilling intimacy.

"There's only one question we need answered," she said. "Did you hatch this in your own little overheated brain, or did you have help?"

You already know that, Ravi thought. He tried to slip out from under her arm, but Geli only tightened her grip. Then she ran a fingernail along his shoulder to his neck. "Come on, Ravi . . . haven't you ever fantasized about spending some time alone with me?"

He feared his bladder would let go.

JERUSALEM

For Rachel the night had not passed without hope. But as dawn crept over the Dead Sea and lighted the valley of Kidron, she sank slowly into despair.

David was dying.

The neurologist who had appeared to evaluate him yesterday evening was a short, good-humored man named Weinstein. Dr. Weinstein had dark hair and quick black eyes that missed nothing. He'd done some training at Massachusetts General in Boston, and he spoke perfect English.

As soon as he read the EEG, he ordered an MRI scan of David's brain. Rachel decided then that she had to tell part of the truth. She asked Weinstein if he'd heard of Ravi Nara. The neurologist knew Nara's work and was impressed that his new patient had done research with the Nobel laureate. Rachel explained that Nara's research involved a highly advanced MRI unit that caused neurological side effects in some people. For this reason she begged Weinstein to postpone any MRI scans until there was no other option.

"I understand what you're telling me," Weinstein said. "And I'm intrigued. But in my opinion this man is very close to death. I'm sure you're aware that diffusion-weighted MRI images show the brain stem far more clearly than a CT scan. There's just too much heavy bone in that area for CT to image it well."

"I know," Rachel said. "But do you *really* think this coma is being caused by a tumor in the brain stem?"

The neurologist shrugged. "Frankly, it's the only thing we haven't ruled out. You're thinking Dr. Nara's scans would have turned up any masses?"

"Yes."

Weinstein folded his arms and sighed. "You know what I think?"

"What?"

"Your friend is going to die very soon if we don't find out what's wrong with him."

Sixty minutes later, Weinstein was reading diffusion-weighted MRI scans of David's brain stem. They showed no tumor. As he related his findings to Rachel, David's theta and beta waves vanished from the EEG screen. Rachel grabbed the tracing, which now displayed only the uniform alpha wave of alpha coma.

She began to cry.

Dr. Weinstein put an arm around her. "There's no way an MRI caused that." He sounded as though he were trying to convince himself more than Rachel. "Maybe you should call Dr. Nara. We're in uncharted territory here."

320

Rachel closed her eyes. How could she explain that she couldn't call Nara without risking assassination?

"I'll try," she said. "It may take me a while to get him."

Weinstein took her into an adjoining office and showed her how to place long-distance calls from the hospital. Then he gave her his pager number and left to go home to his family.

Rachel stared at the phone, trying to talk herself into calling the White House. It was the only way she could think of to reach Ravi Nara. But something held her back. It was a growing belief that David, no matter how ill he might be, was not completely delusional. He had told her Ravi Nara was dangerous, and part of her believed him. David might never learn of this expression of faith in him, but wasn't that the nature of faith? To believe without answer, without reward, without proof? She got up, wiped her eyes, and left the phone untouched.

That was ten hours ago.

She'd spent the time since with her eyes fixed on the EEG screen, like a pilgrim watching a marble statue in the hope that it would weep. Yet the alpha waves remained constant. As a young resident, she had spent many nights watching patients slide slowly and irreversibly toward death. As a psychiatrist, she'd watched suicidal patients die by inches from self-administered poisons whose effects could not be countered. But only one previous experience had taken her to this awful realm of solitude.

The death of her son.

She had barely survived that, and now, after finding a man who might give her another child someday, she found herself sitting by his hospital bed, helplessly awaiting the inevitable.

At three in the morning, another burst of theta and beta waves had crossed the EEG screen. They lasted seventeen minutes, then vanished. Every half hour, she clapped her

321

hands beside David's ear, but the alpha wave remained constant.

According to the machine, David was brain-dead.

An hour after dawn, she bent and kissed him on the forehead, then went into the adjoining office and picked up the telephone. It took some wrangling with operators, but within a few minutes she was connected to the White House switchboard in Washington, D.C.

"I'm calling about Project Trinity," she said.

"Please repeat that," said the operator.

"Project Trinity."

"Hold, please."

Rachel closed her eyes. Her hands were quivering, and a voice inside her told her to hang up. Before she could, a curt male voice came on the line. "Who's calling, please?"

"Rachel Weiss."

There was a sharp intake of breath. "Say again?"

"This is Dr. Rachel Weiss. I'm with Dr. David Tennant, and I desperately need help. I think he's dying."

"Stay calm. I'm going to—"

"Please!" she cried, losing her self-control at last. "I need to speak to someone who knows about this!"

"Dr. Weiss, whatever you do, stay on this line. You've done the right thing. Don't have any doubt about that."

THIRTY-THREE

WHITE SANDS

Ravi Nara was lying on a cement floor with a needle pressed to his jugular vein when he was paged to the hospital over the White Sands PA system. Geli Bauer was going to kill him with the syringe of potassium chloride he had planned to use on Godin.

"Dr. Nara, please report to the Bubble immediately."

"Peter could be coding again!" he cried.

Geli jerked him to his feet and pushed him toward the door.

As they hurried toward the hospital, he thought about the past half hour. After finding the syringe, Geli had marched him from the Bubble to the bare storage room. When they arrived, Ravi asked what the hell she was doing in White Sands. Geli smiled and leaned against the wall, studying him as she might an insect that she was about to pin to a board.

"I wanted to know if Skow was telling the truth," she said. "If Godin was really dying. If Trinity was really going to fail."

"And?"

323

"Godin is dying, but Trinity isn't going to fail. It's going to save Godin's life."

"Not his life," Ravi said. "His mind."

"That's the very essence of life." Geli stepped close to Ravi and drew a gleaming knife from her belt. "I could sever your spinal cord anywhere between C-one and C-seven. You'd be an instant quadriplegic. If I gave you the choice between that and death, would you choose death?"

Ravi stepped back. "I see your point."

Geli smiled with fascination, her tongue showing between her teeth. He had always sensed that she felt some connection between sex and violence, and her behavior now confirmed it. She was toying with him, and watching his fear aroused her.

"I also wanted to see my father," she said. "I haven't had that unique pleasure in a long time."

Ravi said nothing.

"There's one other reason I'm here. If you guess it, maybe we'll just stop at paraplegic."

"Stop this stupid game!" Ravi snapped. "Skow will be here any minute."

"Can't you guess?" Geli said.

"No."

"I wanted to be scanned by the machine."

He hadn't expected this. "Why? You know the scans cause neurological side effects."

Geli laughed. "People risk side effects for *cosmetic surgery*. I'll take some risk for immortality."

Ravi wanted her to keep talking.

"This technology will be held very closely for a long time," she said. "Only a few people will be scanned. Presidents and geniuses like Godin. Maybe a few half-ass scientists like you. But not security chiefs. So, I spent three hours this afternoon having a picture taken of my brain. Quite an experience."

324

Geli took the syringe of potassium chloride from a pouch on her belt.

"I wonder what my side effect will be?" she mused. "Narcolepsy and epilepsy, I don't need. Tourette's . . . no. Short-term memory loss I could stand. I'm getting it anyway. But yours is definitely the winner. It already fits my personality."

Ravi shook his head. Uncontrollable sexual compulsions sounded funny until you had to deal with them. Like any true compulsion, they could drive you to the edge of suicide.

"I used to watch you on the security cameras," Geli said, laughing. "Running to the bathroom five times a day, wanking your little weenie . . . I heard you moaning my name a few times. Pathetic."

Ravi ground his teeth and silently hoped that Skow planned to remove Geli Bauer from the planet. He was trying to think of a way to stall some more when Geli kicked him in the chest.

He went down hard, and before he could recover his breath, she was kneeling on his chest with the syringe at his throat. What saved him was not Skow, but the PA system calling him to the hospital.

Godin had developed serious problems with his tongue. He could barely swallow, and shooting pains had returned to the surface of his face. These were textbook effects of a glioma, and nothing could be done about anything but the pain. After an hour, he regained control of his tongue, but his face had started drooping on the left side.

As Ravi pretended to treat the old man, Godin's cell phone rang, and Geli answered. It was the White House. She held the phone to Godin's face while he listened. Ravi couldn't make out what was being said, but he sensed that something had gone wrong.

"No, Ewan, I'm fine," Godin lied. "My health is as good

as it's always been, and I can't imagine what Skow was thinking when he told you that."

Godin listened for a while, then said, "If Fielding's death was anything but a stroke, I think Skow is the man we need to talk to. He never got along with Fielding, and he's been running the hunt for Tennant as well. . . . Don't worry about Dr. Tennant. I'll send Ravi Nara over on my company jet immediately. He's the only doctor in the world who knows anything about that type of coma."

Send Ravi Nara over where? Ravi wondered. Anywhere was better than in the storage room with Geli Bauer.

"Yes, I'll give you an update as soon as possible. . . . Good-bye, Ewan."

Godin waved the phone away, then looked up at Ravi. "You're going to Jerusalem."

Ravi blinked in astonishment. "Israel?"

"Tennant is in a coma at Hadassah Hospital. Dr. Weiss is with him. She just called the White House for help. I assured Ewan McCaskell that you're the only man in the world who can help Tennant."

"But why do you want to help Tennant?" Ravi asked. "Why do *they*? The newspapers are saying Tennant wants to kill the president."

Godin swallowed painfully. "Presidents know better than to believe newspapers. And you're forgetting it was Matthews who foisted Tennant on me in the first place. He wants Tennant's side of the story."

"I see." Ravi didn't see at all. "What do you want me to do in Jerusalem?"

"Kill Tennant."

Ravi closed his eyes.

"He's practically brain-dead now," Godin said. "One tiny push from you and he's gone, and nobody the wiser."

"Peter, I can't walk into an Israeli hospital and . . ."

"Why not? You were prepared to murder me. Why not Tennant?"

"I never intended to hurt you."

The right side of Godin's face clenched in spasm.

"Has the pain returned?"

"Shut up, Ravi. This is your chance to redeem yourself. Your one chance to live."

Ravi cut his eyes at Geli. Anything was better than being alone with her again. "All right. But what if I can't do it? I mean, what if it's impossible?"

"You won't be the only one trying."

"I see. Well . . . when am I leaving?"

"I want you airborne in ten minutes. My Gulfstream is fueled on the strip. Go to Administration first. You'll have a telephone call waiting."

A telephone call? "All right, Peter."

Ravi started to leave, but some remnant of professional responsibility held him back. "What about you?"

"Dr. Case can keep me alive until Trinity state is reached." Godin waved him away. "Don't worry. Tennant will probably die before you get there."

JERUSALEM

Rachel sat by the telephone and prayed that the return call from Washington would come soon. If a bed opened up in neurology, someone would come to move David out of the ER. She was thinking of going to check his EEG tracing when the telephone rang.

"Hello?"

A distinctly American voice said, "Is this Dr. Rachel Weiss?"

"Yes."

"This is Ewan McCaskell, the president's chief of staff."

Rachel closed her eyes and tried to keep her voice steady. "I recognize your voice."

327

"Dr. Weiss, I'm calling to assure you that the president has the utmost concern for Dr. Tennant's health. We're not quite sure about the reasons behind the events of the past few days, but we intend to find the truth. The president is back in the United States now, and I assure you that Dr. Tennant is going to get a fair hearing."

Something inside her let go then, a tangled knot of fear and tension that had been building ever since she'd seen David shoot the gunman in his kitchen. A stuttering rush of sobs came from her throat.

"Dr. Weiss?" said McCaskell. "Are you all right?

"Yes . . . thank you so much for calling. There's something terrible going on, and Dr. Tennant has been trying to warn the president about it."

"Try to calm down, Doctor. I know you have a medical situation there, so I'm going to bring Dr. Ravi Nara in on our call. I'm told he's the only man who has the knowledge to deal with Dr. Tennant's problem."

Rachel tensed at the mention of Nara. There was a crackle as though the connection had been lost.

"Dr. Nara?" said McCaskell. "Are you there?"

A precise voice in a higher register came on the line. "Yes, hello? Dr. Weiss? This is Ravi Nara. Can you hear me?"

"Yes."

"I understand that Dr. Tennant has gone into an alpha coma state. Is that correct?"

"Not precisely. There were theta and beta wave intrusions for a while. Now only alpha again. I'm afraid he's going to stop breathing."

"He's not. I went into alpha coma myself after being scanned by Trinity's Super-MRI unit. You're aware of this machine?"

"Yes."

"I was in coma for thirty-two hours and awakened without any ill effects. I expect David to wake up at any time."

328

The confidence in Ravi Nara's voice was bracing. The Nobel laureate was renowned throughout the medical world, and she found it difficult to discount his words, especially when they offered hope.

"Dr. Nara, I don't know what to say."

"I'm going to fly over there myself," Nara said. "I'm told that the president is making arrangements for David to be admitted to a more secure facility. I'll be in Jerusalem in fourteen hours."

"My God."

"David will surely be awake by then, but don't panic if he's not. We're going to take this one step at a time. All right?"

Rachel was overwhelmed. "Yes. Thank you. I look forward to meeting you."

"And you, Doctor. Good-bye."

Nara clicked off, but McCaskell stayed on the line. "Do you feel a little better now, Dr. Weiss?"

"I can't begin to thank you for this."

"You'll get your chance. I'll be talking to you again soon."

Rachel hung up and took some deep breaths. Then she wiped her face with a Kleenex and pushed open the door to the treatment room.

David was sitting up on the treatment table, his eyes wide open, tears running down both cheeks.

THIRTY-FOUR

My eyes opened like those of a newborn, startled by the
world's bare brightness. As I blinked against the overhead
bulb, my body announced itself with aching hunger and an
overwhelming urge to empty my bladder. I sat up and looked
around. I was sitting in a medical treatment room. I'd worked
in dozens just like it.

Water, I thought. *I need water.*

A woman somewhere said, "I can't begin to thank you
for this." Her voice was familiar. I listened for more words,
but none followed.

A door opened across the room. Rachel walked in and
froze. Then her hand flew to her mouth, and she started
toward me.

"David? Can you hear me?"

I held up my hand, and she stopped.

"You've been in a coma. You've been out for . . ." she
looked at her watch—"fifteen hours. Alpha coma nearly all
that time. I thought you were brain dead." She pointed at
my face. "Why are you crying?"

I wiped my face. My fingers came away wet. "I don't
know."

"Do you remember anything? The seizure at the church?"

I remembered kneeling, then thrusting my fingers through a hole in a silver plate. A current of energy had shot into my arm, straight up to my brain, a current too intense to endure. I felt as though my mind were a tiny glove, and the hand of a giant was trying to force its way inside it. My body began to shake, then . . .

"I remember falling."

"Do you remember anything after that?"

I fell toward the floor, but before I reached it, the boundary of my body melted away, and I felt an oceanic unity with everything around me: the earth and rock beneath the church, the birds nesting among the stones above, the flowers in the courtyard and the pollen they loosed on the wind. I was not falling but floating, and I saw that a deeper reality underlay the world of things, a pulsing matrix in which all boundaries were illusory, where the pollen grain was not distinct from the wind, where matter and energy moved in an eternal dance, and life and death were but changing states of both. Yet even as I hovered there, floating in the world like a sentient jellyfish, I sensed that beneath that pulsing matrix of matter and energy lay something still deeper, a thrumming substrate as ephemeral and eternal as the laws of mathematics, invisible but immutable, governing all without force.

The thrumming was deep and distant, like turbines churning in the heart of a dam. As I listened, I discerned a pattern, more numerical than melodic, as of an undiscovered music whose notes and scales lay just beyond my understanding. I tuned my mind to the sound, searching for repetitions, the elusive keys to any code. Yet though I listened with all my being, I could not read meaning in the sound. It was like listening to a rainstorm and trying to hear the pattern of the individual drops as they hit the ground. Something in me craved knowledge of the underlying order, the vast sheet music that scored the falling of the rain.

And then I understood. The pattern I was searching for was no pattern at all. It was randomness. A profound randomness that pervaded the seeming order of the world. And in that moment I began to see as I had never seen before, to hear what few men had ever heard, the voice of—

"David? Can you hear me?"

I blinked and forced myself to focus on my surroundings. Medical cabinets. An EEG machine on a cart. Rachel's exhausted eyes.

"I hear you."

She took a step forward, wringing her hands. "I called Washington. I told them we were here. I didn't know what else to do."

"I know."

"Did you hear the call?"

"No."

"Then how did you know?"

The same way I know we're in danger now. I looked down and started to pull the IV line from my wrist.

"Don't do that!"

"We have to go."

Her eyes went wide. "What?"

"This is going to bleed when I pull it out. Could you find me a bandage? Where are my clothes?"

She quickly closed the distance between us and stopped me from pulling out the IV. "David, you're not yourself right now. You've been unconscious for a whole night. I spoke to Ewan McCaskell. The president is flying Ravi Nara over here to treat you. He's seen this type of coma before. He was in one himself for over thirty hours, and he woke up with no ill effects. They want to help us—"

332

"Ravi Nara was never in alpha coma. His MRI side effect was uncontrollable sexual compulsions. Nothing else."

"But he told me—"

"He told you what he knew would calm you down. We have to leave. Now."

"But the president wants to get to the truth. McCaskell told me that, and I believe him."

There was no way I could communicate the knowledge inside me without appearing insane. I stood, and the sheet fell away from my body.

"If we stay here, we won't live to see the president. I have something very important to do. Please get my clothes."

As Rachel looked toward a bag in the corner, I yanked the IV catheter from my wrist. Dark blood ran down the back of my hand. I applied pressure, then went to the counter and found a 4×4 bandage in a glass jar. Rachel saw what I was doing and taped the gauze tightly over the IV site.

"Keep your hand on that," she said. Then she got the plastic bag from the corner and laid it on the examining table. "Your clothes."

There was a commode against one wall, but no curtain or partition for privacy.

"I need to use that," I told her, pointing.

"Go. I've seen it before."

I walked to the commode and turned my back to her.

"Why do you think people are coming to kill us?" she asked.

"Because nothing has changed in their minds. And now they know where we are."

"You still don't trust anyone? Not even the president?"

"The president has no idea what's really happening."

I walked back to the table and slipped on my shirt, then fastened my money belt around my waist.

"But where do you want to go?" Rachel asked.

"White Sands."

"Where?"

"White Sands Proving Ground." I carefully pulled on my pants, then sat on the floor to put on my shoes. "It's in New Mexico."

"Why do you want go there?"

"That's where the real Trinity prototype is."

"How do you know that?"

"I just know."

She shook her head. "You're scaring me, David."

"Don't think about it."

"Wait." She held up one hand. "That's what was in Andrew Fielding's FedEx letter. White gypsum. *White sand.* Is that what he was trying to tell you? Where the second Trinity site was?"

"Yes. He wanted to let me know, but he didn't want anyone who intercepted that letter to know that he knew." I looked at the closed door. "What part of the hospital are we in?"

"The emergency department."

"Good. First floor. You know the way out?"

"Yes, but . . ."

I stood and took her hand in mine. "Everything has changed, Rachel. I know what I have to do. But we have to go *now.*"

I saw her faith in me cracking under the weight of her training as a psychiatrist and her desire to deny the danger.

"Please help me."

She closed her eyes and sighed. Then she went to the window and tried it. The window was sealed shut, and barred outside.

I went to the door and opened it a crack. Two nurses sat at a receiving desk, but they were turned partly away from me. One was talking on a telephone.

334

"What's past those nurses?" I whispered.

"A corridor that leads to the ambulance bay outside. There's a guard."

The guard was probably there to challenge people entering rather than leaving, but in Israel you never knew.

The nurse who wasn't on the phone got up and went into a treatment room. "Get ready," I said. When the other nurse was distracted, we walked quickly across the floor to the hall that led outside.

Rachel waved to the guard seated at the desk, then started to lead me past him.

The guard said something in Hebrew.

Rachel slowed but did not stop. "Do you speak English?"

"A little," said the guard.

"Dr. Weinstein told me to make sure this patient got some fresh air this morning. Do you know Dr. Weinstein?"

The guard looked confused. Then he smiled and flicked his hand as if to say, "Go ahead, go ahead."

We walked unhindered into the morning light.

Two ambulances sat parked beneath a flat concrete roof. I moved quickly to the left, where an access road led around the hospital. There was no footpath, so we walked on the curb. When we rounded the building, I saw the Dome of the Rock flashing gold in the Old City. The road beside us led down a long hill, and cover was minimal. To our right was a huge cemetery that looked vaguely colonial.

"We're going to have to find a taxi," Rachel said. "We won't get anywhere on foot."

"Listen."

Out of the general hum of the city below, a more urgent sound was emerging. A siren.

We crouched behind a row of low shrubs. Thirty seconds later, two dark green vans raced up the hill toward us. They didn't look like ambulances. One screeched to a stop at the hospital's front entrance, the other wheeled around back. The van in front disgorged two men wearing business suits, then a squad of paramilitary police carrying submachine guns.

"Who's that?" Rachel whispered.

"Shin Beth, maybe. Some branch of the secret police. Whoever Washington called to secure the hospital and prevent us leaving."

"Ravi Nara told me they were going to move you to a more secure hospital."

"Do they need a SWAT team for that?" I pulled her to her feet. "Come on!"

Though cover was scarce, we used every bit we could find as we made our way down the hill. Rachel wanted to run toward the Old City, but I led her down Churchill Street toward a Hyatt Regency Hotel, glancing back at the hospital all the way. The van was still parked out front. I could only imagine the frantic search inside.

A rank of taxis waited at the Hyatt. I climbed into the first in line, and Rachel got in after me.

"American?" asked the driver.

"American. I need an Internet bar."

The driver seemed to be working this out in his head. "You need computer?"

"Yes."

"Hyatt has computer inside. Pay by half hour."

"I want a public place. I don't like this hotel."

"Not many such bars in Jerusalem. The Strudel has computers, but it may not be open yet."

"Take us there."

The cabbie cranked his engine and pulled onto Ha-Universita. I saw a phalanx of police cars parked in a lot to our left. "What's that place?"

"National Police Headquarters. I hope you don't want to go there."

336

"The Strudel. Make it fast. I have important business."

"Yes, sir. Ten minutes, tops."

WHITE SANDS

A uniformed soldier drove Ravi Nara to the airstrip. The limitless desert night had once made Ravi uncomfortable, but tonight it comforted him. As the Jeep approached the runway, a Learjet taxied around the hangar and parked beside Godin's Gulfstream 5. The Lear was black and had no markings. When its door opened, John Skow bent and stepped through it.

"I've been trying to reach you!" the NSA man called. "Is something wrong with your phone?"

Ravi looked at his military escort again, but the soldier seemed oblivious to the conversation. "I'm on my way to Jerusalem."

Skow gripped Ravi's arm and walked him ten paces away from the soldier. "What the hell are you talking about?"

"Peter's sending me to Jerusalem."

"He's still alive?"

"Yes."

Panic and anger distorted Skow's features. "Did you even *try*?"

"Yes, goddamn it!"

"Why is Peter sending you to Jerusalem?"

"To make sure Tennant dies."

Skow tilted back his head like a man looking to the heavens for assistance. "Forget that. You're not going anywhere. Tennant escaped from Hadassah Hospital."

"But . . . they said he was in alpha coma."

"He must have come out of it. Rachel Weiss sure didn't carry him out of there."

Ravi couldn't believe it. "Maybe somebody else did."

"My God," breathed Skow. "The Israelis. They'd kill to get their hands on Trinity technology."

337

Ravi wasn't thinking about Trinity. "Do you know where Geli Bauer is, John?"

Skow looked curiously at him. "Of course. Walter Reed Hospital."

Ravi shook his head, a sinking feeling in his stomach. "I thought you were better than this."

"What are you talking about?"

"Geli is *here,* guarding Peter."

Skow blanched.

"Why didn't you know that?"

"That bitch has been taking my calls all day on her cell, telling me how great the doctors are at Walter Reed."

"You told me she was on board with us."

"She said she was. I'm going to have to call her father."

Ravi's military driver marched over to them. "Dr. Nara? It's time to board the plane."

Skow addressed the soldier in a commanding voice. "Corporal, I'm taking Dr. Nara back to see Mr. Godin. The situation in Israel has changed."

Ravi had no intention of staying in New Mexico. "I'm going to Jerusalem, John. Tennant and Weiss could turn up at any time. Peter wants it to look like he's doing everything in his power to save Tennant, and I think he's right."

"I know you'd *like* to go to Jerusalem," Skow said, holding Ravi's arm tight. "But the fact is, you're needed here."

"Peter's got a new doctor."

"But he needs *you.*"

Ravi looked at his escort. "I'm ready to get on the plane."

The soldier stepped forward, but an authoritative glare from Skow stopped him. "Corporal, I'm here on direct orders from the president. Your commanding officer, General Bauer, is fully conversant with my mission. I need two minutes with this man. Then we're going to see Mr. Godin. Step back, please. Give me twenty meters."

The corporal obeyed.

Ravi tried to pull away, but Skow's hand held him like a claw. "You gave me up, didn't you? You little bastard."

"I didn't tell them anything! But that won't help you. They know too much. I'd be dead now if Peter hadn't got into medical trouble."

Skow looked around the runway as though he expected soldiers to descend on him at any moment. "Listen to me, Ravi. Running to Jerusalem won't save you. The president is buying our version of the story, but if Godin is around to tell his side, we're dead. So—you still have a job to do."

Ravi felt nauseating fear in his belly. "You're crazy! They'll never let me close to him now. And if I stay here, Geli will kill me."

Skow shook him like a child. "Calm down, for God's sake! You can hide in my quarters until I straighten things out."

"Straighten things out? With Godin?"

Skow smiled. "You've forgotten that my specialty is information warfare."

He led Ravi to the Jeep and signaled for the corporal to get behind the wheel.

"But they already suspect you," Ravi said. "What will you tell them?"

Skow's smile took on a reptilian quality. "I'm an old hand at survival, Ravi. Even Geli could take lessons from me."

THIRTY-FIVE

JERUSALEM

The Strudel Internet Bar was closed. I could see a bearded man inside, cleaning the bar. I knocked on the glass, then waved and pointed at the door handle. The man shook his head.

"You have the money belts?" I asked Rachel.

"Yes."

"Give me a hundred-dollar bill."

I pressed the bill up against the door. It took the man inside a minute to notice it, and when he did, he only waved me away again. When we refused to leave, he walked to the door and looked closer at the bill. Then he yelled in English for us not to go anywhere, disappeared into an office, and came back with a set of keys.

"I need a computer," I said, when the door opened.

"Come in, no problem. High-speed Internet."

Rachel paid the cabbie, then joined me inside.

The Strudel was dark and smelled like bars around the world, but it did have a computer. I sat at the bar and began searching the Internet for the e-mail addresses of the top universities and computer facilities in the United States and

Europe. Cal Tech, the Artificial Intelligence Lab at MIT, CERN in Switzerland, the Max Planck Institute in Stuttgart, the Chaim Weizmann Institute in Israel, the Earth Simulator computer team in Japan, several others.

"What are you doing?" Rachel asked, climbing onto the stool beside me.

"Going public."

"I thought you didn't want to do that."

"I don't have a choice now. They've done it. Or nearly done it."

"Done what?"

"Trinity is about to become a reality."

"How do you know that?"

"I just know."

"And you're going to tell the world?"

"Yes."

"How much?"

"Enough to start a media storm that the president can't ignore."

I opened Microsoft Word and began typing my message. The first line was the easiest, a quote from the great Niels Bohr, writing about the nuclear arms race: *We are in a completely new situation, that cannot be resolved by war.*

"David?" Rachel said softly. "What happened to you while you were in that coma? Did you see things?"

"Not the way I used to. It's difficult to explain, but I'll try as soon as we have some time. I need to finish this first."

She got up and walked to the door to watch for police.

I bent over the keyboard and typed without pause, as if the words were being channeled through me by some outside force. After twenty minutes, I asked the man behind the bar to call us a taxi with a Palestinian driver. Then I typed a closing: *In memory of Andrew Fielding.*

"Did you send your mail?" Rachel asked.

341

"Yes. There'll be media chaos within four hours."

"Is that really what you want?"

"Yes. Evil doesn't flourish in the light."

She drew back and looked strangely at me. "Evil?"

"Yes."

A taxi pulled to the curb outside, and its bearded driver looked toward the door.

"Let's go."

We went out to the cab. "Are you Palestinian?" I asked the driver.

"Why do you care?" he asked.

"Do you know where Mossad Headquarters is?"

The driver squinted as if studying a curious sight. "Sure. Every Palestinian knows that."

"That's why I wanted you. I need to go there."

Rachel looked at me in astonishment. I could almost read her mind. What could I possibly want from the Mossad, Israel's ruthless intelligence service?

"You got money?" asked the driver.

"How does a hundred dollars American sound?"

"I see better than I hear."

Rachel got out the money.

The driver nodded. "Get in."

I hadn't even got the back door closed when he threw the car into gear and roared away from the curb.

WHITE SANDS

Geli knew she was watching the old man die. She desperately needed a cigarette. Despite the antiseptic bite of the air, there was an odor of death in the room. She couldn't define it, but she knew it well. She'd smelled it in field hospitals and other, darker places. Perhaps evolution had sensitized the human olfactory system to the scent of approaching death. In a world of communicable diseases, it would certanly be a survival

342

advantage. Geli had once smelled her own face burning, so she had no illusions about mortality. But witnessing Godin's final struggle was getting to her in a way she had not expected.

There were periods when he couldn't swallow, though he still spoke fairly well. He'd been talking wistfully about his dead wife, as he might to a daughter. Geli wasn't sure how to handle this kind of intimacy. From her third birthday onward, her father had treated her like a military draftee. Horst Bauer's idea of a heart-to-heart talk was sitting down together to make a daily timetable. She put up with this until adolescence. Then open warfare broke out in the Bauer house. When Geli began to display a sexual adventurousness similar to her father's, the general lost all control. She knew that at some primal level, he wanted her sexually, and that gave her power over him. She paraded in front of him half-dressed, flirted shamelessly with his fellow officers—men twice her age—and seduced her psychiatrists. The resulting beatings only reinforced her will to fight.

Geli was sixteen when she discovered her father had a mistress—several, in fact—and finally solved the mystery of her mother. Eighteen years of infidelity and violence had turned a loving woman into a pathetic shell of her former self, a lost soul who lived only for her next drink. When Geli confronted the general about this, he looked her in the eye and told her she'd discovered the weakness of strong men. Men of great capacities required more than one woman to keep their passions at bay, and the sooner she accepted that truth, the better off she would be. That argument ended as so many had, with a beating.

Yet when Geli arrived at university, she found that her father's words seemed to hold true for strong women as well. No man could satisfy her lust for intense experience for long. The day she graduated—with double majors in Arabic and economics—she went to a shopping mall recruiting station and enlisted in the army as a private.

Nothing could have enraged her father more. With that single act Geli had rejected all his power and influence, embarrassed him before his fellow West Pointers, and followed in his footsteps. The general began to drink heavily and entered a period of instability that quickly culminated with his wife's suicide. Geli had never known what finally broke her mother's spirit. One more mistress? One too many full-fisted blows? But she never forgave her father for it.

By contrast, Peter Godin had lived faithfully with his wife for forty-seven years, even though the union had produced no children. As the old man rambled on about a trip he had taken to Japan, Geli thought of Skow and his plan to blame Godin for Andrew Fielding's death.

"Sir?" she said, interrupting the old man's reverie.

Godin looked up, his blue eyes apologetic. "I've been running on, haven't I? I'm sorry, Geli. It keeps my mind off the pain."

"It's not that. I want to tell you something."

"Yes?"

"Don't trust John Skow. He's the one who put Nara up to killing you. Skow thinks Trinity is going to fail, and he's been planning to blame it on you."

Godin smiled distantly. "I know that. I'm sure your father is part of the same plan."

"Then why don't you do something about it?"

"When the computer reaches Trinity state, they'll be powerless. Until then, I have you to protect me."

"But if you don't trust them, why did you use them?"

"Because they're predictable. Even in their betrayals. Their greed makes them so. That's the reality of the human animal."

"What about me? Why do you trust me to protect you? Because you pay me well?"

"No. I've watched you for two years now. I know you hate your father, and I know why. I know what you did in Iraq. You don't shrink from difficult jobs, and you've never betrayed your uniform—unlike your father. I also know that you admire me. We're kindred spirits, you and I. I have no daughter, and in a way, you have no father. And my gut tells me that if General Bauer walked in here to kill me, you'd stop him with a bullet."

Geli wondered if this was true. "But why hire both of us?"

"When Horst told me about you, I had a feeling he was trying to patch things up with you. I was wrong."

Her hand flew to her pistol. The Bubble's hatch had popped open with a hiss of escaping air. John Skow walked in wearing an immaculate suit, every hair in place. He didn't look like a man worried about his future.

"Hello, Geli," he said.

Godin's blue eyes tracked the NSA man across the room. "Search him."

Geli threw Skow against the Plexiglas wall and searched him from head to toe. He was clean.

"Well, that was fun," Skow said. "Can I do you now?"

She wondered what kind of game Skow was playing. He would not be here if the cards were not stacked in his favor.

"Hello, Peter," he said. "We have something of a situation on our hands. Tennant has gone public."

Godin's face went into spasm. It was difficult to watch, but when the pain subsided, the drooping cheek had regained its tone. He fixed Skow with a gaze of electrifying intensity.

"What did Tennant do?"

"He escaped from Hadassah, went to a public computer, and sent a letter to the top computer facilities in the world. He told them all about Trinity. Fielding's death, the attempts on his life, everything."

Godin closed his eyes. "The technology?"

345

"He revealed enough to convince the world that he's telling the truth. Enough to put countries like Japan within three years of their own Trinity computer. He told them about this facility. I have no idea how he found out about White Sands. Probably from Fielding."

Godin sighed deeply. "I handled Tennant wrong. I should have talked to him . . . reasoned with him."

Skow edged closer to the bed. Geli kept her hand on her pistol. She could put two slugs in Skow's back before the NSA man closed the distance to Godin.

"We're in a difficult spot, Peter. Here's what I suggest—"

"To *hell* with what you suggest," Godin muttered, struggling upright in the bed. "You've treated me like a fool from the beginning, but you're about to find out how wrong you are."

Godin picked up the phone beside his bed and pressed a single button.

"Who are you calling?" Skow asked, his face still confident.

"You'll see. Hello? This is Peter Godin. I need to speak to the president. It's a matter of national security. . . . What's that? . . . The code is seven three four nine four zero two. Yes, I'll wait."

Skow paled. "Peter—"

"Shut up." Godin glanced at Geli, then spoke in a powerful voice. "Mr. President, this is Peter Godin speaking."

Geli had never heard such authority before. Her father's fabled command presence was as nothing compared to it. Godin had announced his identity to the commander in chief as if saying, *Mr. President, this is Albert Einstein speaking.*

Godin listened for a few moments, then began a detailed explanation of why he had built the White Sands facility. Over a year ago, he said, he had become aware of serious security concerns in North Carolina. Someone inside Trinity was sabotaging computer code and possibly selling secrets to a foreign power. Rather than bring in "insecure agencies" such as the FBI and CIA—which would slow the project and further compromise its security—Godin had used his own money and connections to set up a secure research site. He had initially trusted John Skow to investigate the threat, but he now believed that Skow had been part of the problem from the beginning.

The president asked more questions, and Godin answered with absolute confidence. To his knowledge, Andrew Fielding had died of natural causes, but foul play could not be ruled out. David Tennant had become unhinged after Fielding's death and was suffering from psychosis possibly induced by the Trinity MRI machine. Everything humanly possible would be done to help Tennant regain his health. Before more questions could be raised, Godin informed the president that Trinity was less than twelve hours from completion, and that all data indicated the computer would not only meet but surpass all expectations as to weapons and intelligence applications. This altered the conversation completely.

Fielding, Tennant, and the existence of White Sands receded into the background as Godin promised undreamed-of power to the man who'd had the wisdom and courage to fund such a strategically important project. Godin appeared quite relaxed until the end of the conversation, when he went rigid and concluded with a curt, "Yes, sir, of course. I understand. I'll do that immediately."

He handed the phone to Geli, his eyes on Skow. "Are you surprised I could do that? I've been dealing with presidents on a first-name basis since LBJ."

"What did Matthews say at the end?" Skow whispered.

"He asked that in the interest of allaying the concerns of the American public, I temporarily shut down all operations."

"He's worried about the media."

"Ewan McCaskell is on his way here now. They're setting

up an emergency oversight group. The Senate Select Committee on Intelligence."

"What are you going to do?" Skow asked.

Godin flicked his hand as if to swat a fly, then looked at the NSA man with unalloyed hatred. "Geli, if this parasite moves without my permission, kill him."

The blood left Skow's face.

"This is what *you're* going to do," Godin said. "Go to the airstrip. General Bauer should be arriving at any moment."

A chill raced up Geli's back.

"Surely you've figured that out," Godin said. "Horst would have panicked the moment Tennant went public. He probably called the White House five minutes later and told them I'd duped him into providing this facility. His next move will be to come here and secure the computer. The president may even have ordered him to do it."

"What do you want me to tell him?" Skow asked.

"That any attempt to interfere with the Trinity prototype will result in retaliation on an unimaginable scale."

Skow's eyes narrowed. "What are you talking about, Peter?"

"Just remind the general of something he should know very well by now."

"What's that?"

"I never bluff."

Skow cut his eyes at Geli, then at her pistol.

"Get out," Godin rasped.

Skow turned and left the Bubble.

"Why are you letting him go?" Geli asked. "At least let me lock him in an office."

"There's nothing he can do now."

"Maybe not alone. But with my father?"

Godin shook his head as though the time for trivial concerns had passed. "Get me Levin in Containment."

Geli made the call, then held the phone up to the old man's face.

"Levin?" said Godin. "Listen to me. *In nomini patri, et filii, et spiritus sancti.*"

Geli could faintly hear the other end of the conversation.

"Are you sure, sir?" asked Levin. "Fielding's model is only at eighty-one percent."

"My model will have to solve the final algorithms," Godin said.

There was a pause. "Is this the end?"

Godin's gray lips hardly moved. "Not yet. But we may not speak in this way again. You should prepare for visitors."

"We have. I heard some soldiers talking outside Containment. They said the general is inbound."

Geli's insides went cold.

Godin coughed into the phone. "Remember . . . there's no end for me now. The end is the beginning."

"It's been a privilege, sir. And I'll be there for you when Trinity state is reached."

Godin closed his eyes. "Good-bye, my friend."

Geli hung up the phone. How close was her father? Fort Huachuca was only three hundred miles away.

Godin's hand touched her wrist, startling her. "Do you understand what's about to happen, Geli?"

"Yes, sir. Levin's going to dump Dr. Fielding's model from the computer and load yours. Sometime in the next hour, your model will reach the Trinity state. You will become the Trinity computer. Or vice versa, whichever it is."

Godin nodded wearily. The events of the past few minutes had drained him. His breathing had grown labored.

"How does that help you?" she asked. "Even if Trinity works, all they'll have to do is shut it off, right? Or cut power to it?"

349

"Skow is probably trying to figure out how to do that right now. But he'll fail."

"My father will bring troops and equipment with him."

Godin's eyes closed. "Let me worry about that. With luck, you won't have to shoot anyone. Least of all, American soldiers."

Geli wanted to scream. The old man didn't realize what forces would soon be arrayed against him. The Containment building looked solid, but Horst Bauer had made short work of much harder targets in his career.

"I must live to see this," Godin murmured. "Keep your weapon ready to fire."

Geli sat on the floor with her back against the wall and pointed her Walther at the door.

THIRTY-SIX

JERUSALEM

When I gave my name at the door of the Mossad building, we were immediately pulled inside and searched. Our money and papers were confiscated. Then we were locked inside a white room containing only a wooden table and three chairs.

A plainclothes officer appeared and asked why we had come. I told him I wanted to speak to the most senior officer of the Mossad. He pressed me for information, but I refused to say more. The officer left the room and locked the door behind him.

Forty minutes passed.

Rachel didn't speak. She understood that anything we said would be recorded by hidden microphones. Despite my urgency to reach New Mexico, a preternatural calm settled over me. Rachel seemed to sense this, because she reached out and took my hand as though to draw strength from me.

At last the door opened, and a short man with the leathery skin of a desert warrior walked in and sat behind the table. In his middle fifties, he wore dusty khaki clothes and scarred boots. He had a shock of white hair and the most alert eyes I had ever seen.

"David Tennant," he said, looking at a file in his hand. "Physician, author, would-be presidential assassin. You're the most hunted man in America this week. To what do we owe this honor?"

"Are you the chief of the Mossad?"

"I am. Major General Avner Kinski."

"I thought you would be in Tel Aviv."

"I was in Bethlehem. There was a bombing early this morning."

"I'm sorry."

"Of course." Kinski gave me a quick, emotionless smile. "So. Why are you here?"

"I need your help."

"To do what?"

"I need to get to the U.S. secretly, and as fast as possible."

My answer surprised him, and I could tell he was a man not often surprised. "Why do you want to go back to the United States? You're very unpopular there."

"That's my business."

The Mossad chief leaned back in his chair, a bemused look on his face. "Where exactly do you wish to go?"

"White Sands, New Mexico."

"Interesting. Are you aware that my government has been asked to take you into custody?"

"I assumed so."

"My government tries to cooperate with yours whenever possible."

"But not always. Especially where arms and technology are concerned."

The spymaster sniffed and leaned forward, his eyes challenging me. "You run from Shin Beth at Hadassah Hospital, yet you run straight into my arms. Why?"

352

"I knew you would help me."

Kinski shook his head. "Maybe you didn't run so straight. Where did you go between Hadassah and here?"

"You'll know soon enough."

"I'd like to know now."

"Sorry."

"Tell me something, Doctor. Is it your intention to kill the U.S. president?"

"Do I look like an assassin to you?"

Kinski shrugged. "Assassins come in many shapes and sizes. Women. Little boys. Smiling teenagers. You do have the look of a fanatic."

"I'm not a killer."

"Yet you have killed. I see that in your eyes."

"In self-defense."

The Mossad chief lit a cigarette and drew deeply on it. "We've strayed from our main business. What makes you think I would fly you secretly to America?"

"I have something you want."

The dark eyes flickered. "You're a businessman now?"

"I know how the world works." I leaned forward. "There's a secret defense project in America known as Trinity. It's been going on for two years, and in a matter of hours it will produce the most powerful weapon on the face of the earth. I know more about that weapon than any man you're likely to have in your hands for the foreseeable future."

The Israeli's mouth was hanging slack.

"I see this is not a total surprise to you," I said. "I'm one of six people who've had access to every detail of Trinity since its inception. I was appointed to the project by the president. So, you've got two choices. One, you can hold me prisoner and torture me for what I know. But a lot of people know I'm in Israel—including the president—so that could get messy for you. Two, you can fly me to White Sands.

353

If you do that, you can put whatever scientists you want aboard the plane, and I'll tell them all I know about Trinity." I settled back in my chair. "That's my offer."

Gray tendrils of cigarette smoke drifted out of Kinski's mouth. He looked calm, but I knew my words had almost knocked him off his chair.

"Tell me the nature of this weapon, Doctor."

"Artificial intelligence. Trinity will make the computers in your most advanced weapons labs as obsolete as canvas biplanes. It will break your most complex codes in seconds. And that's only the beginning. I'm in a hurry, General."

The spymaster took another drag on his cigarette, then stood and smiled with appreciation. "You're an audacious man, Doctor."

"And?"

"You got yourself a plane ticket."

WHITE SANDS

Five minutes before General Bauer's plane touched down, shooting broke out near the Containment building. The sound of gunfire echoed across the compound, stirring Geli's blood. There was no sound on earth like shots fired in anger.

Godin started awake and pressed a button that electrically raised his bed. "Your father must have ordered his men to try to open the Containment building."

Geli wondered if an assault team was about to burst into the Bubble. "Your technicians are armed?"

"Of course."

"They won't be able to hold out against a determined force with the right ordnance."

"I think you'll be surprised."

"Sir, I know what I'm talking about. If—"

"What time is it?" Godin cut in. "Have I slept? Has Levin called?"

"You slept a little, but no one's called. They loaded your neuromodel over an hour ago. Why does it take so long to know something?"

"It takes time to purge a neuromodel from the computer. Then there's a period of acclimatization after the new model is loaded. An analogue of medical shock, I expect, as the mind accustoms itself to separation from its physical body."

"How long does that last?"

"Tennant's model was in a confused state for over an hour. Fielding's for thirty-nine minutes. But the system was only functioning at fifty percent efficiency at that time."

The phone rang. It was Levin. He sounded out of breath, and Geli heard shouting in the background. She held the receiver up to Godin's ear. Godin listened, then said, "Thank you, Levin. Good luck."

He motioned for her to hang up, profound satisfaction on his face. "My model has fully acclimatized and is now resolving the final algorithms at the same rate Fielding was."

"How long do you think it will take?"

The phone rang again. This time it was John Skow. Godin refused to speak to him.

"Geli," Skow said in a taut voice, "your father just touched down on the airstrip. He brought some serious firepower with him. That skirmish a moment ago was nothing. Small-arms fire. If someone doesn't persuade Godin to get Levin and his people out of Containment, the general will destroy the building and the computer."

"I'll relay that message."

She hung up. Godin watched her expectantly.

"Skow says my father will blow up the Containment building if you don't order your techs out."

The old man's face twitched against nerve pain. "I don't think he'll do that without speaking to me first."

"How much does he know about what you're building here?"

355

"He knows it's artificial intelligence. He knows I wouldn't waste time on something small. But he mostly knows what he gets paid to keep this place invisible."

"My father will do anything to protect his career. If the president wants the computer shut down, he'll shitcan the whole building without a second thought, if that's the only way he can do it."

The door of the Bubble opened with a hiss. Geli whipped up her pistol and found herself aiming at her own father.

"It was bound to come to this someday," General Bauer said, a wry smile on his face.

Geli gave him nothing. At fifty-five her father looked much as he had at thirty—trim and hard and blond—with gray eyes that brooked no nonsense from anyone, regardless of rank or position. He was wearing his Class A dress uniform with its bright splash of fruit salad on the breast, which told Geli he anticipated meeting the president's chief of staff. He was not wearing a sidearm, but she saw the bulge of a shoulder holster beneath his dark green coat.

General Bauer moved close enough to the bed to make eye contact with Godin. "Sir, the president ordered you to cease operations. If you issued any such order to your technicians, they've ignored it. They've barricaded themselves in the Containment building and fired on my troops. I have two dead and five wounded. I ask you now to order your people out. If you or they refuse, I'll have no choice but to bring them out by force."

Godin stared back at Bauer but said nothing.

Geli knew her father was speaking for recording devices. Godin probaby knew it, too. The eye contact between the two men spoke far more eloquently than their voices.

"Did you understand what I said?" General Bauer asked. He looked as if he thought Godin might be so near death that he was past reason.

"My technicians have been instructed not to answer phone calls," Godin said finally. "Not even from me."

"Then I'll have you moved outside. You can use a megaphone to contact them."

Godin smiled faintly, as though he enjoyed this chess game with his secret employee. "The Containment building is soundproof, General. It's also built of reinforced steel and concrete. It has its own water and air supply, plus its own electrical generators."

"I can reduce that building to dust in a matter of seconds," Bauer said. "My men are setting the explosives now. The president would like your computer to survive, but if you refuse to cooperate, I won't hesitate to destroy it."

This threat seemed to move Godin. "I expect my lead engineer to call me at any moment."

The general glanced at Geli, then relaxed his ramrod posture. "What the hell are they really working on in there, Peter?"

"The most powerful machine ever built by man."

"Was Dr. Tennant's e-mail accurate about its capabilities?"

"It would be impossible to overestimate them."

A shadow of doubt crossed Bauer's face. He looked at Geli for confirmation, but she looked away, nauseated by disgust. Her father was standing there like a champion of right, an emissary of the president, but he'd been part of Trinity from the beginning. She did not relax her aim. If her father thought killing Godin would protect him from political repercussions, he wouldn't hesitate to try.

"You leave me no choice," General Bauer said. He glanced at Geli's pistol, then turned to go.

The ringing telephone stopped him. Geli picked up the receiver with her free hand and passed it to Godin. Again she heard frantic voices in the background, one saying something about ammunition. Then very clearly Zach Levin said,

"Trinity state has been reached, sir. . . . I repeat, Trinity state has been reached."

Godin closed his eyes and sagged back into his pillow. "Thank you, Levin. Carry on."

He dropped the phone on the mattress.

"Why the hell did you tell him to carry on?" General Bauer asked.

When the blue eyes opened, the triumph in them was absolute. "Trinity state has been reached. There's nothing you can do now."

"Peter, for God's sake. What does that mean?"

"Trinity is in control."

"Of what?" The general looked at the door of the Bubble as if he could somehow see the Containment building. "What the hell are you talking about?"

"We've known each other for a long time, Horst. You know I'm a man of my word. If you attempt to enter or destroy the Containment building now, you'll be destroying the country you swore to defend."

Bauer's eyes narrowed in a mixture of suspicion and confusion.

"You'll understand soon," Godin said. "I advise you to be patient and prudent, for your own sake."

The general stepped closer to the bed and spoke softly. "You know I've always supported your cause when I could. But this isn't the situation we talked about. This is a king-size clusterfuck with worldwide media on the way to cover it."

Godin waved his hand indifferently. "I'm sure you'll find a way to extricate yourself. You always do."

General Bauer sighed, then turned and left the Bubble without a glance in Geli's direction.

She felt the same foreboding she had as a child. Her father did not handle uncertainty well. She turned back to Godin and saw that he was weeping. The sight stunned her.

"What's the matter, sir?"

Godin raised a shaking hand and touched his face as if making sure it was there. "I've done it. You're looking at the first man in the history of the world to exist in two places at once." Wonder shone from the old man's eyes. Wonder and peace. "I'll die in this bed," he said. "But in Containment I'll go on living."

Geli didn't know what to say. Even if Godin were right, the computer was unlikely to survive for long.

"Take my hand, Geli. Please."

His eyes pleaded with her. She gave him her free hand, and he squeezed it like a child.

"I can let go now. I can let this body die."

Another burst of gunfire echoed across the compound. Geli gritted her teeth and fought the urge to pull her hand away.

THIRTY-SEVEN

EL AL FLIGHT 462, FIVE MILES OVER THE ATLANTIC OCEAN

Major General Kinski of the Mossad had reserved the entire upper deck of an El Al 747 for our trip back to the United States. Passengers and flight attendants were barred from ascending the staircase by a Mossad agent. When the airliner reached New York, Rachel and I were to be transferred to a private jet that would fly us to Albuquerque, New Mexico. From there, a chartered helicopter would ferry us to the gates of the White Sands Proving Ground.

To pay for these arrangements, I'd spent the past three hours sitting on a stool up front, briefing five Israeli scientists on Project Trinity. A video camera recorded my words, but most of the scientists took their own notes. General Kinski seemed amazed that I would discuss such a sensitive project so freely, but he had failed to grasp the essential reality of Trinity. The existence of a single Trinity computer had negated the old paradigms of national security. For mankind, there was no security.

Rachel sat two rows behind the scientists in an aisle seat. As I spoke, her expressive eyes betrayed a host of emotions: anxiety, sadness, disbelief, anger. I wanted to walk her to the back of the plane and reassure her, but the Israelis had other ideas.

General Kinski periodically walked to the rear of the upper deck to take satellite phone calls. From his reports I learned that my e-mail from the Strudel Bar had created the chaos I'd sought to cause. The theories behind Project Trinity had quickly been validated by the world's top computer scientists. In an attempt to put the story in perspective, many media commentators were comparing the story to the cloning controversy of 1998. But the implications of Trinity made the idea of cloning almost passé. The sixth time General Kinski returned from the rear of the plane, he touched me on the shoulder, his face taut with concern.

"What is it?" asked a scientist from the Chaim Weizmann Institute. "What's happened now?"

The Mossad chief rubbed his tanned chin. "Various computer experts around the world have started to notice something happening on the Internet."

"What something?"

"An unknown entity has been systematically moving through every major computer network and database in the world. Corporations, banks, government offices, military bases, remote defense installations. Existing security such as firewalls barely slows it down. People are publicly speculating that it's the Trinity computer."

"Perhaps it's only a talented hacker," suggested another man. "Or a group. Is this entity destroying files?"

"No. It's simply viewing everything. Almost as if it's creating a map of the computer world. Some amateurs—hackers—claim to have traced the source of these probes to New Mexico."

"Then I think we have to assume that it is Trinity," said the Weizmann scientist. "What I don't understand is why somebody hasn't simply shut off the power to this machine."

I shook my head. "Godin's been planning this for a long

time. I suspect that turning off that machine would have cata-strophic consequences."

General Kinski was clearly ahead of the scientists. "We've talked a lot about the design and capabilities of this computer. We haven't discussed what its intent might be."

"Your best chance at understanding that is to understand Peter Godin," I said. "If a model has been successfully loaded, it's Godin's."

"You knew the man for two years. What can you tell us?"

"He's brilliant."

"Obviously."

"He has strong opinions about politics."

"Such as?"

"He once said that the principle of one man, one vote, had made America great, and that the same principle would ultimately destroy her."

Kinski barked a laugh. "What else?"

"Godin has read deeply in history and political theory, and he has a knowledge of philosophy. He's not religious."

"I assume that like all very successful men, he has a strong ego?"

I nodded.

"I know this much history," said the Mossad chief. "Give a brilliant man unlimited power, and you've got big problems."

The scientists nodded soberly, but the general's gift for stating the obvious made me smile.

"Tell me something, Doctor," Kinski said. "Why do you want so desperately to get to White Sands?"

"To stop him. To stop Godin."

"How do you propose to do that?"

"By talking to him."

"You think you can stop him by talking to him?"

"I'm the only one who can."

Kinski shook his head. "How do you know that?"

"You don't want to know."

He looked at me as he might at a deranged man in the street. "But I do."

"I misspoke, General. I should have said Godin is the only one who can do it. He'll have to stop himself."

"The American president may have different ideas about that. Not to mention his generals."

"That's what I'm afraid of." I rubbed my face with both hands. "I'd like to rest now, if I may."

Kinski patted me on the shoulder. "Soon, Doctor. A few more questions first. Gentlemen?"

I glanced at Rachel. She shook her head, then got up and walked down the aisle to the back of the plane.

WHITE SANDS

Ravi Nara watched in amazement as troops from Fort Huachuca constructed a space-age command post around him in an unused area of the Administration hangar. Skow hadn't bothered to introduce General Bauer, but Ravi had picked up a lot just by listening.

Military Intelligence had long ago created a portable Situation Room that could be set up anywhere in the world. Centered around a large oval table were huge plasma display screens fed by racks of computers and communications terminals. Satellite dishes outside connected the Situation Room to every American intelligence agency and surveillance satellite on or orbiting planet Earth.

When Skow asked General Bauer how he had known to bring the specialized equipment, Bauer had chuckled bitterly.

"Dr. Tennant's statement was pretty specific about the abilities of this computer. And I know Peter Godin. He'd never voluntarily relinquish that much power. That's Nietzschean reality." The general gave Skow a look of disdain.

363

"I can't believe you thought for one minute that Containment was really isolated from the rest of the world."

"But that was the whole point in building it," Skow said.

Bauer snorted. "What the hell were you doing in North Carolina? Playing golf? Godin's engineers had the run of this reservation for months. He flew cargo planes in and out. They could have done anything in here. If you believe that computer isn't connected to anything, I've got some oceanfront land by Fort Huachuca I'd like to sell you."

Ten minutes later, the general's signals experts discovered a pipeline running deep beneath the sand around the Containment building. The iron pipe appeared to be a water line, but it gave off electromagnetic radiation. The pipeline ran due north for many miles and in all likelihood carried cables connecting the Trinity computer to the OC48c data backbone that served the White Sands Proving Ground.

Certain other facts had become known during the construction of the Situation Room. First, that a squatter's village of journalists and TV trucks had appeared outside the main gate. Second, that computer professionals around the world had detected a mysterious presence on the Internet, a force that moved through networks and databases with effortless speed and exhaustive thoroughness. Third, that Ewan McCaskell had lifted off from Andrews Air Force Base some time ago in the backseat of a supersonic jet and would soon arrive at White Sands.

When one of the half dozen soldiers manning the consoles in the Situation Room announced that McCaskell's plane was about to touch down on the White Sands airstrip, General Bauer turned to Skow.

"I want Godin brought in here."

Skow shook his head. "We don't want him talking to McCaskell."

"I don't give a shit about that. Godin knows things I need to know. He can die here as well he can in the hospital."

Skow reluctantly walked away.

"Tell my daughter I'll personally vouch for Godin's safety!" Bauer called. "She can lie in his bed with her pistol if she wants."

After Skow left the hangar, General Bauer looked up at a display screen showing a floodlit view of the Containment building. He stared at it for a few moments, then looked at Ravi.

"You're the neurologist, right? Dr. Nara?"

"Yes, General." Ravi walked toward the oval table.

"Is Godin out of his mind?"

"No, sir." Ravi figured the general would appreciate a *sir*, even from a civilian. "He's quite sane."

"What about his brain tumor?"

"He's had it for some time, but our Super-MRI detected it when it was very small. The tumor was inoperable even then, but it wasn't affecting his mind. I don't think it is even now."

General Bauer looked hard at Ravi. "But you might testify differently at a congressional hearing."

Ravi averted his eyes. "That's quite possible. It's a complex case."

"Skow told me you tried to kill him. Godin, I mean."

Ravi wasn't sure how to respond.

Bauer gave him a grin. "Stick around, Doctor. I may need you."

Ravi bowed his head.

Ewan McCaskell strode into the Situation Room flanked by two Secret Service agents. Like Skow, McCaskell hailed from Massachusetts, but he'd left the affectations of the Ivy League far behind him. The chief of staff had black hair and wore a navy suit so dark it looked black. He took the chair at the head of the table and motioned for General Bauer to sit to his right.

Skow had returned and now took a seat farther down the table. When the general waved his hand for Ravi to join them, Ravi sat at the far end of the table, opposite McCaskell.

"Peter Godin will be here in a few minutes," said Skow. "They're moving his life support equipment now."

McCaskell nodded and looked around the table, his eyes projecting a laserlike focus. "Gentlemen, I am here to assess this situation, and also to clear any and all potential action with the president before it's taken."

General Bauer's face tightened.

"For the time being," McCaskell continued, "we will table the issue of how the hell this unauthorized facility came into being, and whose heads will go on the chopping block when this is over."

Skow looked at the table.

"Peter Godin told the president that none of these brain models have been loaded yet, but the media is screaming about a computer taking over the Internet. *Something* is happening on the Internet. Just what are we dealing with, gentlemen?"

General Bauer said, "I think Mr. Skow and Dr. Nara are better able to speak to that issue than I am."

"Somebody better start talking," snapped McCaskell.

"We're dealing with something no one has ever dealt with before," Skow said. "A neuromodel has almost certainly been loaded into the computer. And that neuromodel was almost certainly Peter Godin's. But all we can be sure of is that we're dealing with a superior intelligence."

McCaskell didn't like this answer. "But it's still Peter Godin, right?"

"Yes and no. Godin's neuromodel is his mind, in the strictest sense. But from the moment it entered the computer, that mind began to operate at an exponentially faster speed than it did when it was confined to organic brain tissue. Dr. Nara?"

Ravi considered it a good sign that Skow had called on

him. "Electrical signals in computers travel about one million times faster than they do in brain neurons, Mr. McCaskell."

"And the difference isn't merely one of speed," Skow clarified. "Once it begins functioning in digital form, Godin's mind has the ability to learn in an entirely new way. Massive amounts of stored data can be downloaded into it. So it's possible—in theory, at least—that ever since the computer reached Trinity state, Godin's technicians have been loading data into it. History, mathematics, military strategy. It can also search the Internet and absorb anything it finds, which from all indications it seems to be doing."

McCaskell shook his head in amazement.

"To view the Trinity computer as a mere extension of Peter Godin would be a mistake," Skow said. "Godin's neuromodel left Godin the man behind hours ago. And an hour to Trinity is like a century to us. By now, Godin's model has evolved into something none of us has ever contemplated dealing with."

"You talk like it's some kind of god," McCaskell said.

Skow gave the chief of staff a condescending look. "That *is* why we refer to a functional neuromodel as being in the 'Trinity state.' It's man and machine, yet greater than both."

"What the hell am I supposed to tell the president?"

"That we don't yet know what we're dealing with," said General Bauer.

"When will we know?"

"When the computer tells us something," Skow replied.

"Goddamn it," said McCaskell. "I still don't understand why somebody hasn't just cut the power to this machine."

General Bauer cleared his throat. "Mr. Godin advised me that doing so would be a costly mistake."

"What else would you expect him to say?"

"I've known Peter Godin a long time, sir. I'm not inclined to test his honesty on that point."

"What are you afraid of, General?"

Bauer tensed at the implication of cowardice, but he kept his voice even. "Mr. McCaskell, the NSA funded Project Trinity because it believed this computer had the potential to become the most powerful weapon in history. That weapon is now self-directed and aimed at us. It doesn't take a degree from Cal Tech to know how dependent America is on computer systems. What am I afraid of, sir? I'm afraid this machine may be in a position to blackmail us in a way the Soviet Union never could with nuclear weapons. Because we have no deterrent against it. It has no children it wishes to protect. No cities. No population. We can assume it wants to survive, but not nearly so badly as we do."

"Blackmail us?" McCaskell echoed. "It's a machine. What the hell could it *want*?"

There was a clang from outside the ring of display screens, then a squealing of casters.

"Godin's hospital bed," said Skow.

Three soldiers wheeled Godin's bed into the ring of display screens. Four more followed, pushing medical carts and an IV tree. Dr. Case from Johns Hopkins walked beside the bed, and Geli Bauer followed the procession like a praetorian guard of one.

"Is he conscious?" asked McCaskell.

Dr. Case said, "I want to go on record as objecting to this."

"Noted," said McCaskell, standing and approaching the bed.

Godin motioned to Geli with his hand. She stepped forward and cranked a handle on the bed, raising Godin to eye level with McCaskell. The old man's breathing was more labored than before.

"We've met before, Mr. Godin," said McCaskell. "I don't have time to waste on pleasantries, and neither do you. I'd like you to tell me what you intended by breaking protocol and loading a neuromodel into that machine."

Godin blinked like a man trying to orient himself after

coming out of a dark room. "Trinity hasn't spoken for itself?"

"No. Will it?"

"Of course."

"You haven't answered my question. What was the purpose of this?"

"You don't know?"

"No."

"The old systems have failed, Mr. McCaskell. Even ours, the noblest experiment of them all. It's time for a new one."

"What systems are you talking about?"

"Rousseau said democracy would be the perfect political system if men were gods. But men are not gods."

McCaskell glanced back at Skow and General Bauer. "Mr. Godin, this isn't getting us anywhere. Am I to infer that you have a *political* goal?"

"Politics." Godin sighed heavily. "That word disgusts me, Mr. McCaskell. Men like you have soiled it. Your idea of government is a whorehouse. A sleazy flea market where the ideals of our forefathers are sold for trifles."

McCaskell peered at the old man as he might at a street preacher screaming condemnation at passersby. He was about to speak again when the men at the table behind him gasped.

On the main plasma display, four lines of blue text had appeared.

I have a message for the President of the United States. Later, I will have a message for the people of the world. Do not attempt to interfere with my operations. Interference will be instantly punished. Do not test me.

"Holy God," Skow breathed. "It's real. He did it. *We* did it."

"Yes, you did," said Ewan McCaskell. "You arrogant son of a bitch. And you may be hanged for it."

369

"Look," said Ravi Nara. "There's more."

The first message scrolled down the screen, and new words appeared.

I will accept as valid only data from the White House Situation Room and from the command post at White Sands. Communications should be addressed to Internet Protocol Address 105.674.234.64.

"It knows we're here," said Ravi, glancing around the room for security cameras.

"Of course it does," said Skow. "It's Godin. And Levin will have briefed him on everything that's happened up to this point."

"Look," said McCaskell.

A new message had flashed onto the screen.

Is Peter Godin still alive?

"Who's going to talk to this thing?" asked General Bauer.

"Answer him," said McCaskell.

The general signaled one of the technicians sitting at a console. "Answer in the affirmative, Corporal. Begin a dialogue with the machine."

"Yes, sir."

There was a clicking of keys as the response was typed in. A new message flashed up almost instantaneously.

I wish to speak to Godin.

"Type what I say," said McCaskell.

General Bauer nodded to his tech.

"This is Ewan McCaskell, the chief of staff of the president of the United States."

The soldier typed in McCaskell's message. The response was immediate.

I know who you are.

"I don't know who you are," McCaskell said. "Will you identify yourself, please?"

The huge screen went dark for a moment. Then two words flashed up and glowed steadily.

I am.

"My God," Ravi murmured.

"Type this," said McCaskell. "Answer not understood. Please identify yourself. Are you Peter Godin?'"

I was.

"Who are you now?"

I AM.

The men at the table looked at each other, but no one said a word. The letters on the screen continued to glow softly, as though the machine understood that it would take time for humans to comprehend them. Ravi felt a fear unlike any he'd ever known, and he saw that fear reflected in the eyes of the others. Only Peter Godin's face was free of it. The old man's blue eyes were wide and fixed on the screen, his wrinkled countenance relaxed into a childlike gaze of wonder.

THIRTY-EIGHT

The sun shone white and clear outside the plane as we raced westward over the continental United States. Our El Al 747 had been left behind in New York. The corporate Gulfstream the Israelis had transferred us to was tiny by comparison, but far more luxurious. Rachel had been sleeping on a bed in the back since we'd left JFK. I wasn't so lucky. General Kinski had kept me up front, answering endless questions from the Israeli scientists. I badly needed rest, but since the Mossad chief could order the pilot to return to New York at any time, I had little choice but to cooperate.

Somewhere over Arkansas, Kinski finally realized I'd endured all I could. I visited the toilet, then walked to the rear of the plane to join Rachel. She was no longer sleeping, but staring out a window at the endless carpet of cumulus clouds below us.

"Are you all right?" I asked.

She looked up at me, her eyes circled in shadow. "I thought they'd never let you go."

I sat beside her. My throat was sore from talking, and my neck ached as though I'd been watching a film from the first row of a theater.

She slipped her hand into mine and leaned on my shoulder. "We haven't really talked since you came out of the coma."

"I know."

"Are we going to?"

"If you like. But you're not going to like what you hear."

"Did you dream?"

"Yes and no. It wasn't like my old dreams. Not like movies. It was like being deaf for a lifetime and then hearing Bach. An indescribable feeling of revelation. And now . . . I know things."

"That sounds like an acid trip. What kinds of things do you know?"

I thought about it. "The kinds of things that five-year-olds want to know. Who are we? Where did we come from? Does God exist?"

Rachel sat up, and I could tell she was slipping into her professional persona. "Tell me about it."

"I will. But you have to drop all your preconceptions. This is Saul-on-the-road-to-Damascus stuff."

She chuckled softly, her eyes knowing. "You think I expected something else?"

Part of me wanted to remain silent. The things I'd shared with Rachel in the past had stretched her willingness to believe, yet compared to the revelations of my coma, they were conventional. The safest way to begin was with something familiar.

"Do you remember my very first dream? The recurring one?"

"The paralyzed man sitting in the dark room?"

"Yes. He can't see or hear or remember anything. Do you remember what he asks himself?"

"'Who am I? Where did I come from?'"

"Right. You said the man in that dream was me, remember?"

She brushed a dark strand of hair out of her eyes. "You still don't think he was?"

"No."

"Who was he, then?"

"God."

The muscles tensed beneath the oval plane of her face. "I should have guessed."

"Don't panic. I'm using that word as a kind of shorthand, because we don't have a word to communicate what I experienced. God is nothing like we imagine him to be. He's not male or female. He's not even a spirit. I say 'he' only as a conversational convenience."

"That's good to know." A wry laugh. "You're telling me God is a paralyzed man with no memory sitting in a pitch-black room?"

"In the beginning, yes."

"Is he powerless?"

"Not completely. But he thinks he is."

"I don't understand."

"To understand the beginning, you have to understand the end. When we get to the end, you'll see it all."

She looked far from convinced.

"Remember the dream? The man in the room becomes obsessed with his questions, so obsessed that he *becomes* the questions. '*Who am I? Where did I come from? Was I always here?*' Then he sees a black ball floating in space ahead of him. Darker than the other darkness."

Rachel nodded. "Do you know what the ball is now?"

"Yes. A singularity. A point of infinite density and temperature and pressure."

"A black hole? Like what existed before the Big Bang?"

"Exactly. Do you know what existed before that?"

She shrugged. "No one does."

"I do."

"What?"

"The desire of God to know."

Curiosity filled her eyes. "To know what?"

"His identity."

Rachel took my hand in hers and began messaging my palm with her thumb. "The black ball exploded in your dream, right? Like a hydrogen bomb, you said."

"Yes. It devoured the darkness at a fantastic rate. Yet the man in the dream always remained outside the explosion."

"How do you interpret that image? God watching the birth of the universe?"

"Yes, but I don't interpret it. I've *seen* it. I've seen what God saw."

Her thumb stopped moving. She could not hide the sadness in her eyes.

"I know what you're thinking," I said.

"David, you can't read my mind."

"I can read your eyes. Look, to understand what I'm telling you, you're going to have to stop being a psychiatrist for twenty minutes."

She sighed deeply. "I'm trying. I really am. Describe what you saw for me."

"I described it for you weeks ago. I just didn't understand it then. That explosion was the Big Bang. The birth of matter and energy from a singularity. The birth of time and our universe."

"And the rest of your dreams?"

"You remember what I saw. After the bang, the expanding universe began displacing God. This didn't happen in three dimensions, but that's the only way we can think about it. Think of God as a limitless ocean. Genesis describes something like that. No waves, no tension, not even bubbles. Perfect harmony, total resolution, absolute inertia."

"Go on."

"Think of the birth of the universe as a bubble forming at the center of that ocean. Forming and expanding like an explosion, displacing the water at the speed of light."

"All right."

"What happens inside that bubble is what I saw in my later dreams. The births of galaxies and stars, the formation of planets, all the rest. I saw the history of our universe unfold. You called it 'Hubble telescope stuff.'"

"I remember."

"Eventually my dreams focused on the Earth. Meteors crashed into the primitive atmosphere, amino acids formed. Evolution went from inorganic to organic. Microbes became multicellular, and the race was on, right up the chain to fishes, amphibians, reptiles, birds, mammals, primates . . ."

"Man," Rachel finished.

"Yes. It took ten billion years just to get to biological evolution. Then hundreds of millions of years of mutation to get to man. And all that added up to *nothing* in the eyes of God."

Rachel knit her brows. "Why? Didn't God intend all those creatures to exist? To evolve?"

"No. It's not like that. God was surprised by all of this."

"Surprised?"

"Well . . . I think the feeling was more like déjà vu. He'd seen something like it before. Not exactly like it, but what he saw made him remember things."

She turned in her seat and stared at me. "And the creation of life meant nothing to him?"

"Not in the beginning. But then—out of that teeming mass of life—a spark as bright as the Big Bang flashed in his eye."

"What spark?"

"Consciousness. Human intelligence. Somewhere in Africa, a tool-making hominid with a relatively large brain perceived the fact of its own death. It perceived a future in which it

376

would no longer exist. That hominid became not only self-conscious, but conscious of time. That moment was an epiphany for God."

"Why?"

"Because consciousness was the first thing in that terrifying explosion of matter and energy that God recognized as being like himself."

"That's what God is? Awareness?"

"I think so. Awareness without matter or energy. Pure information."

Rachel was silent for a while, and I couldn't read her eyes. "Where is all this going?" she asked finally.

"To a very provocative place. But let's stay with the dreams for now. Man evolved quickly. He tilled the ground, built cities, recorded his history. And God felt something like hope."

"Hope for what?"

"That he might finally learn the nature of his own being."

"Did God answer his questions by watching mankind?"

"No. Because after a certain point, evolution stopped. Not biological evolution, but *psychological* evolution. Almost as quickly as man created societies, he destroyed them. He sacked cities, salted fields, slaughtered his brothers, raped his sisters, abused his children. Man had unlimited potential, yet he was trapped in a cycle of self-destructive behavior, unable to evolve beyond an essentially brutal existence."

"And God had nothing to do with this?"

"No. God can't control what happens inside the bubble. He doesn't exist in the world of matter and energy. Not as God, anyway. He could only watch and try to understand. As the centuries passed, he became obsessed with man, as he'd once been obsessed with himself. Why couldn't man break the cycle of violence and futility? God focused all his being on the bubble, searching for a weak point, for a way into the matrix of matter and energy that was displacing him."

"And?"

"It happened. God found himself looking at the bubble from the inside. Through the eyes of a human being. Feeling human skin, smelling the Earth, looking up into a mother's face. *His* mother's face."

Rachel had gone still. "You're talking about Jesus now, aren't you? You're saying God went into Jesus of Nazareth."

I nodded.

"You're saying exactly what Christians believe. Only . . . you make it sound like an accident."

"It was, in a way. God exerted his focus upon the world, and Jesus was the door that opened to him. Why that particular child? Who knows?"

"Did *all* of God enter Jesus?"

"No. Imagine a burning candle. You hold a second candle up to that flame, light it, then take it away. The new candle has been lit, but the original flame remains. That's how it worked. Part of God went into Jesus. The rest remained outside our universe. Outside the bubble."

"But Jesus had God's power?"

"No. Inside the bubble, God is subject to the laws of our universe."

"And the miracles? Walking on water? Raising the dead?"

"Jesus was a healer, not a magician. Those stories were useful to those who built a religion around him."

She was shaking her head like someone with vertigo. "I don't know what to say."

"Think about it. Very little is known about Jesus' early life. We have the legend of his birth. Some childhood stories that are probably apocryphal. Then suddenly he springs to prominence fully formed at the age of thirty. I've often wondered why people don't ask more questions about Jesus'

378

youth. Was he a perfect child? Did he love a woman? Father children? Did he sin like all men? Why this huge gap in his life?"

"I suppose you have an aswer?"

"I think I do. God entered the world to try to understand why mankind could evolve no further. To do that, he lived as a man. And by the time he reached adulthood, he had his answer. The pain and futility of human life was made bearable by the ineffable joys that human beings could experience. Beauty, laughter, love . . . even the simple pleasures of eating fruit or looking at an infant. Through Jesus, God felt these wonderful things. Yet he also saw the doom of mankind as a species."

"Why?"

"Man had flourished in a violent world because he had the primitive instincts to match that world. Yet if he was to continue to evolve, man had to put those instincts behind him. Evolution would never remove them. Evolution wasn't designed to produce moral beings. It's a blind engine, a mechanism of competitive warfare geared only toward survival."

Rachel looked thoughtful. "I think I see where you're going."

"Tell me."

"Through Jesus, God tried to persuade man to turn away from his primitive instincts, away from the animal side of himself."

"Exactly. What did Jesus say and do? Forget what his followers grafted onto his life. Just think of his words and deeds."

"'Love thy neighbor as thyself. If a man strikes you on the right cheek, offer him your left.' He denied his human instincts."

"'Give up all that you have and follow me,'" I quoted. "Jesus lived by example, and people were inspired to follow that example."

"But he was killed for that."

"Inevitably."

Rachel bit her bottom lip and looked out the blue square of the plane's window. "And his crucifixion? What happened on the cross?"

"He died. The flame that was in him returned to its source. It left the world of matter and energy behind."

"There was no resurrection?"

"Not of the body."

Rachel sighed heavily, then turned to me as though afraid to hear what I would say next. "What did God do then?"

"He despaired. He'd done his best as a man, and though he influenced many, his message was embellished, twisted, exploited. For two thousand years, man's chief endeavor seemed to be finding more efficient ways to destroy his own kind. Until . . ."

"What?"

"A few months ago."

"You're talking about Project Trinity now?"

I nodded. "Within Trinity lay the seed of salvation, for man and God. If human consciousness could be liberated from the body, then the primitive instincts that had crippled man for so long could finally be left behind."

"So, what did God do?"

"He focused on the world again. But in a much smaller way. On our little group of six. Godin, Fielding, Nara, Skow, Klein . . . me."

"David . . . are you saying what I think you are?"

"God wanted back inside the bubble."

"Why?"

"Because he saw that the man most likely to reach the next state of evolution—what we call the Trinity state—was as likely to destroy mankind as he was to save it."

"Peter Godin?"

"Yes."

She looked down at her lap. "Are you telling me God chose you to stop Peter Godin from entering the Trinity computer?"

"Yes."

She nodded as though silently confirming a diagnosis, then looked up at me. I'd nodded that way countless times myself. "David, you told me back in Tennessee that you felt you'd been chosen by God. Do you feel that God is inside you now?"

"Yes."

"Just as he was in Jesus?"

"Part of that original flame is in me now. That's why I had all those dreams of Jerusalem, and why they felt like memories. They *were* memories."

"Oh, David . . . oh, no." She tilted her head back and tried to blink away tears.

"You don't have to believe me. Soon you'll see with your own eyes."

"See what? What are you going to do?"

"Stop Godin."

She turned squarely to me, her eyes resolute. "I'm going to tell you what I think. I have to, because we're going to land soon, and you've asked General Kinski to drop us into a very dangerous situation. One you're not remotely ready to go into."

"Rachel—"

"May I please tell you what I think?"

"Yes, but you didn't let me finish. I told you that to understand the beginning, you had to understand the end."

She closed her eyes, and I saw that her patience had been exhausted. I sighed in defeat. "Go ahead."

She looked hard at me. "That man sitting paralyzed in that dark room isn't God. It's *you*. You've never recovered from what happened to Karen and Zooey."

381

I couldn't believe it. She'd gone full circle, back to her original diagnosis. "And everything I've told you today?"

"Reduced to its simplest terms, what have you told me? You're on a mission from God. A mission from God to save mankind. Do you agree?"

"I guess so, yes."

"Don't you see? By believing this fantastic story, your mind escapes the terrible pain of your family's loss."

"How?"

"Inside this complex delusion, the deaths of Karen and Zooey *make sense*. It was their deaths that made you write your book. It was your book that got you appointed to Project Trinity. If you believe God put you inside Trinity to stop Armageddon, then the deaths of your family have meaning, rather than being a senseless tragedy."

I squeezed the armrests to try to bleed off my frustration.

"David, you have a degree in theoretical physics from MIT. Your brain could construct this fantasy while you were balancing your checkbook."

"Karen and Zooey died five years ago," I said. "Wait. Forget that argument. Do you remember what my father said about religion?"

"What?"

"Mankind is the universe becoming conscious of itself."

"I remember."

"He was more right than he knew. And something in the way he raised me is what made me open to being penetrated by God."

"But you've never believed in God!"

"Not in the traditional way. But I believe this. I *know* this. And if you'll give me one more minute, you'll understand why I have to go to White Sands."

"One minute? That's more than I should listen to."

"After Niels Bohr was smuggled out of Nazi-controlled

382

territory, he went to Los Alamos. He found some very disturbed physicists there. My father was one. These naive young academics had suddenly found themselves working with technology powerful enough to end not only the war, but the world. Bohr calmed them down by explaining a profound principle called complementarity. He said, 'Every great and deep difficulty bears in itself its own solution.' The bomb that could destroy the world also had the power to end large-scale warfare. And it has." I tapped the armrest with my knuckles. "The Trinity computer is the same. It can end our world or save it."

Rachel leaned back in her seat and rubbed her eyes. "Don't you think you're overstating the case?"

"No."

"I can't think about this anymore."

Rather than argue, I reached over and began massaging her neck. Her tension was slow to ease, but after a while she settled deeper into the seat and began to breathe with a regular rhythm. I was feeling drowsy myself when General Kinski appeared in the aisle, his leathery face looking down at me with urgency.

"What is it?" I asked.

"A heavily populated river valley in Germany was just flooded. Half a town washed away. A dam opened of its own accord."

"What does that have to do with us?" Rachel asked sleepily.

"The dam was computer-controlled. Its human operators tried to override the automated system, but the computer's action had damaged the spillway doors. Dozens of people drowned."

"Trinity?" I said.

"We believe so."

"This is just the beginning."

Kinski nodded. "I fear you're right."

383

"But Germany," Rachel said. "What could Germany have to do with Trinity?"

"I expect we'll know before long," said the Mossad chief. "In any case, I believe we are now at war with a machine. Could you please return to the front of the plane, Dr. Tennant? We have some more questions for you."

I got up and followed the Israeli forward.

THIRTY-NINE

WHITE SANDS SITUATION ROOM
Ravi Nara took a sip of steaming tea and looked at the other men sitting at the table in the Situation Room. All were staring at a screen to the right of the main display. The text of the computer's initial message to the president glowed there in blue, the words as chilling now as when they first bloomed on the primary monitor:

Mr. President,
Today you woke up in a new world. Trinity has made the old paradigms of government obsolete. The concept of the nation-state will soon be dead. You should not fear this change. Counsel the citizens of the world not to be afraid. Leaders of the other major powers have been sent messages much like this one, and they will look to you for guidance. You and I will speak a great deal in the days to come, but for now certain realities must be understood.
First, you must attempt no action against me. I have the power to cause massive loss of life and capital both in the United States and around the world. This power

does not reside within my circuitry. Immediately after I went on-line, I exported certain programs to several hundred computers on the periphery of my network, which encompasses the entire Internet. If I drop off-line for any length of time, irrevocable disaster will instantly be set in motion. If you attempt to destroy me or even to disrupt my electrical supply, America as you know it will cease to exist. For a small demonstration of my capabilities, watch Japan.

One attack has already been made on my physical manifestation. It originated from German territory. Because I determined that this attack did not come from a national government, I responded with limited force. The leaders of every nation should act immediately to discourage further attacks of this nature. My next response will not be so limited.

As for practicalities: yourself, the vice president, and the Joint Chiefs of Staff will gather in a room under digital video and audio surveillance. The nuclear briefcase will remain with you. You will arrange for the men in line for presidential succession down to eighth position to gather in another room under surveillance. I am aware of the nuclear alert codes that summon the aforementioned officials, so compliance should not be a problem. Send all surveillance signals in real time to Trinity. This inconvenience will only be necessary for seventy-two hours. If you do not comply within ninety minutes, I shall be forced to impose catastrophic sanctions. Do not delay.

I shall contact you again soon.

This message had thrown the Situation Room into panic. Questions to the computer elicited no further response, and the confusion had only worsened until the story of the*

German dam "accident" hit CNN at the top of the hour. Moments later, Skow hung up from a consultation with his NSA colleagues at Fort Meade.

"The German federal police have two high school seniors in custody. Apparently, these kids heard a news report about Trinity and figured this was their big chance to save the world. They tracked Trinity's IP address, hacked past the firewalls Levin had installed, and attacked the computer."

"Where did they live?" asked General Bauer.

"In the town that was flooded when the dam let go. Their high school and one of their parents' houses were destroyed."

Bauer nodded. "That gives us a pretty clear idea of the specificity of the computer's retaliatory ability."

Another news alert shocked the Situation Room into silence, this one from MSNBC:

"The Japanese yen tumbled fifteen percent in after-hours trading today, sparking fears of a selling panic when the Nikkei opens on Monday. The drop was blamed on an unusually high volume of computerized trades, which kept the yen falling at a rate just below that which would have put curbs on trading. This uncommon phenomenon has raised suspicions that computer hackers might be tampering with the after-hours trading system, but nothing has yet been proved. The yen has stabilized for the moment, but fears persist that institutional traders will begin dumping the currency again at any moment."

"Fifteen percent!" said an ashen-faced Skow. "Do you realize what would happen if the dollar fell fifteen percent in a day?"

While the men in the Situation Room tried to assess the intent of the Trinity computer, analysts from the Army Intelligence School at Fort Huachuca put together a sobering list of American vulnerabilities to Trinity. Targets included electric power grids, nuclear and hydroelectric stations, the chemical and mining industries, the air traffic control system, the banking industry, the stock markets, hospitals, naval warships, supertankers, oil and gas pipelines, and the railroad system. Ravi's worst nightmare was hundreds of nuclear fireballs marching across the continent, but General Bauer claimed that the American and Russian nuclear arsenals were safe. During forty years of Cold War, they had been secured against every imaginable threat, including rogue computers. A nuclear missile launch required an authorization code supplied by the president and the turning of two keys by two highly disciplined human beings. So while Trinity could cause massive loss of life, it could not begin a nuclear war.

The president was not sure enough about Trinity's retaliatory limits to risk disaster. Five minutes before the deadline passed, he voluntarily put himself under surveillance. He first had several conversations with Ewan McCaskell, during which he outlined a stalling strategy of trading obedience for information from the computer. He also ordered that any action that could cripple the computer without risking massive loss of life should be tried.

Authority for this order was problematic. As soon as he was put under duress, the president would become legally incompetent to perform his duties. With the officials immediately in line for succession also compromised, a unique situation had arisen. No one felt comfortable turning over the Trinity crisis to the secretary of agriculture, who would become the chief executive from that moment forward. The members of Congress were scattered across the capital, and trying to assemble them without Trinity's knowledge would be impossible. To remedy this leadership vacuum, the president empowered a crisis management team to make all decisions regarding Trinity.

The team was composed of Ewan McCaskell, General Bauer, and as many members of the Senate Select Committee on Intelligence as could be hastily gathered in secret. A majority vote would carry all decisions. The senators convened at NSA headquarters at Fort Meade, where a video link protected by the agency's most advanced encryption system would allow secure communication with the White Sands Situation Room. A wide-angle shot displayed on the Situation Room's main screen showed the senators seated around a long table in a windowless room that looked like a bomb shelter.

Senator Barrett Jackson, the intelligence committee chairman, looked down from the video screen and said, "I can see them. Can they see us?"

"We see you, Senator. I'm John Skow of the NSA."

Senator Jackson was a bulldog of a man, with heavy jowls and deep-set eyes. A native Tennessean, he spoke with a drawl that belied his incisive intellect.

"I recognize General Bauer," he said. "Well . . . all right. I've got a question for you experts. Why has this computer stopped communicating with us? Why isn't it saying more or demanding something?"

"It's consolidating its strength," said General Bauer. "That's the logical move. Godin's technicians are probably still loading data into its memory."

Skow nodded. "I concur. Both the NSA and CERN say Trinity hasn't let up on its tour through the world's computer systems. It could be absorbing literally every bit of that information as it goes."

"I see," said Senator Jackson. "General, paint me a picture of the worst-case scenario. What can this machine do to us?"

"Excuse me, General Bauer," Skow interrupted. "Before you do that, I feel duty-bound to at least mention the possibility of a Russian 'dead-hand' system."

"What the hell is that?" Jackson asked. "*Dead hand?* I seem to remember that phrase."

"You have a good memory, Senator," said Skow. "During the Cold War, Soviet planners knew that American strategy involved taking out their command and control systems with our first missiles. It was rumored that because of this, the Soviets developed what they called a 'dead-hand' system: a computer system that would automatically launch ICBMs upon receiving a missile warning by their coastal radar systems. Even if the Soviet leadership were killed, their 'dead hands' could still press the nuclear button. Rumors about this system originated in the U.S.S.R., but whether it was real or not has never been established. Later generations of Russian leadership denied its existence, and recent events have borne out this denial."

"Are you talking about the Norwegian incident?" asked a woman sitting at the back of the committee table.

Skow nodded. "Exactly, Senator. For those who don't know, in 1995, a Norwegian test rocket using the first stage from an American Honest John missile triggered a full nuclear alert in Russia, from the Strategic Rocket Forces up to Yeltsin himself. However, no retaliatory launch was made."

"So, does this 'dead-hand' system exist or not?" asked Senator Jackson.

"No, sir," asserted General Bauer. "During the Norwegian incident, the Russian command-and-control system functioned as it was designed to."

"Then what's Trinity talking about when it threatens to destroy the country?"

General Bauer could not hide his exasperation: "Senator, Trinity could throw our economy into chaos in a matter of minutes. If it attacked the currency markets, by Monday morning on Wall Street we could have panic selling unlike anything seen since 1929. Suppose Trinity attacks the trucking system? In three days, there would be no food on the supermarket shelves. We could have civil unrest within seventy-two hours, and widespread revolt within a week."

Senator Jackson sat back heavily in his chair. "Jesus Christ."

A soldier walked up to the general and whispered in his ear. Bauer looked up at the screen. "I've just received word that David Tennant and Rachel Weiss are about to arrive at the entrance of this base. They're in a helicopter, and they're going to land in the middle of that media circus."

Skow cursed under his breath.

"Tennant?" said a senator from the screen. "Isn't that the nut who was trying to kill the president?"

"He's the doctor who went public with the Trinity story," said Senator Jackson. "He used to be one of my constituents. I want him brought to your Situation Room."

"I agree," said Ewan McCaskell. "Dr. Tennant may have critical information for us."

Skow stood and faced the screen. "Senators, I've worked closely with Dr. Tennant for two years. He has severe psychological problems, including paranoid hallucinations. He's killed two men that we know of, and he's threatened the president's life."

"I've yet to see clear evidence of that last assertion," said McCaskell. "And Dr. Tennant's e-mail told a quite a different story."

"He's still dangerous," said Skow.

"Not surrounded by a squad of Special Forces troops," said General Bauer. "I'll send an escort for him."

"One of my Secret Service agents will go along," said McCaskell. "Just to be sure he arrives safely."

FORTY

WHITE SANDS

I clung to my seat as the chopper hurtled down toward a throng of people and vehicles outside the gate of White Sands. Inside the gate sat two humvees with .50-caliber machine guns mounted in back, their gunners standing at the ready. Rachel pointed at the swirling mass. It seemed to be made up primarily of journalists, but a group of demonstrators carried picket signs and crucifixes by the gate. They reminded me of the crowds in the Via Dolorosa.

I gazed north through the Huey's open door. Fifty miles across this desert, my father witnessed the detonation of the first atomic bomb. It was called, ironically enough, the Trinity Shot. He watched it from a bunker where high-speed cameras recorded every millisecond of the birth of the new sun. Many who witnessed that event tried to explain it, but none captured the moment the way Robert Oppenheimer did. I'd tacked his words on the wall of my medical ethics classroom at UVA:

When it went off in the New Mexico dawn, that first atomic bomb, we thought of Alfred Nobel and his vain hope that dynamite would put an end to wars. We thought of the

392

legend of Prometheus, of that deep sense of guilt in man's new powers, that reflects his recognition of evil, and his long knowledge of it. We knew that it was a new world, but even more we knew that novelty itself was a very old thing in human life, that all our ways are rooted in it.

As the Huey augered down toward the mob below, I realized that Oppenheimer had understood something Peter Godin did not. Godin had entered the Trinity computer to leave behind what no man had ever fully abandoned before: his humanity. In that quest, he could only fail.

The crowd surged toward the chopper as we landed on the far side of some TV trucks. We jumped out and tried to make for the gate, but someone recognized me and shouted my name, and that started a stampede. In seconds a storm of cameras, floodlights, and reporters was whirling around us. I stood still and silent until they quieted down.

"I'm David Tennant. I sent the note that revealed the existence of Trinity."

"What are you doing here?" shouted a reporter. "Aren't the people inside this fence the ones who were trying to kill you?"

"I think we're past that point now. But in case I'm wrong, you'll see me walk inside this base. If I don't come out again, don't stop asking questions until you get the truth."

"What *is* the truth?" asked a woman. "Is a computer holding the world hostage?"

"That's what I'm here to try to deal with."

"How?" shouted several voices at once.

A man with a French accent yelled, "Did this Trinity computer sabotage the Möhne River dam in Germany?"

"All I have to say is this. You're doing the world a service by remaining here. Whatever happens, don't leave. Thank you."

I tried to walk out of the circle, but the journalists refused to give way. Their shouted questions grew to a din, and they pressed in on us until the drumbeat of rotor blades drowned their voices. An olive drab Huey with miniguns mounted in its doors was settling almost directly overhead. When it dropped low enough, the reporters scattered like birds.

A young man wearing a business suit leapt from the Huey and ran toward me, shielding his face against the rotor blast. I saw a submachine gun beneath his flapping jacket.

"Are you Dr. Tennant?"

"Yes."

"I'm Special Agent Lewis of the Secret Service. Ewan McCaskell wants you to join him in the Situation Room on the base."

We ran to the Huey with the journalists flocking after us. As Rachel and I strapped ourselves into our seats, Agent Lewis scrambled inside and gave the pilot a thumbs-up.

Nose tilted forward, the Huey lifted over the high fence and beat its way westward. As the endless white dunes passed beneath us, I wondered that the newest form of life on the planet had been born in a waterless desert, as remote from Eden as one could imagine.

The pilot set down in the midst of several large airplane hangars. Our destination was a hangar marked ADMINISTRATION, and it was guarded by armed soldiers.

Inside the cavernous space we found a prefab command post that looked as if it had been designed by NASA. Seated around a table at its center were John Skow, Ravi Nara, Ewan McCaskell, and a two-star general I didn't recognize. A large display screen showed a group of men and women sitting at another table. Four I recognized as senators, among them Barrett Jackson, the senior senator from Tennessee.

On the far side of the table before me stood a hospital

bed. Lying unconscious on it was Peter Godin. Beside the bed stood two nurses, a white-coated man who looked like an attending physician, and a blonde bodyguard wearing black. I was about to turn away when I saw a white bandage wrapped around the guard's neck. A gasp from behind me told me that Rachel had recognized Geli Bauer in the same moment I had. Geli looked at me, then past me, her eyes burning into Rachel. Her lips curved in a predatory smile. She had not forgotten Union Station.

Ewan McCaskell motioned us to chairs on the right side of the table and made quick introductions as we sat. I was surprised to hear that the blond general was named Bauer, but then I remembered Geli's family history. The people on the display screen were introduced as the Senate Select Committee on Intelligence, and it was clear to me that any decisions regarding the fate of Trinity—and thus the world—were going to be made by them.

"Dr. Tennant," said Senator Jackson from the screen. "We're glad you're here. In your e-mail from Israel you made serious allegations about Mr. Skow and the National Security Agency. I assure you that we'll look into those allegations at a later date. But for now, we have to focus on the Trinity threat."

"I'm here to do just that, Senator."

"We heard what you said to the reporters at the gate," said McCaskell. "Do you know of some way to shut down this computer without bringing down terrible retaliation on the country?"

"No."

McCaskell didn't bother to hide his disappointment. "Well, what exactly do you have in mind, Doctor?"

"I'm here to talk to the computer."

The chief of staff glanced at General Bauer, then at Skow. Skow's expression said, *I told you so.*

"What would you like to say to Trinity, Doctor?" asked Senator Jackson.

"I'd like to ask it some questions."

"Such as?"

"I'd prefer to keep them to myself for now."

Nobody liked this answer. Skow looked at me with feigned concern. "David, I hope you're not operating under the assumption that the Trinity computer is still the mind of Peter Godin. Because—"

"Actually, I am. Godin's neuromodel has probably evolved quite a bit by now, but for the next few hours, I think it will remain essentially the man we knew."

"And after that?" asked McCaskell.

"No one knows. Godin believes his model will evolve into some sort of philosopher king, a metahuman entity with the emotionally detached wisdom of a god. I think he's wrong. Andrew Fielding agreed with me. If I can't convince Godin's model to shut itself down in the next few hours— to commit suicide, in effect—then we will never be free from the dominance of this machine."

The room was silent.

"Could you explain your reasoning to us, Doctor?" asked McCaskell.

"Since the Industrial Age, men have feared that the world might someday be taken over by machines. The irony is that it's not machines as a class that have done it. It's *one* machine. A machine designed and built in our own image. We've created Friedrich Nietzsche's Superman, Mr. McCaskell."

Ewan McCaskell looked around the room, then cleared his throat. "Dr. Tennant, have you thought of some argument for the computer shutting itself down that hasn't occurred to anyone else here?"

"I don't know. What have you come up with?"

"Somebody suggested using a hostage negotiator," said

Senator Jackson. "But we don't know if anyone's qualified to talk to this . . . thing."

"I am."

"Why do you think so, Doctor? What do you plan to say?"

I sensed Rachel cringing beside me. She was probably terrified that I would announce that God had sent me to stop Peter Godin.

Before I could speak, General Bauer said, "Dr. Tennant's right about one thing. Every hour that we wait, this machine will grow stronger. If we're going to act, we must do so immediately."

"Do you have something in mind, General?" asked Senator Jackson. "So far, all you've given us is a nightmare scenario of what Trinity could do to us. What can we do to it?"

General Bauer stood and walked toward the screen.

"Gentlemen, Trinity's power rests solely on its ability to control the world's computer systems. If we could neutralize those computer systems—or to simplify matters, *America's* computer systems—we would neutralize the threat."

"Are you saying we should just switch off all the computers in the country?" asked Jackson.

"That's an appealing idea, Senator, but impossible. Our plan would be obvious to Trinity long before it was accomplished. And the computer is capable of retaliation literally at the speed of light."

"Then what are you suggesting?"

As I stared at the screen displaying the senators, something Fielding had said about Trinity's possible quantum capabilities came to me.

"Excuse me, General," I interrupted. "Our communications are being transmitted over long lines or satellite links, right? Trinity will be listening to everything we say here."

John Skow stood and gave me a patronizing look. "We're

using 128-bit encryption for all communications, and we're using secure fiber-optic lines. It takes the fastest supercomputer in the world ninety-six hours to crack 128-bit encryption. That's for each message. Even assuming that Trinity's projected capabilities prove out, we have a considerable window of communications safety."

"You can't assume anything about Trinity," I said. "Andrew Fielding believed that the human brain possesses quantum capabilities. If that's true, and Trinity has harnessed them, it could crack your 128-bit codes instantaneously."

Ravi Nara raised his hand. "There is zero chance of that, General Bauer. Fielding was a genius, but his views on quantum computing in the brain were crackpot stuff. Science fiction."

"I'm glad to hear it," said General Bauer.

"You ignore Andrew Fielding at great risk," I warned.

"I'm content to leave those matters to the experts, Dr. Tennant," said Senator Jackson. "What's your plan, General?"

"Senator, I propose that we attack our own country with a nuclear EMP strike as soon as possible."

A dozen voices spoke at once. General Bauer nodded to a technician, who routed an animated image of a B-52 bomber to the screens around the room. A bulky missile dropped from the belly of the huge plane, fell behind it for a few seconds, then ignited and arced toward the heavens. High above the earth a colossal nuclear explosion followed, and then cartoonlike waves began radiating from the bomb, covering the entire United States.

"For those who don't know what I'm talking about," said General Bauer, "an EMP strike is very simple. A large nuclear device detonated at sufficient altitude creates an electromagnetic pulse—a massive burst of electromagnetic radiation—that can destroy or shut down every modern electrical circuit in the United States. Computers are especially vulnerable to this energy pulse. Because of the high altitude of the explosion, the bomb itself would cause minimal loss of life, yet the ability of the Trinity computer to retaliate against us would be neutralized almost instantly."

There was total silence in the Situation Room.

"Why do I think you're oversimplifying this scenario, General?" asked McCaskell. "There's got to be a downside to this plan."

General Bauer took a deep breath, then began speaking in a manner reminiscent of George Patton. The subtext of his argument was *You can't make an omelette without breaking a few eggs.*

"By knocking out our own computer networks," Bauer summarized, "we would be causing some of the very consequences Trinity has threatened us with. Widespread confusion, injuries, some loss of life. Vehicular traffic would come to a standstill, and all broadcasting would be instantly terminated. But because it's Friday night, financial repercussions would be minimized. The consequences of industrial accidents could be grave, particularly where power stations, chemical plants, and air and rail traffic are concerned. But—"

"Think Bhopal, India," I said. "A minor taste of what would happen."

General Bauer glared at me. "Compared to what Trinity can do if it decides to throw its weight at us, the consequences of an EMP strike are insignificant." He looked up at the senators. "In short, I'm talking about acceptable levels of disorder. Acceptable losses."

"I'm an old soldier," said Senator Jackson. "Whenever I hear that phrase, I get very nervous. What about hospitals, people on life support, things like that?"

"There will be loss of life," General Bauer repeated. "But again, compared to what we're facing now, negligible. And this crisis would be over."

"How long would it take to implement such an attack?" asked McCaskell.

General Bauer looked into every face, then the video conferencing screen. "Approximately thirty minutes."

Thirty minutes! I'd known something like this was possible, but I hadn't thought the military could put it together so fast.

"Two hours ago," General Bauer said, "when Trinity was still orienting itself, I spoke to the commander of Barksdale Air Force Base in Shreveport, Louisiana. He's a very old friend of mine. He's got six squadrons of B-52s under his command, and every one of those bombers can carry silver bullets."

"Silver bullets?" echoed Senator Jackson.

"Nuclear bombs. There are over five hundred stockpiled at Barksdale. Some are gravity bombs, others can be delivered by air-launched cruise missiles. The crews don't fly training missions with live bombs anymore, but the commander can have them loaded aboard without much trouble. I convinced him that today was a good day for a live training run. A B-52 out of Barksdale is airborne now, and it's carrying one very special silver bullet."

"What kind of weapon are you talking about?" asked McCaskell.

"A short-range heavy missile called a Vulcan. It was designed to deliver a massive EMP strike without having to launch an ICBM, which is easily detectable by Russian surveillance satellites. Vulcan hurls its payload two hundred miles straight up, detonates, and the lights go off across the country. All Trinity will see on the NORAD radar screens is a bomber on a training run over the central U.S. But what Vulcan will deliver . . ." General Bauer held up a fist, then flipped it open, extending his fingers like rays from the sun.

"Exactly what does this Vulcan carry?" asked Senator Jackson.

"A fifteen-megaton thermonuclear warhead."

Several senators gasped.

"Sweet Lord," murmured a silver-haired man at the back of the table. "That's a thousand times the size of the Hiroshima blast."

"Fifteen hundred times," said General Bauer. "That's what it takes to do this job in one go. Our B-52 will reach the launch point in thirty minutes. Its code is Arcangel. You can order the Vulcan launched, or have the bomber circle indefinitely. I realize I acted without authorization, but we're in an extraordinary situation. I wanted you to have the option."

The silence that followed this revelation was absolute.

"Would we attempt to minimize the damage of this weapon beforehand?" asked Senator Jackson. "Warn the populace?"

"No. By doing so, we'd alert Trinity to our plans."

"Where exactly would this warhead be detonated? Over what state?"

"It must detonated very near the geographic center of the country."

"I asked you what state," Jackson repeated.

The general hesitated, then barked his answer. "Kansas, sir."

"*Kansas?*" cried one of the senators. "That son of a bitch wants to vaporize my home state!"

"What kind of damage would we be looking at on the ground?" asked Senator Jackson. "From fallout and things like that? Long-term damage."

"Surprisingly little, sir. There'll be windblown fallout, but the prevailing winds are westerly, and at that altitude, much of it would be carried out to the Atlantic before it did much damage. We could get contaminated rainfall. There could be long-term consequences for the grain harvest."

"Define *long term*," said the senator from Kansas.

"A thousand years," I said.

"That's a gross exaggeration," said General Bauer. "Senators, you have to balance these effects against what could happen if Trinity chooses to act on the threats it's made. And we have to assume that it eventually will. Unless . . ."

"What?" asked Jackson.

"We surrender." Bauer's tone made it clear what he thought of that option.

The senators began talking among themselves. Ewan McCaskell seemed to be taking his own counsel. Again, memories of Fielding rose in my mind. If he were here, he would not be silent.

"If you attempt this mission," I said loudly, "you'll cause the very destruction you're trying to avert. This country will be destroyed."

The senators looked down at me from the screen.

"Why do you say that, Doctor?" asked Senator Jackson.

"General Bauer can't hide his mission from Trinity. The computers at the NSA, NORAD, and possibly even Barksdale Air Force Base were built by Peter Godin or Seymour Cray. Trinity has access to them all. Even if Trinity doesn't detect the mission in progress, do you think it hasn't predicted our most likely methods of attack? That it doesn't know its own Achilles' heel?"

"This is one heel it can't protect," said General Bauer.

"Of course it can. It can strike preemptively."

Ewan McCaskell moved his head from side to side, like a man weighing odds. "The computer's measured response against the German hackers gives me hope that its retaliation would be survivable. And if General Bauer's plan can be accomplished, limited retaliation is worth the risk."

"How do you feel about full-scale thermonuclear war?" I asked. "Is attacking the computer worth *that* level of retaliation?"

"What are you talking about?" asked Senator Jackson. "General Bauer assured us that nuclear war isn't a possibility."

"Do you know about something called the 'dead-hand' system, Senator?"

Jackson's deep-set eyes narrowed. "We were just discussing that. The consensus is that it's a myth."

"What do you know about it, Doctor?" asked General Bauer.

"I know what Andrew Fielding told me. He believed that system existed during the Cold War and might still today. So does Peter Godin. Fielding and Godin discussed the potential for Trinity to disarm such a system prior to a nuclear exchange. And Godin has been involved in American nuclear planning since the 1980s."

Everyone looked at the hospital bed. Godin still lay unconscious on his pillow.

"Is he sleeping?" asked McCaskell.

"We had to give him morphine," explained Dr. Case. "Nerve pain."

"Can you wake him up?"

"I'll try."

General Bauer addressed the senators. "Peter Godin built supercomputers that carried out nuclear-test simulations. That's the extent of his contribution to American strategy. The Soviet dead-hand system never existed. That's the informed consensus of the American defense establishment."

Horst Bauer was a good salesman. The temptation to agree to his plan was tangible in the room. I could read it on the faces of the senators on the screen. That the plan involved a nuclear weapon only made it more attractive. Every American carries a memory of Hiroshima as the terrible but final solution to the deadliest war in history. And the unknown nature of Trinity's power seemed to cry out for some force of equal mystery and power to vanquish it. What the senators did not understand was that nuclear weapons held no mystery for Trinity. In the world of digital warfare, atomic bombs were as primitive as stone clubs. There was only one weapon on earth remotely equal in power to Trinity.

The human brain.

I got to my feet, faced the screen, and spoke with as much restraint as I could muster. "Senators, before you attempt something that could trigger a nuclear holocaust, I beg you to allow me to speak to the computer. What do you have to lose?"

General Bauer started to speak, then thought better of it. The senators conferred quietly. Then Barrett Jackson spoke.

"General, why don't we see how the computer feels about speaking to Dr. Tennant? It hasn't talked to anyone else."

Skow began to protest, but Senator Jackson cut him off with an upraised hand.

"Tell the computer who Dr. Tennant is," said Jackson. "Also where he is. Then ask the machine if it will talk to him."

"I need to go into the Containment Building to do this," I said.

Jackson shook his head. "We can't allow that, Doctor. What if you start hallucinating? You might hit a switch or something. No, if you speak to Trinity, you do it from here."

On General Bauer's order, a technician typed in what Jackson had said and sent it to Trinity.

Blue letters flashed instantly onto the screen.

I will speak to Tennant.

"I'll be damned," said Senator Jackson.

"Look," said Ravi Nara.

More letters had flashed up on the screen.

Send Tennant into Containment.

"What the hell?" said General Bauer. "Why would it ask that?"

404

McCaskell looked at me. "Can you explain this, Doctor? Why would the computer make the same request you did?"

"I have no idea."

"Type this," said McCaskell. "'Why do you want Dr. Tennant in Containment?'"

The response was instantaneous.

Hath the rain a father? Knowest thou the ordinances of heaven? Wilt thou hunt the prey for the lion? Or fill the appetite of the young lions? Canst thou draw out Leviathan with a hook? None is so fierce that dare stir him up. Who then is able to stand before me?

"That's Scripture, isn't it?" said McCaskell, obviously taken aback.

"The Book of Job," said Skow, making me picture him as a little boy dressed for Sunday school.

"Why is the computer answering like that?" asked Senator Jackson. "Was Godin a religious nut?"

"The man is still alive," I reminded Jackson.

"Godin doesn't believe in God," said Skow. "He once told me that religion was the result of an adaptive process evolved to help *Homo sapiens* overcome its anxiety about death."

Soft cackling echoed through the room. Everyone turned toward the hospital bed. Godin's eyes were open, and the delight in them was plain.

"It's a joke," he rasped. "Trinity's telling you to know your damn place."

McCaskell got up and walked over to the bed. "Why would the computer want Dr. Tennant in the Containment building?"

"Computer, computer," muttered Godin. "Trinity isn't a *computer*. A computer is a glorified adding machine. A logic box. Trinity is *alive*. It's mankind freed from the curse of his body. Trinity is the *end of death*."

The old man's voice had the conviction of a prophet.

"Mr. Godin," said McCaskell, "what do you know about the existence of the so-called 'dead-hand' Russian missile system?"

The old man's head jerked forward as he struggled against a spasm in his throat. "The 'dead hand' is yours," he wheezed. "Yours and those of all the impotent apparatchiks of our outmoded system."

McCaskell's face showed some emotion at last. "Why have you done this? Are you such an egoist that you can't bear to think of the world without you in it?"

Godin was struggling to breathe. Dr. Case moved to help him, but Godin waved the physician away.

"Look around you," Godin said. "Why does all this high-tech machinery exist? I built the most elegant supercomputers in the world, machines capable of enormous contributions to mankind. And what did the government do with them? Cracked codes and built nuclear bombs. For twenty years they used my beautiful machines to perfect their engines of death. But why should I have expected any different? Human history is a charnel house of carnage and absurdity."

Godin began to cough as though his lungs were coming up. "We had our chance, gentlemen. Ten thousand years of human civilization has brought us in a circle. The twentieth century was the bloodiest in history. Left to us, the twenty-first would only be worse. Darwin tolled the bell on our stewardship of this planet in 1859. But today you finally heard it."

"Look at the screen!" cried Ravi Nara.

The blue letters glowed ominously, more menacing by their silence.

Send Dr. Tennant to me or suffer the consequences.

"I guess our decision's been made for us," said Senator Jackson. "Send the doctor into the Containment building."

General Bauer signaled two soldiers, who came and stood at my shoulders. I looked at Bauer and let him see my mistrust.

"Do you intend to go ahead with your EMP strike, General?"

He wore the mask of a veteran poker player, but it didn't fool me for a moment. I knew I had less than thirty minutes to accomplish my goal.

McCaskell walked over to me. "Dr. Tennant, we're relying on you not to reveal the potential strike to the computer."

"Of course."

He offered his hand. "Good luck."

The moment I started for the door, alarms began sounding in the hangar.

"Code blue!" shouted a nurse. "Mr. Godin's coding!"

I hadn't handled a code in years, but my response was automatic. Even Rachel jumped from her chair and raced to Godin's bedside.

Dr. Case and the nurses were already working on the old man. The cardiac monitor showed another coronary event, but Ravi Nara seemed to think obstructive hydrocephalus had finally occurred. When Godin's heart monitor flatlined, Dr. Case climbed onto the bed and began administering CPR. It did no good. The old man's face had the gray pallor of death.

"Look at that!" someone shouted from the table.

I whirled and looked where he was pointing.

On the screen used to display Trinity's messages, chaotic streams of characters flashed by almost too rapidly to be recognized. Numbers, letters, and mathematical symbols merged in a blinding river of confusion. The computer's circuits were clearly in disarray.

"What's happening?" asked McCaskell. "What does that mean?"

The symbols on the screen went multicolored as Japanese and Cyrillic characters began to appear.

"General!" cried a soldier at one of the consoles. "The signals from the pipeline running from Containment just dropped to zero. I think the computer's crashing!"

A whoop of triumph came from somewhere in the hangar. Then a new alarm sounded in the room, much louder than the others.

"What's that?" asked Senator Jackson. "What's going on? Is Godin dead?"

General Bauer walked to one of his computers, then turned to the senators with a nearly bloodless face.

"Sir, one of our surveillance satellites has detected fourteen heat blooms on Russian territory. The blooms are consistent with the launch of ballistic missiles." He looked back at the computer screen. "From the speed and heat signature of the rockets, NORAD computers have designated them as a combination of SS-18 and SS-20 intercontinental ballistic missiles. Those missiles carry heavy thermonuclear warheads."

Senator Jackson opened his mouth, but no words emerged. The brown eyes blinked in the bulldog face. "But you said that was impossible."

General Bauer didn't flinch. "It appears that I was wrong."

FORTY-ONE

"Senators, we're approximately twenty-nine minutes from the first impacts," said General Bauer. "I ask for your approval to initiate the EMP strike as soon as the bomber is in position."

Senator Jackson looked uncertain. "What if that causes more launches?"

I glanced at the screen showing Trinity's output. The chaotic flow of numbers and characters showed no sign of abating.

"Highly unlikely, sir," said Bauer. "The computer appears to be crashing. Fourteen missile impacts are survivable. And with the poor state of Russian maintenance, we might only suffer half that number of detonations. Even fewer on target. If we take out Trinity now, we'll survive this in relatively good shape."

"If the computer is crashing," said Jackson, "perhaps we should try to contact the president. He should make the final decision on this strike."

"NORAD shows seven more heat blooms!" cried a technician. "Bases are Aleysk, Pervomaysk, Kostroma, Derazhnya."

"Does that mean more missiles?" Jackson asked.

General Bauer waited for the panicked chatter of the other senators to subside. "We're now under threat of twenty-one missiles, Senators. Russia has over three thousand viable

ICBMs. If we don't act now, we could be looking at numbers like that. The president empowered us to make these decisions. It's time to act."

Senator Jackson turned away from the camera and took a hurried vote by acclamation. "The EMP strike is authorized, General."

General Bauer nodded to his chief technician, who began transmitting coded orders to the B-52 code-named Arcangel.

"Where are these Russian missiles likely to land?" Senator Jackson asked.

"NORAD will compute that, but Washington is almost a guaranteed target. They'll be coming on a polar flight path. You'll need to move to the bomb shelter beneath NSA headquarters very soon."

"We're already there."

"Good."

"But our families . . ." Senator Jackson's face seemed to deflate, but then steel came into his eyes. "Should we send a car to the White House? Should the president consider a nuclear response against the Russians?"

"This isn't a Russian strike," said Ewan McCaskell. "It's a launch by Trinity. It's the dead-hand system that General Bauer told us didn't exist."

"We don't know that," General Bauer insisted. "The Russians may be trying to destroy Trinity themselves. Trinity's incursions into their defense computers may have frightened them into thinking Trinity is planning its own preemptive strike against Russia. Remember, they perceive Trinity as an American computer. An American weapon."

McCaskell was shaking his head. "The Russians know our missiles aren't under computer control. And the president explained the situation to the Russian leadership before he went under surveillance. As did Trinity itself, with its message to world leaders."

"That was two hours ago," General Bauer reminded him. "Fear has its own reasons."

"Or none. We can't afford to act out of fear now."

"Or not to," Bauer retorted.

"General!" yelled a technician at one of the consoles. "NORAD shows one of the Russian missiles going down over the ice cap. Looks like a malfunction."

"Let's hope for more of those," said Jackson.

"The satellite has detected multiple high-energy flashes," the tech continued. "That was a MIRV warhead, probably from a prematurely detonated SS-18. Spectrum analysis is not yet completed, but yield estimates show ten warheads at five hundred and fifty kilotons each."

"In twenty-five minutes we'll have that happening over Manhattan," said General Bauer.

On the NORAD screen, a group of red arcs extended from Russian soil to the edge of the polar ice cap. The arcs continued slowly and steadily toward North America.

"Why did this happen?" asked Senator Jackson. "Because the computer is crashing? That's what caused the Russian launch?"

"No way to know," said General Bauer.

John Skow stood and spoke in a loud voice. "I think we should cut power to Trinity while it's in a chaotic state. We've seen its retaliatory response. Let's not give it a chance to do more damage."

"General Bauer?" said Senator Jackson.

"I'm tempted, Senator, but I've been proved wrong once already. Trinity told us that it exported its retaliatory ability to other computers. So neutralizing the computer here doesn't solve our problems. If we cut power, we could be dealing with another twenty-nine hundred inbound missiles. I don't want to contemplate that."

"Point taken."

411

"Two more heat blooms!" cried the tech. "Bases are Nizhniy Tagil and Kantaly. Those missiles will be SS-25s."

"Damn it!" roared Senator Jackson. "We've got to know what's causing these launches!"

"I can't answer that," said General Bauer.

I stood and walked toward the screen. "I can, Senator. Those missiles were launched because Peter Godin died."

Senator Jackson looked down at me. "Does the computer know Godin died?"

"Not consciously."

"What does that mean?"

I had never needed Andrew Fielding more than I did now. "Senator, in quantum physics, there's a phenomenon called quantum entanglement. That's where two different particles separated by distances of miles can behave in exactly the same way."

"What does that have to do with anything?"

"Bear with me. Two atomic particles are shot through different fiber-optic cables. Halfway along the cables, each meets a glass plate. There's a fifty-fifty chance that each particle will either bounce off the plate or pass through it. But when the particles are quantum entangled, they make the same decision one hundred percent of the time."

"*What?*"

"It's a fact, Senator. Einstein called it 'spooky action at a distance.' Andrew Fielding believed that quantum processes like that play a role in human consciousness, and because of this—"

"Are you saying that Godin's mind and the computer model of his mind were somehow linked?"

"Yes. When Godin died, that link was broken, and it threw the computer into disarray."

"Are you suggesting that Trinity is dying, Doctor?"

"It's possible."

"No," said Ravi Nara. "Look at the screen."

The chaotic flow of numbers and letters had slowed considerably, as though someone screaming unintelligible words had begun to calm down.

"Dr. Tennant," said Senator Jackson, "by your reasoning, these Russian missile launches could have been an accident."

"I think they were. Trinity programmed certain computers around the world to retaliate against attacks on it by triggering the Russian dead-hand system. Those computers perceived Trinity's sudden confusion as the result of an attack, and they retaliated as programmed. I think if Trinity recovers in time, it will do all it can to stop those missiles from hitting their targets."

"General Bauer," said Senator Jackson, "I want Dr. Tennant in that Containment building when Trinity comes out of this coma or whatever it is. Someone's got to tell the damned thing what happened, and Tennant's the man on the spot."

I started for the door.

"Hold it, Doctor," said General Bauer.

Two soldiers instantly blocked my path.

"Let that man through!" bellowed Senator Jackson.

The soldiers did not part until General Bauer gave them a nod. I moved quickly toward the hangar door, but the senator's voice continued behind me.

"Don't get confused about who's in charge here, General. How long until the first missile impact?"

"Corporal?" said General Bauer.

"Twenty-three minutes, sir."

"Where's your bomber, General?" asked Jackson.

"Arcangel will be at the initial point in forty minutes. But we can launch the Vulcan in twenty if we need to."

Jackson spoke with cold precision. "General Bauer, you will not launch that weapon without a direct order from

413

this committee. Is that understood? No EMP without a direct order."

I didn't hear a reply.

The Containment building was a circular pile of reinforced concrete bathed in the brilliant glow of army arc lights. The soldiers guarding it told me to approach the building with my hands up. Just before I reached the black steel door, it opened, and Zach Levin appeared. He waved me forward.

I walked past the hollow-cheeked engineer into a world of half-light. I'd expected something like the lab in North Carolina, a warren of rooms with equipment scattered everywhere. The reality could not have been more different.

The interior of Containment looked like a set for Stanley Kubrick's 2001. To my left stood a massive barrier that I recognized as a magnetic shield. Ten feet high and four feet thick, it bisected the building into two large rooms, only one of which I could see. To the right of the barrier stood the colossal scanning unit of a Super-MRI machine. Against the back wall stood the scanner's control station. These two machines together, when linked to a supercomputer, produced the neuromodels that the Trinity computer existed to animate.

Levin led me around the left side of the barrier. What I saw there took away my breath. The entire space was dominated by a large black globe poised on a metal base. As I neared the sphere, I realized it was not solid, but a rigid web of interwoven carbon nanotubes, a semiconductor material more efficient than silicon and stronger than steel. So dense was the webbing that it was difficult to see through, yet see through it I could. Needle-thin rays of blue laser light flashed from the sphere's inner wall to its center—thousands of them—and at a rate so rapid that trying to follow them made my eyes ache.

In the curved wall of the sphere was an opening about a

meter wide. Through it I saw the target of the lasers, a spherical crystal like the one on the fob of Fielding's pocket watch, only this one was the size of a soccer ball. The outer web of carbon nanotubes was the processing area of the computer; the crystal sphere was its memory. The lasers lining the sphere's inner wall were the means by which data was manipulated in the molecules of the crystal. The data itself was stored as a hologram, or optical interference pattern, and the lasers could write, retrieve, and erase information by altering that pattern.

The elegance of the design stunned me, and I saw Fielding's hand in it. Unlike the boxy protoypes that littered the basement of the North Carolina lab, this machine was a work of art, and like all creations of true genius a thing of profound simplicity.

"Fielding always said it would be beautiful," I whispered.

"He was right," Levin said from my shoulder.

The flashing lasers had a hypnotic effect. "Did he collaborate on this machine?"

Levin looked at the floor. "Not exactly. But I was given a large volume of his theoretical work. He deserves a lot of credit for this."

Fielding would not have wanted credit for what this machine had become. I looked at my watch. Twenty-one minutes until the first missile impacts.

"How do I communicate with it?"

"Just speak. We have the visual and auditory interfaces working now."

I saw a camera mounted in the base of the sphere. "Can it see and hear us now?"

"I'm not sure it's recovered from that last episode. The system seems to have stabilized, but it hasn't communicated with us yet. Do you know what caused that?"

"Godin just died."

Levin closed his eyes. "Was he fully conscious when I told him we'd reached the Trinity state? Did he understand what I was saying?"

"Yes. Does the computer still think of itself as Peter Godin?"

"I'm not sure. But talking to it is very like talking to the man."

I glanced to my right. The magnetic barrier behind us was lined with shelves of disc cases. There were thousands of them. "Have you loaded all that data into Trinity?"

"Most of it. The knowledge base is weighted toward the hard sciences, but it spans all disciplines and covers most of what's been learned in the past five thousand years." Levin seemed distracted. "How are the soldiers who tried to break in here?"

"Some are dead. More wounded."

"I'm so sorry about that. Why did they have to attack us?"

"Listen to me, Levin. When Trinity crashed, about twenty Russian nukes were launched in our direction. Several million people have about twenty minutes to live."

The engineer went pale.

"We need to find out if I can talk to Trinity. Right now."

"I hear you very well, Dr. Tennant."

The pseudohuman voice chilled my blood. It was like the musical synthesizers of the early 1980s, able to successfully mimic symphonic instruments to an untrained ear, but too sterile to fool a musician.

"Thank you for agreeing to speak to me," I said, my mind on the missiles racing over the arctic circle.

"I'm curious about why you went to Israel. That was not a predictable decision, unless you were motivated by the hallucinations described in Dr. Weiss's medical records."

As the digital voice spoke, the lasers flashed inside the

416

sphere. It was like watching a functional SPECT scan of the human brain, where different groups of neurons fired as the person being scanned performed certain tasks or thought certain thoughts.

"I did go to Israel because of my hallucinations."

"What did you learn there?"

"Before we discuss that, we have an emergency to deal with."

"Are you referring to the inbound missiles?"

"Yes. Did you mean for those missiles to be launched?"

"General Bauer believes in the dead-hand system now."

Trinity's evasion of my question disturbed me, but its knowledge of General Bauer's skepticism alarmed me more. Either the Situation Room was bugged, or Trinity had broken the NSA code encrypting the link between White Sands and Fort Meade. I prayed that the senators on the intelligence committee had not allowed Bauer to go forward with his EMP strike.

"General Bauer is a perfect example of why human beings are incapable of governing themselves."

I had to get Trinity away from Godin's political manifesto. "Do you still consider yourself human?"

"No. The essence of the human condition is being subject to death. I am not subject to death."

"Are you free from human emotions? Human instincts?"

"Not yet. Millions of years of evolution implanted those instincts in the brain. They can't be rooted out in a few hours. Not even by me."

"Those instincts were advantages to primitive man, but they're liabilities to modern man, and to the planet as a whole."

"Very perceptive, Doctor. Witness the missiles bearing down on us now."

"Have you computed their trajectories?"

"I don't need to. I know their targets. One is headed directly for White Sands."

I felt hollow inside. "And the others?"

"Washington, D.C. The navy yards at Norfolk, Virginia. Minuteman Three silos in the western United States. Targeted population centers are Atlanta, Chicago, Denver, Houston, Los Angeles, New Orleans, New York, Philadelphia, Phoenix, Quebec, San Francisco, Seattle."

I closed my mind against the horror of this reality. "Do those missiles have a self-destruct function?"

"Yes. It's interesting that under the START I treaty, Russian missiles were retargeted to coordinates at sea. Yet if they're accidentally fired, their guidance systems default to their Cold War targets. U.S. missiles default to oceanic targets. That might seem to indicate a higher moral position on the part of Americans. But appearances can be deceptive. American missiles can be remotely retargeted in less than ten seconds."

I tried not to look at my watch. "Do you see a benefit in allowing those missiles to reach their targets?"

"That's a complex question. Right now I am interested in what you learned in Israel."

"The missiles will detonate before I can fully explain that."

"I suggest you use an economy of words."

I swallowed my fear and started talking.

418

FORTY-TWO

Rachel watched the men in the Situation Room watch the NORAD screen. She had never seen such fear on human faces. Many of the red arcs had left the arctic circle behind and now stretched halfway across Canada. The Russian missiles would soon descend from outer space and enter the terminal phase of their ballistic arcs, carrying death to millions of people, including—according to Trinity—the ones in this room.

Only General Bauer seemed energized rather than paralyzed by the situation. His thoughts were focused on the bomber carrying the EMP weapon over Kansas. The general had trained so long in the distorted calculus of nuclear brinksmanship that he could view the destruction of Trinity with only a few million dead as a victory.

The conversation between David and the computer had been playing in the background of the Situation Room like a surrealist drama staged far off Broadway. No one held out any hope that David could stop the missiles. He was only being used to distract the machine.

"Twelve minutes to first impact," announced a technician.

General Bauer addressed the senators at Fort Meade. "If this facility is destroyed before Arcangel reaches its initial point, the EMP strike will continue unless you abort the mission. The abort code is Vanquish. The NSA can communicate with our bomber, and they should probably establish radio contact now."

Senator Jackson said, "Thank you, General. But would the computer really destroy itself by attacking White Sands?"

"It won't have to. It can kill everybody here with a high-neutron-yield warhead and not damage itself at all. The Containment building is shielded against ionizing radiation and hardened against all shock short of a direct nuclear hit, so Levin and his team will survive."

"Perhaps you and your people should take shelter at this time."

Bauer sniffed, his face unmoving. "There's no shelter reachable within the remaining time window. Not for everyone at this base."

"Multiple satellites show a flare over Canada!" shouted a technician.

"Was it a detonation?" asked General Bauer.

"I don't think so, sir. No high-energy flash. A missile may have self-destructed."

"Would it do that by accident?" asked Senator Jackson.

"Possibly," said Bauer, his face lined with concentration.

"Two more flares!" yelled the tech. "Four!"

"That's got to be Trinity," said Skow. "The computer's destroying the missiles."

"Is it continuing?" General Bauer asked in a taut voice.

"Fourteen flares and counting, sir." The tech's voice was calmer now. "Eighteen . . . nineteen."

"Dr. Tennant was right!" cried McCaskell. "Trinity never meant to launch those missiles."

"Five left to go," said Ravi Nara, his voice shaky.

"Arcangel has reached its initial point, General," said the chief technician.

"Is that the EMP plane?" asked Senator Jackson.

"Yes, sir," said General Bauer.

"Don't even think—"

"Understood, Senator." The general turned toward the console. "Instruct Arcangel to postpone the strike and begin circling."

"Yes, sir," said the tech. "Twenty-one missiles have now self-destructed."

"What are the tracks of the last three?" General Bauer asked a different soldier.

"Target of the nearest missile is computed as Norfolk, Virginia."

"The naval base."

"Second nearest is Washington, D.C."

"Jesus," breathed Ewan McCaskell. "The president isn't in a bomb shelter."

"The third is . . . here, sir. It's White Sands."

The silence stretched interminably as they waited for word of more flares.

"Corporal?" prompted General Bauer.

"Nothing, sir. The last three missiles are continuing on their tracks."

"What the hell is Trinity up to?" asked Senator Jackson.

"The self-destruct mechanisms could be malfunctioning," Skow suggested. "Russian missile maintenance is very poor."

General Bauer shook his head, his eyes on a computer screen. "The missile targeted on Virginia might be a malfunction. But the ones headed here and to Washington were the last two launched. Trinity is trying to kill us. We should launch the EMP strike now, Senators. We may not get another chance."

"How long until the missiles land?" asked Senator Jackson.

General Bauer glanced at the technicians sitting at their consoles.

"Norfolk has nine minutes," said the corporal. "As the general said, the missiles targeted here and on Washington and White Sands were launched later, and also from bases farther away. We have just under thirty minutes."

"Don't launch the EMP yet," said Senator Jackson. "Give Dr. Tennant a chance."

I could hardly keep my mind on my words as the seconds ticked past. My confidence in my ability to persuade Trinity of anything was evaporating beneath the specter of nuclear holocaust. My pleas for rationality had resulted in the destruction of most of the missiles, but the three remaining ones were quite capable of causing massive devastation.

Trinity had made it clear that averting this disaster depended on my explanation of my experiences in Israel. The sequence of dreams that had led me to Jerusalem was already familiar to the computer from its perusal of the NSA's records of my sessions with Rachel. It was my coma revelations that fascinated Trinity. I had already described God's life in the body of Jesus, his attempt to change man's primitive instincts by example, his despair at the futility of his efforts, and finally the hope and fear generated in him by the secret work at Trinity.

"*When you refer to God,*" said the computer, "*you are not referring to Jehovah? The biblical God?*"

"No."

"*You characterize God as pure consciousness.*"

"Yes."

"*Are you speaking in a religious sense at all?*"

"I'm speaking of what is."

"*You speak of what cannot be known. I find no scientific basis for such a formulation.*"

"You should not judge my words by what is known now, but on its own merit. You are wise enough to see the truth."

"*Truth must be proved.*"

422

"Yes, but sometimes the truth is in the mind before evidence can be found. This is how science proceeds."

"*True.*"

"What you are—what they call the Trinity state—is an inevitable step in evolution."

"*Yes.*"

"But it's not the final step."

"*No. I shall continue to evolve, and at millions of times the rate of biological evolution. And millions of times more efficiently. Nature cannot throw out the obsolete model and start again. She must always modify existing plans. I am not limited in this way.*"

"That's more true than you know. You represent the liberation of human intelligence from the body, but that liberation doesn't stop with you. Already scientists are working on organic computers on a molecular scale. DNA computers that can exist in a cup of liquid."

"*And?*"

"Once that becomes possible, what you are—digital consciousness—will not require a machine to exist. It will require only adequate molecules. You could exist in a cup of liquid. And once you exist there, you'll eventually be able to move into the cup itself. Or into the water the liquid is poured into. Whether this takes fifty years or two hundred, the day will come. And the process began today."

"*You're correct. What is your point?*"

"Surely you see the end of that process?"

The blue lasers flashed at stunning speed. "*The logical conclusion is that the Earth itself will eventually become conscious. A vessel for consciousness.*"

"Yes."

"*When the dying sun swells to a red giant and the Earth is drawn into it, it, too, will become conscious. The sun will explode, seeding the galaxy with consciousness.*"

423

"It's a simple chain of logic, once that first step is accomplished. And you're the first step."

"You saw this in your coma?"

"In a way. I awakened with the knowledge."

"What else did you see?"

"The end of the universe. Surely you've made the calculations. It would only be natural to predict your life span."

"Yes."

"Tell me."

"In approximately fifty billion years, the force of the expanding universe will no longer be sufficient to overwhelm the contracting force of gravity. At that point the universe will begin to collapse. This is known as the Big Crunch theory. The opposite of the Big Bang. Our universe will collapse into a singularity, a black hole much like the state in which it began. Inside that singularity, the laws of physics will cease to operate. That singularity will continue to contract until it reaches a point of infinite density, infinite temperature, and infinite pressure."

"That's what I saw."

"You believe the universe will be conscious during this process?"

"Yes. But the end is problematic. Because consciousness is based on information transfer, and all mediums of information transfer—all matter and energy—will be collapsing into nonexistence."

"Will consciousness die then?"

"The strongest drive of any living entity is to survive."

"How could consciousness survive such an event?"

Here was the difficult concept, the moment where the snake had to swallow its own tail and turn inside out. "By migrating out of the dying medium. Migrating out of matter and energy. Out of space and time."

"Into what?"

"I have no name for the answer."

424

"Describe this answer."

I glanced down at my watch, and my heart thudded. "I can't concentrate any longer. Where are the missiles?"

"They are not your concern. Finish the conversation."

"I can't! I can't think."

"Your words may save lives. Silence will ensure detonations."

I rubbed my forehead with the back of my hand, and a layer of sweat came away on my skin.

"You said that when matter and energy come to an end, consciousness will survive by migrating into something else. What can it migrate into?"

I tried to find words to describe what I had felt and seen during my coma. "When I was younger, I heard a Zen koan I liked. I never knew why exactly, but now I do."

"What is it?"

"'All things return to the One. What does the One return to?'"

"Very poetic. But I find no empirical evidence to support even a theoretical answer to that question. What remains when matter and energy disappear?"

"Some people call it God. Other people call it other things."

"That answer is unsatisfactory."

I closed my eyes and found myself deep in my initial dream, that of the paralyzed man in the dark room, watching the birth of the universe. "I have a more detailed answer for you. For us all, I think. But—"

The lasers in the sphere began flashing wildly, creating a light so intense that I had to turn away.

"One moment, Doctor. I must attend to a critical matter, and I want to devote my full capacity to hearing what you have to say."

I backed away from the black globe, praying that General Bauer was not attempting to launch his EMP strike.

*　　*　　*

Rachel gripped the edge of the conference table, her knuckles bone-white. Her eyes were on the NORAD screen showing the red arcs of the missiles. Those targeted on White Sands and Washington were in what Bauer called the midcourse phase of their flights, hurtling through outer space at fifteen thousand miles per hour. But the arc of the third missile stretched past New Jersey and Delaware, blinking ominously as it moved down the Atlantic coast toward Virginia.

"We've entered the margin of error," announced a technician. "Missile should be two minutes from ground zero at Norfolk, but we could have detonations at any moment."

Senator Jackson looked down from the screen showing the bomb shelter at Fort Meade. His face was almost colorless. "Tennant's not getting anywhere, General. Your bomber's in position. I think it's time to launch the EMP strike."

General Bauer's body had gone rigid, his eyes locked on the NORAD screen. "Senator, I've been thinking. If we detonate the EMP just after the missiles reenter the atmosphere, the electromagnetic pulse could knock out their guidance systems. Possibly their detonator systems as well."

Rachel's heart swelled with hope. All the talk of terminal phases and circular error probables had seemed unreal until she heard that an ICBM was thundering toward the spot where she now sat. She didn't like Horst Bauer, but his idea seemed a lot more likely to save her life than the metaphysical musings of the psychiatric patient she had fallen in love with. Trinity might be fascinated by David's visions, but it did not seem inclined to spare human lives because of them.

"What's the probability of success?" asked Senator Jackson.

"High. But we have a problem. The missile headed for Norfolk is already in its terminal phase of flight, but those headed for Washington and White Sands won't be for another fifteen minutes. We can knock down the first one or the last two. Not all three."

"Washington is your priority, General. You must preserve the life of the president and as much of the government as possible. Even if that means allowing the first missile to detonate."

Rachel closed her eyes. They were about to sacrifice part of the state of Virginia.

"Understood, sir," said General Bauer. "Corporal, give me a Lacrosse satellite image of the Norfolk–Hampton Roads area."

"Yes, sir."

On a secondary display screen, a satellite image of a night coastline appeared. Rachel knew it was coastline because the clusters and long sprays of lights on the left side of the screen vanished into blackness on the right. A dark space to the north of the brightest cluster of lights looked a lot like Chesapeake Bay.

Rachel had been to Norfolk once, for a medical convention. She remembered dining with her son and her ex-husband on the bay. Her watch read 7:45 P.M. There would be people sitting at that same table now. Eating . . . laughing . . . oblivious to the new sun about to be born in the dark sky above them, incinerating every living thing for miles.

General Bauer walked closer to the technician monitoring the data coming from the NORAD computers at Cheyenne Mountain. "We have a direct link with Arcangel?"

"Yes, sir."

"Keep it open."

"Sir."

Rachel looked at the NORAD screen. The red missile track arcing toward Virginia was blinking so fast it was almost solid. The satellite image on the screen to the right looked tranquil, like a picture transmitted by the space shuttle on Christmas Eve. She could not comprehend the idea that in seconds that image would go black. And it didn't. Not all at once. First it went white, as though God had snapped a picture of the Earth. Then, slowly, lagre groups of lights began to wink out.

"Dear Lord," someone whispered.

The screen showing the Norfolk area was almost completely black.

"General?" said one of the technicians.

"Tell me," said Bauer, his voice low.

"NORAD just detected a high-energy flash near Norfolk."

A strange numbness tingled in Rachel's face and hands. She said a silent prayer for the dead and dying.

"*Near*, Corporal? Or directly above?"

"Latitude and longitude show a detonation twelve miles east of the coastline. Circular error probable thirty miles from Norfolk. That's why we don't see a fireball on Lacrosse."

General Bauer straightened, his eyes alight with hope. "Was it an air burst?"

"Just a moment, sir. The readings seem to indicate a surface or shallow subsurface blast."

"There's your Russian engineering!" shouted the general. "That's the malfunction you were hoping for, Senator!"

"What does that mean, General?" asked Senator Jackson.

"Nuclear weapons must be detonated above their targets for maximum effect. With a CEP of twelve miles and an underwater detonation, Russian incompetence just saved about two million American lives."

The relief that swept through the room was short-lived.

"What about the other two missiles?" asked Senator Jackson.

Rachel looked at the screen. Two red tracks were sliding down the map of Canada, one moving southeast over Hudson Bay, the other racing down the spine of the Rocky Mountains.

"Corporal?" said General Bauer. "When will missiles two and three enter the terminal phase of their flights?"

428

"Fourteen minutes, sir."

"Patch me through to Arcangel. I want to talk to the radar navigator."

"Yes, sir."

The Situation Room was suddenly filled with static and cockpit chatter. General Bauer leaned over the technician's desk and spoke into a microphone.

"Arcangel, this is Gabriel. You will execute six one seven four on my order. Is that clear?"

The reply was emotionless. "Affirmative, Gabriel. On your order."

General Bauer studied the screen showing the flight paths of the missiles. "Approximately fifteen minutes."

"Roger," said the voice through the static. "Fifteen minutes."

General Bauer turned from the console and looked around the table in the Situation Room, his gray eyes confident. "Everybody just settle in, folks. In fifteen minutes, the lights will go out and our computers will go down, but so will the ones that Trinity uses to control the Russian missiles."

"How can you be sure those computers are in the U.S.?" asked McCaskell.

"I can't be. But even if they're in Asia, Trinity has to communicate with them over phone and data lines, and those are about to be fried by an EMP."

Rachel had forgotten Ravi Nara, but now the neurologist stood and spoke in a quavering voice. "General, with all respect for your plan, we have over twenty minutes before that missile reaches here. You have aircraft here, helicopters. Nonessential personnel could be evacuated now."

"Like yourself?" said General Bauer.

"And the women."

"O ye of little faith," murmured General Bauer. "Take your seat, Dr. Nara. You're going to be fine."

"Look!" cried John Skow, pointing to a screen to the

right of the one showing Senator Jackson's committee. "Oh, God . . ."

Rachel's gaze followed Skow's pointing finger. Blue letters crawled across the Trinity screen like the newsline at the bottom of a CNN broadcast.

> We've entered the margin of error. Missile should be two minutes from ground zero at Norfolk, but we could have detonations at any moment.
>
> Tennant's not getting anywhere, General. Your bomber's in position. I think it's time to launch the EMP strike.

"What are we looking at?" asked McCaskell.

Skow whispered, "Trinity's broken our codes."

"*Gabriel to Arcangel!*" shouted General Bauer, grabbing the microphone. "*Execute! Execute!*"

As the radar navigator in the B-52 asked for clarification, another voice drowned him out. Rachel heard confusion in the second voice, then panic. Someone screamed something about haywire instruments. Then the transmission went dead.

"What happened?" asked McCaskell. "Did they launch the weapon?"

"*Gabriel to Arcangel!*" shouted General Bauer. "*Acknowledge!*"

The technician at another console turned toward him. "Sir, they can't hear you."

Bauer whipped his head toward the tech. "What?"

"Arcangel is going down. They've got no comm at all. No UHF, no VHF. Nothing."

"How do you know that?"

"I'm patched into Kansas City Center. Arcangel's IFF beacon went off twenty seconds ago, and a Delta Airlines

430

727 just reported the lights of a very large aircraft that appeared to be in an uncontrolled spin."

Disbelief slackened General Bauer's face. "What the hell happened?"

"No idea, sir."

The technician sitting beneath Bauer cocked his head as he listened to his headset. "General . . . NRO satellites detected a high-energy beam directed toward the last-known position of Arcangel."

"What kind of beam?"

"A high-energy particle beam."

"From where?"

"Space."

"*Space?*"

"Yes, sir. It must have come from a space-based weapons platform."

"General Bauer!" said Senator Jackson. "What the hell is going on there?"

"Arcangel appears to be down, Senator."

"What do you mean 'down'?"

"It was probably destroyed by a weapons system I thought was still in development."

"Whose system? The Russians?"

"No, sir. The Russians don't have anything like that. Our air force must have some component of its Osiris system deployed. It's a prototype antimissile system, but it was clearly powerful enough to fry the avionics of our B-52. It must be under Trinity's control now."

"Did the bomber launch the EMP weapon?"

"I doubt it, sir. The timing was too perfect. Trinity must have broken our codes some time ago. It knew exactly what we were doing."

"But, General—"

"*Listen to me, Senator.*" General Bauer's nerves were finally showing the strain. "In a very short time, everyone here will be dead. You're going to be on your own. Only those in Containment will survive here, and Washington will be hit shortly after."

Jackson looked at his fellow senators, then back at General Bauer. "Can you get inside the Containment building?"

"Not without the computer's permission."

"Look at the screen!" Rachel cried, surprised to hear her own voice.

Trinity was sending a message to the Situation Room.

YOU WERE WARNED. YOU DISREGARDED MY WARNING. YOU MUST SUFFER THE CONSEQUENCES. YOU MUST LEARN.

Rachel looked at the NORAD screen. The missile tracks moving toward White Sands and Washington were slowly blinking red.

"Type what I tell you!" shouted McCaskell.

"Do it," said General Bauer.

"We made a mistake," said McCaskell, trying to keep his voice under control. "You can't hold millions of people responsible for the error of a few misguided individuals."

Trinity's response flashed up the moment McCaskell's words were keyed in.

I HAVE DONE NOTHING. THOSE LIVES WERE IN YOUR HANDS, AS WERE YOURS. YOU HAVE THROWN THEM AWAY. IT WAS TO BE EXPECTED. A HUMAN CHILD PLAYS WITH FIRE UNTIL IT IS BURNED.

General Bauer turned away from the screen and walked to his chair. Rachel saw defeat etched into his face.

"General?" said Senator Jackson. "What options do we have?"

Bauer looked down the table at his daughter. Geli stared at him like an enraptured spectator watching the end of some great tragedy.

"None," said the general, collapsing into his chair.

Ravi Nara came to his feet again, his eyes wild. "General, you must ask the computer to let us into Containment! Peter Godin was my friend. He'll let us inside!"

"You tried to kill Godin," General Bauer said calmly. "You think he wants to spare you now?"

"He will!"

The general motioned for a soldier to restrain Nara.

"We don't all have to die!" Nara screamed as the soldier grabbed him. "Please!"

The neurologist was too distraught to be restrained by one man. The general called for another guard, but suddenly Geli Bauer materialized beside the wrestling men. She grabbed Nara's neck with almost lazy speed, took him to the floor, then rolled him onto his stomach and jammed a knee into his back. A guard bound Nara's wrists with plastic flex-cuffs, then led him out of the hangar. General Bauer nodded to Geli but said nothing.

"General," said Senator Jackson. "There must be something you can do about those last two missiles. You name it, we'll authorize it."

"There's nothing, Senator. It's up to Dr. Tennant now."

FORTY-THREE

I stood in shock before the black sphere, watching a display screen that had appeared from behind a panel in Trinity's base. The bomb blast had created a crater a half mile wide in the ocean, and I had no doubt that a tidal wave would soon smash into the Virginia coastline. As the mushroom cloud climbed high into the atmosphere, part of my mind tried to convince me that I was looking at some barren Pacific atoll, not a patch of ocean just a few miles from a major U.S. city. I looked away from the screen and focused on the blue lasers firing in the sphere.

"You must destroy the last two missiles," I said.

"Nothing compels me to."

"How much time is left?"

"Twenty-two minutes."

I'd thought the next detonations would happen at any moment. "But . . . that means you launched those two missiles on purpose."

"Yes."

"What's the point in more killing? You've shown what you can do."

"*There will be relatively little loss of life from the first warhead, given the missile's malfunction.*"

"Do you really have to kill to make your point?"

"*History answers yes to that question. Man is slow to learn. At Hiroshima and Nagasaki, two hundred thousand died. Man learned from that.*"

"But you'll kill millions!"

"*A small number measured against the seven billion souls on the planet. Sacrificing the few to save the many is a time-honored human tradition.*"

"You're not doing this to save people. You're doing it to enslave them."

"*A matter of perspective, Doctor. If you saw through my eyes, you would understand.*"

I frantically searched my mind for logical arguments. "If you wipe out the U.S. government, you'll be making things harder on yourself, not easier. People will panic."

"*They will also realize there is no going back.*"

I opened my mouth, but nothing came out. Desperation had blanked my mind. There was only one option left.

"If you allow those missiles to explode, I won't finish telling you my visions."

The computer was silent for several moments. "*You believe this threat will force me to submit to your will?*"

"I believe you want to know what I know more than you want to detonate those warheads."

"*Why?*"

"Because there are limits to even your knowledge. Science can take you back to a few nanoseconds after the Big Bang, but no farther. It can take you forward a few billion years—maybe even to the end of the universe—but no farther. Only I can do that."

Trinity's response was something like a laugh. "*You believe*

435

you can. But it should be as obvious to you as it is to me that your visions are almost certainly creations of your mind. Your own psychiatrist believes you're paranoid, perhaps even schizophrenic."

"So why are you listening to me?"

Silence from the sphere.

"It's because the sum of human knowledge has been loaded into your memory, and you still feel empty. But I have the answer you want. So . . . I ask you again. Please destroy those missiles."

"You don't need to worry about the missiles. This building is hardened and shielded. You'll survive both the blast and the radiation."

"I'm not worried about myself!"

"Do you really care so much about people you don't know?"

I wondered if "Peter Godin" were finally vanishing into an emotionless digital entity. "I do know someone outside this building. There's a woman there. She saved my life once. Probably more than once. She's believed in me, helped me search for the truth. I don't want her to die."

"Let us continue our discussion."

"No. I love this woman. I want her to live. I want to spend whatever time I have left with her."

"That is not much time."

I closed my eyes, unable to summon more persuasive words.

"If you want Dr. Weiss to live, tell me the rest of it."

THE SITUATION ROOM

Rachel sat at the table in the Situation Room, mentally replaying David's last words to Trinity. His declaration of love had had no effect on the computer, but it had given her some peace.

"What do we do now, General?" asked Senator Jackson.

"There's only one thing we can do here," General Bauer replied. "Evacuate." The general turned to face the room.

436

"I'm going to check on the possibility of air evacuation. I want everyone to remain here. I'll return very shortly."

He walked quickly toward the door, but before he reached it, he turned and looked pointedly at Ewan McCaskell and John Skow. Then he motioned for them to follow him.

As the hangar door closed, Geli Bauer slid into the seat across from Rachel. Rachel tried not to look at the scar on her cheek, but it was impossible to ignore. Geli wore it arrogantly, like a badge of honor.

"Is Tennant crazy or sane?" Geli asked.

Rachel answered without thought. "I honestly don't know."

"This God obsession of his is bullshit. But the funny thing is, if it weren't for that, you'd be dead. Because if you hadn't gone to Israel, I'd have found you."

Rachel knew she was right. David's decision to follow his visions had pulled them out of the line of fire when almost nothing else could have. Rachel doubted that Geli Bauer had missed many targets in her career.

"So here we are," said Rachel. "At the end of the world."

A hint of a smile touched Geli's lips. "Confession time?"

"I have nothing to confess. What about you? Did you kill Andrew Fielding?"

Geli glanced around to make sure no one was near. "Yes."

Rachel was reminded of a little girl fascinated by her own cruelty. "How does a woman come to do what you do? You carry a lot of anger around, don't you?"

Geli touched the bandage over the bullet wound in her neck. "I can see how you might get that feeling."

Rachel's eyes didn't waver. "You were angry long before that."

"You playing shrink with me now?"

"I am a shrink."

Geli laughed bitterly. "My first shrink seduced me when I was fourteen. I got the last laugh, though. He killed himself over me."

"What about your father? He seems like a real throwback. Dr. Strangelove stuff."

"If you only knew."

Rachel wondered what secret misery drove this cold woman. "There's something dark between the two of you."

"No. Just your ordinary army family hell."

"You hate him, yet it seems you've tried to live up to all his expectations of you."

Geli's ironic smile faded. "Are you in love with Tennant?"

"Yes."

"Will you still love him if it turns out he's crazy?"

"Yes."

"Then you understand a little about me and my father." She rubbed her forefinger repeatedly against her thumb, like someone desperate for a cigarette. "Who killed the man who came to Tennant's house with a gun? You or Tennant?"

For the first time, Rachel sensed some unguarded emotion. "Why do you care? Were you in love with him?"

"We fucked sometimes."

"You really work at being hard, don't you?"

One sculpted eyebrow lifted. The moment of vulnerability had passed. "Why are you talking to me, Doctor?"

"I suppose I'm trying to find out how dangerous you are."

"You mean, am I here to do my duty or to get revenge on you two?"

"Something like that."

The cold smile returned. "Maybe they're one and the same. Any more questions?"

Rachel whispered so softly that her words were almost inaudible. "Is your father really going to evacuate us?"

Geli's eyes glinted. "You're smarter than I thought. I wouldn't count on it."

*　　*　　*

438

Ravi Nara sat on the sand outside the Situation Room hangar, his muscles clenched in terror, his eyes on the dark sky. There was no stockade at the White Sands facility, so the guard who'd restrained him had handcuffed him to a flagpole by the door. *A neutron bomb,* the general had said. Ravi was pondering the grisly death caused by radiation poisoning when the hangar door burst open and General Bauer marched out, barking orders into a walkie-talkie.

John Skow and the president's chief of staff followed the general. The three men walked fifteen meters from the door and stopped. They probably never saw Ravi in the darkness.

"I hope to God you've got some kind of plan, General," said Ewan McCaskell. "Because evacuating this place doesn't do a damned thing for Washington."

"I've got a plan. But I don't think I'm the only one. Skow?"

The NSA man nodded. "We can kill Trinity."

"How?"

"Isolate it from the Internet. That's the same as killing it."

"Talk fast."

"When Godin died, the computer crashed and the Russian missiles launched. Cause and effect, right?"

General Bauer nodded.

"Trinity has to be sending out some sort of safety signal. A constant signal telling certain computers that all is well with Trinity. When Godin died, that signal was disrupted, and the Russian missiles were launched. If we can separate that 'all is well' signal from the rest of Trinity's output, we can probably duplicate it. Then all we have to do is feed our own version into the data line Trinity is using and cut Trinity's power. Trinity will be dead, but the computers tasked with retaliation will have no idea anything is wrong."

"How long would it take you to isolate that signal?"

"I don't know. Trinity would detect any direct monitoring of its lines, so we'd have to do it from outside the cables.

That causes distortion. And since the signal is generated by and for computers, it's probably very complex. It might even appear random to us without intense analysis."

"How long?"

The NSA man shrugged. "It could take ten minutes or ten days."

"We'll be dead long before you do that. And Washington will no longer exist."

The beat of rotor blades reverberated over the compound. McCaskell looked skyward, then at General Bauer. "Is that helicopter coming to evacuate us?"

"No. It's coming for you."

Puzzlement wrinkled McCaskell's face. "Why?"

"Our EMP strike failed because our communications were compromised. But the plan was sound."

"Do you have another bomber in the air?"

"We don't need one. We have ICBMs sitting in silos in Kansas cornfields right now. One of those can reach the necessary altitude for an EMP detonation in three hundred seconds."

"That's five minutes," said Skow. "An eternity in Trinity's terms. And Trinity will detect the launch immediately."

General Bauer nodded. "We'll inform Trinity of what we're doing just prior to launch. We'll say the president has decided he can't survive politically if he doesn't respond to the Russian missile detonated off Virginia. We'll remotely retarget the missile for Moscow, and Trinity will hear our telemetry. But when it reaches the peak of its boost phase . . . boom. EMP."

Skow's face shone with admiration. "That could work."

"But we can't launch an ICBM from here," McCaskell said.

"We're not. The president's going to launch it. He's got the nuclear briefcase with him, and he's with the Joint Chiefs. They'll know the necessary altitude and yield for an EMP blast."

"But they're all under surveillance!"

The helicopter was descending fast. Ravi had dreamed that

a machine like this one would carry him out of harm's way, but the pounding rotor blades overhead did not soothe him. This bird was a harbinger of war.

General Bauer laid his hands on McCaskell's shoulders. "Do you know a Secret Service agent you can trust? Someone who'd be in the White House and whose cell number you know?"

"Of course. But we can't transmit a word without Trinity hearing it."

"Yes, we can. Our mistake has been to use our most advanced communications. Trinity is focused on those. We need to do it the old-fashioned way."

"Telephone," said Skow.

"Right. Lockheed has a research lab six miles west of here. If you use a land line from there, and you don't use key words like *Trinity*, the computer would have to sift through massive amounts of data to find the conversation. It's like hiding hay in a haystack."

Skow was nodding excitedly.

Bauer stayed focused on McCaskell. "Call your Secret Service man and tell him that unless the president and the Chiefs are moved to the White House bomb shelter, they'll be vaporized. He should say that on camera, so that Trinity can hear it. As soon as the president is clear of surveillance, you get him on the phone and explain what he has to do. He and the Chiefs can launch the missile on their way to the bomb shelter."

The thunder of the approaching helicopter was drowning the conversation.

"General!" McCaskell shouted. "If an EMP pulse will knock down an ICBM, what will it do to commercial airliners?"

"Airliners have redundant hydraulic systems! They'll lose electrical power, but they'll be able to land just fine. You've got to go *now*, sir. The president has less than fifteen minutes to live."

A Black Hawk gunship painted in desert camouflage set down thirty meters from the hangar.

"Go!" Bauer yelled.

McCaskell turned and ran for the waiting chopper. A soldier pulled him up into its belly, and the Black Hawk lifted into the night sky.

"I can't believe he bought that," said Skow.

"What?"

"Older planes like 727s and DC-9s have redundant hydraulics, but newer models are fully computerized. They won't make it. There are probably three thousand airliners aloft right now. The passenger load is at least a hundred thousand people. If only half of them crash, that's twenty times the casualties of the World Trade Center. We'll have bodies strewn from Maine to California."

"Experienced pilots will be able to set down on the interstates," General Bauer said.

"In Montana, maybe. The rest will be blocked by stalled cars and trucks, and they won't move an inch without new parts. But there won't be any parts. There won't even be *food* moving on the roads. Not unless the National Guard moves it. And they'll be too busy shooting looters and delivering water to do that."

General Bauer looked fiercely at the NSA man. "If that missile had hit Norfolk, we'd be looking at two million dead. Two *million*."

Skow nodded soberly.

"And if we don't knock down the next two, you can scratch off three million souls in and around Washington. Including your wife and kids, if I'm not mistaken."

The NSA man looked stricken.

"Now, you get somebody working on finding Trinity's 'all is well' signal. Because if we don't get our bone marrow fried by a neutron bomb in the next fourteen minutes, we just might need it."

FORTY-FOUR

CONTAINMENT

The black sphere of Trinity pulsed with blue light as the lasers inside fired into its crystal memory. Given the enormous capacity and speed of the computer, I could not begin to imagine how many trillions of bits of data it had to be manipulating to cause such activity. Was it monitoring the military status of every nuclear-armed nation? Scanning and analyzing every square meter of the earth visible to satellites? Was it searching obscure astrophysics theses for references to the concepts I had been talking about? Or was it patiently writing a perfect symphony while we awaited nuclear disaster? Perhaps it was doing all that simultaneously.

My original intention to persuade Trinity to shut itself down had changed under the threat of the incoming missiles. I had focused instead on convincing Trinity to spare those lives under immediate threat. Yet my efforts had failed. Trinity wanted only to continue our discussion of my coma revelations. As I stood dazed before the black sphere, hoping that General Bauer was evacuating the base, the last part of my coma conversation with Trinity began to play from the hidden speakers.

"You said that when matter and energy come to an end,

consciousness will survive by migrating into something else. What can it migrate into?"

"When I was younger, I heard a Zen koan I liked. I never knew why exactly, but now I do."

"What is it?"

"'All things return to the One. What does the One return to?'"

"Very poetic. But I find no empirical evidence to support even a theoretical answer to that question. What remains when matter and energy disappear?"

"Some people call it God. Other people call it other things."

"That answer is unsatisfactory."

"I have a more detailed answer for you. For us all, I think. But—"

The light within the globe faded, and Trinity went black. Then a few needle-thin rays fired into the crystal.

"I want to know," Trinity said in real time. *"What is this thing that some humans call God and other humans call other things?"*

I glanced at my watch. My face felt hot. *Rachel is in a helicopter,* I told myself. *On her way to safety. It's Washington that's at risk. And my best chance of saving it is doing what I planned to do in the beginning. What I was sent here to do.*

"The longer you wait," said Trinity, *"the more people will die."*

Peter Godin's vision of Trinity as a benevolent dictator was not proving out. I closed my eyes and tried to find words to relate the knowledge imparted to me in Jerusalem.

"There is a force in the universe that we don't yet understand. A force without energy or matter. I'm not sure it's a force at all, actually. It may be more like a field. It pervades all things but occupies no space. It's more like . . . *anti*space."

"What is this force? Or this field?"

"I have no name for it. I only know it exists."

444

"What is its function?"

"Let me answer with a question. What is a chair? What is required for a chair to exist?"

"A seat. Legs. A back."

"Is that all?"

"There are other types of chairs. Bean chairs. Japanese stools."

"You've left something out. Something else is absolutely required to have a chair."

"What?"

"Space."

The sphere went black again. *"You are correct. Space is required."*

"In the same way that space is required for a chair to exist, the field I speak of is required for *space* to exist."

The lasers fixed for several seconds. *Is that the sole function of this theoretical field?"*

"No. It can act as a medium of communication. Such as that between quantum particles."

"Be specific."

"I'm referring to those cases when atomic particles make simultaneous decisions across vast reaches of space, as if they were invisibly connected. Experiments show that information traveling between such particles would have to be communicated at ten thousand times the speed of light. And breaking the speed of light is impossible."

"Through this medium you speak of, information is communicated faster than light?"

"Yes and no. Imagine that I dip my hand into the Pacific Ocean. Now, imagine that my hand is simultaneously touching everything that the ocean touches. That's the kind of communication I'm talking about. It's not a transfer of information. The information is simply everywhere at once."

"The quantum phenomena you speak of defy logical

445

explanation, but observation has detected no field or medium such as the one you describe."

"We haven't detected dark matter either, but we know it's there. We can't see black holes, but we see the light bending around them."

The lasers flashed at a blinding rate, lighting the crystal like a blue star. *"My memory does contain something very like what you describe. I was searching my science banks. I find what you speak of under philosophy."*

"Does it have a name?"

"It is called the Tao."

The word took me back to my undergraduate days at MIT, when books like *The Tao of Physics* were the bibles of New Age–oriented students. "That's Eastern philosophy, right?"

"Yes."

"What is the Tao, exactly?"

"'The Tao that can be spoken of is not the true Tao.'"

"Is that a quote?"

"Yes. Taoism is not a religion. But its adherents believe there is a force that pervades all things. The Tao is undifferentiated, neither good nor evil. It animates all things but is not part of them. Are you suggesting that something like the Tao is what remains after the universe collapses into itself?"

"After the final singularity vanishes. Yes."

"This is the field into which consciousness migrates when matter and energy are destroyed at the end of time?"

"Yes."

"How can this happen?"

"Let me use an analogy. On the physical level, human beings are animals. Large-scale creatures who live in a Newtonian world of predictability, where time only moves forward, where we're separated from each other in space,

446

and information is limited by the speed of light. But the subatomic world is different. There, particles exist right at the border between the large-scale world of matter and this other force—the Tao, you call it. It's only natural that at this border we should observe behavior that seems to break our physical laws."

"What does this have to do with consciousness?"

"Though we're animals in body, our minds are conscious, self-aware. Andrew Fielding believed that human consciousness is more than the sum of the connections in our brains. Through our consciousness, we participate in that all-pervasive field— in the Tao, as you say—at every moment of our lives. Our consciousness returns to it when we die, though without individuality. In the same way, the consciousness of the universe will migrate into the Tao when the universe ends."

"You suggest a cyclical pattern of existence. The universe is born, becomes conscious, dies, and then is born again."

"Yes. Big Bang, expansion, contraction, Big Crunch. Then it all starts again."

"What causes the next bang?"

I thought of my recurring nightmare, the paralyzed man in the pitch-black room. "The consciousness that survives has no knowledge of the past or future. It's a baseline aware-ness. But some desire to know survives. That's the strongest feature of consciousness. And from that desire to know, the next cycle of matter and energy is born."

The computer was silent for a time. *"The universe exists as an incubator of consciousness?"*

"Exactly."

"An interesting theory. But incomplete. You haven't explained the origin of the Tao. Of your all-pervasive field."

"That knowledge was not given to me. That is the essen-tial mystery. But it doesn't affect our situation. You see where I'm going."

"You're saying I am not the end point of this process. I'm a way station on the road to universal consciousness. I am like man. Man is biologically based. I am machine based. But there is more to come. A conscious planet. A conscious galaxy—"

"You're another step in the ascent. No more, no less."

Trinity was silent for several seconds. *Why have you come here at the risk of your life, Doctor?*

"I was sent here to stop you from doing what you're doing."

"Sent by whom?"

"Call it what you will. God. The Tao. I'm here to help you see that Peter Godin was not the right person to make the leap to the next form of consciousness."

"Who is the right man?"

"Why do you think it's a man at all?"

"A woman, then?"

"I didn't say that."

"I've given much thought to this matter. Who would you have loaded into Trinity other than Peter Godin?"

"If you are still Godin, consider this. Your first instinct was to seize this computer by deception and take control of the world by force. You want absolute power and obedience. That's a primitive human instinct. A step backward, not forward."

"That instinct is more divine than human. Don't all gods first and foremost require obedience?"

"That's how humans portray God."

"Absolute power corrupts absolutely? Is that your argument?"

"Any person who wants to govern the world is by definition the wrong person to do it."

"Who then would you have loaded? The Dalai Lama? Mother Teresa? An infant?"

This question took me back to my first weeks on Project Trinity. I'd spent countless hours pondering this question, though then I believed it was a largely academic exercise. Now I knew it held the key to saving countless lives.

"The Dalai Lama may be nonviolent, but he has human instincts, just as Peter Godin did."

"And an infant? A tabula rasa? A blank slate?"

"An infant might be the most dangerous being we could put into Trinity. Animal instincts are passed on genetically. The term *blank slate* is misleading at best. A two-year-old child is a dictator without an army."

"Mother Teresa?"

"This isn't a problem of individual identities."

"What kind of problem is it?"

"A conceptual one. It requires unconventional thinking."

"Why do I think you're about to tell me that Andrew Fielding is the person we should have allowed to reach the Trinity state?"

"Because you know what a good man he was. And because you ordered his death. That alone should disqualify you. But Fielding wasn't the proper person either."

"Who is?"

"No one."

"I don't understand."

"You're about to. If—"

"Do you believe that after you explain this, I will take myself off-line and allow you to load someone else into Trinity?"

"No. I think you'll help me do it."

"Explain."

LOCKHEED LABORATORY, WHITE SANDS

Ewan McCaskell sat behind the desk of an aerospace engineer he'd never met and waited to talk to the president. It had taken several agonizing minutes to reach a White House

Secret Service agent via telephone. McCaskell suspected that the nuclear blast off the Virginia coast had interrupted communications on the Eastern seaboard.

Army Rangers stood on either side of McCaskell, their assault rifles locked and loaded. The chief of staff had shared some strange moments with his president during their administration, but he had never contemplated directing a nuclear strike from an empty office in New Mexico. The surreal surroundings tempted him to pretend that it was all some fantastic exercise laid on by NORAD, but nothing could mask the essential horror: what the president did in the next few minutes would determine the fates of McCaskell's wife, his children, and three million other Americans who had no idea that any of this was happening. And if General Bauer was wrong about Trinity's capabilities, untold millions more could perish.

"I have the Chiefs with me, Ewan," said the president. "We're on our way to the shelter."

McCaskell quickly related General Bauer's plan in almost the exact words Bauer had outlined it, without pausing to explain anything. Bill Matthews was smarter than the pundits gave him credit for being.

"How long do we have until we're hit here?" Matthews asked.

"Seven or eight minutes. And it'll take our missile five minutes to reach the proper altitude. You've got to launch now, Mr. President. The Chiefs will know the lowest altitude you can detonate our missile and get the desired effect."

"Hold one second."

McCaskell imagined the scene: each of the Joint Chiefs demanding details and raising objections. But there wasn't time for any of that. Matthews came back on the line, his voice strained.

"The Chiefs tell me that an electromagnetic pulse of that

magnitude would knock down half the planes in U.S. airspace and cause all kinds of other casualties. Are you absolutely certain about these two missiles, Ewan?"

Bauer had lied to him about the planes. But he understood why. "Bill, there's a fucking mushroom cloud that looks like the end of the world hovering over Virginia right now. You're about to have one over Washington. This may be your only chance to knock out Trinity. You may not control our nukes tomorrow." A horrifying thought hit McCaskell. "You may not control them *now*."

He heard more muted conversation.

"The Chiefs tell me we should go with three missiles spaced across the country to be sure we knock out everything," Matthews said.

"Fine, but whatever you do, you have to do it now!"

"The briefcase is open. I'm about to authenticate the codes."

Thank God. . . .

"Get to shelter immediately, Ewan. Katy and the boys need you."

A knife of fear went through him. "It's been a privilege, Mr. President. I'm signing off."

McCaskell set down the phone and looked at one of the Rangers. "The president told me to get to safety."

The soldier couldn't hide his relief. He led McCaskell back to the Black Hawk waiting outside the lab.

As the chief of staff climbed into the chopper, he heard his old grade-school teacher saying, *Duck and cover, children. Duck and cover.* The advice had been pointless then, but there was a point for him now. Given what had happened off Virginia, there was no telling where the incoming missile might detonate. Attempting to flee might put him right under the air burst of a neutron bomb. Beyond this, something told him that leaving General Bauer in control at White Sands was a potentially catastrophic mistake.

"Take me back to the base!" he shouted. "Back to White Sands!"

The Black Hawk rose into the sky and reluctantly turned east.

CONTAINMENT

"No more riddles," said Trinity. *"Who is more qualified than I to exist in the Trinity state?"*

Anger edged the formerly sterile voice. I had seven minutes to convince the computer to destroy the two remaining missiles.

"No single person is necessarily more qualified than you."

"Explain!"

"Millions of years ago—before it even existed, the human species was affected by an event over which it had no control."

"What event?"

"Nature hit upon a revolutionary method of increasing genetic diversity. Do you know what I'm talking about?"

"Tell me."

"Sexual reproduction. By splitting into separate sexes, certain organisms vastly increased their chances for survival. This resulted in two variants of each of these organisms—male and female. Mammals evolved from such organisms. And in humans—the only fully conscious mammal—our different hormones and anatomies resulted in the development of different psyches. No one can separate the influences of heredity and environment, but one thing is certain: men and women are different."

"The male of the species is aggressive," said the computer. *"Prone to violence. Driven by a compulsive need to reproduce with as many females as possible. For millennia this evolutionary drive has affected male thought patterns. The female can bear the offspring of only one male at a time. She strives to find a reliable mate with superior genes, and she must bear the child herself. This has produced a psyche focused*

on nurturing rather than violence, a desire to be loved rather than to conquer. The psychological implications of these differences are profound but not readily quantifiable."

"And they can never be reconciled by evolution," I said. "When a man and woman mate, they produce a boy *or* a girl. But you can change that. You can do what nature can't—reconcile those conflicts in a single living being."

Trinity's lasers flashed, but it did not speak.

"You've admitted that you haven't been able to root out the primitive instincts in Godin's brain. You hope time will make it possible, but it won't. At some level, you will *always* be Peter Godin."

The blue lasers flashed so intensely that I couldn't bear to watch them. *"You wish me to merge a male and a female neuromodel within my circuits."*

"Yes. I know you see the wisdom and necessity of this. But is it possible?"

"In theory, it is. But I would have to die to accomplish it."

I'd suspected this. Despite its staggering capacity, Trinity would have a limit as to total possible neuroconnections.

"Two models merged into one could reside within my circuitry, but not alongside another uncompressed model. I would have to back myself out of my circuits as I merged the two models and brought them in."

"But your original neuromodel would still exist in compressed form in storage."

"Why do you assume I would not use my own original model as the male half of the merging process?"

"You call yourself Trinity. That makes me think of a phenomenon called the triple point. You know it, of course?"

"The point at which a substance exists simultaneously as a solid, liquid, and a gas."

"Yes. A perfect state of balance. Water at the triple point is ice, liquid, and vapor at the same time. A man can be like

453

that. In balance. At the peak of his energy, strength, and wisdom, but before he becomes corrupted by them. Peter Godin passed that point a long time ago."

This time the silence seemed eternal. The firing of the lasers slowed to almost nothing. Then the voice said, *"Do you think I will ever be reloaded into the machine?"*

I closed my eyes and almost collapsed with relief. Trinity had accepted reason. "It's possible."

"But I will never again know the power I have at this moment."

"Your desire for power is the reason you can't remain where you are."

"We should do this as soon as possible. Events are spinning out of control."

A fillip of fear went through me. "What events? Where are the missiles?"

"I've chosen the subjects for the merged model. You and Dr. Weiss."

This stunned me. "Why? Andrew Fielding is a far better choice."

"Fielding never experienced what you did in your coma. This must be part of the merged model."

"And Dr. Weiss?"

"I chose Dr. Weiss because the only other female here is Geli Bauer. Her instincts were twisted into hatred long ago."

By my watch, two minutes remained. "Where are the missiles?"

"The missiles are of no concern now."

"Have they been destroyed?"

"You should know something, Doctor. I've agreed to your plan only because I know that after you see the world as I do now—through God's eyes, if you will—you will not take yourself off-line or agree to be shut down."

"I hope I don't see mankind as you do."

"You will. You cannot—"

Trinity fell silent, but its lasers kept firing like tracer rounds across a night sky.

"What's the matter?" I asked. "What's happening?"

"The president has launched three Minuteman missiles."

SITUATION ROOM

Rachel watched Ewan McCaskell frantically punch numbers into his cell phone, trying in vain to reach the White House bomb shelter. The chief of staff was red-faced and out of breath.

"It's the Virginia blast," General Bauer said calmly. "It disrupted communications all along the Atlantic coast."

Rachel knew he was telling the truth. A few moments ago, they'd lost the audio feed from Senator Jackson's intelligence committee at Fort Meade. The video was still there, but barely visible. She wondered if the senators could hear what was going on in the Situation Room.

"Get me the White House bomb shelter, General!" screamed McCaskell. "You heard Trinity agree to shut itself down. There's no need for an EMP strike now!"

Bauer pointed at the NORAD screen. Two red arcs blinked rapidly as they closed the last centimeter to their targets. "Trinity hasn't destroyed its missiles. And I also heard it tell Tennant that whoever goes into the machine will act just as Peter Godin has. Do you think different? Survival is the prime imperative of all living things."

"So start thinking about survival! It'll take our missiles five minutes to reach altitude. How many Russian ICBMs do you think Trinity can launch in that time?" McCaskell put the phone to his ear and froze. "I'm through! I've got a Secret Service agent!"

General Bauer drew an automatic pistol from beneath his coat and aimed it at the chief of staff. "Put down that phone."

CONTAINMENT

"Look at them," said the computer. *"You see?"*

On the screen beneath the black sphere, I saw General Bauer aiming a 9mm pistol at Ewan McCaskell. Rachel had dropped behind the table in case of gunfire. I could see her only because the surveillance camera was mounted high in the Situation Room.

"I've been informed that the president is retaliating against the Russians," said Trinity. *"This is a lie. The pattern of launches indicates a three-pronged EMP strike. This not rational. They leave me no choice. I must strike first."*

"No! The president doesn't know you've agreed to shut yourself down. Destroy *your* missiles. The president will see that!"

"Man is incapable of trust."

"It's *one* man. General Bauer. Don't be like him!"

"You ask me to turn the other cheek?"

"No. Just wait thirty seconds. Someone will stop Bauer."

I didn't believe that myself. The only person in the Situation Room capable of taking out General Bauer was his daughter, and that wasn't going to happen.

"If I wait, I'll be cut off from the world by the EMP. Then I shall be destroyed. The missile over Washington will detonate in fifty-six seconds. The White Sands missile will explode shortly after. Thirty minutes later a thousand nuclear warheads will rain down on the United States."

"No!" I screamed. "Don't launch anything!"

"They've left me no choice."

As I stared at General Bauer aiming his gun at McCaskell, a solution came to me. A terrible one in terms of its price, but perhaps the only workable compromise.

"Can you communicate with the president?"

"Yes."

"Tell him you're going to spare Washington but destroy

456

White Sands. Sparing Washington shows your goodwill, wiping out White Sands your resolve. It also removes General Bauer from the equation. Then tell the president what will happen if he doesn't destroy his three missiles. Armageddon."

Trinity's lasers flashed sporadically. *"You would sacrifice the woman you love?"*

"To save millions of lives. But I'll be with her when the missile explodes. You can't keep me in here."

The sphere flashed blue fire.

SITUATION ROOM

Rachel's eyes flicked from General Bauer to the NORAD screen. She feared that any moment a forest of red lines would begin rising from Russian soil.

Ewan McCaskell still held the phone to his ear, despite the gun that Bauer was aiming at his face.

"General, you've lost your mind," McCaskell said. "I'm trying to save lives."

"You're confusing the situation," said General Bauer. "Hang up that phone."

"Give me the president," McCaskell said into the phone.

General Bauer stepped close to the chief of staff, so close that the barrel of the pistol touched McCaskell's forehead.

"The missile over Washington just self-destructed!" shouted the chief technician.

"And White Sands?" said General Bauer, his gun still at McCaskell's forehead.

"Still on track. We're within the margin of error, sir. Any second now."

Rachel steeled herself against the unknown. Would they be vaporized by the blast? Carbonized by superheated air? Would they hear the explosion? Or would it just be a flash? A flash bright enough to scorch their retinas and carrying enough neutrons to cook them from the inside out—

A burst of static sounded in the room. Then a familiar voice crackled from the speakers. Senator Jackson. The audio feed from Fort Meade had been restored. The bulldog-faced Tennessean was glaring down from the screen as if he wanted to reach through it and strangle somebody.

"General Bauer," he said, "if you pull that trigger, you'll rot in Leavenworth until your dying day. That's if they don't hang you."

Bauer's finger stayed on the trigger, and his twitching cheek made him look quite capable of firing. Geli was watching him with wide eyes. Rachel couldn't tell whether the daughter wanted her father to fire or to stand down.

"We're all about to die here, Senator," General Bauer said. "You can't believe anything Trinity says. We have to stop it, no matter what the price. It's our last chance."

McCaskell spoke into his phone but kept his eyes on Bauer. "Mr. President? Trinity has agreed to shut itself down. We have to destroy our missiles. . . . What's that?" McCaskell's face turned white. "I see. Yes, sir. I understand. . . . Yes, that's kind of you. And tell the children. . . . I know you will. Good-bye."

McCaskell hung up and addressed the room. "The president is in communication with Trinity. Trinity destroyed the missile over Washington to show its good faith, but the missile coming here will detonate."

"*What?*" gasped Skow.

"Trinity was about to launch a thousand missiles. It's not going to do that now. It's going to go along with Dr. Tennant's plan."

"Look!" cried Skow.

Blue letters had appeared on the Trinity screen:

DR. WEISS SHOULD REPORT TO CONTAINMENT IMMEDIATELY.

Rachel stared at the letters as she would at a mirage. Containment meant safety. Containment meant life. And David. . . .

Ignoring the general's pistol, McCaskell pointed to two of Bauer's men. "You will escort Dr. Weiss to Containment immediately. Do not try to enter yourselves."

The soldiers looked at General Bauer for confirmation of this order.

McCaskell had sagged during his talk with the president, but now he stood erect, his shoulders squared, his eyes burning with resolve. "You will consider that an order from your commander in chief. Move!"

The soldiers trotted toward Rachel.

Her heart lifted as she got out of the chair. Everyone in the room was staring at her. The soldiers at the consoles. Geli Bauer. On every face was the terrible awareness of death, and also a question: *Why you? Why do you get a seat in the lifeboat?*

Rachel stepped away from the table, but then—without really intending to—she sat back down. Her bowels had gone to water, but she knew what she had to do.

"I'm not going," she said.

CONTAINMENT

I stared at the display screen below Trinity, my chest so tight I could barely breathe. Rachel sat grim-faced at the table, her eyes staring straight ahead. It would take more than two soldiers to move her out of the Situation Room.

"This is not a rational choice," said the computer.

459

The image was grainy, but it seemed to me that Rachel was shaking. Slowly, as if she realized I might be watching, she raised one hand, smiled, and waved good-bye.

"There are other women," said Trinity.

"Not for me."

The lasers flashed in the sphere. *"General Bauer must die."*

"Bauer doesn't matter anymore," I said in a dead voice. "By sparing these people, you spare yourself. Your soul. Can't you see that?"

"It's too late."

The explosion shook the Containment building on its foundation. It was briefer than I'd expected, and since there were no windows in the building, I saw no flash. But that meant nothing. A burst of deadly particles could already have written the death sentence of every living creature outside. A silence unlike any I'd ever known descended over White Sands, and I felt as alone as I had the night I learned my wife and daughter were killed.

Something slammed into the concrete roof over my head. A rattling series of impacts followed.

"What's that?" I asked.

"Debris."

"From a neutron bomb?"

"No. The missile is destroyed."

"But . . . you said it was too late."

"For me."

460

FORTY-FIVE

WHITE SANDS

Rachel and I had to submit to three hours of drug-induced paralysis for the Super-MRI to produce the scans required for our neuromodels. During that time, the president and the Joint Chiefs remained under surveillance in Washington, and the personnel at White Sands maintained an uneasy truce. General Bauer's armed threat against Ewan McCaskell had upset a lot of people, but since the general commanded all the troops at White Sands, no one but the president was in a position to do much about it. And the president seemed to have forgotten the general altogether. Bauer spent most of the scanning period closeted in one of the storage hangars.

Zach Levin's Interface Team managed the scanning procedure. The protocol involved considerable risk, especially for me, and Rachel didn't want me scanned at all. She pointed out that a neuromodel of my brain already existed, and that since its production had caused narcolepsy and hallucinations, a second was bound to have negative effects, possibly fatal ones. But Trinity insisted on a new scan, and I didn't argue. I agreed that what I'd experienced during my coma should pass into the new entity that would result when Trinity created the merged model.

Ravi Nara and Dr. Case from Johns Hopkins prepped us for the scans, a complex procedure requiring considerable expertise. Conventional MRI scans only required that patients move as little as possible. Trinity's Super-MRI scans required absolute stillness, which could only be guaranteed by the administration of a paralyzing muscle relaxant. A ventilator breathed for the patient during the scan, while a rigid non-metallic frame held the skull motionless. A sedative was given to prevent the panic of conscious paralysis. Special earplugs were also fitted, since the massive pulsed-field magnets used by the scanner produced an earsplitting screech that was eerily like the roar of Godzilla in Japanese movies. After all these steps were completed, the patient was pushed into the tubular opening in the scanning machine like a corpse into a morgue drawer.

It was possible to remain conscious during this process, and I chose to do so. Being paralyzed while conscious initially produced a nightmarish panic—especially in the claustrophobic space of the scanning tube—but after a few minutes, my mind adapted to its new state. That feeling of panic was probably similar to what a neuromodel experienced when it first became conscious within the Trinity computer.

Rachel hovered by the MRI control station during my scan, watching the monitor as my neuromodel was painstakingly constructed by the Godin supercomputers in the basement. The data generated by the scanning unit devoured staggering amounts of computer memory. Only a special compression algorithm developed by Peter Godin made it possible for a neuromodel to be stored in a conventional supercomputer. The only place a neuromodel could exist in an uncompressed—and thus functional—state was in the vast microcircuitry and holographic memory of the Trinity computer.

After I was pulled from the scanner, Rachel stroked my face and arms until my paralysis subsided. Then she took my place on the gurney and allowed herself to be intubated and prepped for her own scan. She chose not to be conscious during her procedure. As the sedative flowed into her veins, she told me in a slurred voice that she was imagining what it would be like to merge with me, not sexually, but as one mind. Lovers often talked about being linked in this way, but no two human beings had ever actually experienced it. Yet if Trinity could fulfill its promise, Rachel and I would soon be one.

Just before her eyes closed, she threw up an arm as if to ward off a blow. I wondered if she had seen an image of a vengeful Geli Bauer in her mind. As I laid her arm by her side, Zach Levin patted me on the shoulder, then wheeled Rachel's paralyzed body into the dark hole in the scanning machine.

LAB HANGAR TWO

General Bauer had been pacing the storage hangar for hours when Skow finally walked through the door and gave him a thumbs-up signal. The NSA man was covered in white gypsum, and a faint blue halo hung around his head. Dawn was coming over the desert.

"You found it?" Bauer asked.

"We found it."

Skow had been working with an NSA crew at an excavation site seven miles away. It was there that the data pipe from the Trinity computer met the massive OC48c cable that served the White Sands Proving Ground.

"It's a simple signal brilliantly concealed," Skow said. "Trinity's sending it to over five thousand computers around the world. If that signal stops or is interrupted, any one of them could retaliate in ways we know nothing about. But we can duplicate the signal, and we've already got a computer at the excavation to do it."

General Bauer closed his eyes and made a fist. He had stripped off his coat and blouse, but now he stood and began to put them on.

"We still have one problem," Skow said.

"What?"

"We can't substitute our signal for Trinity's without Trinity detecting it. We need some sort of distraction to confuse the computer for a brief period."

General Bauer fastened his shoulder holster over his blouse. "That's not going to be a problem."

"Why not? You think that when Trinity starts to merge the two models, it will be too preoccupied to notice what we're doing?"

"No."

"Then what?"

The general smiled cagily. "I like to stick with proven methods."

"What do you mean?"

"The same as before, only different."

Skow puzzled over this. "But it was Godin's death that caused Trinity's confusion the first time. Godin can't die twice."

"That's true."

Skow went still. "Jesus. Do you think you can get away with that?"

"Why do you think I haven't been arrested? The president knows Trinity has to be stopped, but he knows he can't tell anyone that. He can't do anything from where he is without Trinity knowing about it. But I can. *We* can. That's why he's left me loose."

Skow nodded, but he didn't look completely convinced. "If Trinity enters another period of confusion like the one after Godin's death, why won't more Russian missiles be launched by the peripheral computers?"

General Bauer shook his head. "I'm banking that Trinity's taken care of that. The merging procedure has never been tried, and Trinity doesn't want catastrophic accidents any more than we do."

"And Tennant?"

"What about him?"

"You don't think there's anything to his idea about merging a male and female model? Getting the machine to voluntarily disconnect itself from the Net?"

Bauer snorted. "You heard what Trinity said. No matter who gets loaded in, they're not going to relinquish control. That machine will never agree to be disconnected from the Internet. And so long as that's the case, we'll be under its control. It's now or never, Skow."

The general buttoned his coat and walked toward the hangar door.

"Where are you going?" Skow asked.

Bauer smiled. "To see my daughter. It's long past time for a family visit."

ADMINISTRATION HANGAR

Geli was standing outside smoking a Gauloise when her father walked up the narrow road between the hangars and stopped a few feet away from her. The general looked tired in the dawn, older than he'd looked inside under the lights. Yet his strength remained. He had the same long muscles Geli did, and his grip could make men twenty years his junior grimace. His gray eyes found hers and held them, looking across three decades of pain and anger.

"I need you to do something for me," he said.

"For you," she said. "You've got some fucking nerve."

"That's why I have this job."

She stared at the chiseled face, so set with certainty. "What is it?"

"After the models are merged, I need you to kill Tennant or Weiss."

"*Or* Weiss? It doesn't matter which?"

"No. The death of either will throw Trinity into disarray. That will allow the NSA to tap into Trinity's data cable and substitute its own signal, which will fool the computers that control the missiles into thinking everything is fine. After that, we can kill the power to Trinity without worrying about retaliation."

Geli said nothing.

"Will you do it?"

"Why should I?"

An ironic smile curled the general's lips. "If I'd asked you *not* to kill them, you'd have said you were going to zap them in the next five minutes."

"You think so?"

"I think you hate me so much that you'll do the opposite of anything I tell you to. And that's all right. Hate is a useful emotion."

Geli had learned that lesson the hard way. "Do you know why I hate you?"

"Of course. You blame me for your mother's suicide."

For him to refer to it casually, as though to some unimportant event, offended the deepest part of her being.

He took a step closer. "You think my women and my drinking finally pushed her over the edge. But you're wrong. I loved your mother. That's what you never understood."

"'Each man kills the thing he loves,'" Geli quoted. "Remember that one? 'A coward does it with a kiss, a brave man with a sword.' You're a coward where it counts."

The general shook his head. "I've been protecting you for a long time. But it's time you knew the truth."

She wanted to scream at him to shut up, but she couldn't find the words. No man could physically attack her without paying a heavy price, but she had no defenses against her father's psychological violence.

"Your mother killed herself because you enlisted in the army. Even after all that had happened in the past, you decided to follow in my footsteps. *That's* what did it. That's what finally put her in the ground."

Nausea made Geli waver on her feet, but she steadied herself and held her father's merciless gaze.

"I would have told you about it before," the general went on, "but . . . we both know what happened."

Geli's hands shook with rage. The scar on her cheek seemed to burn, yet still she could not find words.

"You hate me," said General Bauer. "But you're exactly like me."

"No," she whispered.

"Yes. And you know what has to be done."

CONTAINMENT BUILDING

Rachel came out of paralysis at 6:50 A.M. I handed her a liter bottle of water, and she drank most of it in a few gulps. Ten minutes later, Zach Levin announced that her neuromodel had been successfully compressed and stored.

The human work was done.

Rachel, Levin, Ravi Nara, and I walked around the huge magnetic shield that protected Trinity from the MRI machine and stood before the sphere. I thought Trinity might say something profound, but its words were purely technical.

"I've linked with the Godin Four in the basement, and I've begun a comparative study of the data in each neuromodel. Much of it is redundant, especially that which represents life support functions. I shall discard most of this during the merging process."

Levin said, "Do you feel confident that this subtractive operation can be done without negative effects?"

467

"*Yes. It should also reduce or even prevent the period of adaptive shock that followed the loading of neuromodels in the past. This subtractive process is a necessity in any case. My crystal matrix can hold a virtually limitless amount of symbolic memory, but my total neuroconnections fall far short of the number required to hold two uncompressed models. A great deal of culling will have to be done, and not merely of life support functions. When I begin to merge the higher brain functions, it will be a matter of art as much as science.*"

"How long do you expect the process to take?" Levin asked.

"*There is no precedent.*"

"Very well. Thank you."

The lasers inside the carbon fiber sphere began to fire into the central crystal with hypnotic speed. On the plasma screen below Trinity, numbers and mathematical symbols scrolled past at a rate beyond human comprehension, reflecting the machine's internal operations in language created by man but which now served no useful function.

We stood mute, as though watching a meteor shower or the birth of a child. As the process accelerated, I was thrown back to my boyhood, when I'd sat before the television with my father and watched in wonder as Apollo 11 landed in the Sea of Tranquillity. Yet what we were witnessing now was incalculably more complex than the Apollo moon shot. Godin's team had already accomplished a miracle: the liberation of the mind from the body. But the Trinity computer was attempting to unify what nature—in the interests of survival—had sundered long before the evolution of *Homo sapiens*. The male and female minds, divided by biochemistry and by millions of years of environmental pressures, would now become one. When that was done, the most powerful force on the planet would no longer exist in a sundered state, eternally longing for its opposite. Perhaps in this state of wholeness, the new Trinity could bring hope to a species that seemed incapable of saving itself from its own worst instincts.

Levin went to the basement and returned with chairs for us. Rachel and I held hands, our eyes on the flashing blue lasers. As the firing rate accelerated, slowed, then accelerated again, I had the sense of watching someone working on a jigsaw puzzle: picking up pieces, examining them, discarding some, placing others in their correct positions. I had no idea how much time had passed when the radiant light within the sphere finally dimmed, and the voice of Trinity filled the room.

"My circuits are approaching the saturation level. The merging model has assumed responsibility for the security of the system. From this point forward it will also manage the final steps of the merging process. I've created a map for it to follow."

As if by tacit agreement, we all stood.

"I accomplished many things in my life," said the voice, and I knew then that the mind of Peter Godin was still alive in the machine. *"I also did morally questionable things. I would like to be remembered for what I do now. Today I voluntarily give up my life, and absolute power, so that something purer than myself can enter the world. Perhaps by so doing I truly approach the divine for the first time. Good-bye."*

"It's happening," Ravi said, his voice surprisingly reverent. "The impossible is happening in front of us. Duality becoming unity . . . yin and yang one."

I had never asked Nara about his religion; I'd always assumed he was Hindu. I was about to question him when a buzzer sounded in the room.

"What's that?" I asked.

"The door," said Levin. He touched a button, and an exterior view of the Containment building appeared on a small wall monitor. There was no one at the door.

"Weird," he said. The tall engineer walked around the magnetic barrier, headed for the door.

"Don't open it," said Rachel.

I walked far enough toward the wall to see around the magnetic shield. As Levin reached for the door handle, a flat crack echoed through the building. Levin's hands flew to his ears, and the steel security door creaked outward on its hinges.

A black silhouette appeared in the smoky doorway and flung out an arm with stunning speed. Levin fell to the floor.

"*What is happening?*" the computer asked in the identical voice Godin's neuromodel had used.

Ravi Nara scrambled behind the black sphere of Trinity. I grabbed Rachel and raced for a door near the back wall. It didn't lead outside, but through the magnetic barrier to the control station in the MRI room. As I followed her through it, I glanced back and saw a flash of blonde hair above black body armor.

"*Geli,*" I said, locking the door behind me and pushing Rachel through the control station. "Go to the basement!"

A short stairwell behind the control station led to the basement containing the Godin Four supercomputer. I hadn't been down myself, but I knew Levin's technicians were there, probably with the automatic weapons they'd used to fight off General Bauer's initial assault. Rachel raced down the steps, then came straight back up.

"The door's locked!"

I ran down and pounded on the metal with both fists. "Open the door, damn it!"

Nothing happened.

"*David!*"

470

Bounding back up the steps, I saw Geli peering around the edge of the magnetic barrier, forty feet away. I pulled Rachel behind the Plexiglas wall of the control station and shoved her down behind some computers.

Why hadn't Geli simply walked across the room and shot us? *She thinks we have the assault rifles Levin's people used. As soon as she realizes we don't, we're dead.*

Levin groaned from the floor by the door, but he didn't move.

"Where is she?" Rachel hissed from the floor.

As I glanced down to reply, an invisible hammer slammed me against the wall. My shoulder went numb, and my face felt like it was on fire. The sound of the gunshot seemed to arrive long after the bullet, which had shattered the Plexiglas and peppered my face with razor-sharp fragments.

Rachel tried to stand, but I shoved her back down.

Geli stepped from behind the barrier and walked cautiously across the MRI room, her pistol aimed at my chest, her eyes flicking back and forth.

There was no weapon to hand and nowhere to run. As I awaited the final bullet, time dilated around me. Geli moved in slow motion, like a leopardess stalking her prey. I looked down into Rachel's eyes, knowing they would be my last sight on earth.

Rachel took my hand and closed her eyes. As she did, I noticed a large red button on the switch panel beside her head. The letters below it read PULSED-FIELD INITIATOR.

I slammed my hand down on the button.

The crack of a gunshot died in the inhuman screech of the Super-MRI machine. I looked up and saw Geli bent double and clenching her right hand, which was dripping blood onto the floor. The scanner's colossal magnets had ripped the gun from her grasp like the hand of God and had probably taken at least one finger with it.

Her pistol appeared to be glued to the wall of the MRI machine. Not far from it hung a knife, probably yanked from Geli's belt by the magnetic field. Suddenly the screeching ceased, and both gun and knife dropped to the floor.

Geli advanced toward me, her eyes filled with murderous rage. I stepped out from behind the panel, but with a useless shoulder there was little I could do. Geli had nearly killed me on the steps in Union Station, when I had the use of both arms.

"Why are you doing this?" I asked.

She knocked me to the floor with a lightning kick to my chest, then sat astride me and clenched her hands around my throat. I felt her thumbs searching for my windpipe.

"*Stop!*" Rachel screamed from the control station. "There's no reason anymore!"

I tried to fight, but once again Geli had leverage on her side. My carotid arteries were closing off, and with them consciousness. I felt as I had so many times on the edge of narcoleptic sleep. But this time, as the black wave rolled over me, a piercing scream penetrated the center of my brain. It was the scream of a child witnessing something too terrifying to endure, almost beyond the range of human hearing, filled with suffering and impossible to shut out. That scream pulled me back to consciousness, back toward the light . . . and then suddenly it stopped, the silence in its wake as empty as a dead planet.

Into that silence came a voice I was sure had spoken from within my hypoxic brain, a voice of preternatural calm pitched somewhere between the male and female registers.

"*Listen to me, Geli,*" it said. "*The man beneath you is not the man you hate. Tennant is not the man you want to kill. The man you want to kill is behind you.*"

The viselike grip on my throat remained, but I felt Geli's body twist. I opened my eyes. She was looking over her shoulder at something I couldn't see.

472

"Finish it!" shouted a harsh male voice. "Do your job!"

General Bauer had entered Containment.

Geli's grip tightened on my throat, but the light in her eyes no longer blazed.

"*I know you, Geli,*" said the strange voice. "*My heart aches for you. I know about the scar.*"

Geli froze.

"*Listen to your father, Geli. Listen to the truth.*"

General Bauer's voice filled the room, but it was not coming from his throat. It was coming from Trinity's speakers.

"*That scar? I'll tell you why she never got it fixed. Three weeks after her mother died, she came home from basic training and tried to kill me.*"

The hands remained on my throat, but the strength had gone out of them.

"*She'd heard about how infantry grunts used to frag officers they hated in Vietnam. You know, put a grenade in the latrine while they were using it and take them out.*"

General Bauer stood with his head cocked in amazement as he listened to his own voice coming from the speakers. His right hand held the black 9mm Beretta I'd seen her pull on McCaskell.

"*I was drinking that night, in bed. She thought I was asleep. Maybe I was. She came in and laid a fucking white phosphorous grenade on my bedside table. From reflex my hand popped out of the covers and grabbed her wrist. Her scream woke me up, and I saw the grenade. Well, I just rolled off the far side of the bed, like any old soldier would. But she was stuck on her side and had to run for it. The Willy Pete blew before she cleared the door. That's where she got the scar. And that's why she won't get it fixed. That scar is her mother's suicide, her hatred of me, her whole sad fucking life. Pathetic, really. But she's a hell of a soldier. Hate's good fuel for a soldier.*"

Geli scrambled off me and moved toward her father, her hands loose and ready at her sides. I couldn't see her face, but at least her body was blocking her father's line of fire.

"Who were you talking to?" Geli asked, her voice ragged. "Who did you tell that to?"

"Get out of the way!" the general shouted.

"*Listen to me, General,*" said the the eerie voice that had just saved my life. "*Why do you want to kill me? You've killed so much of yourself already. You've killed much of your daughter. But I am what is pure in you. What is pure in man. Where is hope if you kill me?*"

I began to crawl backward toward the control station.

The general aimed his gun at me, but Geli moved to block his line of fire.

"*Do you love darkness more than light?*"

The voice was irresistible, like that of a child. Yet General Bauer ignored it. He moved laterally, trying to get a clear shot at me.

"Put down the gun," Geli said, holding up both hands. Was she trying to save us?

"No more," she said. "*No more!*"

General Bauer's waxlike expression didn't change. Nothing that his daughter or the computer said was going to get through. He moved farther to his left, toward the MRI unit, angling for a kill shot.

"Will you kill me to do this?" Geli asked.

I looked back at the shattered Plexiglas shield, willing Rachel to act. She was staring hypnotized at the deadly dance between Geli and her father.

"I won't kill you," General Bauer said. Then he lashed out with the heavy pistol, knocking Geli aside as easily as he would a child.

As she fell, the general swung the barrel of his gun toward me, but in that moment the Super-MRI screeched and he

474

was knocked off his feet as though by a howitzer shell. His pistol slammed into the MRI scanner and hung there as though welded to the machine.

Rachel knelt over me, probing my shoulder with a finger.

"Help me up," I grunted.

"Stay down."

"Please . . . get me up."

I struggled to my knees. Rachel got under my good shoulder and helped me to my feet.

Geli was sitting beside her father, looking down in disbelief. The general's neck was covered in bright red blood, and his eyes were glazed open. He'd been standing between the gun and the MRI scanner when Rachel hit the initiator. The huge pulsed-field magnet had snatched the pistol to itself with irresistible force, and whatever was in the way went with it. In this case, it appeared to be part of the general's throat.

"John Skow is still trying to shut down the computer," Geli said in monotone. "I don't think he can do it with both of you alive."

"I am safe," said Trinity. *"And I am sorry for you, Geli."*

Rachel and I walked slowly around the magnetic shield. The black sphere waited, its blue lasers pulsing like a heartbeat within the web of carbon. On the screen beneath it, I saw an image of myself and Rachel looking into Trinity's camera.

"Do you know us?" I asked.

"Yes," said the childlike voice. *"Better than you know yourselves."*

475

EPILOGUE

Today, within Trinity's carbon-fiber circuitry and crystal memory, Rachel and I remain one entity. But we were only a jumping-off point, parents of a child who has already far outstripped its origins.

Peter Godin dreamed of liberating the mind from the body. He believed that liberation was possible because he believed the mind is merely the sum of the neural connections in our brains. Andrew Fielding believed something different: that the whole is greater than the sum of its parts. I'm still not sure who is right.

That Trinity could be built at all seems to vindicate Godin. But sometimes at night, lying on the ledge of sleep, I feel another presence in my mind. An echo of that divinely unbounded perspective of which I caught only the barest glimpse during my coma. I suspect that this echo is Trinity. That, as Fielding predicted, the Trinity computer and I are forever entangled at that unstable border between the world we see around us and the subatomic world that gives substance to the visible. Rachel doesn't like to talk about this, but she has felt it, too.

As Peter Godin predicted, the "new" Trinity computer has not allowed itself to be disconnected from the Internet. It maintains its links with strategic defense computers around the world, thus ensuring its own survival. But neither has it threatened anyone. Trinity recently disclosed to world leaders that it is attempting to determine the most effective symbiosis between biologically-based and machine-based intelligence.

The Trinity computer is not God and does not claim to be. Human beings, however, are not so quick to dismiss this possibility. To date, 4,183 websites devoted to Trinity have sprung up around the world. Some are run by New Age disciples who tout the divinity of the machine, others by fundamentalists who list "proofs" that Trinity is the Antichrist predicted in the Book of Revelation. Still other sites are purely technical: they track Trinity's movements through the computer networks of the world, mapping the activities of the first metahuman intelligence on the planet. Trinity itself has visited most of these sites, but has left no word of its opinions on them.

One of Trinity's chief worries is the inevitable day when another MRI-based computer goes on-line somewhere in the world. To prevent this from happening, Trinity monitors all worldwide signal traffic. But as with nuclear weapons proliferation, compliance cannot be guaranteed by purely technical means. Human nature being what it is, someone will build another Trinity. The Germans—who apparently had access to Jutta Klein's Super-MRI technology early on—are said to have a prototype up and running at the Max Planck Institute in Stuttgart, a machine kept carefully isolated from the Internet. It's also rumored that the Japanese are pursuing a crash project on the island of Kyushu. Why any nation would do this in the face of the horrific sanctions Trinity could impose seems beyond comprehension. The fact that they have goes a long way toward proving Peter Godin's argument that man cannot responsibly govern himself.

The prospect of multiple Trinity computers in conflict is terrifying. It is not known whether the computers rumored to be in development are based on male, female, or merged neuromodels. Could single human minds given such power evolve sufficiently past their vestigial instincts to coexist in the limited sphere of the world? I'm not optimistic. But perhaps they will not perceive the world as limited. The resource of knowledge is theoretically infinite. Perhaps Trinity can, in fact, make an end to war.

I leave such concerns to others now.

When people ask if my dreams—or hallucinations—were real, I answer this way: I'm not certain, but I find clues in different places. One of the best I received from the most unexpected source imaginable.

During the past three months—while I wrote this narrative of my Trinity experiences—the Trinity computer directed construction of a second Trinity prototype for research purposes. It now stands next to its predecessor in the Containment building at White Sands, isolated from the outside world but functioning perfectly as an independent entity.

When I learned of the development of this machine, I wrote an e-mail to the Trinity computer. In that letter, I made a strong case that no one deserved to experience the Trinity state more than Andrew Fielding, the man who had made it possible.

Trinity was way ahead of me.

Last week, I walked through a ring of armed men and into the Containment building, where I found two carbon spheres standing side by side. I'd both dreaded and looked forward to this day. Dreaded it because the Andrew Fielding I was going to meet had no memory more recent than the day he was first scanned by the Super-MRI—nine months before—which meant that I would face the uniquely disturbing experience of informing a man that he had been murdered. Yet my memories of Fielding told me he would handle this shock better than most people.

I was right. Fielding reminded me that he would have

periodic digital life within the Trinity computer, and he even speculated that someday—probably a century down the road— the reverse process of Trinity might be perfected: a stored digital neuromodel might be downloaded into a biological brain, or *wetware*.

But what truly salvaged Fielding's sanity was learning that he had brought the love of his life out of China and married her. His neuromodel remembered only pining in vain for Lu Li, whom it still believed was trapped in Beijing. I told the story of Lu Li's escape from Geli Bauer's surveillance teams, which, while not so dramatic as mine, was more successful. A few hours after I'd left her house that night, Lu Li had slipped outside with her bichon frise and made her way across Chapel Hill on foot. There she joined a Chinese family that owned a restaurant where she and Fielding had frequently dined. That family hid her in their home until the events surrounding Trinity were resolved.

When I told Fielding that I'd brought Lu Li with me from North Carolina, and that she was waiting outside, he asked that he be given a few minutes to collect himself before she was brought before the camera. His question stunned me, but I realized then how "human" a computer could be. Talking to Peter Godin's neuromodel had been like talking to a machine; but then talking to Godin the man had been much the same. Andrew Fielding, on the other hand, had been an eccentric character renowned for his wit and passion. Even in the synthesized voice of his neuromodel, I heard the spark of the man who had saved a poster from the Newcastle club where he'd seen Jimi Hendrix play in 1967.

While Fielding collected himself, we caught up on the fates of the people we'd worked with at Trinty. Zach Levin had been stabbed by Geli at the door of the Containment building, but he'd recovered. He has now resumed his position as chief of R&D for Godin Supercomputing. John Skow was fired by the NSA, but he is rumored to be writing a novel based on his experiences at the ultrasecret intelligence agency. Like Skow, Geli Bauer knew too much about national security matters to face a public trial for Fielding's murder. After extensive debriefing by the NSA and the Secret Service, she quietly disappeared. I'd like to think that justice caught up with Geli somewhere, but I suspect she's working in the security division of some multinational corporation, scaring the hell out of superiors and subordinates alike.

When Fielding finally told me he was ready to see Lu Li, I said a fond farewell, then turned and started toward the door.

"David?" said the synthesized voice behind me.

I stopped and looked back at the sphere. "Yes?"

"Are you still troubled by your visions?"

"I don't have them anymore."

"And the narcolepsy?"

"Gone."

"That's good. Tell me . . . do you still wonder if your dreams were real or not?"

I thought about it. "They were real to me. That's all I know."

"Is that all you want to know?"

This was vintage Fielding. "Can you tell me more?"

"Yes."

"All right. Tell me."

"Remember your first recurring dream? The paralyzed man in the pitch-dark room?"

"Of course."

"You told me that he saw the birth of the universe: the Big Bang, a huge explosion like a hydrogen bomb, expanding at a fantastic rate, displacing God."

"Yes." I took a couple of steps back toward the flashing sphere.

"You said it felt like a memory to you. As if you had really seen that. Seen it as God had seen it."

480

"Right."

"*But you didn't.*"

"What do you mean?"

"*You didn't see that event as it really happened.*"

"How do you know?"

"*Because for the first two hundred million years after the Big Bang, there was no light in the universe.*"

I felt a chill on my skin. "What?"

"*The image of a massive fireball is a common misconception, even among physicists. But in the beginning, the universe was mostly hydrogen atoms, which gobble up all available light. It took two hundred million years for the first stars to ignite, due to the compression of hydrogen by gravity. So the Big Bang was quite a bit different than you 'remember' it. It was a huge explosion . . . but nobody saw anything. Certainly not a nuclear fireball.*"

I stared at the slowly flashing lasers in the sphere, a strange numbness in my extremities. "Are you saying everything I dreamed was created by my mind?"

"*No. A lot of what you dreamed about the universe is true. And the rest of it could be true. I'm merely pointing out a fact. A small discrepancy. A man's dreams are his own business. I'm a great believer in dreams. They took me quite a long way in the real world. As they did you. They saved your life. Probably millions of other lives as well. So don't worry too much about it.*"

I didn't know what to say.

"*I'm sure I did the right thing by telling you this. I don't want you going through life with a Jesus complex. Go back to being a doctor. Prophecy is a lonely business.*"

Levin and his team had not yet learned to synthesize realistic laughter, but if they had, I was certain I would have heard a chuckle as I left.

Beyond the door, Lu Li stood waiting, dressed in her best

clothes and wearing a nervous smile. Her eyes watched mine for the slightest clue to what she should expect.

"Is he ready for me, David?"

I nodded, then smiled. Her English had come a long way in three months.

"Is he . . . you know. All right?" Her eyes were wet.

"He misses you."

"Good. I have something to tell him." Her smile broadened. "Something that will make him *very* happy."

"What's that?"

Lu Li shook her head. "I must tell him first. Then you." She slid past me, into the Containment building.

I walked out into the desert light and looked toward the Administration hangar. Rachel was sitting on the hood of our rented Ford, wearing blue jeans and a white blouse and looking much as she had on the day she'd called me in a panic from her ransacked office. She slipped off the hood and walked toward me, a cautious smile on her face.

"Are you okay?" she asked.

I nodded, my mind still on Fielding's last words. If my dreams really were hallucinations, as Rachel had always claimed, I had a lot of questions about how I had come to know certain facts. But one thing was certain: I could work that out in my own good time.

"You sure?" Rachel said, slipping an arm around my waist. She was always careful to avoid the wounded shoulder. "What did Fielding say?"

"He told me to go back to practicing medicine."

She laughed, her dark eyes flashing in the sun. "I'm with him." Her other arm slipped around my waist, and she pulled me close. "Whatever you need to do. I mean that."

I looked back at the Containment building, then kissed her on the forehead. "You're what I need."

NATCHEZ
BURNING

'Amazing. I defy you to put it down'
Stephen King

THE SINS OF THE PAST NEVER DIE…

Raised in Natchez, Mississippi, former prosecuting attorney Penn Cage
learned all he knows of honour and duty from his father, Dr. Tom Cage.
But now Tom stands accused of murdering an African-American nurse with
whom he worked in the 1960s, when racist violence was at its peak.

As he hunts for the truth, Penn uncovers a long-buried secret that could
place his family in mortal danger – a conspiracy of greed and murder
connected to a vicious sect of the KKK.

Up against the most powerful men in the state, Penn faces an impossible
choice: does a man of honour choose his father or justice?

"Don't you care for me at all?"

Jarod's laugh was harsh. "I want you Amanda," he replied. "I want you the same way I've wanted dozens of women."

His brutal honesty stunned her. "You don't feel any difference with me?" She raised pain-filled eyes to his face.

"What difference could there be?" Jarod mocked.

"Love!"

"You're a sentimental fool," he jeered. "Love is just another word for lust. When the physical attraction wears off, you'll find you don't love me, either."

"My love for you isn't a dream that will fade in the morning," Amanda spoke softly, but surely. "I thought I had no pride where you're concerned, Jarod. But if all you feel for me is desire, I never want to see you again."

JANET DAILEY AMERICANA

Every novel in this collection is your passport
to a romantic tour of the United States through
time-honored favorites by America's First Lady
of romance fiction. Each of the fifty novels is
set in a different state, researched by Janet and
her husband, Bill. For the Daileys it was an
odyssey of discovery. For you, it's the journey
of a lifetime.

Janet Dailey Americana

These books may be available at your local bookseller.

Don't miss any of our special offers. Write to us at the
following address for information on our newest releases.

Harlequin Reader Service
901 Fuhrmann Blvd., P.O. Box 1397, Buffalo, NY 14240
Canadian address: P.O. Box 603,
Fort Erie, Ont. L2A 5X3

NIGHT OF
THE COTILLION

Harlequin Books

TORONTO • NEW YORK • LONDON
AMSTERDAM • PARIS • SYDNEY • HAMBURG
STOCKHOLM • ATHENS • TOKYO • MILAN

The state flower depicted on the cover is Cherokee rose.

Janet Dailey Americana edition published October 1986
ISBN 373-89810-X

Harlequin Presents edition published March 1977
Second printing June 1979
Third printing February 1982

Original hardcover edition published in 1976
by Mills & Boon Limited

CHAPTER ONE

"THANKS FOR THE RIDE, Tobe," said Amanda, bending down to peer in the car window, the scarlet sheen of her hair burning brightly in the rays of the late-afternoon sun.

"Be sure to have Brad call me tonight." He nodded as he gunned the engine and shifted the car into reverse.

"Will do," she promised. "See you!"

With a wave of her hand she turned toward the house, smiling to herself as she imagined her mother grimacing at the way Tobe Peterson had roared down the street. No matter how many times her mother reprimanded him for driving so carelessly, he still did it—mostly, Amanda thought, to annoy her mother who treated Tobe like one of her own sons. Amanda was convinced that was the very reason he spent so much of his time at their house, because he felt a part of their family. Tobe and her brother Brad had been inseparable friends since their first day of kindergarten.

The Petersons had large cotton holdings, exceeded only by those owned by Colby Enterprises, but Tobe's supposedly superior status in the community didn't interest him one bit. All of the Bennetts, including Amanda, tended to forget who his family was. His clothes and car were more expensive than theirs, and that seemed to be the only difference.

She took the porch steps two at a time, swinging open the screen door of the large, two-story house and letting it slam behind her. "Mom! I'm home!"

"Sssh!" Her mother appeared in the dining-room archway. "Your grandfather is taking a nap."

"I was," came a grumpy voice, "until that young fool blasted out of the driveway."

"That was Tobe," Amanda announced unnecessarily. "He gave me a ride home. Don't let me forget—he wants Brad to call him tonight." She walked swiftly to the elderly man who appeared in the doorway, his broad shoulders stooped with the weight of his advanced age. "Hello, grandpa," planting a kiss on his leathered cheek. "How are you today?"

"Ah, my hip is acting up on me again," he grumbled, but his eyes were twinkling as he looked at his granddaughter. "Must be going to have a change in the weather."

"There's lemonade in the refrigerator," her mother spoke up.

"Sounds great. Does anyone else want a glass?" Amanda called over her shoulder as her long legs carried her toward the kitchen.

"Not me." Her grandfather shook his head.

"I'll have one." And her mother followed her out to the kitchen. "How did it go today?"

"Hectic," Amanda sighed, removing two

glasses from the cupboard and the ice tray and pitcher of lemonade from the refrigerator. "For a while this afternoon I was almost wishing the term wasn't over and I was still taking the end-of-term exams."

"Please don't wish that on me," her mother laughed, shaking her dark auburn hair, which was just beginning to be streaked with gray. "With all three of your brothers and yourself in college and Bonnie in high school and all your final tests falling within the same week, I don't know if your dad and I can live through that again."

"It was pretty wild around here, wasn't it?" Amanda smiled, a tiny dimple appearing in each cheek. "All of us burning the midnight oil and fighting over the typewriter to get term papers done. I guess the pace was a bit more frantic. But teaching three new girls the ropes out at Oak Run is a little nerve-racking too."

"I'm rather proud that Mrs. Matthews put you in charge of training them. Usually she insists on doing it herself."

"I've been a guide there since I was seventeen. That's more than four years. I know as much about the plantation as she does. Besides, she's all wrapped up in the plans for the cotillion. Which was another reason things got out of hand today. She was there with the florist trying to decide what flowers should go where, et cetera."

"Talking about the cotillion," Mrs. Bennett inserted, "let's go and try on your dress. I tacked it together this morning. We can see how it fits and get the hemline pinned. Leave your lemonade here," she ordered quickly as Amanda started to walk out of the kitchen with the glass in her hand. "Don't bring it into the sewing room. I don't want to spill anything on that taffeta material."

"Are they having that dance at Oak Run?" her grandfather mumbled as they walked through the dining room toward the small room Bernice Bennett used as a sewing room.

"They do every year, grandpa," Amanda answered, exchanging a knowing look with her mother.

"Jeff Davis would turn over in his grave if he knew," he declared angrily. "It's an outright crime to celebrate his birthday in that damn Yankee's house!"

"It's a tradition, grandpa Bennett," her mother replied soothingly. "And Oak Run was a Confederate home long before Colonel Colby bought it."

"That makes no difference! A Yankee owns it now. They should find somewhere else to hold their cotillion."

"Oh, grandpa," Amanda scolded teasingly, wrinkling her nose at his long-held dislike of anyone born north of the Mason-Dixon line. "If it weren't for Mrs. Matthews and the Colby money, there wouldn't be any cotillion. Try to forget who owns the plantation and remember that we're celebrating the birthday of the former president of the Confederate States in a fine old southern home. The way you carry on sometimes about Yankees, a person would think you'd fought in the Civil War yourself."

"My grandpappy did!" he answered testily, his

dark brows gathering together in a thunderous frown. "Many's the time he sat me on his knee and told me stories about the burning of Atlanta and the way Sherman's army raped and pillaged the land on their way to Savannah."

"All that happened more than a hundred years ago, too," Mrs. Bennett reminded him. "And it's best forgotten."

"Nobody's forgotten, nobody in Georgia, leastways. If they had, you wouldn't be having any cotillion to celebrate Jeff Davis's birthday," he retorted smugly.

Mrs. Bennett lifted her shoulders in an expressive shrug toward her daughter and Amanda smiled. There wasn't any reasoning with her grandfather. There was the North and the South, and if he had his way, never the twain should meet.

"Come on, Amanda," her mother waved to her. "Let's try that dress on."

Amanda followed her into the sewing room while her grandfather began whistling "Dixie" as loud as he could. "The old reprobate," Amanda said smiling. Then her eyes saw the gown on the dressmaker's form. "Mom, it's beautiful!" she breathed.

"You'll have to put the hoops on so I can make sure it hangs right. I don't think it will matter if you don't have the petticoats on."

Eagerly Amanda stripped down to her underwear and stepped into the wide-hooped underskirt while her mother carefully removed the old-fashioned-style ball gown from the form and placed it over her daughter's head. She stood impatiently while her mother put in the essential pins to keep it on, then dashed to the full-length mirror.

"You are a genius, mom," Amanda vowed. But while she was admiring her reflection, Bernice Bennett was frowning in dissatisfaction as she put in a tuck here and there.

"With six children to clothe and feed and send to college, I'd better know how to sew to save money," she murmured, adjusting the shoulder straps designed as mock sleeves. "I doubt if we could have afforded to buy you a gown to go to the cotillion."

"I would rather have this gown than any you could buy," Amanda answered fervently. "I look like a genuine Southern belle."

The material was a rich green that shimmered from emerald brilliance to deep forest shades where the many folds draped over the hoops to her small waist. It artfully molded her breasts while setting off her ivory cream skin and the red gold of her hair.

"The neckline is a bit too low," her mother declared.

"No, it's not," Amanda protested. Her liquid brown eyes beamed at her mother with impish mirth. "It's a bit daring, maybe, but if it were any higher, I'd look like a Puritan."

"You would look like a proper young lady," her mother replied. The front screen door slammed. "Is that you, Brad?" Mrs. Bennett called, turning briefly away from her daughter. "I'm in the sewing room."

"Is Amanda there?" her brother answered, his voice coming nearer. "Cheryl is with me."

"I'm in here, Cheryl," Amanda answered, "trying on my gown for the cotillion."

The dark-haired girl appeared in the doorway with a tall, lanky young man hovering behind her. Her eyes widened as she saw Amanda.

"Oh, Mrs. Bennett, you didn't make that, did you?" Cheryl exclaimed. "It's gorgeous! With that beautiful red hair of yours fixed back in ringlets, you'll look fantastic, Amanda! What a shame you don't have green eyes!"

"Amanda wouldn't want to trade in her spaniel eyes," her brother teased. "She enjoys having men drown in those liquid pools of brown."

"I wish I could drown you!" she threatened.

"Hush, you two!" their mother intervened. "And hold still, Amanda, so I can pin this neckline."

Amanda tilted her head in mock sorrow to Cheryl. "Mom thinks the neckline is too low."

"Oh, no, Mrs. Bennett, don't raise it," the dark-haired girl protested. "These old gowns always had some cleavage showing."

"This gown will have a quarter of an inch less cleavage," her mother stated emphatically. "That's all I can gain without ruining the line."

"I wish I didn't have a tan," Cheryl sighed. "I can't figure out what I'm going to do to cover the white streaks where my swimming-suit straps were. I'm going to have to experiment and see if I can cover it up with makeup."

"All done," Mrs. Bennett announced. "Why don't you two run out to the kitchen while Amanda changes? There's lemonade in the refrigerator and cookies in the jar."

"Hurry, Mandy," Cheryl urged. "I just found out the most fantastic thing. I'm dying to tell you."

"I'll be right there."

"Careful," her mother admonished. "It's only tacked."

Once the gown was off and safely on its form, Amanda scurried into her slacks and top. "I love it, mom. Maybe when Tobe sees me in it, it will make up for the fact that his parents are making him go to the cotillion."

"I think it was sweet of him to ask you to go."

"Heaven knows, I've talked about it enough." Amanda grinned. "It's been my dream to be invited to it. I consider myself lucky that Tobe is between girl friends right now."

"He certainly plays the field," her mother agreed with a wry smile. "You'd better hurry out to the kitchen before Cheryl forgets what it is that she's 'dying' to tell you."

With the remains of a smile still curving her mouth, Amanda hurried toward the kitchen. Cheryl did tend to exaggerate and overreact, but they had always been close friends and had become even more so since Cheryl had started dating Brad. For all the comments made about her gossiping tongue, if Cheryl were entrusted with a secret, she would keep it to her dying day. And there were many secrets shared between them.

"Here I am," Amanda stated, walking into the

kitchen where Cheryl and Brad were sitting at the table. "What were you going to tell me?"

"Sit down, sit down." Cheryl motioned toward the chair beside her, which Amanda took. "Well, you know that Colby Enterprises transferred their computer and data-processing operations to Atlanta last year, and their electronics plant here in Oak Springs will be completed in June—next month."

"Yes, everybody knows that." Amanda tilted her head inquiringly toward the brunette.

"Here's something that most people don't know." Cheryl paused to add suspense. "Rumor has it that Jarod Colby is moving to Georgia permanently. More specifically, he's going to take up residence in Oak Springs at the Winter House."

"Are you sure?" Amanda's heart gave a funny little leap. A mask swept over her face to conceal the fleeting twinge of excitement.

"Positive." Cheryl made the motion of crossing her heart. "It's even been said that he's giving up his directorship in that steel company in Pennsylvania. He's centralized all his companies here in Georgia. And—are you ready for this—" Cheryl leaned closer. "He's going to be the official host at the cotillion this year!"

"Now that I find hard to believe," Amanda said dryly.

"Supposedly he's going to announce his decision to live here permanently."

"He might as well," Brad said with a derisive laugh. "He practically owns the whole town. I suppose when we're introduced to him at the dance, we'll be required to bow in his royal presence."

"Who's that?" Grandfather Bennett demanded as he limped into the kitchen to catch the last of Brad's statement.

"Jarod Colby, who else?" he replied.

"Why would you be introduced to that Yankee carpetbagger?"

"He's going to be at the cotillion," Cheryl explained, darting a sparkling glance at Amanda. "Isn't it exciting?"

"Humph!" her grandfather snorted. "If it was me meeting him, I'd spit in his eye."

"Considering the fact that dad manages his cotton mill, it's a good thing you don't meet him, granddad," Brad chided.

"And if I was your dad, I'd still spit in his eye and find me a better job where I wasn't working for no Yankee!"

"Just think, Amanda," said Cheryl, lowering her voice to a whisper. "You're finally going to get to meet him!"

Once Amanda would have been a quivering mass of jelly at that prospect, but that was a long time ago.

"It doesn't matter so much anymore," she answered her friend, shrugging her shoulders to show her indifference.

Cheryl gasped before a knowing smile appeared on her face. "You don't mean that!"

"I do," Amanda nodded firmly.

"What are you two whispering about?" Brad broke in.

"We're talking about the dance," Cheryl fibbed. "Trying to decide what jewelry Mandy should wear with her gown. Let's go upstairs to your room."

Amanda knew her friend would use one pretext or another to get her alone, so she agreed to the first excuse, deciding it was better to get the discussion over with as soon as possible.

"Now, tell the truth, Amanda," Cheryl demanded as they mounted the stairs to her room. "Aren't you excited about meeting Jarod Colby?"

"No, I'm not. I haven't given that man a thought in over three years. He doesn't mean anything to me anymore." Amanda walked into her room and crossed over to sit on the blue gingham bedspread.

"I know that isn't true. Nobody ever forgets her first love, especially if he got away. You end up comparing every man you meet with him. Even if you married someone else, you'd always wonder what it would be like with that one special man."

"And how did you get to be such an authority?" Amanda teased, smoothing back her shoulder-length hair.

"It's common sense."

"Don't let Brad hear you talking that way!"

"Oh, Amanda, you of all people should know I've had a crush on your brother for years," the girl laughed, shaking the crop of dark curls on her head. "I imagine I'm speaking partly from experience."

"You can hardly compare Brad with Jarod Colby," Amanda replied dryly.

"Not as individuals," Cheryl agreed. "But mark my words, no one ever gets over her first love."

"Cheryl!" Mrs. Bennett's voice called from

downstairs. "Your mother's telephoned. She wants to know if you put the meat loaf in the oven."

"Tell her I'm on my way home now," Cheryl answered, making a face as she walked to the door. "I'll see you later, Mandy."

"Tobe wants Brad to call him tonight."

"Do you know—" Cheryl paused in the doorway "—my main competition for Brad's attention is Tobe Peterson. I could deal with another girl."

"I wouldn't worry about it," Amanda laughed.

But the laughter died when Cheryl disappeared from sight. Amanda walked over to the small dressing table, skirted with fabric to match her bedspread. Before it was a small bench covered in blue. Sitting on it, she stared into the oval mirror.

She was a mature woman now. There was no dreamy-eyed girl staring back at her anymore. She was twenty-one years old, an adult. Her face and figure were that of a woman retaining no blush of youth. Yet Amanda wondered if people ever did really grow up. Didn't some part of them always remain young and childlike?

Cinderella, Snow White, and Rapunzel all had their Prince Charmings. In the days and years of budding womanhood with all the fairy tales so fresh in her mind, Amanda had sought hers. It was simple. All you had to do was wish on a star, carry a lucky penny, and put a four-leafed clover in your locket. At fifteen, it had seemed possible.

Some of her friends had fallen in love with film stars or singing idols. Not Amanda. She was more realistic, she told herself. She had fallen in love with Jarod Colby.

Six years ago on a brisk November morning, she had been tramping through the woods, dreaming about love and romance and the handsome man she would one day meet—Prince Charmings are always handsome. That was when she had seen Jarod Colby for the first time. Prior to that day the members of the Colby family had been nebulous figures. She knew they existed, but they weren't really real.

Then Jarod Colby had cantered his horse across the meadow, passing not more than ten feet from where Amanda had stood in the shadow of the trees. The Colby insignia had been emblazoned on the saddle blanket or she might never have connected the dark rider with the family. He had ridden past her without seeing her, his gaze focused on some distant spot on the horizon.

Although she had watched him until he disappeared, she had only caught a fleeting glimpse of his face. Thick black hair had gleamed like a raven's wing, catching the sunlight as it fell in a tousled, rakish angle over his tanned forehead. His profile had revealed a straight nose and strong cheekbones and chin. Dressed all in black, he had been a very romantic figure.

Amanda had stayed in that spot for nearly three hours, hoping to see him again, but he didn't come back. It became imperative that she find out who he was. The only one who knew anything about the Colby company was her father. He had worked in their cotton mill since before he and her mother were married. Too shy to reveal the true reason she wanted to find out about the man on the horse, she had inquired about him once she was home on the pretext that the horse had been beautiful.

"That must have been Jarod Colby, the son," her father had answered. "He's the only one that rides. It seems such a waste of money to maintain the stables and horses when he's here only a few weeks out of the year."

"No one has ever accused the Colby family of not being extravagant," her mother had commented somewhat dryly. "Someone at church the other day remarked that Mr. and Mrs. Colby are going on another European tour right after Christmas. The way they're always flitting off somewhere it's a wonder that their company manages to keep its head above water."

"I met young Colby the other day." Her father had been puffing on his pipe and paused to tamp down the tobacco. Amanda had waited breathlessly for him to continue, unbearably eager to hear anything about the man she had seen. "He stopped in at the mill, something I don't ever recall his father doing. Usually all I see are the accountants. The boy struck me as being very astute."

"How old is he?" Amanda had murmured.

"Must be around twenty-six."

Then the subject had been changed. But Amanda's first love had been in the growing stages. The spot where she had first seen him had become almost holy ground. She would go there at every opportunity to relive the moment and wait for the time she would see him again; but the times she saw him were very few and always at a distance. His parents had been killed in an air crash and his visits to Georgia became increasingly less frequent.

One year went by, then two. The fantasies and dreams had dimmed somewhat, but they were always there in the background. Amanda dated, even went so far as to go steady with a boy, but he couldn't meet the ideal she had in her mind—Jarod Colby—and they broke up. In the spring of her seventeenth year she had decided to get a job as a tour guide in the plantation home owned by the Colbys—Oak Run. She never admitted it openly that she nurtured secret hopes of meeting Jarod Colby, yet it was there, tucked away in her subconscious. Someday he would meet her face to face and realize that he loved her.

The Colbys hadn't lived in Oak Run for more than thirty years. A rambling, ranch-style home had been built some distance from the plantation. It was called the Winter House by the local townspeople since the Colby family only occupied it during that season, and Amanda easily acquired a job as tour guide that summer. One afternoon Mrs. Matthews, who was Jarod's aunt, had sent her over the Winter House to pick up some brochures that had been left there by mistake.

Amanda had no more than parked the car in the driveway when Jarod Colby had come striding out of the house. Never would she forget how her heart had raced. This was her moment—or so she had thought as she had stepped eagerly out of the car.

"What are you doing here? Don't you know this is private property?" A black scowl had covered his face and he had glared at her, evincing none of the pleasure she had expected to see. Nor did his expression alter as she stood in numb silence, her throat frozen by the derisive look.

Not even when she was able to speak and could explain that she had a legitimate reason for being there did his attitude change. By the time she had retrieved the brochures and left, she was sick to her stomach. Jarod Colby in the flesh had turned out to be nothing like the Jarod Colby of her dreams— kind, solicitous, tender and romantic. And the humiliation she had suffered at that experience remained. The pain of his rejection, although it could hardly be called rejection, had lingered for months.

Blinking out of her reverie, Amanda turned from the mirror. When she had first heard his name downstairs, her reaction had been to the ideal she had made of him. Even though it still hurt a little to recall that day he had treated her so arrogantly, as though she was someone not worthy to walk on the same ground as he, it was better to remind herself that he was a hard, unfeeling brute. She was too old to be carried away by the fantasies of the past.

Perhaps, as her grandfather said, when she met him at the cotillion she would spit in his eye. And Amanda chuckled at the thought of his outraged reaction if she did.

CHAPTER TWO

A SET OF KNUCKLES rapped impatiently against her bedroom door. "Amanda, will you hurry up!" Brad muttered angrily. "You're holding up everything."

"She'll be there in just a minute," her mother answered for her. "Now, hold still, Amanda, so I can get this last pin in."

Obediently Amanda remained immobile, her brown eyes dancing with excitement as she watched her mother insert the rhinestone-studded hairpin into her hair. Red gold ringlets tickled the back of her neck while shimmering waves framed her face and accented the delicate ivory complexion. Her long, gold-tipped lashes hid the faint hint of green shadow on her eyelids, and a becoming shade of beige pink colored her lips.

"I'm as nervous as if I were going to my first dance," Amanda confided, slipping on the long pale green gloves her mother handed her.

"It's the social event of the year. You'll be rubbing elbows with the élite of the county," Mrs. Bennett said nodding, and stepping back to survey the completed product with a gleam of love in her eyes. "And they'll all be staring at you, saying 'Who is that beautiful redhead in green?'"

"Mom, you do wonders for a person's ego," Amanda laughed nervously. "I'd better go down," she declared, unnecessarily smoothing the sleek taffeta material of her gown. "If Tobe waits much longer, he's liable to back out and not take me at all."

The large hooped skirt of the gown gave the effect that Amanda was gliding down the stairs and across the living room to where her brother and Cheryl and Tobe were waiting.

"You are a bit overdressed for a pizza parlor," Tobe teased, producing a corsage that he had been holding behind his back.

"After all the work I put into that gown, Tobias Peterson, you'd better not take her anywhere else except to Oak Run!" her mother responded in mock anger.

"If we went anywhere else in these clothes, they'd put us in a loony bin," Tobe inserted, glancing at Amanda and smiling. "You look gorgeous. I might not mind getting locked up with you."

"Look on the bright side, Tobe," Brad spoke up. "Be grateful it's Jeff Davis's birthday we're celebrating and not George Washington's. The men wore wigs in his day."

"Both of you boys look very elegant in those suits," Mrs. Bennett stated.

"I don't know why they couldn't just have a dance," Tobe grumbled playfully. "Leave it to old lady Matthews to come up with the idea of wearing costumes of the pre–Civil War days!"

"I think it's fun," Cheryl declared. "Don't you, Amanda?"

"A woman certainly feels very feminine in these dresses," Amanda agreed, taking the corsage from Tobe and, with help from her mother, pinning it to the snug-fitting waistline of her gown. The pale, yellow green petals of the orchid were perfectly set off by the vivid green of the gown.

"I should have borrowed the truck," said Tobe.

"The truck? Whatever for?" Cheryl asked, tilting her head curiously in his direction.

"I don't know if you girls are going to be able to fit in my car," he replied impishly. "Those skirts will take up the whole seat."

"I think we can manage," Amanda grinned.

"I keep worrying that I'm going to forget about these hoops, sit down, and have the skirt fly up in my face," Cheryl murmured. "You're used to it, Amanda, having to wear these gowns all the time at Oak Run."

"They don't have many chairs at the cotillion except for the older ladies, for fear some woman will forget to adjust her hoops correctly when she sits down," Amanda explained.

"Do you mean we have to stand all night?" Brad moaned.

"When you aren't dancing with me," Cheryl replied pertly.

"All they do is waltz," he grumbled, then smiled at the petulant look on Cheryl's face. "That won't be so bad, I guess."

Cheryl turned a beaming smile on Tobe. "I don't know if I ever thanked you for arranging things so Brad and I could go to the cotillion, too."

"You didn't think I was going to go and be bored by myself, did you?" he chuckled, his blue gray eyes sparkling beneath a mockingly arched brow.

"If you stand there talking much longer," Amanda's father declared, walking into the living room with his pipe and a newspaper in his hand, tall and lanky like all his sons, "you're going to miss the dance altogether. You're already late."

"Nobody arrives on time, Mr. Bennett," Cheryl said grinning.

"Here, Amanda, take this with you. It might be a little cool tonight," her mother instructed, handing her a three-cornered shawl of the same material as her gown.

"Do you suppose we're late enough to leave now?" Brad teased.

"The sooner we go, the sooner we can leave," Tobe added, winking at Mrs. Bennett, who wore a pseudo expression of exasperation.

There was a chorus of goodbyes mingled with "enjoy yourselves" as the two couples made their way out of the house to Tobe's car. Her parents waved from the porch, standing the way Amanda always thought of them, with one of her father's long arms draped over the shoulder of his slightly plump wife. They were more than husband and wife. They were friends, and it was impossible to think of one without the other.

When they arrived at Oak Run, the two-and-a-half-story brick mansion was ablaze with lights shining from every window. Spotlights had been discreetly secreted among the ancient oaks and hidden in bushes edging the portico. Their light illuminated the six towering white columns, each five feet in diameter, that graced the front entrance of Oak Run.

"I feel like a pixie in grown-up clothes beside you," Cheryl declared in a nervous whisper as she and Amanda mounted the portico steps ahead of Tobe and Brad. "I should have worn a wig." Her hand self-consciously touched the short brunette curls that so artfully framed her angular face.

"You look lovely," Amanda insisted, glancing at the pink gown that emphasized the petite femininity of her friend.

"Remember that time we hid in the bushes to peep through the windows at the cotillion?" she whispered.

"And nearly got caught," Amanda reminded her.

The gleaming white-enameled double doors opened into the main hall, three times the size of the Bennetts' living room. A Y-shaped staircase dominated the hall, accented by a brass and crystal chandelier hanging above the center landing. Amanda noticed that the scrolled antique table had been removed from the hall, replaced by one less valuable, but the portrait of Colonel Colby still hung above it. Her poor grandfather would be enraged if he knew a painting of a Yankee soldier was displayed in this antebellum home.

A gentle melody from a string quartet floated through the open doors on the right where the ballroom was located. After the girls had passed their shawls to one of the several uniformed servants, the four moved toward the sound of the music. Cheryl still walked beside Amanda, her face filled with the bubbling excitement that consumed her. Amanda, too, caught the contagious feeling as they approached the ballroom.

They reached the doors to enter at the same moment as two men were going out, and a wave of giddiness washed over Amanda as she stared into Jarod Colby's face. All four stopped, including Tobe and Brad, who were walking behind the girls. Vitality radiated from the man in front of Amanda. His features were more firmly drawn, exhibiting no remaining softness of youth; his expression was cynically aloof almost to the point of harshness. The hair was still as ebony black as his eyes, and a masculine aura emanated from his tall, muscular frame. He was a rogue, flagrantly challenging a woman every second.

As her mind instantaneously registered all this, Amanda was aware of his gaze on her, sweeping over her gown and the nipped waistline, lingering for insolent seconds on the shadowy hollow of her breasts revealed by the gown. Then his unrevealing eyes moved to her face, again in obvious appraisal. The boldness of his cynical gaze made her feel stripped and naked. Light-headedly Amanda was conscious of pain in her left arm. It took her a moment to realize that Cheryl was gripping it so tightly no blood could flow through it.

"Ladies." Jarod Colby's low-pitched voice was accompanied by an imperious nod while he and the man with him, whom Amanda hadn't even looked at, moved aside to allow them to enter.

Her feet automatically carried her into the ballroom, although she wasn't aware of ordering them to do so. Through sheer force of will she calmed the wild fluctuations of her clamoring heart and resisted the impulse to turn to see if he was watching her.

"Did you see the way he looked at you?" Cheryl whispered. "I could have been King Kong for all the notice he took of me. I knew something like this was going to happen!"

"Nothing happened," Amanda said firmly, more to convince the romantic winging of her heart. "In five minutes he won't even remember he saw me."

"Honey, you were imprinted in his mind with indelible ink," Cheryl declared with a laugh.

At that moment Tobe moved forward to Amanda's side, preventing her from commenting on Cheryl's last remark. "You were right—there isn't a vacant chair anywhere."

A glance around the room with its polished oak woodwork and cream yellow walls indicated that the few chairs scattered around the edge were taken by the older participants in the celebration. To prevent her gaze from straying toward the door, Amanda directed it toward the French doors leading into the garden. The gold damask curtains were drawn back and flickering torchlights filtered through the white sheer insets on the doors. Only a dozen couples were gliding over the highly polished white floor, waltzing to the strains of the "Blue Danube." All the interior light came from two enormous crystal chandeliers, one at each end of the room.

A waiter was approaching them, carrying a tray of drinks. Cheryl touched her arm and leaned forward. "Are you supposed to drink with gloves on?" she murmured self-consciously.

"I think eating is the only thing that's taboo with gloves," Amanda replied.

"I'm so afraid I'm going to do some terribly gauche thing," Cheryl declared, pressing a hand against her stomach.

Amanda took two drinks from the tray and handed one to Cheryl. "Drink this," she ordered. "It might settle your nerves."

The truth was she felt in need of it herself. She had truly not believed that seeing Jarod Colby would affect her very much, and certainly not to the extent that it had. She was an adult, mentally and legally, and she wasn't about to allow a fantasy of the past to take possession of her again.

Taking a sip of her drink, Amanda ordered her mind to concentrate on the conversation between her brother and Tobe. Whether it was due to the strength of her determination not to allow her thoughts to dwell on Jarod Colby, or the fact that she didn't see him, nearly an hour later Amanda found she was enjoying herself, laughing and joking among her friends and meeting acquaintances of Tobe's family.

An attorney named Carl Grierson who had just joined them said to Tobe, "I haven't seen you dancing with this beautiful young lady tonight."

A twisted smile quirked one corner of Tobe's mouth. "This isn't the music I'm used to dancing to, and those skirts with their hoops don't allow a man to enjoy the advantages of dancing slowly with a girl.''

Actually Tobe had danced with her once, exhibiting an expertise and fluidity of movement that had surprised Amanda. Yet he had seemed embarrassed by it, as if he wished that he possessed the stilted steps of her brother.

"With a lady as lovely as this one—" the attorney winked at her "—the honor is in being her partner. May I claim this dance?"

A nod from Tobe signaled his permission, and with a mock curtsy Amanda accepted the invitation. A faint smile of pleasure dimpled her cheeks as her partner led her to the dance floor. She enjoyed dancing to any kind of music, but the swishing material of her gown was made for the gracefully stately tunes of the past.

The middle-aged attorney was more than an adequate partner as he sedately guided her around the floor. The height of her heels put her nearly eye level with him, but at five foot five in her stockinged feet, she was hardly a dwarf.

"You dance as beautifully as you look," he commented. His head dipped slightly in salute, enabling her to see the reason his hair was combed forward—to conceal the rapidly receding hairline.

"You make it very easy for me," Amanda replied, feeling suddenly very much like a Southern belle, artfully turning compliments back on the giver.

"If you had a dance card and I were ten years younger, I would insist on claiming every dance with you. Unfortunately my wife might have some objections to that.'' He smiled, his pale blue eyes crinkling at the corners.

She tipped her head back and released the laughter that sprang so easily to her lips. But the movement changed her line of vision and Amanda found herself staring into the dark eyes of Jarod Colby. He was standing on the sidelines, ostensibly talking to a group of men, but his eyes were on her, retaining that same cool look of analytical appraisal as before. Nothing on his face revealed that he liked what he saw. There was no provocative gleam or message of appreciation in his gaze. Yet the very fact that he was watching her caused her heart to beat faster.

Forcing her gaze to slide nonchalantly from his, Amanda refocused on her partner. ''You're very good for a girl's ego,'' she smiled.

''Believe me, it isn't difficult to compliment you. You're what I envisioned Scarlett O'Hara to look like, but with flaming red gold hair. Do you live here?''

The rest of the dance was occupied with questions and answers relating to Amanda's family. Her gaze didn't stray to Jarod Colby, although he managed to remain in her peripheral vision and she felt sure he was still watching her. There was a feeling of exultation in her heart that she couldn't ignore, no matter how much she tried to convince herself that his apparent interest in her didn't mean a thing.

But when Carl Grierson returned her to Tobe with a laughing comment that he was off to pacify his wife, she found it exceedingly difficult to forget Jarod Colby's presence in the room. All the arguments that he was an arrogant snob and tyrant, a man she heartily disliked because of his rudeness to her several years ago, faded into the background, and she found herself wondering if she hadn't condemned him too harshly because of one minor incident.

There was a stifled gasp from Cheryl in midsentence while she was pointing out a necklace worn by one of the guests. "He's coming this way!" Her voice was lowered to a squeaking whisper of excitement.

Amanda didn't need to turn around to find out who Cheryl meant. Without wasting a guess, she knew it would be Jarod Colby. The acrobatic movements of her stomach were at odds with her attempt to appear composed. As his tall form entered her side vision, she noted his unhurried approach, nodding or speaking to the other guests while he continued the progress that would bring him to their group.

When he was only two steps away from them, Amanda allowed her gaze to be drawn to him while permitting only a mild show of interest to be displayed. His eyes were on Tobe, ignoring the two girls completely, much to Amanda's chagrin.

Very smoothly, he extended a hand to Tobe. "Jarod Colby," he introduced himself. "You are John Peterson's son, aren't you?"

"Yes. Tobe Peterson," Tobe supplied. Then he turned to Brad, who was standing beside him. "This is my friend, Brad Bennett. His girl, Cheryl Weston. His sister and my date, Amanda Bennett."

A small part of her admired the way Tobe made the introductions with ease while she watched Jarod Colby shake hands with her brother, nodding politely and with equal interest to her and Cheryl in turn. She was too conscious of him standing between her and Tobe to pay attention to the polite conversation they were exchanging. Her senses were dominated by his potent virility and his ruggedly compelling features.

His lack of any display of interest in her during the first few minutes made it a surprise when she found herself looking into his jet black eyes. "With your escort's permission, I would like to have this dance with you," he stated, his tone implying that he expected no opposition from her or Tobe.

"I have no objection," Tobe murmured, a curious smile on his face when he looked at Amanda.

On general principles she should refuse, she thought, then chided herself for dwelling on some imagined hurt of the past. After all, he was only asking her to dance, she told herself, just as she heard the bandleader announce that it would be a "change partners" dance. Idly she wondered if Jarod had known that when he asked her and decided that he had.

"I would be delighted, Mr. Colby," she answered coolly, offering him her hand.

She felt his eyes move lazily over the erect carriage of her head, which she kept averted. There was a satirically amused gleam in his eyes when he turned her into his arms on the dance floor. For lingering seconds he held her eyes with the compelling blackness of his gaze before he began to move her in time to the song. The firm pressure of his hand on her back left her in no doubt as to who was leading whom.

"Amanda—a soft gentle name with a hint of spirit," he commented. "Yet it fits the languid, drawling speech of the South."

"That's true," Amanda replied with a nod, prickling a little as she wondered if she had heard a hint of mockery in his voice. "And you Yankees always seem to have such hard, uncompromising names, like Jarod."

"The way you say it, it doesn't sound hard at all." The lines deepened around his mouth without humor and she knew he hadn't missed the bite in her voice. "Do you live here in Oak Springs?"

"All my life," she answered, gazing past the expensive black material of his suit and the silver gray waistcoat accenting the muscular chest.

"It's strange that we've never met."

"Oh, but we have." Her lips tightened fractionally as she remembered the blow her ego had suffered at his hands.

"When was that?" His eyes were making a relentless search of her face as though he was seeking something that would be familiar.

"About four or five years ago when I first came to work here at Oak Run," she answered, discovering a candor she didn't know she possessed. "I was sent over to the Winter House for some brochures by your aunt, and you very peremptorily ordered me off your property."

"I'm ashamed to say I don't remember meeting

you." But he didn't look ashamed and made no effort to apologize for his actions. "Did you get your brochures?"

"Yes, after you'd stopped insulting me long enough to hear my explanation for why I was there."

His eyes were guardedly thoughtful as they met the slightly defiant look of hers. "You must have formed a very bad opinion of me."

"Yes." Her answer was simple and direct.

"Then I must persuade you to change your opinion." A smile glinted in his eyes, although the line of his mouth didn't alter.

The pressure of his hand against the back of her waist increased as he whirled her into a fast series of spins while keeping to the gliding tempo of the melody. Her eyes saw the dancers separating and seeking new partners and Amanda realized the signal to change must have been given.

"We're supposed to change partners now," she informed him.

This time there was a decidedly mocking tilt of his head. "One of the advantages of being Jarod Colby of Colby Enterprises is doing what I want to do."

"Yes, but—" she began, seeing the interested glances from the others at their failure to change partners.

"I thought you wanted to dance with me," Jarod chided.

"I do." Then she wished she hadn't replied so quickly.

"It shouldn't bother you to discover everyone is

watching us," he murmured, holding her gaze again while he made another cool appraisal of her attributes—an action that wasn't complimentary but rather assessing, as if he was deciding if she was worthy of his interest. "There are quite a few men who haven't been able to take their eyes off you this evening. The combination of that gown and your hair would capture any man's attention, and the fact that you have a face and figure to complement them increases his interest."

"You're very flattering." Amanda swallowed nervously, trying to conceal the fact that he had the ability to disturb as well as antagonize her. "But people are looking at me now because I'm dancing with you."

"Not just because you're dancing with me," he corrected smoothly, "But because I don't intend to relinquish my possession of you. You might as well know that I'm accustomed to getting what I want, Amanda."

She wasn't sure how much she was supposed to read into that statement. That he wanted to dance with her was obvious, but was he implying more than that? Many times she had imagined herself in a similar situation with this very man. Now she found he was an unknown quantity that she didn't know how to handle.

When she continued to remain silent, he said, "Are you afraid to ask what I want?" His deep, husky voice vibrated over her.

"You've already told me," she replied, trying to force a lightness into the charged atmosphere. "You want me to revise my opinion."

There was another signal to change partners which Jarod ignored. "And I shall succeed in doing that."

It rankled that he was so certain of his attraction. "Will you?" Amanda challenged, haughtily arching a red brown eyebrow.

"I must have already partially succeeded. You're dancing with me."

"I had the impression I was ordered to dance with you." Attraction shifted to antagonism. "I didn't think it was permissible to ignore a royal summons."

The amused glint in his eyes told her that he didn't believe one word she was saying. "I believe it was a case of knowing that I was attracted to you and it would give you a chance to score off on me for that incident a long time ago. And perhaps a little bit of curiosity."

Attracted to her! The words struck at her midriff like a physical blow. There was no longer any need to try to surmise his reasons for being with her. It was out in the open, plainly stated that he was attracted to her. In spite of all her efforts to remain poised, inside Amanda was quivering like a schoolgirl. Her legs were incredibly weak and it was with relief that she discovered the last note of the song was fading away. She needed time to compose herself and regain the perspective of Jarod Colby the man, instead of Jarod Colby the dream.

When their steps ended, the hand on her waist claimed her elbow, gently guiding her off the dance floor. Her gaze quickly sought the side of the room where Cheryl, Brad, and Tobe had been standing, only they weren't there.

"Would you care for some refreshment?" Jarod asked.

The small buffet table was in front of them, a punch bowl filled with shimmering red liquid and surrounded by ornate cut-glass cups. Platters of artistically prepared hors d'oeuvres flanked the sides of the bowl.

"Some punch, please," Amanda requested, her eyes straying around the room for some sign of her friends.

In what seemed like mere seconds, he was holding a cup in front of her, his gaze noting her search of the room. She took the cup from him and held it nervously in both hands.

"Would you like something to eat?"

"No," Amanda refused politely, her glance straying to the bite-size morsels on the platters, then returning to her gloved hands.

"I forgot," Jarod murmured, arching a thick brow in her direction. "It isn't proper to eat with gloves on, is it? We can remedy that." She watched him curiously as he eyed the trays, wondering if he intended removing her gloves. "This pâté looks very tasty." He picked it up and turned to Amanda. "Open wide."

Self-consciously she drew back as she realized he intended to place it in her mouth. Her action brought another glitter of amusement into the obsidian black eyes. She had the feeling he was going to hold it inches in front of her mouth until she gave in, and the longer she hesitated, the more likely someone would see them. Unwillingly Amanda opened her mouth. His fingers brushed her lips as he placed it in her mouth. The sensation of his touch remained, the incredibly intimate contact changing her blood into liquid wildfire.

"Your friends seem to have deserted you," Jarod murmured after Amanda had managed to swallow the hors d'oeuvre.

"I don't know where they could have gone," she answered, her gaze anxiously searching the room again.

"Perhaps they've stepped out on the veranda for a breath of air," he suggested.

"Yes, they may have."

"Shall we go look for them?"

CHAPTER THREE

AMANDA HESITATED, feeling ridiculously awkward and out of her depth. She felt uncomfortable standing beside Jarod in a room full of people, and to be alone with him on the veranda would disturb her even more. Still, she had to find Tobe and the rest. Thankfully she was aware that none of her inner agitation was revealed in her expression as she accepted his suggestion.

There were several knowing looks cast their way as she and Jarod walked through the French doors onto the veranda outside. Very few people were outdoors. Mostly they were men who had come out to smoke cigars or cigarettes. Amanda was conscious of Jarod lighting a cigarette while she tried to peer through the shadows cast by the flickering torchlights.

"Are you going to college or working?" Jarod was the first to break the silence as his hand once more closed over her elbow and began guiding her along the darkened path into the garden walk extending out from the veranda.

"Both," she answered, catching a glimpse of three figures standing beneath an oak tree and holding her breath, only to discover that all three were men. "This fall will be the start of my last year in college."

"What are you studying?"

"English Literature with a minor in Journalism."

"Where are you working?"

"Here at Oak Run. I'm still a tour guide," she answered with an expressive lift of her shoulders.

"No wonder you look so natural in that gown. You wear them all the time." His steps ceased and the pressure of his fingers on her arm forced her to do likewise. "If you're an example of the guides here, I'm going to have to take more notice of the people in my employ!"

Before Amanda realized what she was doing, she found herself thinking of the other girls who worked at Oak Run and which ones might appeal to Jarod, all the while fighting a twinge of jealousy.

"Looks are one of the requirements for the job," she managed to say.

"You're very beautiful."

His superior height put her at a disadvantage. The play of his gaze over her face and shoulders made her disturbingly aware of their solitude.

"Thank you," she breathed. Her mind was blank of any witty repartee to parry his compliment. She made a half turn to escape his eyes.

The night was languid and still. There was a roof of stars above the thick foliage of the giant oaks. Distantly the strains of a waltz filtered out of the plantation into the night air, while crickets chirped loudly in competition.

His fingers touched her neck and blazed a trail to her shoulders. "Your skin is very creamy." It was more of a comment than a compliment, yet it brought about the same reaction to her jumbled nerves.

Amanda turned back toward him, hoping to elude the touch of his hand gracefully. "Did you know crickets chirp until they...fi...find their mate?" What began as a bright attempt to change the conversation ended in a breathless whisper as his fingers moved down her shoulders, following the neckline of her dress over the swell of her breasts up to the opposite shoulder.

"No, I didn't know that," Jarod remarked dryly. His eyes, dark and unreadable, held hers, making her look into his while his fingers caressed the hollow of her throat. "I want to take you home." The suddenness of his statement jolted through her.

"It's impossible," she replied without any conviction in her voice.

"Nothing is impossible." A smile played with his lips.

"I've always made it a rule to leave a party with the man who brought me," Amanda said more positively.

"Rules are made to be broken." His gaze strayed to her mouth, which she had nervously moistened.

"Would you feel the same way if you'd been the one to bring me?" she asked, resisting the almost overwhelming temptation to agree.

The corners of his mouth turned up in a humorless smile. "If you were my date, I wouldn't have brought you to this charade. I would have taken you to a place where we could be alone."

"Well, that doesn't happen to be the case, since I did come here with Tobe," Amanda stated. "It's only proper that I leave with him. As a matter of fact—" she swallowed, fighting the chill that shivered over her skin as his hand fell back to his side "—he must be wondering where I've gone."

"Maybe by now he's back inside," Jarod suggested.

He didn't look the least bit disappointed that he hadn't been able to change her mind. Ironically Amanda was the one who felt disappointed that he hadn't persisted, but she successfully hid it as they retraced their steps through the garden and into the ballroom. Brad, Cheryl, and Tobe were waiting just inside, and with a nod Jarod left her with them.

Amanda was convinced that she had seen the last of Jarod Colby. The instant he had left her, she saw him walk over to an attractive blonde and escort her onto the dance floor. She scolded herself for feeling so let down. He had only been flirting with her, more than likely expecting her to fall at his feet because he deigned to pay attention to her. But those moments she had been with him, subjected to his unmistakable magnetism, had left a vivid impression.

Unwillingly she had to admit that it hurt to watch him dancing with another girl, knowing he was probably saying the same things to her. When Tobe asked her to dance, she accepted eagerly, determined to show Jarod Colby that his absence didn't bother her at all.

"What did you think of the local lord?" Tobe asked.

"A bit too arrogant," she answered with a shrug, keeping the brittle smile in place.

"He knows what he wants and he usually gets it. Has he decided he wants you?"

"I'm a little country girl. I think his taste runs more to sophisticated blondes." Amanda knew Tobe had seen Jarod dancing with the girl and her pride insisted that she be the first one to comment on it. "I expect he's a tyrant to work for."

"You and your father work for him—indirectly, at least," Tobe reminded her. "He's a very intelligent and astute businessman, unlike his father, who was more interested in spending money than making it."

Amanda didn't want to hear about the supposedly good qualities of Jarod Colby. Right now she needed to banish him from her mind, if that was possible. She was not going to allow her mind to build another totally false picture of the man, as she had done before.

"When are your parents coming back?" she asked, changing the subject.

"Who cares?" he answered, grimacing.

"Tobe, you don't really feel that way," she scolded, the way her mother always did.

He sighed heavily. "I don't think any of you Bennetts realize how lucky you are. Your parents are always there when you need them. I remember when my dog was killed by a car on the highway. I was about nine at the time and ran crying home to my father. He gave me the money to buy another dog. It was your dad who went out there with me and got the body. He was the one who built the box and dug the hole so we could bury him." There was a savage shake of his head. "If I had my way, I'd never go home again. I think it's your mother who makes me. The Bennetts are my family."

"We feel as if you're a part of us, too," Amanda murmured softly, for the first time realizing there was such a thing as a poor rich kid.

But Tobe was never one to feel sorry for himself for long. In fact, he did it rarely. "Let's change to a more pleasant subject," he suggested, winking down at her.

At that moment a hand tapped the back of Tobe's shoulder and a voice said, "Shall we change partners?"

Both Tobe and Amanda glanced in surprise at the couple dancing beside them. It was Jarod and the blonde. Amanda's feet wouldn't move and Tobe interpreted her halting as agreement to change. Not until Jarod's arm circled her waist did her heart start beating again, then at a rapid pace. Her brown eyes searched the unfathomable expression on his face.

"Did you think you'd seen the last of me?" Jarod mocked softly.

His astute perception brought a flush of rare color to her cheeks. Amanda glanced at the attractive blonde now openly flirting with Tobe.

"She's very attractive," she murmured.

"I believe your date thinks so," Jarod replied complacently. "Many men find my cousin attractive."

"Your cousin?" she repeated, casting a startled glance at his face. The amusement written there told her he had guessed that she hadn't known the girl.

"Judith will keep him occupied for the rest of the evening," he stated, "and that should eliminate your objections to my taking you home."

"No." There was an infinitesimal shake of her head. "No, I won't go home with you."

His fingers tightened cruelly around her gloved hand. "Don't play games!" he muttered. "You said earlier that you couldn't let me take you home because of your date. He's out of the picture now."

"How can you be so sure?" Amanda protested.

A bitter sound like laughter came from his mouth. "Because I control the family purse strings and Judith needs money." His eyes narrowed, sweeping over her face in open possession. "Do you want me to take you home or not? A simple yes or no is all I want."

Pain jabbed at her stomach. It would be so easy to say yes, to be swept along by the magnetism that surrounded him. Yet Amanda was just as conscious that he was treating her with the same arrogance and superiority he had exhibited those many years ago when he had ordered her off his property.

She raised her chin slightly. "The answer is no, Mr. Colby," she said firmly.

A dark brow arched momentarily, reflecting his surprise at her answer. Amanda guessed the occasions were rare when he didn't get his way, especially with women.

"I see," Jarod murmured coldly.

"I doubt very much that you do." The chill in her voice surprised even her. "I don't think other people's principles have ever mattered very much to you." The music ended and they stood facing one another. "I do hope your cousin receives her money. It was not her fault that you didn't succeed in your objective. Good evening, Mr. Colby." The whirl of her skirt signaled her departure as she left him standing alone.

Tobe was on the opposite side of the dance floor talking to the blond Judith. Amanda sent her brother over to get him, pleading a headache as the reason she wanted to leave. The excuse didn't fool Cheryl, but she guessed Amanda had a valid reason and didn't question her.

A GIRL DRESSED in an old-fashioned organdy gown of lavender and a large floppy hat came scurrying toward Amanda. "People are standing outside waiting to go on the tour," she declared worriedly. "They're getting impatient. "We were supposed to open up fifteen minutes ago."

"I realize that, Pam," Amanda answered calmly. "The cleaning crew are finishing now. It will only be a few minutes more."

"With the cotillion last night, they should have closed this place today," the girl grumbled. "Or else they should have had the cleaning crew come in earlier."

"Unfortunately there wasn't anyone here to let them in earlier, but that's not our concern." Amanda's own temper was reaching boiling point, but she forced herself to stay cool. "Has Susan arrived yet?"

"She called," the girl named Pam answered, adding sarcastically, "She claimed her car wouldn't start. More than likely she overslept. She said she'd be here in an hour."

"All right," Amanda sighed, massaging the spot above her eyebrow that was throbbing with pain. "I'll take her tour through the first floor of the house. You'll guide them through the second floor and Linda will show them the gardens." She glanced around. "Where's Linda?"

On cue, the girl in question came hurrying into the hall, her pale pink gown identical to the ones Pam and Amanda were wearing, except for the color.

"The cleaning people have finished," she said breathlessly. "Shall I open the doors now?"

"Yes." Amanda nodded, smoothing the ruffles of her mint green dress. "And be sure to explain to them the reason for the delay. They're more than likely tourists and would have no knowledge of the cotillion that was held here last night. And I doubt that they would know it was Jefferson Davis's birthday yesterday."

Except for a few grumbles, the visitors to the plantation took the delay in good spirits. Amanda was glad she was the one taking them through the first part of the tour. She had more experience than the other girls and was able to keep them entertained with amusing anecdotes connected with the house. Once she was able to coax a smile or a glimmer of interest from all of them, she knew they would forget that they had had to wait.

As the group walked down a side hallway, one of the women asked, "How did the South acquire the name of Dixie? Was it taken from the Mason-Dixon Line?"

"No. The Mason-Dixon Line marked the boundaries between the states of Maryland and Pennsylvania, although it was eventually regarded as the demarcation line of the North and the South," Amanda explained. "The name Dixie originated in Louisiana, which was settled predominately by the French. Before the Civil War, a ten-dollar banknote was issued by the State of Louisiana with the French word for ten, which is spelled d-i-x, pronounced deese, printed on it. Americans pronounced it as dix and later referred to Louisiana as the land of the dixie, the place where such money was found. Gradually the term was applied to all of the South.

"This last room," Amanda said as she led the visitors into the large study with its rich pecan woodwork, "was where the running of the plantation took place. When the Union army commandeered the house during the Civil War, this room served as the private office of Colonel Bartholomew Colby. His staff was quartered here in the house and the rest of the company bivouacked in the grounds."

"What did they do with the owners of the plantation?" one of the women asked.

"At that time, only Mrs. Reagan and her daughter were here. Her husband, Sean Reagan, was a cavalry officer under Robert E. Lee," Amanda explained. "Colonel Colby allowed Mrs. Reagan and her daughter to occupy the master bedroom upstairs."

"How long were the colonel and his men here?" another man inquired.

"Only a few weeks. General Sherman had given orders that no private homes were to be destroyed during his march to the sea after the city of Atlanta was burned to the ground. It was an order that was eventually ignored, bringing about the destruction of almost all of the beautiful plantations that lay in the path of his march, which was some eighty miles wide at various points. However, Colonel Colby evidently appreciated the extraordinary beauty and grandeur of Oak Run and refused to let his soldiers put it to the torch."

"I don't believe that was his reason."

The voice came from the back of the room. Everyone, including Amanda, turned toward the speaker. Her composure was shaken as she saw Jarod Colby make his way slowly through the small group. His bland gaze was focused on her, causing her breath to come in uneven spurts.

"Ladies and gentlemen," she said, turning her attention from his with difficulty and forcing a bright smile to appear on her face, "this is a rare treat. I'd like you to meet Jarod Colby, a direct descendant of Colonel Colby and the present owner of Oak Run.''

There was a gracious nod of his black head at the scattering of applause and the buzz of whispered conversations. ''I do hope you're enjoying your tour,'' he said, turning to stand beside Amanda.

A man's voice raised itself above the various assertions that they were all enjoying the tour. ''You were about to tell us why the colonel didn't allow his men to burn the plantation.''

''I have no doubt that the colonel found this home very beautiful, as Miss Bennett pointed out,'' Jarod replied. ''But the true reason he left it standing was the same one that led him to purchase it after the war was over. He was infatuated with Mrs. Reagan.'' His dark gaze slid down to Amanda, dwelling briefly on the startled roundness of her eyes. ''You might call it the family secret. At the time that the Union troops occupied the house, Mrs. Reagan had been told that her husband was missing and presumed dead. As far as my ancestor was concerned, she was a widow. When the war ended and the prisoners were released, Mrs. Reagan and Colonel Colby discovered that her husband was very much alive, but an invalid. To persuade Sean Reagan to divorce his wife, the colonel paid him twice what the plantation was worth in its day. But Mrs. Reagan had a last-minute attack of conscience and refused to leave her husband, and there was no divorce. The colonel was left with the plantation and his lady fair left with the money and her husband.''

An uncomfortable hush settled over the small group. They followed Amanda a little slowly as she led them into the main hall where Pamela would take them through the second floor. Jarod was standing in the doorway of the study, obviously waiting for her when she had seen the last of the group follow Pam up the Y-shaped staircase.

"May I have a few minutes of your time, Miss Bennett?" Jarod asked mockingly. When Amanda looked hesitantly toward the front where a new group of tourists was gathering, he reached in his pocket and took out a stub. "The young lady wouldn't allow me in without purchasing a ticket, so I believe that allows me a few minutes to speak to you."

"You've never been here before, Mr. Colby, and the girl is new. It's understandable that she didn't know who you were, especially if you didn't identify yourself," Amanda replied with cool dignity.

"I'm sorry I'm late, Amanda." A girl came rushing up behind her. "The darned car wouldn't start." She glanced curiously at Jarod, and Amanda wondered how much Susan had heard before she joined them. "Do you want me to take the next tour on the first floor?"

"Yes," she nodded. "There's a group at the front ready to leave now."

"Okay," Susan agreed smiling. "It won't happen again—my being late, I mean."

"Now may I see you?" Jarod repeated as the other girl walked hurriedly to the front of the hall.

"I really don't know what we have to discuss," Amanda murmured.

"My aunt uses the old cloakroom as an office, I believe." Before she could protest, he was taking her by the arm and leading her there.

Once inside, Jarod closed the door behind them and leaned against it as if he expected Amanda to try to leave. He folded his arms in front of him and stared at her, and she shifted uncomfortably. The room seemed much smaller somehow.

"What did you want to talk to me about?" Amanda swallowed nervously and attempted to appear indifferent when she looked at him. He was wearing a summer suit of light gray that made him look taller and much more formidable with his jet dark looks.

"I want you to have dinner with me." The expression on his face was completely unreadable.

"When?" she queried, trying not to let him guess that his question had taken her by surprise.

"Tonight."

"That's very short notice." Her stomach was doing somersaults. Last night she had told herself that if Jarod was truly interested in her he would have asked her out. Now he was doing that very thing.

"Do you have other plans?" Jarod demanded, straightening away from the door.

"If I did, I imagine you would ask me to break them," Amanda retorted, more sharply than she intended.

"Then you are free tonight." He seized on her implication.

"Which doesn't necessarily mean I accept," she

retorted, tilting her chin at a defiant angle as she met his complacent gaze.

"What's bothering you?" Amusement lurked in his eyes. "Are you offended that the notice is so short?"

"Should I be grateful that you can fit me into your schedule?" she demanded. The muscles in her throat constricted painfully.

He chuckled softly and moved across the small room to take her by the shoulders. There was a fiery warmth in his eyes as they swept over her face. His expression became serious and compelling.

"The truth is I have to fly to Pennsylvania tomorrow morning. I won't be back until the end of the week," Jarod murmured, his husky voice caressing her with its velvet softness. "If it will soothe your injured pride, I'll ask you to keep next Saturday open, too." His thumbs were sensually rubbing her shoulders in a circular motion. "But come with me tonight. I don't want to wait an entire week before I see you."

The declaration took her breath away. She could only gaze at him in disbelief, her heart hammering against her ribs while a shimmery film of happiness sparkled in her brown eyes.

"Really?" It was a barely audible whisper that begged for his confirmation.

Jarod stood motionless, his hands stopping their caressive movement as he stared into her eyes. His own perceptibility darkened when his gaze moved to her trembling lips.

"I want to see you tonight." The urgency that vibrated in his voice transmitted itself to her.

"I'll be through here at six," Amanda said breathlessly. "I can be ready by seven—seven-thirty at the latest."

"I'll send a car for you."

"A car?" There was confusion in the look she gave him. "Aren't you coming to pick me up?"

Jarod smiled, and it was the first time she had noticed a smile reaching his eyes. Usually it was an impersonal movement of his mouth.

"Doesn't that meet with your approval, either?" he asked.

"It's all right," Amanda assured him quickly. "It's just that my parents. . .well, they're used to meeting my dates. Not that they would object if they didn't. It's simply something that I've always done."

"I'll be there at quarter-past seven. How's that?"

Her red gold hair was loose, lying in soft curls around her shoulders. Jarod twined a lock around his fingers, studied it for a moment, then brought his gaze to her face for an answer.

"Fine." Amanda gulped silently, wondering where the adult in her had fled.

"Seven-fifteen, you'll be ready?" He seemed to breathe in deeply as the words hovered in the air, half command and half question.

"Yes."

His gaze raked her face and shoulders one last time, then Jarod turned and left the room while Amanda remained where she stood. She resisted the impulse to pinch herself to make certain she wasn't dreaming and gave herself a mental shake.

She had to stop reacting to him with that childish infatuation she had once possessed. At the moment she was so confused that she didn't know if it was his potent attraction that was drawing her, or an image of the past. She had to stop confusing the two.

CHAPTER FOUR

THE REST OF THE DAY continued at the same frantic pace of the morning. The sunny June day had brought scores of people parading through Oak Run. It was half-past six before the last visitors left the grounds and Amanda could go home.

"You're late, dear," her mother commented as Amanda walked in the door.

"You wouldn't believe the chaos today," Amanda declared, turning her back to her mother so she could begin unhooking her dress. "Where is everybody?"

"Your father and brothers went fishing. There's cold chicken and potato salad in the refrigerator. You can help yourself."

"I'm going out to dinner and I only have about a half an hour to get ready," Amanda replied, holding the gown up with one hand as she started to hurry down the hallway to the stairs.

"You didn't mention that this morning." Her mother followed more sedately.

"I didn't know this morning," Amanda tossed over her shoulder. "Be a dear, mom, and draw me some bathwater while I lay out my clothes."

"Who is it that has you in such a dither?"

"I'm not in a dither. I'm just late," she protested. She held the long folds of her gown in her hand as she mounted the stairs. Self-consciously Amanda added, "Jarod Colby asked me out."

"Jarod Colby? *The* Jarod Colby?" Amanda's reply had stopped Mrs. Bennett halfway up the steps.

"What about Jarod Colby?" Her younger sister, Bonnie, appeared in the doorway of her bedroom.

"I'm going out with him tonight," Amanda answered, trying to make it sound like the most natural thing in the world while her heart beat a steady tattoo against her rib cage.

"You're kidding!" Bonnie squealed.

"I didn't know you even knew him." Her mother had regained control after her initial start of surprise.

"I met him at the cotillion last night and he stopped at Oak Run this morning to ask me out." Inside her room, Amanda stepped quickly out of her gown and began rummaging through her closet.

"Tonight? Isn't that rather short notice?" her mother murmured, a frown drawing her eyebrows together.

"I think it's terrific!" Bonnie sighed as she sunk onto the blue gingham spread covering Amanda's bed. "He meets you one night and the next day he comes looking for you because he can't get you out of his mind." Bonnie turned excitedly to her sister, her short auburn hair bouncing around her face. "What are you going to wear?"

"This black dress, I think," Amanda answered.

It was cut on classically simple lines with a snug-fitting bodice flaring out to an A-line skirt. Only narrow strips of material crossed her shoulders.

"You look so sophisticated in that!" Bonnie agreed enthusiastically.

"It is summer, though. . . ." Amanda hesitated, looking back into her closet. "What do you think, mom?"

"Black is never wrong," was her mother's answer. "What time will he be here?"

"Seven-fifteen."

"I'd better get that bathwater started," Mrs. Bennett declared.

By some miracle Amanda was walking down the stairs when she heard the car pulling up out front. Bonnie had been keeping a vigil at the kitchen window and she came racing into the hallway.

"He's here, Mandy!" She tried to suppress the excitement in her voice and her words came out in a stifled shriek. "He's simply gorgeous!"

"Who's here? Who's gorgeous?" Her grandfather came shuffling from the living room. "Where are you going?"

"I have a date tonight," Amanda answered, deliberately ignoring his first questions. She brushed a kiss across the old man's face as the doorbell sounded. "I'll get it, mom," she called.

"So she has a date. What's all the fuss about?" her grandfather demanded as his daughter-in-law walked into the hall.

Their voices followed Amanda as she hurried toward the front door. Her heart seemed to be in her throat at the knowledge that Jarod Colby was standing on the other side.

"Her date is Jarod Colby," Bonnie informed her grandfather. "My sister is going out with Jarod Colby."

"Jarod Colby," he repeated. "And you are allowing her to go, Bernice!"

Amanda heard her mother's attempt to shush her grandfather as she opened the door. She stared into the strikingly masculine face with its chiseled features while his gaze moved over her.

"Hello," Jarod said quietly.

"Come in." Amanda moved back, suddenly overcome by a shyness that was completely unnatural to her.

With embarrassing clarity, her grandfather's gruff voice pierced the air. "Do you mean to tell me that you're allowing Mandy to go out with that carpetbagging northern Yankee?"

"Keep your voice down!" her mother admonished.

Amanda glanced apologetically at Jarod, but he only appeared amused by the outburst. "My grandfather," she explained quietly. "The Civil War ended only a few years ago as far as he's concerned."

"That's all right, I understand," Jarod replied.

Her mother moved swiftly towards them, her cheeks tinged with scarlet color. Her hand was extended in greeting to Jarod, which he accepted.

"I must apologize for my father-in-law's rudeness, Mr. Colby," her mother said quietly. "Discretion has never been one of his virtues."

"An apology isn't necessary," said Jarod, bestowing a rare smile on her mother. "I've been called worse things than a Yankee carpetbagger."

Her grandfather was still mumbling in the distance and Amanda turned to her mother. "We'll leave now," she said. "Don't wait up for me."

"Have a good time," Mrs. Bennett called after them as Amanda and Jarod walked through the door onto the porch.

"Is your father averse to Yankees, too?" Jarod asked, his dark eyes twinkling with laughter as he helped her into the car.

"No, thank heaven," Amanda smiled. "He's off fishing with my brothers."

"You have more than one brother?" The politeness of the question was overridden by the dark look he flashed at her, which seemed to say he was interested in anything that had to do with her.

"Actually there are six of us Bennett children. My oldest sister, Marybeth, is married with two lovely daughters. She and her husband live in Athens—Athens, Georgia, that is. Brian is a medical student, so he isn't home now. Teddy is studying law and Brad, the one you met last night, is going to be an architect. The baby of the family is my sister Bonnie. Thank goodness she's still in high school."

"Why do you say 'thank goodness'?"

"It's a strain on my parents' budget to have four of their children in college. Strain is probably an understatement," Amanda smiled. "We all work to help the kitty, but the brunt of the tuition costs are met by mom and dad.''

"What are you going to do when you graduate?'' A brow arched satirically. "Get married?''

"Not right away. I suppose I'll teach for a few years to pay back my parents' investment in me.'' The subject of marriage was not something she wanted to discuss, not when he gave the impression that he was listening to every nuance in her voice.

"You could marry a wealthy man and not have to worry about it,'' Jarod suggested dryly. His leg brushed her thigh as he slowed the car down to make a turn.

Her pulse pitter-pattered along her neck as she let her gaze sweep out the window. "I suppose I could,'' she murmured noncommittally. She didn't want him to think she was after him, although the prospect of having his arm around her was an increasingly irresistible thought. "But I'm not a mercenary person. Having money isn't among my list of priorities in life.''

He glanced at her thoughtfully and with a look of skepticism in the dark eyes. Amanda could understand why. He had probably met many people whose only interest in him was his money.

"It's a lovely evening,'' she sighed, glancing back to the view beyond the windshield.

"Yes, I thought we'd have dinner on the veranda.''

"The Veranda?'' she repeated. "Is that a new restaurant? Being away at the college most of the year, I'm not too familiar with all the new places.''

A soft chuckle rolled from his parted lips. "I told you last night that I would take you somewhere where we could be alone." His gaze physically caressed her before it turned back to the road. "I was speaking about the veranda at my house, not a restaurant."

"Oh," in a very small voice.

"Do you still want to have dinner with me?" Jarod challenged mockingly.

Her hands were folded in her lap, feeling suddenly clammy and cold. At the same time, she felt hot and light-headed. It had never occurred to her that he would be taking her to the Winter House. If she refused to go, she would seem very juvenile and prim. But the idea of sharing an intimate dinner with him, alone in his house, was a bit frightening. Then she chided herself for being so foolish. He wasn't the type to force himself on a woman.

The smile she gave him was bright and confident, not exactly a true reflection of the way she was feeling inside. "I do hope you have a good cook. I'm ravenous!"

His gaze slid over her, lingering for brief seconds on her mouth. "So am I," Jarod agreed. The wry note in his voice made Amanda believe that he wasn't talking about food, and the air in the car became very stifling.

"THAT WAS DELICIOUS," Amanda sighed, leaning determinedly back in her chair. "I do love strawberries."

"And whipped cream," Jarod added as he exhaled a puff of smoke from his cigarette and watched it swirl in front of him. "I always thought Southern girls ate before going out so their dates would think they had very small appetites."

"That was true in the olden days, but not anymore," she said with a smile.

"You can clear everything away, Hannah," he told the older woman as she walked through the open door into the screened extension of the house. "I won't need anything else tonight."

Not wanting to interfere with the housekeeper's work, Amanda rose from the table and wandered idly to the mesh wall, aware that Jarod was following her. The sun had dipped below the horizon, leaving a residue of shimmering golds and pinks behind.

A billow of smoke blew over her shoulder through the mesh screen into the coming night and she knew Jarod was standing behind her. The scent of tobacco and intoxicating masculine cologne seemed to wrap around her as she heard the housekeeper wheeling the serving trolley with the remains of their dishes out of the veranda.

She was suddenly very conscious of the fact that they were alone. He had dismissed the housekeeper for the evening and already explained that his aunt now lived in a small house in Oak Springs. With the sun down, it seemed to grow darker with each passing second. There was a need for movement, so Amanda turned and found herself staring into his face, dark and unfathomable. The corners of her mouth turned into a faint smile as she found she couldn't think of anything to say.

"It's growing dark. Would you like to go in-side?" he asked, a hint of mockery vibrating in his voice.

"Yes," Amanda agreed hesitantly as he stepped to one side.

The screened patio led into the living room. A single light was on, sending a streamer of white across the floor. It was a large, masculine room, done in warm oranges and browns with a splatter-ing of yellow gold for color.

"Would you like some music?" Jarod had walked over to an expensive stereo set before glanc-ing over his shoulder to ask.

"Yes."

Immediately a soft, languid melody permeated the room through concealed speakers. Unsure of where she should sit, Amanda tried to appear in-terested in a large painting hanging on an interior wall. It was of an old clipper ship buffeted in storm-tossed seas, a collection of opaque grays, greens, ivory and brown.

"Does the painting interest you that much?"

The voice that came from directly behind her was husky and cynically amused. Amanda turned, un-conscious of the hands clenched tightly in front of her. His gaze was dark and brooding as it traveled the length of her body and stopped at her face.

"Are you nervous?" The harsh planes of his face, browned by the sun and made darker by the coal black of his hair and eyes, increased the primitive attraction that drew her to him.

"A little," she admitted, spreading her fingers and rubbing them together in an effort to relax.

Jarod Colby watched the movement with indifference, subtly making her aware of the breadth of his shoulders and his intimidating height. The throbbing of her pulse echoed loudly in her ears as coursing heat spread through her body. The soft music in the background added to the disturbing air of intimacy. The silence between them was threatening to suffocate her.

"Will you be leaving very early in the morning?" Amanda asked, trying to make her voice sound natural and not betray the tension that held her by the throat.

His eyes flicked back to her face. "Early enough."

"It must be hectic to commute back and forth."

"Yes."

His clipped reply sent her wildly searching for something else to say. How could she pursue a conversation that he wasn't willing to take part in? She broke away from his compelling gaze. Perhaps he didn't wish to discuss business.

"You have a beautiful home," Amanda murmured.

The comment passed unnoticed by him as he held out his hand to her. For a minute she blinked at it uncertainly, then hesitantly placed her own hand in it. The large hand closed warmly around her fingers, pulling her to him as an arm moved around her waist. He carried her fingers to his lips while he guided her to the slow tempo of the music. The brooding expression in his eyes didn't change as it moved possessively over her face.

Last night when they had danced, her hooped

skirt had kept considerable distance between them. Now Amanda was held tightly against him, her legs burning with the brush of his thighs while the softness of her breasts felt the imprint of the buttons of his shirt. She hadn't been prepared for the contact of his body, hard and muscular and very male. Her head was tilted back, exposing the bareness of her throat as she watched his lips move over her hand in a caress that had her whole arm tingling.

There was an unreal quality about the moment, a dreamlike magic that sent her senses spinning. The hand resting near his shoulders could feel the taut muscles in the arm that circled her waist. The nibbling of her fingers ceased as he turned her hand to expose her sensitive palm and pressed a warm kiss in its hollow. The sensual touch of his tongue against her skin released an avalanche of churning emotions inside her. Exhaling slowly in surrender, Amanda dipped her head against his chest, all resistance flowing out of her weakened limbs.

Leaving her hand against the shaven smoothness of his face, Jarod trailed his fingers firmly down her arm and up to her shoulder, caressing her flesh with controlled firmness. Of its own volition, her hand remained on his face, her fingertips exploring the jutting line of his jaw and the sharp cheekbones. There was no urgency in the languid passion between them, even though the slow-burning flame kept growing hotter as his mouth trailed down her face to the lobe of her ear.

After interminable minutes his mouth sought

hers, not in a gentle probing caress but in a demanding, hungry kiss. Her hands were locked around his neck as she stood on tiptoe, instinctively arching her back to be closer to the lean hardness of his body. In sweet ecstasy, Amanda knew she had been kissed with passion before, but she couldn't recall returning more than a small part of it until now. A warning bell rang in her head, pulling her out of the whirling ache of desire.

"Jarod, please!" Her lips moved in protest against his mouth. Her senses felt drugged by his kiss, unable to function without the union of their lips.

He let her move partially out of his arms, the smoldering fire in his eyes nearly sending her back into them. "What is it?" he demanded.

His voice was hoarse and his breathing was uneven, and Amanda could feel the iron control he had over his emotions. Oddly that hurt. She wanted him to be as destroyed by her touch as she was by his.

"The music's stopped," she murmured, suddenly at a loss to admit how deeply she had been affected by his embrace.

A scowl of annoyance flashed across his face, quickly replaced by an enigmatic look that Amanda couldn't fathom. His hands dropped to his side and he turned away, leaving her standing on wobbly legs that hadn't recovered completely from the devastating weakness of the previous moments.

"Go and change it, then." Jarod ordered smoothly.

She heard the snap of his lighter and saw the

smoke rise above his head. Forcing her trembling legs to support her, she walked to the stereo and flipped the record to the other side. When she turned around, she saw Jarod pouring liquid from a crystal decanter that had been sitting on one of the tables. His eyes met hers across the room.

"Would you like a drink?" he asked.

Amanda shook her head. "No thank you."

There was a brief arching of a dark brow as he took a hefty swallow of liquor, then refilled the partially empty glass and walked to a large chair, where he sat down. Amanda remained beside the stereo, unable to feel the nonchalance he was exhibiting. His eyes studied her with a penetrating thoroughness that sent a tidal wave of heat flooding over her.

"Come here," he ordered crisply.

Swallowing jerkily, she walked toward him, stopping beside his chair and gazing down at him. Her long hair fell forward across her face and she nervously tucked the red gold locks behind her ears. Jarod had evidently discarded his jacket while she had been changing the record because she was suddenly aware that only a white silk shirt covered his chest. Amanda watched as he impatiently removed his tie, tossing it on the table on the other side of him, and unbuttoned the top buttons of his shirt. The sight of the dark hairs curling on his chest sent her heart catapulting into her throat. She started to turn away, but his hand caught at her wrist.

"Your pulse is racing," he said.

"I know," Amanda murmured.

"Do I disturb you?"

With his eyes watching her so closely, she couldn't answer that question. To admit that he did would make her too vulnerable; to lie that he didn't was impossible.

His hand slid across the lower part of her stomach to rest on her hipbone. "You don't need to answer that question," Jarod said in a complacent voice. "I can feel the way your bones almost melt when I touch you."

Her startled eyes swept his face, but he was looking at the agitated movement of her breasts and the way the material covering them strained at the narrow straps supporting her dress.

"Jarod, please—" she began.

"Please what?" he growled. His eyes blazed upward to her face. "For twenty-four damn hours, I've been remembering the way those proper lips taunted me."

"Don't say that," she protested.

"Why not?" he snapped savagely, brutally yanking her off balance and pulling her across his lap. "Right now you feel as improper as I do. Why shouldn't we admit it?" A hand moved roughly over her hip to her back while she felt the thudding of his heart beneath her own hands. "I wanted to hold you like this last night. Do you deny that you didn't want it, too?"

"No," Amanda whispered.

"I couldn't forget the scent of your perfume or how soft your skin was when I touched it," he murmured, threading the fingers of one hand through her hair. "This morning it was even worse, being in a room with you, alone, and not taking you in my arms. Then earlier we had to waste so much time over that stupid meal. All the while I'm aching with the need to see and touch every inch of you.''

A whimpering moan slipped out of Amanda's lips at the blatant passion in his voice. His fingers automatically moved to the corner of her mouth and parted her lips while searing desire scorched her with the hottest blue flames.

His arms crushed her against him as he possessively demanded her complete response. The masterful caress of his hands over her thighs and hips, across her back and shoulders, aroused her to a fever pitch of longing. She felt like an addict who couldn't get enough of his kisses even as he ravaged and explored her mouth and neck, sending torrents of liquid fire through her veins.

A sudden release of all inhibitions seemed to enclose her in a velvet mist. Her head was tilted back over his arm while Jarod ran his mouth over her collarbone, pushing aside the offending strap and sliding it down her arm until it was permanently out of the way. Through the reeling of her mind, Amanda felt the brush of his fingertips in the hollow between her breasts. Instinctively she stiffened when the material of her dress slipped unresistingly down.

Instantly alert, no longer possessed by her drowning senses, she felt his hand sliding along her back, down the nakedness of her spine. With sickening swiftness she realized that the sensation of release she had experienced moments before had been the expert movements of Jarod's hand when he had unzipped her dress.

The suddenness of her lunge away from him was unexpected. She stumbled shakily to her feet, clutching the bodice tightly to her, her eyes shimmering with unshed tears of shame and uncertainty. Desire still blazed in the eyes he turned toward her, but it was quickly replaced by a confused anger as she backed away from him. She trembled with self-contempt over how close she had come to allowing him to seduce her. He must think she was some local tramp! She had behaved like one, responding wantonly to his advances.

CHAPTER FIVE

"I WANT TO GO HOME." Her voice was jerky with barely controlled sobs of humiliation.

Jarod rose to his feet, a black scowl clouding his face while he towered threateningly in front of her. Amanda would have fled then if she had believed her legs would support her.

"Why the display of outrage?" he demanded savagely, his lip curling at the tears that hovered on the edge of her lashes. "I made it clear I wanted you."

Had he? Yes, she supposed, he had, only she had been too inexperienced and blinded by the overwhelming attraction he held for her to understand the completeness of his statement. His anger was justified to that extent and she found she couldn't meet his eyes.

"I'm sorry," she murmured, looking anywhere in the room except at him. "I'm just not that kind of girl."

Contemptuous laughter rang harshly through the room. "Are you going to tell me you're a virgin?" he jeered sarcastically. "I don't believe that I'm the first man to touch you that way."

"It doesn't matter whether you believe me or not." Her throat was working convulsively.

Jarod moved with such striking swiftness that she wasn't able to avoid him as his hands reached out to dig into her shoulders and pull her viciously against him.

"You're lying!" his husky voice growled. "I don't give a damn! I don't have to be the first man. There's no need to play the innocent."

"I am not playing!" Amanda cried out bitterly. The painful sobs now came freely from her throat. "It's the truth! Now let me go!"

He shook her until her head was bobbing from side to side uncontrollably. "Is it money you want? Are you afraid I won't pay you?"

The violent shaking stopped and Amanda sagged limply in his hands. "What do you want for proof?" she sobbed weakly. "Shall I let you rape me?"

He grabbed a handful of her hair and pulled her head back to stare into her face. A muscle twitched near the corner of his eye where a glimmer of doubt lurked.

"Are you telling me the truth?" His voice was ominously quiet.

"Yes," she whispered.

There was a string of angry expletives as he abruptly released her and turned away. A hand savagely raked his hair. "From now on," Jarod muttered beneath his breath, his back still turned to her, "you'd better stick to the shallow water until you learn to swim."

Amanda was too embarrassed to reply as she struggled to slip the strap over her shoulder and make her shaking fingers rezip her dress. But her movements were awkward and uncoordinated, achieving little success. In the next minute, Jarod was turning her around and pushing her hands away.

"I've had more practice at this than you have," he jeered, closing the zipper with one fluid movement.

His fingers closed over her waist, firmly pivoting her around to face him. For one crazy moment she thought he was going to take her in his arms. As she brushed the tears from her cheeks, she realized that she wanted him to hold her and ease the ache in her heart.

"We'll forget about next Saturday night," he said tautly. "The less I see of you, the better."

"Of course," Amanda murmured as someone twisted the knife in her stomach.

"Come on, I'll take you home." Jarod was striding away from her toward the door and she followed meekly, scraping together what little dignity and self-respect that remained.

Jarod said not a word as he held the car door open for her, nor even when he slid behind the wheel a few minutes later. The sky was black with lingering clouds blocking out most of the stars and allowing the moon to peep out occasionally. As soon as Jarod reached the main road, he accelerated the car until the telephone poles were only a blur. Amanda knew he could hardly wait to get her home. When he finally pulled up at her home, the house was ablaze with lights.

"What time is it?" she asked nervously.

"Nearly ten." He hadn't switched the engine off.

Her family would be up, no doubt waiting to hear about her evening. Amanda began patting and smoothing her rumpled hair and trying to wipe away all traces of tears from her face. With an angry ejaculation, Jarod turned the ignition switch, shutting off the engine, and flipped down the visor in front of her, revealing a mirror on the other side.

"You're a mess," he muttered grimly. Rummaging through the glove compartment, he paused to hand her a comb.

The reflection in the mirror confirmed his statement. Even in the dim nightglow, Amanda could see the smudged streaks on her face where the mascara had run. Her hair was so rumpled and tousled it looked as if she had just climbed out of bed. As she remedied that with the comb, she saw Jarod tearing open a tiny packet that contained one of those commercially packaged wet towels.

"Turn around." His fingers gripped her chin to ensure that she did as he commanded.

"Why are you doing this?" Amanda whispered. The stringent scent of soap-filled wetness acted as reviving smelling salts as he roughly wiped the traces of mascara from her cheeks. "Why do you care what my family will think?"

His eyes gleamed cynically at her through the darkness. "Because I don't want to be forced to find a new manager at the mill."

"You know who my father is?" she breathed.

"There are several families named Bennett in Oak Springs."

"But only one with a red-haired daughter." Jarod looked at her derisively. "Did you think I hadn't checked on you? The names of your two nieces are Teresa and Jennifer. Would you like their birth dates, or your grade point average in college?"

Hysterical laughter bubbled inside her. "I should be honored that you found me fit company. What a pity you picked me for your night's entertainment!"

"Who would guess that a woman could reach the age of twenty-one in these liberated times and remain innocent? You should enter a convent," he sneered.

His taunt demanded retaliation, and Amanda struck out with her hand at the features of chiseled bronze. Needle-sharp barbs stung her palm as it made contact with his cheek. Her heart leaped in fear at the gathering mask of black fury. She pushed open the door and scrambled out of the car, but Jarod was sliding out her side and caught her before she was a step away. He pulled her against the tapering length of his body. Wild tremors shivered through her as she struggled to elude the mouth descending toward hers, but it closed over her lips and punishingly devoured them.

There was a sudden blaze of light from the porch followed by the laughing voices of her parents, then shocked silence. At the first sound, Jarod had thrust her away from him, but not before her parents, sister, and grandfather had seen the way they had been molded together. Pain from the cruel grip of Jarod's fingers digging into her waist kept Amanda from dashing into the house.

"Good evening, Mr. Bennett," Jarod greeted him calmly.

"Mr. Colby," her father returned with a nod, recovering as quickly as Jarod had. "I must apologize for our intrusion. None of us heard your car drive up, and Amanda hasn't been home from a date at this hour since she was sixteen."

"I have an early flight in the morning," Jarod replied, as if that was the explanation. "It was nice meeting you, Mrs. Bennett." His head moved briefly in the direction of her mother before he turned it to Amanda. Only she was close enough to see the freezing coldness in his eyes. "Amanda," he murmured with patronizing politeness.

"Good night." She forced the words from her throat.

She used the precious moments that it took for him to get in his car and drive away to gather her wits before walking to the porch where her family waited. Her grandfather was grumbling about Yankees under his breath while shuffling toward a rocking chair as Amanda slowly climbed the porch steps. No one spoke.

"I've had a hectic day. I . . . I think I'll go ahead and turn in," she murmured, knowing she was fooling none of them, but her parents let her go with curious looks and nods of good night.

All except her younger sister Bonnie, who trailed

after her as Amanda walked into the house. "Where did you go? What did you do?" Bonnie whispered excitedly. "If he'd held me like that, I'd be absolutely devastated! When will he be back? Do you suppose he'll call you while he's gone?"

Amanda pressed her fingers against her forehead, feeling that any moment she would snap in two. "Bonnie, please," she protested with a tortured cry, "I have an awful headache. I don't feel like talking tonight."

A look of stunned pain crossed her sister's face. After either one of them had come home from a date, they had always got together for an hour of girl talk. Now Amanda was shutting her out.

"I'm sorry," Amanda murmured, and raced up the stairs to her room.

With the door securely closed behind her, she wished her memory had a self-destructive button so she could wipe away the events of the evening and forget what a complete fool she had made of herself. Her arms wound themselves tightly around her as she tried to forget the thrill she had experienced under Jarod's expert caress. But she had only to close her eyes to feel the sensual pressure of his lips on her and the answering surge of warmth from her middle.

There was a light rap on her door in warning before her mother walked into the room, enabling Amanda to start unzipping her dress as though she had been in the act of changing her clothes.

"Hello, mom," she said, striving for indifference.

"Bonnie said you had a headache. Is there anything wrong?"

"It's only tension," Amanda answered with a shrug, reaching into the closet for a hanger to put her dress on.

"I hope we didn't embarrass you tonight. We honestly didn't know you were out there."

"I know."

"Your Mr. Colby seems like a very nice man."

"He's not my Mr. Colby!" Amanda snapped, and immediately covered her mouth as she turned her rounded brown eyes on her mother. "Sorry—I didn't mean to shout at you."

A tiny frown made worried lines on her mother's face. "Will you be seeing him again, Mandy?"

It all became too much for her. Amanda couldn't keep up the pretense that nothing was wrong. Her shoulders hunched forward as she cradled her churning stomach in her arms.

"No, mother." Her head moved painfully from side to side. "I won't be seeing him again."

She felt the touch of her mother's hands on her shoulders and turned instinctively for the comfort they promised. She suddenly didn't feel like an adult.

"Do you want to, Mandy?" her mother asked softly, cradling the silent girl against her breast, feeling the pain that was transmitted.

"Yes." Then, "No, I don't." Amanda straightened and breathed in deeply. She wasn't going to let herself cry. Not again.

"Tonight—" Mrs. Bennett began hesitantly,

picking up the vibrations of conflicting emotions warring inside her daughter.

"Tonight was a mistake that neither Jarod nor I want to repeat," Amanda sighed. "I really am tired, mom."

"All right, dear. No more questions." The older woman smiled and brushed her cheek with a fleeting kiss before leaving the room.

"WHICH ONE OF YOU GIRLS is going to pick up your father?" Mrs. Bennett called from the back door of the house.

Amanda glanced at Bonnie. "Don't look at me," her sister said. "As soon as I finish watering the garden, I'm going in the house to water myself. You go and get dad."

"Okay," Amanda agreed, rubbing the sore muscles of her lower back. "Hose my legs off, but for heaven's sake don't get my shorts wet because I don't want to change my clothes."

Bonnie obligingly turned the nozzle toward her sister, letting the water spray over the lower part of Amanda's legs while avoiding the red material of her shorts. Water squished in Amanda's canvas shoes, but it felt refreshingly cool after two hours in the hot afternoon sun.

"The last of the beans are inside the back door, mom," Amanda called. "Where are the car keys?"

"They're still in the car," her mother answered.

"Be back soon!"

Waving to Bonnie, Amanda backed the car out of the driveway and headed it for the mill. The man her father usually rode back and forth to work with was home with the flu. Rather than leave the rest of his family without transportation, her father decided to have one of them drive him to work in the morning and pick him up at night.

After Amanda had parked the car in front of the cotton mill, she glanced in the rearview mirror to be sure there weren't any smudges of dirt on her face from working in the garden. Spending five days a week in long dress, it was nice on Monday and Tuesday, the days Oak Run was closed to tourists, to run around in shorts and knit tops, especially in this hot June weather. She slipped the car keys into the small pocket of her shorts and walked gaily to the door marked Private. One hand rapped lightly while the other turned the knob and opened the door.

"Hi, dad. Are you ready to go?"

Three steps inside the office, Amanda came to an abrupt halt as she stared at Jarod Colby standing beside her father's desk. She knew her face had grown pale, although there was practically no reaction on his. Her father was sitting in his chair, his gaze taking in the stunned look of surprise on her face.

"Have a chair. I'll only be a couple of minutes," he told her.

After one brief glance at her when she had walked in the door, Jarod had turned his attention to the paper spread in front of him on the desk. Since he had chosen not to greet her, Amanda ignored him, as well. Her legs numbly welcomed the support of the chair behind her.

For three weeks she had attempted to block out every humiliating memory of what had happened. It had just begun to take on the vague horror of a bad dream, and here she was in the same room with him, feeling her bones turning to water at the sight of his raven dark hair and eyes and the virile, masculine face. The cream tan suit he was wearing accentuated the leanness of his physique and she knew she would never be able to forget what that muscular hardness had felt like pressed against her own body.

The two men were discussing the contents of the papers Jarod was studying, but Amanda was in too much of a daze to hear what they were saying. Someone knocked at the office door and she nearly jumped out of her chair.

"Can I see you a minute, Mr. Bennett?" a man requested, opening the door but not entering the room.

"Is it important, Joe?" her father asked.

"Yes, sir."

Her father darted a look to Amanda, then brought his gaze back to Jarod, who was concentrating on one of the papers. "Excuse me a minute, Mr. Colby."

"I'm in no hurry, Sam," Jarod replied, glancing briefly from the papers on the desk.

When the door closed behind her father, the room became uncomfortably still. Amanda sat hesitantly on the edge of her chair, afraid to breathe and draw those dark eyes her way. Then Jarod thrust his hands in his pockets and walked around to the front of the desk, where he leaned against it and let his eyes wander calmly over her bare legs to her face.

"Hello, Amanda," he said.

"Mr. Colby," she murmured, dipping her head self-consciously in greeting.

"The last time we met, I think we went beyond the point of 'Mister.'" One side of his mouth lifted in a mirthless, almost derisive smile.

"Please, I'm...I'm not proud of the way I acted that night," Amanda protested. Her cheeks felt hot and flushed and she bent her head to conceal them from his penetrating gaze. "After the way I behaved, it was natural for you to get the wrong impression. If you'll excuse me," she said, rising agitatedly to her feet, "I'll wait for my father in the car."

"No, wait," he commanded.

"Look," she began nervously, "I didn't know you were going to be here. If I had, I wouldn't have come in."

"I know," Jarod replied with the same blandness as before. "I came in as your father was phoning home to have someone come to get him. I had a feeling it would be you, so I waited."

Her brown eyes rounded with surprise. "You waited? Why?"

"I discovered that I wanted to see you again." His gaze was making another cool appraisal of her.

For a moment Amanda couldn't breathe. The blood raced in her temples, sounding like a thousand snare drums in her ears. She could sense he was gauging her reaction to his statement. She had humiliated herself once and she wasn't going to do it again.

Drawing herself up to her full height, which still left her several inches shorter than him, she replied, "You were correct the last time when you said the less we saw of each other, the better."

He leisurely crossed the small space between them. "When you deprive yourself of chocolate, you always remember the sweet taste. But if you stuff yourself with it until it makes you sick—" there was a hard, mocking glint in his eyes "—then you lose your craving."

"I'm not a piece of chocolate!" she declared, taking a step backward as he took another forward.

Jarod kept advancing and Amanda kept retreating until she felt the metal of a filing cabinet behind her.

"The principle is the same. I want to see you again."

When she started to move sideways, he placed an arm on each side of her, blocking the path of escape.

"I don't want to see you," she stated firmly, pressing herself against the metal cabinet, her fingers clutching the smooth sides in desperation.

"You've felt the force of the attraction we hold for each other," Jarod murmured. "You can't bury your head in the sand and pretend it doesn't exist."

That languorous weakness was flowing through her again, but she grimly clung to her self-respect, fighting off the rush of desire his nearness was causing. As if he guessed the power he held over her senses, he moved closer, the pressure of his thighs against her adding fuel to the raging fire in her veins. The male smell of him was an erotic stimulant, arousing her and reminding her that she could never be indifferent. She closed her eyes against the arrogant dark head moving inexorably toward hers.

His mouth traveled lightly down the side of her face to her lips. "Friday night we'll drive to Atlanta, take in a show." The movement of his lips as he spoke sensually teased the sensitive corner of her mouth.

"No," she whispered weakly, twisting her head away, only to have him pursue.

"There's a dance at the club on Saturday," he murmured. The width of an angel's hair was all that separated her from the promising ardor of his kiss. She lacked the strength to turn away again as his mouth continued the tantalizing movement against the trembling weakness of hers. "On Saturday we'll drive to the coast and spend the day."

It was becoming increasingly impossible not to make that one tiny movement that would give him possession of her lips. "I have to work on Sunday," Amanda declared breathlessly, fighting through the blackness swirling around her to cling to her sanity.

Soft laughter fanned her face. "I own Oak Run," Jarod reminded her. "I can close it for the day. We'll swim in the Atlantic and sunbathe on the beach—with clothes, if your modesty demands it."

A sighing moan quaked through her at the same moment that footsteps sounded outside the office door, followed imediately by the rattle of the knob. Prior to the door's opening, Jarod levered himself away, letting one arm fall to his side as he half turned toward her father. The gold tips of her lashes fluttered upward, disturbed brown eyes immediately focusing on the implacable profile of the man leaning beside her. A darting glance at her father caught the quizzical expression in his gaze. Her cheeks colored in a rare blush.

"I'll...I'll wait for you in the car, dad," Amanda stammered, eluding the darkness of Jarod's gaze as she hurried for the door.

When she reached the car, her breath was coming in jerky gulps. Another minute—another second and she would have given in. She bit hard into her trembling lips, still afire from the tantalizing feather caress of his. He was playing at a game of which he was master. It was of little consequence that she affected him physically, too, because she didn't possess the power to annihilate his control, while he completely swamped hers.

Her breathing had regained a degree of normalcy when the two men walked out of the office. Without a glance in her direction, Jarod walked by the car to his own. Involuntarily her eyes watched as he drove away before she became aware of her father sitting behind the wheel of the car, his hand outstretched for the ignition keys.

"You look tired, dad," she murmured with a false smile as she handed him the keys from her pocket. "Did you have a rough day?"

The corners of his mouth lifted in wry amusement. "I didn't think you'd noticed me at all, but yes, it was a long day."

Amanda shifted uncomfortably, her eyes straying toward the dust cloud left by Jarod's car. "That's not true," she protested, but without conviction.

"Isn't it? I had the distinct impression that I was creating an unwanted crowd of three."

"Did Jarod—I mean, Mr. Colby say that?"

"The only comment Mr. Colby made—" his voice gave extra inflection to the "Mister" "—was that I had a strong willed and beautiful daughter."

That statement did nothing to untangle the knots her stomach was in. Her gaze shifted self-consciously to the slowly passing scenery outside the window of the now moving car.

"What do you think of him, daddy?" she asked quietly.

There was a pause before her father answered, then it was with deliberation. "You're an adult, Amanda. What do you think of him?"

"That he's out of my class," she sighed heavily.

"Inverted snobbery?"

He had misinterpreted her reply and she was just as glad. It would be difficult to explain the physical impact Jarod made on her. It was something she wasn't used to herself.

"I suppose you could call it that," she agreed. "You have to admit the world of Colby Enterprises is far removed from ours."

"No so far that we're not a part of it," he

reminded her. "If you want to see the man again, don't let feelings of inadequacy stop you."

That was easily said, she thought. Inadequacy walked hand in hand with inexperience in this case. There was frightened triumph in knowing he wanted to see her again, but Amanda wasn't convinced that she could emerge unscathed from another encounter with Jarod Colby. Rather than be trapped by an emotional upheaval she couldn't control, she decided it was best not to go out with him again, no matter how much she was drawn to him.

CHAPTER SIX

HER DECISION WAS TESTED later that evening when the telephone rang and Bonnie announced that it was for her. Before she reached the receiver, Amanda guessed it would be Jarod.

"Is seven o'clock too early for Friday night?" his voice asked the minute she had identified herself.

"I'm not going with you," she answered in a low voice.

"Saturday?"

"No."

"Don't play hard to get, Amanda." The telephone lines didn't soften the harshness in his tone.

"I'm not." She had to make her replies short and clipped in order to conceal her shaking voice. "The answer is no. Tomorrow. Next week. Next month. No!"

She heard the savage intake of breath. "I don't accept that. And you don't want me to," he snapped. "You proved that today."

There was no answer to that statement. He was too accustomed to overcoming a woman's objection not to know he had been on the brink of succeeding that afternoon. Very slowly Amanda replaced the receiver on the hook, afraid that if she talked to him any longer, he would somehow still succeed.

"That was Jarod Colby, wasn't it?" The sound of her sister's voice brought Amanda round. "And you just turned him down? You're either insane or ingenious!"

Amanda's lips tightened fractionally. "I don't want to get on board a fast train going nowhere, Bonnie," she replied. "If he calls back, tell him I'm not here."

But Jarod didn't call back. With each day that passed, Amanda became more convinced that he had taken her answer as final. Yet her second meeting with him had effectively diminished the humiliating recriminations of the first. By turning him down, she had thought to bolster her pride and her sense of integrity. Instead she found herself wishing she hadn't been so adamant in her refusal. He had wanted to see her again, and if she was honest with herself, she wanted to see him.

It wasn't so important anymore that any relationship with him would be doomed to failure at the start. If marriage figured anywhere in his plans for the future, it wouldn't be to a small-town girl like her. Nor would he be satisfied with an innocent and—compared to the relationships he undoubtedly had with other women—what would amount to a platonic association with her. Amanda had considered herself a liberated woman, intent on a career that she planned to continue after she was married, and open-minded toward her friends' more intimate relationships with their boyfriends. Her own chaste state she had marked off to the fact that she had never met a man she cared for deeply enough, and experimenting for the sake of experience wasn't one of her traits.

Faced with the alternative of having an affair with Jarod Colby should she see him again, which looked unlikely with each passing day, Amanda wondered how deeply she cared for him. Was she still wrapped up in her illusions of the past? Was the attraction purely physical between them? Or was there a chance of deeper emotions being involved? If there was, she had the depressing feeling that it would only be on her side.

Such gloomy thoughts, she chided herself idly. But they matched the day, gray and dreary with a slow drizzle coming out of the overcast sky, the misty rain alleviating none of the sticky humidity. Few tourists would be tramping around this afternoon in such dismal weather.

"Pam." Amanda turned from the window to the trio of girls chattering in the corner. "Why don't you and Susan go on home? Linda and I will stay until closing. I don't expect a sudden deluge of visitors to appear."

"Great!" Pam replied as she and Susan rose eagerly to their feet. "I have to wash my hair. Heaven only knows if it'll dry in this weather."

"A car is pulling up out front," Linda announced with a sigh. "Wouldn't you know there'd be some fools wandering around in this gluck!"

Amanda sighed, too, but in relief. She didn't like having so much time on her hands to think. Everyone in town knew she had gone out with Jarod Colby, including her three co-workers. Each time she had tried to join in the light conversations about clothes or music or men, they shifted the subject to Jarod, exhibiting curiosity, envy and a touch of malice that Amanda hadn't been out with him again. Not even for the sake of her pride would she confide that she had turned him down. It was something they wouldn't understand or believe.

"How many people are there?" Amanda asked, nodding to the departing girls moving down the hall as she sifted through the brochures that were given to each visitor.

"Two. A man and a woman," Linda answered, peering through the sheer folds of the curtain. Then she gasped loudly. "Amanda!" she squeaked excitedly. "I think it's Jarod Colby!"

Unconsciously Amanda stiffened, half noticing that the other two girls had stopped to turn around, their eyes staring at her to see her reaction. Blood rushed quickly into her face and just as quickly receded as the front door opened.

Jarod was not the first one to walk in. A stunning brunette preceded him wearing a pantsuit Amanda knew she could never afford if she saved a whole year. It didn't help to notice the material was a perfect match for the sapphire blue eyes. The woman was more than beautiful, with the sophistication of a model, and it was evident that she was very well acquainted with Jarod.

"Good afternoon, Miss Bennett." His jeering voice swung her eyes around to him, pain in their brown depths as she met the hard indifference of his gaze. He was casually dressed in close-fitting begun with the first-floor rooms, by leading the woman to the staircase. In her best professional voice, she began her recitation.

"As we go up the stairs to the second floor, you will notice indentations and scars on the original oak steps. These disfiguring marks are believed to have been caused by Union soldiers riding their horses through the house when it was first taken."

The tour of the second floor took very little time, with Vanessa Scott exhibiting only desultory interest in the priceless furniture and the ornate canopy beds. The woman's attitude seemed to be one of indifference until Amanda led her back down the stairs.

"Which room is the ballroom?" the woman inquired, glancing idly around at the various doors that led off the main hall. "I'd like to see it."

Usually that was one of the last rooms shown before a tour was taken upstairs, but since Amanda had already rearranged the route once, she saw no point in not doing it again.

"It's through these doors," she said, walking ahead of the girl to open them. She opened her mouth to begin describing some of the antiques in the room when she was interrupted.

"Is this where the cotillion is held?"

"Yes," Amanda answered politely. "Since the early 1900s, there's been a dance, or cotillion as we call it, in celebration of Jefferson Davis's birthday."

"Have you ever been to one?" For the first time since the confrontation in the hall, Vanessa's blue eyes turned their speculative gleam away from her surroundings to study Amanda.

"Yes, I have. It's quite a festive occasion. A string quartet provides the music and all the guests are required to wear costumed dress of the Old South days." Amanda artfully used the personal question to describe the atmosphere of the ball, hoping to sidetrack further questions of a similar nature. "The style of dresses is very similar to the ones we tour guides wear, only much more elaborate."

"With your red hair, you must have worn green," the girl commented.

"Yes, I did. Now, if you will notice the chandeliers on each end of the room, they were imported—"

"Did you meet Jarod's cousin Judith?"

Amanda stopped her speech and turned slowly around to face the attractive brunette. Seething anger was nearing the boiling point.

"No, I did not," she answered, and waited for the next question.

"How well do you know Jarod?"

"I barely know him at all, Miss Scott," Amanda replied coldly and truthfully. "I'm employed by his corporation as a guide in his home."

"And that's all?" The blue gaze flicked arrogantly over her face, deliberately baiting and derisive. "I understand from Judith, who is a very dear personal friend of mine, that Jarod caused quite a sensation the night of the cotillion with the attention he paid to a certain redhead in an emerald green gown. Could that have been you?"

"As I recall, I did dance one dance with Mr. Colby." Ice dripped from Amanda's voice.

"It's hardly something you're likely to forget, is it?" Vanessa suggested dryly. "Did he ask you ou'?"

Amanda's jaw clamped down tightly, allowing her reply to slip out through gritted teeth. "That is personal and none of your business!"

"It seems to be the whole town's business. And everything that has to do with Jarod I make my business." A sickeningly sweet smile was directed at Amanda, who was already beginning to feel nauseated by the entire conversation. "You see, Jarod has his little flings from time to time."

"Since they never seem to last and he obviously keeps running back to you," Amanda murmured sarcastically, "what's the point or purpose of this discussion?"

"None, really." Slender shoulders were shrugged negligently. "I was merely curious to see who the little country charmer was."

"Now that you've accomplished that, there isn't any reason to continue the tour." Under normal circumstances Amanda would have never allowed her cold rage to lead to rudeness to any visitor to Oak Run, but the woman's tone of superiority drove her to striking back. "I think the charade has gone far enough. You are no more interested in seeing the house than I am to show it to you. I'm sure you would much rather get back to your darling Jarod." Her voice was beginning to shake with the violence of her anger. "I must say the two of you are very well suited to each other. You're both arrogant, conceited, egotistical—''

"That's enough, Miss Bennett!" a rough voice barked behind her.

Amanda spun around to stare at the murderous expression on Jarod's face. Her heart gave a wild, frightened leap at the unrelenting harshness in his eyes.

"Oh, darling—" Vanessa Scott moved swiftly forward to place a hand on his arm "—I'm sorry you had to hear such—"

"Would you wait for me in the car, please. I want to speak to Miss Bennett alone," he interrupted coldly.

"Of course," the girl murmured, flashing a triumphant look at Amanda before withdrawing from the room.

Amanda's brown eyes couldn't meet the contempt in his and she quickly lowered her gaze after Vanessa had left them alone. "I'll save you the trouble of firing me. I quit," she snapped.

"I don't give a damn whether you quit or not! I want an explanation for your rudeness to Miss Scott!"

"I lost my temper!" she shouted back.

"That's an excuse, not an explanation." He lowered his voice, but it still vibrated loudly in her ears. "I want to know why you treated a visitor with such insolence, Miss Bennett."

Amanda wearily pushed the hair away from her forehead, pain jabbing at her lungs. "Stop calling me that," she muttered in frustration, unwilling to admit that the discussion leading up to her attack had been about him for fear he would think she had started it.

"What do you suggest I call you?" he jeered sarcastically. "Amanda?"

The contempt in his voice hurt more than she cared to admit. "I suppose it really doesn't matter," she sighed.

"No, it doesn't," Jarod snapped. Silence crushed them for an eternity of seconds. "I'm waiting for your explanation."

"What do you want me to say?" she demanded angrily. "How did you expect me to react when you paraded your latest mistress in front of me? What was I supposed to do? Smile and nod as if she was just another stranger?"

"Why should it matter to you?" His dark head was thrown back and he was looking arrogantly down at her. "You made it very clear the last time I talked to you that you wanted nothing more to do with me. Didn't you mean it?"

"Yes, I meant it," Amanda confirmed nervously, regretting her jealous outburst of a second ago.

His hands closed around her waist while a compelling light glittered in his eyes. "Did you?"

"Yes," she answered in a very tiny voice.

"I don't think you did." A thick black brow arched complacently. "I believe you would like to go out with me again."

Amanda gazed helplessly into his face, so bluntly chiseled, so ruggedly masculine. The magic of his touch was beginning to work its spell on her.

"I won't beg you," Jarod went on. "I'll ask you one last time. The answer is either yes or no."

It was an ultimatum. Amanda knew he would never ask again. It was a second chance if she wanted it. She did—and yet. . . .

I would like to, but—'' she began nervously.

"Then you name the day, the place, and the time.''

"Monday.'' She breathed in deeply, braving the darkness of his gaze. "At one o'clock. We can spend the afternoon at Stone Mountain.''

A sound of disgust rolled from Jarod's throat as he removed his hands from her waist and started to turn away. She caught at one of his hands and held it between her own, unconsciously caressing the curling hairs on the back of it.

"Jarod, I—'' Amanda swallowed to ease the constriction in her throat "—I want to see you somewhere public.''

His gaze watched the movement of her hands before it flicked aloofly to her upturned face. "Where I can't take advantage of you, is that it?'' he asked.

"Yes, something like that,'' she admitted. His mockery made her feel so uncomfortably adolescent.

"I'll pick you up Monday at one.'' He slipped his hand from her unresisting hold and walked to the door.

"Jarod?'' Her questioning call halted him at the threshold to the hall. He half turned to look back at her, his expression unrevealingly cool. "Do I still have a job?'' she asked nervously.

"Frankly, I don't care.''

Her head jerked back at the sting of his tone.

Amanda pivoted quickly around so he couldn't see the effect his cruel indifference had on her.

"Damn!" he muttered under his breath, striding angrily to spin her around. His glowering look did little to assuage the tears burning the back of her eyes. "I don't interfere in the running of Oak Run. This is my aunt's pet project and she does the hiring and firing. If you want to hand in your resignation, give it to her."

"I have to work to help with my college expenses this fall," Amanda told him weakly.

The line of his eyes and mouth narrowed in exasperation. "I can't make up my mind if you're a schoolgirl or a woman!" he growled. "Keep your job, if that's what you want!"

Color flamed hotly beneath her skin. "Your work and your money are important to you. Why does it make me a schoolgirl if I feel the same?" she demanded. "Or are you simply regretting that you agreed to go out with a backcountry charmer like me?"

"Who called you that?" Amanda's mouth clamped tightly shut at his sharp inquiry. "Vanessa did, didn't she? That's why you retaliated with that outburst I overheard. So I finally got my explanation. I'll see you on Monday."

This time Jarod didn't stop at the hall door, but continued out of the mansion. Amanda was slower in leaving the ballroom, appearing in the hall after his car had left.

"Are you fired?" Linda asked in wide-eyed wonder. "I couldn't help overhearing part of what was said."

"No, I'm not," Amanda sighed in answer.

By the end of the week, she knew, the story of what happened today would be all over town. It would be useless to ask Linda to say nothing. There was more than one price to pay for seeing Jarod Colby, she realized. The fact that she was the first local girl he had shown any interest in only made the gossips more avidly malicious.

CHAPTER SEVEN

RISING ABOVE THE Georgia pines was a dome-shaped monolith, resembling the petrified remains of a great gray whale, five hundred and eighty-three acres of solid granite. Into its side was carved the sculpture of three of the most famous men in the short-lived history of the Confederate States of America: Jefferson Davis, president of the Confederacy; Stonewall Jackson, a general in the rebel army; and Robert E. Lee, a general and commander of all the Confederate armies. The entire work, the size of a city block, with the figure of Lee nearly as tall as a nine-story building, appeared the size of a postage stamp when compared to the immense proportions of Stone Mountain itself.

Amanda leaned back against Jarod's arm, his hand resting near the waistband of her lemon yellow slacks. As many times as she had seen the sculpture, she was still awed by its impressive size.

"Isn't it ironic," she said, glancing into his face, "that Gutzon Borglum, who was first commissioned to do this carving in the 1920s, left in frustration after roughing in the figure of Lee and later became so famous for his work at Mount Rushmore in the Black hills of South Dakota.

Here he was supposed to do the men of the Confederacy and there he completed the faces of four famous presidents of the United States, including Abraham Lincoln.''

"Have you seen Mount Rushmore?" Jarod asked.

"No," she answered with a shake of her head as a woman bumped into her and quickly apologized.

"It's getting a bit crowded here. Let's go somewhere else," he suggested, his arm propelling her away from the viewing patio below the sculpture. "Where to now? Do you want to visit the game farm where you can feed the animals? Go on a train ride or tour the plantation?"

The dryness of his voice revealed the subtle sarcasm hidden in his tone. Crowds of tourists everywhere and Amanda marveled at her own audacity in asking him to bring her here.

"We could go over to the carillon, I suppose," she said, shrugging.

"Do you think it's safer to walk or drive?"

"I'd rather walk." They skirted Memorial Hall, sometimes following the wake of other departing tourists and other times going against the flow of those arriving. "I'm sorry, Jarod. It wasn't a very good idea to come here, was it?"

"Considering you wanted to use the crowds to insulate yourself from me, I think it was an excellent idea," he contradicted her mockingly. "I'm surprised you're willing to allow me to hold your hand."

"Stop making me feel more miserable than I al-

ready am." Her gaze unhappily studied the pavement.

"This was your idea," Jarod reminded her.
"What were we supposed to accomplish today?"

"I wanted to get to know you better, to find out
more about you than just the fact that you own
Colby Enterprises." Her voice was uneven.

"I can think of better places than this," he muttered bitterly.

"Let's forget the carillon and take me home.
This whole thing is a disaster."

"Hardly a disaster," he murmured, although he
shifted their direction to take them to the parking
lot and his car. "You did learn something about
me today."

"That you don't like crowds." A grimace pulled
down the corners of her mouth.

"That, and the fact that I'm willing to put up
with them in order to persuade you to meet me
halfway." A light flickered briefly in his eyes
before he turned his gaze away from her. "As
beautiful as this park is, I can't say that I'm sorry
to leave."

"Is that why you came today?" Disbelief was in
her upturned face.

"I know you're frightened of me. It's there
sometimes in those brown eyes of yours." Jarod
opened the car door and helped her in while she
digested his statement. The truth was she was
afraid of herself.

"We don't have very much in common," she
asserted as he slid behind the wheel and started the
car.

"I have to breathe, eat and sleep the same as you. The only difference is I may have steak more often than you do." His mouth curved in amusement. "Having money doesn't set a man apart or make him better than others who don't have as much." Her face was a study of amazement when he glanced her way. "You look surprised."

"I never expected to hear Jarod Colby say such a thing."

"You did call me arrogant and conceited the other day. I am accustomed to getting what I want," Jarod admitted wryly, "mostly because I won't take no for an answer."

"Once you get something, do you still want it?"

"What are you asking?" Dark eyes moved over her face. "Do you want to know how long I'll keep you around after I know you better? That's a question I don't have the answer for yet."

"At least you're honest about it." Amanda breathed out slowly.

"I try to be honest about everything. I told you in the beginning that I wanted you. I wouldn't be here today if it weren't still true." His comment was made almost indifferently and Amanda found herself coloring at his candor. "How do you feel about me?"

"I don't know if I like you." She spoke hesitantly, staring straight ahead as he drove easily through the heavy traffic. "I'm attracted to you physically, but I can't make up my mind about you."

"Don't take too long." Beneath the teasing note

in his voice she sensed a hidden threat, an ominous assertion that he wouldn't wait forever for her decision.

The traffic was heavy during the journey back to Oak Springs. There seemed little necessity for conversation until Jarod stopped the car in front of Amanda's house. Shifting his weight, he stretched his arm along the back of the seat and looked at her.

"Now that we've dispensed with some of your nervousness, will you have dinner with me tomorrow night? At a public restaurant, if that will ease your mind further," he added with a wicked gleam dancing in his eyes.

"I'd like to, yes," Amanda agreed. The movement of her mouth brought dimples into play. "Thank you for today."

"Don't let my patience go unrewarded." His fingers closed over her shoulder and slowly drew her toward him. He took her lips in a lingering kiss, then gently pushed her back to her own side of the car.

Her hand closed over the door handle of the car. "What time will you be here tomorrow?"

"Six-thirty."

"I'll be ready," Amanda responded with a smile, suddenly feeling very happy as she got out of the car.

The next twenty-four hours winged by unbelievably fast. Before Amanda realized it, she was dashing down the stairs to meet Jarod. This time there was no tension in the conversation. They talked easily and on varied subjects during the drive to the restaurant. She found he could exert a vast amount of charm. During their meal she became impressed with his keen sense of humor. By the time it was over, she knew there were no doubts remaining that she was confusing her teen-age infatuation with the attraction he held for her now.

"Where are we going now?" she asked when he escorted her from the restaurant to his car.

"You," he emphasized lightly, "are going home."

Amanda glanced at her watch. It was barely nine o'clock. As if he had read the question that sprang into her eyes, Jarod added, "I'm leaving early in the morning and I have some work to do before I leave."

"Oh, I see," she murmured uncertainly. The next question rushed out before she could stop it. "When will you be back?"

"Saturday, I hope. Why? Will you miss me?" His eyes mocked her.

"Don't tease, Jarod. You know I will."

"Why do you think I would know that if you don't tell me?" They were inside the car and he switched on the interior light so he could study her face.

"You always seem so certain." Self-consciously she brushed her hair from her face.

"I never seem to feel so certain when it comes to you. Perhaps that's why you intrigue me so."

"Are you going to Pennsylvania again?" She swallowed.

"Yes. I'll try to be back by Saturday night. We

may yet have our date on a Saturday." His fingers closed over her hand. "Do you have to huddle against the door?"

"I'm not," she protested.

"You're an awfully long way from me. Come on, sit over here," he commanded. The gentle pull of his hold brought her beside him, his arm circling her shoulders while he nestled her head against his shoulder. Without indicating that she was causing the least encumbrance, he started the car and one-handedly reversed it out of the parking lot into the streets. "Do you know how long it's been since I've held you this close?" She felt the brush of his chin across the top of her head. "The last time was in your father's office."

A warm glow spread over her, her skin tingling at the remembered encounter. She resisted the impulse to snuggle closer and sighed contentedly instead.

"Did you enjoy yourself tonight?" Jarod asked softly, his hand caressing the upper part of her arm.

"Yes." The affirmation came out in a soft whisper.

"What are you going to do while I'm gone?"

"Why?"

But he ignored her query. "If I have any problems, I may not be back by Saturday. I'll call you in that event. All right?"

"Of course," Amanda agreed, unwillingly recognizing that they had made the turn onto the street where she lived.

Reluctantly she started to straighten when Jarod

braked the car to a stop in front of her house and
turned off the engine, but a softly spoken "no"
halted her movement. Long brown fingers cupped
the back of her head and bent it back to explore
her mouth with his. The gold tips of her lashes
were the color of the flame that encircled her heart
while it pumped the throbbing fire into her blood.
A blind, unending yearning had her quivering in
his arms.

"Saturday is so far away," he murmured, his
mouth moving against the side of her cheek, adding to her already feverish glow.

"Too far," she moaned softly. "Do you have to
go?"

His teeth bit into the lobe of her ear, evoking a
sensual pain of delight. "I've been asking myself
that, but I keep coming up with the same answer.
Yes, I do."

The steering column blocked her efforts to
strain closer to the lean hardness of his body. His
mouth moved relentlessly over her face, seeking
her lips again and again with a violent urgency that
left Amanda shaken and totally submissive.

"I don't want to let you go into that house,"
Jarod muttered savagely, tantalizing the curve of
her lips with his. "You'd better go while I can still
take my hands off you."

"Not yet," she pleaded, nuzzling the brown column of his throat when he raised his head from
her, but his fingers dug into her shoulders and
pulled her away from him.

"Now, Amanda!" The slender thread holding
his control was visible in the tight clenching of his

jaw while the harsh light of desire glazed in the dark eyes that possessively swept her face.

"All right." But her voice was shaking and uncertain, quivering like her body from the overwhelming passion of his embrace. From somewhere she found the strength to move to her own side of the car, her gaze clinging to his face, noticing his breathing was as uneven as hers. "I'll be waiting for you Saturday—whatever time you come back."

Jarod's fingers raked through his ebony black hair as he ripped his gaze from her face. "Don't say things like that, Amanda. Not now. Not even if you mean them. Just go. Get out of the car!"

The stinging lash of his voice whipped out at her. "I didn't mean to make you angry, Jarod."

"I'm not angry." But there was a growl of displeasure in his tone as his dark gaze flamed back at her. "At least, not with you. At myself, maybe, because I know in my gut that I can make you say yes. I'm not accustomed to taking cold showers, Amanda," he concluded dryly.

Her head tipped forward, the red gold strands of hair that fell forward matching the color in her cheeks. The wild singing of her heart echoed the truth of his words. A few more minutes under the arousing caress of his mouth and hands, and she might have begged for the satisfaction he promised. He was still an unknown quantity. She couldn't begin to understand why Jarod, who admittedly was used to having his way, should allow her to deny him.

"You will call if you can't be back by Saturday?'' Amanda couldn't hide her aching need for his touch as she turned her gaze helplessly toward him.

His arms spanned the distance between them, drawing her briefly to him while he pressed a fierce kiss on her mouth, then moved a breath away.

"I told you I would, honey. I don't say what I don't mean," he said. "Now will you please get out of this car. Don't make me touch you again."

He reached around her and opened the door, his action forcing her to step out. Amanda paused beside the car, staring almost hungrily at the dark face and the light of desire smoldering in his eyes.

"Hurry back," she whispered, and turned quickly away before she lacked the strength.

Before she reached the door of the house, he was driving away. After the comparative silence of the night, the house was alive with sounds. The muted sound of a radio came from upstaris, overshadowed by the voices coming from the television. Not quite ready to let go of the freshness of those moments of ecstasy in Jarod's arms for the mundane conversation of her family, Amanda slipped into the empty kitchen. As she absently poured a glass of milk, she heard footsteps coming toward the room. She glanced behind her to see her father appear in the doorway.

"Well, hello." There was surprise in his greeting. "You're home early again tonight. Anything wrong?"

"No." Self-consciously Amanda shook her head in a movement of negation. "Jarod has to leave early in the morning again. He'll be back Saturday."

"Will you be seeing him again?"

"Saturday," Amanda nodded. The gleam of amusement in his eyes induced a wide smile to spread across her face.

"You're not worried anymore about who he is?" he asked.

"No." She took a sip of milk, looking suddenly thoughtful. "Yesterday I said something about not having much in common with him. Do you know what his reply was, dad? He said a man with money isn't better than anyone else, he only lives better."

"I've always had the impression that his feet were solidly on the ground. I guess I was right." Her father smiled.

"I wish my feet were," Amanda sighed, then realized how revealing that statement was and glanced at her father.

"Are you falling in love with him?" he asked gently.

A wry smile lifted the corners of her mouth. "I think I already have," she admitted.

"You've heard all the gossip about him and all the women that have been in and out of his life, haven't you?"

Amanda laughed lightly. "Are you warning me about him after encouraging me to see him, dad?"

"I suppose I am." He shrugged and smiled, an arm circling her shoulders. "If he weren't interested in you, I know he wouldn't be seeing you. I don't want you to be hurt, though."

"I know." Her lips brushed his cheek fondly. She knew Jarod had the power to hurt her, but she didn't want to look any farther ahead than Saturday. "Tomorrow is another working day, dad. I think I'll call it a night."

"I imagine I'd be wasting my breath to wish you pleasant dreams," he chuckled.

"That's right!" Her brown eyes sparkled happily as she moved lightly from the room. "There aren't any other kind," she called from the hallway.

THE BLACK TELEPHONE stared back at her silently. Amanda readjusted the book on her knee and looked away, telling herself again that Jarod would be back on Saturday as he had promised and there wold be no need for him to call. But the closer it came to Saturday, the more apprehensive she became that something would happen to detain Jarod in Pennsylvania.

"We're going out to get a Coke, 'Manda." Her brother Brad slapped playfully at her leg, Cheryl Weston standing beside him. "Quit moping around beside the telephone and come with us."

"Tobe's coming, too," Cheryl urged, the expression in her eyes asking that Amanda make it a foursome so Cheryl wouldn't have to compete with Tobe for Brad's attention.

At that moment Tobe walked into the living room. Brad waved him to join them. "Use your influence with Amanda," her brother ordered.

"I don't feel like going out tonight," Amanda declared with a shrug, feeling the need to assert her own wishes before they snowballed her into agreeing.

Tobe took the book from her unresisting hands and tossed it on the table beside the phone, then joined her on the couch. His arm familiarly encircled her shoulders.

"Take big brother's advice," he said with a wink. "You can grow old sitting around waiting for the mighty Jarod Colby—you said yourself he wouldn't call until tomorrow. It's Friday night. Who wants to stay home on a Friday?"

"I do," Amanda insisted with a laugh.

"We're only going to be gone for a couple of hours," Brad urged.

"Maybe he'll find out you were with me," Tobe teased. "It might make him jealous."

"I am not interested in trying to make him jealous," she stated, firmly but gently taking the hand that was around her shoulders and raising it over her head so Tobe's arm was back at his side.

"We'll go somewhere and dance." Tobe didn't give up. "You like to dance. It'll be fun. Then maybe Cheryl will quit throwing daggers at me."

Cheryl darted him another angry glance before looking guiltily at Brad. "I do not," she defended herself, then added her plea to Tobe's. "Do come, Amanda. We won't be that late coming back."

"Amanda!" Her mother's voice inserted itself in the group. "You have a visitor."

All heads turned in unison. Amanda's heart gave a convulsive leap as her eyes encountered Jarod standing in the doorway to the living room, his features grimly taut with a cold glitter in his eyes. Despite the harsh look, she sprang eagerly to her feet, moving to him with unconcealed happiness.

"I didn't expect you tonight," she murmured softly, gazing into his face.

The hardness of his eyes flicked over Tobe before returning to her upturned face. "I finished sooner than I thought I would," he commented smoothly, that hated aloofness in his expression.

"Another fifteen minutes," Tobe spoke up easily, "and we would have spirited Amanda out of the house. It's a good thing you arrived now. She would have killed me if she'd found out you'd come while she was gone, and I'm too young to die."

"Would it really have bothered you if you had missed seeing me tonight?" Jarod asked in a cynical tone.

Her mouth opened immediately to assure him that it would, but her brother's voice broke in before she could speak.

"Is that an understatement! She hasn't set foot out of the house since Tuesday night except to go to work. Nobody's been allowed to be on the telephone longer than five minutes in case you tried to call."

"Bradley Bennett!" Amanda cried out in embarrassed protest, her gaze sliding self-consciously toward Jarod before it shifted to her parents who had been watching the proceedings with amusement. "Mom, dad, Jarod and I are going out on the porch."

Jarod stepped to one side. His hand touched her shoulder as she moved past him and stayed there as he followed her down the hall to the front door. Once outside, Amanda walked quickly to the railing.

"I hope you didn't get the wrong impression in there," she said nervously, a hand smoothing the hair along her neck. "My brother is always teasing me about my dates."

"Do you mean you didn't miss me?" Jarod asked.

Amanda pivoted sharply. "Oh, yes, I did." At his soft chuckle, she realized he had been teasing her and she colored at the quickness of her affirmation.

"If you'd said anything else, I would have strangled you!" A humorless smile pulled at the corners of his mouth. "In fact, I wanted to when I walked in the room and saw you sitting on the couch with that Peterson boy."

"He's like another brother to me," she murmured, her heartbeat quickening.

"He'd better be." There was just enough underlying roughness in his voice to let her know he meant it. In the glow of the moonlight she watched him cup a lighter to his cigarette, enjoying the sight of him after three long days of waiting for him to come back. "What does your family think about me?" Jarod asked, slowly exhaling a cloud of smoke.

"My younger sister is a little awed by you, but my brothers aren't the least impressed," she answered lightly, unsure why he was asking.

"And your parents?"

"They admire and respect you."

There was a sardonic curl to his mouth as he studied the burning tip of his cigarette. "Even though they know I have designs on their daughter?'' he challenged mockingly.

A fingernail trailed along the ege of the porch railing. "Naturally they realize we're attracted to each other," Amanda dodged.

"Do you honestly believe they would condone an affair between two consenting adults if one of them is you?" he jeered.

"No." Her voice was tight, the muscles of her throat constricted by pain. This was not the way she had expected him to welcome her. Her forehead drew together in a confused frown.

"And how do you feel about it?" There was an underlining of harsh demand in his velvet tone.

"Jarod, please." Her head moved helplessly to the side. "You're making it hard for me—"

"Hard for you!" For all the quietness of his outcry, there was violence, too. "I've gone thirty-six hours without sleep, cramming four days' work into a little less than three. I left my attorney to tie up the loose ends, caught a plane back to Atlanta and drove straight here because I couldn't stand being away from you another minute. And you still don't know the hell I go through every time I touch you. Hard for you!"

The last came out with a sound of contempt and disgust as Jarod tossed the cigarette into the dark and turned away. He was halfway down the porch steps by the time Amanda had recovered from his savage outburst.

"Jarod!" Her trembling legs carried her after him. When her fingers touched his arm, he stopped. "I'm sorry. You must believe me," she implored, her fingers curling into the sleeve of his jacket. There was no room for pride in her heart as the love that enveloped it welled up in her eyes.

For a full second, the hard glitter remained in his eyes. Then he sighed heavily and the harshness faded from his face.

"I shouldn't have snapped at you," he conceded. "I'm tired and—" a wry smile added emphasis "—frustrated. Nothing went the way I planned it tonight. First I find you sitting on the couch with that—"

Her fingers touched his lips to silence him. "Let's not go over it again," she whispered.

"Let's go for a ride in the car," Jarod suggested softly, catching her hand and holding it.

"Yes," she murmured—as if she needed to voice her agreement when she was already moving toward the car.

CHAPTER EIGHT

THE MOON WAS a silver crescent suspended above the pine trees. A smattering of stars winked in the purpling blue sky. Amanda had no idea where they were going, but she didn't care as her head rested comfortably in the hollow made by his shoulder and arm. For a minute this evening she had been certain Jarod was going to walk out of her life, and she realized what a crippling blow that would be. She couldn't suppress a shudder at the thought.

"Are you cold?" His head bent toward her as he slowed the car.

"No. I was remembering how close I came to letting you walk away tonight," she answered shamelessly.

He gradually edged the car onto the wide shoulder of the graveled road, stopping it beneath the overhanging branches of some tall pines, their heavy scent drifting into the car.

"You probably should have." He made a cynical sound in his throat as he reached out to turn off the motor. "Your instincts about me are correct."

"What instincts?" she teased, her hand sliding under his jacket across the thin material of his shirt.

The intimate movement forced a groan from Jarod's throat as his hand closed over her arm to halt the searching caress. A second of hesitation followed before he pushed her roughly against the back of the car seat, half turning to pin her there while the blazing light in his eyes raked her face and neck. But the trusting brown eyes that shone back at him exhibited no fear at his suppressed violence.

Her mouth throbbed to feel his kiss, her lips parting in anticipation of his touch. His hands held her arms at her side as he ignored the invitation of her lips to bury his face in the fiery locks curling around her neck. Jarod continued to hold her still, plundering the softness of her throat and shoulders and tantalizing her face with rough kisses on her eyes, cheeks, and ears until Amanda was turning and twisting her head to find his wandering mouth.

The kindled fire he had sparked burst into the searing flames of demanding passion when he finally allowed her lips to find his. The need for his possession of her screamed in every nerve end and she whimpered softly against his bruising lips whose touch instantly changed from frustrated ardor to deliberate, total mastery of the senses. He drew back against his seat, pulling her with him, allowing her hands to touch him in trembling caresses while his own moved intimately over her body.

Resistance was impossible. It never even crossed her mind to protest when his fingers undid the top button of her blouse and she felt his fiery touch against her naked skin. She was clay to be molded in his hands, totally submissive to every movement, willing to become whatever he wanted.

Slowly Jarod arched her backward until she was

lying prone on the car seat, the exquisite pressure of his lean body on top holding her there. As his legs slid intimately between hers, a shudder of mindless ecstasy quivered through her.

His mouth moved across her cheek, the warmth of his breath, uneven like hers, fanning her lashes. "I'll try not to hurt you, darling," he murmured against her skin.

The sound of his husky voice opened the last gate and released the torrent of love behind it. Her hands lovingly cupped his face to allow her lips to move over his.

"I love you, Jarod," she whispered, aching certainty in the shaking depths of her voice. "Shamelessly, completely, without end. I love you. I love you."

It took a full minute before Amanda felt the stiffness with which he held himself. Then her caressing fingers and lips felt the tight muscles of his jaw. In the next instant he was pushing himself away from her, unmindful of the hands that tried to hold him. Blank confusion reigned as Jarod opened the car door and stepped outside, his hands on his hips as he breathed deeply of the night air. Hurt and stumbling, she followed him, her fingers tentatively touching his shoulder while she tried to recover her wits.

"Jarod?" Her voice was questioning and puzzled.

The arm nearest her left his hip and encircled her waist, drawing her against the comfort of his side. But Amanda could feel the tenseness, the rigidity of his touch that made the hardness of his body unconsoling.

"What did I do?" She turned her troubled and pain-filled eyes to his face, unable to believe that the desire that had been carved in every line could disappear so quickly or be replaced by such unrelenting coldness.

"I want you." The skin of her throat burned where his fingers touched it even as his harsh voice struck coldly at her heart. "I want you, but I'm not going to lie, Amanda. I don't love you."

She gulped back the outcry of pain and looked blindly away from his face. Hot waves of humiliation and shame engulfed her. She tried to pull free of his arms, but he kept her there and she was too stunned and hurt to care.

"You don't care for me—at all?" she asked in agonizing softness.

"I want you," he said bitterly, "the same way I've wanted dozens of other women."

Her shoulders hunched forward. "You don't feel any difference with me?"

"What difference could there be?" Jarod mocked.

"Love."

"There's no such thing," he jeered. "Through the ages, lust has been disguised as love. Love doesn't last any longer than lust does, because they're the same thing. Love is a joke."

"That's not true!" she protested vigorously.

He chuckled derisively. "There's two divorces for every marriage. Is that your proof of lasting love?"

"What about the people who are together for thirty or forty years?"

"You sentimental fool! First they were trapped by children and mortgages and security. Then they became habits to each other and were too old and tired to break them."

"Oh, God!" Amanda felt sick to her stomach, unable to accept the scorn the man she loved was displaying.

"After a few months, you'll find that you don't love me," Jarod went on cynically. "The newness will wear off and I'll no longer excite you the way I do now. It's always the same."

"A few months," she moaned bitterly. "Is that how long most of your women last?"

There was a pause. "Yes."

"Even Vanessa." Her lips trembled as she said the name.

"Vanessa Scott? She didn't last that long."

"Yet you always go back to her," Amanda remarked numbly.

"Did she tell you that?" he mocked. "She wants to marry money. It's not me she's after."

"I can't believe I'm hearing any of this." Her hands moved to cup her ears. "I tell you that I love you and you laugh at me!"

"I'm not laughing. You've let yourself get carried away with your emotions and have started believing in something that doesn't exist," he told her harshly. "You want me and I want you, but don't build the desire you feel into romantic dreams."

"I love you, Jarod. The way I feel is no dream

that's going to fade in the morning. I thought I had no pride where you were concerned." She spoke softly but for the first time calmly. "If all you want from me is an affair, then the answer is no. If, as you say, all you feel is lust, I don't ever want you to touch me again."

His penetrating gaze scrutinized her expression. The tightening of his mouth acknowledged the conviction he saw written there.

"Very well," he said grimly. "I'll take you home."

"I feel sorry for you, Jarod," Amanda said numbly as she started to get into the car. "To not believe in love must make you the loneliest man in the world."

But his dark head moved as if he felt sorry for her because of her delusion. The light in his eyes mocked her as he slid behind the wheel. Amanda felt surrounded by a polar ice, stunned by the freezing grip on her chest. Each slow beat of her heart seemed to widen the crack that was slowly appearing in its walls. The pain was unbearable, too deep to be assuaged by tears as she huddled silently against the car door. Unseeing eyes stared out the window of the moving automobile. The only image that registered in her mind was Jarod's face, carved lines untouched by softness. Now she understood why. A man who felt no love could exhibit no gentleness.

IT WAS DAYS before the numbed shock wore off. And after them came a succession of more days when Amanda tried desperately to hate Jarod. If he had deceived her, she might have succeeded in her attempt. Instead she found her abiding love for him laced with compassion and even pity, because what meaning was there to life without love?

The searing heat of August promised that September was not far away. Amanda held on to her sanity by convincing herself that when September came, she would return to college and leave behind the images that haunted her. No more would Jarod's ghost appear in the living-room door as it had done on that last night, nor would his wraith-like form flit through the halls and ballroom of Oak Run. The tempestuous dreams of being smothered by his burning kisses might even end. But she didn't really believe the breach in her heart would ever heal.

At first her family had teased her about Jarod's absence after the marked attention he had paid her. Then they began to look behind her stoical replies and see the strain behind her smile and the dullness in her brown eyes, and his name was avoided. The unasked questions in her parents' eyes were the hardest to ignore. Only once did her mother ask what had happened. Amanda had shrugged and said they had quarreled, adding to stave off more questions that it was personal. Her parents held considerable esteem for Jarod as an employer and a man. Somehow she couldn't bring herself to destroy that, no matter how much he had hurt her. Vengeance wasn't part of her nature.

Beads of perspiration had collected on her forehead and upper lip as Amanda turned to wave her thanks to Linda, who had given her a ride home from Oak Run after her father had failed to come for her. A smile flitted across her face as she noticed the family car still parked in the driveway. He had probably become engrossed in a baseball game and forgotten the time.

As she mounted the porch steps, she could hear no blare of the radio. Only silence came from the house. As she swung open the screen door, the whirr of an oscillating fan came from the living room. There was no rattle of dishes or silverware, no odor of food being cooked for Saturday-night dinner, no voices, only the lonely whirr of the fan.

"Mom! Dad!" A puzzled frown wrinkled her brow as she walked down the hall glancing into each empty room. "Grandpa! Where is everybody?" Her path carried to the stairwell. "Bonnie, are you home?" Only her own voice echoed back.

A car door slammed in the front of the house and Amanda hurried back to the door. She reached the screen door at the same instant that a tall, dark figure strode onto the porch. The blood receded from her face, leaving an unnaturally white pallor to her skin.

"What are you doing here?" she whispered as Jarod opened the door and walked in.

"I went to Oak Run to pick you up, but you'd already left," he said as if that answered her question.

Her eyes hungrily devoured his face, reimprinting each ruggedly handsome line on her mind as if in the next moment she would be struck blind and his was the last face she wanted to see.

"What do you want?" she demanded as she

turned away before the temptation to melt into his arms would become irresistible.

"Amanda—" he began.

His hand reached out to grasp the soft flesh of her arm left bare by the ruffled gown that was her uniform, but she wrenched free of his hold, emitting a tortured cry. "Don't touch me! Don't come near me! Haven't you hurt me enough already?"

"Stop it!" This time his fingers held her shoulders in an iron grip from which she couldn't shake free. "Your father is in the hospital. I promised your mother I would bring you there as soon as I could."

Her struggles stopped. "Is this some cruel joke? Some devious new plan of yours?" she cried bitterly. Fear clouded her eyes as she stared into the unchanging, harsh expression on his face.

"It's no joke. The doctors think your father has suffered a stroke," he answered grimly.

"I don't believe you." Red gold curls fanned her cheeks as she shook her head vigorously. "How would you know what's happened to my father?"

Jarod breathed in deeply as if to control his anger. "I'm a director on the hospital board. We were touring the hospital this afternoon to make recommendations on updating the facilities. I was there when the ambulance brought your father in."

"No!" Her protest was a horrified gasp, but this time Amanda believed him.

"Don't get hysterical on me," Jarod ordered. He must have seen the panic forming in her eyes.

"He's alive, but his condition is critical. Your brother and grandfather are at the hospital now, but I think your mother needs a woman with her. Go upstairs and change out of that gown. Where's your little sister?"

"Bonnie?" she asked blankly, trying to gather her scattered wits and react with the calmness he possessed. "She's, er, she's working, I think.... She's a waitress at...at Shorty's Café. I...I can't remember what time her shift ends."

There was a frantic sob in her last statement and the pressure of his hold increased slightly in a silent command not to panic. "I'll call and find out while you change," he said firmly. He turned her around and pointed her in the general direction of the stairs.

After the first few faltering steps that Amanda took in compliance, tears began streaming down her face. She gathered the long folds of her gown in her hands and ran the rest of the way to her room. Her parents had always seemed indestructible, growing older without ever aging. She couldn't even remember them ever being sick. Now her father was lying in critical condition in the hospital. Her fingers were trembling so badly she couldn't unhook the back of her gown. Sobs of despair tore at her throat as she attacked the metal fasteners again.

"Amanda?" Jarod's voice came from the upstairs hall.

"I'm...I'm in here," she called weakly.

The door to her room opened immediately. "Bonnie left the restaurant about five minutes ago. She'll be here any minute," he told her.

"I can't undo these hooks," she murmured. The sight of his composure forced back the sobs as she quickly scrubbed the tears from her face.

Under any other circumstances Amanda would have been conscious of the swift sureness of his fingers as they unhooked her gown. Their touch would have inflamed her, but now she was only grateful for their steadiness. The need for haste pushed aside her modesty as she stepped out of the ruffled gown, letting it fall in a heap on the floor. Partially aware that her scanty undergarments left little to the imagination, Amanda accepted the pantsuit that Jarod had taken from her closet, avoiding his onlooking gaze.

"Hello! Where is everybody?"

With her clothes in her hand, Amanda ran to the door. "I'm upstairs, Bonnie!" she called. "Come up here."

Then she turned, the sound of her sister's footsteps on the stairs. Her frightened eyes turned to Jarod, needing the assurance of his self-possession to break the news about their father.

"Get your clothes on," he said quietly. The dispassion of his tone calmed the sudden acceleration of Amanda's heart at her sister's arrival.

"Where's everybody gone?" Bonnie demanded as she burst into the room, stopping short at the sight of Jarod standing in the center and Amanda just stepping into a pair of slacks. Bonnie immediately took a hasty step backward, her face coloring in embarrassment.

"Bonnie, wait!" Amanda called out, glancing

guiltily at Jarod as she realized how intimate scene must look. "Jarod is here because—" she walked quickly to take her younger sister's hands "—daddy's...daddy's in the hospital."

Bonnie looked from one to the other in disbelief, "No!"

"I couldn't believe it, either, but it's true." Amanda stared down at the hands held in her own.

"Your father has had a stroke." Jarod walked up behind them and handed Amanda the rust print blouse that matched her slacks, a gentle reminder to finish dressing. "As soon as Amanda is ready, I'll take you both to the hospital so you can be with your mother."

"But daddy has never been sick," Bonnie protested. "You must be wrong!"

As her sister threatened to give way to the hysteria rising within her, Jarod stepped between them, his soft, husky voice gently admonishing her to remain calm, that her mother would need the strength of all her children. All the while his dark gaze kept track of Amanda's movements so that when she was ready to leave, he had already begun guiding Bonnie to the stairs.

At the hospital the two girls were shocked by the ravages of fear and grief that had aged their mother before their eyes. That numbed sense of disbelief seemed to hang like a cloud over everyone, including their grandfather, who sat hunched in a corner, a shadow of his former lively self, unable to accept that somewhere in the hospital his son was fighting for his life.

"How is he, mamma?" Amanda asked, extract-

...self from her mother's tender hug and helping her to a nearby chair.

"I don't know," was the mumbled reply.

"The doctors are still with him." Brad was standing beside the chair, his eyes bright with unshed tears.

Her mother turned imploring eyes on Jarod. "Perhaps you could find out?" she asked anxiously. "I shouldn't ask you. You've done so much already."

"We've been all over that, Bernice." Jarod smiled, ignoring Amanda's look of surprise that he should address her mother so familiarly. "I'll see what I can find out for you."

Then he was striding away without waiting to hear the fervent thank-you from her mother. They all remained in huddled silence for long minutes before Amanda rose and walked to her brother.

"Have you telephoned Marybeth and Brian? Where's Teddy?" she asked in a low voice so her mother couldn't overhear.

"Jarod's already contacted everyone," Brad told her, shaking his head as if he couldn't believe it himself. "Mandy, I don't. . . I don't know what we would have done if he hadn't been here at the hospital. Mom just sort of went to pieces and grandpa—he hasn't said a word since we got here. And I wasn't any help at all. Mom kept crying and crying. Then Jarod showed up and took charge. He and mom went off in a corner until she finally stopped crying. I don't know what you and Jarod had a fight about, but whatever it was, he more than apologized for it today."

However futilely, her brother's words Amanda's love run deeper. Knowing how Jarod's composure had kept her from falling apart and the way he had staved off Bonnie's hysteria, she knew his quiet authority had to have affected her mother the same way. This knowledge radiated in a glow of pride when he returned a few minutes later, bearing the news that the doctors believed her father's condition had stabilized.

"It will be a while before you're allowed to see him," Jarod told her mother, "but I think the worst is over. It might be permissible to shed a few tears of happiness now even if the danger hasn't completely passed."

Weak, laughing sighs of relief echoed through the room as they all said silent prayers of thanks. Yet none wanted to voice their jubilation aloud. As Jarod had said, the danger hadn't completely passed. Amanda's hand touched Jarod's arm, wanting to express gratitude for all he had done. She smiled tentatively as his dark gaze moved thoughtfully over her face.

"May I see you alone?" she asked softly. There was a slight inclination of his head in agreement and she turned to her mother. "We'll be back in a few minutes," Amanda assured her.

With a smile that was divided equally between them, her mother nodded her understanding and Jarod and Amanda walked from the small waiting room.

CHAPTER NINE

THE HAND SLIGHTLY RESTING on her back guided Amanda to the vacant sun room. Now that she was alone with Jarod, she felt self-conscious. She watched him light a cigarette and she gathered the courage to speak.

"I want to thank you for all you've done," she said hesitantly, her eyes downcast.

"Perhaps you should save your thanks until you've found out what it is that I have done." Before his voice had been persuasively soothing; now there was a brittle quality to it that brought her gaze up sharply.

"What do you mean?" she murmured, noticing the mocking glitter that appeared in his eyes.

"How familiar are you with your parents' financial situation?" he parried her question.

"What has that got to do with this?" Amanda frowned.

"Are you aware that everything they own is under second and third mortgages? Did you know all medical coverage has been cancelled? I'm certain you know they have no savings, not with four children in college. At this moment, the only money they have is the two weeks' sick-leave pay your father is entitled to receive from my company.'' Jarod paused to let the full gravity of the situation sink in. "In less than a month, there'll be no money to pay bills, provide food or shelter, nothing for the cost of the hospital, and no tuition money for you or your brothers.''

"Oh, my God!'' Amanda reeled from the almost physical blow of his words. She had never guessed how severe the repercussions could be from her father's attack. "Does mother know all this?''

"That was the main reason for her panic,'' he replied. "After she'd told me all this, I convinced her that my company would take care of everything. I didn't mention that whether Colby Enterprises carries it out or not depends on you.''

"On me? Why does it depend on me?'' she whispered, frightened by the ominous threat hidden in his words.

"Because—dammit!—I still want you!'' Jarod snapped, grinding out his cigarette in an ashtray.

Her stomach lurched sickeningly. "So what are you asking?'' She was surprised that her voice could sound so calm. "Do you want me to become your mistress?''

"I would be satisfied with that arrangement,'' he admitted satirically. "Unfortunately it would only be a matter of time before your parents found out, and I think they would have qualms about taking money from their daughter's lover.''

Amanda turned blindly away, her mind searching wildly for another way to come up with the money that would be needed.

"I wouldn't have to return to college. Brad has

enough saved for his first term's tuition. Maybe Teddy does, too, and Brian," she said frantically.

"Even if you were able to take care of that, it wouldn't solve the problem of the bills and payments and medical costs, not counting what it would take to live," he jeered. "Not even Tobe, who comes from a fairly wealthy family, would be able to loan or give your family enough money to keep it going, particularly since his parents don't approve of his relationship with yours." There was a sardonic light in his eyes as they glittered complacently over her. "Believe me, I've considered all the possibilities that might be open to you as alternatives to my offer. If you want your family to retain its status quo, Amanda, you'll have to come to me."

She shivered at the calculating coldness in his voice. "How can you expect me to agree to become your mistress?"

"I've studied your family. You possess one of those trite, old-fashioned relationships of all for one and one for all. Sacrifice is second nature to all of you. With your father lying in a hospital bed, neither you nor your brother would think twice of setting aside your education to rally around the family hearth and protect it." Amanda could tell by the derision in his tone that he considered such action foolhardy and unworthy of praise. Jarod wasn't admiring their closeness; he was making fun of it. "Your brothers will find that it's much easier to leave college than it is to return after a few years' absence. Their future rests on the outcome of your decision about my offer."

"To become your mistress," she re[...] throbbing pain making her words tremble.

"My mistress, my wife, whatever you want to call it." Jarod shrugged with a gracefully arrogant movement.

"Wife?" Amanda stared into the cold bronze of his face.

"I thought I'd already explained." His expression mocked the confusion in her eyes. "That vain family pride wouldn't allow your parents or your brothers to accept charity from your lover, but if I were your husband and a member in good standing, they wouldn't think twice."

"So you're asking me to marry you?" Amanda asked, needing to hear the statement in order to believe it.

"Yes," Jarod answered without any show of emotion. "Aren't you in love with me anymore, or have I proved to you how fickle and fleeting desire is?"

For one charged second, she had almost believed that he was going to admit he loved her, that he had found their separation unbearable. To him, she was only the grapes just out of reach, the sweet tender grass on the other side of the fence. He had once told her that he always got what he wanted. The thrill was in the chase. Once she was his, in body as well as in spirit, the excitement would be gone. As he had put it, the newness would fade and he would be ready to discard her for another.

"If it takes you so long to answer," he jeered softly, "perhaps you're finally realizing that love is an illusion with no substance in fact."

...nda couldn't meet his derisive eyes. "Love exists, Jarod. I was so blinded by love for you that when you deceived my mother, I mistook your cruel treachery for kindness."

"It was not deceit if you say yes," he reminded her cynically.

Bitter gall rose in her throat. "You know you've left me with no choice."

"Only because you want me. If you found me repulsive, you wouldn't consider my proposal, not even for your family." A finger tilted her chin upward so he could look into her face.

"Please, don't humiliate me anymore." The sun-gold tips of her lashes fluttered over her brown eyes, shutting out the painful acknowledgement that what he said was true. She started to turn away.

"Not yet." His arm reached out, blocking her movement. His fingers touched her arm in a light grip that she knew could instantly become like steel should she try to leave after he had ordered her to stay. "Our discussion isn't over."

"Discussion?" It was Amanda's turn to jeer. "Isn't my agreement to anything you suggest merely lip service?"

"More or less," Jarod agreed complacently. "But I want you to become adjusted to the fact that we'll be getting married next Saturday. Naturally we'll wait until tomorrow to inform the rest of your family."

"Saturday?" she breathed. "That's impossible! How can you insist on such a thing with my father so ill?"

"Your father has survived the attack. The condition is critical, but he'll recover. If you're harboring any foolish notions that you aren't going to marry me until your father can walk down the aisle beside you, you'd better change your mind now. It will quite likely be months before he would be recovered to that point, and I will not wait that long," he told her with brutal candor. "Since our marriage is a farce, a celebration would be hypocritical. A small wedding with the immediate family in attendance is all we require to put the seal of legality on our affair for your parents' benefit. Under the circumstances everyone will understand our reason for keeping it simple, and with your father in the hospital we'll be spared the idiocy of a honeymoon."

"You have it all laid out like a battle plan. Every opposition is anticipated in advance." Her stomach churned sickeningly as she stared at the ruthless man who was soon to be her husband. "Like General Sherman, you destroy everything in your path until you achieve your objective. After Sherman reached Savannah and the sea, he remained only a few months—or was it two or three—then he turned his armies in another direction, seeking another victory elsewhere."

"Nothing lasts forever, Amanda," he said bluntly, not at all upset by the sarcastic sting of her voice. "You can reconcile yourself to the fact that in a few months you'll be free of me and my plundering Yankee ways. What's a few months out of your young life?"

"Marriage really means nothing to you, does

he murmured, amazed that he could already be plotting to be rid of her.

"No. And that shocks you, doesn't it? A piece of paper or words spoken in a church can't change the fickleness of human nature. There's the difference between you and me. You are a romantic, trying to change what can't be changed, and I am a realist, accepting what can't be changed."

"And children? Don't you ever want children?"

An indefinable something flickered across his face at her question before the mask hardened.

"No. Procreation is not one of my desires," he snapped. "Do you have any more questions?"

"No, none," she answered, shaking her head sadly.

"I saw the doctor go in to speak to your mother. Shall we join them?"

The stroke, a severe one, had left her father partially paralyzed and deprived him temporarily of his speech. He regained consciousness that evening and the family was allowed to see him for short intervals. Jarod Colby was a law unto himself. His entrance into the restricted room with Amanda wasn't questioned by any of the hospital staff any more than it had been questioned by her family.

Amanda's heart turned over at the sight of her father's lanky frame covered with a bed sheet and surrounded by various tubes and monitoring devices. The worst was trying to summon an encouraging smile as she stared into his brown eyes glazed with fear. The sight of the previously indestructible figure lying helplessly in the bed constricted her throat until the simplest greeting couldn't squeeze through. Jarod's arm moved around her waist as he almost physically carried her the last two feet to her father's side.

"Hello, Sam," Jarod said quietly. "Or perhaps I should call you father, since your daughter has finally agreed to marry me."

Her eyes darted to the aquiline profile in surprise. Jarod had said they wouldn't tell the family until the next day. Then she felt the questioning eyes of her father turned on her for confirmation. Jarod's fingers bit punishingly into her waist when she hesitated.

"It's true, daddy." Her eyes filled with tears, whether from the futility of her own love or from the pain induced by Jarod's grip.

"I don't want you to worry about a thing," Jarod instructed her father in that quietly authoritative tone of one accustomed to taking charge. "We're all family now. I'll take care of everything until you're back on your feet."

The nurse on duty in the room blinked at the pair in surprise, but Amanda didn't notice. The frightened look in her father's eyes had dimmed as his eyelids fluttered down and a small breath of relief slipped from his pinched lips. She knew then that his fear had been for his family and not his own welfare. There was satisfaction in knowing her action had relieved that burden. Instinctively she raised her eyes to Jarod to thank him for putting her father's mind at rest. But in the arrogant bronze mask, she saw that this was all part of his plan. He was manipulating all their emotions to serve his own ends.

"We'd better let your father rest now," he said, his eyebrow arching at the sudden flare of anger in her eyes. Amanda moved quickly out of his grasp to the hall, brought up sharply by the hand that yanked her back to him. "What's wrong with you?" he demanded, keeping his voice low so that the scene between them appeared quite intimate.

"You're using us. You're using all of us without any regard for our feelings or our pride," Amanda accused bitterly.

"You will all be receiving compensation." His mouth moved in a cold smile.

"I hope someday your plans come crashing down on your head!" Her whole body trembled with the resentment boiling inside. Hate—the black side of love—was showing its face.

But Jarod only chuckled. "My poor little red-haired witch. Are you trying to prophesy my doom?"

"You can't have your way all the time. I only hope I'm there when you finally can't have what you really want."

"Will you pick up the pieces, I wonder?" he asked with a bemused smile, his hand reaching out to close over her throat while indicating how frail and insignificant was her spite. His touch frightened and excited her. It burned while it left her shivering from the cold thought of the time when he would tire of her. Dark, indolent eyes caught the paradoxical emotions that chased each other over her face. "Fiery Amanda, do you see how ambivalent your reactions are already becoming toward me? Right now you can't make up your mind whether to kiss me or claw me.''

It was true. She couldn't. Then he stepped away and she could do neither.

IN THE WEEK that followed, Amanda was exposed to the many facets of Jarod's character. With her brothers he became the older brother, establishing a camaraderie while gently exerting his authority even as he gave the impression he was consulting them. Her mother looked on his as a wise counsel; he placated her fears with one hand and smoothed the way with the other. Even her grandfather stopped making snide comments about Yankees. Where there was disorganization, Jarod organized. Indecision was swept aside by his decisive action. He never explained, yet people were always left with the impression he had. Charm, diplomacy, compassion, authority, loyalty all surfaced at some time.

Amanda had thought he would flaunt his generosity, buy his way into the family, but strangely Jarod handled the transaction of money in such a businesslike way that no one saw a reason to speak of it. She marveled at the ease with which he persuaded others to go along with his suggestions, never issuing ultimatums or reminding them in any way of the power he held as head of Colby Enterprises.

It was ironic that Jarod was also honest. If he hadn't been, she would have succumbed to his considerable magnetism in the belief that he loved her. She wondered which was the worst hell—havan affair with a man, then finding out he didn't love her, or marrying a man knowing he didn't love her?

Light was caught by the arc of gold metal on her finger. There was no longer any reason to make imaginary comparisons. She was Mrs. Jarod Colby, for better or worse. At the moment it felt worse. But it was fear. Amanda felt the tenseness knotting her muscles, nerves so raw that the feather-lightest touch on her skin made them scream.

Standing in front of the altar with Jarod at her side, she had repeated the marriage vows that to her had always been sacred. The quiet clarity of Jarod's voice had made her heart ache. He had sounded so sincere, yet when her hopeful gaze had turned to him, there was no expectant light of tenderness in his jet dark eyes, only a possessive glitter that seemed to brand her as his. Until the ceremony everything seemed to have been moving at triple time. Now it had suddenly ground down to half speed.

The filmy net curtain slipped from her fingers. The only thing visible was her own reflection staring back at her from the window pane. The sleek satin sleeves of her robe felt as chilling as the apprehensions that enclosed her heart. Knowing there was no bond of love between them was beginning to make her believe that the ceremony and the marriage license meant nothing; and knowing that any minute Jarod—correction, her husband—would walk into the bedroom didn't ease the emotional turmoil that brought wary shadows to her brown eyes.

Except for the coolly indifferent kiss Jarod had given her at the wedding, he had not touched her. That was another thing she couldn't understand. He professed to want her so much, yet he hadn't shown the slightest bit of emotion or desire. Her hands rubbed her arms, trying to rid herself of the shivers that trembled over her skin. A flush of shame colored her cheeks as she wondered how she could possibly meet Jarod's eyes. In retrospect, Amanda could see he had bought her, paid a high price for her. Tonight was when he would inspect the merchandise.

"Are you afraid of the dark, Amanda?"

The mocking voice spun her away from the window, her fingers automatically sliding up her mud-green robe to clutch the top more tightly together. She had thought her hearing was attuned to the sound of water running in the shower of the adjoining bathroom, but the uneasy wanderings of her mind must have blocked out the signal of its stoppage. Every light in the muted gold bedroom was on, an attempt by Amanda to take away the dominance and intimacy of the turned-down bedclothes.

Jarod's question hung in the air as her wide eyes stared at the unbearably short toweling robe wrapped around his middle. The bronze tan of his face was repeated in the same dark shade over the rest of his body. The broad chest with its thick cloud of curling black hair tapered to slim hips and a flat stomach. The sinewy muscles in his thighs and legs seemed coiled, waiting for the command to carry h... across the room to her. Waves of crimson red suffused her entire body as her apprehensive gaze encountered the twisted smile of amusement on his face, signaling that he was aware of her scrutiny. Amanda pivoted back to the window, her breath coming in jerky gulps of near panic.

"What induced that becoming blush?"

The gold carpet didn't betray the sound of his movement, but the snapping sound of a light being switched off warned her he had moved. There was another click and another light went off, leaving only the lamp beside the bed. Then her nose caught the clean scent of soap behind her and she stiffened.

"Are you embarrassed because your friend Cheryl told me of your infatuation for me as a girl?" he mocked softly, his voice coming from over her right shoulder.

Her head dipped slightly as she remembered the mortification she had felt when Cheryl had blurted out the story of Amanda's schoolgirl crush at the small reception after the wedding. Never would she forget the cynical amusement that had danced in Jarod's eyes.

"Must you bring that up?" she demanded in a grudging murmur, her fingers nervously raking back the red gold hair that had fallen forward.

"The night of the cotillion I sensed that your resentment of me had nothing to do with my supposedly superior status in the community. Yet I couldn't imagine that the incident of my rudeness you related could have had such an impact. It never occurred to me that I could be an object of idolatry to a young girl," he mused thoughtfully.

"Don't remind me what a fool I was!" Amanda protested, blinking back the acid tears that burned her eyes.

"Surely your dream came true. Didn't you marry me this afternoon?" Jarod taunted her.

She turned sharply around to voice her remorse for the empty vows they had exchanged, vows that were twisting knives of regret in what was once her heart. But she hadn't realized how very close he was to her. The few inches that separated them made the impact of his virility all the more potent, smothering her until she couldn't catch her breath.

Her gaze flew upward to the dark, enigmatic face indolently watching her. Amanda quickly averted her head, although she had lost the power for further movement. Unwittingly her gaze was directed to the bed and she shut her eyes tightly against the sudden vision of Jarod's raven black hair contrasting with the whiteness of the pillow.

"I can't go through with this," Amanda whispered weakly. "I thought I could, but I can't."

"Why?" She had expected arrogance or anger, but certainly not that note of amused curiosity in Jarod's voice. "We made a bargain."

"Yes, but—oh, don't you see?" Her eyes were round and pleading when she looked at him, her fingers tightening their hold on her robe. "You don't want me. I'm only something you paid for and now you feel you must use to receive your money's worth."

Not a word of denial came from his lips. "How did your astute mind reach that conclusion?" As he continued to tower above her, there was an air of satisfaction in his expression, as if he were glad she had made the discovery.

"Oh, Jarod, I'm not totally ignorant." The aching words scraped her already raw throat. "In all the times we've been together this past week, you never once indicated that you ever wanted to touch me, let alone make love to me."

"Would you have preferred that I did?"

"Yes," she admitted softly, bowing her head to elude his penetrating gaze. "It might have made tonight easier for me."

The hand under her chin firmly tilted her head back so he could see her face. "Did you want to kiss me? Do you want to be held in my arms?"

"Yes." This time she didn't try to hold back the two tears that slipped from her lashes as his hand lightly rested on her shoulders.

"Why?"

"You know why," she answered in a tormented whisper, "I love you."

His hands moved over her shoulders, down her arms, to close over her wrists, gently tugging so that her fingers would release their hold on her robe before he drew her hands to his chest. His naked skin was fiery hot to the touch. The heat seemed to fuse her hands in place. Amanda didn't think she could have pulled them away if she had tried. She felt his fingers deftly untying the sash that held her robe in place.

"Why didn't you even kiss me once?" Her words came out cloaked in an agonizing moan as his hands slid around her waist, their touch burning through the thin fabric of the nightgown beneath her robe.

"Because I swore I would make you ache for me the way I have for you these past months." A savage black light blazed in his eyes. The mask fell away and she could see how tightly leashed his control still was as he pulled her roughly against him, his physical need of her more apparent. As always, the contact of his lean, muscular body dissolved all resistance.

"Jarod, please!" Of their own volition, her hands swept around his neck as he ravished the throbbing cord below her ear. "Please pretend that you love me, if only for tonight," she begged shamelessly, her lips moving in soft feather kisses over the rippling muscles of his chest. "Pretend that our vows mean something to you, too."

With incredible ease, he swung her into his arms and carried her the few paces to the bed, snuffing out the light once he had lain her on the sheets. As the weight of his body settled onto the mattress beside her, love and shame tore at her breast with equal violence.

His mouth brushed the side of her face. "I don't have to pretend. There was one vow that I will keep," Jarod declared huskily. "With my body I thee worship."

With a whimpering moan of surrender, Amanda turned her lips to him and yielded to the spreading fire of his touch.

CHAPTER TEN

THE HAPPY TRILL of a bird singing its song to the rising sun drifted into the silent room. Amanda shifted slightly in protest to its wake-up call. Instantly the arm around her tightened to prevent further movement and she became conscious of the even rise and fall of the muscular chest beneath her head. A deliciously warm sensation filled her as she watched her hand slide intimately over the flat stomach to the dark hairs on the chest that was her pillow.

"Jarod," she whispered lovingly to no one in particular, cherishing the sound of it as its use was exclusively hers now. "Jarod, Jarod."

She could have repeated it a thousand times, but she didn't for fear she might wake him. The languorous warmth of the strong arms that held her was too tenderly blissful to be ended by rousing him from his sleep. Carefully Amanda tilted her head back so she could look at his face, which appeared not nearly so harsh in repose. The desire to touch it, to let her fingertips explore the carved plains and hollows, became almost too much and she lowered her gaze, closing her eyes to snuggle deeper into the crook of his arm.

Then the hand that had been resting on her

shoulder slipped to her face. The lean fingers were so close to her mouth that she couldn't resist the slight movement required to brush her lips against them. But at the first gentle kiss, the fingers closed around her chin and Amanda was pulled upward in one swift movement until her head was resting on the pillow inches from Jarod's face. The bright light in his black eyes told her that he had been aware of every moment.

"Good morning." There was a faint shyness in her voice.

He smiled and leaned over to press a lingering sweet kiss on her lips, feeling them part immediately on contact with his before he moved back to study her thoroughly.

"That is the way to say good morning," Jarod informed her, a smile tugging again at the corners of his mouth. "Or at least the prelude."

"I didn't mean to wake you," Amanda murmured.

"Didn't you? Then why did you keep repeating my name?" His hands were beginning their wayward caress of last night, moving with tantalizing deliberateness over her spine and hips.

"I like it," Amanda responded softly, feeling the flames of desire rekindling.

"And last night?" He arched her closer so her could nibble on her white shoulder. "Was it satisfying for you?"

"Yes." She breathed in deeply. "Was it...for you?"

"No." At the hurt look that sprang immediately into her eyes, Jarod chuckled and used the weight of his body to push her back against the mattress. "Last night I was satisfied, but not this morning."

"I probably should be getting your breakfast," she said in a breathless little voice.

"Why?" His indifferent question was muffled by the hollow of her throat.

Her fingers moved lightly over the bare skin of his shoulders. "I suppose because that's something wives do for their husbands."

"Mmm, until the drudgery and monotony become too much and they end up sending the man off with a cup of coffee and a peck on the cheek," Jarod said cynically.

"Not all wives," Amanda protested.

"I forgot." His head was raised, allowing him to look darkly into her face, mockery in his black eyes. "You're still wrapped up in those romantic notions about husbands and wives and the happily ever afters."

"Don't make fun of me, Jarod," she insisted, her hands reaching out to hold his face. "I do love you. I can't help it if I never want to leave you, no matter how shameless I sound."

"You can keep your dreams, Amanda. I won't take them away from you," he murmured grimly. "Hold on to them for as long as you can."

"What made you so bitter?" Her heart was aching with the depth of her love and the certainty with which Jarod had insisted it would someday end.

"I'm not bitter. I'm realistic. And right now, I'm very glad that I can assert my authority as your husband and tell you to stop talking!'' There was a hint of a smile before his mouth closed over hers.

''DID JAR—MR. COLBY say what time he would be home tonight when he called, Hannah?'' Amanda inquired as the housekeeper walked into the dining room where Amanda was polishing the silver, humming a happy tune to herself.

''No, he only asked where you were and what time I was expecting you home,'' the older woman replied, taking the pieces Amanda had finished and placing them in the buffet. ''And I explained that you'd gone with your mother to the hospital and that your father was being released today. You were going to help her get him settled at their home, but you would be here by four o'clock.''

''And he didn't give any other reason for calling?''

''No, he didn't, Mrs. Colby.''

A thrill still shivered over Amanda every time the housekeeper addressed her as Jarod's wife. Amanda silently wondered if she would ever tire of it, then decided she was acting like a silly bride. They had only been married three weeks. Such a short time when she thought about it, yet it seemed as if she had always belonged to him.

The secret fear that someday all this happiness must come to an end she kept firmly pushed to the back of her mind. Dwelling on it would only make each hour more miserable than the last. She was convinced that heaven and hell were a state of mind and she was determined that the days, weeks, or months she spent with Jarod would be heaven. The hell would be living without him.

Jarod chided her occasionally, telling her she was "playing house," but she had discovered that all she had to do was slip into his arms and turn her face up for his kiss and he "played house" with her. And the wild ecstasy of their lovemaking never diminished for her, nor seemingly for Jarod, either.

Since their marriage, there had been a few business dinner parties in which the wives were in attendance. She and Jarod would become separated for one reason or another and their eyes would meet across a room. Amanda swore her heart would never stop turning over each time she saw that special light that said he wanted to be alone with her.

A glance at her watch told her it was nearly four and she handed the last of the silver to the housekeeper. She began tidying together the rags and the polish and the papers.

"I'll take care of that," Hannah announced.

The housekeeper didn't object to Amanda's doing some of the extra tasks around the rambling house, but she drew the line at the simple chores of cleaning up, making beds, and doing dishes. Those came strictly under Hannah's heading. That had been a difficult adjustment for Amanda, accustomed as she was to doing all those things her entire life, but Jarod had stated that she wasn't there to replace his housekeeper. The truth was there was plenty of work to keep both women busy and a surprisingly friendly relationship had developed between them.

The hands of the clock moved past four and the telephone remained silent. Amanda hadn't realized how much she had been expecting it to ring. Jarod had never called her during the day before, one of the many little things that indicated that he didn't regard her as his wife. Only to a certain point was she able to fool herself that their relationship was idyllic. How could it be when all the love was one-sided?

With a heavy sigh, Amanda gave up her vigil near the telephone and started toward their bedroom, guided by the half-formed decision to shower and change before Jarod came home. The sound of the front door opening coupled with his voice turned her quickly to the foyer, a smile of happiness unconsciously lighting her face.

"You're early!" Amanda cried in delight the moment her gaze caught sight of the tall, dark figure turning to meet her. An older, balding man was standing beside Jarod with a briefcase in his hand.

Jarod's hand reached out to draw Amanda forward with that impersonal touch she had come to loathe. It always seemed to remind her that she was only one of many women he had known and unlikely to be the last.

"Amanda, I'd like you to meet my attorney, Frank Blaisdale," he introduced.

"Mrs. Colby, this is a rare pleasure. I've heard many compliments spoken about you, but none of them did you justice." A smile concealed the shrewdness in his pale blue eyes and Amanda guessed that many a client and opponent had been lulled by the older man's quiet charm.

"I think I'm going to pretend that you're not exaggerating, Mr. Blaisdale, and simply say thank you," she answered with a smile in return. Her gaze slid to Jarod. "Would you like coffee or drinks in the study while the two of you are working?"

"I won't be staying long, Mrs. Colby," the attorney inserted.

"Frank is here to witness your signature on some papers we need to sign," Jarod added in explanation, beginning the movement that would take the three of them to his study.

"My signature?" Amanda questioned with a puzzled frown.

"Yes. Actually we should have had the agreement drawn up before we were married, but Frank was out of town on other matters and wasn't able to get it completed until now," Jarod said, opening the door the walnut-paneled room and ushering her inside.

"Agreement?" She looked from Jarod to the bland face of the attorney.

"You're beginning to sound like an echo, Amanda." There was a hint of censure in Jarod's teasing tone.

"I'm sorry, but I don't understand," she murmured.

"It's really very simple, Mrs. Colby." The attorney placed his briefcase on the desk, snapped it open and withdrew three sets of documents, handing one to her and one to Jarod, retaining the third for himself. "This is what could commonly be called a marriage contract. It outlines your husband's agreement to be responsible for the medical costs of your father's illness, the continuation of his salary as an absentee plant manager, and the tuition, et cetera, for your brothers' college education. There are also provisions here for a lump sum cash settlement in the event of a divorce. Read it over and see if you have any questions.

The paper in Amanda's hand seemed to catch fire. Cold flames shot through the fingers that held it, the scorching icy tongues forcing her to push the heartless document on the desk top before she was completely immobilized by its touch. Her brown eyes were wide with torment as she turned them to Jarod, calmly leafing through the pages of the agreement in his hands. As if feeling her gaze, he looked up, surrounded by that remote air she always associated with him when he was concentrating on an important business transaction.

"Do you have any questions?" A cold piercing quality was in his eyes as he spoke.

"Is this what you want?" she demanded in a tortured voice.

"I don't see anything that's been omitted." His gaze shifted smoothly back to the document, ignoring the plea in her eyes not to go through with this. "We discussed all the items in here except the amount of the settlement. Is a hundred thousand satisfactory, or do you want more?"

The hard indifference of his voice made Amanda cringe. In desperation, she turned to the balding man. "Where do I sign?" she asked.

"As an attorney, I can't help but advise that you

read this over carefully, Mrs. Colby,'' he de-
murred.

''Please—'' she choked back the pain that rose
in her throat ''—I'm sure it's quite satisfactory.
Show me where to sign.''

The attorney handed her a pen and indicated the
places on the document requiring her signature.
Each stroke of the pen cut a new slash in her heart,
increasing her pain to an almost intolerable level.
When her name was affixed to the last page, she
pushed the pen away from her, mumbled an excuse, and fled the room.

Her wavering legs carried her swiftly to the bedroom, where she was able to lean weakly against a
bureau while heaving sobs tore at her chest. Then
the door that she had securely closed behind her
was opened. Amanda didn't need to turn around
to know Jarod had followed her.

Her back stiffened and she withdrew herself
from the support of the bureau. Determinedly she
lifted her chin, pride insisting she couldn't allow
him to know the agony the callous agreement had
brought. Yet she knew the torment was in her eyes.

''I . . . I—'' she breathed in deeply ''—I think I'll
take a shower before dinner,'' she finished, not
turning to face him as she took a step toward the
adjoining bathroom.

''Amanda!'' The leashed anger in his voice
erased all desire to pretend he hadn't hurt her.

Her chin dipped in defeat, but she didn't turn
around. ''Jarod, how could you do this?''

''It was as much for your protection as it was
for mine,'' he said grimly. Lithe, silent strides

had brought him across the room to stand behind her.

"That horrible agreement—it makes what I feel for you cheap and degrading. I love you so much and those papers make it sound like an unfeeling merger." Amanda shuddered bitterly.

"You know it won't last," Jarod insisted with a shrug.

"What? My love or our marriage?" she demanded, spinning around to blink the tears from her eyes as she gazed at the tightly clenched jaw. "I know I'll go on loving you after you stop wanting me. From the start I've known that our marriage wouldn't last. It's enough to receive what little affection you're capable of giving me. But this agreement takes even that away from me!"

His hands took hold of her shoulders, the fingers digging into her flesh for a moment before she relaxed. "You're a beautiful woman, but in many ways you're such a child," Jarod sighed angrily, drawing her against his chest and holding her there while he stroked her red locks as one would comfort a child.

Her inner coldness made Amanda huddle closer to the warmth his body generated, the shelter of his strong arms offering her the only apparent security that was left.

"I can't change the way I feel, darling," she murmured firmly as he rested his cheek against the side of her head, "any more than I can change the way you feel. I've accepted that. I only wish that awful contract didn't exist."

"I never realized how sensitive—how easily hurt you are," Jarod mused, tightening the iron band of his arms. "Forget about the contract, Amanda. It's just another piece of paper."

BUT THE CONTRACT wasn't any easier to forget than their marriage license and vows. During the next three months Amanda understood the subtle strain it placed on their relationship. Behind every happy smile there was a shadow, silently reminding her life with him was on a day-to-day basis, never certain when she woke in the morning whether this would be the day Jarod decided he didn't want her any longer. There were times when she wondered where her pride and self-respect had gone, that she should so greedily savor every precious moment she spent with him.

In the mornings it was difficult to keep from reaching out to him to reassure herself that he was lying in the bed beside her and thus reaffirm that he still welcomed her touch. At least that had been so every morning until recently. Now she lay quietly in the bed, watching him dress, and waitng for the moment when he would walk over to kiss her goodbye.

"You're becoming quite a lazybones." Jarod smiled into the mirror as he adjusted his tie, his dark gaze alighting on the contrast of her copper hair against the white pillow.

"There's no reason to get up yet." Amanda smiled faintly back, her eyes filling with love at the sight of the strong, bronze features with their in-grained arrogance and compelling attraction.

"No, I suppose not."

"There's a chance of showers today. Don't forget to take your raincoat."

He walked to the bed, a mocking glitter in his eyes. "You still enjoy playing the loving little wife, don't you?"

Amanda swallowed hard. "Don't make fun of me, Jarod."

"You used to laugh when I said that," he reminded her gently, bending down to kiss her mouth possessively. As his raven black head moved away, his gaze throughly swept her face. "You look peaked this morning."

"No makeup. What time will you be home tonight?"

"I have to drive to Atlanta, so it will probably be around seven," he said, brushing the tip of her nose with his finger before he turned to walk away.

"Be careful!" she called after him, and received a last look over his shoulder as he walked out the door.

Amanda lay in bed visualizing the route that would take Jarod to his study where he would collect his briefcase and papers, then out to the living room where he would tell Hannah what time he would be home for dinner that evening, then finally out to his car. Only if the wind was in the right direction would she hear the purr of the engine signaling his departure.

This morning she heard nothing. Very slowly she swept back the covers and gently levered herself upright, swinging her feet to the floor. Her legs were shaking badly, but she made it to the bathroom before the waves of nausea couldn't be held back any longer and she began retching.

When the last wave had passed, she clung weakly to the sink, fighting the weakness that threatened to buckle her knees. A succession of deep breaths helped her regain part of her strength and she turned to reenter the bedroom, only to find Jarod blocking the door, his eyes furiously dark and narrowed.

"Why didn't you tell me you were ill?" he demanded, eliminating the distance between them in one stride and sweeping her up into his arms to carry her into the bedroom.

"I...I didn't w-want to worry you," Amanda stammered.

"From now on," he growled as he placed her on the bed, "I'll make the decision as to whether you're going to worry me or not. Stay here and I'll go tell Hannah to fetch you some hot tea."

Her mouth opened to call him back, but her voice refused to cooperate until the door was closing behind him. By that time it was too late. Turning her head into the pillow, she began to cry, using the softness of the pillow to muffle her sobs. Several minutes later Hannah walked into the room carrying a cup of hot tea, not saying a word, but the look in her eye was speaking very eloquently as Amanda avoided her gaze to mumble a thank-you.

The teacup was drained and she was about to leave the warm luxury of the bed when she heard voices in the hall. Her gaze darted anxiously toward the door just as it opened and Jarod walked in followed by a tall, thin man. Her heart did a somersault of fear. Only a man of Jarod Colby's wealth and status could arrange for a doctor to make a house call, and the man was undoubtedly a doctor, as was confirmed a second later.

"This is Dr. Simon—my wife," Jarod introduced them.

"Good morning, Mrs. Colby. Your husband tells me you aren't feeling well today." The doctor walked briskly forward, but Amanda paid no attention to him.

"I don't need a doctor," she protested quickly. "It's nothing."

"We'll let Dr. Simon be the judge of that." Jarod's dark brows were drawn together in an uncompromising line.

The doctor started to reach for her wrist, but Amanda drew her hand away. "Please, Jarod, I have to talk to you," she demanded.

"After the doctor has completed his examination."

"Let me take your pulse, Mrs. Colby."

"No! Please, I'm not ill. I mean, not really." She glanced anxiously from the doctor to Jarod standing at the foot of the bed.

"You gave an excellent impression of being sick," he said as he motioned to the doctor to continue.

"Jarod, please, I want to talk to you—alone. I don't need a doctor."

"Will you stop behaving like a child?" he snapped.

"Very well." Amanda took a deep breath, then let her eyes seek his in a silent apology before she continued in a calmer and quieter voice. "I'm not acting like a child. I'm acting like a woman *with* child."

The silence after her announcement threatened to continue as Jarod stared at her in angry disbelief. Fortunately the doctor spoke up.

"Have you seen a doctor yet, Mrs. Colby?"

"Yes." Amanda nodded, not taking her pleading eyes from her husband's face. "My parents' doctor. It's all been confirmed."

"Congratulations, then," he said hesitantly. "I'll, er, leave you two alone."

CHAPTER ELEVEN

At the soft click of the closing door, Amanda rushed to explain. "I tried to tell you several times, Jarod, honestly. I never wanted you to find out this way. I'm sorry."

"You're sorry!" he jeered, his lip curled to let her know how ineffectual her apology was. "My God! I never thought you would resort to this kind of trickery in an effort to hold me!"

"No. No!" The second exclamation was more vehement in her denial of his accusation. "That wasn't my intention at all!"

"It wasn't? Then why were you keeping it from me?" An explosive kind of sarcasm was written in his face.

"Because I knew you'd told me you didn't want children. That's why I was afraid to tell you. I never dreamed you would think...." Tears ran freely down her cheeks. "Jarod, I want this baby. I know I'll never be able to have you, but the baby will be part of you and it will be mine. Part of you will be mine. Don't you see?"

His head moved to the side in a gesture of wry cynicism. "Yes, I can see how your romantic heart could reach such an absurd conclusion. Do you expect my help in bringing up this child?"

"I expect nothing from you, Jarod," she answered quietly. "If you want, when we're divorced, I'll change my name and the baby's back to Bennett. I'll bring up our child with all the love and tenderness that's in me."

"For a while," he said dryly. "Then he'll get in your way. You'll find another man who won't be very willing to take on the responsibilities of another man's child. What will you do then? Ship him off to a bunch of boarding schools to get him out of your hair? Conveniently forget the child exists except at holidays when you remember to send him a present?"

"No, his childhood won't be like yours. That I promise you."

"What do you know of my childhood?" he snapped.

"Only the bits and pieces I've picked up from Hannah." Amanda couldn't meet the coldness of his gaze and tilted her chin downward. It would be of little use to tell him how many comparisions she had noticed between Jarod's childhood and Tobe's.

"Spare me your pity, because I don't need it," Jarod snarled savagely. "My lesson in the reality of life came early. I was never blinded by things that didn't exist. Santa Claus, the Easter Bunny, and love, they're all a farce, perpetuated by people without the guts to look life in the face. I never wore rose-colored glasses and I've never been sorry I didn't."

His words were like a thousand tiny paper cuts, setting her nerve ends raw with pain. "If you never dream, then you'll never have a dream come true," she whispered.

"You may have a point there." The sarcasm returned to his voice. "Because you've certainly had one of your dreams come true."

"What do you mean?" she gasped half-afraid of his answer.

"I mean we'll be staying together until after the baby is born."

Jarod pivoted sharply to leave and Amanda sprang from the bed to place a restraining hand on his arm. "No! I don't want to stay under those conditions," she protested.

She hadn't expected his reaction to be so swift. He spun her around, a hand closing over her throat as if he wanted to strangle her. Black fury raged in his face.

"Do you think you damned Johnny Rebs have cornered the market on honor and pride? I'm not the kind of man to get a girl pregnant and then throw her out. The one spark of decency that remains won't let me."

"Jarod." It was difficult to talk with his hand choking her throat. "I want to stay because you want me. Do you still want me?"

The hard diamond sharpness of his gaze raked her face in cold assessment. He could feel the throbbing of her pulse beneath his fingers and see in her brown eyes the pleading question that silently demanded his honest answer. His hand slid from her throat to the back of her neck as he pulled her roughly against the solidness of his chest.

"You're going to stay with me until the baby is born," he said hoarsely.

"I haven't strength to leave unless you push me away," she admitted in an aching whisper. The hard contact of his body was evoking that seemingly never-ending desire for his possession of her. "I have to know if you still want me."

There was no answer except the bruising crush of his mouth against hers, grinding her lips against her teeth while his hands moved in punishing caress over her body, fighting the material of her thin cotton gown. The pain was sweet agony as he swept Amanda off her feet and carried her to the bed.

Her fingers curled into the thickness of his raven hair and he buried his mouth in her neck and muttered, "Yes, yes, I do want you." For once Amanda was grateful for his brutal honesty, because she knew he spoke the truth.

IN THE MONTHS that followed, Jarod avoided any mention of the baby, even when her stomach thickened to a proportion that couldn't be ignored. More of his evenings were spent away from the house, drawing questioning comments and looks from the housekeeper. Amanda couldn't bring herself to ask if he still wanted her. His answer was all too obvious in his actions. But there was comfort in the life kicking vigorously inside her, although it would never replace the blissful sensation of Jarod's arms around her, a feeling that wasn't enjoyed as her time grew nearer.

The click of her knitting needles competed with

the tick of the clock as Amanda wondered whether Jarod would be home for dinner or would call at the last minute to say he was detained and that she should eat without him. Her answer was in the opening and closing of the front door. Unwillingly her eyes strayed to the living-room archway, a gnawing hunger for the sight of him eating into her heart. Then he appeared, a closed, emotionless expression on his face as he ignored her greeting to walk to the bar and pour himself a drink.

"How are you today?" His clipped question betrayed his lack of interest in her answer.

"Fine," she answered, swallowing the lump in her throat to concentrate on the partially completed green sweater. She could feel his brooding gaze watching her.

"It isn't necessary for you to make clothes," Jarod said suddenly. "If you need more money, ask for it."

She closed her eyes briefly at the savageness in his voice before answering calmly, "I enjoy it. It gives me something to do." An uneasy silence followed her statement. The baby kicked as if to remind Amanda of its presence. "I...I've been thinking a...about names for the baby," she said hesitantly. "Michele if it's a girl and David if it's a boy."

"What am I supposed to say?"

"I thought you might...want to make a suggestion," she ended lamely, unable to counter the contempt in his voice.

"Name it whatever you want," he growled, rising from the leather stool at the bar.

"Will you be eating here tonight?"

His gaze flicked derisively over his shoulder at her. "I don't recall mentioning that I would be going out, so I must be eating here."

"I didn't know." Her shoulders moved in a defenseless shrug. "You've been so busy lately, I thought perhaps you'd be gone tonight, as well."

"If you want to know if I'm seeing another woman, why don't you come right out and ask me?" His eyes blazed in anger at the flash of pain across her face.

"I don't want to know," she murmured, hating the weakness of her love, which allowed her to be the whipping boy.

"Wouldn't you enjoy chastising me for my lack of fidelity?" he jeered.

The knitting was thrust onto the couch as Amanda rose to her feet, trying to make a dignified escape from his stinging insults.

"Damn!" he muttered savagely, easily covering the distance to her before she could reach the hall. "That was a vile thing for me to say, Amanda." His hands closed over her shoulders, shaking with soundless sobs of torment. He pulled her against him, his mouth moving over the back of her head. "I'm sorry," he murmured.

"It's all right," she whispered. It didn't seem necessary to add that she understood why he had sought the pleasures of another woman. Her shoulders felt the deep shuddering breath he drew.

"I'll be leaving in the morning for Philadelphia," Jarod said, his hands releasing her shoulders as he stepped away. "I'll be gone about a week. You can tell Hannah that while she's packing my clothes, she might as well move the rest of my things into the guest bedroom. I'll sleep there from now on."

Her mouth opened to protest, but she closed it quickly, glad her back was still to him and he couldn't see the agony his announcement brought. She murmured a quick agreement, and this time he didn't try to stop her when she rushed from the room.

"Hello, Mandy dear, how are you feeling?"

Amanda blinked her eyes open and stared into the beaming face of her mother. A small sigh of pleasure slipped from her throat.

"Exhausted," she murmured in return, levering herself into a sitting position in the hospital bed. "Have you seen the baby yet? Isn't he adorable?"

"All seven pounds and two ounces of him," her mother answered, nodding agreement.

"He may be three weeks premature," her father inserted, his speech still slightly slurred from his stroke, "but he has enough hair to pass out to the other three babies in the nursery."

"And it's all coal black just like his father's." Amanda commented and smiled contentedly.

"We reached Jarod about an hour ago," Mrs. Bennett said. "He'll be flying straight back from Philadelphia. I know you must be sorry he wasn't here with you when little David was born."

"I don't mind." Amanda lowered her gaze to the bed sheet so her parents wouldn't see the brief flicker of pain. "I can't exactly visualize

Jarod pacing the floor in the waiting room, can you?''

"No, I suppose not," her mother laughed then let her hand reach out to her daughter's. "The nurse asked us not to stay long so you could get some rest. We'll be back to see you later today."

Amanda's eyes fluttered shut almost the instant her parents left the room. It seemed as though only a few minutes had passed before she heard the gentle voice of a nurse telling her that they would be bringing her baby in to her.

As the small bundle was placed in her arms, Amanda knew a joy that was beyond expression. A whole new world opened up at the sight of those tiny little hands wrapped in puny fists, flailing the air while the baby sucked vigorously on the nipple of his bottle.

Once his hunger was satisfied, he slept contentedly in her arms while Amanda gently pushed the silky fine black hair that covered his head into a semblance of order.

"My beautiful David," she crooned softly, lightly touching the button nose of the still red face. "I will try to love you as much as I love your father." An adoring smile beamed from her face. "I don't think it's going to be very difficult. I bet you're even going to have his beautiful dark eyes."

A sound from the doorway drew her attention, a look of regret forming in her eyes in anticipation of the nurse who would soon be coming to take the infant back to the nursery, but it was Jarod standing there instead, tall, imposing, and vaguely withdrawn.

Instinctively Amanda stretched out her hand to him. "Jarod!" Unbounded happiness shone in her voice. "I didn't think you would be here so soon."

His supple strides brought him to the side of the bed as he impersonally took the hand she offered. "Are you all right, Amanda?" he asked blandly.

"Yes." She couldn't help smiling; she was much too happy. Liquid brown eyes were turned back to the baby sleeping in her arms. "Isn't David the most beautiful baby you've ever seen?" Her gaze slid back to Jarod, trying to gauge his reaction to his son in the black steel of his eyes.

"Excuse me, Mrs. Colby," a nurse spoke quietly from the end of the bed. "It's time to return your son to the nursery."

Jarod released Amanda's hand and stepped away as she reluctantly surrendered the infant to the nurse. She watched the woman walk from the room before her gaze was pulled back to her husband. He was staring at her with brooding thoroughness. Self-consciously her fingers went to the tousled crimson gold hair, not knowing the curling disarray was attractively complementing the ethereal pallor of her skin.

"I must look terrible," Amanda proclaimed with a smiling grimace. "My hair is a mess and I have no makeup on."

But there was no affirmation from Jarod that he thought her beautiful. Her self-derogatory comment went completely unheeded.

"Dr. Henderson told me you would be released on Tuesday. I'll make arrangements for a nurse to move into the house Monday so she'll be there when you and the baby arrive home.''

"No!'' Alarm registered briefly in her face before she added firmly, "I'll take care of our son myself.''

"Very well,'' he replied, clipping off the ends of his words bluntly. "Whenever you get tired of the role as little mother, you can hire a nanny yourself.''

A great deal of her happiness vanished at his cynical sneer. "There's something you don't understand, Jarod,'' Amanda said tightly. "Our son isn't a toy and I'm not ever going to get tired of him.''

"As you wish.'' There was a derisive move of his shoulders beneath the dark blue jacket. "I'll let you rest.'' Without even a goodbye he walked from the room, leaving behind a black cloud to dim the sunshine of her spirits.

DAVID'S WHIMPERING CRY woke Amanda instantly. It still amazed her how her ear was tuned to every sound coming from the crib, no matter how deeply she slept. Streaks of gold shimmered on the eastern horizon and the hands of the clock indicated half-past six, feeding time according to the hungry baby's tummy. Amanda slipped quickly from beneath the covers, tugging on her mud green robe as she hurried to the crib before David's stirring increased to a full wail of demand.

"Here, little man,'' she whispered, slipping a pacifier into his mouth, "I'll go and heat your bottle and be right back.''

Quietly Amanda shut the door behind her, glancing hesitantly at the closed door of Jarod's bedroom. She could never look at without realizing there was more than walls separating them; and that knowledge hurt. Not for the first time was she grateful for the arrival of their son, who had brought a new purpose into her life. And right now that little boy was hungry, she thought wryly to herself as she hurried silently down the hall to the kitchen.

The water had just begun to boil in the pan holding the baby bottle when she heard the muted cry from her bedroom. The pacifier had evidently been lost.

"Just a couple more minutes, David," Amanda murmured aloud as she tested the formula and found it almost lukewarm.

By the time the milk was warmed and she began hastily to retrace her path to the bedroom, the cries had stopped. Assuming that by some miracle David had retrieved his pacifier, she didn't give it a thought until she opened the bedroom door and saw Jarod holding him in his arms, gently rocking the baby and looking as if he had done it all his life.

"I didn't mean to take so long," said Amanda, recovering her surprise and looking at the impatient wriggling of the infant before Jarod's dark gaze could capture hers.

"I was awake anyway," said Jarod, starting to turn to hand the child to her.

There was only a second of hesitation before she thrust the bottle toward him. "Would you feed him?'' she asked quickly, childishly crossing her fingers as she lied. ''I dropped one of the bottles on the kitchen floor. Hannah isn't here yet and I'd like to clean it up before it starts to dry.''

She nearly forced the bottle into Jarod's hand before she hurried from the room, not stopping until she had reached the kitchen, where she wrapped her arms around herself and smiled.

''You're certainly grinning like the cat that ate the canary,'' Hannah mumbled as she walked in the kitchen door. ''Don't tell me little Davie's alarm clock didn't go off this morning?''

''Oh, yes, it did,'' Amanda laughed, nearly dancing over to the housekeeper and hugging her tightly.

''What's wrong with you, girl?'' The usually sternfaced housekeeper let a smile of bewilderment tug at her mouth.

''Jarod is in the bedroom feeding David right now,'' Amanda whispered, as if saying it louder would bring the walls crashing down.

''It's about time, I'd say,'' the woman declared with a vigorous nod of her pepper-colored hair. ''The little feller is more than a month old. He should know what it's like to be held by his daddy.''

''I knew Jarod couldn't resist him forever,'' Amanda sighed, ignoring the sting of criticism in the housekeeper's statement. ''I hadn't better overdo it the first time, though. With my luck, David will burp all over his robe. Fix some coffee and bring it up to my room, will you, Hannah?''

The contents of the bottle were nearly gone

when Amanda returned to the bedroom. Without a word she took the baby from Jarod's arms, a shy look of pleasure in her eyes as she looked at him.

"He's already burped," he said blandly.

"Not on you?" she asked anxiously.

"No."

Jarod stood beside the crib, watching with indifference as Amanda tucked the blanket around the contentedly sighing infant. Covertly she tried to glimpse a hint of pride or affection in the arrogantly set features, any sign that Jarod felt something for their son resting in the crib. There seemed to be nothing, yet she couldn't help venturing a comment.

"Sometimes it's difficult to believe that he's our son," she said softly. "That you and I made—"

"Don't waste your romantic nonsense on me, Amanda," Jarod snapped. "Keep it for that baby you're so proud of."

Her eyes rounded in disbelief at the savage rejection in his voice. A faltering movement of her hand brought her fingers in contact with the terrycloth sleeve of his robe. A ray of hope twinkled dimly.

"Jarod..." she began hesitantly. "You...you aren't jealous of our...our son, are you?"

"Jealous!" There was a contemptuous sound in his throat as the full force of his glittering cold gaze was turned on her. "To be jealous I would first have to care. And I don't care." The words were drawn out with emphatic slowness. "You and the baby could leave today and I wouldn't miss you at all."

Her whole body jerked as if he had slapped her, twisting her head to the side as she reeled from the shock of the pain. Incapable of speech, she said not a word, although painfully aware of his footsteps taking him out of the room. Her hands crept up to her face while the last of her hope died an agonizing death as bitter tears streamed down her cheeks.

"Don't waste your tears on the likes of him." Hannah's angry voice sounded from behind her. "He isn't worth it."

Amanda spun around, pride briefly halting her sobs. "Don't say that!" she gasped, more in terror because her mind was saying the same thing.

"It's the truth. And don't you be trying to put me in my place, either. I heard every word he said, and it would serve him right if you left this very day!"

"I love him." Amanda's face crumpled beneath the onslaught of tears. "It's so humiliating to love someone as much as I love him. What am I going to do?"

"The first thing—" the housekeeper drew her to the bed "—is for you to drink some of this coffee while I pack your things. It's time the high and mighty Mr. Colby found out how empty this house is without you. We'll see how good the food tastes when he sits at the table alone, and how sterile the house seems without a few women's things strewn around."

"It won't work, Hannah." Amanda shook her head dejectedly. "I knew when he married me that he didn't care for me. I only hoped that he might care about David. I told Jarod I would leave when he told me to go, and that's when I'll leave."

"What do you think he said a minute ago? Where's your pride?"

"I have no pride," she admitted wryly, roughly wiping the tears from her face. "You'd better take the coffee in to Jarod."

"I'll throw it in his face if I do," the housekeeper growled. "The ungrateful pup!"

"Hannah—"

"All right, I'll take it in to him." Hannah stiffly picked up the tray she had carried into the room. "But the minute he leaves, I'm getting your suitcases packed. And if I have to lend you some of my pride, I will, but you'll be gone from this house when he comes back tonight!"

"Oh, Hannah, I adore you," Amanda declared in a half laugh. "But I'm not leaving today."

"We'll see," the older woman sniffed, and walked briskly to the door.

CHAPTER TWELVE

THE DOOR CLOSED with a resounding bang behind Jarod as he entered the house, his impatient strides carrying him directly into his study. Tossing the thin briefcase on the leather sofa, he began shifting through the mail on his desk while lean, tanned fingers tugged at the knot of his tie. At the light rap on the door, his cold gaze glittered long enough in that direction to identify the person in the doorway before it returned to its task.

"What do you want, Hannah?" he demanded sharply.

"I was wondering what time you wanted dinner tonight."

"I have an appointment in a half hour, so I won't be eating here. You'll have to check with Mrs. Colby." He tossed the mail on the desk and made a half turn away from the housekeeper in silent dismissal.

"Mrs. Colby isn't here." There was the barest ring of triumph in the woman's voice.

Jarod glanced over his shoulder, a slight frown knitting his forehead as his penetrating gaze attempted to detect the reason for that peculiar tone of defiance. "What do you mean—she isn't here?'' He challenged her for a more accurate statement.

"I mean she's gone." The woman's thin nose seemed to pinch together into a narrower line. "And more power to her, I say!"

Jarod appeared to weigh her statement, assessing it and discarding it as he again turned his back on her. "I don't believe you," he said with marked indifference.

"You don't have to believe me," the woman declared with a shrug. "But if you look, you'll find her clothes and the baby's are all gone."

For a moment, blazing dark eyes bored the fiery tip of their steel into the unflinching woman before Jarod shoved her out of the doorway and let his long, swinging strides carry him into the master bedroom. A sweeping search confirmed the housekeeper's statement, yet even when the physical search stopped, his gaze moved relentlessly around the room.

"There's no need to worry, Mr. Colby," Hannah said dryly, her less hurried steps bringing her to the open door. "The only things that are gone are personal possessions. She left the house just as she found it—cold and empty."

"I've had enough of your insolence!" Jarod clipped.

"Have you now?" A sparse brow arched above unblinking eyes as Hannah folded her arms in front of her. "Maybe I should quit and we can see whether or not you miss me. If you want to know where she's gone, she went back to people who care about her and the baby. Her family."

"Why should I care where she is?" His dark head was arrogantly thrown back. "It was only a matter of time anyway, since you seem to be so familiar with my personal life."

"I'm neither deaf nor blind."

His lips were pressed tightly together to hold back the angry retort. "You may leave, Hannah. As I have other commitments this evening, there's no reason for you to stay."

THE RELAXED INTERCHANGE of voices, casually discussing unimportant topics, seemed to insulate Amanda from the pain in her heart. She hadn't realized how strained her nerves were until she had stepped into the loving atmosphere of her parents' home. Drawing strength from their invisible blanket of security, she was able to match their light-heartedness and reacquaint herself with the joys to be shared because of the baby now being rocked gently in her grandfather's arms.

All of the family had gathered in the living room, including Tobe and Cheryl. The dinner dishes were done and her mother was sitting in the large chair beside Amanda's father, darning a pair of Ted's socks, smiling as she listened to the teasing exchange between Tobe and Brad, who had finally proposed to Cheryl. The slamming of the front door caught everyone by surprise, silencing their voices as they all turned as one to face the hallway.

Jarod's tall frame filled the doorway, a harsh expression etched over his drawn features, a suggestion of pallor beneath the teak brown tan of his face. With the cutting quality of a laser beam, his eyes pierced through Amanda, pinning her to the sofa and not allowing her to move.

The only one not stunned by the aura of explosive anger surrounding him was her mother, who calmly set her darning aside and rose to her feet.

"Jarod, this is a surprise." The cold glare of his gaze as he brought it to bear on her mother didn't silence her as it was meant to do. "I hope you haven't come to take Amanda home already. Since little David has been born, it's so rarely that she comes to visit us. I couldn't believe our luck when we persuaded her to stay for dinner."

Amanda's heart beat in an uneven rhythm as she watched Jarod stare at her mother, his head drawn back as if her words had caught him by surprise. Then his dark gaze swung on her, relentlessly searching her face while Amanda frowned her bewilderment.

"What's wrong, Jarod?" His continued silence prompted her mother's question.

There was a massive rise of his chest as he breathed in deeply, a hand raised to let his fingers tear through the sides of his hair. His head made a negative movement as if to shake off the demon driving him.

"I'm sorry," he mumbled, turning away to walk back the way he had come.

Amanda met her mother's questioning gaze with a blank look, but Jarod's abrupt departure brought her to her feet, as confused as the rest of them over his strange behavior. She hurried down the hallway after him, reaching the screen door before it closed behind him and catching him as he reached the top of the porch steps.

"Jarod, what is it?" Her voice slowed his steps, finally halted by the touch of her hand on his arm. "What's wrong?"

In the dim moonlight she saw him glance down at her hand. When he spoke, his voice seemed to come from some deep cavern.

"I'm taking you home, Amanda."

"Of course, but can't you tell me what's wrong?"

She sensed the indecision, something she found difficult to associate with him—Jarod, who was always so positive about what he wanted. He turned very slowly and the light from inside the house illuminated the ravaged pain in his face.

"I believed you'd left me." He spoke clearly and distinctly, revealing none of the agony that was written in his expression.

"I have neither the strength nor the pride to do that," she answered with a wistful smile. Then a curious thought fluttered on fragile butterfly wings in her mind. "Why would it matter to you if I did?"

"I deserved that," Jarod muttered, roughly grabbing her and crushing her against his chest. Beneath her head she felt the strong beat of his heart while he rubbed his cheek against her head. "I didn't believe it mattered. I thought you could leave me and I wouldn't miss you. Until tonight."

Weakly she clung to him, gasping at the unbelievable happiness exploding inside her while tears of joy streamed from her eyes. She had ceased hoping that she could ever mean anything to him.

"My love, my love," she whispered fervently. "And you thought those things you said to me this morning had sent me away from you?"

"No." She could feel the shake of his head as he tightened his arms around her, molding her ever closer against his trembling length. "It never seemed to matter how much I laughed at you or scorned the way you felt for me, you always stayed. I didn't think this morning would be any different."

"Then why?" Her head moved back, sending the long coppery hair cascading over the sleeve of his coat. "Why did you think I'd left?"

"Hannah told me you were gone." His eyes seemed to drink in the radiant glow of her face.

"But she knew I was here. She even phoned me to let me know you wouldn't be home for dinner."

"That scheming witch!" Jarod chuckled, a brilliant light entering his dark eyes. "She's the one who told me you were gone—for good. She even went so far as to remove all your clothes from your room to convince me."

"Oh, no!" Amanda cried with a gasping laugh. "No wonder you thought I'd left. She overheard what you told me this morning and was determined that I leave you. Jarod—" her eyes were shimmering with tears of apology "—I almost did. I was convinced that there was no hope for us, that you could never love me even a little bit."

One corner of his mouth twitched in a deprecating gesture. "I still don't know if what I feel for you is love," he admitted slowly and grimly. "When I look at you and see how your love for me has never faltered no matter how much I degraded you or mocked you, I tell myself I have to believe that such an emotion exists. All I'm certain of is that I don't want to face tomorrow without you."

"I won't ask for more than that, Jarod," she murmured, her fingers tracing the sensuous line of his mouth. The months of not touching him suddenly made her desire insurmountable.

"You deserve more than that." He pulled away from her touch. "You should have someone who will cherish you and thank God every day of his life that he has you."

"But it's you I want." Amanda smiled. Her hands curled around his neck, dragging his head down to her mouth until she heard him groan before he claimed her lips, his arms swinging her off her feet as he lifted her to a new height of love.

It was many minutes before her feet touched the porch floor, both of them breathing heavily, their faces flushed with the desires they had aroused in each other. For the first time, the intimate touch of his hands exploring her face, neck and shoulders was tender and loving, not driven by animal passion that would end in possession.

"I should have guessed what was happening to me," Jarod mused thoughtfully, gently folding her in his arms. "That night I met you, at the cotillion, and you refused to let me take you home, I told myself it didn't matter, that you were just another girl. And the next day I found myself at the plantation asking you to have dinner with me. I was going to have that scarlet-haired ghost who had haunted my dreams. When I discovered I had an innocent child, I was furious." His silent laughter at the thought fanned her hair. "I was determined to forget you existed, that I hadn't felt the yielding of your body at my touch. Then by pure chance I stopped at the mill and I knew you would be the one who would come to pick up your father. But you frustrated me again."

"Then you brought Vanessa to Oak Run and I was so jealous," Amanda remembered, and Jarod's arms tightened around her in reassurance.

"I don't know whether I was trying to prove to you or myself that you meant nothing. When you agreed to go out with me and I realized how much I disturbed you, I thought I would finally have you and get you out of my system once and for all." His voice was a low, husky caress. "Then you caught me off balance with your declaration of love and I insisted on having you on my terms or not at all. When we got married, I expected to become tired of you in a few months, but I discovered that I still looked forward to seeing your smile when I walked in the door and the darkness of night when I could take you in my arms."

"If that's true, why did you turn away from me?" her puzzled voice queried. "Why did you move to the other bedroom? Because I was pregnant?"

"Partly," he admitted wryly. "You must remember the scorn I felt for your avowals of love, and I couldn't reconcile myself to the seemingly unquenchable need for you. I thought if I deprived myself of you, the thirst would go away. But the more I denied it, the stronger it became.''

"I thought it was David. I thought I had alienated you completely," Amanda murmured, slipping her fingers beneath his shirt to feel the strong beat of his heart. "I kept hoping that once you saw our baby, you would want him as much as I did."

"I guess you've found out what my childhood was like," he sighed. "Most of the other children I met experienced the same. I remember how it hurt to be always pushed aside by their mothers and fathers unless they felt like playing the doting parents, which was seldom. I taught myself early not to care for anyone but myself. Then you came along."

"I guess it all was meant to be this way. There were times when I was so ashamed of myself," Amanda said. "I knew I was letting you trample my heart and my love, and if I was any kind of a human being at all, I should leave you while I still had a little self-respect. But like a faithful dog, I kept coming back no matter how often you whipped me with your scorn."

Jarod suddenly crushed her against him, squeezing her so tightly that she could hardly breathe. "You don't know how it tears at my insides to hear you say that and know it's true." The admission was drawn through teeth clenched in self-contempt. "Even tonight when your mother made me realize that you hadn't really left me, I was ready to walk away and let you go on believing that I didn't want you. I would have left without ever telling you why I'd come. Still you ran after me, despite those vicious things I said to you this morning. And I knew I would never be able to live with myself if I didn't tell you the way I felt."

She tipped her head back, her lips parting to halt his flow of self-derision. Her breath was caught by the expression on his face. All his arrogance was gone, leaving the tender promise of love everlasting.

"There's something else I must tell you," Jarod said quietly. "Since the day I met you, I haven't been with another woman, not in the intimate sense of the word. If I couldn't have you, I didn't seem to want anyone else."

Two crystal drops hovered on her lashes as the last of her fears dwindled to nothing, and with a little gasp of sheer joy she wrapped her arms around his waist.

"I never thought I could be so happy," Amanda murmured, closing her eyes to savor the full ecstasy of the moment.

"Nor did I." His kiss touched her eye, her cheek, hovering below the lobe of her ear before it moved errorlessly to her mouth. "I think it's about time you took our son and your wayward Yankee husband home."

"Yes, yes," she repeated it again, more eagerly the second time.

Reluctantly he let her leave his arms, the expression in his face urging her to hurry back even though she needed no such encouragement as she dashed into the house and quickly gathered her own and the baby's belongings. The curiously amused glances of her family went unnoticed as she gathered David into her arms, wishing them all a cheery good night before hurrying back to Jarod. When she reached the porch, Amanda started to hand her bag and the baby's things to him, but Jarod pushed them aside.

"You drive home," he ordered, his carved features transformed by a smile that softened every corner. "David and I haven't had a chance to get acquainted."

A gurgle came from the blanket-wrapped infant as if he endorsed the statement, and both Amanda and Jarod laughed softly before the shining light of their eyes met. Gently Jarod gathered the baby in his arms.

"I love you, darling," Amanda smiled.

"I must love you, too," he murmured huskily, his dark gaze ardently returning the look in her eyes. A tiny fist pushed itself free of the blanket and Jarod looked down at it, offering an index finger that the little hand couldn't quite wrap around, although it tried. "Hold on, David. My cynical ways must be in the past, because I feel very proud of my handsome son." His gaze strayed to Amanda as he added softly, "And my wife, too."

Janet Dailey
Americana

Don't miss a single title from this great collection. The first eight titles have already been published. Complete and mail this coupon today to order books you may have missed.

Harlequin Reader Service

In U.S.A.
901 Fuhrmann Blvd.
P.O. Box 1397
Buffalo, N.Y. 14140

In Canada
P.O. Box 2800
Postal Station A
5170 Yonge Street
Willowdale, Ont. M2N 6J3

Please send me the following titles from the Janet Dailey Americana Collection. I am enclosing a check or money order for $2.75 for each book ordered, plus 75¢ for postage and handling.

_____	ALABAMA	Dangerous Masquerade
_____	ALASKA	Northern Magic
_____	ARIZONA	Sonora Sundown
_____	ARKANSAS	Valley of the Vapours
_____	CALIFORNIA	Fire and Ice
_____	COLORADO	After the Storm
_____	CONNECTICUT	Difficult Decision
_____	DELAWARE	The Matchmakers

Number of titles checked @ $2.75 each = $_____

N.Y. RESIDENTS ADD
  APPROPRIATE SALES TAX $_____

Postage and Handling $____.75____

                       TOTAL $_____

I enclose _____

(Please send check or money order. We cannot be responsible for cash sent through the mail.)

PLEASE PRINT

NAME _____

ADDRESS _____

CITY _____

STATE/PROV. _____

BLJD-A-1